DEDICATION

In loving memory of the best father a girl could have,
Brian Montgomery Hanson

To my husband Don, my children David, Cody, Victoria and
Nicole, without your love and support this book would never
have left my computer.

To Carol

Slainte

Jennifer Dake

ACKNOWLEDGMENTS

It has taken me many years to write this book, the first of the three-part trilogy. During that time, I have asked my Irish friends many, many, many questions. Since I have asked questions of anyone willing to answer, I am sorry to say I cannot remember everyone I pestered. Therefore, I owe all those people an enormous thank you.

I would like to thank the ones who were stuck answering my questions the most. Questions like, how would someone from Northern Ireland say this, or what is a Catholic surname.

Angeleen and Brian Carnduff, who have been a great source of information about Ireland over many years, I appreciate all your help. Brian, I thank you for putting up with all my late night Facebook questions. Angeleen, thank you for giving me all the history of English rule in Ireland, which gave me the idea of the family estate being granted to Michael.

Rebecca McCreedy, even though you will not let me hear your accent, I still want to thank you for your help to describe how something would be said and the many other questions I asked.

My Irish dance moms, thank you for describing different areas of Ireland, talking about the culture and putting up with me rambling on about a novel that never seemed to be finished.

Tracy and Dave Herron, Dave for telling me things such as, 'that is a Protestant last name,' and for answering all the other questions I asked the both of you. Thanks to Tracy for describing to me where the Blarney Stone was located in the castle and how to get to it. I still have two more books in the series so be prepared.

Rachel McGibbon, thank you for answering the questions I had. It was helpful getting the perceptive of a person actually living in Ireland.

Faith Casement, you have been a great sounding board and a great source of inspiration.

Last but definitely not least.

My wonderful husband who listened patiently to me rambling on about this novel for many years. Never knowing if I am talking about real people or my characters, whom by the way are real to me.

My beautiful daughters Victoria and Nicole thank you for all your support and for reading my manuscript and telling me how hot Declan was. To Victoria for taking my headshot that appears on the back cover.

My wonderful sons David and Cody thank you for putting up with my endless nights at the computer. I appreciate all the times you went to get us dinner.

My parents Brian and Dore Hanson, who gave me the love of reading.

To my mother-in-law Barb Dickinson, thank you for your support and belief in me.

All my other family for your support over the years.

Deadly Legacy

A Brother's Betrayal

Jennifer Dickinson

Trafford rev.   02/24/2014

 www.trafford.com

North America & international
toll-free: 1 888 232 4444 (USA & Canada)
fax: 812 355 4082

The overpowering aroma of death hung in the air like a shroud, filling Meghan's soul with a deep loss, a loss that had only been an irrepressible gnawing deep in her stomach. She could no longer deny the sensation, now that she was in a room that even as a medical student she hated to enter. However, at that time, she was part of a group of fresh-faced eager students, and she could never connect a personality or a soul to any of the lifeless forms that lay flat on the icy metal slabs. Now she could. It was her love, her soul, and her heart that rested in one of the cold dark shelves awaiting identification.

The stark white floor felt fluid under her feet, as she leaned firmly against Fabrizio, hoping that somehow he could change the outcome of what had become the most horrifying day of her life. Fabrizio was struggling to keep control of his own emotions, and the devastating loss he felt had vanquished his normally smug cynical attitude, leaving him on the verge of tears.

The small greying man in the immaculately white cloak wandered a few feet ahead of them, his demeanour was cold and detached. Not unlike her reaction to the countless families that funnelled through the morgue when she had worked her rotation in the death pit.

"Fabrizio, I can't do this," Meghan mumbled and glanced around the cold, sterile room, allowing her dark green eyes to settle on the row of metal drawers. Her hand swept across her tear-stained face, corralling a wild auburn curl, which refused to stay out of her eyes.

"Meghan, you have to do this. I know it's hard, but if you don't see for yourself, you will . . ." Fabrizio's voice was stern as the words lodged behind the lump in his throat. His dark brown eyes glazed over; his emotions were out of control. Over the years, he had seen many dead bodies, but the thought of seeing his friend's corpse was overwhelming.

"Fabrizio," Meghan whimpered, her knees resembling the consistency of pudding. "It can't be him."

"Oh, Boo . . . !" Fabrizio sighed, unsure what to say to console her. He ran his large hand through his wavy dark brown hair.

"I can't believe this is happening! Everyone I come in contact with is being slaughtered." Meghan's face dropped into her hands, and her voice was barely audible.

Fabrizio attempted a comforting smile as his mocha eyes settled on the long drawer that the cloaked man was opening with slow precision. A low groan filled the room as the silver tray emerged from the cupboard, the draped body as still as a sleeping child.

"Ma'am, if y' would please come over and identify the body. I have a lot of paperwork to complete before we can release the body for y' to take back to the United States," the cloaked man muttered through his crooked teeth. His voice was as dead as his ward's.

Fabrizio smiled softly and kissed Meghan's forehead, causing her eyes to close as the sensation of Declan's lips on her forehead came rushing back. How many times had he kissed her forehead, a thousand, maybe a hundred thousand, and with that thought, the tears exploded from her big green eyes.

"This can't be happening?" Meghan cried, collapsing into Fabrizio, unable to control her devastation any longer.

Fabrizio sighed and tucked her under his arm, positioning her in front of the long body, draped with a white sheet.

Her eyes scanned the broad frame of the corpse lying lifelessly on the metal shelf, and she felt the blood draining from her face. The white-cloaked man nodded, and then slowly pulled back the ghostly white sheet, forcing a loud gasp from Meghan before everything in her view faded into a calm blackness.

CHAPTER ONE

Whether Meghan was a willing participant or not, it appeared to her that, the acquaintance of Ms. Eliza Pettigrew was a burden she would have to endure. Eliza was a bizarrely inquisitive woman, who took a liking to Meghan on the terribly long bus ride to the Colorado Rocky Mountain Chalet. Meghan, being taller than most, was not difficult to locate once she stepped off the bus onto the crisp November snow, but before she could collect her luggage and escape, the round face was directly in her path.

"If I didn't know better, I would think you were trying to get away from me." The woman's big blue eyes fixed on Meghan through her quickly fogging glasses.

Meghan smiled politely and reached for her luggage, which the driver had finally removed from the bottom compartment of the bus. "No, Eliza, I am just excited to see my friends."

Eliza eyed Meghan with interest and then lifted her own suitcase. "I am so pleased that I met you today. I was afraid I would be lonely until my companions arrived. But now I have you," Eliza smiled and followed quickly behind Meghan.

Meghan cringed slightly at the thought of spending one more second with the invasive woman, who had constantly questioned her throughout the extremely long trip from Los Angeles. Even with Meghan's many attempts to change seats along the way, the woman always managed to seat herself either next to Meghan or across the aisle. The chatty woman was possibly in her early sixties but had aged poorly due to her self-confessed hard living in the past few years. Meghan had to admit that on some level she did feel sorry for the woman, whose husband abandoned her, taking her child and leaving her destitute and alone. However, Meghan had her own worries to deal with at that moment, and the last thing she needed was to befriend a nut case like Eliza.

"Well, it was nice meeting you, but I have to find my friends," Meghan blurted out as she stopped at the foot of the steps and surveyed her surroundings.

Encircling the lodge were evergreens that reached up to embrace the clear blue sky, as if the two were somehow connected. The soft wind blew the newly fallen snow off the roof, creating a magical ambiance on the rustic log building that stood ahead of her.

A group of young men wrapped in heavy down jackets greeted the crowd at the bottom of the steps and then struggled with the multitude of baggage towards the front desk. Meghan's breath caught in her throat as she gazed around the room. Magnificent wildlife paintings and sizeable lighting sconces hung on the log walls of the large open room. Various couches scattered throughout the lobby gave the room a warm and inviting presence and enhanced the beautiful Navajo rug that centred the gleaming oak floor. The sitting area in the middle of the room was sunken down one step, and in the centre of the space was a four-sided fireplace, constructed of large stones with a chimney that slowly narrowed towards the roof. On each side of the fireplace, a couch faced the fire, inviting the guests to warm themselves after a day of skiing.

The dark red poinsettias on the lobby desk drew Meghan's attention and her thoughts filled of the stories her father had told her of her mother's love for the Christmas flower. However, sadness soon overtook her, as it always did when she thought about her mother. Meghan remembered very little of her mother, and the older she became, the fewer memories existed.

"Oh, how I love poinsettias, when I see them I know that Christmas is coming, and that brings families closer together, no matter what has happened in the past. Don't you agree?" Eliza's blue gaze settled on Meghan, awaiting a response.

"I guess so. That is, if you have a family," Meghan sighed and focused on the check-in counter, remembering once again that it was going to be her first Christmas completely alone.

Eliza cringed at the expression on Meghan's face, but before she could speak, Meghan turned back around to face her. "Eliza, if you have family somewhere, you should make an effort to mend the past. Once everyone is gone and you are left alone, it will be too late." Meghan's smile was so kind, it tugged at Eliza's heart.

"Thank you, dear." Eliza patted Meghan's face then turned and scanned the room. "I wonder if my companions have arrived yet."

Eliza's gaze settled on a large dark-haired man leaning against the wall, his arms folded across his broad chest, his gaze directed towards her.

Meghan's attention turned to the woman at the counter who had waved her over. "Hi, I'm Meghan Delaney, I have a reservation." Meghan introduced herself, her dark green eyes sparkling with delight.

"Oh, Miss Delaney, your friends have already checked in, dear." The grey-haired woman smiled warmly, softening her time-weathered skin. "They're waiting in the dining room for you. I will have your luggage taken to your room if you would like to go meet them right away?"

"That would be wonderful," Meghan smiled with excitement in anticipation of seeing her friends. While she waited for the key to her room, Meghan watched Eliza glide across the lobby towards the lounge. Meghan could not help but notice the underlying beauty of the woman even though her dark black curls washed out her pale, aged skin. She had a delicate frame under the twenty extra pounds she carried, and her dark blue eyes were large and quite stunning with her glasses removed.

Meghan gently brushed the remaining snow off her long auburn hair and removed her jacket, laying it across her luggage for the bellman to bring to her room. Anxiously she pulled at her fitted dark red sweater, rubbed at her jeans, and fussed with her hair, hoping the bellman would move a little faster, she was anxious to see her friends.

Cassie's twenty-fifth birthday was a perfect reason for a reunion and the lodge provided a cozy backdrop for the week. It had been quite some time since Meghan had seen the group of misfits she called friends, and excitement was beginning to well inside her.

Cassie was the beauty amongst them, and most likely; she would be wearing something tight, accentuating her large breasts and tiny waist. Meghan giggled as she made the comparison to a walking Barbie doll.

Unfortunately, for Cassie, her appearance left her with few girl friends. Meghan, however, could see past Cassie's outer beauty and found a great friend in her. Pete was the stabilizer of the troop and had a great many friends. Most of them computer geeks and number junkies, and he always seemed to be out, making it hard to keep in touch with him. Meghan decided that at that moment, he was most likely checking his watch every five minutes, annoyed that she was once again late. The creases on his forehead would be evident, as he looked from his watch to the door, totally ignoring Cassie as she, ten to one odds, flirted with the waiter. Pete had a methodical mind and found Meghan's "fly by the seat of her pants" attitude trying. Nevertheless, she loved him. Nathan, no doubt, had not yet arrived since he was always more tardy than Meghan. There is Pacific time, standard time, mountain time, and Nathan time. Meghan giggled as the thought occurred to her.

The tall, dark-haired man was quite enthralled with Meghan's facial expressions as she leaned against the counter. What thoughts were entertaining her, bringing her so much joy?

"Excuse me?" Eliza stopped directly in front of him. "I'm Eliza." Her dark blue eyes scanned the chiselled face. She did not realize he would be so handsome.

The man eyed her shortly. "Nice to meet you." He sounded disinterested, his gaze switching back towards Meghan.

Eliza sensed his apathy. "You wouldn't happen to be Liam?"

"No." His response was quick. "I think y' have me confused with someone else." He turned slightly away from her.

"Oh, terribly sorry," Eliza muttered and turned to leave.

"But there might be something y' can help me with." The man's hand landed on her arm.

Eliza turned and eyed his large hand gripping her arm. "What would that be?"

"That girl y' were talking to when y' came in. Do y' know her?" His eyes raked Meghan's body, the soft curves of her hip and breast torturing his mind. She was the most beautiful woman he had ever seen, and that awareness intrigued him.

Eliza eyed him with concern. What was his interest in Meghan? "Yes."

"What's her name and is she married?" The man blurted out before he could stop himself.

"I think you need to ask her that." Eliza pulled her arm from his hand. "It's not my place to give out any of her information to a total stranger." Eliza quickly glided down the hall towards her room to await her companions.

The man scowled at Eliza, but when he noticed Meghan passing by him, his breath caught in his throat, and his heart raced with adrenaline. His eyes narrowed slightly when she did notice him, but they never left her until she disappeared into the dining room.

Meghan eagerly glanced around the enchanting dining room. It was as marvellous as the lobby, large but still maintained a rustic charm. Pale cream tablecloths covered the tables, and the centrepieces were a mixture of dried flowers and evergreen boughs with a cream pillar candle in the centre.

Gleaming pale oak floors and the multitude of old oak hutches scattered around the room gave it the appearance of a large country kitchen. White wooden shutters on the windows were open slightly to allow the soft morning sun to spill into the room. The scent of vanilla floated through the air, overpowering the scent of brewing coffee. Nonetheless, Meghan's nose detected the aroma, causing her nerves to settle inadvertently.

Meghan anxiously scanned the tables, searching for her friends before a loud scream of excitement came from across the room. Cassie jumped from the table causing her long blonde hair to fly up around her narrow face.

"Meghan!" Her voice was loud and cheerful. "We're over here!"

Meghan and Cassie had met in high school when Cassie took an instant liking to the tall gawky girl with the long auburn hair. Meghan reminded her of Pippy Longstockings, with her braided hair and her freckled nose. Meghan found that comparison less flattering than Cassie had intended, nonetheless, their friendship blossomed.

"Meg, I'm so glad you came. You seemed so uncertain whether you were going to make it." A large toothy smile filled Cassie's narrow face, and her arms swung around Meghan in greeting.

"Bad roads?" A loud voice spoke up from behind Cassie. "Between you and Nat, I will grow old, waiting." A grin twisted Pete's thin lips as he swept a hand across his balding head, the short hairs, still present, bouncing back into place with rebellion. "But I'm glad you came."

5

Meghan laughed with pleasure and flew into Pete's welcoming arms. He was one of the most decent men she had ever known, and she valued her friendship with him and his wife, Marlene. Oddly enough, Meghan had first met Marlene when they sat next to each other in a biology course during her first semester at university. When Pete and Meghan met, they became fast friends, and even though Marlene dropped out when she had their second child, their friendship endured.

"So you decided to grace us with your presence, did you?" Pete joked, gripping her around the waist and holding her hostage to his lean chest.

Meghan laughed at his comment remembering how funny he could be. "Well, someone had to bring some class to this party, now didn't they? Hey, where's Marlene?"

"She had to stay home with the girls. Rebecca is sick, and we did not want to leave her with a sitter for a week when she is not feeling well. A wild five-year old and a sick dramatic nine-year-old are a handful." Pete's mouth twisted wryly. "So you're stuck with me."

"Oh, that's too bad. I was looking forward to seeing her," Meghan commented with slight disappointment but could not control the smile curling her lips. "But you'll do."

Pete smiled and looked over at Cassie as she glanced around the room. "I sure hope that this next baby is a boy. I am surrounded by girls."

Meghan giggled and took a sip of her coffee that a scowling young woman had poured for her while they were talking. "You always have, Nat."

Pete shot her an amused gaze before his slanted blue eyes settled on something across the room. "I don't suppose that this will make your day, but guess who else is here." He bobbed his head towards the tall, slim blonde woman sauntering across the dining room.

"Kaye is here? Why did you invite her?" Meghan whispered fiercely towards Cassie, her eyes narrowing with agitation. It should not have surprised Meghan that Cassie would have invited her cousin. Their mothers were sisters, and the pair had grown up spending every summer together and most of the other school holidays. Unfortunately, Meghan had an ongoing hatred for Kaye since university. Kaye was constantly luring Meghan's boyfriends into bed, and she was at a loss as to why Kaye constantly made everyone Meghan dated her target.

"Relax, Meg, I'm sure she has changed a lot in the past few years. The baby seems to have anchored her. Besides, you're single at the moment, so you have no worries," Cassie smiled sweetly, glancing at Kaye as she dashed out into the lobby.

"Lucky me!" Meghan said with a forced smile, happy that Kaye seemed uninterested in joining them for breakfast.

"Did Kaye bring Ayden with her?" Pete questioned, glancing over at Cassie.

"No, he lives with his father. Kaye's career is so busy, and she does not have time for him. It's a shame," Cassie sighed.

"Kaye is modelling in Paris. I saw her on one of those fashion channels." Pete appeared to be rather star-struck with Kaye.

"Yes, I know. I ran into her at a party last month," Meghan remarked blandly, she was uninterested in Kay's life.

Before Pete could give them any more tidbits of Kaye's life, the waiter bounced over to take their order. The amiable young man's blue eyes settled on Cassie.

"I would like eggs Benedict, please," Meghan said softly, unsure if she could get the waiter's attention off Cassie long enough to place her order. Men rarely noticed her with Cassie around. She wished she had Cassie's ability to flirt; maybe she would not have such a hard time dealing with men.

"Meg, are you listening to me?" Cassie questioned, staring across the table at Meghan who was in quiet thought.

"Pardon?" Meghan asked, refocusing on the conversation that had started up once the waiter left the table.

"I asked how your residency was going." Annoyance slightly edged Cassie's voice. It drove her crazy when Meghan withdrew into herself in thought and did not pay attention to her.

"Great, I am working in paediatrics right now. I love working with the children." Meghan smiled at her accomplishment: a doctor, who would have thought?

A loud crash across the room interrupted their conversation when a flustered young waitress knocked over a tray of empty glasses. She seemed distracted by something out in the lobby, and a few of the guests stood and moved towards the entrance for a better look at the cause of her clumsiness.

A short, slender waitress hurried by the table, her acne blotched face aglow with excitement, Pete caught her attention. "What's all the commotion out there?" he questioned, looking towards the entrance and the giggling girls that had gathered.

"Oh, it's Colton Barrett and Declan Montgomery. They're here filming a movie, and they're staying here at the lodge." The waitress's voice crackled with excitement as she tried to appear unfazed by the famous guests.

"Declan Montgomery?" Cassie exclaimed. "How can you stay so calm, he's gorgeous?"

The waitress hurried away, and Cassie jumped to her feet to catch a glimpse of the two men.

"I don't mean to seem dense, Cass, but who is Declan Montgomery?" Meghan questioned as she watched her friend's face fill with anticipation.

"You don't know who Declan Montgomery is?" Cassie asked in amazement.

"I haven't got a clue," Meghan confessed with a self-conscious grin. Her eyes scanned the entrance for a view of the men. "I've seen some movies with Colton Barrett but not the other guy."

"He's the hottest thing in Hollywood right now. He's in that new movie, *The Trial's End*." Cassie babbled with excitement as she sat back down in her chair.

"They say he's the next Harrison Ford," Pete continued, glad that he had read the Hollywood magazine on his flight. "Marlene loves him."

"What's wrong with the Harrison Ford we have now? No one can replace him!" Meghan stated with an impish grin curling her lips. She glanced towards Cassie and could not help but giggle at Cassie's facial expression. Cassie was still so star-struck.

"Marlene is going to be so choked that she didn't come," Pete laughed and took a sip of his orange juice. "She knows everything about him. I bet she could tell you what he eats for breakfast."

Within minutes, the crowd settled, and the waiter was back with their breakfasts. He seemed unfazed by the presence of the two men in the lobby.

"Is Declan Montgomery here at the lodge quite often?" Cassie asked, still fascinated by the famous guest.

"Yes, they come and go. We are very isolated, and this lodge gives them easy access to the mountain where they are filming. Maybe you will run into him around here somewhere." The waiter said evenly. "Not that he'll talk to you, though, he's pretty arrogant."

"Oh, I thought he was supposed to be nice?" Cassie questioned, an expression of disappointment crossing her face.

"Well, he's not rude, but he just doesn't seem interested in talking to anyone that's not involved in the movie," The waiter explained and then turned towards a table with an older woman waving her arm wildly at him.

"Well, I guess you're out of luck, Cass," Pete laughed as he watched the waiter disappear from the table. Meghan giggled and threw Cassie a consoling glance before her eyes settled on the extremely thin blonde woman that had arrived at their table.

"You will never believe who I just saw in the lobby!" Kaye blurted out rudely.

"Let me guess!" Pete grinned tauntingly. "Declan Montgomery and Colton Barrett!"

"Yes, how did you know?" Kaye asked, raising her ring-clad eyebrow, and then waved her hand dismissing him. "Well, I'm going to make that gorgeous man mine this week," she commented in a very confident voice, brushing back her platinum blonde hair and smirking at Meghan.

"Which one? Or both?" Pete laughed and slightly chocked on the piece of bacon he had in his mouth.

"Declan Montgomery of course, I've already had Colton," Kaye responded with a tone of annoyance.

Cassie scowled and handed Meghan a strawberry from her plate. "Get in line, Kaye."

Kaye shot her an irritated look and sat down in the empty chair next to Meghan. "Well, Meghan, I hear you and Ian broke up. He's very upset," Kaye said smugly, resting her narrow hand on the table and flashing party invitations.

"We were never dating, he's stalking me," Meghan grumbled, annoyed that Kaye was interfering into her life by pushing Ian on her. "You didn't tell him I was coming up here, did you?"

"No, why would I? I give little thought to you, Meghan." Kaye's brow rose slightly, then she waved the invitations towards Cassie.

"Aren't you going to ask what these are? You're going to be indebted to your dear cousin forever."

Cassie leaned towards the table to see what Kaye was so determined to show her. "Oh my God!" she blurted out, eyeing the cast party invitations. "How did you get those?"

"Colton, of course, I guess he thinks we're going to hook up again. I even got one for you, Meghan," Kaye said smugly.

Meghan cringed, fighting the urge to tell Kaye where she could shove her invitations, but she really wanted to go to the party to meet Colton Barrett.

Kaye's attention broke when the large old grandfather clock in the corner of the dining room reverberated out the eleven chimes announcing the hour.

"Well, I must be off." With no more explanation, Kaye left the table with the same flamboyant air she arrived.

Meghan was exhausted after her long bus ride, so she excused herself and headed for her room to have a much-needed nap. As she ascended the stairs from the dining room, she noticed her waiter waving at her from the hostess station.

"Have a great day." A smile filled the young waiter's warm face as he continued to overzealously wave at her.

"Thanks, you too," Meghan replied and gave one last wave. She giggled to herself, turned towards the lobby desk and crashed into a large man in her path. Her hands flew up to protect herself, and they landed firmly on his broad chest with quite a force. "Excuse me!" she blurted out as she tried to steady herself.

"I should say so." His voice was deep and edged with arrogance, the Irish lilt very evident.

A slight gasp escaped Meghan's mouth as she gazed up at the handsome chiselled face, dusted with a few days of black beard growth. His haunting grey eyes had an expression of aloofness, which caused her unease.

"Sorry," Meghan blurted out, lowered her gaze, and began to back away. However, his hands stayed firmly on her hips, holding her in place. A slight smirk twisted his full lips when Meghan's face began to flush into a deep pink.

"Y' should really be more careful. Y' could have damaged me," he smirked and tightened his grip on her hips.

"Sorry, but you obviously weren't watching either," Meghan mumbled weakly before a loud voice down the hall broke her comment.

"Monty," the tall dark-haired man hollered and gestured towards them, "come on, we're going to be late."

"Aye, I'm coming." The handsome man broke his gaze on Meghan and glanced at the man down the hall. When his grey gaze settled back on Meghan, a smile curled his lips causing a long dimple to appear on his left cheek, giving him a very boyish appeal. "I think that y' should be offering to take me for a drink tonight to apologize." His voice was firm and quite demanding.

"I'm sorry I can't, I have plans," Meghan muttered and backed away from him, worry filling her eyes.

"Oh." No woman had ever turned down an invitation from him before. She must have not heard him. "I think y' misunderstood me. I'm asking y' to have a drink with me tonight."

"I didn't misunderstand!" Meghan replied sharply, annoyed at the arrogance that surrounded him. "I have plans."

He grabbed her left hand and glanced down at her bare knuckles. "Y' don't seem to be wearing a ring, so what could be more important than spending time with me?"

Meghan glowered at him; her dark green eyes were flaring like molten flames. "Spending time with my friends!" Her voice was cold and harsh. "And you are definitely no friend of mine."

His brow rose slightly, and it took every ounce of restraint he had not to smile. Her eyes were so magnificent when she flared. Who was this woman who had the nerve to talk to him in such a way? Who would reject an offer for an evening with him? She was not going to get away so easily now that she struck his ego. In his mind, she had set the challenge, and he was up to the task. He would have her, no matter what it took.

"Y' have a sharp tongue, Freckles, but I don't mind." His grin was far too smug for her, and she opened her mouth to speak, but he rested his finger across her lips. "And a good friend I'll be to y', I will guarantee that." His finger brushed across her lips to her cheek before he removed his hand from her skin. "Aye, you'll see."

As he sauntered towards the door, he glanced over his shoulder at Meghan who still watched him intently. Her dark blue jeans and tight red sweater accentuated her curvaceous figure, capturing his attention. He stopped and turned back towards her. "I'll be seeing y' again," He smiled, his eyes scanning her body with interest. "You're mighty tall, a beautiful Amazon."

Meghan's brows crumpled with annoyance, her green eyes flickering with subdued anger, not quite certain if he meant the comment as an insult or compliment. Her mouth opened, and then shut, the words not coming.

"Monty!" The deep voice spoke again. "Let's go!"

The man winked at Meghan as a smirk spread across his chiselled face, and then he turned and walked through the large wooden doors in the middle of the hall.

CHAPTER TWO

The day passed quickly while Meghan wandered the lodge, hoping to catch a glimpse of the man she had met earlier in the day. As arrogant as he was, she could not stop the overwhelming attraction she felt for him, and she could not get him out of her mind.

Meghan's mind kept wandering as she and Cassie headed for the lounge to meet Declan Montgomery and Colton Barrett. Meghan had to admit that she was excited about meeting the movie stars, but she was not as excited as Cassie, who had gone to a great deal of trouble to ensure she looked fabulous without appearing to have spent a large amount of time trying to do so. Her long blonde hair was curled and shaped softly around her narrow face, and her makeup accentuated her big blue eyes to their fullest advantage.

As the two women reached the lobby, Kaye and Pete were waiting impatiently. Cassie fussed with her short purple dress as she watched Meghan scanning the room. Her attention on Meghan was short-lived, however, since she was too anxious to meet Declan to worry about what Meghan was doing at that moment.

Nathan's familiar laugh filled the room as he tormented the woman at the lobby desk, and Meghan turned towards the ruckus and eyed him with pleasure. He had not changed a bit; he was big and loud. His russet hair was long and tied back into a ponytail, and he had grown a goatee since she had last seen him. The faded blue jeans and black leather jacket that concealed a dark blue button-up shirt appeared to be identical to his attire in college. In addition, coming as no surprise to anyone, he still adorned his customary scuffed cowboy boots and the large silver buckle on his belt. Nathan joined the group of friends in their second year at university. He was law student that spent more time in the pub than in class. His law career predominantly focused on pro-bono cases in Dallas. He believed strongly that the underdogs needed protection.

"Hey, you losers, you still can't function without me, so here you all are standing around waiting for me!" he hollered, his voice booming throughout the room.

"I see you are still as conceited as ever," Pete laughed, his narrow frame shaking with humour.

"Yeah, I'm still the man!" The large man laughed and sauntered across the room, appearing to be a member of a renegade motorcycle gang.

"Nat, couldn't you clean up for the occasion, you look like a biker," Cassie joked as she eyed his attire.

"All part of my charm, darlin'. My clients love it. They don't feel intimidated by a lawyer that looks like them," he joked and yanked at the waistband of his jeans, slightly hidden by a small paunch.

"You defend bikers?" Cassie questioned, her narrow blonde brow rising slightly.

"Yeah, drug-dealing bikers, horse thieves, pretty much any riffraff that comes along!" he joked, embracing Cassie in a bear hug.

"Only drug-dealing bikers?" Pete questioned, trying to rile Nathan.

"Well, the clean ones don't need defending," Nathan laughed as he glanced over at Meghan, who was off to the side of the group.

"So, Megs, you came," Nathan chuckled, his brown eyes shimmering at the sight of her. He scooped her into his arms and spun her in a circle. "Fantastic."

Meghan's attention quickly switched to Kaye's annoyed voice. "Good you're all here. We are wasting time!"

"Yes, we are," Cassie blurted out, anxious to get into the party. She had always been star-struck and would fill Meghan's nights at the private Beverly Hills Boarding School they attended with stories of whom she had seen or talked to that day.

Kaye forced her way to the front of the group, knocking Cassie backwards towards Meghan. Cassie grunted with annoyance and then squeezed in-between Nathan and Pete; she was as determined as Kaye was to meet Declan.

Kaye slithered towards the tall, dark-haired man and caressed her very thin torso seductively. The dark blue sweater clung to her body like a second skin, and her micro mini skirt revealed her long reedy legs, one of which she had pressed up against Declan's thigh. "Oh hello, Declan, it's great to see you again."

"Oh my God!" Cassie muttered, completely annoyed that Kaye would be so overt. She was also hoping to capture the man's attention, but with Kaye clinging to him, that seemed impossible. "You are unbelievable, Kaye!"

As Kaye pressed her body against Declan, he backed away slightly, before a large ruggedly handsome man, with dark brown hair and mocha eyes, appeared from behind him. Fabrizio's large hand gripped Kaye by the arm and hauled her away from Declan.

"I'm sorry, do I know y'?" Declan raised his brow in annoyance.

"Yes, we met this morning!" Kaye glanced at Cassie, before regaining her composure. "Colton introduced us."

"That's right. Sorry, Colton introduces me to so many women." Declan's voice mirrored the disinterest in his eyes.

"Hi, I'm Cassie." She reached out her hand to him.

Declan eyed her with interest, and then took her out stretched hand. "It's nice to meet y'." His eyes raked her slim build.

Cassie smiled smugly, knowing she had taken his interest from Kaye. Actually, he did not appear interested in Kaye in the least.

Cassie managed to get a few suggestive compliments in before Declan's attention abruptly shifted from her to Meghan. She was standing just inside the doors, gazing out into the lobby, her exquisite auburn hair swaying slightly as she moved her head from side to side. His breath caught in his throat when Nathan moved towards Meghan, gripped her around the waist, and tugged her towards the group and him. The short, black flowing skirt she wore revealed her long slender legs and sent waves of desire through his entire body.

"Nat, stop it!" Meghan giggled and took a swing at his head. "I am looking for someone."

"Who?" Nathan pressed his face against her cheek.

"Nobody." Meghan turned in his arms, resting her hands on his chest. "Just someone I met today."

Nathan's brow rose slightly. "Man or woman?"

"Man," Meghan smiled and kissed Nathan's cheek. "Stay close to me tonight. I might need you later to keep Kaye occupied."

Declan could only make out bits and pieces of what she was saying, but he did hear that she was looking for someone she had met that day. Could it be him? She must have known whom she was meeting.

Nathan grinned and released her. "It will be my pleasure, darlin', but I don't think Kaye will be interested in your new man, she seems to have found one of her own." Nathan bobbed his head towards the group.

When Meghan lifted her eyes towards Declan, she gasped, as the breath emptied from her body. Her mouth was slightly ajar, causing her bottom lip to appear somewhat sultry just right for kissing, Declan thought. He fought the urge to grab her and kiss her until she collapsed into him with breathless pleasure. Declan's smile was uncontrollable, and his eyes glimmered with excitement. He had thought about her since he left her in the lobby that morning.

"Yo, that's her, the girl from the lobby," Fabrizio blurted out, smacking Declan on the shoulder.

"You're not going to hit me again, are y', Freckles?" A slight grin crossed Declan's face, and his hand stroked the spot on his chest where Meghan's hands had landed earlier.

"I just might," Meghan said abruptly, taking a step away from him, her eyes caught in the dark grey gaze.

Declan's laughter filled the area, causing the little group to stare bewilderedly at Meghan.

"I see you're still cross with me," Declan's voice was surprisingly playful. "Well, I'm sure your friends here . . ." His emphasis on the word friends made her cringe. "I'm sure they will attest to my acceptability. Seeing is how y' are very particular who y' keep company with."

Meghan was slightly embarrassed at the direction the conversation was heading. Her big mouth always got her into difficult situations. Now, she was in a battle of egos with a man that apparently every woman in the world would give up their firstborn to spend time with, Cassie included. Meghan eyed her shocked friends, and then turned her gaze back to the smug man. She could not back down now since he had just made the next move.

"I'm sure that your acceptability with my friends has more to do with what you are than who you are." Meghan forced calmness into her voice.

"Are y' saying that if I wasn't an actor, y' wouldn't find me attractive?" Declan pushed, unconcerned with Kaye's growing agitation at his side. "I have a proposition for y'. Y' agree to allow me the honour of buying y' a drink, and I'll try hard not to get under your skin."

"Declan, I don't understand what the problem is, have you two met before?" Kaye grumbled, anxious to decipher the bantering between Meghan and Declan.

"There's no problem, we are just ribbing each other," Declan blurted out, noticing the distress on Meghan's face and the anxiety clouding the beautiful green eyes. "All in good fun." Declan gripped her hand lifting it to his lips. "You have a quick wit, Freckles, I like that."

Every instinct Declan had told him that Meghan was interested in him, even though she was displaying a strong aversion towards him. Had he scared her that morning, or did he intimidate her? No, she did not seem to have any recognition of him that morning, and she appeared shocked moments earlier when she put the name to the face. He watched her back up towards Cassie and the door, and he panicked, he did not want her to leave. Why was she leaving?

"And where do y' think y' are going, Freckles?" Declan blurted out, jumping towards her and gripping her by the slender arm.

Meghan, startled at his sudden movement, "Nowhere," she blurted out, not sure what to say to him.

"I thought you promised to have a drink with me." Declan forced his most alluring smile.

"Well, I . . ." Meghan babbled, her gaze switching from Declan to Cassie, who was glaring at her.

"What the hell is wrong with you?" Cassie blurted out with annoyance.

"I'll have a drink with you," Kaye intervened and gripped Declan's arm, trying to dislodge his hand from Meghan's wrist.

"Are y' forfeiting the offer?" His eyes settled on Meghan. She had the most amazing eyes he had ever seen, big and expressive and fixed on him with a slight expression of curiosity shadowing them.

"What is going on, Meg? Is he the guy you met this morning?" Cassie whispered, her gaze switching from Declan to Meghan.

"Yes," Meghan whispered back, her knees beginning to tremble with excitement.

"Oh my God!" Cassie blurted out, directing her gaze back on Declan. He was watching curiously as the women whispered.

"Last chance." Declan released her arm and turned towards Kaye.

"I'm going to go sit with Nat. I haven't seen him in a long time, and I want to visit with him for a while," Meghan babbled, her eyes settling on Pete and Nat, who had started a game of pool. She did not want to get into a battle with Kaye over him, knowing Kaye would end up winning. Meghan forced a smile, then slid past Cassie towards Fabrizio, who was watching her with interest. "Excuse me," she muttered and brushed up against Declan to get past him and over to Nathan.

Declan, however, did not move, forcing her to squeeze in-between him and Fabrizio. Her eyes fluttered nervously as she squished through the cramped space. When Meghan got between the two men, Declan moved his foot slightly, causing her to stumble into Fabrizio. Unprepared for the collision, the beer in Fabrizio's hand smashed to the floor, spraying most of the people within a two-foot radius. Before she caught her footing, Declan had hold of her around the waist, and Fabrizio was clinging to her back to keep her from falling.

"Dammit, Meghan, what the hell are you doing?" Kaye snorted. "Look at my skirt, it's covered in beer. You're like a bull in a china shop."

Declan's brow rose with humour as he watched her face filling with embarrassment. "I'm so sorry," Declan laughed. He doubled over, still clinging to her, causing her to sway with him. "I . . ." He could not finish what he was saying as he gasped for breath.

Meghan's face filled with distress, her eyes sharp green. She broke Declan's gaze and glanced at Fabrizio, who had crouched down and was picking up the broken pieces of his bottle.

"I'm sorry," Meghan muttered. She pulled loose from Declan and squatted down to assist Fabrizio in the cleanup. "I tripped."

"No, sweetheart, you were tripped," Fabrizio grunted and glanced up at Declan's amused face. "Don't touch that, you're going to cut yourself," He ordered, noticing the agitation building in her.

"No, I made the mess." Meghan's mind was spinning as she tried to understand why Declan would have tripped her. Why embarrass her in front of everyone in the bar? Anger was brewing, and unfortunately, she gripped a jagged piece of the bottle a little too tightly. "Ouch!" she blurted out and dropped the glass shard to the floor.

"Leave that be, the cleaning staff can handle it," Declan grunted as his arm snaked around her waist from behind. He lifted her to her feet and away from the glass. "Let me see that?" He turned her towards him and gripped her finger, examining the cut. "Y' will need a bandage on this." Regret replaced the humour in his eyes as they settled on her. Unfortunately, he did not miss the expression in her eyes. Anger and humiliation were tangling together fighting for superiority. "I'm really sorry."

"It's fine," Meghan said softly, pulling her hand from Declan's grip. She turned towards Cassie who was also watching, unsure what had just happened.

"Meg, come with me, we'll get a bandage from the bartender," Cassie blurted out, making a move towards Meghan.

Meghan nodded and took a step back away from Declan and rested her hand on Fabrizio's arm. "Sorry about the beer, I'll buy you another one."

Fabrizio smiled and rested his hand on hers. "Don't worry, sweetheart. He caused it, he can replace it." He bobbed his head towards Declan.

"Well, just let me know if you change your mind," Meghan smiled and stepped through the opening that was now between Declan and Fabrizio.

"What the hell was that about?" Fabrizio grunted after he ordered a new beer from the waitress.

"I could be asking y' the same question. Don't worry, sweetheart?" Declan's brow rose slightly. "Why were y' making moves on her?"

"I wasn't," Fabrizio snorted and glanced over at Meghan as she made her way across the room. "I just felt that someone should show her that all men aren't jerks."

Declan, startled by the comment, glanced at her departing back. "Is that what she thinks of me?"

"Well, she certainly isn't thinking you're a nice guy. Why did you trip her?"

Declan's shoulders rose in a shrug. "I wanted her to fall into me again." A slight grin curled his lips as he thought about her hands on his chest and her warm sweet breath on his face. "I just wanted to hold her again."

"You're a warped man, has anyone ever told you that? You embarrassed her in front of her friends. If she ever talks to you again, I'll be surprised."

"She will." A smile twisted Declan's lips. "She loves me, she just doesn't know it yet."

"You're unbelievable." Fabrizio shook his head and wandered away as he noticed a group of women eyeing Declan with desire. He chuckled when it occurred to him that with the entire female population in the bar after him, Declan chose the one woman that appeared to hate him.

The lounge was small with no more than twenty tables spread throughout the room. The long bar on the far wall was the focal point of the room and off to the right was a large fireplace surrounded by couches. A small dance floor was sandwiched between the pool tables, and a few tables were tucked up in the back corner next to the bar.

The mixture of perfume and cooking grease filled Meghan's nose as she manoeuvred her way through the mass of people that watched her as she passed. Apparently, most of the guests noticed the kafuffle moments earlier.

"I hate it when people stare at me," Meghan whispered to Cassie, who was now at her side.

Cassie's brow rose slightly as they reached the counter. Congested with people down the entire length, Cassie struggled to manoeuvre them in-between two groups of women. One woman glanced over her shoulder, her eyes resting on Meghan with interest. Meghan smiled pleasantly, but the woman turned her head and re-entered the conversation with her companions.

"Well, you seem to have annoyed a good percentage of the women in here," Cassie blurted out with a slight laugh. "It's nice not to be the one the women hate for a change."

Meghan scowled and glanced over at Declan as he leaned against the bar counter a few feet away. His eyes were set on her. "That guy is unbelievable."

"Who? Declan?" Cassie questioned, glancing in the direction Meghan was staring. "I can't believe he teased you like that."

Meghan nodded and lowered her eyes to the counter top. Her finger traced out one of the long dents made by people slamming the bottles into the hard wood. "Why can't every man be like Nat?"

Meghan sighed and glanced over towards Nathan and his harem of women.

Cassie giggled as she finished attaching the bandage to Meghan's finger. "Women love Nat so much because he is one."

"Cass!" Meghan grumbled. "Why must you say things like that about him? He's gay, he's not a woman."

Cassie smiled with apology, and the knowledge, that he did have a feminine side to him, which allowed him to understand how women felt. From all outer appearances, he was the portrait of a cowboy. His upbringing on a large horse ranch in southern Texas showed strongly in his demeanour. Nathan was in his late twenties and had never told anyone in his family of his preference for men. He assumed his dad would disown him and his poor mother, the deeply Baptist woman she was, would feel the devil possessed him.

"Meg, let's go play pool, Colton Barrett is over there," Cassie suggested, spotting the very handsome blond man over at the pool table next to where Nathan and Pete were playing. Apparently, she had no chance with Declan. "If I don't hurry up, Nathan might snag him. Sorry." She amended after noticing the look of disapproval cross Meghan's face. "Shit, you're grumpy today. Normally you would have found that funny."

"I'm sorry; I'm just not in the best of moods right now. I think I might sneak out," Meghan said softly, glancing over at Declan who was still staring at her. "I'm just going to finish my cooler and leave?"

"All right," Cassie agreed. "But don't you want to see what he is up to now." She bobbed her head towards Declan as he approached, a smug expression crossing his face.

His advance was cautious, he was unsure if Meghan was angry with him or not. He had not meant to embarrass her. All he wanted to do was to hold her, but his plan backfired. It never occurred to him that she would turn down his offer to buy her a drink, not once but twice.

"Hi," Declan said nervously. "May I talk with y' for a moment?"

Meghan looked up at his handsome face and felt her body melt, but luckily, the bar was supporting her. "I guess so," she mumbled quietly. She eyed him apprehensively, then switched her gaze to Cassie.

"Can we start over?" he questioned, lifting his hand out towards her, his palm up and inviting.

Meghan eyed him with distrust and did not take his hand. "What is it you want?"

Cassie gasped at the insolent tone Meghan had used and backed away from them. "Excuse me," she blurted out and disappeared into the crowd.

Meghan shook her head and scowled at her departing back, then forced her gaze back to Declan and his incredible eyes.

"Did I scare her off?" Declan moved in beside Meghan and leaned against the bar. His hand brushed against her arm, the feel of her was intoxicating. He was fighting the urge to surround her in his arms and kiss her with abandon.

"No, I think it was me," Meghan admitted, holding back the smile that was trying to escape. "She said I'm being grumpy today."

"Are y'?" Declan chuckled and tapped the end of her nose. "I only ask because I'm trying to decide if I'm as big a jerk as y' think I am or if it's just that you're grumpy."

Meghan giggled and took a nervous sip of her cooler. "I guess I am. I've had a bad week."

"I certainly didn't make it any better, did I?" He rested his hand on hers as she traced out the dents in the counter top. "I didn't hurt y' this morning, did I?"

"No, I was just startled, that's all." Meghan's smile was uncomfortable. She was fighting the urge to pull her hand away from his. Her heart was racing with excitement, and she was painfully aware that her face was flushing with colour. She suddenly dropped her gaze, and her loose hand began to pick nervously at the label on the bottle in front of her.

"I have to admit I saw y' talking to the waiter, I just didn't expect y' to turn around so quickly," Declan confessed, a grin forming on his chiselled face. His mind was reeling from the feel of her hand under his, her skin was soft and warm, and the slight trembling was driving him to the edge.

"Oh."

His soft deep voice was lulling her into a daze that she had never experienced before. His damn eyes, she was unable to break his gaze. This could not happen. She could not let herself feel this way, especially with a total stranger.

"I upset y', and I'm sorry. I wasn't trying to trip you." An impish grin curled his full lips as she forced an uneasy smile. "Ah well, that's a lie." His hand tightened over hers when she tried to pull away. "I wasn't trying to hurt y', I just wanted you to, well, has anyone ever told y' that y' have gorgeous eyes?"

A smile spread across her lips at his inept apology. "Not lately, but thank you."

Declan nodded with acceptance, then glanced around the room as if looking for something. "I guess I should introduce meself properly. I'm Declan Montgomery."

Meghan smiled softly and held his gaze. "I'm Meghan Delaney."

"It's a pleasure to make your acquaintance, Meggie. So this was your big plans for tonight?"

"Well, yes," Meghan smiled smugly as she watched his eyes filling with confusion. She could play games too, and if he were determined to keep her on edge, she would at least keep him confused.

"Oh, and y' didn't figure I'd be here?" A slight smirk crossed Declan's lips. The disbelief that it was a surprise to her that he was there, showing strong in his eyes.

"No, not a clue." Her voice was cool and somewhat disinterested. She had had enough of him and his condescending tones, and all she wanted to do was to retreat to her room and escape his piercing eyes. "Well, it's been nice meeting you, but . . ."

"Brushing me off again?" His voice seemed slight annoyed.

"No, I . . ." She paused as he released her hand, resting his only inches away.

His head turned, and he glanced around the room, his eyes searching for something. "I suppose I could go cozy up to those lovely ladies over there." His head bobbed in the direction of a table full of gawking women.

"Go ahead." With forced calmness, Meghan waved her hand out to her side daring him to go. "I won't stop you."

His brow rose slightly, her words and her face were telling two different stories. "Ah well, if I walk all the way over there . . ." his voice lowered and his eyes settled on Kaye who was quickly approaching them. "Then I'll have to pass by that woman, and I really don't want to talk to her again."

"Really?" Meghan sighed, hoping for disinterest. "Then go around that way."

His grin widened into a smile, causing the dimple to appear down the side of his face. "You're a terrible liar, y' are."

Meghan crinkled her nose and turned her head away, slightly annoyed that he could read her so easily. Damn man! She forced calmness back into her demeanour, then forced her eyes back to his. "I'm sure you are a very nice guy, but I'm really not interested . . ." She stopped when he choked on his beer.

He threw his head back and laughed loudly, drawing the attention of the women right next to them.

"Come, dance with me." He pushed through his laughter, trying to avoid the curious looks from the women. "No interest in me needed. I just don't want to talk to her again." His head bobbed towards Kaye.

"I'd rather not," Meghan grumbled on her way to the dance floor.

"Well, that's of little consequence to me at the moment, since I have y' in my arms."

"I suppose you don't care what I want," Meghan grunted, glancing over at Cassie, who was standing by the pool table, watching them.

"I care," he jerked her towards him, crushing her up against his chest. "As long as it benefits me, and right now, having y' pressed up against me like this definitely benefits me."

"Do you always get what you want?" Meghan grumbled but fell into step with him.

"Aye," he smiled and pressed his face against hers. "I think this makes up for crashing into me," he whispered into her ear. His breath was warm as his soft lips brushed against her skin.

She smiled nervously but said nothing. The slow beat of the music was thumping through her, offsetting the fast rate her heart was beating. Being so close to him was causing her to quiver with excitement. Everything from the feel of him under her hand to the scent of him; his musky cologne was strong and fragrant in her nose.

"Your hair smells lovely," he commented evenly. "It smells like kiwi."

Meghan giggled slightly that he was thinking the same thing as her, but as she gazed into the deep grey eyes, she lost any form of speech she had.

"Why are y' so quiet all of a sudden?" Declan questioned, pressing his face up against hers. "I won't bite y'. Well, not unless y' want me to."

A loud laugh exited Meghan at his comment, and she began to stumble as he swept her around the floor. He pulled her tightly against his chest until she caught her footing, the smooth rhythm returning.

"Do you ever say anything serious?" she questioned.

"Not if I can help it," Declan smirked, coming to a stop in the middle of the dance floor as the song ended. "Well, I've had me one dance." He released her and bowed mockingly towards the counter. "May I escort y' back to your stool?"

"Yes." She giggled and took his bent arm.

"So how about that drink? Would y' care to join me for Guinness?" Declan waved towards the bartender.

"My grandpa drank that all the time, but I never developed much of a taste for it." Meghan eyed the bartender pouring the first pint. The precision in which he poured the dark ale was remarkable, slowly allowing the slanted glass to fill and then he set it upright until the perfect head formed; it was a perfect work of art.

"He has poured a grand pint," Declan smiled and handed the glass to Meghan.

Meghan crinkled her nose but did not argue. She had learned early in life that you do not insult an Irishman by refusing a pint of Guinness. The taste of the thick malt made her quiver, but she managed to swallow a couple sips before Declan received his own pint.

"Brilliant," he smiled and clinked his glass against hers. "Sláinte!"

Meghan giggled and repeated the cheer. This man could be her grandfather's twin, a younger twin, mind you.

Declan's smile quickly faded when Kaye shoved her narrow frame right up against him. "I thought you were buying me a drink, Declan."

Declan eyed Meghan's anxious expression. "Meggie never forfeited the offer I made to her, so the offer never transferred to y'."

"Is that so?" Kaye was annoyed that he was attracted to Meghan, but he would not be for long. "Oh, Meghan, I almost forgot to tell you," Kaye smirked as she slid in beside Declan, dislodging a young girl from her stool. "I was visiting my cousin Deirdre, and I asked her about that locket of yours that you claim is an heirloom."

"Did you?" Meghan muttered with a scowl developing on her normally pleasant face.

"Deirdre and my friend Liam said that it is probably nothing of any historical value." Kaye's eyes settled on Declan.

Declan turned to Kaye with a questioning gaze.

"How could he make an evaluation without seeing the locket?" Meghan grumbled at Kaye's attack of her locket's history. She wanted to believe her grandfather when he told her that the locket was the key to her past.

"The O'Briens are very prominent in Ireland, and Deirdre is a historian, and they both think that the locket is nothing more than a replica," Kaye smirked almost cruelly.

"This Liam, do y' happen to know his da's name?" Declan questioned as the hair on the back of his neck rose.

"Fergus," she said evenly.

Declan stiffened, his face flushing with what appeared to be worry. "How do y' know that family?"

"They are old friends," Kaye said, not understanding the tone of Declan's voice.

"Hmm," Declan muttered and turned towards Meghan.

Meghan smiled softly, sensing the tension in him. "Declan, are you okay?" she questioned, resting her hand on his shoulder.

"Aye fine." He forced a smile, trying to hide his concern. "I would love to see the locket."

Meghan smiled and lifted it out from under her turtleneck sweater. "I never take it off." She held it out in her fingers.

"That's a lovely locket," Declan commented, lifting the triangle-shaped silver locket into his fingers. The solid piece of silver that was rounded on the bottom side and had a raised Celtic knot covering the majority of the surface. A pale purple quartz stone was set in the bottom right corner, carved with a Gaelic symbol of three lines, each swirling out from a point on a small triangle in the middle. His eyes settled on Meghan with interest. "So, Miss Delaney, does your family come from Ireland?" he questioned, wanting to find out more about her family.

"My grandfather did, but he was banished." Meghan giggled when Declan's brow shot up with surprise.

"Banished! What did he do?" Declan's tone sounded rather disturbed.

"I don't know, he would never tell me. All I know is that my grandma died and papa took my dad and fled to the States. My dad always joked that it must have been pretty bad to be banished from a country," Meghan smirked. "Maybe he was a famous outlaw, like Robin Hood."

A grin curled Declan's lips. "Aye, or he could have been Jack the Ripper."

Meghan scowled, looking slightly affronted and smacked him on the shoulder. "He was not! Anyway, those guys were English."

"Have y' ever been to Ireland?" Declan questioned glancing down at her hand that was still on his shoulder.

"No," Meghan murmured quietly, wondering if he was annoyed that she hit him.

"Well, y' should. Its' spectacular." Declan's smile returned, his gaze was on her. "You'd love it there."

"If everyone sounds like you, I would imagine I would." Meghan gazed up at him, but his eyes were stuck on her locket.

"Y' enjoy me accent, do y'?" he said, quietly trying to keep their conversation between them.

Her eyes lit with humour. "It's very sexy."

"Really?" He grinned at her admission. "So y' think I'm sexy?"

An unmistakable blush crossed her face, but she held her senses. "I said your accent was sexy, not you."

"Fair enough." He had no interest in provoking her further on the subject, with Kaye listening to their conversation. "So where did you get the locket?"

"My grandpa gave me this. It was my great-grandmother's." Meghan felt oddly uncomfortable with his interest in her locket. His hand was resting against her chest, the locket held between his fingers, as his eyes studying the markings.

"It's very beautiful." His brows were crumbling with obvious distress, and she was sure his hand was slightly shaking. "Meggie?"

"What?" she questioned rather startled by his facial expression.

"Have y' ever had this appraised or searched its history?"

"Why?" Her eyes rose to Kaye, who was now staring at them with definite interest.

"Me grandmother had an amulet almost identical to this, it's very old. But hers has a quartz carving of three lines instead of this one. She said it represents the male and female energy with the third one as a balance. Hers was not a locket though." He brushed him thumb across the small piece of purple quarts.

"Oh," Meghan lifted the locket from his hands and examined the marking. "I'm sure it's just a coincidence." She forced a smile as an odd sensation engulfed her. Should she tell him that Nathan was searching her family's history because he felt that her grandfather had been hiding something from her about her family's past?

"Well, y' never know," Declan muttered, not noticing her attention was elsewhere. He was still busy examining the markings. "I loved that locket."

"Did you?" Meghan chuckled as her attention returned to his softened face that was almost childlike at the thought of his grandmother.

"Aye." His eyes fixed on hers. "I played with it as a lad. I would pin it to me shirt and pretend I was a king."

Meghan started to giggle at his facial expression. "So you were quite the actor even back then."

"Aye," he laughed. "Me grandma would get cross with me for playing with her fine jewelry. She said I was a wee puff and no good would come of a boy wearing jewelry."

"Is that right?" Meghan smiled. "My dad wore an earring."

"Hmm." Declan chuckled. "She would have called him a puff."

"Well then it's a good thing those puffy men in my family passed this down to me," Meghan said, resting her hand on her locket.

"You're pathetic, Meghan, trying to pass off that ugly piece of junk as an ancient artefact. Liam said . . ." Kaye grumbled, wondering why Declan was so interested in the locket.

"Well, I don't really care what your friend thinks, Kaye, I know that it belonged to my family, and that's all that matters to me," Meghan said strongly, trying to draw Declan's attention back to her and away from Kaye and her bony hand, which was now on his shoulder.

"Well, it certainly doesn't date back to 1500s," Kaye snorted with a menacing chuckle and began rubbing Declan's shoulder.

"I never said it did." Meghan looked up at Declan, but her eyes kept inadvertently resting on Kaye's hand, which was still caressing his muscular shoulder.

"Where did y' come up with that time period?" Declan's eyes were hard and dark. Kaye knew more than she was saying. Declan jerked his shoulder dislodging Kaye's hand.

Kaye realized she had said too much, and she shrugged. "I don't know, I thought that is what Meghan claimed."

A feeling of concern filled Declan's thoughts. Was this the missing amulet? If so, was this woman the third member of the triad, Michael's line? Did Meghan know what the significance of the amulet was, or was she being honest about it just being important to her because it was an heirloom?

Declan's attention switched from Meghan to an older woman with grey-streaked hair that pushed in front of Meghan, blocking her from his view.

"I don't mean to bother you, but my daughter . . . she's right over there." The woman waved a flabby arm towards a table filled with young giggling women.

The young women were very plain in comparison to the other women in the bar, even Meghan felt ordinary in her black skirt and sweater.

"Well, she won a contest to come to this party tonight and she was told that she would get to meet you and she is very excited, so I was wondering if you could take a few minutes to come over to the table." The woman eyed Meghan and smiled nervously.

"Oh, I am terribly sorry, I wasn't told anything about that. It would be grand to meet your daughter." Declan forced interest and eyed the girls as they moved quickly towards him. "Promise me y' won't go anywhere until I'm done."

"I promise," Meghan smiled as he turned back towards the mother and young girls.

"I see you have managed to draw Declan's attention to you for now, but don't get too comfortable. I want him, and I always get what I want." Kaye brushed her hand down her ribs with the appearance of straightening her sweater. "You know very well, I can take any man away from you. You're dull, and when he realizes that, he will be mine for the taking."

"Shut up," Meghan growled and turned her back on Kaye.

"Admit it, Meghan, you can't keep your men."

"Not with a slut like you around," Meghan snarled just before Kaye's hand crashed across her face.

Meghan recoiled from the blow and stumbled backwards, gripping her burning cheek with her hand. When Meghan regained her thoughts, she slammed both hands into Kay's shoulders, sending her flying backwards.

"You bitch!" Anger shot from Kay's eyes as she lunged at Meghan and gripped her hair in her hands.

Meghan struggled and shrieked, trying to pry Kaye's bony fingers from her hair before she pulled it out by the roots. "Kaye, let go!"

"No not until you apologize." Kaye's voice was loud and forceful.

"Ladies, ladies." Declan was between them and pulling Kaye from Meghan. "As much as I love to see a good cat fight, this is not the place." Declan glanced at Meghan with a smug expression. "Y' enjoy causing trouble, don't you?"

"I didn't start this," Meghan argued and kept her eyes glued on Kaye.

"Yes, you did. You called me a slut, and you said that Declan said I was a dirty whore." Kaye lied as her eyes settled on Declan.

"I did not!" Meghan blurted out in her defence.

"Are you saying you didn't call me a slut? I bet that these women heard you." Kaye pointed to the nodding women.

"I . . . well, you are twisting my words." Meghan felt the walls closing in on her as she tried to explain what happened. Declan was eyeing her with an expression that worried her. "I didn't say Declan called you anything." Meghan eyed her accusers one last time before she turned and pushed her way through the gawking crowd.

"Meggie, wait," Declan yelled as he pushed through the crowd after her.

Meghan was already down one of the hallways, struggling with the door to her room when he emerged from the crowded bar. He slowly approached her; he was very aware of the sobs that accompanied the curses she was directing at the door and the small key card in her hand.

"Are y' okay?" His voice was soft with concern, the urge to engulf her in his arms was overpowering. "Are y' in need of some help?"

Meghan jumped at the voice and turned her tear-stained face towards him. "No, thank you, I'm fine." What the hell was he doing there? She hated the thought of him seeing her crying over what Kaye had done. It was bad enough that she had let Kaye goad her into a physical fight, but she did not need this arrogant man around to mock her.

"Y' don't appear to be fine." Declan's voice was soft as he tugged the key card from her hand. "Here, let me help y'."

"No, please just give me my key." Meghan panicked, not wanting him in her room.

Declan grinned at the expression in her eyes, he unnerved her. "I'm not intending to molest y', I was just planning on opening the door for y'."

Meghan cringed at the comment. Why would she think he wanted anything from her in the first place? He had a room full of very beautiful women to choose from and all more than willing.

Declan nudged her out of the way of the door, but before he slipped the key card into the slot, he turned to her. His large hand rested gently on her shoulder, and he fixed his soft eyes on hers. She tensed slightly under his hand, but she quickly relaxed as his thumb brushed softly back and forth across her collarbone.

"I'm sorry that she hurt y'. She's a horrible woman to torment y' until y' retaliated."

"You know what we were saying?" Meghan appeared shocked.

"Well, y' both were yelling very loudly. I think most of the people close by heard the two of y'," he said softly, his head tilted slightly to the side as if in an attempt to comfort her.

"Oh my God, I'm so embarrassed!" Meghan sniffed and covered her face with her hand.

"Don't be. She should be the one that's embarrassed. Bragging about how she seduces all of your boyfriends. I have to say, though, that they must have all been daft to cheat on y' with the likes of her. She is a dirty whore." Declan rested his other hand on her shoulder.

Meghan lowered her hands from her face and looked up at him. "I didn't say that!"

"I know, Freckles, I believe the word y' used was slut," he laughed and caressed her shoulder softly.

Cassie had finally pushed her way out of the lounge after she watched Meghan running out the door. She turned down the hall but came to an abrupt stop when she realized who Meghan was standing with, his large hand stroking her hair.

"Meg, there you are." Cassie walked as calmly as she could down the hall, her eyes inadvertently resting on Declan.

"Hi, Cass."

"Are you okay?" Cassie questioned, her eyes returning to her friend and noticing for the first time that she had been crying. "What happened?"

"It's nothing." Meghan forced a smile, not wanting to repeat the incident.

Cassie raised her brow and eyed Declan. Had he done or said something to upset Meghan? It did not appear to be the case, since Meghan did not appear bothered by Declan's hand in her hair.

"Is this about Ian?" Cassie blurted out.

"Ian? This doesn't have anything to do with him," Meghan growled as annoyance set in that Cassie would bring him up. She was trying to forget about the last few months the psychopath stalked her.

Declan noticed the tension building in Meghan, and he became agitated. Why did her friend have to show up now? He was making headway with Meghan. "Actually, it was that horrible woman Kaye that upset her."

Meghan jerked from his arms and stared at him with shock.

"What?" Cassie barked. "What could Kaye possibly have done?"

"Never mind," Meghan muttered, lowering her gaze, not wanting to meet Cassie's angry eyes. "It was nothing."

"Why do you let her get to you?" Cassie sighed. She had hoped that over the years, Meghan and Kaye would stop their fighting and be friends for her sake. It was hard choosing sides between your cousin and your best friend.

"I would venture to say it's because the lass enjoys bedding Meggie's boyfriends." Declan's eyes were directed at Cassie. "As Meggie's friend, I would assume y' are privy to that information."

Cassie jerked from the comment and eyed Meghan with annoyance. "You told him that?"

"No," Meghan blurted out. "Your stupid cousin did. She decided that mocking me in front of a bar full of people would be fun."

"Oh," Cassie sighed and hugged Meghan. "I'm sorry. I thought that she had changed. It was her idea to come this week because she wanted to mend fences with you and Nat. Apparently she forgot about that."

"It's all right, Cass, Kaye and I are never going to be friends."

"I should say not," Declan spoke up reminding the women of his presence. They seemed to have forgotten that he was there. "Now that we have all had hugs and the tears are dried, why don't y' ladies join me outside for a game of football?"

"Football? Out in the snow?" Meghan blurted out in shock. "I don't think so."

"Why not?" Cassie blurted out. "Who's playing?"

"The crew and some of the cast, and I promised I would join them tonight," Declan commented and glanced down the hall.

"Meg, you need to come play," Cassie blurted out, she knew Meghan hated being cold, but she did not want to play by herself.

"Come on, let's go play, it will cheer y' up." Declan grabbed Meghan's hand and pulled her towards him and the door.

Meghan stumbled and fell into him, caught off balance by his sudden movement. Her loose hand smacked down on his chest as she plummeted into him totally off balance. His large hand had involuntarily gripped her hip to steady her, and he was apparently in no hurry to remove it. His heart was racing under her hand, and she could not fight the twinge of gratification that she held a physical power over him.

"Sorry!" Meghan mumbled and pulled away.

"Don't be." An animated smile filled his lips as he released her hand and scrubbed his firm chest. "I'm getting used to it."

"Come on, Meg, we're wasting time. We need to get our coats," Cassie said, noticing the awkward moment.

"Aye, get your coats," Declan agreed, slipping the card into the slot. When it did not open, he pulled out the card and studied it. "Well," he grinned and held up the card towards Meghan. "Y' must have the wrong key."

Cassie laughed. "No, you have the wrong room." She rolled her eyes towards Meghan, but Meghan's anxious gaze was stuck on Declan.

"Oh, my mistake," he smiled and winked at Meghan.

She forced a smile, unsure why he did not tease her. "Thank you for your help."

"Aye." His smile was unmoving. "I'll see y' out there, I must go back into the pub and visit with those girls from the contest." One side of his mouth rose slightly, causing the dimple to appear.

"Don't hurry on my account because I'm not going." Meghan forced out of her mouth, unsure why she did. She wanted to spend more time with this incredible man, yet she was rather embarrassed about her outburst in the bar. She was a little worried about being near any of the people who witnessed it.

"Why not?" Cassie blurted out sharply, slightly annoyed at Meghan's refusal. "I can't go by myself."

"Sure you can, go with him," Meghan muttered, bobbing her head towards Declan.

"He doesn't care if I go. It's you he wants to go," Cassie grumbled through her clenched teeth; she was not used to being the third wheel, and she did not like it.

Declan moved towards the women and stared at Meghan with slight agitation. "Why don't y' want to play?"

"I . . . I just don't," she mumbled, keeping her eyes purposely off him. "I'm not feeling well."

His brow rose slightly, and his hand rested on her shoulder. "If y' change your mind, y' know where I'll be," he said, with a hint of arrogance. "But don't keep me waiting too long."

She did keep him waiting.

CHAPTER THREE

The next evening, the air was crisp, but not particularly cold, as Meghan and her friends wandered through the snow towards the lake. A few men were standing in a circle, the majority of them with their backs turned towards the approaching group. However, Fabrizio noticed them and waved them over, causing the rest of the group to turn and look.

Meghan's eyes settled on Declan as he turned towards her, his hand landing on the back of Fabrizio's shoulder and a slight smile curling his lips.

"Are y' two big men going to play tonight?" Declan questioned, moving towards the group, his gaze on Nathan. "We could use a couple more players."

Nathan eyed the women, assessing their opinion. Meghan slightly shrugged and backed away when Declan stopped in front of them. "Go ahead, we can go to the lake by ourselves," she blurted out, turning towards the lake.

"Aren't you ladies going to join us tonight?" Fabrizio questioned, moving quickly towards them, his hand settling on Cassie's arm.

Cassie looked over at Meghan, but she was shaking her head as she took another step backwards. "Go ahead."

"Do y' think you're too good to play with us?" Declan blurted out, a slight smirk filling his lips, his eyes glued to Cassie's face. He was deliberately not looking at Meghan, and that made her slightly uncomfortable.

"No," Cassie blurted out, not wanting to upset Declan; he was fair game after all. "She'll play too."

"Cassie!" Meghan whispered fiercely. "What are you doing? I really don't want to have anything to do with Kaye." Meghan's eyes settled on Kaye, who was heading towards them.

"It will be okay, he obviously wants you to play. Why are you letting Kaye ruin your fun?" Cassie pleaded, more interested in her own agenda.

Declan was standing close by, but he had turned his attention to Kaye who was now pressing her narrow frame up against him. Kaye's hand was on Declan's arm, and her face was right up against his ear. Declan and Kaye seemed quite friendly with each other, and Meghan could not help but wonder if they had spent the day together. Meghan knew Kaye well enough not to underestimate her powers of seduction, and most likely, she made her move after Meghan went back to her room the night before.

Kaye's eyes narrowed as she glared at Meghan. "You better behave yourself, Meghan. I don't want a repeat of last night," Kaye snorted and turned, flipping her long blonde hair as she spun.

"Leave me alone, Kaye! How dare you even speak to me, after what you did last night?" Meghan growled, feeling quite safe with Nathan and Pete standing beside her. They disliked Kaye as much as she did, so she knew they would back her up.

"You know, Meghan, jealousy doesn't become you," Kaye smirked and rested her arm around Declan's waist.

"Megs, she is trying to rile you into saying something," Nathan warned and slipped his arm around her waist from behind. "Just walk away."

Meghan smiled softly at Nathan and rested her head back onto his chest. "You're right." She glanced over at Kaye, who was trying her best to keep her hand on Declan, but every time she touched him, he dislodged her hand. "I'm sorry, Kaye, we are ruining this week for Cassie with all of our fighting. Why don't we try to get along?"

Kaye laughed smugly, stretched up, and kissed Declan's cheek. "At least, you're a good loser, Meghan. Nevertheless, I have to admit that I am so accustomed to women being jealous of me that I tend to get defensive. It's a curse to be this beautiful, and sometimes I wish I was uglier, so I could be like a normal woman."

"Nicely put, Queen Narcissistic." Nathan laughed loudly. "That is the biggest pile of crap I have ever heard."

Cassie stood shocked at Meghan's side; she had never before heard Kaye make such a horrible comment, and she was dumfounded. Cassie glanced over at Meghan and shook her head. "All right, I get it."

Meghan nodded and turned in Nathan's arms, resting her hands against his chest. "I'm taking her down."

"Go for it, Megs," Nathan whispered back and kissed her cheek.

When Meghan glanced over at Declan, his eyes were piercing through her. The dark grey eyes were intense and causing her unease. Meghan's gaze left him and scanned the rest of the group, but no one else seemed to be noticing the expression on his face. She sensed something in him that the others could not.

Declan took a step towards her, which caused her to turn away from him and focus on Cassie. "Well, are we playing, or what? I want to go to the lake at some point."

Nathan chuckled at her facial expression and gripped her arm pulling her to his side of the field. "Darlin' you can be on my team. With that look on your face, I don't want to be your opponent."

A few of the men finished arguing about who was ahead in the score, and the group lined up, ready for the next play. Once in the line, the girls began to growl at each other and stamp their feet in the snow like two wolves about to do battle. However, when Meghan caught a glimpse of the short thin man standing next to Cassie, staring at them as if they were idiots, she froze. Embarrassment shot through her, and she abruptly halted the noise, and glanced up the line, to find the rest of the players watching them curiously.

"What would y' be doing?" Declan asked, grinning over at them, his head tilted to the side.

"Sorry, we just don't know much about football, and we were goofing around," Cassie blurted out, while Meghan stood quietly, trying desperately to keep her face from enflaming with colour.

Declan's gaze settled on Meghan, and a smirk curled his lips. He was finding her very amusing. Sauntering towards them, he stopped right in the middle of the two women. Declan let out a large sigh, then eyed the burly man standing beside Meghan. "I'd imagine this is exactly why women aren't capable of playing ball." His mouth twisted into a mischievous grin. "I guess it's true enough that a woman's place is in the bedroom."

"I thought it was in the kitchen," the man laughed and eyed the women.

"Aye well, the bedroom is all that matters to me," Declan grinned and patted Meghan's backside.

She jerked away, her eyes flaring with anger. Her lips pursed together, and she appeared to be ready to explode.

"Okay, ladies, we'll give y' quick instructions. This would be a football." Declan held it up in front of them, his sizeable hand gripping it easily, as he turned it from side to side. He was determined to provoke Meghan and watch her flare. Her eyes excited him, so expressive and full of life.

"Oh football, is that what we're playing? Well, I'm glad you took the time to explain it to us bedroom dwellers," Meghan blurted out, with slight annoyance.

Cassie immediately started to laugh at her friend's sarcasm.

Declan choked down the laughter that threatened to explode, and then eyed Meghan dubiously, his brow rising slightly. "Are y' making fun of me?"

Confrontation crossed Meghan's brow. "I guess you would think that, since you feel everything revolves around you." Her voice was cool, but her eyes flared with green flames. She was unsure why she was reacting to him so heatedly, but he seemed to send her emotions into a tailspin, and it frightened her.

"You're a natural redhead, are y' not?" Declan's face was expressionless. "Y' have a sharp tongue, Freckles."

Cassie was already gripping Meghan's arm, trying to calm her. She had seen this behaviour in Meghan before, but Meghan's target concerned her.

"That may be." Meghan's eyes never left him as she tried to calm herself. This was jealously rearing its ugly head, she suspected. When she saw him with Kaye, her stomach twisted into knots. Why did Kaye always manage to get the man she wanted? "But I would be thankful if I were you, I haven't sharpened it yet."

A smug, satisfied smile curled Declan's lips, and he took a step towards Meghan, reached out, and touched her hair. "So that's the way of it?" His fingers stayed occupied in her auburn curls. "Well, I never back down from a challenge, so if y' think there is anything y' can tell me that I haven't already heard, go right ahead, Freckles."

Meghan felt Cassie shake her slightly, and she turned towards her, not wanting to engage in an argument with him while everyone watched. "I'm sure there is nothing I can say," she conceded and turned her back on him.

"I didn't think so." Declan chuckled smugly and slapped her backside again, causing her to whirl around, her eyes flaming again.

"If you do that again, Mr. Montgomery, I will flatten you!" Meghan snarled. "You may be accustomed to getting what you want, but my ass is not something you have any right to."

A loud roar exited Declan, and he took no trouble to conceal his amusement as the rest of the players' mouths gaped from her comment. "Meggie, you're a beautiful sight when y' spit fire." His hands gripped her shoulders, and he leaned forwards, almost buckling over from his laugher.

"I'm glad you find so much amusement in this," she scowled; slightly embarrassed that she let him rile her. "But if you will kindly get your hands off me."

"Wow, what a bitch you are, Meghan. It's no wonder you are still single," Kaye blurted out cruelly.

Declan swung towards Kaye, a scowl building across his face. "We're just having a wee bit of fun, and I don't appreciate y' talking to her that way," he grumbled, looking sideways at Meghan, but she was backing away from the group.

"Meggie, where are y' going?" Declan moved towards her and gripped her wrists in his hands.

"I'm getting cold," she muttered, her eyes switching from Cassie to Kaye to Declan, seemingly unsure whom to be watching. "I'm sorry for being so rude," her voice was so soft that only Declan heard her.

Declan's brow rose slightly as he watched the embarrassment shooting from her green eyes. "Y' weren't rude." He rested his hand on her face, trying to refocus her on him. "If it's a habit you're making of berating me, I best be on me finest behaviour." His grin turned into a smile as her eyes settled on him, the life returning to the dark green eyes. "I shouldn't have teased y' so, but I wanted to see the fire in your eyes."

Meghan cringed slightly and chewed at her bottom lip, unsure what to say to him. It was easy arguing with him, but to have a calm conversation, she found herself at a loss for words.

His mouth rose to one side as he watched the concern explode from her eyes. He could not believe how transparent she was. Every thought she had showed clearly on her face with an illuminating presence.

"Stay and play," Declan softly asked as he brushed his thumb across her wrist, sending sparks of desire up her arm. "I promise I'll keep me hands off that beautiful arse of yours."

The expression on her face confused him, and he forced a smile, released her wrist, and held out his hand towards her. "Truce?"

She smiled softly and took his outstretched hand. "All right, but no more touching."

"Aye." He raised his loose hand in front of him in retreat. "I'll do me best. If I can control meself," he added as an afterthought before he turned and headed towards his original position.

As the game continued, it became clear to Meghan that the men were definitely dominating the plays, and she had little chance to be involved. She stopped paying attention to the game and began watching a gaggle of Canada Geese flying overhead towards their resting grounds. The moon was casting a glow around their outstretched wings as they flew across the dark sky. The honking clamour they generated was bouncing off the snow-covered ground and blurring the screams coming from the wannabe football players down the field.

"Meghan, catch!" A loud voice yelled from the other side of the field, drawing her shocked attention to a spinning brown object heading at great speeds towards her head. She threw up her hands with panic, and to her amazement, when she brought them down, the ball was between them.

Quickly scanning her surroundings, she observed her teammates pointing frantically in the direction of some large fir trees. With further examination, she noticed there was also a pack of very large men running towards her. She gripped the ball firmly in her hands and ran towards the trees.

"Watch out!" was all Meghan heard, before she hit the ground in the shadows of the large fir trees. She felt a crushing weight on top of her, pinning her to the snowy ground and a loud laugh in her ear. The ball flew out of her hands, and the commotion around her disappeared as the hollering group headed up the field with the ball. When the snow finally settled, she saw that her attacker was none other than Declan, lying on top of her, laughing uncontrollably.

"What's so funny?" Meghan grumbled. Her voice was irritated as she pushed at his shoulders, trying to remove him from on top of her.

"I'm sorry, but the look on your face is priceless," Declan declared with a twisted grin, curling his lips that were dangerously close to her.

"I thought this was supposed to be touch?" Meghan questioned, a scowl forming on her brow.

"We're touching, are we not?" Declan smiled, one brow cocked in apparent amusement. "And be thankful, me hand is not on your arse."

Fire shot from Meghan's eyes as she stared at his smug face. "Get off me!" she grumbled. The feel of his hand that had so casually rested against her face sent shivers down her spine.

He shook his head slightly, and his mouth rose to one side, forcing the dimple to appear. "I've angered me red prickly beauty again."

"I'm not your anything," Meghan's voice was weaker than she had intended. "Please get off me."

As the fingers of one hand entwined in her hair and the other hand gently caressed her face, she began to settle, and he was aware of it. "Well, that will teach y' for standing me up last night."

"I didn't stand you up." She pushed past the lump in her throat, which had developed the minute he touched her. "I told you I wasn't going."

"So y' did." He rose up on his elbows when he noticed her squirming slightly under him.

Declan laughed at her facial expression and shook his head. He was amazed at how drawn he was to her, as she laid in the snow beneath him. Her hair was fanning out like a ground cover of fire and her dark green eyes flashing with life. He moved his face closer to hers, wanting to feel her soft lips against his.

"I do believe y' are going to be the death of me," he mumbled as his lips claimed hers with little resistance. Her body shuddered as his thumb began to slowly stroke her cheek, his hands cradling her face.

His kiss was soft but demanding, and her lips responded in turn, allowing him to take what he needed. She was surprised and slightly agitated that she was reacting to him with such passion, but she could not stop her needing compliance any more than she could stop the sun from coming up in the morning. He was in control, and she knew it.

Without her realizing it, her hands had slipped around his back, holding him tightly. She pressed herself against him as he filled her with a desire so deep, it hit her soul. The sounds in the distance faded into a low murmur as he plunged her senses deeper into the kiss, demanding her total surrender. This had to stop, she thought painfully, as the kiss continued to attack her senses, leaving her confused and desirous.

Declan could feel her surrender to him, her body shuddering under him. No woman had ever brought him to the point of pleasure so quickly, with only a kiss; he had to pull away before he took her right there on the snowy ground. Her green eyes smouldered with desire, fluttered open, and gazed at him with surprise.

"Declan," Meghan breathlessly mumbled against his lips.

"Wow." A twisted smile curled Declan's lips, and he bent down and kissed her forehead. "Where have y' been all me life?"

Meghan swallowed painfully, somewhat overwhelmed with the comment. She struggled to get out from underneath him, unable to think of a response to his question. The deep snow was difficult to stand in, but she was desperate to get away from him.

"And where do y' think you're going. Freckles, without helping me up?" Declan reached up and yanked her back down towards him, her body slamming into him with quite a force. "I think I'm going to need to wear some protective padding when you're around," Declan smirked, gripping her shoulders holding her hostage to him.

"Shut up!" Meghan snorted, smacking her hands against his shoulders, pushing him back into the snow.

"Hey." Declan reached up, grabbed her arms, and flipped her into the snow beside him, then scooped a handful of snow at her head.

"Stop that!" she screamed and batted a handful of the cold substance into his smirking face.

He had manoeuvred himself on top of her before she had time to react. Not that she would have been able to stop him in any case. "Now you're asking for a fight, I never back down from a challenge."

"I've already heard this speech," Meghan said evenly. "I'm not scared."

"Well, y' should be." Declan adjusted himself on top of her and rested his hands in the snow.

"Don't you dare!" Meghan muttered when her eyes fixed on his hands that were sliding down the side of her, scooping snow as they went.

"I think y' owe me an apology," Declan taunted, his cupped hands resting full of snow on his legs.

"Declan," she laughed. "Get off."

"Not until y' say you're sorry."

"For what?" Meghan questioned as her dark lashes fluttered across her eyes, very innocently.

He made no attempt to hide his delight, his head shaking with amazement. "If y' think that face will save y', you're mistaken."

Suddenly her hands were in the snow, and with that action; the snow was flying around them in a haze of white chaos. When the cloud retreated, leaving the two of them covered in snow, Declan leaned down and kissed her nose.

"I do believe y' are going to be the death of me," he laughed loudly.

"So you've said," Meghan giggled and pushed at his shoulders. "Declan, I need to get up, I have snow down my jacket."

"I'll get it," Declan grinned and shoved his hand up her jacket.

"Stop that!" Meghan squealed and pulled at his arm. "Declan!"

Declan jerked up suddenly when he heard voices approaching, but he did not remove his hand.

"Monty, there you are." Fabrizio and Kaye stopped beside them.

"What the hell are you doing?" Kaye grumbled, eyeing their positioning and their snow-covered bodies.

"Aye well, we had a wee accident." Declan's tone was light and amused.

"Is your hand stuck?" Fabrizio questioned, his dark brown eyes landing judgmentally on Declan's arm that was still stuffed up Meghan's jacket.

Declan chuckled as embarrassment flushed Meghan's face. "I was just helping her get the snow out of her jacket," Declan said calmly and pulled his hand from her jacket.

"For Christ's sake, Meghan, get a bit of class!" Kaye blurted out.

"Bloody hell!" Declan muttered as he climbed off Meghan. His hand lowered towards her to help her off the ground. "Meggie!"

Meghan refocused and took his hand, but made no eye contact with him. "Thank you."

"Aye, my pleasure," Declan said offhandedly, his attention now on Fabrizio. "Do you have a problem too?"

"If he doesn't, I certainly do!" Kaye blurted out and glanced around at the group of men surrounding them. "And you called me a slut last night. At least, I wasn't caught screwing him in the bushes."

"We weren't screwing, Kaye!" Declan growled. "We fell."

Fabrizio laughed slightly, but he stopped when he noticed the expression on Meghan's face. She had moved towards Nathan, and he would have sworn she had tears in her eyes. "Meghan, the big lug didn't hurt you, did he?"

"No, I'm fine." Her voice was weak, and her eyes never left Nathan.

"Well, then, I guess we are all fine," Declan blurted out, his eyes still glued to the back of Meghan's head. "Let's get on with the game."

It did not take long for the men to start bickering again about the field position of the ball, and while their backs were turned, Meghan took the opportunity to slip away.

The lounge was peculiarly quiet that evening, and in the solitude, Meghan stared into the dancing flames, which seemed to be talking to her, slowly lulling her into a peaceful calmness. The Irish coffee she had ordered was overflowing with whipping cream, resembling snow-covered mountains, which she found rather soothing.

"Sorry for the overkill on the cream, but you look like you could use some cheering up." The aging bartender's dark brown eyes crinkled as he placed the mug on the table in front of her. "It's quite slow in here tonight. Most of the guests prefer the night club on the other side of the lodge, it's livelier."

Meghan glanced over at the two other tables of guests and Eliza sitting at the bar, her gaze on Meghan. "I guess you will be able to leave early?"

He smiled and laid a few small napkins on the table. "Well, don't feel you need to hurry off, we are open until midnight."

"Thanks," Meghan smiled and settled herself into the couch deliberately keeping her eyes off Eliza. That last thing she wanted was to talk to her. She seemed to be everywhere Meghan went.

"Well, enjoy," he said as he wandered back behind the bar.

Meghan lifted the satisfyingly hot cup to her lips but inadvertently stuck her nose into the mountain of cream. The napkin was rough against her skin, as she wiped the sweet white cream away, but it was even harder when she banged it against her nose.

"I'll lick that off for y'," Declan's familiar lilt startled her.

She turned around to find Declan standing directly behind her, which startled her. For such a large man, he seemed to move with an unnerving covertness that she could not understand. She turned her back on him, hoping he would not come any closer. She was terrified of her feelings for him.

"May I sit down with y'?" Declan asked, with hesitation.

"I'd rather you didn't!" Meghan mumbled, her passion and embarrassment spinning together in a flurry of emotions. She flipped her head around blocking him from her view. "Mr. Montgomery, I'm sure there are plenty of places you could be tonight instead of here tormenting me."

"I'm sure there are!" Declan's temper rose with her dismissal of him. Why was he so intent on possessing her? He could not vanquish the memory of the kiss they shared from his overburdened mind. Her soft needing lips pulsed against his skin, and her hands clung to him with desire. He was confident that she was attracted to him, but how was he going to convince her of that fact? With the possibility that she could be somehow involved in the triad or lead him to whoever was, he needed her in more than just a physical way.

"Before y' thrash me with that sharp tongue of yours any further, I would like to express me sincere apology for anything I have done to upset y'." Declan bowed towards her in a mocking jester, which infuriated her further.

"You're unbelievable!" Meghan's dark green eyes were smouldering with life, waiting to exploded and consume him in a burning eruption of fire.

"So y' told me," he grinned and tweaked her nose.

Declan's smugness ignited her as he had intended. "Don't take it as a compliment, it certainly was not meant as one. You are the most—" Her comment was cut short when the bartender approached to take Declan's order. "He's not ordering," Meghan blurted out, "he's not staying."

"You're a prickly wee thing, are y' not?" Declan commented as he dropped to the couch beside her. "I'll have a Guinness."

As the bartender moved away quickly, not wanting to get in the middle of their argument, Meghan turned to Declan, anger shooting from her eyes. "Why are you here?"

"Because y' are." His calm answers were sending her into a tizzy. It took every ounce of self-restraint she had not to clobber him across the head, and he knew it.

Meghan's eyes fixed on the fire, hoping that it would soothe her exposed nerves, but that was not to happen as he began to blow softly in her ear.

"Stop that!" Meghan grumbled and batted at his face with her hand. "I'm not going to be your play toy."

"Me play toy?" he laughed at the comment. "Is that what y' think I'm after?" He paused, his fingers occupying themselves by twisting in her curls. "Well, you're mighty pretty lass, but a play toy you're not." He sensed the slight withdrawal in her, and he grabbed her hand and held it up to his chest. "Freckles, you're far too dangerous for any man to toy with."

Declan eyed her curiously. The tension in her eyes was building with every blink of her long dark lashes. She was definitely struggling with something, and he was getting very anxious, wondering which way she was going to decide.

"Meggie, what are y' thinking?" Declan finally questioned, getting impatient with her thought process.

Her eyes left his face, and she lowered her gaze once more to the table, not knowing how to answer his question. Her emotions were whirling out of control, and she could barely keep herself composed in the haze of uncertainty this man created in her.

"I'm sorry. I had no right to behave that way," Meghan mumbled so quietly, he could barely hear her.

"No right? What do y' mean by that?" Concern edged Declan's voice as he stared at her.

Meghan shook her head and casually adjusted herself on the couch, moving slightly away from him.

Declan noticed her slight shift and turned towards her, raising his brow. "Do y' think by moving over a few inches you're going to accomplish anything?" he asked, a large smirk curling his lips. His eyes were dancing with amusement over top of the long dimple that appeared on his cheek.

"No, I . . ." she mumbled. "I was just getting comfortable," she said, with a tone of complacency.

"Oh, is that what y' were doing?" he joked, his grey eyes fixed on her face as she nervously fussed with a strand of hair, which she was twisting around her finger. "Meggie, why are y' so uncomfortable with me again?" His eyes were serious now with a slight sign of worry.

"I'm not."

"Aye, y' are. I can feel the tension in y'."

"Sorry," Meghan muttered and lowered her eyes to the table.

"Stop saying sorry and tell me what's upsetting y'?" He placed his finger under her chin and lifted her head towards him.

"I know I have no right to say whom you . . . well, spend time with, but if you and Kaye have something going on, I am not getting in the middle. I just thought that you might be, well, I was wrong, and I'm sorry," Meghan rambled then jerked her head away from his hand and stared at the fire, hoping it would somehow calm her surging emotions.

"Well, I'm sorry I asked," Declan joked.

Meghan turned on him, with annoyance building in her. "Well, then why did you?" she grunted, rose to her feet, and started to move past him to leave.

"Where do y' think you're going?" Declan grabbed onto her arm.

"Back to my room," she replied coldly.

"Meggie, you're not going anywhere," he informed her as he pulled her down onto his lap.

"Declan, let me go!" Meghan demanded and tugged her arm, trying to loosen his grip.

"No, but it's nice to see we're back to Declan. Mr. Montgomery is me da." His voice was light and teasing, but she refused to be baited again.

"Why are you doing this to me?" Meghan questioned as his hand slipped across her face, his fingers massaging behind her ear.

"Doing what, Freckles?" he smiled as his lips moved towards her. "I'm not doing anything to y' that y' don't want."

His lips were around hers, stifling the complaint she was about to throw at him. Her body shuddered, and her arms wrapped around his neck totally overwhelmed with the sensation. This trip through his passion was no less alarming than the last, but her resolve to end the kiss seemed to have heightened at the same time his hand slipped up the back of her sweater to caress her flushed skin.

"Please stop that." Her voice was uncommonly weak, her eyes glazing over.

"Meggie, what's wrong?" Softness crossed his face startling her.

"I can't do this, it's too, you're too . . ." She stopped, not liking the position she had put herself in. It was much easier dealing with him confrontationally than emotionally.

"Meggie, I'm sorry for the way Kaye behaved tonight, and the way I reacted." Declan voice was soft and apologetic.

"It's fine," Meghan said quietly, turning towards him. "I understand."

"No, I don't think y' do, or y' wouldn't be acting this way," Declan responded, not liking the tone of her voice. "I was just cross with the way they reacted. I'm sorry I hurt your feelings, but I wasn't worried about anyone finding out about us."

"What about us?" Meghan questioned, not sure, why she did.

"Well, y' know," Declan smirked and twisted slightly on the couch. "That we are . . . well, attracted to each other."

Meghan's brow rose slightly at the comment. "Are we?"

"Aye." His voice was confident and strong. "That is exactly what we are," he grinned slightly. "And as for Kaye, there is nothing going on with her and never will be."

Meghan smiled and looked up at him, but his eyes were focused across the bar. "There is that crazy old woman again," Declan muttered. "Everywhere I go, she seems to be there."

Meghan turned and glanced at her. "That's Eliza. I met her on the bus up here. She has been sitting, staring at me since I came in."

"Well, let's give her something to stare at." Declan grinned mischievously and pulled her towards him. Meghan shuddered as his lips descended upon hers. He was doing it again, breaking down her resolve and plunging her deep into his web. His kiss caused a rush of need and longing to well inside her, and her body shuddered as her mind wandered to a place she had never been before. A place where she found herself wanting him with an unrelenting passion, that rushed through her veins like a poison. Panic forced her to pull back and eye him with trepidation.

"Meggie, let's go back to me room," Declan suggested, as he ran his hand from her face into her hair. "I want y'."

He could feel her trembling in his arms, and he knew that she would be his in every way; she could not deny it. His eyes fixed on hers as passion and fear continued to do battle in her brilliant eyes.

Suddenly, she jerked away from him as her fear won out. "No, this is moving too fast. I think I better go to my room tonight." There was no possibility of letting herself make love to him, now or anytime in the future. He was a dangerous man who had a firm grip on her heart. He could destroy her without a thought.

He stared at her shortly, quite surprised by her response. No woman had turned him down since high school, and he was not sure what to think. He was sure that she wanted him as much as he wanted her; what was her problem?

"Fine!" Declan blurted out.

"I'll see you tomorrow?" Meghan's voice sounded uncertain at best. Damn, she was hoping for calmness.

"Aye, whatever," Declan mumbled, his ego slammed from her refusal.

Meghan slipped off his lap rather awkwardly, trying desperately not to make eye contact with his frustrated dark grey eyes. Once to the safety of the floor, she pulled at her black cashmere sweater and moved quickly towards the door, deliberately not looking back at him. She knew she had annoyed him, but she was not ready to be his next conquest. Her mind was in turmoil, wondering if she had done the right thing.

Declan watched with confusion as she bolted from the lounge and from him with an overpowering air of fear. What could have possibly frightened her? The growing awareness inside him, which was telling him not to let her leave on those terms won out, and he darted towards the door after her.

Once right behind her, his large hand swung up and clasped her arm, jolting her to a stop before she was half way through the lobby. His loose hand softly landed on her shoulder, and he turned her towards him, with a gentle but commanding force.

Her head was down, deliberately being evasive to his gaze. When he lowered his head under hers and looked up at her, her eyes seemed distant and hurt.

"I apologize, I shouldn't have reacted that way." Declan gently kissed her on the forehead and wrapped his arms around her stiff unwelcoming body. He held her tightly, the need to have her in his arms was overpowering. She was pulling him into a spiral of desire, but her refusal to give in to the passion confused him.

"Meggie, please don't be cross with me," he begged, tilting his head to the side, his mouth rising in a half smile.

She sighed deeply, her eyes still locked on his. "I just feel like I have been caught up in a whirlwind that is spinning me out of control." Out of control was putting it mildly. She was long past control and dangerously close to a total melt down.

"I didn't mean to frighten y'. I just want y' so badly that I guess I've pushed y' too hard." Declan's face lightened, and the tension seemed to vanish.

"I want . . ." Meghan stopped to censor her words, not wanting to admit she desired to feel his warm pulsing flesh against her skin as well. "I just need more time."

"Aye. I promise I won't push y' to do anything y' don't want to do." A smirk filled his face. "But I don't think y' can deny that y' want me as badly as I want y'."

Meghan stared at his smirking face and began to see the arrogance returning, and it scared her. She did not intend to be his next conquest, only to be tossed aside, and the longer she thought about his comment, the more annoyed she became.

"You have a lot of nerve assuming that!" she snorted, pulling out of his arms.

"Well, it's true," he said sharply, bracing himself against her attack.

"I should have stuck with my first impression of you!" she growled as her emotions exploded to the surface.

"And what would that be?" he said coolly.

Meghan's eyes narrowed as she watched his face harden and his eyes become cold. "That you're an arrogant jerk!" she snorted and turned towards the hall, but his grip on her arm stopped her retreat.

"Oh, that's nice. Is that what y' thought?" Declan muttered through his clenched teeth. "Well, apparently I did something to redeem meself in your eyes over the past few days."

"Well, I was mistaken," Meghan mumbled, becoming uncomfortable with his large hand on her arm. He had a firm grip on her wrist, but he was not hurting her; which surprised her.

"Meggie?" Declan sighed, unsure why she was reacting so explosively to his comment, which he meant as a compliment.

"What type of woman do you think I am that I would sleep with you anyway? I just met you, and I have no intentions of sleeping with you!"

His brow rose at her attack, and he began to smile. "Well, I've been told."

"Yes, you have! I suggest if you're just looking for someone to have sex with, then you go find Kaye," she blurted out seemingly as surprised by the comment as Declan was. Her eyes widened, and her face began to show signs of distress.

"Meggie," Declan laughed and gripped her other arm; he now had hold of them both. "Where did y' get a daft idea like that? I don't want that wacky woman, I want y'."

"Don't make fun of me!" Meghan snarled and attempted to yank her arms loose.

A broad grin broke across Declan's lips, even though he was trying hard to stop laughing. "I'm sorry."

"Is everything okay, Meghan dear?" Eliza questioned as she came to a stop beside them, eyeing Declan's large hands wrapped around her wrists.

"Yes," Meghan muttered, her gaze still glued to Declan's humour-filled eyes. "I'm fine."

"We were just having a wee disagreement," Declan smirked, brushing his thumb across the underside of her wrist.

Her brow rose slightly, and she broke her gaze on him and focused on Eliza. "I'm fine."

"All right, dear. I just wanted to make sure he wasn't harming you." Eliza stared at Meghan for a few awkward minutes before wandering across the lobby.

"She is a weird duck," Declan mumbled before refocusing on Meghan. "So will y' do me the honour of accompanying me for breakfast?"

"I don't know," she mumbled, breaking her gaze on him. He was making her very uncomfortable. She had never felt so strongly for anyone before, and she was quite frightened of her feelings.

"Please, I'm begging y'," Declan grinned and kissed her hand. "If y' don't, I might have to kill meself," he laughed, released her hands, and wrapped his hands around his throat. "It won't be a pretty sight. I can see the headlines now. *Declan Montgomery takes his own life over the lack of a breakfast companion.*"

Meghan laughed despite herself. "All right, I wouldn't want to face the scorn of the entire country."

"So I can call you in the morning?" Declan's voice trailed off near the end when he saw Eliza approaching again. "Christ, here she comes again!"

"Oh my God. What is with her?" Meghan gripped Declan's hand and pulled at him. "Walk me to my room. She freaks me out!"

Before Eliza got to them, they disappeared down the hallway.

CHAPTER FOUR

Loud thumping on the door early the next morning startled Meghan, while she sat on the sleigh bed, brushing her wet hair. Her excitement of seeing Declan that morning for breakfast had her frazzled. She darted across the light oak floor and swung the door open but stumbled backwards at the sight of Ian's agitated face.

He grunted, pushed her aside, and then lumbered into the room, glancing in all directions as if searching for something. His large muscular frame ridged, and his dirty blond hair was a mess of curls; apparently, he had not taken the time to clean up from his trip. His pale blue eyes pierced her as they settled on her terrified face.

Anxiety surged through her as he paced and scrubbed a large hand across his stumbled chin. "Ian, what are you doing here?" Meghan finally questioned, trying to break his concentration. "I have a restraining order. You are not allowed to be here."

"Do you think a stupid piece of paper is going to stop me?" He eyed her with annoyance.

"I am going to call security." She backed away, having the overwhelming urge to put some distance between them.

"Go ahead, they're not going to do anything," Ian laughed cruelly and took a menacing step towards her.

Meghan was startled when the phone rang halting Ian's advance towards her. "Hello." Her voice slightly edged with panic.

"Good morning to y', can I assume that y' might be willing to talk to me today?" The very sexy voice questioned, calming her slightly.

"I need you to come here," Meghan muttered, as she caught sight of Ian's angry face in the mirror. "Please."

"Meggie, is something wrong?" Declan questioned, hearing the terror in her voice.

"Yes," she blurted out before Ian grabbed the phone and flung it across the room.

"Who was that?" Ian asked fiercely, his blue eyes dark and threatening.

Meghan's eyes widened with worry. "It was my friend, Declan, and he is really big, so you better get out before he gets here," She blurted out, making a move towards the door.

Ian appeared startled but settled quickly. "That didn't take you long, you whore. Where did you meet him?"

"Ian, please get out," Meghan begged and backed away towards the bathroom.

"Meghan, when are you going to learn that you belong to me?" Ian sighed and reached forward, gripping her arm tightly.

"Let go," Meghan begged pulling at her arm. "I didn't do anything."

"Don't lie to me, you stupid bitch!" Ian hollered and threw her to the floor, causing her to slam her back up against the bed frame.

Meghan curled into a ball and covered her face with her hands as he approached in an absolute rage. "Ian, please!" she shrieked as his foot crashed against her ribs. "Ian!"

"Meghan, you had your chance. I told you that you would regret your decision. Now give me the locket. I need that locket." His tone edged with something close to panic.

"No, it's mine," Meghan shrieked and gripped the locket in her hand as she huddled against the wall, trembling with fear and pain. She was gasping for breath, every fibre in her stomach burning, his blow striking her to her core.

An anxious knock on the door interrupted Ian's rage, and he groaned with annoyance. "Dammit." He pulled her to her feet. "Get the door," he growled and slammed her against the hard wooden door, completely forgetting about retrieving the locket.

"Meggie, is everything okay in there?" Declan's deep concerned voice penetrated the door.

Ian grimaced at the sound of the voice out in the hall. "Get rid of him!"

Meghan stepped back from the door and slowly opened it a few inches. She gazed out at the worried face with terror exploding from her eyes, tears dripping down her face.

"Meggie, what's going on?" Declan mumbled, lines of worry creasing his forehead. The dark gaze left her face and scanned the room through the small opening.

"I need . . ." she muttered in a shaky voice. Blood was draining from her face, leaving her ashen coloured.

"Are y' going to let me in?" Declan placed his hand on the door and gave it a slight shove. The door swung wide open, exposing Meghan and the empty room behind her.

When Declan got to the open window he eyed the footprints in the newly fallen snow, but no one was in sight. He grunted slammed the window shut and returned his gaze to Meghan's tear-stained face.

"Meggie?" Declan shouted and rushed to her side. "Are y' okay?"

"No!" she cried, the pain surging through her like shards of glass, slicing every fibre in her midsection.

"Christ, what has happened to y'?" Declan's hand slid down her shoulder to her hand that was clutching her ribs with a protective presence. His hand was strong and determined as he pulled her housecoat open, exposing her rapidly bruising ribs.

"Bloody hell!" he snorted, scooped her into his arms and carried her to the sleigh bed, resting her gently down. "Who did this to y'?"

"Ian," she muttered and took a deep breath, trying to calm the pain.

His hand slid softly across her skin, examining the dark patches that were forming on the delicate skin of her stomach. "Does that hurt?" he asked, pushing slightly on her ribs around the bruises. "I'm taking y' to the hospital."

"No. I don't think anything is broken." She sniffed and swabbed her eyes with her shaking hand.

"Oh, Meggie," Declan sighed gently, sliding his hand across her stomach. "How could he do this?"

"It's okay," Meghan muttered, pulling her housecoat closed, suddenly feeling embarrassed about her exposed bra and panties. She glanced over at him and smiled softly. "Thank you for coming."

"You're welcome, Freckles. It's a good thing I did," Declan sighed and brushed his hand down her hair. "So who is this Ian?"

"I met him at a party a few months ago, and now he's stalking me. I didn't think he knew where I was. I have a restraining order," she rambled, completely terrified that Ian had come after her. "I have to call the police."

The room seemed eerily quiet while Declan sat silently on the bed beside her, stroking her hair as she talked to the police officer on the phone. It was taking everything in him not to go find Ian and beat him to a pulp for what he had done.

"Meggie, do y' want to go to the hospital?" Declan questioned once she hung up the phone. His hand was still stroking her hair down her back with gentle precision, lulling her into calmness.

"No, I'm okay, I just need to . . ." she paused and tried to control her embarrassment.

"What possessed y' to let that man in your room?" Declan's voice was full of confusion.

"I thought it was Cassie." Meghan jumped from the bed but buckled over as a sharp pain shot through her stomach like a fiery sword. "How did he find me?"

"What are y' doing? Lie down," Declan ordered, leaping across the bed towards her as she leaned against the wall for support.

"No, I'm fine, just leave me alone." Meghan waved her hand dismissing him.

"Damn, you're a stubborn woman," Declan grumbled, his movements towards her slow and cautious.

"I think you better leave," Meghan said, much quieter than she had intended.

Declan's face changed from annoyance to bewildered surprise. "Y' want me to go?"

Meghan swallowed hard, her eyes fixed on the dark grey that were quickly filling with concern. "You're scaring me."

"I'm sorry," he said, taking a few steps towards her. "I don't know why I'm getting so upset." His hand reached for her face, but she jerked back before he touched her. "Meggie?" Declan sighed lowering his hand to his side, his eyes shutting softly. "Please lie down, you're obviously in pain."

She broke her gaze, swung around, and stared out the window at a group of people skating on the cleared patch of ice on the frozen lake. Ashes and soot landing on the snow surrounding the large fire pit flaming on the shoreline.

"Meggie, please don't push me away." Declan stepped in behind her and wrapped his arms around her from behind. His six-foot-four frame was much taller than she was, so when she rested her head back, it was resting in the upper curve of his shoulder. His face rested against the topside of her head, his breath gentle in her hair.

"Kiwi," he whispered, enchanted by the aroma that surrounded her. "And maybe apples."

"What?" Meghan glanced up at his face that was buried in her hair.

"Your hair," Declan grinned removing his face. "I love the smell of your hair."

"I'm glad I smell like a fruit salad," Meghan giggled, leaning into him. She felt so at home in his arms, almost as if she had been there forever.

"This is nice," she whispered and closed her eyes allowing herself to enjoy the sensation.

"Aye," he whispered softly. "I can't believe I've found y'."

Meghan glanced up at him with interest. "Found me?"

She thought she detected a slight tensing of his arms, but it faded quickly, it must have been her imagination.

"I mean that I found a woman that fits so well in me arms," Declan said with forced calmness. He kissed the side of her head and directed her back to the bed. "It worries me that he would come after y'," Declan blurted out as the thought occurred to him.

Tears began to drip down Meghan's cheeks as she painfully lowered herself down. "He says he owns me, and our families are destined to unite."

Declan, startled at the comment, and eyed her with concern, "What the hell does that mean?"

Meghan shrugged and slowly lowered herself to the bed. "I don't know. But I think it has something to do with this locket."

"Why would y' think that?" Declan's voice sounded panicked even to him.

"Well, two weeks ago, he tried stealing it. He said it belonged to his family, and if I wasn't going to be part of it, then I couldn't keep it. And just now he told me to give it to him."

"I thought y' said it was your grandma's?" Declan's voice was sharper than he had intended.

"It was. I have no idea what he meant." Meghan eyed him wearily. "I guess he just wants to steal it because he knows how much it means to me. Maybe Kaye told him about it."

"Kaye knows the lad?" Declan was growing concerned about Kaye's involvement. Why was she in the centre of all the issues with Meghan's locket?

"She is the one that introduced us. To be honest, I am not sure why she did, but she seemed determined for me to meet him. Maybe she wanted to get him out of her hair."

On the other hand, maybe she was setting her up for some other reason. Declan nodded, not wanting to push her any further at that point. She was opening up to him, and soon he would find out all he needed to know.

He dropped to the bed beside her and stared down at her as she adjusted herself on the pillow. A soft smile spread across his lips, and he lay down beside her, his face up next to hers. She returned the smile, her eyes flashing with life. Then she suddenly reached out, resting her hand on his face.

"Thank you," Meghan muttered and leaned over and kissed him quickly.

"For what?" Declan questioned, staying completely still, enjoying the feel of her hand stroking his face.

She broke her gaze and stared at the wall, as if she could see something he could not. "When I was little, I thought my father was a hero. He kept me safe, and I always knew that he would be there if I ever needed him. I thought that no man could ever be as wonderful as him." Her eyes returned to Declan. "I haven't . . ." She stopped and eyed him with a questioning gaze.

"Y' haven't what?" His hand rested on her face, and his thumb brushed across her cheek so gently she closed her eyes.

She suddenly opened her eyes and stared at him. "I don't know how to trust people anymore."

"So I've noticed," Declan chuckled and tickled her under the chin. "You're as guarded as I am arrogant," he laughed.

She stared at him for a moment, then broke her gaze and sighed heavily, not finding the humour in his comment. "Freckles, I was kidding," he muttered, continuing to stroke her face. "Y' need to relax and not take everything I say so literally."

"Declan, you're not understanding what I am saying."

"Well, then y' better spell it out for me, Meggie."

"I try very hard to give people my trust, but when I do, I always end up getting hurt. The only people I have ever been able to trust is Cassie, Nat, and Pete."

"Meggie, y' can't live your life expecting people to let you down. There have been plenty of times that I have given me trust to people undeserving of it, but there have been just as many people that have kept me trust."

"Really?" Her voice begged for reassurance.

"Aye. I consider meself very astute when it comes to judging people, but I always want to see the best in people, and sometimes I get burned."

Meghan sighed and closed her eyes. "I get burned a lot."

"As does everyone. Meggie, please let down your walls and let me in. I promise I will do everything in me power to be deserving." Declan knew all about walls, he had build up a fortress around himself to safeguard him from the multitudes of people wanting something from him. Women that appeared to have ulterior motives for everything they did. Now he had stumbled upon Meghan, she has brought that wall crashing down, and that amazed him.

Meghan's dark green gaze settled on him with interest. "Declan, why don't y' have a girlfriend?" she blurted out, seemingly from out of nowhere.

A grin broke across his lips. "Y' were right when y' said I was an arrogant jerk," he laughed and pulled her towards him encircling her in his arms. "Since I began to achieve a level of notoriety, I have found that most women I have met are so intent on pleasing me that they lose themselves, and when they do, I lose interest."

"Well, apparently that is not a problem I have," she smiled slightly when he began to laugh.

"So I've noticed," Declan laughed harder. "I have never met anyone in all my life that has as sharp a tongue as y', Freckles."

Her brow rose, and she buried her face in his shoulder, the manly scent of him strong in her nose. "I was trying to scare you away."

"Well, it's not working." He kissed her forehead. "So, when y' leave here, what are y' going to do? Y' obviously can't go back to where y' were living before if Ian knows where you live," he questioned with concern, not wanting her to go anywhere near Ian again.

"I'm going to stay with Nat for a while, but then we are moving to my ranch in Montana."

"That explains it. Y' don't sound like you're from LA."

"Well, I'm originally from Calgary."

"So you're a Canadian?" he smirked. "I've been to Calgary on me way to the Banff film festival."

"Really?" Meghan smiled and adjusted herself slightly.

"That's great, eh?" His accent mimicked a Maritimer's.

Meghan glowered at him. "Is that the only thing people think of when they think of Canadians?"

"No." He chuckled. "I have actually been to a few places in Canada. I love Jasper and Whistler. They were very quaint little towns. I have also been to Vancouver, Toronto, Quebec City, and I travelled throughout the Maritimes for a few weeks, that's where I heard it the most." He smiled, proud of his travels in Canada. "As a matter of fact, I don't believe I have heard y' use that term."

Meghan giggled and pushed at his shoulder. "Well, now I am going to be insecure about saying it."

Declan smiled and tweaked her nose. "Y' never need to be insecure around me."

"Well, I think that word is the fault of the Irish and Scottish anyway," Meghan giggled.

"How so?" Declan smirked, wondering how she could put the blame on his countrymen.

"Well, eastern Canada was settled by a great number of Irish and Scottish families, and I think over the years the 'aye' that they used turned into 'eh' as the way of speaking adapted."

"Well, that is a very interesting thought," he laughed.

"It's not so farfetched. They both are a way of saying yes or asking for agreement."

"Aye," Declan laughed and tweaked her noise. "So y' own a ranch. Are y' rich?" He was slightly curious about her past.

"No." She giggled and batted at his hand. "My grandfather owned an oil company, and when my father was killed in an accident on the rigs, he was devastated, and he sold the company and moved us to the ranch in Montana."

"Where does your mother live?" Declan questioned, an overwhelming sense of sorrow for her rushed through him.

"I don't know. I haven't seen her since I was five," Meghan muttered quietly. "When my parents met, she thought she would be well looked after."

"Wasn't she?" Declan questioned, his brow rising slightly.

"Well, we didn't starve, but my father was very proud, and he wouldn't take any money from my grandpa. So we lived off his rig pay. She was about ten years older than my dad, and she saw in him as way to be a socialite." Meghan shuffled on the bed and glanced back at him. "When she left us, she told him she didn't marry him to be a rig pig's wife."

Declan's brow crumpled slightly as he watched her struggle with the memory. "She didn't take y' with her?"

"No, she . . ." Meghan lowered her eyes to the bed, slightly embarrassed. "She was close to forty when I was born, and she said the only reason why she had me was to force my dad into leaving the rigs and work with his father. She told my dad that he could be burdened with me, her new boyfriend didn't want a kid."

"Oh, Meggie," Declan sighed and rested his hand on her face. "Did your da—" He stopped, unsure how to ask.

"Did my dad step up and take care of me?" She finished for him. "Yes, he did, he was a terrific dad. But when he died . . . ," she paused and eyed him hesitantly. "Well, my grandpa took on that role. My mother was nowhere to be found."

"How old were y'?" he asked, a look of sympathy crossing his face.

"Sixteen, I lived at the ranch in Montana summers and on school holidays. He sent me to a private school in Beverly Hills while he fought with his demons."

"Where was your Ma?"

"She turned up at the funeral, and I thought for a short time that she was back to . . ." She stopped and sniffed. "Well, it turned out that she was looking for the inheritance she thought she would receive, and my grandpa never let me see her. Papa said she was a conniving she-devil."

Declan jerked from the comment. "A she-devil?" His voice was light with humour. "I'm sorry to laugh, but that is something me da would have said."

Meghan chuckled slightly, but the lightness of her laugh was missing. "I never got to see her or ask her why she left me. I really wanted to know that."

"Maybe it's best that y' don't," Declan said softly. "Sometimes people do things that let us down, and it's best not knowing their selfish reasons. Just be grateful that y' had a da and a grandda that loved y' enough to protect y' from further hurt."

Meghan nodded, closed her eyes, and pressed her face against his firm chest. "After all these years, I still want to believe that she came back for me and not the money, but I know that's not true. Whenever I go to a new city, I always look in the phone book to see if there is an Elizabeth Delaney listed, but there never is."

Declan grabbed her hand and tucked it up against his chest. She could not believe how gentle his hands were, even though they seemed to engulf hers as he held them.

"Where do your parents live?" Meghan questioned.

"Boston. We moved from Northern Ireland when I was about fourteen."

"Why did you move away?"

"Well, it's a long story, but the gist of it is me ma was a devout Catholic and me da converted to marry her, which wasn't well accepted. Then to make matters worse, his sister Mary married a Catholic man that was rumoured to have ties to the IRA at the time."

"That caused a problem?"

Declan tilted his head and raised his brow. "Y' don't know much about the troubles that have plagued the country in the past, do y'?"

"Well, I know enough to know that using religion as an excuse to kill each other is horrible," Meghan blurted out, trying to defend her question.

"Aye, it is, but religion had very little to do with the fighting when y' get right down to it. It was more about power and years of oppression to the Catholic people."

She nodded slightly, not wanting to get into an intense argument about the underlying issues in Ireland.

Declan grinned slightly. "But Uncle Mick is pretty cool, I always like his stories he had growing up, and I loved hanging out with me cousin Eamon. When I was about twelve, me da got into some dealings with a man that wasn't well liked. As y' could imagine at that time, members of the community were not too interested in having much to do with us after that. So after about two years, me ma made us move to Boston. She had an auntie there." His brow rose slightly. "Do y' recall the man Kaye was talking about?"

"Her friend Liam?"

"Aye, that's the one." He dropped his hand to her leg. "Well, his da Fergus O'Brien threatened me family."

"Why?"

"Well, I'm not quite sure," Declan said abruptly, his eyes settled on her and a shadow of distrust appeared. His dark grey eyes scanned her face as if he had just noticed that she was present, and he was not sure if she could be trusted with his life history. "Me parents never told me."

Meghan noticed his hesitation and an overwhelming feeling of foolishness was consuming her. She had rambled on about her life and yet he seemed hesitant to reveal too much information about his.

His brow rose slightly, and he eyed her curiously. He knew that she was not accepting his excuse, but he did not want to get into his family history with her. It would bring up to many questions, and he was unprepared to divulge that information. He was not even sure why he mentioned Fergus to her, he should not have. He needed to tread carefully. He never imagined that he would encounter her family line; he thought it had died off. It must be fate.

The tension in her, however, was escalating, and he desperately tried to think of something to say to break the silence that had developed over the past few minutes.

"I think you better get going. I have to meet Cassie," Meghan blurted out, breaking the dreaded silence. However, pushing him away was not the icebreaker he wanted.

He sighed and stared at her shortly. "Please tell me what I did to upset y'?"

"Nothing, I just . . ." she babbled, trying to get off the bed.

"Where did y' develop that flight trait that y' have?" he questioned, gripping her arm holding her hostage to the bed and him.

"What do you mean by that?" Meghan's eyes narrowed with annoyance.

"Every time y' don't know how to deal with something, y' try to run," he commented evenly.

"Are you a shrink now?" Meghan questioned, still squirming in his arms.

"No, I just noticed it, that's all," Declan said calmly, brushing his thumb across her wrist that he was still clutching. "Y' never have to run from me, I will never hurt y'."

She nodded her head and forced a painful smile.

A deep-seeded fear crept through him as he realized that she could sense his hesitation in telling her the truth. She understood him better than most people did, and that thought worried him slightly.

"Maybe me brother will dig up what the big secret is," Declan said evenly, hoping that she would believe he was not hiding anything from her. "He's over in Ireland now."

"If your parents are so secretive about your past, won't they be upset if he discovers the truth?" Meghan questioned cautiously, her overpowering curiosity taking over.

His brow rose slightly, his mouth twitched at the corners. "That's why he's there. Rory is the kind of person who goes against the grain."

"Really, he's not a straight arrow like you?" she joked, resting her hand on his chest and brushing away the imaginary wrinkles on his shirt.

His brow rose slightly, and he grabbed her hands, giving them a slight squeeze. "No, if he can find a way to cause trouble, he will."

"You don't get along with him?"

"I try because I feel sorry for him, but he makes it very difficult to like him sometimes."

"Why do you feel sorry for him?"

"Me da always treated him differently than the rest of us. It was as if he didn't belong. I would hear me parents talking about him sometimes, and it was like me da hated him," he continued, trying to explain his reasoning for feeling guilty.

"Is it because he likes to cause trouble?" Meghan questioned with interest.

"No, I don't think so. It was something else. But I'm sure Rory could feel it, and that is why I feel the need to make up for it."

"How many brothers do you have?" Meghan questioned curiously.

"I have two brothers and two sisters. Moiré is the eldest, then there is me, then Rory, and then Claire and Colin, they are twins.

"Wow, that's a big family." Meghan gasped.

"Aye," Declan smiled with delight. "I have to say that some days I would prefer to be an only child, but it is nice having family."

Meghan nodded and glanced up at Declan. "So how old are you?"

"Twenty-eight." Declan scratched his chin.

"Oh," Meghan grinned. "An older man."

Declan grunted and pinned her to the bed. "I'm not old."

Meghan could not help but giggle at his annoyed facial expression.

"Well, if y' prefer younger men. Rory would be just about the right age for y'. He's twenty-four."

"I love the way you say that." Meghan giggled.

"What?"

"Rory. It is such a sexy name," Meghan smirked, feeling more at ease the more he talked about his family. Maybe he was not being evasive and felt he could trust her.

"Well, I think y' would find him far from sexy," Declan informed her with a wink.

Meghan laughed at his objection to her finding the name sexy, and she was rewarded by Declan squeezing her hands in retaliation. "You're not jealous, are you, that he has the better name?"

"I'm not jealous," Declan grinned, knowing she was trying to provoke him. "I have been told by many that Declan is a very sexy name."

Meghan broke into hysterical laughter and pushed herself to a sitting position on the bed.

"Well, Declan, the 'oh so sexy'," Meghan muttered as she climbed off the bed.

"Well, what?" Declan chuckled, rolling on to his side so he could follow her with his gaze.

"I have to admit when you say it, it sounds sexy," she teased as she headed towards her discarded coffee cup on the table by the window.

"Aye, that's because I pronounce it properly." Declan jumped from the bed and adjusted his clothing.

"And I don't?" Meghan stared at him as he glanced from his watch to her.

"Aye, y' say it perfectly," he smiled with pleasure.

"Would you like some coffee? I never thought to ask you earlier," Meghan smiled and lifted the decanter towards him in offering.

"No, I actually have to get going. I just wanted to see y' this morning. So will y' honour me with your presence at dinner?" He bowed slightly, then glanced up at her with a smile, twisting his full lips.

"Sure." Meghan giggled before gulping down a mouthful of coffee.

"Great, then I'll see y' tonight." Before she noticed, he was across the room and right up behind her.

Meghan jumped slightly when he put his hand on her shoulder. "Would you stop doing that!"

"Doing what?" Declan asked, quite startled by her jumpiness.

"Sneaking up on me."

"I'm sorry, I didn't mean to. It's just a habit."

"It's a habit to sneak up on people?" She giggled.

"Aye." Declan's arms wrapped around her waist, his lips moving closer to hers. "Freckles, are y' still scared of me?"

"Yes," Meghan admitted but could not hold back a smile.

He sighed and eyed her softly. "Well, then I guess I will have to do everything in me power to change your mind," he said quietly as his lips touched hers, causing an overflowing passion to flow into her, her body trembling with anticipation. "I want y' to think of me all day," he announced, with an air of arrogance as he released her and turned towards the door.

"And you think that will do it?" she replied dryly.

Declan's mouth twitched into a slight smile as he watched her eyes dancing with mischief, and he grabbed hold of her arm and pulled her towards him.

"Let go, that's not fair. You're bigger than me!" Meghan shrieked as his hand snaked around her waist, pulling her securely to his chest.

"Aye, and I'm going to take advantage of that fact," he told her sternly as he spun her around to face him. He grabbed her face in his hands, holding it still as his lips locked around her mouth. Electricity shot through her as one of his hands left her face and slid gently down her neck with a tingling force that made her tremble.

"If that doesn't get you to think of me, nothing will," he smiled softly, then released her from his grasp, leaving her to catch her breath. "And as for the trust issue. You'll trust me soon."

Declan could not control the smile as he headed towards the door very aware of the effect he had on her. He could make her tremble with passion.

"Do y' want Fabs to stay with y' today?"

"No, I'll be fine," Meghan mumbled uncomfortably. "Don't you need him?"

"No," Declan laughed. "He's around more to keep me out of trouble and make sure I get where I'm supposed to be than for protection."

"Oh," she giggled. "He's your assistant."

"Sort of, but don't call him that," Declan laughed louder. "I hired him last year because after me first movie, I found it hard to go out in public without being followed by the paparazzi, who were trying to find some dirt to use against me da. Fabs has been a good friend for years, and I like having him around because I know I can trust him, and that's important in this business."

"I guess so," she agreed, wondering how much he trusted her. "Why would they need dirt on your dad?"

"Oh, he's the Senator for Massachusetts."

"Really?" Meghan sounded shocked.

"Aye," Declan smiled, content that his father's career was not her driving force for her interest in him. Unlike Georgia, the woman his mother wants him to marry. All she cared about was going to the parties and associating with the right people.

"So are y' sure y' don't want Fabs to stay with y'? He wouldn't mind. I think he is getting sick of coming to the set, and it would make me feel better," he smiled, pressing her to allow Fabrizio to stay with her.

"All right." Meghan begrudgingly agreed. Why was he so determined to have Fabrizio follow her around all day?

"Good, I'll see y' when I get back." Declan's grin filled with triumph. She was finally bending to his will. Maybe she was not as headstrong as he thought.

CHAPTER FIVE

Meghan occupied the rest of her morning with the documents that Nathan had given her regarding her family lineage. Nathan had been researching Meghan's family history because she did not have any information before 1956 when her grandfather moved to the United States. The records Nathan found in Ireland were sparse since the church that had all the birth records burned down in 1945. He was convinced that there was property somewhere in Ireland that was hidden in her grandfather's estate. Income was entering Meghan's trust, and her grandfather's lawyer refused to explain the source.

Meghan sighed and dropped the file to the nightstand to read after she got back from lunch.

Fabrizio was supposed to meet her over half an hour earlier and since he had not shown up, she was going on her own.

Only one light in the hallway was illuminated and casting a dim glow around the stocky man standing at the end of the hall. It was Ian. Could she get back into her room before he caught her? What if she couldn't get the key out of her purse fast enough? Should she scream?

"Meghan, I have come to take you home." Ian's voice was low and pierced through her, sending chills of terror through her.

Panic set in, and she swung around and slammed into a large frame in her path. "Holy shit!" she blurted out.

"Meghan, what's wrong?" Fabrizio's voice startled her as his dark brown eyes scanned over her shoulder, looking for what had frightened her.

"It's Ian," she blurted out and buried her face in Fabrizio's chest. "Please don't let him near me."

Fabrizio eyed her curiously and glanced once more down the empty hall. "I don't see anyone."

"He was right there!" Meghan sniffed and turned to look down the hallway. "He was."

"I believe you." Fabrizio's voice sounded disbelieving. "You look like you have seen a ghost."

"I must have," Meghan muttered and eyed the empty hall again.

"Well." Fabrizio chuckled and tweaked her nose. "I think I have found your nickname."

"What?" Meghan blurted out.

"Well, I like to give people nicknames, and I think I am going to call you Boo."

"Please don't," Meghan begged.

Fabrizio laughed at her facial expression. "Oh, I am afraid you are stuck with it."

Meghan crinkled her nose at him. "What is yours?"

"That depends on who you ask. My mother calls me Fabrizio Antonio Stagliano, but everyone else calls me Fabs."

"So that's your name," Meghan smiled. "Declan always calls you Fabs. Well, it's nice to meet you, Fabrizio," Meghan smiled warmly up at him.

"You are the only person on this earth, other than my mother, that I will allow to call me Fabrizio."

Meghan giggled. "I guess then I will have to allow you to call me Boo."

"All right, look at me," Fabrizio smiled. "I'll take you under one condition."

"What's that?" Meghan smiled, her bright green eyes fixed on him.

"That you don't leave my side today. If you saw Ian, then I don't want to take any chances . . ."

"If!" Meghan snorted, interrupting his comment. "You don't believe that I saw him, do you?"

Fabrizio laughed at her expression. "Declan is right, everything you think shows on your face. You want to smack me right now, don't you?"

Meghan scowled at him, her eyes burning through him. "You're pretty close." She swung around to leave, but she was stopped by Fabrizio's hand gripping her arm.

"Listen to me, Boo, I'm not saying that I don't believe you."

Meghan sighed and eyed him with regret. "I'm sorry, I don't mean to freak out."

"No problem," Fabrizio smiled and bent his arm towards her. "Let me escort you to your friends."

Declan arrived in the lounge late in the evening, with Colton Barrett and a couple members of the crew. He had told Meghan he would have dinner with her, but dinnertime had long passed, and it was getting late. His concern was that Meghan had gone to her room, not wanting to wait any longer. Georgia would have gone home, but Declan used that to his advantage and constantly made her wait. She would go home, and he was off the hook. His mother constantly forced Georgia into his life, and he wanted nothing to do with her. How would his mother react to his relationship with Meghan? Not very well, he assumed.

Meghan partnered with Nathan against Cassie and Pete, and they had been playing pool for a few hours. Fabrizio was over by the bar, more interested in talking with a group of women that seemed very interested in him.

Declan's eyes immediately rested on Meghan who was tormenting Pete as he took his shot, causing him to miss the pocket by only inches.

"Meg, stop cheating," Pete joked and grabbed her from behind, running his fingers up her ribs, forcing loud shrieks out of her mouth.

Declan chuckled slightly at her reaction to Pete's attack. Her interaction with her friends was no different than it was with him, and an overwhelming feeling of contentment swept through him.

Fabrizio wandered up and eyed Declan with a slight grin filling his lips. "She is a terrific lady."

Declan turned his eyes on Fabrizio. "Y' had an enjoyable afternoon with her?"

"Yes, they are all very nice. It's good to see that you're finally attracted to a woman with substance."

"I'm not sure if that's a blessing or a curse," Declan chuckled and smacked Fabrizio's shoulder. "She'll keep me on me toes."

"She will," Fabrizio smirked and then focused on Meghan.

"Eight ball in the left corner pocket," Meghan announced, bending over the pool table. She eyed Pete with a rebellious glance, grinned, and then stuck out her tongue.

"You better hope that goes in after that!" Pete grumbled, shaking his head at her.

Meghan grinned and eyed the ball with an appearance of skill, then lined up her long, narrow queue and shot. It bounced off the pine green felt on the side and rolled slowly into the pocket.

Meghan shrieked when Nathan lifted her into the air, swinging her in a circle. "We won!" She shouted throwing her arms up in the air over her head.

"We are the champions, we are the champions." Nathan started to sing.

"That girl is smoking hot!" Colton blurted out, his sky blue eyes settling on Meghan. His hand ran through his short blond hair in preparation of introducing himself. "If you will excuse me, I must meet her."

"Give it up, Colton, she's mine." Declan boasted as his dark grey eyes sparkled with delight.

"She's yours?" Colton replied, scratching his stumbled square chin and his full lips tuned up into a smile exposing his larges white teeth.

"Aye, I met her three days ago," Declan informed him with a tone of pride in his voice.

"Wow, three whole days!" Colton teased. His eyes danced with humour as he watched his friend talking about the new woman in his life. "So she's the one you have been babbling about all day."

"I've heard enough from y', I'm going to kiss me beautiful lady," Declan snorted, focusing his eyes back on Meghan.

"Don't tease him, Colton, he is very sensitive when it comes to her, she is his soul mate," Fabrizio mocked and batted his dark brown eyes at Declan.

"Oh, your soul mate, you really believe that crap?" Colton joked as he turned his attention to the waitress to order his drink.

"Colton, until y' stop dating shallow vain women and find a woman like her, you'll never know what I'm talking about," Declan muttered, his attention drawn back to Meghan and her friends.

"Oh, and you have dated such well rounded women in the past." Colton snorted a laugh. "I believe the last girl could even spell her full name."

Declan grunted with amusement. "Aye, well, I'm a changed man. Meggie is perfect."

Colton laughed and eyed Cassie. "Well, what about the stunning blonde?"

"That's Cassie, and I do believe that she is available." Declan pushed at Colton's shoulder. "Come on, I'll introduce y'."

Apparently aggravated by Nathan's championship song, Cassie had run around the side of the table and jumped onto his back, cupping her hand over his mouth. He lowered Meghan to the ground, finding the weight of the two women overwhelming, and he reached around, grabbing at Cassie to remove her from his back.

Meghan was laughing uncontrollably as she watched Nathan spinning in circles like a bronco trying to remove the unwelcome rider. Her attention, however, was broken when a large pair of hands slipped around her ribs from behind. She swung around and came face to face with Declan's smirking face. Her brow rose slightly, but before she could complain about his sneaking up on her, his hand was on her face, and his lips were heading towards her.

"So did y' miss me?" he questioned, his face only inches from hers.

"Terribly." Meghan giggled and rested her hands on his chest.

"Good." His lips pressed against hers with a force that let everyone know that she was his. "I missed y' too."

She smiled and patted his chest slightly, noticing that the majority of the people in the lounge were now watching them, including Kaye. "Maybe we should sit down."

"Good plan," he said quietly, noticing the gawking patrons as well. "I'll get us a drink."

Meghan nodded and eyed the chair beside Cassie. "Fine, abandon me already," Meghan grumbled, a slight grin curling her lips.

Declan chuckled, his brow rising slightly. "Don't y' be worrying yourself about that." He leaned towards her and kissed her upturned face. "But if y' get lonely, y' can look at this." He pulled a picture out of his coat pocket and handed it to her.

Meghan eyed it, then looked up at him with amazement. "Oh my God, you carry signed pictures around with you?"

He looked startled by her comment but settled quickly. "No, I just thought y' might like it."

Her brow rose slightly as she held it tightly against her chest. "I'll treasure it forever." She giggled.

Declan appeared rather insulted and made a grab for the picture. "If y' are going to make fun."

"Declan!" Meghan grumbled as he wrapped his arm around her shoulders, his loose hand prying at her hands that she had pressed up against her chest. "I wasn't making fun."

Declan's face pressed into the side of her neck from behind, and his fingers slid down her ribs. "Do I need to use me secret weapon?" Declan mumbled against her neck as she began to flail around in his arms.

"No, here, have it." Meghan giggled and smacked him in the head with the picture.

Declan gripped the picture and bent back the corners she had bent in her struggles. "Thank y', but I must say y' are very ungrateful," he smirked.

"Well, next time try and get my name right," she laughed and smacked his arm. "I'm Meghan, not Candy."

"Ah well," Declan laughed and glanced at the bartender. "She asked me for it the other night."

Meghan smirked and pushed at his arm. "Then I suggest you get over there with it."

"Aye," Declan smiled and rested his hand on her shoulder. "Oh, Meggie, I would like y' to meet Colton." Declan turned to the side, exposing the tall blond man to her.

Colton smiled and reached out his hand towards her. "Hi, Meghan, it's nice to meet you."

"It's nice to meet you too." Meghan forced an uneasy smile.

"So, Declan tells me that you are a big fan of mine," Colton grinned as her face enflamed with colour.

Meghan glared at Declan, then turned back to Colton. "Well, I have seen some of your movies, but I can't claim to be a big movie fan."

Colton smiled and turned to Declan when he started to laugh. "She hasn't even seen any of my movies."

"Really?" Colton sounded surprised.

"Aye." Declan slipped his arm around her waist. "She didn't even know who I was until the other day."

Meghan giggled as his fingers tickled her ribs. "Well, you will be happy to know I watched your last movie this morning." Meghan glanced up at Declan with a smirk crossing her lips.

"Really?" Declan sounded slightly shocked. "What did you think?"

"Well, I felt it was unrealistic and demeaning in its portrayal of the First Nations people, depicting them as ignorant savages, who hunted the buffalo almost into extinction. That is completely wrong. They were a very intelligent and resourceful people that only killed what they could use. It was the Europeans that almost annihilated the buffalo, hunting them for their pelts and leaving the rest to rot. In addition, it didn't even talk about the government's role in killing off the buffalo to drive the native people onto reserves."

Colton snorted a laugh and glanced over at Declan. "I have to agree with her. It was a very cheesy movie."

"Aye," Declan agreed. "But it made a lot of money at the box office."

"That's because you spent the whole movie in a loincloth," Colton laughed.

"Well, that part I found rather appealing." Meghan giggled and rested her hand on his firm chest.

"I'm glad to hear y' found something agreeable about the film. I hope this one will be more to your liking."

"Are you undressed?" Meghan giggled and pressed up against him.

"Are y' daft? It is a film about a group of explorers trapped on a mountain pass over the winter." Declan was slightly offended that she felt his only acting skill was exposing his body. "This is a very intellectual film, and I resent the fact that y' think the only way it will succeed is if I undress."

Meghan eyed him shortly, then she glanced over at Colton. "I'm sorry. I didn't mean to suggest anything of the sort. I'm sure it is a very life-altering movie," Meghan sighed and turned towards Cassie. "Cassie, have you met Colton?"

Cassie jumped from her chair and took his outstretched hand. "It's nice to meet you."

Meghan forced a smile and moved away slightly as Cassie gave her opinion of Colton's last movie. She raved of course, seeming to have a bit more common sense than Meghan had.

"Boo, what's wrong?" Fabrizio questioned as he noticed her facial expression.

"Nothing." Meghan forced a smile, wandered past him, and headed for the washroom.

Declan noticed her walking away from them, and he followed closely behind her. He knew he had upset her once again. Why did he keep letting his ego get the better of him? He knew that the movie was ridiculous, and she was correct with her facts. She was just telling him the truth, and it was her inability to lie that he found so appealing about her. Her blatantly honest answers to his questions grounded him. He needed to apologize.

Meghan stared at her reflection in the mirror, wondering why she would have told him the things she had. Why couldn't she keep her mouth shut and tell him she loved his movie. She was completely embarrassed by his reaction, and she wanted to escape to her room.

Meghan mustered up the courage and pulled open the door to the ladies' room. She was half way across the room before she noticed that Declan was not with the others. Colton was sitting beside Cassie, wooing her with his charms, and the rest of the group seemed unconcerned with her whereabouts. Maybe she could sneak out without anyone noticing.

"Where do y' think y' are going?" Declan's voice was soft in her ear. "Bolting again, are y'?"

Meghan stopped her retreat to the door and turned towards the voice. "No, I was just . . . well."

"Meggie, I'm sorry. I shouldn't have reacted like that." He gripped her hand, pulling her towards him. "I know that was a daft movie." He eyed her shortly. "I know that I get parts because of the way I look, and for now, I have to accept that."

"Declan, I didn't say you weren't a good actor. I said the movie sucked. You were very good." Meghan kissed his cheek. "I'm sorry I was nervous, and I was rambling."

Declan's brow rose slightly. "Are y' unnerved by Colton?"

Meghan giggled at his facial expression. "Yes. It's not every day you meet a movie star, let alone be . . ." She stopped not knowing how to finish the sentence.

Declan smirked and kissed her forehead. "Dating one."

Meghan eyed him with a smile curling her lips. "Yes."

Declan winked at her and pulled her towards the table. "Sit down, and I'll get the drinks."

Declan sauntered over to the bar and leaned against the counter next to Fabrizio. He began to banter with the bartender and did not notice Kaye's approach. She pushed past the two women that had moved over and were now standing directly next to Declan, their eyes glued to the back of his head.

"Watch it!" snorted a short brunette, when Kaye's wiry frame shoved her slightly, dislodging her from her position next to Declan.

"Well, then get out of my way," Kaye said harshly, eyeing the woman up and down. "Like you have any chance with him."

Declan turned around at the sound of the commotion to find Fabrizio pulling Kaye and the brunette apart, while the blonde used the opportunity to get right up next to him. His brow crumpled at the women, and he fixed his gaze on Kaye.

"What are y' doing?" Declan was aggravated by Kaye's presence at his side. "Do y' need to fight with everyone?"

"I need to talk to you," Kaye blurted out, gripping his arm.

"I'm busy right now," he said firmly and began to push past the women.

"Declan, please listen to me," Kaye pleaded, her voice sounding slightly panicked. "You need to keep your distance from Meghan."

Declan's brow shot up with vague surprise. "Why?"

"She's not who you think she is."

Declan grunted with slight annoyance. "Let me clear something up for y'. I have no intentions of staying away from Meggie now or in the future, so y' better just accept it."

Kaye eyed him narrowly. "Fine, but don't blame me when . . ." She stopped and turned away from him.

Declan made a grab for Kaye's arm to question her about the comment, but Fabrizio intervened, gripping his arm. "Monty, she is trying to rile you, leave it be."

Declan nodded, his cold eyes still fixed on Kaye as she wandered back towards the table. "I have to say I dislike that woman."

Fabrizio laughed and nodded towards Meghan, who was also glaring at Kaye; evidently she had been watching the exchange going on. "That makes two of you."

"I hope she isn't cross with me again," Declan grinned, smacking Fabrizio on the shoulder. "That woman seems to bring out the worst in Meggie."

Fabrizio laughed as his gaze settled on Meghan. "Kaye definitely knows how to push Meghan's buttons. Monty, I'm not sure if I should say anything about this or not, but something happened today, and I think you should know." Fabrizio's eyes switched back and forth from Declan to Meghan.

"What?" Declan blurted out, trying to keep his voice low.

"Well, I found her in the hallway, and she was freaking out about some guy named Ian. She said she saw him at the end of the hall, but I didn't see anyone."

Declan glanced over at Meghan with interest. "He was the guy in her room this morning, the one that hit her."

"That would explain her panic, but it was her description of the guy that concerns me."

"Why?"

"She described Rory," Fabrizio blurted out.

"She said it was Rory? My brother Rory?" Declan's voice rose with worry.

"No, but she described Rory perfectly right down to the birthmark on his neck."

Declan sighed and glanced back at Meghan. "So Rory has a double. It can't be him because he's in Ireland."

"I know, I doubt it was him, but I suggest you don't introduce her to him for a while."

"Don't worry. I have no intentions of inflicting me family on her any time soon. I want her to like me," Declan laughed and smacked Fabrizio's shoulder. "Thanks for the warning."

CHAPTER SIX

Meghan quietly staggered down the hall, leaning in to Declan, trying not to focus on anything since she could not stop the spinning. Even in her intoxicated state, she had unease about allowing him to escort her back to her room. If he was just interested in taking her to bed, she was definitely going to be vulnerable against his unyielding strength.

"Thanks for helping me back," Meghan announced, with a tone of dismissal.

"You're welcome, but I'm not leaving y' standing out in the hall." Declan snatched the key from her hand and opened the door to the brightly decorated room.

"I'll be fine." Meghan panicked, wondering how far he would push the situation.

"Meggie, stop trying to get rid of me. I'm not leaving y' until I get y' tucked into bed."

"That's what I'm afraid of," she mumbled, not realizing how loud she had said it.

Declan's brow rose with amusement, and he released her arm, allowing her to stumble through the door onto the gleaming oak floor. When she got to the sleigh bed, she flung the floral comforter back, flopped down, and tumbled forward.

Declan darted towards her and gently pushed her back to a sitting position. "Meggie y' need to lie down," he ordered firmly, pushing on her shoulders until she obliged and lay back on the crisp white sheets.

"The room is spinning," she blurted out as she tried to focus on the two wing chairs over by the window.

"Aye, Freckles, it will for a while," Declan laughed and brushed back a wild wave behind her ear.

"You're finding this funny?" Meghan blinked at him, trying to focus, but his face was spinning along with the rest of the room.

He smiled and pulled her shoes off, then lifted the blankets over her shivering body. "I'll get y' a damp cloth."

When he returned to the bed, he laid the cloth across her forehead and then reached for the light. His chest tightened when he noticed the bundle of papers lying next to the lamp. Curiosity got the better of him, and he glanced down at Meghan; her eyes were closed, and her head was turned towards the window.

He cringed slightly when the paper crinkled as he spread it open; why he had the urge to read it he did not know, but it was strong.

"Bloody hell," Declan muttered as his eyes scanned the paper. "I'm too late. She is searching for her genealogy." He glanced down at the unconscious woman on the bed, the only one that could unite the families. Did she know about the triad? He did not think so, she would have told him. Did she even know she owned a large estate in Ireland?

Time was running out, and if she left the lodge without committing to him, that would destroy his plans. Once Nathan links her father's side of the family together, she will learn of her legacy, then it might be too late, and what little trust she has in him would be gone.

Once he had returned the papers to the nightstand, he bent and kissed her forehead, causing her lashes to flutter open as she gazed up at him. A slight smile grew across her face as he ran his hands through her hair, smoothing it behind her ear, repeatedly in a rhythmic motion.

"Are y' feeling better?" Declan asked softly.

"No, not really," she whispered, her eyes wide and childlike, as she gazed up at him hovering over her.

"Did y' eat today?" he asked softly.

Her face crumpled in thought. "Not since lunch," she admitted.

He grunted with amusement. "I'll order y' something."

"No! I couldn't eat anything," she begged, her face turning a slight shade of green.

"Freckles, y' have to get something into your stomach. I'll order some soup and toast." He gently insisted, lifting the phone and placing the call.

"I'll stay with y' until y' feel better." He lay down besides her, staring at her with amusement.

"You don't have to. I'll be fine, I just need some sleep." She was fighting to keep her eyes open as she glanced at him through the narrow slits.

Declan smiled softly and stroked her hair behind her ears again. "I don't mind."

"Declan, why are you staying?" Meghan gazed up at him, with one eye open.

"Because I find y' very attractive when y' look at me like a pirate," he joked but quickly realized she was not finding it amusing. "What do y' mean, Freckles?"

"I just don't understand why you would want to waste your night here with me?" She could hear the words exiting her mouth, but she was not sure why she was asking him a question so loaded.

"Meggie, time spent with y' isn't a waste," he whispered and kissed her forehead.

"I'm sorry."

"What are y' sorry for?" His tone was gentle and caring.

"For ruining your night, I know you were expecting . . ." She stopped, realizing she was pushing the line again.

Declan looked down at her with amusement growing across his face. "So that's what this is all about." He mused. "Y' still think me only interest in y' is to take y' to bed?"

Meghan's eyes widened at his comment. What the hell had she done? "No," she blurted out with an overwhelming tone of embarrassment.

"Meggie, if I was only interested in sex, I wouldn't have any trouble finding a woman to take to bed," he informed her with a tone of arrogance.

"I see," she muttered and rolled onto her side, trying to avoid his irritated eyes.

"Meggie?"

"What?"

"Why are y' cross with me?" Declan pulled her onto her back, leaving her no choice but to look at him.

"Why don't you want to make love to me? Don't you find me attractive?" she blurted out irrationally, but quickly regretted doing so.

"Y' think that I don't find y' attractive? Meggie, I find it hard not to take y' in me arms and make love to y'. I just don't want to push y', especially after the way y' reacted last night." As long as he lived, he would never understand the way women think.

Meghan's face crumpled as she thought about what she had said. Her stomach began to churn once again as she mulled over her comments, and mortification took hold. She repeatedly swallowed, trying to hold down the rebelling contents of her stomach, her eyes closed, and her breath was deep and laboured.

"Are y' okay?" he questioned, noticing the change in her behaviour.

"No," she muttered, keeping her eyes closed, trying to control the fermenting alcohol in her stomach that was tumbling out of control.

"Oh no!" She bolted from the bed and darted across the slippery wooden floor to the bathroom, coming to an abrupt stop as she hit the floor with a terrible thud.

Struggling to get up, she felt Declan lifting her effortlessly to her feet and ushering her to the toilet, where she proceeded to relieve the discomfort in her belly, by regurgitating the remainder of the night's indulgence. Exhaustion finally took hold, and she collapsed to the floor in a heap of distress as her eyes filled with tears, and she sobbed.

"Meggie?" Declan whispered scooping her into his arms and holding her close to his comforting chest. "Why are y' crying?"

She shook her head into his chest, not wanting to say anymore to him, since she had already said more than enough. He stroked her hair back off her face while he waited patiently for her to calm down.

"I need to brush my teeth." Meghan sniffed, trying to regain some composure.

"Aye," Declan lifted her to her feet and helped her to the sink, "do y' need help?"

"No."

Declan smiled softly and left the bathroom, closing the door behind him. She could hear him moving around in the room; then she felt her heart drop as the door to her room opened, then the distinct sound of it closing came resonating back to her. A foreboding feeling overcame her as she struggled with the fact that he walked out the door, leaving her to wonder what had happened that evening.

It took her quite some time before she managed to brush her teeth, wash her face, and slip into the tank top and shorts she wore to bed.

Stumbling out of the bathroom, she kicked at the waist basket that she had knocked over when she fell. It skidded across the room, coming to a clanging stop against the wall.

"Shit!" Meghan blurted out, as a sharp pain shot through her foot. She bent down and rubbed her toe, with growing annoyance.

"Are y' blaming that for your falling?" Declan smirked as she took out her aggression on the white metal basket.

"You're still here?" Meghan babbled, her eyes settling on him with shock.

"Aye."

"I thought you left." A smile curled her lips and the tension in her face lessened.

"No, room service came. Did y' want me to leave?" he questioned with a tone of worry.

"No!" Meghan blurted out. "I mean . . ."

Declan smiled softly and jumped from the chair to help her back to the bed. She immediately pulled up her foot and examined the throbbing toe.

"Hurt?" Declan chuckled and dropped to the bed beside her, stroking her hair down her back, enjoying the feel of her bare shoulders against his hand.

"Yes," she grumbled and rubbed the reddened appendage, keeping her eyes deliberately off him.

He had turned off the overhead lights, and the only light in the room was coming from the lamp on the other side of her bed. Meghan found the dimmed light more pleasant for her burning eyes, but she was worried about the implication. Logically, with everything she knew about him, she did not think he would take advantage of her in her intoxicated state. However, she reminded herself that she had only known him for a few days, and there were still times he seemed so self-absorbed.

"Are y' okay?" Declan questioned, trying to keep a straight face while she scrubbed her toe, as if the motion would somehow soothe it.

"Yes." Meghan released her toe and slid back on the bed.

He could not hold the laughter in any longer, and he burst into hysterics as she fluffed her pillow, trying to find a comfortable position.

"I can't believe y' barfed in front of me," Declan blurted out as he continued to laugh.

"Don't make fun of me!" Meghan snorted, still fighting to keep her eyes open.

"Sorry." Declan agreed, kissing her forehead.

She sighed and closed her eyes, trying to stop the spinning caused not only by the alcohol but by the roller coaster her emotions seemed to be on. Warm moist air was surrounding her face, and she abruptly opened her eyes finding his face hovering over hers.

"What?" she blurted out.

"Nothing, I was just watching y'."

"Why?" she questioned, rather concerned.

He shrugged and kissed her forehead. "I just can't believe y' are real."

A concerned expression crossed her face as she forced both eyes on him. "What do you mean by that?"

Amusement shadowed his face as he watched her becoming more anxious. "Don't get yourself all worked up. I just meant that you're an incredible woman. If I didn't know better, I would think that y' somehow found out what I was looking for in a woman and moulded yourself to fit the part."

She jerked from the comment, her eyes suddenly alert. "That's what you think of me?"

"No!" Declan said firmly, regretting making the comment. She was in no condition to grasp his meaning. "Please, don't misunderstand me."

She swallowed hard, her eyes fluttering with worry. "I think it's very unfair of you to judge me when I'm in this condition, considering you contributed to it." Her voice was shaky and full of distress.

"Meggie, I'm not judging y'," he consoled, sliding his hand down her head. "I'm sorry I shouldn't have made that comment while y' are . . ."

"While I'm what?" she blurted out, interrupting his comment. "This is why I didn't want you coming in. I knew I would scare you away."

"Meggie," he said softly, as her eyes closed, blocking out his face. "What did I say to make y' think y' have scared me off?" he asked firmly, resting his hand on her face.

Her eyes opened slowly, embarrassment shooting from them. "Never mind," she mumbled, shaking her head with distress.

"Y' will have to do a lot more than get drunk to scare me off."

"I'm sorry," she whispered, her eyes closed again as she tried to hide her anguish.

He smiled slightly and kissed her lips softly. "Y' have nothing to be sorry for."

He was amazed at the level of emotions that was surrounding them. They both seemed caught up in something stronger than common sense, and he felt a slight tug at his heart. Meghan appeared completely caught off guard by her feelings for him, and her irrational response to his comments worried him slightly. How was he going to calm her down enough so she would accept her feeling for him before it was too late?

"Meggie." His voice was soft and low as his lips headed towards her, landing gently against her startled mouth.

His earlier kiss was quick and undemanding, but this time he was letting her know that he was serious about her, and he wanted more. Not only was the room spinning, sending her equilibrium into havoc, but also her entire body felt foreign somehow. As if she was trapped in someone else's shell, and she could not break free. The feel of his hand sliding up her tank top and across her breast startled her back to reality, and she panicked. She wanted to be more in control when or if they made love.

"Declan," she blurted out, pulling her mouth away from his. "Please, I—"

"Shh, Freckles," he whispered, kissing the nape of her neck, his fingers circling her breast.

"Please, I don't want our first time . . . ," she sniffed as a tremor ran through her. "I want . . ."

His head lifted, his hand moving out from her tank top. "What is it y' want?"

She stared at him with worry, not confident that pushing him away again was the right thing to do. On the other hand, the last thing she wanted to do was make love for the first time, drunk. The words to tell him were not materializing in her mind, and the longer it took, the more impatient he became.

"Meggie, I just want to feel you next to me, I've been able to think of nothing else since I first saw y'. Please let me touch y'. I promise I won't take it any further," he begged.

"I can't," she blurted out, pushing at his shoulders. "Please, I feel so sick, and I want to experience it properly."

A slight grin spread across his face as he watched her trying to explain her feelings. His hand slid across her cheek and rested in her hair. "All right, Freckles, I guess I can wait," he smiled and kissed her forehead. "You're driving me crazy, do y' know that?" he sighed and gently covered her with the quilt. "I'll stay until you're asleep. If that's all right with y'?" he asked, staring down at her with tenderness.

"I would like that, thank you," she mumbled and stared up at him. "You're not mad at me?"

"No," he whispered and kissed her forehead. "I'm a little uncomfortable at the moment, but mad, I'm not." He chuckled and pulled at the crotch on his jeans.

She smiled softly, her green eyes finally settled. "Declan."

"Aye."

"I'm not scared of you anymore," she whispered.

CHAPTER SEVEN

The aspirin soothed Meghan's headache slightly after her and Cassie's panicked day of shopping. The sight of herself in the extraordinary emerald green dress cut to fit her like a glove pushed Meghan over the edge into excitement. The jeweled neckline plunged down just above her breasts, and the bodice accentuated her tiny waist. Her long legs, covered to her ankles, readily seen through the slits cut up each side, to just below her hips. She looked fantastic, and she knew it.

Cassie paced back and forth, her pale blue strapless gown swaying as she moved. The colour of her gown complimented her bright blue eyes that gazed out the large picture window in the lobby. Declan had promised the night before that a limousine would pick them up, but as the five minutes it was late turned into fifteen, the women became rather anxious.

"Are you sure he said six o'clock?" Cassie blurted out and adjusted the shawl around her shoulders.

"I'm pretty sure," Meghan said, with little confidence. "Maybe he didn't send it. Maybe he decided he doesn't want me coming."

"Why do you keep saying that? What could you have possibly done last night that would make him change his mind?" Cassie grumbled; the thought of missing the party was causing her attitude to become very hostile.

"Never mind," Meghan muttered and glanced back out the window as a glow floated across the snow, announcing a car approaching the lodge.

"Finally," Cassie muttered and pulled her shawl around her shoulders. "Let's go."

The long black limousine was thankfully warm, as the biting wind nipped at their exposed arms. Cassie's thin shawl provided as little protection as Meghan's.

The driver shut the door behind them and made a hasty retreat around to the front of the car, causing a sudden gush of cold air to fill the car. He slammed his door closed and began fussing with something on the seat beside him.

"Which one of you is Meggie?" he questioned as he turned to face the two women.

"I am," Meghan said hesitantly.

"This is for you," he smiled, handing her a large square box.

Meghan stared at the driver shortly as he gestured it towards her with impatience. She smiled and grabbed the box from his hand and flipped back the lid and gasped at the sight of the thick gold necklace inlaid with small diamonds down the centre. As she lifted it out of the box, a large tear-shaped emerald swung from the middle, swaying back and forth.

"Oh my gosh!" Meghan muttered, searching the box for a note, finally finding it under the emerald earrings that matched perfectly to the necklace. A tear trickled down her cheek as she read his wonderful words.

"Meggie, you shared your tears with me. Now I am sharing a tear with you. You are the most amazing woman I have ever met. You have captured my heart and soul. Love, Declan."

Meghan passed the note to Cassie, her hands shaking with excitement. He loved her; the man she loves, loves her back.

Cassie finished reading the note and looked over at Meghan, her blues eyes filled with envy. "Wow, he's a keeper! Aren't you going to put it on? Here, give me your locket and the earrings you have on, I'll put them in my purse," Cassie babbled, fumbling with the latch to her small black purse.

The necklace fit perfectly landing just above the delicate curve of the dress. Her heart was beating so strongly, she laid her hand over the throbbing pulse to settle it before it jumped from her chest.

"Cass," Meghan muttered, looking over at her friend who was staring out the window, watching the vast pine forest pass by in the fading light.

"Hmm?" she said as she turned towards Meghan.

"What am I going to do?" Meghan mumbled, her eyes glazing over.

"What do you mean?" Cassie questioned, resting her hand on Meghan's arm.

"I mean that I love him with all my heart, and I can't—" She stopped and glanced sightlessly out the window.

"Meg," Cassie soothed, patting her arm with a gentle presence. "I think he's made it perfectly clear that he loves you too," she smiled.

Meghan sighed and rested her hand on the emerald. "I just keep getting the overwhelming feeling that this is too good to be true. What if I am Cinderella, and I wake up when midnight strikes?"

"That's okay; remember the prince searches high and low until he finds her," Cassie smirked. "Then they get married and live happily ever after."

The limousine pulled onto a snow-cover road and continued up the hill until it reached a majestic old hotel, standing aloft over the town site. The enormous monarch was made of sizeable sandstone blocks, painstakingly placed one by one into their proper position. There was a great turret on each corner, with narrow windows encircling the top floors. Tangled vines criss-crossed the walls like spider webs that lay dormant for their winter sleep.

The arrival of the limousine at the front entrance caused the group of paparazzi to leap into action; the camera's began to flash but quickly stopped when the overzealous paparazzi decided the women were of no importance. It was all very exciting, nonetheless, and the women found themselves still giggling as they walked through the doors. An attendant dressed in a uniform similar to the Royal Guards, held the doors, allowing them entry.

Decorated very opulently in a Victorian theme, the spacious lobby proved to be an exquisite room with floral wingback chairs placed throughout its expanse. A gold and cream carpet centred the white marble floor, accentuated with a large maple table; that had an enormous centrepiece of gold and dark mauve flowers.

Meghan could not conceal her excitement, and she smiled wildly as she glanced around the room. In all her years of attending the private school in Beverly Hill, she was never invited to the many lavish parties her classmates held. She was the outsider, and she was never welcomed in. Cassie had made it to a few, but that was only when she was dating someone of importance. Cassie figured out early in high school what boys to attach herself to so she would be included. Her father was very wealthy, but his business of junk removal was not glamorous enough for the elite at their school, and the kids would tease her. However, as Cassie grew older, it stopped bothering her because it afforded her the ability to live a life of leisure and the ability to travel the world without the worry of having to work. She had her degree in horticulture, but she only dabbled in it.

Meghan's thoughts were broken, however, when a large bald man with a neck the size of a tree trunk came towards them, holding a clipboard in one hand and fussing with his earpiece with the other.

"May I have your names please?" he asked in a gruff voice, his eyes never leaving the paper.

"I'm Meghan Delaney, and this is Cassie Williams. We are guests of Declan Montgomery."

The man scanned the list, then looked up at the two women with slight exasperation. "Sorry, your names are not here, I can't allow you in."

"Their names were put on the list this morning. You must not have an up-to-date list." Fabrizio's voice was loud as he moved towards the women and the security guard.

"I have my instructions, and you're not on the list, so you can't go inside," he said, raising his large arm to block Cassie's way.

"Let's just go, Cass." Meghan started to back away from the large man, not wanting to cause a scene in front of the other guests that were waiting behind them.

"Meghan, stay here, you two are coming in with me!" Fabrizio said firmly, as his annoyance built towards the guard, and the large blond man standing behind him grunting with impatience was not improving his mood either.

The security guard was becoming very agitated at Fabrizio's insistence and pushed on the red button attached to his belt.

"There are people up here thinking they should be on the list," he mumbled into his gear. "What's your name?" he said, glaring at Fabrizio and then at the man now standing at Fabrizio's side.

"My name is Fabrizio Stagliano."

The overzealous guard repeated the information to the man on the other end and then listened intently to the increasingly loud voice coming from his earpiece.

"Please just wait here, my supervisor is coming right up," he said, with a snarl.

The impatient guess was now standing right up in the guard's face, waving a security pass under his nose. "I shall not wait while these people try and gain entry," he said, with a particularly demeaning tone, but his strong Irish accent drew Meghan's attention.

"My supervisor will be here momentarily, please be patient," the guard grunted, apparently unimpressed with the man's credentials.

A slight chill ran through Meghan as the Irishman's pale blue eyes settled on her with interest. A slight smirk curled his lips spreading out the well-trimmed golden beard. She abruptly turned and moved in front of Fabrizio, seeking refuge from the piercing eyes of the stranger.

Fabrizio seemed unfazed by her nervousness and continued to argue with the security guard as a continuous stream of the guests arrived at the entrance. The large blond man moved back in the face of the security guard, and as the two men argued with him, the tension in him began to escalate.

Meghan wandered over to the window that was across the hall, trying to avoid any confrontation that was going to arise between the three agitated men. Her mind quickly embraced the astonishing view of the large fir trees that surround the hotel, creating a natural hedge between the building and the river below. The river gently weaved its way through the forest as it headed to the lake downstream. The river was only partially frozen leaving a large area down the middle, against which the moonlight shimmered.

A short stocky man bolted up the stairs with Declan in tow. "What is going on out here?" the man questioned, his bushy moustache twitching with displeasure.

"These people say that they are supposed to be on the list. But they aren't, so I can't let them in," the security guard said, trying to defend his actions.

"I put them on the list today, and Fabs is my security officer. He has already been through your check. Don't y' remember him?" Declan said sharply.

The big blond man smirked at Declan and searched the area for the tall redhead that was trying to get into the party. He turned abruptly and sauntered towards the back of the line up.

The flustered security guard's eyes switched from one face to the other. "No, can't say as I do!"

Declan shook his head at Fabrizio and scanned the area for Meghan. "Where's Meggie?"

"She is over by the window," Cassie said as she turned to find her friend missing.

"Fabs, where is she?" Declan asked, getting rather worried.

"She was right there. She couldn't have gone far, I will go look for her." Fabrizio soothed, turning to go towards the lobby.

"No, I'll find her," Declan announced, resting his hand on Fabrizio's shoulder. "Y' let them in right now!" he snapped at the guard and then he moved quickly past the smiling guests.

Meghan glanced in the direction of the ballroom, spotting the large blond man standing over by the wall, on the far side of the hallway, watching her with interest.

"What are y' doing over here?" Declan questioned, his voice slightly agitated.

She jumped as Declan materialized at her side. "Declan," she sighed. "Jeez, I hate it when you do that."

He shrugged, not particularly interested in her reaction. "Meggie, why are y' not with Fabs?" he questioned again with forced calmness.

"I was waiting for Fabrizio to clear up the problems. I decided if we were worthy and granted access, Cassie would come and get me. If not, we could go back to the lodge," she told him looking rather innocently at him, sensing his annoyance.

"Y' are unbelievable." Declan shook his head and slipped his hand around her waist.

"Why?"

"Sometimes y' are so determined and strong, and other times y' are so childlike." The grin on his face was very mocking, and she was unsure how to take his comment.

"Declan, do you know that man?" Meghan questioned, turning in his arms.

"Which man?" Declan questioned and scanned the crowd.

"Where did he go?" Meghan muttered and chewed at her bottom lip. "He was standing right there."

Declan's brow rose slightly, and he turned back towards her. "Well, I guess he left."

"Apparently." Meghan shrugged, deciding she was overreacting.

Declan's smile spread from ear to ear as he scanned her for the first time. "You're cutting a fine figure this evening, if I do say so meself."

"Thank you, so are you. You look very handsome in a tux," Meghan responded, kissing his cheek. "You shaved."

"Aye, I couldn't come all scruffy now, could I?" he smiled, one corner of his mouth rising higher than the other, causing the long dimple to appear. "Anyway, we are done shooting the pass scenes, so I could shave. I went from full beard a month ago. Be thankful you didn't meet me then. I looked like a Sasquatch"

"I guess not," she replied, unable to control a smile as she stared at his handsome face.

"I see y' got me gift?" Declan placed his hand on her bare shoulder. His thumb brushing across the gold chain that lay flat against her creamy skin, while the emerald teasingly lay just above her breasts.

"Yes, it's beautiful, thank you. But it's too much, I can't accept it." Meghan lifted her hand, gently placing it on the emerald.

"Aye, y' can. It's your birthstone, right?"

"Yes, how do you know?" she smiled curiously.

"I have me ways," he grinned. "Anyway, it matches your dress." He ran his hand down her shoulder to her arm.

"How did you know what my dress was going to look like?" A slight grin crossed her face when the expression of complete guilt filled his eyes.

He smirked, then bent over and kissed her quickly. "Well, there are only a few dress shops in town, and I knew y' were going shopping, so I phoned around. Then luckily I found the necklace to match this afternoon."

It took every ounce of self-control she had not to break down and cry, and thankfully, only one tear escaped her eye.

Declan's hands slid across her shoulders and up her neck, coming to a stop on her face. "Meggie, I hope y' know how much I care for y'. I know that we have only known each other a few days, but I feel like I have known y' forever. It's like you're the missing piece of me."

Tears came then, clouding her eye, but her smile was bright and excited. "Oh, I've done it again," he chuckled, kissing her forehead. "Y' are the weepiest woman I know."

Meghan crinkled her nose but said nothing in response, knowing she had no defence.

"Well, I guess we should get inside before y' have your makeup running down your cheeks." He shook his head slightly, as she dabbed her eyes trying not to smudge her makeup, and he could not help but laugh. "Now I see why you don't normally wear a lot of eye makeup, Freckles. With the amount y' blubber, y' would look like a raccoon most of the time."

"You're very funny!" she grunted, taking his outstretched hand. "I'm glad you enjoy making fun of me."

A loud boom of laughter exited his mouth, and he lifted her hand and kissed her knuckles. "Well, if y' didn't have so many unique characteristics, I wouldn't be able to now, would I?"

"Well, at least I'm not boring," she grumbled, following beside him as he led her back to the ballroom.

"That y' aren't, Freckles," he said, with pleasure.

As they passed the bank of windows that lined the hallway, she glanced out and saw a herd of elk grazing in an open area in the trees. She slowed, and Declan could feel the resistance on his arm.

"What are y' looking at?"

"Those elk, look at them, they don't even notice those two men with the cameras." Her voice was soft as she stared out the window.

The two dark-haired men appeared to be taking pictures of the wild elk, and the animals seemed oblivious to their presence. They were busy pawing at the ground, displacing the snow to reveal the remnants of the summer grasses.

"That's unbelievable. They can't be more than five or six feet from the elk," she said in amazement.

One of the two men moved closer to the large male over by the trees, causing the elk to lift his head towards the moving man. Suddenly the elk's head lowered, and before the man could react, the beast leapt towards the man as he stood frozen with fear. The blow from the large antlers struck the small man square in the chest, sending him flying a few feet into the air like a rag doll. Without breaking stride, the elk bolted into the trees, with the rest of the herd on his heels.

"Oh my God!" Meghan shrieked as she watched in horror as the man lay in the snow, not moving. "He needs help!" She turned towards the lobby but stopped when Declan gripped her arm.

"Meggie, wait." Declan pointed back out the window, as the smarter of the two men ran over to his fallen friend.

A large gathering of people immediately surrounded the dazed man and helped him to his feet. There seemed to be no visible signs of any injuries, other than maybe shock. His friend pulled the camera from a snow bank and then the crowd disappeared inside the building, hopefully a little smarter about the dangers of approaching wildlife.

"Well, that will teach him to do such a stupid thing," Declan announced, with no sympathy for the man, as he turned her towards the stairs.

"That's not a very nice thing to say. He could have been hurt!" Meghan scolded him, rather disturbed at his lack of empathy.

"Aye, he could have been. Y' would think that he would know better than to approach a wild animal. They can turn on y' without any provocation," Declan grunted, defending his attitude.

Meghan's brow rose slightly, not knowing how to defend the man's bad judgment against Declan's obvious demeaning attitude. She had noticed that he tended to be rather judgmental towards people in certain situations, and she found that trait disturbing. She forced a smile, not wanting to dwell on his attitude and allowed him to lead her back towards the big man at the entrance to the ballroom.

"May I have your name please?" the big guard asked, having no recollection of Declan.

"What?" Declan's voice rose slightly with astonishment.

"Your name, you need to be on the list."

"I'm Declan Montgomery!" He looked over at Meghan with a smirk that quickly turned into cocky laughter.

"I'm sorry, sir, that name has already been marked off as in attendance," the thick-necked man said, his eyes rising to Declan's quickly annoying face.

"I came out to meet me girlfriend!" Declan grunted, his voice cold and aggressive. "Do I need to bring your supervisor up here again?"

"No," mumbled the clueless man, his gaze switching to Meghan. "Oh yes, sir, I remember you, go right in," he said as he moved out of the way and let the two pass.

Meghan giggled as she watched Declan trying to control his annoyance. "He had no clue who you are."

Declan's dark eyes settled on her with agitation. "Apparently."

"Did he hurt your feelings?" Meghan teased, trying to calm him down, but all she managed to do was agitate him further.

"That's not funny!" Declan grumbled and pulled her to a stop at the end of the hall. "How pathetic is it when the security guards hired to protect us don't even know who they are protecting."

Meghan shrugged but could not control the smile that was threatening to break. "Declan, I'm sure everyone downstairs will know who you are."

He was startled at her tone and glanced at the couple that was heading towards them. The young woman smiling pleasantly, her eyes never leaving him. His eyes settled back on Meghan, who was watching him with interest. A smile curled his lips as he realized what his comment must have appeared to mean.

"I'm not annoyed that he didn't recognize me, I just meant that he—" He stopped his comment when a slight giggle left her mouth and her hand pressed against his chest. "Meggie, stop it."

"Fine." Meghan turned towards the ballroom. "Mr. Montgomery, are you going to escort me to the party or should I go back to the lodge?"

His brows scrunched as he gripped her hand and tugged her towards the stairs. He had controlled his anger by the time they reached the enormous marble staircase. It was edged with thick maple banisters, supported by pillars, placed every two feet, as the staircase twisted its way to the floor.

As they slowly descended the deep red carpet that was attached down the middle of the stairs, time seemed to pause as the guests stopped to watch her entering the room on Declan's arm.

At the bottom of the staircase that gracefully turned and opened into the room, Declan proudly brushed the top of her head with a kiss. "I knew y' would make a grand entrance."

The enormous ornate room was magnificent, and she could not help but notice its beauty. The chandlers, methodically placed down the length of the extremely high ceiling, not only provided optimum lighting but also gave the room a very opulent appearance. The multitudes of decorative bulbs were casting a soft light across the room. A set of double doors on the far side of the room led to a patio, and a few guests were venturing out into the cold to sneak a quick smoke.

Deep red carpet runners, placed strategically around the room, covered the white marble floor. Large pillars from floor to ceiling graced the room, every ten feet up the length, placed in those positions for no other obvious reason than for decoration.

Declan could feel the hesitation in her as they walked, and when he glanced at her, he became very aware of a group of women that were watching them with obvious interest.

"What are y' looking at now?" he questioned, wondering if she had noticed the women's interest.

"Nothing, I was just admiring the room," Meghan smiled and patted her hand against his arm.

He shook his head and continued on his way to the bar. "I thought that y' were watching those women."

Meghan looked in the direction his head was bobbing and saw a group of three women looking directly at her. Her eyes settled on the brunette woman standing in the middle of the group, and she gasped with recognition.

"Oh my gosh, that's Tina Wolf," Meghan blurted out, her eyes glued to the woman.

"Aye." Declan chuckled at her excitement.

"Declan," she muttered, gazing at him with worry. "Why are they staring at us?"

"They're checking y' out," he smirked and wrapped his arm around her waist, noticing her anxiety.

"Why?" Her voice was slightly shaky as she glanced back at the women, who were still watching them.

Declan smirked and kissed her on the forehead. "I guess they are interested in who I brought. It has been quite the topic of conversation lately."

"Hmm, did you have a relationship with any of them?" Meghan questioned, not completely sure why she did.

"The blonde one." His voice seemed uninterested. "We spent a few nights together, but nothing ever came of it."

"Oh," Meghan muttered and settled her eyes on the thin blonde.

Declan's eyes settled on Meghan's concerned face, and a smile broke at the corners of his mouth. "She was just a pretty shell. She is not a very nice person, and she is quite daft."

Meghan's mouth twitched, and she gazed up into the dark eyes. "What about Tina Wolf?"

"No, we are just friends, but Tina is me love interest in the movie." Declan kissed the side of her head.

"Your love interest? Do you kiss her a lot?" Meghan questioned, forcing her voice to be light and whimsical.

"Aye," he smirked, his mouth rising to one side. "Y' don't have to worry, though. Your kisses are what I desire."

A smile curled Meghan's lips, and she shook her head at his comment. How he came up with such flippant responses so quickly was beyond her.

"Come on, I'll introduce y'." Declan chuckled and changed direction, leading her towards the group of women.

"Hi, ladies." Declan stopped beside the group of attentive women but glanced over at Meghan when her fingers dug into his arm.

"Hi," they all said, their eyes focused on Meghan.

"So this is the woman that you haven't stopped talking about," Tina smiled and extended her tiny hand towards Meghan.

"This is Meghan," Declan smiled with pleasure. "Meggie, this is Tina and that's Sammy, and I'm sorry I don't know your name," he commented to the stocky brunette standing beside Tina.

"Oh, this is Gabriel. She's the new PA on the movie." Tina smiled a bright smile towards the nervous woman at her side. Gabriel seemed equally as uncomfortable as Meghan did. "Keep your eye on this woman, Declan, she will be a great director one day."

"Nice to meet you." Meghan shook every woman's hand, her gaze lingering on Gabriel.

"I have been looking forward to meeting the woman who has stolen our Declan from us," Sammy said sharply, settling her gaze on Meghan.

Meghan jerked slightly, but she forced a pleasant smile, not wanting to reveal her complete unease with the situation. Declan laid his hand on hers that was still draped over his arm; he could feel the tension building in her.

"So, Meghan, Declan tells us that you are up here on holidays for the week," Tina asked, trying to break the tension.

"Yes, I came up with my friend from college," Meghan smiled and focused on Tina's friendly face.

"College, what did you study?" Tina questioned, with interest.

"Medicine," Meghan muttered and gazed at Declan, watching his face fill with surprise.

"Medicine?" Sammy blurted out rather surprised. "You're a doctor?"

"'Yes, I'm a resident," Meghan admitted focusing on Tina, whose blue eyes had fixed on Declan, with a smile twisting her full lips.

"Well, I think I need a drink," Declan announced as he began to turn towards the bar, anxious to get away from the women.

"Oh, Declan, don't drag her away so soon," Tina begged. "I would like to talk to her more."

He glanced at Meghan, then released her arm. "I'll be right back. I'll get us a drink." An expression of terror shot across Meghan's face, and he gripped her hand, pulling her towards him. "Do y' want to come with me?"

"Of course, she does, I wouldn't let you out of my sight if I was her. With you being so fickle," Sammy goaded, her dark brown eyes settling on Meghan.

"Sammy!" Tina snorted, quite shocked at her comment.

Declan shot Sammy an irritated glance, then turned back towards Meghan, who seemed almost amused by the remark.

"I would like a glass of white wine," Meghan smiled calmly, determined not to let the woman upset her.

"Are y' sure?" Declan was slightly concerned with leaving Meghan alone with Sammy. Who knows what Sammy would say about their affair, and Declan did not want anything or anyone to drive Meghan away from him. He had her right where he wanted her.

"Yes, I'll be fine," Meghan smiled and patted his chest.

"All right, Freckles." Declan kissed her forehead and headed towards the bar.

"Thank goodness, he's gone," Tina smirked and moved towards Meghan. "Tell me how you did it," she questioned, with excitement, her blue eyes darting back and forth between Meghan and Declan's departing back.

"Did what?" Meghan questioned, not completely sure what Tina was asking her.

"How did you manage to get him to fall in love with you? Every woman in Hollywood has been trying, and no one has managed to keep him interested for very long," Tina informed her, glancing over at Sammy with a slightly mocking gaze.

"I don't know," Meghan said offhandedly, noticing the annoyance building on Sammy's face. "We only met a few days ago." She shrugged.

"I know, and all I have heard coming out of his mouth since is your name," Tina said, with excitement.

Meghan blushed slightly as she watched Tina's eyes probing her for information.

"I think he is gay," Sammy's voice was edged with antipathy, her dark eyes glued on Declan as he leaned up against the bar. As Gabriel choked on her wine, Sammy continued, "How else would you explain his lack of interest in me?"

Tina and Gabriel's laughter filled the room, their eyes switching back and forth from Meghan's shocked face to Sammy's smug one.

"Well, maybe you're just not what he is looking for. Why don't you try calling him an arrogant jerk?" Tina's voice edged with subdued humour.

Meghan gasped at the comment, her face completely flushing with embarrassment. How much did Tina know about their relationship, and why would Declan tell her that piece of information?

"Why would I want to do something as stupid as that?" Sammy snorted. "Only an idiot would tell him that, he would never talk to me again."

Tina glanced over at Meghan with a slight smirk on her face. "You think so, do you?" Tina's voice was full of humour, but she did not reveal any other information.

"So, are y' ladies behaving yourselves?" Declan commented as he came to a stop beside Meghan, with a Guinness and a glass of white wine for her. He knew the conversation between the women would deteriorate to the level of sex the minute he turned his back, since Sammy felt she was mistreated and made a point of telling Tina that he was a lousy lover.

"Well, we were just asking Meghan her secret," Sammy commented with a seductive grin.

"Do y' have a secret, Freckles?" Declan smirked, gazing at Meghan.

"Apparently." Meghan shrugged and nervously sipped her wine.

Declan kissed her forehead and chuckled with amusement. "I'm starting to wish I never brought her over here. Y' ladies are going to have her thinking that I'm some sort of wacko."

"No, just gay," Meghan said evenly.

Declan's mouth flew open, and a loud laugh exited him as he watched Sammy's face flush with embarrassment. "Oh, Meggie, y' are funny."

Meghan lifted her brow. "Well, I don't believe it, though," she smirked and kissed his cheek.

"I guess that's all that matters," Declan smiled and slipped his hand around her waist, pulling her in to him. However, his sudden movement startled her, causing her to splatter her wine across her dress and the arm of his tuxedo.

"Oh," Meghan muttered, looking down at her dress with worry.

"Sorry, Meggie," Declan blurted out taking the glass from her hand and placing it on the small table within reach. "I'm really sorry."

"It's all right," Meghan muttered, blotting it with a napkin.

His eyes left the stain on her dress and settled on her face, then back to her dress. "I'm really sorry," he repeated, his voice slightly panicked. "I'll get some soda water." He turned to leave, but she grabbed his arm.

"It's all right, Declan." Meghan soothed, wondering why he was so panicked about a small stain on the dress. "I'm sure it will come out."

Sammy laughed with pleasure, as a young woman with a small spray bottle and a white cloth came out from behind the bar and began dabbing at the stain. "See, miss, no harm done," she smiled and glanced up at Meghan. "Once it dries, it will hardly be noticeable."

"Thank you," Meghan smiled and looked down at the spot at her hip. "I guess I'm lucky that it wasn't red wine." A slight smirk curled Meghan's lips as she watched the other women staring at her in horror.

"Aye." Declan's voice lightened as he stared at Meghan.

"Was that your way of monitoring my alcohol intake?" Meghan giggled.

Declan's brow rose slightly. "I didn't want to repeat last night, as cute as y' were staring at me through one eye, I prefer seeing them both." Declan chuckled.

Meghan giggled and slapped his arm slightly. "A pirate is what you called me."

"Aye, mate," he teased as a slight smile twisted his mouth. She was not annoyed about the stain. He was expecting her to blow up, that he caused her to spill her wine, but she did not seem at all upset. Georgia would have been furious. "Freckles, you're one of a kind."

Meghan's cheeks flushed into a pale pink, as she gazed into the dark grey eyes that were fixed on her.

"Well, Freckles, I guess we need to get over to Cassie before she feels abandoned," Declan suggested as he tugged on her arm gently, trying to get her away from the women.

"Yes, you're right," Meghan smiled, relieved to be leaving the group. "It was nice meeting you."

"Nice meeting you too," Tina said as she watched Declan escort Meghan down the bar to where their friends were standing.

Declan manoeuvred Meghan through the crowd towards the long oak counter, which stretched the length of the room. Smoked glass covered the wall, and a multitude of shelves filled with liquor bottles shrouded the wall. Over top of the bar, hanging from the ceiling, was a smoked brass rack full of glassware.

When they reached Cassie and Fabrizio at the bar, Declan wrapped his arms around Meghan's waist from behind and rested his head against hers.

"I see you found her. Where did you go, Meg?" Cassie asked, eyeing the wet spot on her dress, which seemed to be causing such a disruption earlier.

"I just didn't want to get caught up in a fight. He was quite adamant that we weren't getting in."

"Aye, he was quite an idiot, wasn't he? Where did they find him?" Declan questioned, his eyes settling on Fabrizio.

"He works for the security company they hired. They told us that their staff was well trained," Fabrizio assured him, not wanting to be blamed for the overeager employee.

"Well, he takes his job very seriously, he asked for me name," Declan grumbled, the annoyance of the man not recognizing him building again.

"What?" Fabrizio asked in amazement.

"Aye, he said, *'What is your name, sir? You need to be on the list,'*" Declan said, trying to imitate the man's voice as closely as possible, his tone was quite demeaning.

He looked down at Meghan who had her face turned towards him, giving him a disapproving look. She was finding his attitude towards people irritating, and she could not help but scowl at him.

"See, Fabs, look at her. Do y' see what I mean?" Declan lifted his hand and pointed towards her with the glass of Guinness clutched in the sizeable grip.

"I know, I saw her do it yesterday," Fabrizio smirked and eyed her with interest, "when she thought she saw a ghost."

"I didn't think I saw a ghost. I saw Ian," Meghan grumbled. She didn't appreciate the fact that Fabrizio felt she was seeing things.

"Whatever, Boo," Fabrizio laughed and leaned back against the bar.

Declan joined in on the laughter until Meghan elbowed him in the ribs. "I see he found your nickname."

"I'm glad you find it so funny," Meghan scowled at Fabrizio; she had hoped he had forgotten about the name.

"If I can't use that one, I can always think of something else." Fabrizio eyed her confrontationally.

"Keep the one y' got, Freckles, he can come up with some daft ones. I won't repeat in mixed company what he calls Sammy."

Meghan smirked and then turned to Fabrizio. "All right, Fabrizio, have your fun."

"He allows y' to call him that?" Declan eyed Fabrizio with interest. "I don't believe he has ever allowed anyone to call him that but his mother. His father and brothers call him Rizzo."

Fabrizio winked at Meghan, then took a slow thoughtful sip of his beer. "Well, at least, you know she can't lie to you." Fabrizio chuckled, noticing the confused expression crossing Meghan's face.

"Aye," Declan's brow rose slightly, "that's grand, because I have no tolerance for lying."

"You have little tolerance for a lot of things," Meghan muttered before she could stop herself.

"Pardon?" His gaze settled on her, and he released his grip from around her waist.

Meghan cringed and took a step away from him, the anxiety of what she had said completely overtaking her ability to think. "I . . . I was kidding," she blurted out, her eyes settling on Cassie's shocked face.

"No, y' weren't! Y' think I'm intolerant of people. This isn't the first time y' have mentioned this."

She stared at him, trying to recall what she had said in the last few days that would have implied she disapproved of that personality trait. Her eyes left his face and settled on Cassie, who was shaking her head slightly, wondering how Meghan managed to get herself into such explosive situations.

"Well, you do tend to act superior around some people," Meghan blurted out, deciding the only way out was to go on the offensive. "You can be very dismissive."

His brow shot up, but his attention quickly changed to Fabrizio, who was laughing uncontrollably. "God help you, Monty."

A slight smirk curled Declan's lips as he contemplated her comments. "Aye, I guess I can be." His hand went out towards her; she had moved out of his reach. "Come here."

Meghan eyed his hand and slowly took it, allowing him to pull her towards him. Once she was in his arms, he laughed and kissed her forehead. "You're going to be the death of me."

"So you've told me," Meghan giggled and glanced at him as he shook his head in disbelief.

"I'll try very hard not to be vain and dismissive. At least when you're around." Declan chuckled. "I'm getting tired of hearing y' tell me how awful I am."

"I didn't say you were awful. If I thought that I wouldn't be here," Meghan smiled and kissed his check.

"Good," he grinned and kissed her lips. "Because I enjoy having y' around, I think that y' might be me conscience. I need someone close to me that tells me the truth." He grinned over at Fabrizio. "Other than his abrasive comments, everyone usually tells me what they think I want to hear, and I seem to have lost touch with reality."

"Well, I could tell you a lot more," Meghan smirked.

"No, I think calling me vain is enough for one night," Declan laughed. "Why don't y' save them for tomorrow?"

"All right, but I didn't call you vain, I called you intolerant," she smiled and kissed his smirking lips, then rested her mouth next to his ear. "Even with your faults, I still can't get you off my mind. You are an incredible man."

"Is that right?" he muttered into her hair. "Well, once I enter there, I'll be happy," he whispered, resting his hand over her heart.

Her face enflamed with colour as she groped for something to say. "You're already there," she said quietly, but he heard her.

"Good," he sighed and kissed her thoroughly.

"Monty, there's your mom," Fabrizio muttered and gave Declan's arm a quick shake.

Declan jerked away from Meghan and glanced in the direction Fabrizio was pointing. "Bloody hell," he grumbled.

The older woman with dark hair, swept back gracefully into a twist, was watching them intently. The woman seemed particularly displeased with something, as her dark eyes scanned Meghan.

"Ma?" Declan muttered as the woman stalked towards him, her dark brows crumpling with annoyance. "I didn't know y' were coming."

"Obviously," she grumbled and eyed Meghan's position in his arms.

"Declan, dear, I thought we had a talk about this?" his mother muttered, her dark blue eyes settled on him.

"Ma!" Declan said sharply. "I told y' where I stand on this, and y' won't change me mind."

Meghan was quickly realizing that she was intruding on the conversation, and she took a step backwards away from Declan, but he held her hand tightly, pulling her back up to his side.

"Ma, this is Meghan. Meggie, meet me Ma, Katie," Declan commented with forced calmness. His arm wrapped around Meghan's waist to keep her next to him.

"Nice to meet you," Meghan forced out of her mouth and extended her hand towards the woman.

His mother eyed her hand, then attempted a shake; it was the consistence of mush, her small hand weak and flimsy in Meghan's grip. Katie forced an obviously fake smile and then pulled her hand away. After a few painful seconds of silence, Katie cleared her throat.

"So y' are the one who is occupying me son's time?" Katie's tone was very accusing and quite abrasive.

"Don't start, Ma!" Declan growled mildly, his features hardening as he glared at his mother.

"Declan, don't use that tone with me. I just have your best interests in mind." Katie's brow rose slightly as she stared at Meghan.

"Ma!" Declan muttered, his dark grey gaze settling on his mother. "Is Da here too, or were y' sent to interfere with me life again?"

"I don't interfere," she smiled sweetly. "I'm your mother, and I'm just here to see y'."

Declan's brow rose slightly, then he kissed the side of Meghan's head, trying to calm the agitation he could feel rising in her.

"Declan, I saw Georgia before I left, and I told her to come out at the end of the week to spend some time with y'."

"Is that so?" Declan said evenly.

Katie nodded, her eyes settling on Meghan. "Aye, she told me that she was here a while back, and y' ignored her and spent all your time in the bar with floozies."

"Did she?" his voice was cool, but not revealing his thoughts. "Well, Ma, Georgia tends to twist the truth to benefit herself."

"How so, dear?" Katie questioned as Declan began to shuffle, appearing agitated.

"Well, she managed to insight y' into coming all the way out here to torment me." He rested his head against Meghan's. "But unfortunately, y' made the trip for nothing, because Meggie and I have other plans this week." His arm tightened around Meghan's waist as she flinched in his arms. "But if y' care to join us for dinner tomorrow night," he added as an afterthought, sensing Meghan's unease with the implications of his comment.

"Hmm," his mother grumbled, her gaze settling back on Meghan. "I see y' have managed to enchant me son."

Meghan forced a nervous smile, pressing her back up against Declan's chest. "I guess so."

"So she has," Declan smiled and kissed the side of her head. "I have never before met a woman as wonderful as her."

Katie forced a smile, but as her eyes settled on Declan, a warm love crossed her face shortly. It quickly faded, however, when she focused back on Meghan.

"That's a lovely necklace, Meghan," Katie blurted out.

"Thank you," Meghan said weakly, her hand nervously twitching on Declan's arm that was still clinging around her waist.

"I gave it to her," Declan said calmly. "It's her birthstone."

Katie grunted and turned her dark eyes on Meghan. "It's lovely to find a man that is gullible enough to waste his hard-earned money on fancy jewelry, is it not?"

"Ma, that's enough!" Declan growled fiercely. "Y' will not talk to her that way."

Meghan jerked in his arms, spinning towards him. "If you will excuse me, I need to go to the ladies' room," she whispered, her voice shaky and her eyes glazing over.

"Meggie," Declan whispered softly, pressing his face against her ear. "I'm sorry she is behaving this way."

Meghan forced a painful smile and nodded slightly. "It's all right."

"No, it's not," he said a little louder. "She's being rude." His eyes settled on his mother, with annoyance building in the cloudy grey eyes.

"Declan, please," Meghan muttered, her hands pressing up against his chest. "It's okay." She could not understand why his mother seemed to dislike her, but it was very evident. "I'll be right back."

"Aye," he smiled and kissed her forehead. "Don't be long."

"I won't." Meghan forced a painful smile and eyed Cassie.

"I'll come with you, Meg," Cassie blurted out, not wanting to be attacked next. She had never seen such a display, and she was as horrified as Meghan was.

"That was uncalled for!" Declan snorted when Meghan disappeared into the crowd. "I can't believe y'."

"I can't believe y' would pursue a relationship with her. Y' know how dangerous it could be," Katie scolded, her blue eyes filling with concern. "I don't want to see y' hurt."

"Ma, I'm not going to get hurt," Declan grumbled, his eyes scanning the surrounding crowd.

"She is going to bring nothing but trouble into your life."

"No, she won't, she doesn't even know about . . ." Declan stopped, remembering Fabrizio's presence, and he certainly did not want him privy to his family's feud.

"Declan, I told y' to just forget about the decree," Katie whispered fiercely. "It will bring y' nothing but trouble. Not to mention the danger y' would put that girl in."

Declan's brow crumpled with annoyance. "I don't plan on putting her in any danger. I really do care for her, Ma, she is amazing. And I don't think we should be discussing this at this time."

"Have y' given any thought to what will happen if Fergus finds out about her? She could be in grave danger," Katie rambled, not interested in his concerns.

"Ma, stop being so dramatic. How are they going to find out about her?" Declan questioned, with exasperation. The entire situation was getting out of control. Not only was his mother interfering and upsetting Meghan, but he also suspected that if Kaye mentioned the locket to Fergus or Liam, they already knew about Meghan, so he had little time.

"Y' found her," Katie said strongly. "And y' figured out who she was almost immediately."

"Well, that's because I saw the locket, then she told me about her grandfather. I don't think she runs about telling everyone her family history," Declan argued, his eyes settling on Fabrizio.

"What is going on here? Are you involved in some sort of trouble that I should know about?" Fabrizio questioned, getting the overwhelming feeling trouble was brewing.

"No, it's just family problems," Declan grumbled, glaring at his mother for her insistence on discussing the situation in front of him.

"Where is the amulet?" Katie questioned, totally ignoring Declan's glare.

Declan shrugged and glanced around the room to ensure Meghan was not around. "I don't know, I guess she left it in her room."

"Declan, dear, please think about what y' are doing. I can see she is a lovely girl and that y' care about her, but I am terribly frightened that y' are digging up the past."

"Ma, I promise I won't do anything foolish. When I first saw her, I knew she was the woman I was meant to be with, and that was before I even saw the locket. Please trust me. I think I'm in love with her."

Katie patted her son's arm and smiled softly. "All right, dear, have your fun. But don't forget your obligation to Georgia."

"Ma, I don't have an obligation to Georgia. How many times do I have to tell y' that I don't want to marry her?" Declan grumbled and eyed Fabrizio with exasperation.

"We'll see, dear. I'm going back to me room now." Katie kissed Declan's cheek.

"Y' are staying here and not at the lodge?" Declan questioned with relief. At least, she wouldn't be in the way.

"Of course, I am staying here. Do y' honestly think I would stay in a place like the lodge? Oh, for heaven's sake, Declan, sometimes I wonder what y' think about." Katie's voice was irritated as she shook her head slightly.

"Bye, Ma." Declan shook his head as he watched her disappear into the crowd.

Fifteen minutes had passed before Meghan returned from the ladies' room. After listening to Cassie voice her opinion on Declan's mother, she sat on one of the sofas in the lounge area and cleared her thoughts. She was terrified to return to Declan and his mother, which also contributed to the long delay in returning to the party.

The crowd had shifted slightly in her absence, and she was unable to see Declan or his mother anywhere, but she spotted Fabrizio and Cassie across the room, and she knew that Declan must be somewhere close by.

The loud murmurs from the voices around her were dulling her senses as she manoeuvred her way towards Cassie, but she was startled to alertness when her eyes settled on the tall blond man a few feet away. His pale blue gaze was on her, causing her to feel unnerved, and as he moved towards her, the feeling changed to worry.

"Good evening," he said pleasantly, his words formed precisely to conceal the Irish accent he spoke with on his arrival.

"Hello," Meghan muttered, her eyes glancing frantically around the room for Declan. She was not sure what was causing her nerves to react, but something about the man was disturbing her.

"I couldn't help overhearing that your last name is Delaney." His eyes stayed fixed on her face, his mouth twisting into a smile. "You wouldn't happen to be related to Michael Delaney from Claire?"

Meghan eyed him quizzically, wondering how a man so young could possibly be acquainted with her grandfather, since he had left Ireland over fifty years earlier.

"Yes," she said, simply not wanting to reveal too much information to him.

He grinned, his white teeth visible beneath the thick growth of golden whiskers, his eyes sparkling with delight. "Could I interest you in a walk, and we could discuss our mutual interests."

"What interests would that be?" Meghan questioned, taking a step away from him.

"Well, I'll tell y', if y' grace me with your presence in the lobby," he said impatiently, the Irish lilt slightly returning.

"I can't leave," Meghan blurted out, her eyes again searching the crowd. "My date would be worried."

His brow rose slightly as he glanced around the surrounding area. "Your date seems to have vanished."

"He'll be back," Meghan said firmly, as her eyes settled on Colton, who was heading towards Cassie.

"I doubt it, I saw him leaving with an older woman." His brow rose slightly, assessing her reaction.

"Colton!" Meghan blurted out as panic surged through her. She didn't know Colton terribly well, but she felt safer with him than with this strange man that seemed intent on removing her from the party.

"Meghan, where have you been hiding?" Colton said loudly, startling the forward man. "Did Declan abandon you?" he joked as he came to a stop beside her.

"I guess so," Meghan muttered as she turned to him, fear building on her face.

Colton's blue gaze settled on the tall blond man with interest. "A friend of yours, my beauty?"

"No, we just met," the blond man said evenly, when Meghan pressed her shoulder up against Colton. "It was nice to meet you," he commented, then turned, disappearing into the crowd.

"What's wrong?" Colton questioned, his expression somewhat concerned. "Where's Declan?"

"I don't know." Meghan sniffed, blinked frantically trying to stay calm and keep the tears from exploding from her embarrassed eyes. "I couldn't find him when I came back from the ladies' room, and that man said he left with his mother."

"He hasn't left," Colton soothed. "Look, there he is," Colton smiled, pointing towards the far side of the room. "And motherless."

"Hmm," Meghan mumbled, catching a glimpse of the blond man who was still watching her from his vantage point by the bar. "Could you say goodbye to him for me? I think it's time I left," she said, with slight panic in her voice.

"Meghan, what are you so upset about? Just come with me, I'll take you over there." Colton chuckled.

"No!" she blurted out. "I just want to go."

Declan was heading across the room, slightly pushing at the people in his path when he noticed she was attempting to leave. His stomach was in knots as he watched the anxiety growing stronger on her face as Colton talked to her and followed her up the stairs.

"Meggie," Declan blurted out half way up the stairs, which he was leaping up two at a time. "Where are y' going'?"

She turned towards him, the glassiness returning to her eyes. "I'm going back to the lodge."

"Why?" Declan panted as he gripped her hands in his.

"I'm not feeling well," she mumbled, dropping her gaze to the third button down on his crisp white shirt that was visible under his undone tuxedo jacket.

Declan eyed her judgmentally. She had used that excuse before when she was uncomfortable with the situation and wanted to bolt. The dark gaze settled on Colton, who shrugged his shoulders slightly and frowned.

"Did y' say something to upset her?" Declan questioned sharply towards Colton.

"No," Colton snorted defending himself.

"He didn't say anything," Meghan muttered. "I just want to go." She took a step backwards, pulling at her hands that were still trapped in Declan's large grip.

"Meggie, I'll take y' back," Declan smiled softly, noticing her anxiety building, as her eyes betrayed her. Pain was shooting from them with an indisputable force. "What the hell is going on here?" he blurted out, glancing back and forth from her to Colton. He was getting the overwhelming feeling that something had gone on between her and Colton, and he was very agitated.

"Calm down, Declan, nothing is going on. Meghan is just scared of that man."

"Colton!" Meghan blurted out as embarrassment filled her face.

"What man?" he asked softly and pulled her over to the edge of the landing, away from Colton.

Her eyes were stuck in his questioning grey gaze, and her lashes began to flutter nervously across her dark green eyes. "That man I saw earlier. He came up to me and was asking me questions and trying to get me to leave with him." Her eyes settled on Colton. "Can we talk about this somewhere else?"

"All right," he sighed and kissed her forehead. "Will y' promise to tell me later?"

Meghan nodded nervously, forcing a smile.

"Well, Freckles, I guess I better not let y' out of me sight from now on if strange men are after y'."

Her brow rose slightly as he chuckled, seemingly unfazed by her concern, but she did not reply. Maybe it was best to forget about what had happened, but she could not help wondering why she kept encountering Irishmen in the last few months, and all of them seemed interested in her family history.

"Declan, I still want to go," Meghan whispered, lifting her eyes to his.

"Aye," Declan smiled and kissed her forehead. "I have had enough too."

"Are you sure? I don't mind taking a cab back," she questioned.

"Don't start that again, Freckles. You're not leaving me sight again tonight," he smirked and pulled her towards the second set of stairs.

The paparazzi were still lingering outside the hotel, hoping for a picture. Tina Wolf was their target, but catching Declan with a new woman would also sell. Declan appeared unfazed by the flurry of activity around them, but Meghan felt judged. She did not appreciate the questions being hurled at Declan, especially the ones regarding her social status. Another Boston debutant, they were calling her. Where would they get that impression?

Meghan refused to turn her head towards the cameras, causing the photographers to holler louder. "Come on, lady, give us a break." A muscular man yelled as they reached the edge of the sidewalk.

Without warning, he lunged towards Meghan, causing her to stumble backwards. She lost her footing and landed in a heap on the sidewalk.

"Meggie?" Declan reached down and lifted her gently to her feet. "Are y' all right?"

"Yes," Meghan mumbled and lowered her gaze to the ground, slightly embarrassed that she had fallen. "I'm sorry."

"What are y' sorry for?" Declan removed his coat, wrapping it around her shoulders. "Is that better?" His eyes were soft and caring when he wrapped his arm around her shoulder.

"Come on, Declan, give us a good shot." The man casually brushed back his shoulder-length blond hair, seeming to have no remorse for his behaviour.

"Bugger off," Declan growled and pushed at the man's broad shoulder when got up in his face. "Y' are despicable."

"I'm sure that's not the first time your date has been on her back." The photographer laughed, then glanced over at his cohorts. They, however, were not laughing with him and neither was Declan. That seemed to anger the man, and he took a swing at Declan's head.

Before Meghan could stop him, Declan lunged at the photographer. The man was unprepared for the attack and landed on the ground with a thud. Declan's fist slammed across his face a few times before the man managed to lay a punch to Declan's eye.

"Stop it," Meghan shrieked as she stared down at the large men wrestling on the snowy ground.

The other paparazzi were jumping out of the way, trying to avoid the mayhem that ensued. The man leaped to his feet and glared at Declan with malevolence, then pulled a switchblade knife from his pocket. He lunged towards Declan frantically trying to stick him with the long shiny blade, but Declan was darting out of the way of the oncoming attacks with the smooth ease of a cat.

Declan's arm shot up, knocking the knife from the man's hand, then his elbow flew up, slamming into the man's unguarded face. The man steadied himself and grabbed a metal post that was holding up the thick red cord partitions and heaved it towards Declan. It slammed against Declan's back, and he raised his arm as he turned trying to avoid the blow. The blood was drumming in Declan's ears as he stumbled backwards trying to regain his balance. He shook his head in an attempt to focus on the man that stood staring at him with a mocking expression on his face.

"Not so tough now, are you!" The man shouted and moved towards Declan's slouched-over frame; then he rammed his knee into Declan's stomach.

"Declan!" Meghan shrieked as Declan buckled over from the crack to his ribs.

The man laughed cruelly and turned towards Meghan temporarily distracted from his attack. Declan gasped for air and spit out the blood that was filling his mouth from his cut lip. As the dark blotches in his vision began to dissolve, he saw the man stalking towards Meghan.

"Leave her alone," Declan snorted.

"Try and stop me," The man laughed, keeping his back towards Declan, which was a fatal mistake, because Declan jumped on him from behind, knocking him to the ground.

The two large men wrestled on the ground, knocking over the metal posts, causing the red cords to crash down around them. Declan's face was full of rage as he laid a strong blow across the man's face, which seemed to pacify him. With a slight grunt, Declan stood up and brushed off his pants, then wiped the blood that was oozing from his cut lip with the back of his hand.

"Declan, look out!" Meghan screamed as the man jumped to his feet and flew towards him.

Declan swung around to the side, lifting his leg, planting his foot squarely on the man's chest, sending him flying backwards to the ground. He shook his head as he watched the man roll onto his hands and knees, gasping for breath.

"How does it feel, y' bastard? Y' think you're so tough, knocking over a woman, but you're nothing but a spineless coward."

The man groaned and fell to the ground, cupping his mouth with his hands. Declan stalked towards him seemingly in an enraged daze. He gripped the man's jacket and repeatedly slammed his fist against his face.

"Declan, stop it, you're going to kill him," Meghan shrieked and gripped his arm halting his attack.

"Meggie, stay out of this," Declan growled, his voice was dangerously cold.

"No, it's enough, he can't even move," Meghan pleaded with him. "Please, Declan, don't be like him."

That comment startled Declan. The last thing he wanted was for her to equate him with this disgusting human being. "Aye, Freckles. I just couldn't let him talk about y' that way." Declan panted.

"I know," Meghan smiled and kissed his cheek that had a cut just under his eye. "Let's just leave."

"Aye," Declan sighed and turned towards the limousine with Meghan tucked under his arm.

"Declan," Meghan shrieked when she felt a large hand grip her arm and pull her away from Declan. "Leave me alone!"

Meghan's shrieks coincided with two large security guards grabbing Declan from behind and pushing him roughly to the ground.

"Stay down!" the short man yelled, then turned his attention to the other guard that was pulling Meghan away.

"You're hurting me," Meghan shrieked as the man twisted her arm behind her back.

"Get your hands off her!" Declan shouted and jumped to his feet but was grabbed by the two officers. The two men had Declan's arms pinned and his face against the trunk of the limousine before he could react. His worry for Meghan had slowed his reflexes.

"This will go a lot easier for you if you don't struggle," the older officer grumbled as he and two other guards struggled with Declan's thrashing body.

Meghan was pinned against the hood of the limousine by the other security guard, his reaction to her very hostile.

"I swear if you hurt her," Declan growled unable to get loose. "Bloody hell, let go of me."

"What the hell is going on here?" Fabrizio shouted when he bolted through the doors with the head of security.

"We are stopping a fight," the security guard holding Meghan spoke up, but as his adrenaline subsided, he began to realize that he had made a mistake. He suddenly released Meghan, and she bolted towards Declan.

"Let him go," the short man snorted, his bushy moustache twitching with anger. His employees appeared to be complete incompetents. "I am terribly sorry, Mr. Montgomery."

Declan grunted and eyed Fabrizio's annoyed face. Meghan was pressing up against his chest, seeking safety from the flashing cameras, and before she could complain, Declan deposited her in the back of the limousine, then climbed in behind her.

"I'm pressing charges," the photographer yelled at Declan's departing back. He sat up and rubbed at his bleeding nose. "You're a psycho."

"Go ahead," Declan yelled out the opened door. "And I suggest y' never talk about my girlfriend like that again."

A commotion began behind them, as the other paparazzi began to phone in the story to their papers. A lucky few had caught the fight on film, so they would have a big payday. The commotion out in front of the hotel had attracted a few guests, and most of them had begun to surround the area. The security guards of the hotel as well as the police had arrived and had taken over from the security company that had been hired for the evening.

"Well, it's a good thing I do me own stunts," Declan laughed and wiped at the cut on his lip.

"This isn't funny. He could have killed you with that knife," Meghan muttered and wiped the blood from his mouth with the handkerchief he had in the pocket of the jacket she still wore. From her new vantage point, a deep red stain was visible on the breast of his shirt, and she began to panic.

"You're bleeding, oh my God, your chest is bleeding," Meghan shrieked, as did a few of the women peering in the open door of the limousine.

"Aye, just a bit, it's just a wee scratch," Declan smirked and glanced up at the growing crowd outside the car. "Could y' please shut the door?" Declan's eyes settled on the police officer that was standing, blocking the door.

"In a minute, sir, we need to straighten out what happened," the officer mumbled, not concerned with the fact that people were taking pictures of Declan and Meghan in the limousine.

Meghan crinkled her nose and turned her focus to his shirt, frantically unbuttoning it to get a better look at the wound. Her hand slid along the inch-long cut, pulling it apart to judge the penetration.

"You're right, you don't need stitches. You're damn lucky that is all that happened."

"Aye, he's a damn lunatic!" Declan said, with a chuckle.

"This isn't funny!" Meghan cried as she groped the rest of his chest and back for additional cuts.

"Meggie, I'm okay, that's the only cut," Declan assured her as he grabbed her frantic hands. "Oh no, the leaky dam is going to burst, isn't it?" Declan smiled softly as she began to sob.

Meghan collapsed into his arms, crying uncontrollably and shaking with fear as he cradled her tightly, trying to console her. "I'm so sorry."

"Freckles, y' have nothing to be sorry for." Declan kissed the top of her head. "I will always protect y'."

"Meghan, calm down until the door is closed," Fabrizio said coolly, when he climbed into the limousine and pulled the door shut behind him. "He did quite a number on you," Fabrizio smirked, pulling Declan's shirt open with his two fingers.

Declan grunted and batted Fabrizio's hand away, his pride being somewhat insulted. He did not want to admit that the man had caused so much physical damage to him, and he was slightly embarrassed that the security guards took him down so easily. "I'm fine. I won, didn't I?"

"Apparently." Fabrizio chuckled focusing on Meghan's tear-stained face. "Are you all right?" His hand rested on her cheek with a familiarity that she found uncomfortable.

"Yes," Meghan muttered, her eyes lowering nervously to Declan's hand that was still clutching hers.

Fabrizio eyed her warily and brushed his thumb across her cheek. "There is never a dull moment with you around, is there?"

"Fabs, leave her alone!" Declan growled. "This wasn't her fault."

"I'm not saying it was." Fabrizio threw back, mirroring Declan's tone. "What's with the attitude?"

"I could be asking y' the same thing!" Declan snorted. "Why are y' treating her this way?"

A slight scowl crossed Fabrizio's face, then he settled his gaze on Meghan. "Monty, there is something not right about this whole situation."

"What's that supposed to mean?" Declan flared.

"Why did that paparazzi attack you? I have known them to be pushy and rude, but I have never come across one that psychically crossed the line," Fabrizio muttered and flopped back into the seat and rested his long legs on the seat across from him.

Declan sighed and glanced over at Meghan who was staring out the back window, watching the crowd and the hotel disappear in the distance.

"The police officer said you will have to fill out a statement tomorrow. They're not pressing charges since some of the other photographers are claiming that he attacked Meghan, and you were just defending her." A slight smile filled Fabrizio's face. "But the police are the least of your worries. Wait until your mother gets a hold of you."

"Aye," Declan sighed, but jerked as Meghan pressed the handkerchief against the cut. "Bloody hell, your hands are cold." He chuckled, grabbing her hands.

"I get cold easily," Meghan said softly, glancing over at Fabrizio.

"And y' want to move to Montana? Y' should stay back in California with me."

Meghan eyed him with amusement. "Well, I doubt you will want to see me again once you see how cut up you are." Declan began to shuffle in the seat as he reached for a small mirror. "Sit still until this cut stops bleeding."

"Oh that's right, y' are a doctor," Declan smiled and eyed her as she concentrated on his cut. "Why didn't y' mention that before?"

Meghan shrugged but kept her eyes focused on the damage to his face. His eye was bruised and cut, and his nose was bruising as well. "I find that it intimidates men."

Declan's brow rose slightly at the comment. "Really?"

Meghan regretted telling him when he began to laugh. She scowled at him and turned her head away. "As funny as you think that is, I can't count the number of men that have dumped me after a few months of the crazy hours. The only men that seem to be able to handle it are other doctors."

"I can handle it," he grinned and gripped her chin forcing her eyes on him. "Freckles, I'm not laughing at your comment. I'm laughing because I find the same problem with women. The only women I seem to attract are the ones that want something from me." He gripped her chin again when she tried to look away. "Finally, I have found a woman that likes me for me, and those stupid paparazzi attacked y'. I hope that it won't scare you away."

Meghan's eyes brightened, and she rested her hands on his chest. "No, it's not like I haven't fallen once or twice before."

Declan started to laugh and kissed her gently. "That's an understatement."

Meghan giggled and smacked his chest. "I am worried . . ." She paused and looked out the window. "Which pictures do you think they will print? The ones with me falling or the ones with you pummelling the jerk?"

"I'm sure they will all show up somewhere." He shook his head. "Well, me mam should be hollering at me by morning." A smirk curled

Declan's lips as he watched her shivering in his arms. "I'm going to have to find some way to warm y' up when we get back," he smiled with an air of expectation for the evening.

Meghan blushed and looked past him out the window at the dark trees as they passed by the vast pine forest on the way back to the lodge.

Declan's mind was spinning, wondering if trapping Meghan into a relationship was the right thing to do? Did he care for her enough to spend his life with her? She was very beautiful and kind, and he had to admit he had feelings for her. His eyes settled on her face as she rested against his chest, and his heart constricted slightly. Could the anxious feelings he was having when he was around her be love? He loved his family, but as for women, he never let anyone get close enough. Women were arm candy and someone to spend an evening with, definitely not someone to care about. What was wrong with him?

CHAPTER EIGHT

Meghan was extremely warm by the time they arrived at her room. Whether her newfound heat was from the events of the evening or that the chill had finally left her, she was unsure. All she knew was that she was uncomfortably hot.

Once free of Declan's jacket, she laid it across the chair by the window and turned towards Declan, his eyes fixed on her, and a wide smile curled his lips. His movement towards her seemed to be in slow motion as the vibration from every step surged through her. His hand rested on her shoulders as he leaned into her, his lips brushed across her cheek and down her neck.

A tremble rippled down her spine as his hand slid up to her neck and fumbled with the clasp to her necklace. By the time the clasp came loose, she was giggling, which he found rather irritating, and he dropped the necklace to the table with abandon.

She jerked, startled by the sound but relaxed quickly as his large hand gripped her face and focused her attention on him. His mouth trailed across her cheek, and he nibbled at the sensitive area behind her ear. His head lifted, the cloudy eyes fixed on her, as his broad shoulders turned in towards her, and his fingers trailed slowly up and down her arms.

"Y' are so beautiful," he mumbled, pressing his face up against her neck.

"Sit down while I get something to disinfect that cut," Meghan mumbled bashfully as she pushed him away from her and towards the bed.

Declan begrudgingly dropped to the bed, watching as she rummaged through a first-aid kit she found in the bathroom. She was so stunning, he could not take his eyes off her. Even in the dishevelled condition she was in, with her hair falling down around her face in a wild way, she was an incredible woman, and the more he learned about her, the more he wanted to learn.

"This might sting a little," she warned and gently wiped the cotton gauze across the inch-long slash just below his collarbone.

Declan flinched slightly, but his shoulders relaxed quickly as she smiled with an apologetic softness. She slid the clean piece of gauze the length of his cut lip, then ran her finger across his mouth and slowly up his cheek.

"You're getting a black eye." Her fingers gently traced the bruise that was forming around his eye.

"Ah, well, it will make me look more fierce," Declan joked and rested his hand on hers that was still on his cheek.

She chuckled, pulled her hand away, and then finished bandaging the small cut on his chest.

"That didn't hurt a bit," he smirked.

"Well, if you wouldn't have jumped a maniac with a knife, this wouldn't have happened. Who do you think you are anyway, Indiana Jones?" she laughed as she finished taping on the gauze.

"Oh, here we go with the Harrison Ford comparisons."

"You've heard them, have you?" Meghan giggled and dropped to the bed beside him.

"Aye."

"Hey, take it as a compliment. He is a very handsome man."

"I don't see the resemblance."

"You don't look like him, it's just you both have the same grin. It drives women wild," Meghan smirked and kissed his cheek.

"So the truth comes out. You're living your fantasy of being with Harrison through me?" he commented as he ran his hand down the soft skin of her arm.

"Damn, you caught me. I have been stalking you for months in hopes of crashing into you in the lobby."

"I knew it! Y' know, I could make this easy for y'. Why don't I just introduce y' to him, then y' don't need me."

"Wow can you do that?" Meghan laughed uncontrollably.

Declan eyed her with a very menacing grin, then reached for her as she darted off the bed and bolted towards the bathroom. He jumped to his feet and grasped her arm, just before she had gotten through the door. She felt her feet leave the floor as he lifted her, spun her around, and dropped her on the bed.

"Stop it. You're going to start that cut bleeding again," Meghan shrieked, her hands flailing wildly, trying to remove his hands that were tickling her with abandon.

"It'll be worth it, Freckles, if I can tickle him out of your mind."

"Okay, okay, he's gone. Just stop, I can't breathe."

With one last movement of his finger up her side, he rolled to the bed and leaned on one elbow facing her, while she tried to catch her breath. His fingers slid through her hair, fanning the loose pieces out over the quilt.

"Y' have such gorgeous hair." His hand was still moving her hair around the bed, allowing it to catch the light from the table lamp.

"Thanks," she replied as her face blushed slightly.

"Is it natural, or do y' colour it?"

"It's natural!" she responded rather abruptly.

"Sore spot, is it?" A grin was forming on his face when she turned her head and eyed him.

"Yes, some people don't like the colour. They think it's too red." She ran her fingers under it, lifting a chunk up into her hand to examine the auburn waves. "I used to get teased a lot about it."

"Aye, people can be cruel. Don't y' be worrying anymore. I won't let anyone harm y' anymore." He soothed, brushing a loose strand behind her ear. Declan placed his large hand on the curve of her shoulder and gently ran his finger across her collarbone to her neck. His thumb rested at the base of her neck, and he spread out his fingers lightly stroking her chest. "I don't understand how anyone could hurt y'."

Silence filled the room for sometime as she relived the events of the evening. Declan seemed so calm now, but the rage on his face as he fought with the paparazzi frightened her; she never thought that he would snap the way he did.

"Meggie are y' all right?" he questioned, apparently reading the expression on her face.

"Yes." She forced a smile. "I was just thinking about the fight."

His brow rose slightly. "What about it?"

"Where did you learn how to fight like that? You seemed to have been well trained." Her brow crumbled slightly as the question exited her.

"I was a Navy Seal," he said casually.

"What?" Meghan looked shocked.

"Aye, that's where I met Fabs. But I have to say that was a pretty poor performance on me part, he got too many shots in," Declan said, simply not wanting to get into his past at that moment.

"Why did you leave?"

"Me time was up, and I didn't re-enlist." Tonight was not the night to tell her why he left. It would definitely spoil the mood.

Meghan nodded and looked away from him, not getting the answer she wanted. She really wanted to know if he would ever turn that anger on her. But as she felt his hand stroking her chest, she remembered the expression of horror on his face when he found her after Ian had beaten her up. A deep sigh exited her, and she turned her face back towards him, a content smile curling her lips.

Declan sensed her relaxing and rolled over so that he was hovering over her.

"So, Freckles, what did y' mean when y' said our grins drive women wild?"

"Well, it's hard to explain. Sometimes you grin and only one side of your mouth rises and that dimple appears. It's adorable."

"Oh, I didn't know I did that."

"You do, you do it quite often," Meghan smiled and rested her hand against his cheek.

"It drives y' wild, does it?" Declan grinned at her with the smile.

"Stop it, I shouldn't have told you. There will be no living with you now." Meghan moaned and smacked him in the chest.

"Oh, y' plan on living with me, do y'?"

"You're putting words in my mouth again!" Meghan grumbled determined not to let him fluster her.

Declan smiled, leaned down, and gently placed his lips on hers. It was time to make her his, time to secure his family's rightful place in Ireland. He was not only excited about the implications of the two of them uniting, but his body ached for her. Touching her, kissing her, making love to her was all that his overburdened mind had thought about since they met. He needed her, wanted her, and now he was going to have her.

Meghan felt their bodies melt together again, and she wanted more, which caused a sudden fear to rush though her body. She was terrified that if she gave herself to him, she would never be able to get over him. He was pressing hard against her; the intensity of his kiss was overwhelming. Meghan's hand rested on his face, and she pushed gently until he lifted his head up and looked down at her.

"I . . ." she started to say how she wanted him, wanted him to be her first, but her fears were too deep. What if she was just the next girl in a long parade of women? She could not give him that power over her. She knew without a doubt that if they made love, she was trapped, giving him her heart, and her innocence was more than she was willing to allow.

Declan smiled with a pretence of understanding and rose up on his arms, pushing himself to a sitting position on the edge of the bed. A deep sigh of disappointment exited him, wondering when she would trust him enough to give herself to him. He could not understand her reluctance, but then he caught the expression of terror in her eyes. It was there all along, her fear of him, he just chose not to see it. She was pure, never made love. He cursed himself for his stupidity and felt a tug in his stomach that he would cause the pain to her that spilled from her eyes.

Meghan nervously pushed herself upright and slid across the bed, her gaze purposely avoiding his. He could see the anxiety in her eyes as she quickly moved over to the window, with no real purpose for going there. With a sigh of remorse, Declan slapped his hands on his knees and stood and then he turned towards her.

"Well, it's getting late, I best be going." Declan slowly moved towards her to retrieve his jacket off the chair, and she took a step back away from him, which stabbed at his heart. Why was she withdrawing from him, did he frighten her so deeply that she wanted to avoid his touch, or was it the desire in her she feared?

His eyes settled on her flushed face as she nervously fussed with the curtains, her eyes darting from him to the window, then back to him. "Will y' have breakfast with me tomorrow?" he asked softly, trying to soothe her embarrassment and reassure himself that he had not pushed her away with his overzealous pursuit of her.

"Sure." She forced a smile, attempting to appear calm, but the inner turmoil was ripping her apart. How she wanted him, what if she was pushing him away. A man like him would only be pushed so far before he walked away, but how far was too far? She bit at her lip when he took another step towards her bypassing his jacket.

He moved slowly towards her, attempting one last grasp at intimacy. The last thing he wanted was to leave her and go to his own room alone, desire gone unfulfilled. He needed to stay with her and hold her close to him as he slept, smelling the fragrance of her when he wakes. "So, do y' think that this bandage will hold?" He spread his shirt apart and looked down towards the dressing she had attached to his firm chest. If he could only direct her attention to his wounds, play on her sympathies.

"Yes, it should," Meghan replied and moved the three steps left between them. Her hand instinctively went to the bandage and began assuring it was secure.

"Well, I worry about it. I wouldn't want it to become infected and have it all pussy and such." Declan glanced at her with mischief brewing in his eyes.

"I disinfected it, but if you are still worried, I could do it again," she offered, the feel of his warm, moist skin pulsing under her touch, breaking down her willpower.

Her eyes rose to meet his, and she could not break the gaze from the dark cloudy eye that seemed to be probing her soul. She slowly ran her open palms across his chest, causing him to twitch as she traced the lines of his sculpted pectoral muscles from the top of the breastbone down and around to his ribs. Could she risk losing him? Did she want to miss the passion that he instilled in her?

Certainly, her father would not begrudge her such pleasure. She was not her mother after all. She had kept her promise to her father up until this point, she would only make love to the man she loved. And by God, she loved Declan with all her heart. She wanted him, desired him, and if she only got one night, it would be an extraordinary night.

Before she could stop herself, she had gripped the edges of his shirt in her fingers and slipped it over his broad shoulders. As she slid the shirt down his arms, the feel of his hard triceps under her fingers caused her to quiver.

Declan's hands landed on her face, and he gazed at her with questioning eyes. "Are y' sure?"

"Yes, I surrender, I'm your prisoner. Do with me what you want," she smiled brightly with no reservations and then fell into him, allowing him to catch her in his arms.

He laughed loudly as he tightened his arms around her waist and laid a soft kiss to her forehead. "I'll be gentle." His voice softened when he realized what she was offering him. She had cherished her virginity all these years, and now she chose to share herself with him. Should he take advantage of her gift? Should he turn her away, set her free, and never stake claim to her again? No, he was selfish, and he wanted her and needed her. He had to admit he had deep feelings for her; she made his heart glad when she was near him, but was it love? Love was such an enigma to him; his mother was cold and manipulating, her love only given when her needs were met; his father's love was earned through achievement. Could this warm loving woman show him true love? Did she have an ulterior motive to her passion, or was she honest with him and herself?

It was now or never; she was offering herself to him, and by God, he was going to take her. Tomorrow he could worry about all the what ifs; tonight he was going to enshroud himself in her.

His lips roamed down her face to her neck, tasting the sweetness of her. A taste and scent he knew he would never forget, it was Meghan, his Meghan. Her body compressed against him when his hand pressed against the soft curve of her back, urging her closer to him. How soft she was, not emaciated like the women he had been with over the past few years. Sammy was not far off with her assessment of him. He was not aroused by her boyish figure; she was so unappealing to him that he had to imagine someone else to become aroused. But now, he savoured the feel of Meghan under his hand, soft, smooth, but delicate, her touch escalating him to a point of explosion.

Her hands explored his torso, her fingers sliding though the sparse black hair covering the firm chest, allowing them to wander across the curve of his shoulder and down his strong arms. He was solidly built; every muscle exquisitely formed and sculpted to enhance his large frame.

Her body instinctively reacted to his, pressing up against him with crushing pressure. He reacted in turn by forcefully gripping her around the ribs, crushing her further; his other hand slid down her back with the zipper between his thumb and forefinger. Without waiting for a response, he pulled back from her slightly and slid the dress over her breasts, letting it fall freely to the floor.

Her body shuddered gently as his hand brushed across her breast, his thumb circling her nipple until it hardened. Her reaction to his touch was intoxicating, sending him into a lust-driven haze. He had to control himself; he had to be careful with her to ensure that her first time was extraordinary. He could give her that much.

A slight gasp exited her as he lowered his head, his mouth surrounding the hard pink nipple. She was amazed at the sensation he caused in her by simply touching her, and she became extremely anxious not to disappoint him. Her hands were trembling slightly as she gripped his belt and yanked a little harder than she had intended.

His head lifted, his eyes full of humour. "Are y' trying to rip it off before I have a chance to use it?"

"No, I . . ."

Before she could finish her comment, his demanding lips pressed against hers with enough force to part her lips, allowing his tongue to move in and flicker across hers. A soft moan filled the air as she pressed her breasts flat against him, her hands returning to his pants.

This time she managed to release the belt without any comment from him and without delay, she had the button undone and the zipper half way down before he gripped her hands.

The corner of his mouth twitched as he watched her eyeing him with confusion.

"What?" she blurted out, taking a step away from him, somewhat embarrassed that he halted her attempts at removing his pants.

The smile finally broke, and he gripped her face in his hands, a gentle expression crossing his face. "Are y' really sure? I don't want to push y'."

"I have never been more sure of anything in my life," she assured him in a breathy voice, the smile returning to her face.

His hands tightened around her face, and he kissed her hard with so much passion, she could hardly breathe. One hand left her face and snaked around her ribs, crushing her up against him, her breasts warm and moist against his skin.

His unfastened pants were beginning to slip down his hips as he took a few steps towards the bed, pulling her along with him. She gasped slightly as she felt the sizeable hardness pulsing against her pelvis.

Declan halted his movements and gazed at her, his eyes ablaze with desire. "I need y'," he muttered, meant neither as an apology or a demand, it was a simple fact. "I need y' now."

She was trembling in his arms as he touched her, and he knew that she needed him as much as he needed her.

"Meggie, can I take y' now?" His breath was short and warm on her face.

"Yes, Declan." She forced over the emotion building in her throat. "Please, I . . ."

Before she could finish her answer, he gathered her into his arms and carried her to the bed, his lips firmly on hers. She clung to him with a need so deep, she could not deny it as he flipped the bedding back with one hand and laid her down with the other.

His movement towards her was slow and controlled, his pinning gaze fixed on her while his hand slid across her chest, cupping her round, firm breast, his thumb brushing across her nipple.

Suckling and kissing, he ran his tongue around the surface of her skin, feeling her quiver from the sensation, her body heaving towards him while he continued to caress and kiss her with utter desire. Her head arched back in welcoming when he fit himself into her with a gentle force that caused a low groan in the back of her throat.

"Meggie," Declan muttered, his movements slow and precise. "I think y' had it wrong."

Meghan gazed up at him, her eyes ablaze but said nothing as she buried her face into his neck when he shifted on top of her.

"Meggie?"

"What?" she mumbled, the annoyance in her voice evident.

He chuckled slightly at her annoyance and kissed her damp forehead. "I just wanted to tell y' that I'm your prisoner. Y' hold me heart in your hands."

She tried to smile as her head arched back once again as every fibre in her body threatened to explode.

"I just wanted you to know. Y' don't need to answer right now," he joked, pressing his face against hers and nipping at her ear.

"Declan." She frantically gripped his face between her hands. "What?"

"Shut up," she muttered and pressed her lips against his.

Her hands slid across his face back through his thick hair as her body burned with a desire so deep, she thought she would implode.

As she drove her hips hard into him, he thrust himself deeper and deeper into her in an attempt to reach her core—the place deep inside her that he wanted to possess. With every quiet moan, with every urgent arch of her hips, he knew he had filled her with complete desire and satisfaction.

Her cry and the shuddering of her body sent him over the edge, and he was so totally swept away in her reaction that he too exploded, as the pleasurable tremors fanned out from his core, leaving him gasping for air. His voice was husky as he called her name repeatedly with unmitigated gratification before he collapsed in a heap of breathless pleasure.

As the night turned into early morning, they were still lying within each other's arms in a tangle of arms and legs. Meghan's head rested on his shoulder, and her fingers twisted in the dark curly hair on his chest as they lay quietly, trying to recover from the experience.

His hand caressed her arm stopping momentarily to tickle the bend of her elbow, then continued to her shoulder, tracing the little brown marks dotting her creamy skin.

"Y' sure do have a lot of freckles?"

"They're not freckles, they're beauty marks," she snorted, rather offended.

"Aye, if y' say so," he replied as he continued his mapping, his focus on the soft tender skin of her shoulder.

Meghan glanced over at him and watched as he ran his finger across her skin, seeming entranced. In a short period, her life had completely changed course with Declan in control. The expression of uncertainty that was present on his face was disturbing her, and the longer she watched him cataloguing every inch of her body, the more anxious she became.

"Declan," she blurted out, her voice sounding strangled. "Was it, I mean was I . . ." She turned her head away as his dark gaze settled on her.

"Freckles?" He soothed, rolled towards her, and rested his hand on her face. "What's wrong?"

"Nothing." She forced back the total humiliation she felt. How could she possibly believe that she could satisfy him in bed? She had no experience.

"Meggie, I'm sorry," he whispered into her hair, the feel of her withdrawal pieced his heart. "I promised I would be careful."

She shuddered and forced herself to a sitting position, her back to him. "It's not that."

"Then what is upsetting y'? Please tell me what I have done," he begged, he could feel her pulling away and he panicked. "Dammit, Meggie, y' said y' were sure."

"I was." She tossed back at him over her shoulder and jumped from the bed, from him. "I just wanted to, well, I hoped that I . . . Damn, I don't know what I thought."

Declan was on his feet right behind her when she covered herself with her dark purple housecoat. "I'm sorry," his voice turned husky, and his hand trembled against her shoulder. What had he done by pushing her into this relationship?

"I'm the one that's sorry. I wanted to be perfect for you, I . . ."

"Oh, Meggie, y' are perfect." He turned her towards him and brushed her forehead with a kiss. "I have never experienced anything like that before. Y' set me aflame with just a touch."

"Really?" Meghan sniffed, holding back tears. "I should have told you I have never."

"Shh, I knew," he kissed her softly. "I knew."

"How?" She sounded slightly panicked. "When?"

"Tonight."

"Was it that bad?" She pulled away from him, devastation clouding her eyes.

"Meggie, it was fantastic. I figured it out when y' were standing over by the curtains." A smug grin curled his lips. "I could see the desire in your eyes, but the fear was more powerful."

Meghan smiled softly and rested her head on his shoulder. "I feel slightly ashamed. I vowed I would save myself for marriage." Her eyes closed as his hand rested against her cheek. "When my mom left with that man, my dad was devastated, and I swore that I would not be like her, a cheap whore."

"Meggie, you're no whore," he said softly. "And y' have nothing to be ashamed of; we made love as two adults that wanted to be with each other."

She nodded and forced calmness into her mind. He was right. She had made love to the man she loved, and there was nothing to be ashamed of. Her actions were pure of heart, and that is all there was to it. It did not matter that she was unsure of Declan's true intentions. Whether she was just another woman to him or not did not change the fact that she gave herself willingly to him and would now deal with the consequences.

"Meggie, come back to bed." Declan tugged on her arm until she obliged and followed behind him. He wasted no time disrobing her so he could smother her with soft kisses. He was the one, she thought as he locked her heart in a prison of desire and he had the only key.

CHAPTER NINE

The lobby was relatively quiet the next morning as Meghan stormed towards the front desk to confront the lodge manager.

Her anger, if she was honest, was more to do with the fact that Declan was gone in the morning when she woke, leaving no note or explanation for his absence. Adding to the lack of a note, the necklace he had given her was gone, and she was deeply concerned that the fairytale was over.

He was not answering his phone, and after leaving a message, she did not want to continue calling, making herself appear somewhat desperate. However, as the hours of the morning ticked by, her pride was beginning to rebel at the obvious dumping she had received.

"I want to speak to the manager please," Meghan said firmly, trying to control her anger as she stopped at the desk.

"What seems to be the problem, dear?" The older woman behind the desk questioned calmly, her greying hair sweeping softly around her face.

"I phoned for room service, and they won't bring me any breakfast. He said he wasn't allowed to service my room," Meghan grumbled.

"Oh, I see," the wrinkled mouth said loudly, disturbing her from her thoughts. "The man you need to speak to is in that room across the lobby." The woman pointed to a room next to the dining room, the French doors partially open to the lobby.

Meghan turned and headed for the doors with a confrontational force.

"Good luck, dear," the woman said, with a rather taunting tone.

Meghan grunted and shoved the door open, allowing it to bang against the wall. She was startled by the sound, but quickly regained her initial intent to rip the manager's head off; she was completely inconvenienced by having to come out to the lobby.

A small table was in the middle of the room, edged with two large chairs on either side. One of the chairs was blocking her view of the table, but she could see that someone was sitting in the chair. She tried to peek around the chair to get a glimpse of who was seated at the table, but the large side wings were too deep and masked the face from view.

"Excuse me, I was told I need to talk to you," Meghan said abruptly, taking a step towards the chair.

"Uh-huh," grunted the man in the chair but made no attempt to talk to her.

"I want to know why I can't get room service today," Meghan questioned in an increasingly annoyed voice as she marched towards him.

"Uh-huh," grunted the man again, but still he made no move.

"Are you even listening to me? I said I want some breakfast brought to my room," Meghan snapped and stormed over to the large chair.

Suddenly a large muscular arm reached out and pulled her across the lap of the man in the chair.

"I want y' for breakfast," Declan chuckled as his face bent towards her neck.

"You're not funny, Declan!" Meghan snapped, swinging her hands wildly, trying to get off his lap. "You scared me."

"Y' sure can be rude to people when y' get mad, can't y'?" Declan laughed and kissed her cheek.

Meghan tried wiggling loose, but he was having no part of it. He held her tightly until she stopped struggling.

"Y' may as well relax. I'm never letting y' go," he grinned. "And you're lucky y' didn't hit me with those hands. I think I have enough bruises on me face, don't y'?"

Meghan eyed his face and grimaced. "Your eye, it's very black. It looks sore," she said, gently resting her hand on his cheek.

"Aye, it does smart at bit."

Meghan softly smiled and kissed his swollen blackened eye. "I'm sorry."

"What are y' sorry for?" he questioned, resting his hand on her face.

"For everything that happened last night," she sighed and pressed her face hard against his hand.

"It's not your fault for what happened at the hotel. And well, what happened after that, y' have nothing to be sorry for," he grinned, his eyes twinkling with mischief.

Meghan smiled and rested her face against his. "When you were gone this morning, I figured . . . well, I assumed that I wouldn't see you again," Meghan said weakly, slightly embarrassed that she had those crazy thoughts.

"Well, you're stuck with me, because I will hunt y' down and hold y' as a prisoner if y' try to leave me," he said, half laughing, but there was enough command in his voice that she knew he was serious.

"I thought you were the prisoner," Meghan smirked.

"So y' did hear me," he teased, a twisted grin overtaking his lips.

"How could I not? Do you always talk so much?"

"Talk so much? I just was making a comment. Y' shouldn't be commenting on the amount I talk, Freckles, you're the one that always has something to say," he joked and kissed her nose.

"Well, since you are holding me hostage here, you better be feeding me, I'm starved. I haven't eaten anything since yesterday," Meghan complained, noticing the increasing sound of rumbling coming from her belly.

"Your wish is my command." He rang a bell that was on the table.

No sooner did the soft tinkle of the bell stop, the waiter from the other day strolled through the door, pushing a cart with various plates. Meghan raised her brow, a wry smirk twisting her mouth.

"Do you think that I'm that big of a pig?"

"No, I just wasn't sure what y' liked, so I ordered a few things on the breakfast menu."

"Eggs Benedict." The smiling waiter informed him quite proud of his knowledge.

"You remembered?" Meghan said, surprised that he would remember what she had ordered days earlier, especially since he was so focused on Cassie.

"You're hard to forget, Meggie," Declan grinned.

The waiter was still standing, smiling at Meghan when the manager came into the room and stood by the table with an air of superiority, his long moustache twitching slightly as his gaze settled on Declan. "I hope everything is to your liking, sir," he asked, his voice rough and low.

"It's brilliant, y' and your staff did a great job," Declan said, shaking the man's hand after Meghan removed herself from his lap and moved into the other large chair across the table.

"Thanks, that will be all for now," Declan smiled politely at the waiter, who still had not left the table.

"Very well, sir." With an annoyed bob of the manager's head towards the young infatuated waiter, the two were gone.

A wide smile grew across Declan's face as he watched Meghan's observation of the exiting men. "What do y' want to do today?" Declan asked, looking around the flowers that were in the centre of the table.

"I would like to go to town and look around. It looked like such a cute little place with some neat shops, but we only got into the clothing shops yesterday." Meghan sipped her orange juice, enjoying the ease at which the conversation had been progressing.

"I should have known, leave the decision up to a woman, shopping always comes into play," Declan chuckled before irritation crossed his face. Without warning, his hand reached out, grabbing for the flower vase and depositing it on the outside edge of the table. "It's blocking me view of y'," he smiled, much more content at his unobstructed view of her.

Meghan laughed and bent over to pick up her napkin that she dropped during his sudden removal of the flower vase, but unfortunately, when she raised her eyes up towards the door, Kaye was wandering by and noticed her.

"Meghan, have you seen Declan today?" Kaye grumbled, her movement towards the table hurried.

Declan's eyes had rolled back in his head. His hands wrapped around his neck and his tongue was sticking out the side of his mouth, causing Meghan to laugh at his antics.

"What are you finding so amusing? Haven't you heard what happened?" Kaye muttered and quickened her pace.

Before she arrived, though, Declan popped his head out from around the chair and stared at her with an irritated gaze.

"Oh, are you all right?" Kaye mumbled, appearing particularly startled by his presence.

"Aye?" A slight smirk curled Declan's full lips.

"How is your girlfriend? I heard a paparazzi attacked her," Kaye smirked, resting her blue eyes on Meghan.

"Why don't y' ask her yourself?" Declan bobbed his head towards Meghan. "How are y', Freckles?"

"I'm perfect," Meghan smiled, with pleasure.

"You're the girlfriend? I heard it was a woman from Boston?"

"I have no girlfriend in Boston, but I guess it makes a better story," Declan laughed. "But it was Meggie that was my date at the party."

"You went to the party last night?" Kaye questioned, shock and jealousy crossing her face.

Meghan nodded, a large smirk twisting her lips. "Yes, we had a lovely time. I didn't see you there. I thought you said you were going?"

Declan was growing tired of the invasion, and he lifted his fork in his hand. "Well, Kaye, if y' would please excuse us, we are having a private breakfast." Declan tone was dismissive.

"Fine, enjoy what time you have left," she growled and stormed out of the room. As she disappeared, Declan glanced back at Meghan who had a disturbed frown on her lips.

"That was rather rude!" Meghan muttered, looking up at him from under her brows.

"Well, she was disturbing us. The sign on the door says private, does it not?" he said, rather arrogantly and then took a sip of his juice.

"Yes," she muttered, gazing down at her plate rather startled by his attitude.

"Meggie, what are y' worrying about now?" he questioned, his mouth twitching with subdued humour. "You're thinking I'm an arse again, are y' not?"

Her brow crumpled slightly that he caught her again, and she began to chew at her lower lip, her eyes darting around, trying to avoid his pinning gaze.

"I think y' were just as rude," he smirked, lowering his gaze to his plate.

"Me?" she blurted out, rather affronted.

"Aye. What was that crack about not seeing her at the party?" His eyes rose and a glimmer of mischief flashed in the dark grey eyes. "I think y' were trying to rub in the fact that y' went and she didn't."

Meghan's mouth dropped open as she groped for a response, but once again, he had her backed into a corner, and she had no way of talking herself out. "All right," she grunted. "I was trying to torment her."

"Aye, I know," he laughed, the lines around his eyes creasing with humour. "Y' may not have been as outright rude as me, but y' got your digs in, Freckles, and don't try to deny it."

She could not help but laugh at him, he was grinning like the cat that ate the canary.

He shook his head, his eyes still fixed on her, as a gratified expression shadowed his face. "You're a perfect fit, Meggie Delaney."

She smiled bashfully at his comment, the feeling of complete satisfaction filling her entire being. He accepted her for who she was—childish imperfections and all.

Her attention settled back on him when he dug in his pants pocket. "I have a slight problem I was hoping that y' could help me with."

"Sure," she smiled, her eyes glued to the large hand, resting closed on the table.

"Meggie, will y' stay with me here?" he blurted out, not knowing how else to ask.

She eyed him curiously, his face bizarre to say the least. "I would like that."

"No, Meggie, I mean, well, I mean, forever." Declan thrust his closed hand towards her and dropped to one knee by her side. "Meghan Delaney, will y' make me the happiest man in the world and be me wife?" His voice cracked slightly as he opened his hand, revealing a ring, the enormous square diamond sparkling brightly in the thick gold band.

"Oh my God!" Meghan mumbled, staring down at the ring, her mouth gaping open with shock.

Declan's dark gaze stayed fixed on her face as she continued to stare at the ring unspeaking. He could see the uncertainty in her eyes as they rose to his.

"Meggie, are y' going to give me an answer?" he questioned, lifting the ring from his hand and grabbing her left hand.

"Declan," she muttered, pulling her hand away from his. "I . . ." She jumped from the table and moved over towards the window, unsure how to answer his question. She wanted to say yes, but she was wary of his timing, especially since his mother was so hostile about the relationship.

"Meggie, I'm sorry, I didn't mean to scare y'," he said softly; his hands landed on her shoulders from behind.

His heart was pounding so loudly, it sounded as if it was going to spring from his chest.

She twisted around, dislodging his hand from her shoulders, and when she faced him, the expression on his face was startling. She froze in place, and time seemed to stand still as his dark pinning gaze stayed fixed on her, and his hand slowly rested on her hip as if he was unsure if he should touch her.

"I'm sorry, I didn't mean to scare y'. It's just that I can't bear to let y' leave on Sunday. If y' don't want to get married, maybe y' could come back for the weekend every couple of weeks," he said, trying to convince her.

"Declan, I do love you, and I can't bear to be without you either. Ever since I saw you in the lobby, you haven't left my thoughts."

"Then why don't y' want to stay with me?" His voice filled with panic.

"I do, nothing would make me happier, but I'm scared that we're moving too fast. I just don't want to get in-between you and your family. You would just grow to resent me for it."

Declan sighed and rested his hand on her face. "My sweet, Meggie." His voice was soft and caring as he leaned towards her, kissing her lips softly. "From the minute I saw y' walk through those lobby doors, I have been lost in y'. I will never be able to love another, because y' own me heart."

Meghan stared at him for what seemed an eternity before she smiled. "I can't leave you. I'll stay."

Declan let out his breath, lifted her into the air, and swung her around before returning her to the floor. "Oh, Meggie," he sighed into her hair.

When he pulled back to look at her, he noticed that her focus quickly changed back to the ring that he pushed onto his pinky finger during their discussion, and he began to twist it around his finger tauntingly.

"Well," he finally said, looking back down at the ring, "I wonder what I'm going to do with this wee ring."

"You could give it to someone," Meghan smirked, leaning up against him.

His eyes rose to meet hers with a slight shimmer of amusement in the dark grey orbs. His mouth turned up slightly on one side as he returned his gaze to the ring.

"Aye, well, I tried that, but she didn't want it," Declan said evenly. "It is very lovely," he mumbled, pulling it off his finger. "And not every woman could wear a ring like this."

"Really?" Meghan's voice was full of curiosity to hear his reasoning.

"Aye. It's very large as y' see, and a woman with a tiny hand could not wear it. It needs to be on a hand with long slender fingers."

"Is that right?" she giggled and lifted her hand examining her fingers.

"Aye. Y' see, it would look very gaudy on a small hand, but on a hand like yours . . ." He gripped her left hand and slipped the ring over her knuckle. "See, on a hand like yours, it looks beautiful."

Meghan spread out her fingers, examining the ring that fit her hand perfectly. Declan smiled, took her hand in his, and lifted it to his face, kissing her knuckles right above the ring.

"Well, I guess y' see what I'm saying," Declan smirked, placing his fingers on the ring, pulling lightly at the band.

Meghan pulled her hand from him, holding it securely in her other hand against her chest. "I think it's stuck."

"Is that so?" Declan chuckled, grabbing her hand. His mouth rose into a one-sided smile as he pretended to attempt to remove the ring from her finger. "I think y' might be right. Well, what do y' think we should do about that?"

"Well, I could keep it on," Meghan smirked.

"Aye, that's a possibility," he grinned. "Or we could try using soap."

"I think soap would ruin it," she said evenly.

"Y' could be right," he laughed. "Well, I guess there is only one thing to be done."

"What's that?"

Declan dropped to his knee in front of her once again. "Meggie, will y' marry me?"

Meghan blinked a few times, trying to clear the tears that were beginning to build in her eyes as she realized that she would never be able to walk away from him. "Yes," she blurted out, prepared to deal with all the problems that they were likely to face jumping into such a deep commitment so soon after meeting. "I will marry you."

CHAPTER TEN

The sun had long set when Meghan and Declan returned to the lodge, their faces flushed from the chilled night air. Meghan glanced down at the eagle statue that Declan had bought in town for good luck, and the story the sleigh driver entertained them with filled her thoughts.

"Oh, Declan, look at that bald eagle," Meghan blurted out, pointing towards the soaring majestic bird.

"It's beautiful." Declan glanced from the bird to Meghan, then back to the bird.

"That eagle is a legend around here." The driver smiled at the soaring bird.

"Why?" Declan questioned, his eyes still fixed on the eagle.

"Well, years ago, he had a mate. Did you know that eagles mate for life?"

"I didn't know that." Meghan spun around in the seat as the eagle soared behind them.

"They do. They were a beautiful pair. They could always be seen soaring together through the sky, so gracefully, but she disappeared about five years ago, poacher probably. He has never taken another mate. He glides through the air, day after day, searching, as if he thinks he will find her. He sits on their nest and calls out for her. The people around here say he is heartbroken. They call his missing mate, the Lost Eagle of Hidden Falls."

"Oh, that is so sad," Meghan sniffed as tears clouded her eyes.

Declan wiped a finger across her cheek, clearing away the escaping tears. He couldn't help but chuckle at the sappy story, wondering how many times the driver would have told it, he had it down perfectly.

"I couldn't imagine being so much in love that the loss of that person would leave me so broken-hearted and without hope," the driver admitted.

"I can," Declan chuckled and watched Meghan anxiously revolving in the seat to keep her eyes on the eagle.

When Meghan noticed his mocking facial expression, she smacked his shoulder and scowled at him. "I don't care what you think. I think it's a beautiful story."

"Hey, I didn't say anything," Declan complained, gripping her hands to avoid another smack. "I am actually enjoying seeing you so exited; you're like a kid at Christmas."

Meghan giggled and kissed Declan's cheek, then turned back to the driver, but Declan could not help but taunt the driver a little. "Y' should market that story. I'm sure there's a movie in there somewhere."

"Wait until you get into town," the driver laughed as Meghan frowned at Declan once again. "Legend has it that if the eagle flies overhead when a couple is getting married, then their love is for life. Most people buy a statue to bring with them to their wedding to ensure their future," the driver smiled, unfazed by Declan's laugher and continued on his way.

Declan cringed when he spotted his mother storming towards them, her face full of thunder. Damn, she was going to explode if she found out what they had done. He had to sideline her until the next day, but before he could think of an excuse to get away, Katie was directly in his path.

"We were supposed to have dinner tonight! Did y' forget?" Katie snapped, her blue eyes settling on Meghan.

"Apparently, I'm in trouble," Declan chuckled, and a large smile brightened his face.

"Apparently," Meghan replied, her brow rising slightly at Katie's angry face.

"I was just having fun, and I figured it wasn't a big deal. Y' stand me up all the time,"

Declan replied, his tone complacent.

"What were y' thinking last night, leaving the party without telling anyone? Then I find out you got into a fight with the paparazzi. Are y' determined to ruin your father's career? Y' are going to get nothing but bad press now!" Katie muttered and glared at Meghan, her eyes piercing her like daggers.

"We are going for dinner, would you like to come?" Meghan decided to defuse the situation before his mother had a meltdown.

"Now, dear, I know you're only inviting me, hoping I will support y' with me son, but I have no intentions of doing so."

Meghan jerked slightly but held her shock to a minimum. "I don't need your support."

Katie's brow rose slightly and a cruel frown filled her face. "Don't y' be snippy with me."

"Ma! How else do you think she is going to react when y' are attacking her? Y' need to stop it!" Declan's voice was stern.

"Did he tell y' that he has a fiancée back home?" Katie blurted out, unconcerned with Declan's annoyance.

"No, he didn't!" Meghan muttered as her pride began to take hold, and she wondered who was playing her for the fool, Katie or Declan.

"She is not my fiancée, Ma. How many times do I have to tell y'!" Declan gripped Meghan by the arm. "Goodnight, Ma." He turned and pulled Meghan down the hall to her room.

"Meggie, I'm sorry she is behaving this way," Declan whispered into her hair as he gathered her to him once they were back in her room.

"Why does she hate me?" she muttered into his chest as she fought back the tears.

"I don't think she hates y', I think she just wants me to marry Georgia."

"Your girlfriend back home?" Meghan questioned, lifting her head off his shoulder and staring at him with a slight hint of anxiety.

"She's not me girlfriend," he blurted out. "She is me sister Moiré's best friend, and me mam seems to think we would make a lovely couple."

"Oh," Meghan muttered, her lashes fluttering slightly, and she tried to pull away from him.

His brow crumpled slightly as an appearance of guilt crossed his face. "We have dated a few times, but I find her stuffy and overbearing.

She has no sense of humour either and gets cross with me for everything. If I would have spilled a glass of wine on her, I would still be hearing about it," Declan babbled and kissed Meghan's forehead. "Georgia is a debutant and behaves as such. It's such a bore."

Meghan eyed him speculatively. "I keep forgetting your family's position in Boston. I guess it was expected of you to marry someone like her."

"Aye, it was also expected of me to go to Harvard and become a lawyer or a powerful businessman. Acting was the last thing they wanted me to do."

"Really?" Meghan questioned with interest. "So you have completely destroyed their plans for you. No wonder your mother hates me. I'm just one more reminder of lost dreams."

Declan's brow rose slightly, and he kissed her forehead. "Most likely." He knew that his mother was not worried about Meghan not being a debutant; Katie was trying to keep him from marrying Meghan and bringing the wrath of the O'Briens down on her family. "Me mam can be an odd bird sometimes."

He laughed and kissed Meghan's nose, trying to reassure her of his love for her. With his mother interfering so deliberately, he was pleased that he had forced the issue that afternoon to ensure the strength of their relationship.

"I got y' something," he smiled and kissed her gently. "It's on the bed." He pushed her towards the bed and the beautifully wrapped silver box that sat in contrast on the floral bedspread. She seemed hesitant as he moved in behind her, wrapping his arms around her and resting his chin on her shoulder.

"Aren't y' going to open it?" Declan whispered, nudging her towards the bed.

"Yes," Meghan mumbled, sat down on the bed, and slowly picked up the gift. Her hand trembled slightly as she tore off the silver wrapping to find a box with the gift shop seal on the lid. She took a deep breath, trying to calm the anxiety that was building to a point of explosion. What if she had made a terrible mistake that afternoon? Declan seemed in no hurry to inform his mother of the news.

Meghan's worried eyes gazed up at Declan who was smiling, looking quite proud of himself, but as he noticed the expression on her face, he dropped to the bed beside her.

"Meggie, what's wrong?" He soothed, resting his hand on her face.

"Nothing," she forced out of her mouth. "I'm just tired. Maybe this was a mistake." The last part of her comment was almost a whisper.

He stiffened at her remark and wrapped his arm around her waist. "No, it wasn't, Meggie, no matter what me mam told y', I love y' and no other."

She cringed slightly that he knew what she was thinking, and her eyes settled on the rings. "I know," She blurted out, trying to hide her thoughts.

"Meggie, open your present," Declan gently ordered, bumping her shoulder softly with his.

"Declan, you didn't need to get me anything," Meghan muttered, staring down at the box. "When you buy me things, it just makes people think." She stopped her comment to collect her thoughts. "Well, your mother."

"Shh, Freckles, I know y' don't expect anything, but I like buying y' things, and I don't care what me mam thinks." He lifted the box off her lap and gestured it towards her. "Please open it."

She bit her bottom lip, and she took the box from his hand and slowly lifted the lid. A smile curled her lips despite her worry when she saw the beautiful wind chimes she had been admiring in the gift shop earlier that day.

"How did you know that I loved this one?" she asked, gazing up at him.

"I was watching y' while y' were looking at them, and y' seemed to be taken with this one," he smiled and kissed her cheek. "I love the way y' get so excited over little things."

"When I looked at it, I thought of the other day. In the morning when I went outside, the new snow had left a fresh face on the world and that was the day my life changed forever. Every time I look at this, I will think of you," Meghan smiled softly and lifted it from the box, swinging it slightly, creating a gently tinkling sound that filled the air as the snowflakes collided with each other.

Declan began to shuffle on the bed, his eyes switching from her to the wind chimes. "I know it's not much, but it's me wedding present to y'. So y' will never forget the love we found up here at the lodge."

"I never will," Meghan smiled and kissed his cheek.

"So, Mrs. Montgomery, when should we break the news to everyone?"

"How about at dinner tomorrow night?" she smiled. "It's my friends' last night here, and I want to tell them we got married before they leave."

"Aye, maybe that would be a good time to tell me mam too. With all those people around, she might hold her tongue."

Meghan nodded with agreement and wrapped her arms around his neck. "Cassie is going to be annoyed that she didn't get to be my maid of honour," she giggled and nuzzled her nose into his neck.

"Freckles, are y' upset that y' didn't have a big wedding?" he questioned, staring down at her with worry.

"Well, I . . . ever since I was a little girl, I wanted a fairy-tale wedding, but I know that having a big wedding would draw too much attention to you at the moment."

Declan sighed and kissed her forehead. His guilt over stealing her dream wedding from her was ripping him apart. Marrying her would have no impact on his career; his only reason for pushing the marriage that day was to ensure that she belonged to him before O'Brien found her.

She was so loving and understanding, when they married in the small church at the end of Main Street, that he felt somewhat like a jerk. The priest was very friendly and willing, after Declan donated a large amount of money to the parish, and it was not hard to acquire a marriage license from the only judge in town, once a few thousand dollars cross his palms. Acquiring the impromptu marriage was costly but worth it. She was his wife, and soon she would be pregnant and bearing him an heir.

"Freckles, we have a long break over Christmas. Why don't we have another ceremony by the waterfalls, and you can invite whomever y' want?"

"Really?" she shrieked with glee. "That would be wonderful. We could stand by the falls under that umbrella of fir trees and then have the reception here at the lodge. I could wear a white faux fox coat over my dress."

She began to ramble, and Declan threw back his head and laughed at her excitement. "Why did y' agree to a simple wedding in the church if you had your heart set on a big wedding?" She was an odd woman he thought as he watched her trying to decide how to answer.

"Well, to be honest, I was scared you would change your mind, you know, with your mother hating me so much, and I was scared that she would convince you that I was not good enough for you."

Declan shook his head and kissed her forehead. "I want y' to know that no one will ever make me change me mind. I love y', and I intend to stay married to y' for the rest of me life." He yanked the wind chimes from her hands, discarding them to the floor, then pulled her down on top of him. "Well, if y' want to be truly Mrs. Montgomery, then we still have some work to complete."

"And such gruelling work it is," she giggled as his fingers entwined in her hair, pulling her face towards his. "I don't know if I can endure it."

"Oh, you'll endure it all right," he grumbled. "And you'll damn well enjoy it."

"If I must," she shrieked as he flipped her over, crushing her with his large frame.

"Y' belong to me now. No one else." His lips descended on hers with more passion than she had ever felt from him before. "Meggie, my Meggie."

"Declan, I love you," she whispered against his lips.

His head lifted and a mischievous smile curled his lips. "How could y' not?"

Declan was relaxed and resting pleasantly on his back as Meghan lay beside him, her leg over his and her head on his chest. She was twisting the hair on his chest with her finger and caught sight of the rings, her engagement ring, and the wedding band. How odd it looked to her, she had awoken that morning bare fingered and full of anxiety and now she was lying in the arms of her husband.

The moonlight was shining into the room and causing her to appear as if she was glowing as he watched her admiring the rings on her hand. She could not take her eyes off it and neither could he. His impulsive decisions over the last few days had gotten him a wife, a beautiful, headstrong, loving wife. He hoped he could live up to her expectations and not cause her a day's regret. Five days was a short time and even shorter when you base your whole future on someone you have known for that short of a time. However, as he watched her, he knew she was the woman God sent to him. It was ordained over four hundred years earlier, and now it was up to him to fulfill his destiny.

Declan's stomach began to complain with loud bursts of rumblings, causing Meghan to giggle. They had forgotten to go for dinner and neither had eaten since that morning.

"Are y' hungry?" Declan buttoned his jeans and pulled up the zipper.

"Yes, I am, but I thought we were going for dinner?"

"Well, we got kind of busy, don't y' think, and neither of us is in any condition to venture out, so I'm going to order room service, would y' like anything?" he asked as he headed for the phone.

"A burger with fries," Meghan said as he lifted the receiver.

When he returned to the bed, she was standing by the window, staring out at the mountain; the lights flickered like stars in the night. The light illuminated the lake and cast a magical glow on the skaters as they circled in a slow leisurely fashion. The night was dark, and the stars shined so brightly that it appeared that the universe was at peace.

"I finally made a wish on my star," she muttered quietly.

"What?" Declan questioned from the other side of the room, only hearing part of her statement, while he poured them a drink.

"I said I finally made a wish on my star. I have been making wishes for years, and they never came true, so I figured I had been wishing on someone else's star," she smiled.

"Y' have the most bizarre way of thinking sometimes, Freckles," he smirked.

"It's not bizarre. Don't you ever make a wish on a star?"

"When I was a lad maybe. I figure wishing something wouldn't make it so. Y' need to make things happen."

"So you don't believe in fate?" Meghan questioned curiously.

"Not really."

"Declan, how can you say that? It was fate that we met." She turned towards him with an amazed look shadowing her face.

"How do y' figure that? We met because I purposely bumped into y', trying to meet y'," he informed her.

"Well, if I hadn't entered the lodge at the exact time I did, you might not have seen me at all," she retorted.

"Aye, but I would have met y' at the party," he countered.

"Maybe you wouldn't have even noticed me," Meghan scowled at him, then turned back to the window and gazed out at the stars. "I don't care how silly you think it is, I believe in fate."

"Come here, Mrs. Montgomery."

"That sounds so weird," Meghan giggled, and she sat down on the bed beside Declan.

"Well, then, I guess I will have to call y' that way every day until y' become accustomed to it."

"Declan, I love you," Meghan muttered as he pulled her towards him and rested his face against hers.

"How could y' not?" he laughed as he kissed her nose.

"God, you're arrogant," she chuckled.

"So y' have told me," he smiled and tightened his grip around her, his lips landing on her forehead. "I was thinking that on Monday, we could contact the movers and have them bring your belongs to the Malibu House."

Meghan smiled at the thought of living on the beach. "I don't really have much, but would you have room for some furniture?"

"Aye, I just bought it a couple of months ago, and it's pretty sparse inside," he grinned. "I haven't spent much time there yet."

"Is it on the beach?" Meghan questioned with excitement as she shifted slightly.

"Aye. It's not as big as some of the other houses on the street, but it has plenty of bedrooms," he grinned, eyeing her intently.

"Wow that's an asset," she laughed. "Do you plan on having a lot of company?"

"No, I just figured that we would need bedrooms for our wee bairns," he smirked.

"Oh," Meghan blurted out with shock, her face mirroring her voice.

"Freckles, don't y' want kids? I thought y' did," Declan's tone was full of worry.

"I do, but . . . ," she mumbled.

"Meggie, what's wrong?" His eyes fixed on her face as he tried to figure out what was disturbing her.

"Nothing, I'm just surprised that you want children." She forced a smile. Within a week, she was married to a man she barely knew, and now he is talking about children. "I just thought that maybe we should get to know each other a bit better first."

"Why?" he questioned with agitation. He needed her to give him an heir, preferably a male to secure the future for his family.

"I . . ." she paused not liking the determination on his face. "I just wanted to spend time together, just the two of us for a while. I need to finish my residency, and I spend a lot of time at the hospital."

He could see the agitation building in her, and he decided not to push. She would become pregnant; he would ensure that, so there was no point in ruining the evening by upsetting her. "Well, that's something we can discuss at a later date."

Her brow rose slightly. "You're just placating me now, aren't you?"

"Aye, if y' think I'm going to spend our first night of marriage arguing, you're wrong. I have other things I would rather be doing." His face buried in her hair, and he nipped at her earlobe.

"Declan," she grumbled, pulling her head from his wandering lips.

"If y' think y' are going to whip me into a frenzy over when we have our children, you're wrong. You're very high-strung."

"I am not," she snorted and took a swat at his smirking face.

"Aye, y' are, so it's a good thing y' met me," he laughed, gripping her hand before it made contact.

"Why, so you could make fun of me?" Meghan's nose crinkled as he kissed her forehead.

"No," he laughed, resting his hand on her face. "Because I love y'."

She snorted a soft chuckle and pressed her forehead against his. "I love you too."

"How could y' not?" he laughed.

A quiet intimate wedding celebration was the plan as they lay in each other's arms, discussing how they would like the day to go. A few close friends and family, but Declan's one wish was for it to be private without the glare of media attention. The falls would provide a perfect sight, being so difficult to access, with only one road leading into the area. December 26, was the day they had decided on, but they were planning to keep the information a secret until closer to the date to avoid publicity.

"We could go to Ireland for our honeymoon," Declan suggested with excitement.

Meghan smiled with delight and kissed his chest that her head was resting on. "I would love to go there with you and see where you came from. Maybe I can track down my family as well."

He stiffened slightly but a smile curled his lips. "Aye, I'm sure they shouldn't be too hard to locate." His brow rose slightly as he thought how easy it would be to locate her family.

Declan's hand slipped down her ribs, pressing her up against his bare chest, but as her hand gripped the button on his pants, a loud knock on the door sounded, startling her.

"It's room service," Declan muttered against her lips and jumped from the bed. "Great, I'm starved, y' wore me out," he laughed as he swung the door open.

With catlike reflexes, Declan jumped back when the door flew open, exposing Ian and a gun, but before he could react, Ian stormed into the room. Declan had steadied himself by the time Ian was through the door, but he knew that Meghan's presence in the bedroom was going to add some level of difficulty to terminate the situation without incident.

"What the hell are you doing here?" Ian grumbled. Dammit, he was supposed to be with his mother, having dinner.

"Rory, what the hell are y' doing?" Declan blurted out.

"Sorry about this, I never wanted to involve you, but I have my orders," Ian smirked and waved the gun towards the far wall. "Now get over there."

"What orders, Rory? Ma has gone too far this time." Declan's eyes scanned the room.

"Oh my God, Ian?" Meghan shrieked as her mind cleared to what was happening.

"Meggie, get back!" Declan shouted to her as panic filled him, his stance mirroring the appearance of a panther about to pounce.

Ian changed his attention to Meghan and pointed the gun at her head. A menacing grin curled Ian's lips as he glanced back at Declan. "Now that I have both of your attention," Ian took a step towards Meghan, "you need to come with me."

"Rory, calm down."

"Rory? That's Ian," Meghan blurted out with confusion.

"No, he's me brother Rory," Declan said calmly, and slowly moved towards him with his usual stealth.

Meghan stared blankly at Declan, not grasping what he was saying. Why did he think Ian was his brother?

"I'm sure we can work out whatever is upsetting y'." Declan kept glancing at Meghan as she stood frozen in place.

"There is nothing to work out. It's nothing personal, but I don't have a choice." Ian eyed Declan's position on the floor, as if he had noticed Declan's slow, quiet movement towards him. The gun was still fixed on Meghan, and Ian was looking anxiously back and forth between the door and Declan.

"Y' always have a choice."

Meghan's eyes fluttered and closed with worry when Declan's voice shook. She could see the fear in his eyes, and she knew that the situation was not going to end well. Her eyes settled on Ian's agitated face as he took another step towards her. "Please, just come with me, no one needs to get hurt here." Ian's voice trembled slightly. "Please."

It only took a split second for Declan to lunge towards Ian, but his action startled Ian, and a thunderous noise shattered the silence.

Meghan watched helplessly as Declan fell to the floor, his blood splattering across her housecoat. Her scream sounded muffled as she lunged towards Declan, throwing herself on top of his lifeless body.

"Declan!" she cried. "Oh God, please."

"Meggie, I love y', don't ever forget that." Declan's voice was weak, and his eye shut heavily.

"No, Declan, wake up, I love you," Meghan sobbed and gripped Declan's cold face.

"How could y' not?" His lip twitched slightly, then there was no more movement, his large frame limp and surprisingly vulnerable.

"Don't you die on me!" Meghan cried, her tears streaming down her cheeks and bouncing off his pale white face. She groped his neck, searching for a pulse and thankfully it was there, it was weak, but still there.

Her eyes darted around the room searching for something to stop the bleeding, and they stopped on a hand towel resting over the back of a chair by the fireplace. She jumped to her feet and lunged for the towel. Ian appeared stunned and was uninterested in stopping her movements.

"What the hell happened?" Eliza blurted out as she darted through the door with a short heavy bearded man trailing behind her. "You weren't supposed to shoot him."

Eliza stared down at Meghan's terrified face. "Christ, what have y' done?"

Ian shook his head with worry. "He jumped at me, the gun went off."

Meghan's mind was spinning so fast, it took her a moment to notice the other two people standing at her side. "Ian? What the hell?"

"Shut up," he hollered at her, then turned to Eliza. "I have to call an ambulance?"

Meghan's panicked eyes switched from Ian to Eliza, then to the bearded man. What was happening?

"Murphy, where is Liam?" Ian growled, his pale blue eyes settling on the bearded man.

"I don't know. He was supposed to be here by now," he grumbled and turned to Eliza. "Have you seen him?"

"No," she mumbled and glanced down at Meghan. "Dear, please move away from him."

"No!" Meghan shrieked. "I'm not leaving him."

"You have that right, sweetheart," the bearded man grumbled and headed towards her, the gun pointing at her head.

"No!" Eliza bolted towards him and grabbed his arm, trying to change the direction of the gun. "He said she would not be harmed."

Ian, startled, shifted from his focus on Declan and glanced up at Eliza. "Well, neither was he. What have I done?"

"What the hell is wrong with both of y'? She knows too much, and I'm not getting nailed for this?" Murphy snapped and waved the gun towards Declan's lifeless body. "Dammit, this is out of control," he growled and fixed the gun on Meghan.

"He doesn't want her dead. He wants to take her with him." Eliza blurted out gripping Murphy's arm again. Her eyes switched to Ian who was nodding his head with agreement.

"Damn," Murphy grumbled and scrubbed his sweaty hand across his brow. "Fine, take her. We need to get out of here."

"I'm phoning for an ambulance," Ian mumbled and headed for the phone. "Get her, and I'll meet you outside."

The bearded man pressed the gun against the back of Meghan's head. "Let's go!"

"No, I need to be with him," Meghan cried, flailing her arms at him. "Damn you."

"Why, he's already dead."

"Stop it!" Eliza screamed and smacked him across his face. "Don't torment her any further."

"Y' stupid bitch." Murphy slammed his hand against Eliza's head, knocking her to the floor.

Eliza climbed to her feet and flew at Murphy in a rage, slamming into him, forcing his hand to clench around the trigger, causing the gun to fire. A loud shriek filled the air when the bullet tore into the muscle of Meghan's left thigh, leaving her screaming in pain.

"Meghan." Eliza darted to her side and dropped to the floor. "Oh my gosh."

"Why?" Meghan mumbled as her surroundings began to blur.

"Eliza, get the hell out of the way," Murphy bellowed and bent down beside Meghan. "We need to make it look like a domestic incident."

Before Eliza knew what he meant, he began to slam the gun into Meghan's face. Every nerve in her face was exploding with sharp, piercing pain, as he struck her with an unrelenting force. Her eyes burned as the blood from the cuts on her forehead spilled over her lashes. He struck her again and again, sending her into a daze.

"Stop it," Eliza screamed and began to hit at Murphy. "That's my baby."

"Big deal, it's not like you care," Murphy snorted and shoved at Eliza.

Murphy did, however, manage to break Meghan's nose before he was interrupted. Her face was cut in so many places that it was impossible to decipher where all the blood was coming from.

"Bloody hell!" A loud booming voice pierced the air. The large blond man stared down at Meghan, examining the bullet wound and her damaged face. "Who the hell did this? I said I wanted her unharmed."

"You said that no one was getting hurt," Ian blurted out from his position by the phone.

"What do y' think y' are doing?" the blond man hollered.

"I'm phoning for an ambulance," Ian yelled back. "He wasn't supposed to get hurt. I didn't sign up for killing him."

"Shut up and get out to the truck," the blond man ordered and shook his head. "Y' are like the three stooges. All y' were supposed to do was bring me the girl. We can't take her like that." He glanced around the room, his eyes settling on Eliza. "This is what we are going to do. Y' stay here and phone the ambulance. Y' tell them y' were walking down the hall and heard the shot," the blond man sighed with impatience.

"What if the police figure out I am lying?" Eliza panicked. "I don't want to go to jail."

The large blond man pondered her question for a long second before a twisted grin curled his full lips. He dropped down beside Meghan and wrapped her hand around the gun. "Don't worry, me love, I'll get y' out."

Meghan was too terrified to speak as the realization of what was happening took hold. They were framing her for Declan's murder.

"Where is it?" The blond man opened the top of her housecoat.

"What?" Meghan mumbled, her voice was weak and quiet.

"The locket, what have you done with it?" His voice was low.

Meghan shook her head; she could not direct him towards Cassie. "I don't know."

The man grunted and nodded his head towards the bathroom. "Go check in there. She might have left it on the counter." His eyes racked her body before he turned abruptly. "Eliza, I want to be kept informed of her movements. We will get her after the authorities are done with her. That way when we remove her from the country, she will be a fugitive, and she will have no choice but to obey me," the big blond man smirked and sauntered out of the room followed by Ian and Murphy.

CHAPTER ELEVEN

Nathan was permitted in to see Meghan before the police interviewed her, but he could not get Meghan to understand what was happening. All she was concerned about was Declan.

"Megs, you need to calm down," Nathan warned. "If you say the wrong thing to these men . . ."

"Nat, I didn't shoot him, Ian did. Once I tell them my side, everything should be all right. Shouldn't it?" she cried, the tears stinging the extensive cuts on her face.

"Well, since Ian disappeared . . ." Nathan paused, trying to think what to say to get her to understand. "Megs, they want to believe you are guilty. Declan's parents are very powerful, and they want this over quickly. Just please stick to the story you just told me and no more." Nathan told her and squeezed her hand just as the door opened, and four men walked through, two well dressed in dark blue suits, and the other two wore slacks and sports jackets that did not match. It wasn't hard to distinguish the FBI agents from the local officers.

"Good morning, Miss Delaney, I'm Detective McKenna, and this is Detective Moriarty," the short stocky man said, bobbing his head towards the tall blond man walking in behind him, totally ignoring the other two men.

"Hi," Meghan sniffed, trying to control her terror; the expression on the men's faces told her that they believed she was guilty. She reached out for Nathan's hand, her hand waving frantically, since she could not turn her head with the thick neck brace attached around her throat.

"We're from the FBI, miss," the tall agent piped up, throwing a cold glare towards the detective. "I'm Agent Brody Spencer, and this is my partner, Agent Andy Gillis."

Meghan eyed him carefully, he seemed so detached and cold, it frightened her. Why was the FBI involved with a murder case? Surely Declan didn't hold enough influence to have the FBI involved.

Nathan finally noticed her hand and gripped it securely before he spoke. "I'm Nathan Coleman. I'm Miss Delaney's legal counsel."

The tall agent nodded and pulled up a chair next to the bed, totally blocking the police detectives from her view. "We have a few questions for you." His sky blue eyes scanned her face, then the badly bruised arm that lay still at her side, an intravenous tube protruding from the slender arm.

"He did quite a number on you." Agent Spencer's eyes focused on the narrow slits. Damn, he really beat the crap out of her. He was finding it hard to blame her for shooting the bastard.

Meghan nodded and glanced up at Nathan, then at the short detective leaning against the wall, writing in his pad. "He was crazy. He shot me, then hit me with the gun."

Agent Spencer's eyes settled on his partner, then back to Meghan. "Whom would you be referring to?"

"I don't know who he was. He came in after Ian shot Declan," Meghan said weakly, knowing that these two men did not believe her either. The officers that Nathan had talked to had already made it clear they believed her to be guilty.

"Hmm." Agent Spencer kept his eyes on Meghan; her dark green eyes barely visibly under her swollen lids seemed honest somehow. She certainly did not give him the gut feelings that she could have shot anyone.

"Miss Delaney, we have a witness that claims she saw you shoot Mr. Montgomery." Detective McKenna blurted out, noticing the hesitation in the FBI agent, "So why don't you just tell us the truth?"

"I am . . . ," Meghan sniffed gripping tightly on Nathan's hand. "Ian shot him."

"Who shot you? Mr. Montgomery?" Agent Spencer questioned in a soft tone.

"The man with the beard." Her voice sounded weak as she described him in detail.

The detective grunted, "So now there was someone else in the room?"

"Yes, there were three others, Ian, the bearded man, and Eliza, I don't know her last name, and the big man."

The agents eyed each other, then refocused on Meghan. "What were they doing there?"

Meghan began to recount her version of the events leading up to the shooting, but she was fuzzy on some of the details, but she was confident that she had given them enough information to drop the charges. However, as she finished, the group seemed unimpressed.

"Miss Delaney, I have to inform you that the witness was reliable and claims she witnessed you shooting Mr. Montgomery, then yourself. I find it highly unlikely that all these other people were in your room without anyone else seeing them, so that would lead me to believe that you did the shooting." Detective McKenna eyed Meghan with interest, awaiting her reaction.

"That's not true," Meghan blurted out. "I never shot anyone."

"We have also been informed that you have made threats against Mr. Montgomery's family, namely his mother, and with his father in the senate, that's a very serious accusation," Agent Gilley piped in.

Nathan stiffened and stared directly at Agent Spencer. "Megs, I don't think you should say anymore at the moment, you are tired and unless these detectives are planning on charging you, you don't have to say anything else."

Agent Spencer rested a large hand on Meghan's cold and trembling hand, causing a tugging at his heart. Something was terribly wrong with the whole scenario, but he could not put his finger on it. "We'll let you rest now, but we'll be back later."

Meghan nodded, her eyes settling on Nathan. He forced a reassuring smile, then stood to walk out with the detectives.

"We are placing an officer at her door," McKenna commented offhandedly. "We wouldn't want her going anywhere."

"Where is she going to go?" Nathan grumbled. "Someone beat her to a pulp, and she has a hole in her leg."

"He's staying. If you have a problem with that, go talk to the judge," McKenna grunted. "We need to see if Mr. Montgomery is awake. His testimony will shut this case."

Nathan bristled at the thought of what Declan might say. He also wanted to find out what Ian, Eliza, and the big Irish man had in common. He needed to link them together and find the motive. Kidnapping seemed unlikely, but Meghan was convinced that is what she heard them talking about. The thought that maybe the detectives' version of what happened was true stuck in Nathan's mind. What if Declan had beaten her up and she shot him in self-defence? It seems a more likely story than a group of mercenaries is after her and her locket. He could not believe, however, that Meghan would lie to him about something so important. No, she was telling the truth, he decided.

The large figure loomed across the room without a sound, but the shadow he or she was casting on the curtain surrounding her bed was vivid. "Who's there?" Meghan questioned over the lump in her throat. "Who is it?"

"It's me, Boo." Fabrizio's voice was husky, hearing the fear in her voice.

"Fabrizio," she blurted out as the tears filled her eyes. "How is he? No one will tell me anything, they think I shot him," she was rambling by the time he pulled back the curtain and stood by the bed.

"It's all right, Meghan, please calm down," he said softly, not wanting to deal with her emotional breakdown. "Listen, Declan hasn't woken up yet, and until he does, it's your word against their witness. I haven't been able to find out what evidence they have."

"Their witness is Eliza. She was the one left in the room to talk to the police."

"Meghan, can you think of anything that would help? I . . ." He looked away, unable to see the extensive damage to her face. He knew that Declan would never have beaten her, and the conclusions that the police had come to were wrong. He needed to get her to remember something to clear Declan of the accusations.

"Nothing more than what I have already told the police." Her voice was shaking horribly. "Eliza told the police that Declan did this." Her hand waved slightly towards her face. "And she said she saw me shoot him. Why is she lying?"

"Meghan, the police believe her. Since she is a good friend of yours, they don't think she would be lying."

"She's not my friend. I met her on the bus." Meghan paused slightly, her mind spinning with every moment she was around Eliza. "She wouldn't leave me alone, Fabrizio, she was determined to talk to me."

"Did you tell the police this?" Fabrizio blurted out as the thought that Eliza's intrusion into Meghan's life was not an accident. "Boo, what's her last name?"

"I don't know. I didn't pay much attention to her." Meghan began to panic and tears clouded her eyes. "What's happening here?"

"I don't know," he sighed. "But I need a favour of you." Meghan nodded her head as he gripped her hand. "If they will let you leave this room, I want you to come see Declan. The doctors feel that he needs familiar voices around him, and I think you will be able to get through to him."

"I can see him?" her voice filled with life. "Yes, I want to see him."

Fabrizio smiled and released her hand. "I'll arrange it."

The smell was something Meghan would never forget, the aroma of dying men and women, some young, others not so young, but all the same, their lives hanging by a thread. Whether the thread was the doctor's or the will of God, it made no difference to Meghan. Her eyes settled on Declan's lifeless body, the breathing tube gasping open with each breath it forced into him. Her hand shook as she reached for his, which lay flat against the bed. How could this have happened?

"Fabrizio?" Her voice was audibly frightened. "He's not doing so well. His pulse is weak, and he can't breathe on his own."

"The bullet hit his lung," Fabrizio whispered and eyed the nurse that was now watching them. "We can't stay long, the officers switch shifts soon and I haven't met the new officers and with you being, well, you know." His voice was quiet as he bent down, resting his face against her ear. "Just talk to him, bring him out of this."

She gazed up at the monitors in her view, reading his heart rate and pulse. She did a rotation in the ICU, but with it being her loved one lying in the bed, it took on a different atmosphere. She always thought it was odd that when family members came to visit the patients, they all seemed so scared to touch them. They stood around, looking at the equipment, the nurses, the charts, everything and anything to avoid looking at their family member or friend that was lying helplessly in the bed.

"He looks worse than he is. The doctors say he should have a full recovery if he would just wake up. Meghan, if anyone can get him to wake up, it's you," Fabrizio assured her as she stroked Declan's hair.

"Fabrizio, have you even looked at him?" she questioned with annoyance. "Look at him."

"Meghan, calm down. I have been here all day."

"No one ever looks at them," she rambled as she ran her hand across his pale face.

"What are you talking about?" Fabrizio questioned, glancing at the nurse, whose attention was drawn to the conversation.

"No one ever looks or touches them. People come to visit, but they never touch them." Her hand slid down his face to his shoulder. "They need to be touched; they need to feel that someone is here. They need to know that someone needs them," she rambled.

"Meghan, are you okay?" Fabrizio soothed, resting his hand on her shoulder. "Maybe you should come back later."

"No, I'm fine," she assured him. "Ask her, she'd know what I'm saying. She'd know how people react to their loved ones when they are in here." Meghan looked over at the nurse that was sitting in the corner of the room, monitoring him. The nurse smiled with agreement and returned her eyes to her paperwork. Meghan leaned over the bed and held onto Declan's hand, it seemed so lifeless and rather cold as she wrapped his large hand around hers. "Declan, it's me, Meghan, you need to wake up now. You have slept long enough." She looked back at Fabrizio. "I don't know what to say to him. I'm so scared."

"Boo, you have to stay strong. It doesn't matter what you say, just talk. The sound of your voice might get him to wake up." Fabrizio was concerned with her mental state, and he was worried that he had made a mistake bringing her in to see Declan.

Meghan sniffed and rested her head on his arm, stifled another sniff and wiped at her eyes. "Please, Declan, I'm quite bored with no one to argue with, please just wake up." Her tears dripped down her face and splashed against his arm. "The dam has broken into pieces, Declan."

Fabrizio eyed her curiously, then rested his hand on her head. "Meghan, it's going to be okay, he's strong and he loves you, he'll pull through."

"He has to, Fabrizio. I . . . We got married yesterday."

"What?" Fabrizio blurted out. "I knew he proposed but married?"

She nodded and glanced up at his shocked face. "Fabrizio, they took my rings, and no one will give them back." She sniffed and rubbed her finger over the spot her rings used to be. "Can you find them?"

He nodded and patted her head. "I saw the rings. I was with him when he bought them," Fabrizio smiled as his hand rested in her hair. "He spent hours trying to decide."

"He did?" Meghan's face brightened somewhat. "They are beautiful, but . . ." she looked back at Declan and rested her hand on his face. "I would give them back if it would make him all right."

"Shh." Fabrizio soothed when she began to sob again.

Footsteps accompanied the angry voice that broke her sobs. "What the hell are y' doing in here? Y' murdering bitch!" Katie's voice was harsh, and her dark eyes could kill.

Meghan withdrew towards Fabrizio when his hands settled on her shoulder. "I was hoping she could get him to wake up. He loves her, and her voice might bring him out of it," Fabrizio blurted out. He did not particularly care for Katie, he found her domineering and somewhat opinionated.

"Who the hell are y' to decide what's good for me son," Katie snarled and gripped her husband's arm. He was a handsome man, tall and lean, his features were well defined and accentuated by the silver streaks in his black hair. Meghan could see where Declan got his good looks.

"I'm his security officer and his friend!" Fabrizio snarled back. It was amazing to him that Declan turned out as well as he had with the parents that he has.

"Go, get security," Katie ordered Paddy, shoving at his arm.

"All right, dear," the nicely dressed man muttered, his dark grey eyes scanning Meghan with interest. "But don't y' think we should deal with this ourselves, what if Fabrizio is right, and this lass can get Declan to wake up?"

Meghan shuddered at the thought of them dragging her back to her room. Fabrizio had snuck her out when the guards were getting coffee.

"I swear to you I didn't shoot your son," Meghan sniffed. "I love him, he's my husband."

"What?" Katie snorted and stormed towards her. "Don't you dare use this situation to insinuate yourself into his life."

"I'm not. We got married yesterday afternoon, just before . . ." She stopped as the tears began to flow once again. "I love him."

"It's true, Katie." Fabrizio interjected in Meghan's defence. "I was with him when he bought the rings, and he told me yesterday that he asked her."

Katie's brow crumbled in thought. "So we have no proof of the marriage except your word." A cruel smirked filled her face. "Can y' produce a marriage license?"

"Declan had it," Meghan sniffed and glanced up at Fabrizio. "It must be in the room."

Fabrizio nodded, but before he could say anything, the police officers from Meghan's room arrived, their attitudes not too friendly.

"What the hell are you doing out of your room?" The tall burly man snarled.

"I came to see my husband," Meghan said defiantly. "You have no right to hold me prisoner."

"We have every right. The DA doesn't want you disappearing," he snarled back and headed towards her.

"Stay away from her." Fabrizio blurted out, his emotions whirling out of control. He believed in his soul that Meghan did not shoot Declan. "I'll take her back. You are not going to humiliate her any further."

Meghan released her grip on Declan's hand, bent over, and kissed his cheek. "I love you Declan, wake up soon. I need you." She sniffed, then leaned back in the wheel chair.

"Get away from me son!" Katie snorted, taking a threatening step towards Meghan, her hand rising in the air.

Meghan recoiled from the implied threat and her hand reached up to grip Fabrizio's arm.

"Katie dear, for goodness sakes," Paddy intervened, grabbing his wife from behind. "Look at the wee lass, someone's obviously done her damage, and maybe we should listen to what she has to say, because if we take the version of that Eliza woman . . . Well, she's saying that our son did that." He bobbed his head towards Meghan's face.

"Declan didn't do this, he would never hurt me," Meghan blurted out, her need to defend him strong. "It was the other man in the room."

Katie glared at Meghan, then back at her husband. "Don't y' dare let this witch convince y' otherwise. She shot me boy, and no one will convince me otherwise."

"Katie, Declan would never do harm to a woman. I raised him better than that," Paddy protested. "Y' want our son labelled as a woman beater?"

"No, I have no problem believing that someone else beat her," Katie smirked. "They probably had the whole thing planned. Get married, then kill Declan."

"Oh my God!" Meghan blurted out. "I would never . . ."

Fabrizio interrupted, cutting her comment short. "You can't have it both ways, Mrs. Montgomery!" Fabrizio snarled. "The police feel that Declan beat her and then she shot him. Declan is going to be furious when he wakes up to find out you are accusing Meghan of such things."

"Get out!" Katie snarled and bobbed her head towards the police officers. "I don't want her anywhere near me son again, or I'll have your jobs."

CHAPTER TWELVE

The tiny dingy cell was freezing; the thin blanket they provided Meghan with was doing little to keep her warm. Her mind was spinning with the events of the day, and she found it hard to believe what was happening around her. The humiliation she suffered after the arrest and removal from the hospital in handcuffs was nothing compared to the moment when the judge refused her bail. Flight risk he had said, they took her Canadian passport, claiming she could flee there and go into hiding. How could it be possible that this nightmare could have gone so far? She was innocent and yet no one believed her. Only Fabrizio and her friends stood by her. Even Declan believed she shot him.

The rough treatment by the female officers who forced her to strip down and change into the horrible orange prison wear was horrific, but no doubt, it was just a sample of the next twenty-five years of her life. The day felt like a nightmare that would not end. Nathan promised her he would not give up until he proved her innocence, but if he had not found evidence to that point, she was not sure what he would find. He had no defence.

The noises and shouts from the other female prisoners drew her attention back to her surroundings, and that's when she saw the dark face peering down over the bunk at her for the first time. Meghan glanced away, not wanting to acknowledge the young woman.

"So what are you in here for?" The woman questioned, noticing Meghan's gaze jump from her to the wall.

"It's a mistake," Meghan muttered, not focusing on the woman.

"It always is," the woman laughed, then lowered her hand down. "I'm Hayley." Her dark brown complexion highlighted the high cheekbones, and her eyes shone dark as coal. She was a very beautiful young woman.

"Meghan," she said nervously and curled up on her bunk.

"What's with the chair? Are you a cripple?"

"No, I was shot in the leg. I can't walk very well yet," Meghan muttered, forcing her heart back into her throat. "I need therapy."

"Hmm, so you're the one that shot the actor. Well, I don't blame you, miss. I killed the bastard that beat me." Her warm brown eyes smiled from under the dark curls that encircled her round face.

"I didn't shoot him, I love him," Meghan claimed, unsure why she was bothering. Her claims of innocence had gone unbelieved for the last three weeks.

Hayley laughed and swung down, landing with a bounce on Meghan's bunk. "Hey, give it up, Meghan, I won't snitch. Most of us on this block are here for that reason." Hayley suddenly looked disturbed. "Stick with us." She reached out and rested her dark hand on Meghan's very pale face. The bruising around her eyes was still very visible against the pastiness of Meghan's skin.

Meghan jerked her face away from the young woman. "Please, don't touch me."

The woman's eyebrow rose slightly before she glanced out the cell door. "I suggest you stick close to me. There are some nasty women in here that would find you quite a treat." Her eyes scanned the very thin frame of Meghan. She had lost weight over the past weeks, and her soft curves were more sharp and lean.

"This is a nightmare," Meghan sniffed, burying her head into the pillow. "I can't believe this."

"You'll get used to it. We all do. Just keep your nose clean and stay away from cellblock D. Those women are nasty." The dark eyes smiled with pleasure. "It's nice to have someone to talk to."

Meghan forced a smile and glanced up at the woman. She was young, surprisingly so, her dark complexion almost perfect. "How long have you been here?"

"Three months. I killed my stepfather. The bastard felt I was part of the deal in marrying my mamma. He raped me almost every night, and then I got pregnant." As she rubbed her belly, Meghan noticed for the first time the swollen stomach. "When my mamma found out, she kicked him out, but he came after us, and he beat my mamma almost to death. Then he came after me. So I shot him."

"Well, that's self-defence," Meghan blurted out, finding herself interested in the young woman's story.

"Well, not when you are a poor black girl and the man is a white businessman," she grumbled, reached up, and pulled a chocolate bar out from under her mattress. "I hide things under there."

Meghan glanced around the small cell. "How old are you?"

"I just turned eighteen," Hayley smiled and gestured the chocolate bar towards Meghan. Meghan eyed it with interest, then took a small piece. She could never refuse chocolate.

"You look so young," Meghan smiled and popped the chocolate into her mouth.

"What about you, miss?"

"Twenty-five," Meghan sighed. "If I'm found guilty I will be fifty by the time I get out of here."

"I'll be almost forty-five."

"Oh," Meghan gasped and eyed the girl. "There has to be something you could do, find a new lawyer."

"Don't be concerning yourself with that. My only concern is my child, my mamma has lost her sight because of the beatings, and she can't take care of it."

"Don't you have any other family?" Meghan questioned with concern.

"None that will take the child of that white bastard. They say my mamma and me deserve everything we get hooking up with the likes of him." Hayley polished off the rest of the chocolate, then flushed the wrapper down the toilet. "The doc says I'm not to be having sugar, I have gestational diabetes."

Meghan nodded and rested her hand on the dark arm. "Well, I'll keep an eye on you. I was studying to be a paediatrician."

"Really?" Hayley sounded impressed.

"I guess I won't be finishing that?"

"Tell doc, I'm sure he could use the help," Hayley grinned. "It's always easier in here if you can find something to do to fill your days and keep you out of trouble."

Meghan sighed, wondering how she was going to survive in this hellhole for twenty-five years. Her only chance at freedom now rested in Declan's hands. It was unfathomable that he could not remember her or their marriage. When he woke up, she thought the nightmare would be over, but his memory lapse had only strengthened the prosecution's case. Their claim was that Declan was so traumatized by the fact that the woman he thought he loved tried to kill him that he blocked it out. His lawyers claimed that he had no memory of the last two or three years, but they were unwilling to allow him to be interviewed by Nathan. What if Declan never got his memory back? She would waste years trapped like a caged animal.

The first few weeks went by reasonably uneventful. Hayley was correct in her assumption that Doc Walton was in need of help in the infirmary, and Meghan spent most of her days taking inventory and patching up small cuts, while Dr. Walton dispensed the meds to the women that came and went.

It was in her fourth week at the prison when a short stocky woman with enormous forearms entered the infirmary demanding to see Doc Walton.

"Listen, sister." The deep gravelly voice startled Meghan. "You're new here, aren't you?" The woman's eye racked over Meghan's thin frame. "And quite the looker."

Meghan forced a smile and kept her eyes on the woman, hoping for confidence. "I just arrived a few weeks ago."

"Hmm," the woman took a step closer. "Well, I haven't seen you around at meal times."

"I eat in here," Meghan said calmly. "Doc keeps me pretty busy."

The woman scanned the room then settled her gaze back on Meghan. "Listen, sweet thing, I have something I need you to do. Doc's last nurse helped me out."

"How so?" Meghan questioned as unease washed over her.

"She supplied me with a good supply of morphine. I need it, you see, and so do some of my ladies." The woman circled the room and scrutinized the locket cupboards.

"Well, I don't have the keys," Meghan muttered as she desperately tried to think of a way out without jeopardizing herself. If she was to spend her life in this hellhole, she needed to stay clear of this woman and her friends. But then she was getting ahead of herself. She hadn't been convicted yet; maybe a jury would find her innocent, after all, she was.

"Then, get the key," the woman grumbled and gripped Meghan's thin arm, giving her a slight shake. "You don't want me as an enemy."

"I'm sure I don't, but . . ." Her comment was cut short when Doc Walton pushed through the door, his blond brows crunching with displeasure.

"Mack, what are you doing in here? I warned you," Dr. Walton snarled, shoved his glasses farther up the bridge of his nose, gripped the woman's arm, and pulled her away from Meghan. "If I find out that you are threatening my new nurse, I'll have you put into confinement." His eyes settled on Meghan's distressed face. "Is everything all right?"

"Yes," Meghan blurted out, her breath laboured at best. "She was just welcoming me." She forced a smile, not wanting any conflict with the woman.

"Good." His voice was cold and unreadable, but he turned back towards Mack, shoving her stocky body out into the hall, then gave the guard a disapproving glance.

"You know, Doc, you hired yourself a sweet thing as a nurse. I would suspect that you would have plenty of competition for her time. And with her in that chair, she is most likely defenceless," she grinned a decaying smile at Meghan, and then sauntered down the hall towards her cellblock.

Meghan shuttered and wrapped her arms around herself, trying to stop the shaking. "I'm in big trouble."

"Meghan," Doc Walton muttered and moved towards her. "I'm sorry. I should have warned you about her and her friends. They terrified my last nurse until she quit."

"She wants me to give her morphine. I can't, it's against everything I believe, but what will happen to me if I don't?"

Doc Walton shrugged and rested his long narrow hand on her shoulder. "I'll talk to the warden."

"What good is that going to do, if they ever get me alone?" Meghan shuddered, forcing back her tears.

"You only have to avoid her for another month. You have managed all right for the last month, and anyway, I'm sure you'll be found not guilty." He soothed, bending down wrapping his arm around her shoulder, holding her close to his lean chest. "Then you can go home."

Meghan relaxed into him, pressing her face up against his shoulder. "You think I'm innocent?"

He nodded and glanced at her with a soft smile. "I have been in here a long time and have seen women come and go, some innocent but most guilty as hell. But you are definitely not someone capable of lying."

Her brow rose slightly at the remark. Was she that easy to read? "You're not the first person to tell me that." She pushed out of his arms and wheeled over to the barred windows. "If Declan doesn't get his memory back, I'll be convicted."

"Let's just take it one step at a time. If your lawyer wants, I will testify on your behalf," Doc Walton said, resting his hand on her shoulder. "As much as I welcome your help here, I don't want to see you waste away in here for something you didn't do. Especially since . . ."

"Since what?" she questioned with worry.

"Since you are going to have a child," he smiled, hoping for a pleasurable reaction from her. "Your blood test came back positive."

"It can't be," Meghan cried. "I haven't . . . Well, it's been almost two months." She stared up at him, disbelieving.

"When was the last time you had a menstrual cycle?" he questioned.

"I don't know," she sniffed, her mind spinning. "I guess it was just before I went to the lodge."

Doc Walton smiled and patted her shoulder. "Well, that would be the time then." He stopped as Meghan's face went completely white. "What's wrong?"

"Nothing, I just didn't expect to . . . my child will be sent to a foster home."

"Don't worry, Meghan. I'm sure they will place it with family until you are out." Doc Watson soothed, but he knew that was of no comfort to her.

Days turned into weeks, weeks turned to months, and during that time, Meghan's friendship with Hayley and the other women on her cellblock blossomed. Christmas had come and gone and she found herself thinking about the last few months of her life. When she arrived at the lodge, she thought the death of her grandfather was the worst thing that could have happened to her. She never would have imagined that one impromptu trip to the mountains would have thrust her life in this direction.

Every day, Meghan would leave the infirmary and head down to the library to help Hayley and a few of the other women work out legal strategies. Most of the women were ethnic and poor, leaving them prey for the legal system. There were two, however, that Meghan felt were as guilty as sin, but nonetheless, she encouraged them to read the books, just to keep their reading skills acute.

Kimberly was a short stocky woman that appeared to be more masculine than feminine, and she seemed to have taken on the role of Meghan's bodyguard. She had heard through the grapevine that Mack was going to go after Meghan, and Kimberly hated Mack enough to get herself involved. Every day she would escort Meghan back and forth to ensure her safety.

The intense rain had kept the majority of the inmates inside, and a large percentage seemed to choose the library as their activity. Meghan had noticed that a couple of Mack's girls were also present, but they seemed uninterested in her, so she wrote it off as a coincidence.

The prison library was well stocked with books and magazines, and Hayley managed to get her hands on a copy of the National Inquisitor from a few months back.

"Look, Meghan, is this you?" Hayley laughed loudly, lifting the picture of Meghan sitting on the snowy sidewalk. "What were you doing?"

"I fell," Meghan grumbled and snatched the magazine away from Hayley. She found it hard not to cry when she gazed down at the picture of Declan lifting her off the ground. "If I only knew then . . . God, I would have run for the hills."

"You don't mean that." Hayley soothed. "Meghan, you love him, and I'm sure once he gets his memory back, you will be released."

"I hope you're right," Meghan sighed and ripped the pages from the magazine that contained any pictures or mention of her and Declan. She glanced over at Hayley with an apologetic smile. "I want to be able to see him."

"I completely understand," Hayley smiled and focused on the law book in front of her.

Meghan forced a smile and collected her books. "I have to get back to the infirmary." Meghan's comment spurred Kimberly to her feet.

The grey and gloomy atmosphere outside had cast a dreariness in the corridor, leading back to the infirmary. Doc Walton had been expecting her over half an hour earlier, and Meghan was anxious about being late. Would there be a punishment for her tardiness? Hayley said that when she was late getting to the kitchen, she was stripped of phone privileges. That would be the last thing she needed. She was supposed to be calling Nathan that evening.

As Meghan and Kimberly rounded the corner, a large female guard was blocking the hall towards the infirmary, and before Meghan could question her, she raised her arm in the other direction.

"Go that way, ladies, this corridor is locked down." Her voice was cold and detached.

Meghan shrugged and pushed at the wheels to her chair. Kimberley, however, did not move, her eyes were focused down the hall, towards the empty corridor.

"Meghan, wait a minute," Kimberly muttered, gripping onto the chair. "I think we should go back to the library."

"Why?" Meghan was unaware of the danger Kimberly sensed.

"Something's wrong. The alarm didn't sound. They always sound the alarm when they lock down the cell blocks." Kimberly backed up, but before she could take a step, three women came up from behind them.

"Well, if it isn't Doc's diligent nurse," a horribly ugly woman commented and shoved Kimberly from Meghan's chair. Kimberly froze when she felt the cold steel against her neck. "Now come with me. Mack has something she wants to discuss with you."

The woman guard had her back turned and after repeated calls, Meghan realized that she was in terrible trouble. Why hadn't she just given the damn woman the drugs? Why did she have to take the moral high road?

The corridor was abandoned; Meghan had never been to that end of the prison before. It was where all the lifers were housed. The women whose crimes were so heinous, they would never be released from this hellhole.

"Well, well, if it isn't the princess," Mack grunted and moved towards Meghan, gripping her face.

"Mack, leave her alone, you know doc won't let her near the drugs," Kimberly spoke up in Meghan's defence. "She's just his lackey."

Mack laughed and glanced over at Kimberly. She smiled with recognition, then nodded her head towards the woman holding Kimberly. Kimberly sighed and reached for the wheel chair, but before her hand reached the handle, the blade of the knife in the ugly woman's hand slid across her neck, slicing through her windpipe.

"Oh my God!" Meghan shrieked when Kimberly's body plummeted across her lap, the blood from her severed artery spraying across Meghan's shirt. "Kimberly!"

"Loose her," Mack grumbled to a dark-haired woman who grabbed the lifeless body and dragged her into a room down the hall. "Now you listen to me, you'll be next if you don't get me the morphine."

Meghan nodded and plucked her saturated shirt from her chest. What the hell was happening? How could they just kill someone in the corridors of a prison without any guards around? Where were the guards?

"What the hell is going on here?" Doc Walton's voice was sharp and demanding. "Let go of her."

"Ladies!" A stern male voice bellowed, and his voice is what made the woman release Meghan. "Get against the wall all of you."

Meghan noticed Hayley standing behind the guards, her expression concerned. One of the guards hauled Meghan out of her wheel chair and shoved her against the wall, but when she released her, Meghan's legs gave way. Doc Walton was the one who caught her before she hit the ground.

In the chaos of the next few minutes, the women were strip-searched, handcuffed, and led to solitary confinement. Meghan, however, was returned to the infirmary to be examined by Doc Walton.

"I'm dead next time," Meghan muttered and glanced over at Hayley's worried face. "Oh God, Kimberly." Meghan shuddered and scrubbed her eyes. "This is a nightmare."

"Meghan, I think that it might be best for you go talk to the warden. Those ladies will be in confinement for a while, but they might have friends." Doc Walton sounded concerned.

"I still have a week until my trial. Then what if I'm convicted, I'm a dead woman."

"Meghan, you need to stay with the group from our cell block. Now that she has killed Kimberly, well, let's just say, she has also made some enemies," Hayley spoke softly, but her gaze held firm on Meghan's terrified eyes.

Meghan nodded and closed her eyes. One week, could she survive that long, and if so, would it make any difference? Time would tell.

CHAPTER THIRTEEN

Meghan arrived at the courthouse a couple hours before the trial was to start and met with Nathan, Fabrizio, Pete, and Cassie. Nathan wanted to prepare her for the prosecution's case against her. They had accumulated an impressive witness list of hotel staff and guests that would testify against Meghan. Some had seen them fighting in the lounge, and two women were going to testify that they saw Declan shaking her violently in the lobby of the lodge. It was out of control.

"They all just want their day in the sun." Nathan soothed as he tried to control Meghan's panic.

"Well, who do we have?" Cassie questioned as she rested her hand on Meghan's shoulder.

"We have a few people, the bartender from the lounge, and the woman from the front desk. I don't know how much help they are going to be, though."

"I haven't found out any information about that Fergus guy I heard Declan and his mother talking about," Fabrizio sighed and leaned against the wall. "Since Declan's family had him fire me, I can't get near him."

"I do have someone that might help, but I am tentative about using her." Nathan bristled and opened a side door, allowing Eliza to wander in, appearing haggard.

"Eliza?" Meghan blurted out. "What the hell are you doing here?" Meghan was furious with the woman who had lied and accused her of shooting Declan. "You have some nerve coming here!"

"Meghan dear, please calm down. I have come to testify on your behalf. I feel responsible for what is happening."

"You should! You are the reason I am in this position," Meghan snorted and turned her head away. "Get out."

"Hear her out, Megs," Nathan said firmly, his hand landing on her shoulder.

Meghan scowled at Eliza but gestured towards her. "Fine, tell me what you must."

Eliza forced a smile and eyed Meghan. She was so thin and pale. What horrors had she endured in prison? "Meghan, I am so sorry for what happened. I . . . well, someone paid me to accuse you."

"What?" Meghan blurted out. Declan's damn mother, she would stop at nothing. "Nat, this proves that Declan's mother is lying."

"It wasn't his mother." Nathan sounded slightly concerned.

"Then who was it?" Meghan blurted out.

"It was Ian. But I am here today to recant my story," Eliza sighed, keeping the other name to herself; his involvement would only put Meghan and herself in more danger. At this point, all he wanted from Eliza was for her to switch the blame from Meghan to Ian. "Meghan, please don't hate me for what I'm about to tell you."

Meghan cringed and slid back in her chair.

"I met Ian a few months ago, at your house as a matter of fact." Eliza eyed Meghan's stunned face, then continued, "After your grandfather died last year, I felt it was time that I got to know you."

Meghan gasped and wheeled her chair back a few feet. What was this woman saying? How did she know her grandfather died, and what did it have to do with her?

"Meghan, I'm your mother."

"No!" Meghan snorted and backed up further. "I don't have a mother. My mother abandoned me years ago."

"I know, dear. You don't know how often I have regretted that decision. But by the time I came to my senses, your father and grandfather had closed ranks and wouldn't let me see you."

"They couldn't stop you if you really wanted to see me," Meghan grumbled.

"I know, but they . . . Well, I needed the money, and it was a large sum," Eliza sighed, knowing Meghan was not going to forgive her.

"I can't deal with this right now! I am about to be tried for murder. Why now, after all these years?"

"Meghan dear, I tried. After your grandfather died, I tracked you down and went to your house. Ian was there, we had a nice talk, and he was very generous. I thought you loved him, and when he said that he was planning a week holiday for you and your friends, I thought it was wonderful. He paid my way to the lodge and told me to stay with you the whole trip."

Meghan shook her head and glanced at Nathan, but he just shook his head. "Hear her out."

"A few days after I got to the lodge, Ian came to my room and told me that the Montgomerys were very interested in getting a hold of your locket and that your grandfather stole it from them years earlier. He told me it was cursed and would only bring you grief, and if I helped him, then you would realize that I only have your best interests at heart."

"This is ridiculous. How is this going to help her case?" Fabrizio was annoyed. "It's just going to give them a motive for shooting Monty."

"Get her out of here!" Meghan growled and wheeled towards Fabrizio.

"Don't you understand? Declan was not the target, you were. Ian is Declan's brother Rory. Declan was in on it the whole time, it just got out of control." Eliza could not understand why they were missing that point; she had to get her to believe this version.

"This is unbelievable?" Meghan stared at her in amazement as the night of the shooting came flooding back. "Ian . . . Declan called him Rory. Oh my God!" Meghan panicked and looked at Nathan. "It's Declan's brother that shot him!"

"No, Rory wouldn't shoot anyone. He's bit of an idiot, but he could never shoot his own brother," Fabrizio blurted out in complete horror. "He was in Ireland until after Declan got shot." Fabrizio tried to convince himself. He remembered the description of Ian that Meghan had given him. What the hell was happening! Were Rory and the parents involved, or was Meghan trying to set up the Montgomery family like the police thought? With Eliza now adding this to the story, it was all too convenient. He had known Declan and his family for a long time, and he found it hard to believe the accusations Eliza was making.

"I can't believe that Declan's parents would try and have me killed?" Meghan covered her face and took a deep breath. "Then explain to me who the other men were?"

"What other men, dear?" Eliza felt her stomach churn. Meghan remembered them.

"I know there were two other men in the room, and one of them beat me. I could see them, and I heard them talking to you."

"Oh no, dear, you are mistaken."

"What?" Meghan blurted out. "You are trying to make me look crazy. I want nothing to do with you, get out!" Meghan screamed and pointed towards the door.

Fabrizio moved towards Eliza, anger shooting from his eyes. "Are you out of your fucking mind? You honestly expect us to believe that the Montgomery family set up this complicated rouse just to get her damn locket?" Fabrizio bellowed, startling Eliza.

"Meghan, I am just trying to help," Eliza cooed, her round face flushing slightly. She was unsure why Meghan was not taking the opportunity to plead self-defence. "I am so sorry that you don't trust me, but I am here today to testify on your behalf, even with the risk to my own life."

"Don't try and portray the loving mother now, Eliza. You have never been a mother to me, and you never will." Meghan was so bitter, she could not and would not accept Eliza's apology.

"Megs, calm down." Nathan soothed. "Eliza is not expecting you to forgive her today. Just please let me do my job, and if I think we need her, I'll put her on the stand." Nathan glanced over at Eliza. "Could you excuse us for a moment?"

Meghan glanced up at Nathan with distress when Eliza left the room. "What is the point, the prosecution is claiming that I shot Declan. We are never going to convince the jury that his brother was an unstable murderer. His parents are two well connected," Meghan sniffed, completely overwhelmed with what she heard. Her mother destroyed her life for money. "Have you had any luck tracking down Ian or should I say Rory?"

"No, but luckily, your landlord caught him breaking into your apartment last week. He is here to testify that when he questioned him on his purpose for being in the hallway, he ran. He described Ian perfectly. Apparently, that is the only proof of his existence. He has no birth certificate, no driver's license, or social security number. He basically doesn't exist, but that should work in our favour. Maybe we should get a subpoena to have Rory come testify."

"You don't honestly believe that woman, do you? She is obviously lying!" Fabrizio blurted out, turned, and looked out the window. Was he backing the wrong side here?

"What about Kaye, she knows him." Meghan glanced up at Cassie.

Cassie's face shadowed something close to terror, and she looked over at Nathan for assistance.

"Kaye is missing." He looked at Fabrizio.

"What? Oh, Cassie, no!" Meghan felt sorry for Cassie and gripped her hand. "What the hell is happening here?"

"She went to Paris, and she hasn't been heard from since," Fabrizio sighed and ran his hand through his thick brown hair. His dark brown eyes settled on Meghan as she hugged Cassie.

"She's done this before, so I am not getting too worked up until I hear otherwise," Cassie sighed and moved over to the window.

"Nat, if Ian was trying to kill me, why didn't he? Do you think he had something to do with Kaye's disappearance?" Meghan questioned.

"I don't think he was trying to kill you. I think he was up to something else. I knew something was not right about the whole situation. The way he lurked around the hotel, only allowing you to see him. I think he was trying to make you appear crazy. However, I don't know if I believe Eliza's story either. I just would like to understand what Kaye's involvement was. She was involved I'm sure of it." He looked apologetically at Cassie.

Meghan sighed and wiped at her eyes with the back of her hand. "Declan felt something was wrong too. He felt that everyone was out to destroy our relationship. That's why he wanted to get married so quickly."

Nathan shrugged and glanced over at Cassie and Pete. "What do you two think?"

"I don't believe a word that woman said," Pete blurted out after sitting quietly, taking in all the information. "It is all too convenient that she showed up now. It reeks of trouble."

Cassie nodded and glanced down at Meghan. "If someone hired Ian to steal the locket, what's to say that they are not paying Eliza to lie for them now by switching the blame to Declan's family?"

"That's what I have been thinking. If we claim self-defence, and she changes her testimony on the stand, we're screwed," Nathan sighed, sat on the table, and scrubbed his eyes. "I'm sorry, Megs, I just find this whole thing overwhelming. I should have brought in other council."

"It's okay, Nat, no one could have done more for me. I have obviously been framed by someone who has planned out everything."

"All right, let's stick with our original plan and tell the truth." Nathan forced a smile. "You wouldn't be able to pull off Eliza's plan anyway. Hopefully, with Fabs testifying on your behalf that he feels that the detectives only collected evidence and testimony to support their case that you are guilty will help. Hopefully the fact that no GSR was found on you anywhere will give the jury enough doubt."

"Thank you for doing this, Fabrizio. I know how close you and Declan are," Cassie smiled softly.

"Were," Fabrizio sighed.

Meghan sighed and closed her eyes. "My only hope now is that Declan will get his memory back."

The door to the room opened, and the bailiff entered looking rather impatient. "It's time, she needs to get into the court room."

Nathan nodded and gripped Meghan's chair. "All right, darlin', this is it. Let's get this over with, and then we can deal with the rest of this." He bobbed his head towards Eliza, who was standing out in the hall. "If I wheel you in, can you stand when the judge comes in?"

"Yes." Meghan rubbed the cream-coloured pantsuit that hid the small bump that was forming in her belly. She had not told anyone about the baby she carried, but she was wondering if she should. She had so much bad publicity over the last few months, and the last thing she wanted was to drag her unborn child into the fray. No, if she was found not guilty, she was going to disappear into Montana and spend her life in peace.

"Mr. Montgomery!" Someone yelled, drawing Meghan's attention to the mass of people in the corridor. Declan was heading down the hall towards her, wearing a dark suit with an olive coloured shirt. A very large man with dark pants and a brown-checkered jacket was in front of him, making a path for Declan to go through. Declan passed through the crowd without a word to anyone; he kept his eyes focused on the back of the man in front of him and kept walking. Meghan could see that his demeanour was cold and detached, and her heart ached for the loss as she watched him manoeuvre through the reporters at the end of the corridor.

The fear was building in her as she watched the hordes of reporters scanning the surrounding area, looking for someone else to interview, and she began to wheel back into the room.

"Nat, I don't think I can do this," Meghan sniffed and wiped at her eyes with her shaking hand.

"Megs, you don't have a choice in the matter." Nathan gripped the handles on her chair and pushed her from the room.

Agent Brody Spencer turned the corner just before Declan and his entourage made it half way down the hall. Brody's dark blue eyes settled on Meghan's terrified face, then focused on Declan. "I guess if he is going to remember it's now or never." His voice was soft with concern.

She nodded but heard little of what he had said. Her focus was completely on Declan as he sauntered towards her. He was getting so close, too close. She wanted to run to him, to hug him, but the guards, the reporters, his damn mother were all barriers to him.

His eyes were the same smoky grey as they scanned the hallway ahead of him. They settled on Fabrizio, with a cold expression, then the cold glare moved to Meghan's face, but something flickered, only for a moment, but it was there. She found herself smiling softly at him, the way she always did in the past, before her nightmare became her life.

Katie noticed Declan's gaze on Meghan, and she blocked Declan's view of her and then pushed him towards the doors to the courtroom.

"That was her, was it not?" Declan muttered, glancing back over his shoulder towards Meghan. "The woman who shot me."

"Yes," Katie grumbled. "She'll pay, don't worry, Declan."

Declan eyed her one last time before he gave Fabrizio a sidelong gaze, then disappeared into the courtroom. She looked familiar. He was confident of that. He was hoping that seeing her would spark some memory of what had happened that night. Fabrizio had pushed him repeatedly to remember, but Declan resented his insistence, and on the advice of his mother, he had fired Fabrizio a few months back. He did not need someone around him that was determined to free the woman who tried to murder him and destroy his family.

Meghan sighed and rested her hand on Fabrizio's that was on her shoulder. "I'm sorry that your friendship has been destroyed over this."

"It's not your fault, Boo, it's his mother's. She has never liked me. I remind her that Declan didn't follow his family's plans for him. They think he is a quitter for leaving the navy and becoming an actor."

Meghan nodded sadly and settled in as Nathan pushed her into the courtroom, followed by Fabrizio, Agent Spencer, Cassie, and Pete.

The courtroom was small, only accommodating a handful of spectators and the jury, who sat in the two rows of dark maple benches on the far side of the courtroom. The DA and his cronies were sitting to the right of where Meghan, Nathan, and his assistants sat. The judge lowered his lean frame onto his lofty perch at the front of the room and gestured for everyone to be seated. He ran his hand through his salt—pepper shoulder-length hair and glanced out at the people in the room.

"There will be no cameras or recording permitted in this courtroom." His instructions were brief before the DA gave his opening statement.

The older plump man was reading over a handful of papers, his round wire-rimmed glasses were slightly askew on his face, and his thinning hair was a tad windblown. If Meghan were not so terrified, she would have found the sight rather comical. This man, labelled as the brightest District Attorney Denver ever had, so closely resembled Mr. Maggo; he seemed almost out of place in the courtroom.

He made himself right at home, however, as he paraded witness after witness across the witness stand, all testifying in one form or another about the tumultuous relationship between Meghan and Declan. Meghan could not believe how the prosecution managed to skew the truth to his advantage. Day after day, she sat in the courtroom listening to the evidence mounting against her, and her life was appearing very bleak.

When the eighth day arrived, Nathan decided to put Meghan on the stand to testify in her own defence after all his witnesses had testified, all except Eliza. Meghan had never been more terrified then she was when the bailiff pushed her to the witness stand to face all the hostile faces in the crowd. Thankfully, there were only people directly involved, but the sight of Declan's parents was enough to cause her to tremble.

The room was intolerably hot, stifling almost, as Meghan forced her way up to the witness box with the help of Nathan. Maybe the group of star-struck jurors would have some sympathy for her since she appeared to be crippled. Their faces over the past few days had shown nothing but contempt for her.

Her gaze settled on Declan, the coldness in his eyes was frightening. He believed all the testimony against her that she planned and carried out his shooting. Meghan could not understand where all the witnesses came from and where they came up with their testimony. She swore some of them were perjuring themselves, but Nathan was unable to break them in cross-examination. The only fact the prosecution's forensic witness could not explain was how she managed to have no trace of GSR on her hands or anywhere else when she was found by police with the gun in her hand.

The bailiff swearing her in drew her attention back to the proceedings, and the fear returned to her eyes. She glanced down the jury box, taking in every face. Only one man in the back row seemed non-judgmental. What if she could not convince the jury of her innocence? What would become of her and her child? She eyed Declan, saying a small prayer that he would regain his memory. The last thing in the world she wanted was to have her child in prison, only to lose custody of it.

Declan eyed her curiously, she was a beautiful woman, and he definitely could see why he pursued a relationship with her. He only wished he could remember her; remember what happened. She looked scared, like a rabbit cornered by a fox. Could she have shot him, then herself, to cover her crime? Could he have beaten her like the DA claims? He had never hit a woman as far back as he could remember. He found it hard to believe that he could hit that beautiful woman on the stand. The outcome of this case could affect the assault charges he was facing. He needed to remember.

Declan gripped his head, another headache. He grunted and reached into his pocket for his medication. Damn, he hated the headaches. His mother glanced over at him as he popped the pills into his mouth.

"Are y' well, Son?" Katie rested her hand on the side of his head.

"Aye, Ma, I just have a wee headache again." He forced a smile and refocused on Meghan and her testimony.

"Miss Delaney, please start from the beginning," Nathan asked as he leaned against the witness box.

Meghan proceeded to recount her meeting with Declan and the basics of their relationship up to the night her life fell apart. She glanced over at Declan, his face appeared somewhat confused, but his mother's was displaying compete outrage. His dad, however, appeared slightly uneasy as he fidgeted with the collar of his crisp white shirt, as if it was too tight.

"Miss Delaney, the prosecution has paraded a long line of guests and staff from the hotel, that claim you and Mr. Montgomery spent the whole week fighting?"

Meghan nodded and glanced over at Declan. "We did argue, I'm not denying that." She blinked, forcing the tears back. "But he never hit me. That bruise that the woman from the dress shop described was from Ian throwing me against the bed frame."

"Objection! We have already proved the non-existence of the man she calls Ian," Mr. DeAngelo, the prosecutor hollered.

"Overruled. I will allow this testimony." The judge eyed her from his perch.

She paused, her eyes straying towards Declan again, then returning to Nathan. "When I first met Declan, I was very rude to him. I thought he was arrogant, and I didn't like the way he was behaving." She glanced back at Declan, his face showed interest as he stared at her. Meghan's account of the week matched Cassie's and Pete's and was surprisingly close to what Fabrizio had told him months earlier when he woke up.

"Meghan, please tell me about the fight outside the hotel the night before the shooting." Nathan refocused her.

Meghan recounted the evening and the situation with the paparazzi. Her stomach was churning with terror; the jury did not believe her testimony, she could see it in their eyes.

"We left the party, and the paparazzi began to chase us down the sidewalk to our car. One of them jumped at me, and I fell backwards into the snow. He made a horrible comment, and Declan snapped and went after him. The man pulled a knife and tried to attack Declan, but Declan knocked him to the ground and took away the knife just before the police arrived." She finished.

"And the night of the shooting?"

"That afternoon, Declan proposed to me and then we went into the town. We took a sleigh ride. It was lovely." She smiled at the thought, her eyes settling on Declan's face before she refocused. "Then Declan suggested we get married."

"That's a lie!" Katie blurted out, shocking everyone around her.

"Ma'am, please keep your comments to yourself!" the judge ordered, then turned to the jury. "The jury will disregard that comment. Please continue, Miss Delaney." He smiled down at her; he was starting to question the prosecution's case. Meghan had touched on every incident that the witnesses had accused her of and most seemed to have been masterly blown out of proportion. The prosecution's case had too many holes. However, he did not want to upset the Montgomery's by allowing Meghan to slander their son.

"Well, we found this beautiful little church at the end of the town. It was a Catholic Church, and we thought that it was fate. It was so adorable, the steeple held a bell that was ringing as we arrived in town. The priest was delighted to marry us, and we had a pianist. She played Ave Maria," Meghan sighed and glanced at Nathan, his facial expression was telling her to move the story forward.

"We went back to the lodge, and his mother was there, and she warned me to stay away from her son. She told me he had a girlfriend back home that was waiting to marry him."

Katie scowled at Meghan, a horrible look that Declan witnessed. "Ma, is that true?"

"Shh!" Katie scolded.

Declan glared at Katie, then turned back towards Meghan.

"We ordered room service," she continued recounting the evening as best as she could remember. "Declan answered the door, and Ian came in with a gun." She shivered at the thought. Her voice was becoming weak and frightened. "He screamed at us, then pointed the gun towards me, but Declan jumped in front of me," she sniffed. "He fell." Tears were dripping down her face, her body trembling horribly.

"Miss Delaney," Nathan soothed, resting his hand on hers, "please continue."

"He fell and blood was everywhere. I tried to stop the bleeding, but he was bleeding so badly . . ." Tears were streaming down her face when her eyes settled on Agent Spencer, who was sitting at the back of the courtroom.

Declan turned to see Agent Spencer nodding his head coaxing her on. Why was he helping Meghan? This whole situation was becoming more confusing the more Declan found out and the more it appeared that everyone was hiding something. He was getting rather agitated that he was being kept in the dark.

"Then Eliza and another man showed up, and they started arguing with Ian about shooting Declan and then the gun went off, and the bullet went into my leg."

"Objection! We have already established that this Ian person does not exist. No one but the accused ever saw him." The prosecutor waved his hand towards the jury.

"Overruled. Mr. DeAngelo, don't raise that objection again."

The DA dropped to his seat and glanced back at the Montgomery family. Katie shook her head, then refocused on Meghan.

"Miss Delaney, please continue." Nathan forced a reassuring smile.

"The man with the beard decided that the police needed to think that Declan beat me up, so he hit me on the face over and over," she blurted out as she refocused on her testimony. "He kept hitting me, calling me names, and my eyes felt like they were going to explode." She brushed away the tears from her cheek. "He didn't stop until Eliza grabbed his arm."

Declan's dark grey eyes were glazing over with sorrow as he watched her describing her horrendous night, and he was unable to help her. He had promised her repeatedly that he would not let Ian harm her again, and he failed her terribly. As the thoughts came to him, he startled, he remembered that he promised he would protect her. He remembered her crying in his arms, on a bed.

"Objection. She is referring to Ms. Eliza Pettigrew, the woman who backed out of her testimony only weeks ago. That woman is not a trustworthy witness."

The judge glanced at Nathan and then at Meghan before his eyes settled on Patrick Montgomery. "I will allow this line of testimony. You will have an opportunity to cross-examine Ms. Delaney on the subject as well as Ms. Pettigrew when she testifies."

"But, Your Honour, this woman is completely fabricating a story." The prosecution stormed towards Meghan. "We know that you manipulated yourself into Mr. Montgomery's life and shot him."

"Your Honour!" Nathan growled.

"Mr. De Angelo, that will be enough! Sit down!" the judge ordered.

"If the court pleases, we would like to enter these pictures of the injuries to Ms. Delaney's face into evidence," Nathan stated as he moved towards the large wooden bench with the pictures clutched in his hand.

The judge nodded and took the pictures but appeared to have little interest in looking at them. However, total horror shadowed his face when he saw the extensive bruises and cuts, but he quickly regained his composure and passed them to the bailiff to show to the jury. Declan was getting very anxious, wondering how badly she had been beaten up. Why had no one told him? However, the horror on the juror's faces answered his question.

"How badly was she hurt?" Declan whispered to Katie, his brows turning down in annoyance.

"Shh," Katie muttered and turned back towards Meghan.

Declan's headache was getting progressively worse, and his stomach was churning with anxiety. Why was her story so upsetting to him? It was breaking his heart, watching her recount the evening of which he had no memory.

"After he beat me, I was dragged back towards Declan, and the big man put the gun in my hand," she muttered with as much calmness as she could muster. "Then he asked me where my locket was."

"Ms. Delaney, are you all right?" Nathan questioned as he leaned on the rail in front of her.

She looked quite startled to see him standing there as she gazed up when he spoke. "What?" she muttered. "Oh, I'm sorry." she chewed at her lip nervously and glanced at all the faces watching her with interest. "I'm sorry," she muttered again before taking a deep breath.

"It's okay. We know this is hard for you. It's almost over." Nathan soothed as he rested his hand on hers that was still stroking her leg. "That's all I have for this witness, but I reserve the right to recall."

The judge nodded and glanced towards the District Attorney. "You may cross examine the witness, Mr. DeAngelo."

"Well, that was a very moving account of the evening," Mr. DeAngelo smiled with a crooked grin. "I hope I can wade through all the drama and get to the truth."

"It was the truth," Meghan muttered through her teeth, which she embedded in her bottom lip.

"It's been a long day for all of us, so I will keep it as short as I can," he smiled, trying to soothe her into a false sense of security. His long narrow hands rested on the rail, and his fingers tapped against the underside. "Your account of the evening appears to have enormous holes, Miss Delaney?"

She glanced over at Fabrizio, looking for reassurance. He flashed her a toothy grin and winked.

Declan noticed the exchange and was becoming agitated; they looked very close. When had that happened? The District Attorney shook his head and regrouped. "So, Miss Delaney, several witnesses claim you and Mr. Montgomery spent most of the week fighting." He paused and began to pace back and forth in front of her. "And you testified that when the reporter was calling you names, Mr. Montgomery snapped. Your words." A twisted grin filled his narrow face. "Did Mr. Montgomery snap that night and beat you up before you shot him?"

"No, he never hit me, he wouldn't hurt me, and I never shot him. It was Ian," Meghan cried, her voice louder than she had intended.

Declan was shocked at the level of emotion she was displaying. She seemed more concerned with the jury thinking he hit her than she was with them believing she shot him.

"Let's be honest here, Miss Delaney, we could understand if you shot him out of self-defence," he continued to badger her.

Declan's head was throbbing to the point of explosion, and the District Attorney's voice was echoing through his head. It was loud and threatening Meghan, his Meghan.

"You shot him and are trying to hide behind a fictitious scorned boyfriend. You shot Mr. Montgomery and then you shot yourself."

"No! Ian shot Declan . . ."

"Miss Delaney!" the DA blurted out. "Tell us the truth, you seduced Mr. Montgomery, then shot him in cold blood, we have all witnessed your charms," Mr. De Angelo badgered.

"Objection!" Nathan yelled, and at the same time, Declan stood and bellowed.

"Leave her alone!" Declan's voice echoed throughout the courtroom.

Meghan's terrified eyes settled on Declan as he stood glaring at Mr. DeAngelo. Katie was tugging on his arm, trying to pull him back down to the bench, but he was having no part of it, and he yanked his arm free from Katie's hand without changing his grey gaze.

"Sit down, Mr. Montgomery," the judge blurted out, his grey brows crumpling with annoyance.

Declan's face was filled with rage as he watched the smug DA turned back towards Meghan. The room was erupting with discussion as the people began to discuss Declan's outburst, and the judge became annoyed at the amount of noise.

"Order!" he hollered. "If you don't quiet down, I'll clear the room!" he screamed, smashing his gavel on the hard wooden desk.

The room quieted quickly, but Declan was still standing glaring at the District Attorney. "Mr. Montgomery, please sit down," the judge ordered.

Declan begrudgingly dropped to the bench, but he was poised on the edge as if ready to attack the DA.

"Now, Ms. Delaney, let me ask you this again." The DA turned his gaze back on her. "Did you shoot yourself before or after you shot Mr. Montgomery?"

"No, I didn't shoot anyone." Meghan panicked and glanced over at Nathan.

Mr. DeAngelo smirked, realizing he had her flustered, and people usually incriminate themselves at that point. "You are a very beautiful woman, Miss Delaney, and I'm sure you use it to your advantage." He glanced back over at Declan, who had his head cupped in his hands. "I guess if I was Mr. Montgomery and I found out that my girlfriend was out to destroy my family, I would have snapped too."

"Bloody hell!" Declan shouted as he jumped to his feet once more. His head was throbbing, but he remembered, he remembered everything.

"Mr. Montgomery," the judge snapped. "Sit down, or I'll have you removed."

"Are y' going to let him talk to her that way? She didn't shoot me!" Declan snorted, causing a loud outburst from the crowd.

"Declan, sit down!" his mother ordered, completely horrified that he would explode the way he did.

"No, Ma, I'm not, this trial is a farce. Meggie didn't shoot me, I remember now. He was going to shoot Meggie, and I got in the way." Declan moved towards the judge. "I will swear to that."

"I want to see the lawyers and you, Mr. Montgomery, in my chambers," Judge Hamel ordered, then stood. "The jury may return to the sequestering room until this is cleared up."

"Meggie, I'm sorry," Declan whispered as he headed towards her.

"Mr. Montgomery, you need to come with me," the bailiff ordered, gripping his arm, halting his movements. Before Declan could protest, he was escorted from the courtroom, leaving Meghan shaking in the witness chair.

Fabrizio was the one that got to her first; his strong arms wrapped around her, holding her close to his chest as he lifted her from the witness stand. "Everything is going to be okay now, please don't cry." He soothed and slid a finger across her cheek. "Please, Boo, you'll see."

"Fabrizio, what is going to happen now? Do I get to go home?" Meghan muttered as he carried her back to Nathan.

"Great news, Meg," Cassie blurted out, hugging her friend. "They have to let you free now."

"Let's not get ahead of ourselves," Agent Spencer piped up. "We have to wait and see if the District Attorney will drop the charges."

"Well, he has to now. Declan said she didn't shoot him." Cassie turned and eyed Declan's mother who was sitting across the room, glaring in their direction. The tall handsome man at her side looked drawn and confused.

"Why aren't they happy that he remembers?" Pete commented also, noticing the scowl on the face of Declan's mother. "You would think that they would be happy that their son will be cleared of beating a woman almost to death."

"You would think. I don't imagine an assault charge hanging over your head is too good for business," Agent Spencer muttered and glanced up at the door as the group re-entered the courtroom.

Declan's gaze settled on Meghan, who was still being held by Fabrizio. Declan appeared haggard, the events of the last hour seeming to have drained the life from him. "Meggie, we need to talk."

Her eyes filled with concern at his tone, but she nodded her head, unable to speak.

"If everyone could take their seats, this court is now in session, the Honourable Judge Hamel presiding," the bailiff announced, then moved to the corner of the room.

Judge Hamel sat down and glanced over at Meghan, his mouth twitching slightly. "Mr. Montgomery has regained his memory and clarified the situation that Miss Delaney was not the person who shot him. He has also signed a sworn statement." Judge Hamel focused his dark brown eyes on Meghan. "The District Attorney's office has agreed to drop the charges against Miss Delaney. Miss Delaney will be returned to the Colorado Women's Correctional Facility pending a new bail hearing regarding the harassment charges filed against her by the Montgomery family."

The court erupted in confusion, and Declan's family and entourage surrounded him blocking his path to Meghan. The bailiff immediately removed her from the room before Declan realized she was gone.

CHAPTER FOURTEEN

Meghan's life was only a shadow of what it had been. Six months ago, she would never have believed that she would have spent the last four months in prison. Thankfully, that nightmare was behind her, but she did miss Hayley and wondered how her pregnancy was progressing. The promise Meghan had made to raise Hayley's child until she served her time was still strong in her mind, and she was struggling with how to explain it to Nathan. He was so determined to move to Montana and start a new life, how would he react now? Not only would she be raising her own child but apparently Hayley's as well.

She shrugged, deciding that it must be done, and if Nathan did not like it, he could stay in Dallas, and she would move out to her ranch by herself. Pine Creek Ranch was her grandfather's home for over fifty years, and now it was hers. It had more than enough room for two adults and two children; in fact, it could be a comfortable home for a family of fifteen. Why her grandfather built the new main house with eight bedrooms was beyond her, but they would come in handy. Her friends could come out to visit whenever they wanted, and Nathan could stay either at the main house or in the old ranch house across the yard, which was his preference.

When the doorbell sounded, breaking her thoughts, she cringed and wheeled her chair across the travertine floor towards the door. "Who is it?" she said loudly, still very wary of opening the door to anyone. Ian had shaken her confidence in her ability to protect herself, right to her core. She was scared to be alone at night, and when someone came to the door when Nathan was not home, she was terrified.

"Meghan, it's Fabrizio." The voice was strong and determined. "I have some news for you about the harassment charges." He listened as she fumbled with the locks. More locks than normally present on apartment doors in this upper-class neighbourhood.

"Hi." Her voice was choked. She gazed up at him; his dark chestnut hair was glimmering under the sunlight streaming in the big picture window at the end of the hall.

"Are you going to let me in?" Fabrizio questioned, a slight smirk curling his full lips.

"Oh yes, sorry." She wheeled back from the door, allowing him access. "Where have you been for the last few weeks?" She eyed him dubiously; she was annoyed with him, and that was evident. He should not have abandoned her the way he did, but he was finding it painful to be around her. Since her arrest, he had spent every ounce of his energy to prove her innocence, but now that she was free, he did not know how to continue with the relationship. Brody Spencer had been spending a lot of time around Meghan since she was released, and Fabrizio was slowly being pushed out. He had hoped that she would turn to him after Declan cut her out of his life, but with Brody interfering, it was unlikely; he was doomed to the friendship pile. Brody had also convinced Meghan that the Montgomerys were covering something up again. Declan testified for the judge that he was mistaken that he thought Ian was Rory. Meghan was convinced that they had something to do with the whole nightmare.

"So, Meghan, why are you are still in that chair?" Fabrizio noticed that she was still wheeling around the large loft apartment.

She shrugged, then turned her face up towards him, with slight animosity crossing her brow. "Because I went to jail!" she blurted out before she could stop herself. Why couldn't she get past that, and it certainly was not Fabrizio's fault that she was set up. Nathan was right; she was lashing out at everyone in her life that was trying to help her. "I'm sorry. That was uncalled for."

"Hmm, well, why aren't you going to therapy now? I thought you were. You know, Meghan, you have been out of prison now for a month, and you have not gotten any better. Do you want to be in that chair for the rest of your life?" Fabrizio ignored her annoyance with him and focused on her situation at present.

Meghan threw him a dark look over her shoulder as she wheeled towards the kitchen. "Would you like some tea?" This was the reason she liked spending time with Brody, he didn't push her. He was just happy to spend time with her.

"Thanks," Fabrizio smiled pleasantly and followed behind her into the kitchen.

"I can do this myself," Meghan muttered, then stared up into his dark brown eyes. "I . . ."

"I know. I wasn't implying you couldn't," Fabrizio smiled, his large white teeth gleaming in the sunlight. God, she was beautiful; his stomach was churning with desire and unleashed need. Was he being a fool, thinking that she would ever be attracted to him? She treated him with restrained resentment, did she somehow blame him for Declan's dishonesty, and if so, how was he going to get her past that?

"Anyway, Meghan, the Montgomerys have dropped the charges. Apparently, Mrs. Montgomery realized she was mistaken, and they don't want any more publicity." He reached out and rested his large hand on her shoulder when he noticed she had begun to tremble. "It will be simple enough for you now."

"Simple?" she grumbled and jerked her shoulder out from under his hand. "Take your tea." She rolled away into the living room, with Fabrizio close behind her.

"Yes, you are free to live your life now, sweetheart." He cringed when she recoiled from him.

"I gave my heart and soul to a man that just discarded me, nothing is simple," Meghan muttered, her hand trembling as she sipped her tea.

"I know sweetheart but, you have a child to consider now, and I will help you in any way I can to get your life back in order."

She glanced up at him, curiosity shadowing her eyes. "Thank you for your offer, but I have Nat." Her voice was cool as ice; she had no interest in having him in her life in any capacity. He reminded her of what she lost.

"Well, all the same, I'll be there." Fabrizio stood and wandered towards the window.

Meghan sipped her tea and eyed him with regret. Why was she being so rude to him? She needed to stop that. "So, Fabrizio, you never told me where you have been."

His brow rose at the interested tone in her voice. "Oh, well, I have been hired by the FBI. I worked so closely with Brody, he recommended me for the position. Apparently, my training in the navy and my sleuth skills in your case have brought me some recognition. You are now looking at Agent Fabrizio Stagliano," he grinned wildly and flashed his shimmering new badge.

"Wow, good for you," Meghan smiled with delight.

"Thanks, but the only thing is I'm working out of the Seattle office. I was hoping for the Dallas office. So I won't be able to see you as often now." He was convinced that Brody had made sure he was as far away from her as possible.

"Well, that's okay, Nathan and I are moving to Montana soon. He just has to finish up a case here. So you won't be that far away. And Cassie lives in Seattle."

"Does Brody know you are moving?" Fabrizio asked curiously.

"I don't think so, I haven't told him yet. I don't need a lecture from him. He doesn't like Nat much and wants me to get my own apartment. He said I will never get my life back under Nat's thumb." Meghan's tone sharpened at the end of the comment, and she hand gripped her leg.

"Are you okay?" Fabrizio questioned, bending down in front of her again.

"I have a pain in my leg," Meghan moaned, rubbing her thigh frantically, trying to stop the burning sensation shooting up her muscle.

Fabrizio put his hand on her leg, lifted it, and gently rubbed the area she was grasping. "Your muscles need to be used more." Why was he torturing himself by allowing himself to enjoy the sensation of her skin under his hand? His mind was tortured by his physical attraction to her.

"I have been going to therapy every day," she stated rather defiantly, startling him back into reality.

"Do you get out of this chair and move around during the day?" Fabrizio's dark gaze settled on her large green eyes.

"No, I can't," she snorted.

"You can't or you won't?" His brow rose slightly as he watched her face inflame with colour.

Meghan frowned at him, pushed his hand off her leg, and then wheeled her chair backwards, away from him. "I can't!" she snorted.

"Didn't your therapist tell you to get up and move around or do exercises at home to strengthen that leg?"

Meghan looked at him as if she had been caught. "Well."

"He did, didn't he? Why aren't you doing that then?" Fabrizio's tone was judgmental, and his face mirrored the sentiment.

"It's none of your business. I think you better leave." She was getting annoyed with his interference, and her face was showing it.

"Okay, I'm sorry that I upset you. But you need to use that leg more. Tell you what, I don't need to be in Seattle for a few days, I can come over and take you for walks." He stood up and gazed at her with amusement, curling his lips.

"Thanks, but I don't think I need your help," she said smiling politely.

"Well, we'll see." He turned and wandered to the window. "Meghan, don't let him ruin your life."

Meghan eyed her leg and knew that he was right; she should be doing more with her leg by now. She was only punishing herself by not trying. Declan obviously did not love her, so why was she letting him ruin her life? Staying trapped in the wheel chair the rest of her life was not going to bring him back. She was rubbing her leg when Fabrizio glanced back at her.

"Fabrizio, do you think Declan was out to hurt me from the beginning?" She glanced sidelong at him.

So that is what she was thinking. "No, I don't. Declan is a good man, and he wouldn't purposely hurt you. I think his parents are just forcing him to lie about Rory. He has a very strange loyalty to them, and I think he would put that before everything else."

"Hmm. Do you think I should try contacting him again to tell him about the baby, or do you agree with Brody and I should stay away from them? Maybe he didn't get the message. The papers could be making it up that he is dating Georgia again." She began to ramble.

Fabrizio smiled softly; he knew that if Declan hadn't returned her first call, he was avoiding her. He had tried a few times too, and he was unable to get through to him. "It wouldn't hurt to try again, and even if he is dating Georgia, he would still want to know he is a dad."

"Do you think he is with her again?" Meghan sighed, her heart breaking a little more.

"I can't say for sure since I haven't had contact with him since he fired me, but I know Declan, and in his weakened state, his mother could probably convince him to do anything."

"Oh," Meghan sighed and rubbed at her leg.

"Is it still sore?"

"No, not really. It is throbbing, though," she informed him.

"I could give it a massage. That should stop the throbbing."

"I . . . Well, I don't think you should." She knew he had feeling for her, and she did not think it was a good idea to encourage his feelings.

"Calm down, Boo, it's just a massage." Fabrizio knew very well that she was uncomfortable with him touching her, she always had been, but he always thought that it was because she was involved with Declan. However, with him out of the picture, she still was very apprehensive.

She looked at him with sadness in her eyes that made his heart ache. He could not help but put his hand up to her face and wipe the tears away.

"I'm so sorry you had to go through all this," Fabrizio sighed. "If I could take away your pain, I would."

"I know you would. I do appreciate everything you have done for me." Meghan reached up and rested her hand on his face. "You are a very special man, and I am sorry I have been such a bitch to you."

Fabrizio smiled warmly. "I will always be here for you." He bent down and kissed her softly. When she did not pull away, he grabbed her face and deepened the kiss. Wholly crap, she was kissing him back. He knew he should stop, but he could not; he was in love with her, and he wanted her. It was not as if he was betraying Declan, after all, he did not want her, so the hell with him.

When Meghan finally pulled back from the kiss, she eyed Fabrizio with shock. She found herself attracted to him. Was this a new feeling, or was it always there? She was not sure. How could she love Declan so deeply but still be physically attracted to Fabrizio? Maybe it was the hormones. Maybe it was revenge towards Declan for abandoning her to be with Georgia. Maybe she needed to feel attractive, to feel that someone loved her, she was not sure. All she knew was that kissing Fabrizio stirred something in her that she had not felt in a long time. She turned towards him and stared at him for a long moment. Then without warning, she propelled herself out of the wheel chair onto him, knocking him onto the floor and landing on top of him. Her lips were on his, and her hands were gripping his face.

His arm wrapped around her as he kissed her with abandon, he had waited for this day a long time. He grabbed the bottom of her T-shirt, pulled it over her head, and discarded it on the floor beside them. He made fast work of removing her bra, releasing her full breast that landed heavily on his chest. They had gotten much larger with the pregnancy and much more sensitive. She groaned with pleasure as he ran his hand over her nipples then cupped the fullness.

Fabrizio sat up with her still on his lap. She stripped his shirt off, exposing his broad chest dusted with dark curly hair. She ran her finger through the hair, resting her hands on his shoulders.

"What about the baby?" Fabrizio questioned, unsure why he did.

Meghan gazed at him for a moment, then smiled. "It's okay you won't hurt it." She reached down and unfastened his jeans and then shimmied them off him and scanned his strong muscular frame. He smirked at her facial expression, flipped her off him onto her back, and lowered himself onto her. His mouth trailed down her body, causing her to moan with pleasure. He definitely knew what he was doing. She was still so inexperienced when it came to sex. She giggled at the thought, considering she was pregnant. Fabrizio eyed her with interest but quickly returned to his kissing, his tongue now trailing across her pelvis. She squirmed slightly as he spread her legs, and his tongue darted into her. A deep moan exited her at the sensation. It was so foreign, yet so exhilarating at the same time; it was incredible. Meghan gripped his hair as the tension in her pelvis spread across her belly and out her limbs. She cried out with pleasure.

Fabrizio smiled at his accomplishment and manoeuvre himself onto her and plunged himself into her, causing her to cry out again. He moved slowly and carefully, concerned about hitting the baby, which gave her time to recover only to be pushed to the brink again. Her body was hypersensitive to his touch; her body heaved towards him, and she released again, which sent him over the edge as he called out her name.

Fabrizio lay on the floor, completely drained with Meghan sprawled out on top of him. He was too scared to move, and he could not believe what just happened. He has fantasized about making love to her since the day he met her in the bar when she rested her hand on his arm. He could lie there forever, but he knew Nathan would soon be home and reality would set back in for her.

CHAPTER FIFTEEN

The buzzing of patients' bells and the humming from the machines around Meghan were annoying her to say the least, and the fact that her doctor had not yet arrived was sending her over the edge of sanity. She knew labour was painful, but she could never have imagined the horrible sharp pains that ripped through her stomach as every contraction hit with a vengeance. Nathan was doing his best to calm her, but his attempts were failing miserably, and she was snapping at him. The placid nurse, who made an appearance every fifteen minutes or so, did not fare much better.

The screaming woman in the next room sent Meghan over the edge, and she turned to Nathan, her face contorted into an unnatural expression. "Shut that woman up, or I'll get out of this bed and strangle her," Meghan snarled.

"Settle down, Megs." Nathan soothed, forcing the smile to stay off his lips. He could not believe how bitchy Meghan was being and wondered how the nurse did not suffocate her with the pillow.

"Nat, get the doctor and tell him to get this thing out of me," Meghan begged and swabbed at her face with the back of her hand. "Please, I'm going to die."

Nathan did chuckle then. "Megs, you are not going to die, women do this all the time."

Meghan crinkled her nose and turned her face away. Why was he taking this so lightly? Damn, it hurt. The thoughts of having Declan's baby was as frightening as it was exciting, maybe she could lure him back. No, that was not a possibility; he was marrying Georgia. Over the last few months, her self-esteem had plummeted after Declan's ruthless treatment of her and her unborn child. How could he have rejected his child? Why did he send his mother to meet her and tell her that he wanted nothing to do with her any longer? Even Fabrizio was surprised that he did not show up to meet her. Fabrizio called him a coward.

Meghan had never felt so cheap and discarded as she did that day two months earlier when she had met with Katie and Declan's fiancée Georgia at the posh Los Angeles restaurant. Meghan was so excited to see Declan again, but with the arrival of the two women, her hopes were shattered and her life destroyed. Katie had made it perfectly clear that Declan would annul their marriage, and Meghan should never claim her child as a Montgomery.

"Miss Delaney, as long as you are in the child's life, we will never accept it as a Montgomery, and if you try to force it on Declan, we will take complete custody, and you will never see your child again. I suggest you disappear and raise that child without any contact with us again. I will not have your bastard child interfering with Declan and Georgia's life together."

If that is what Declan and his family wanted, then she was not going to be treated like a blight on his family. She would raise her child on her own.

Nathan's father was investing in the special needs camp at the newly named Lost Eagle Ranch, her family ranch. Nathan was his father's representative, and she was pleased with that, since Nathan was going to move with her and the baby to Montana and help her start up her dream.

"I can't do this, Nat. It hurts too much," Meghan moaned when she was smacked back into reality by a strong contraction.

"Yes, you can. Just breathe like we learned in the prenatal class we took." Nathan was exhausted, not having slept in over twenty-four hours. She at least had drugs to soothe her, he felt like the walking dead.

"Nat, get the nurse to give me some more drugs. I need them," Meghan complained, pulling at his arm.

"Megs, she just gave you something," Nathan chuckled and brushed back a wild strand of flaming hair.

The next hour was more of the same, and Nathan was fighting to keep his eyes open when the door opened and Cassie flew in, her long blonde hair flying up around her. "I made it," she said in an excited voice, glancing around at the stark white room filled with monitors.

"Good you can take over then. She is getting too freaked out for me," Nathan joked as he backed away from the bed. "I'm waiting for her head to start to spin around."

"You're not funny. This really hurts. You try having something inside you beating the shit out of you, trying to get out," Meghan growled, her head snapping towards him.

"Jeez, Meg, don't you think you're being a bit dramatic?" Cassie laughed but backed away slightly when Meghan turned the evil contorted face on her. "Holy shit, Nat, I see what you mean."

Nathan and Cassie struggled to settle Meghan's temper as her contractions grew stronger and more frequent. The short plump nurse's presence in the room, however, was doing little to help matters as she nonchalantly fussed with the monitor, took Meghan's blood pressure, and examined her cervical dilatation.

"It shouldn't be long now, dear," the nurse muttered, assuming the remark would be well received.

"That's what you said two hours ago!" Meghan snapped and squeezed Nathan's hand harder as once again a contraction struck.

The nurse just smiled and walked over to the fetal monitor and checked the printout. "The baby looks in good shape." She leaned over and flicked at the IV bag to check the drip, then turned and left the room.

Meghan turned to Cassie, her face dripping with sweat, looking exhausted. "Oh, Meg, it will be over soon." Cassie soothed, rubbing her sweat-damped hair.

It was at least another two hours before Meghan was ready to push out the baby, and when the time came, the room was abuzz with activity. The doctor was sitting at the end of the bed, giving her instructions, and the nurse was hovering around the bed, waiting for the baby.

"Okay, Meghan, give me a good push," The doctor ordered gently, her narrow brown eyes glued to her work.

Ten minutes, a few curses and a load of tears later Meghan was holding her tiny daughter. A beautiful, perfect girl with curly black hair and dark grey eyes, her father's eyes.

"She looks just like Declan," Meghan sighed and kissed the soft fuzzy head.

"I think you're right, sweetie." Cassie soothed her, tension releasing at that instant. How she worried for Meghan and her mental state!

"She's beautiful, Megs, I can't believe it. We have a girl. Hi, little darlin', I'm your uncle Nat." Nathan rested a large finger against the baby's little hand.

"Wow, this is fantastic," Cassie whispered, her eyes lighting with delight. "What are you going to name her?" Cassie rested her chin on her folded arms that rested on the bed.

"I think that I am going to call her Caelan, after my grandma," Meghan beamed. "That should appease them somewhat." She glanced up to the heavens. "She's a blessing."

"That's a great idea," Nathan agreed as he sat on the edge of the bed. "Your dad would be proud of you today, you came through like a trouper."

Meghan nodded and glanced towards Cassie, who was on her feet and heading towards the door. "I'm going to call Pete and Marlene. I promised I would call the minute she was born."

Nathan stayed on the bed, stroking Meghan's hair as he snuggled up beside her. "You did good, darlin'. I'm so proud of you."

"It's wonderful, isn't it? She is so beautiful. Hey, I'm a mother."

"Who would have thought?" he joked. "Now I have my two best girls to take care of."

"Don't forget Anisha," Meghan muttered, her eyes fixing on him. "Where is she anyway?"

"With my parents at the ranch. My mother is spoiling her rotten. Megs, are you sure you want the responsibly of another woman's child, especially since you have your own to take care of?"

"Nat, I promised I would look after her until Hayley is released, and I can't break my word. Anyway she is a delightful baby."

Nathan forced a smile and sighed. "But showing up in Montana with a newborn and a little black baby of five months is going to cause talk."

"Nathan, you're the last person I thought would worry about what people thought," Meghan grumbled and scrubbed at her face.

"I'm not worried what people think, I just want to blend in, and you remember what Fabrizio and Agent Spenser said about the Montgomery's connection to the whole mess. It's best you just disappear. We don't want to get in the middle of a custody battle with them."

"Well, we will. Caelan and I will use your last name, no one will find us. I'm not even sure they are looking."

Nathan shrugged and kissed her forehead just before the door opened again, but this time very slowly. The person on the other side appeared weary of entering, and sure enough, when the opening was big enough, a pair of dark blue eyes peered in. "Hi, can I come in?"

"Sure," Meghan said warily, not certain that Brody was someone she wanted to see after he got angry with her for trying to go see Declan.

Brody ignored her facial expression and sauntered across the room, coming to a stop by the bed, his eye fixing on Nathan, who was lying on the bed right next to Meghan, with his head resting on her pillow. He could not understand the bond they shared.

Nathan could see the disturbance in Brody's eyes, and he began to stroke Meghan's hair back behind her ear as she looked up at Brody. Nathan did not like the fact that he was pushing his way into Meghan's life, and it was bad enough Fabrizio was interfering. He liked having her all to himself, and he didn't want Fabrizio or Brody changing their plans.

"So the nurse told me you had a girl," Brody muttered as his eyes darted from her to Nathan's intimate positioning on the bed.

"Yes, she's beautiful. Isn't she, Nat?" she said, turning her face towards him and leaning her head against his forehead that was only inches from her.

"She sure is, darlin'," Nathan whispered and kissed her cheek.

"So where is she?" Brody questioned as he scanned the small room for the child.

"Under here, she is still nursing." Meghan nodded towards the lump under the sheet.

"Can she breathe under there?" Brody asked anxiously.

"Yes," Meghan laughed and reached for his hand.

Nathan rolled his eyes. "What an idiot!" he mumbled under his breath.

"What?" Meghan asked as she turned towards him.

"Nothing, darlin'."

Her attention returned to Brody, and a smile curled her lips. "Thank you for coming. I'm sorry about the way I behaved. I know you were just trying to keep me from getting hurt."

Brody smiled and bent down and kissed her brow. "All is forgiven." A deep tremor surged through him at the sight of her. How could she twist him around her finger with just a smile? Brody's thoughts were broken, however, when the door flew open, and Cassie bolted through, suddenly stopping when she noticed Brody standing next to the bed.

"Hello?" Cassie said in an inquiring tone, wondering why he was there. "Look, who I found outside."

"Hi," Fabrizio glanced around the room, his eyes landing on Brody's annoyed face. "Wow, what a crowd you have collected!"

Meghan smiled with pleasure at the sight of him. "You came. I thought you couldn't."

"Ya, sorry, I've been busy, but when Cassie called and said you were having the baby, I flew right down. How are you, Boo?"

"I'm good." Meghan's smile faded slightly when Cassie wrapped her arm around Fabrizio's waist. "Cass, did you get through to Marlene and Pete?" Meghan was so concerned with Fabrizio, she did not notice the distress on Brody's face.

"Yes, they are so excited, and they are looking forward to seeing the newest addition to our family," Cassie announced as she rested her upper body across Nathan's chest. "Well, Brody, I hear you and Meg have been spending a lot of time together. Doesn't it bother you that she is in love with another man?" Cassie's voice was clipped. She wanted Meghan to get back together with Declan, she really wanted to tag along with Meghan and be part of his lifestyle. Meghan cringed and glanced up at Fabrizio, wondering if Cassie knew about their relationship. She hadn't told anyone. Why was she touching him so much?

Brody shrugged and looked at Meghan, but she was gazing at Fabrizio. What was going on with them? "I'm not too concerned."

"So, Meg, where is the wee Montgomery bairn?" Cassie giggled, her attention leaving Brody. "Hey, I sounded just like him, didn't I?"

"Her last name is Delaney, or should I say Coleman. And no, you don't sound like him."

"Well, I could call y' Meggie, or how about Freckles?"

"Stop it, Cass, I don't think you're funny. It's hard enough without you . . ." Meghan scolded as tears sat on her lower lashes, dangerously close to escaping.

"I'm sorry, sweetie, I was just trying to get you to remember the love that Caelan was created in." Cassie's hand swept across Meghan's face in a smooth motion and wiped away the tears from Meghan's cheek. She still loved Declan, that was clear. Something needed to be done.

Meghan looked down at the gulping lump under the blankets. "I thought so," she said sadly.

"Meg, you . . ." Cassie stopped and looked at Brody.

"It's okay, Cass, he knows all about Declan not acknowledging his child."

Cassie looked over at Brody, wondering why he would be privy to the information. "Oh, I see," she said, raising her brow.

"Cass, stop it." Meghan stared at Cassie with disapproval.

Fabrizio glanced over at Brody and didn't miss the smug expression crossing his face. She was confiding in him. Had he weaselled his way into her life to the point she trusted him that much? He knew how guarded Meghan was.

"Anyway, Meg," Cassie said, going back to her original comments. "I think that you should call Declan. He would want to know, and if he is planning on marrying the rich chick, well, maybe this will screw up his plans."

"Cass, I told you, he already knows about the pregnancy, and he didn't care. I'm not letting Caelan anywhere near that crazy family. They are too powerful, they could take her away from me."

"Megs, that's not going to happen. I won't let it," Nathan piped in.

"Well, they are not getting the chance. Declan has had plenty of time to talk to me. I gave his mother my number, and if he wanted anything to do with me, he would have phoned by now."

"What would you have done if he did?" Cassie questioned, trying to provoke a reaction from Brody. She was convinced more was going on than either one would admit.

Caelan released Meghan's nipple with a snort, startling Meghan, which she was pleased about, she had no intentions of answering Cassie's question, with Fabrizio around. She flipped the sheet back and stared at the little grey eyes gazing up at her, not noticing where Brody's eyes had landed.

Brody's eyes left her breast and moved from Fabrizio to Cassie to Nathan, none of them seeming disturbed by the bare breast. Meghan reached for Fabrizio's hand, pulling him closer to her until he was sitting on the side of the bed.

"Caelan, this is Uncle Fabrizio, he is a friend of Mommy," she said as she laid Caelan in the bend of her arm and pulled at her gown until her breast was covered.

Fabrizio smiled and glanced down at the little girl with the ample black curly hair. She was the spitting image of Declan, her little lips full and her cat eyes were dark grey. He could feel the distance between him and Meghan growing as she stared down at the child that she and Declan had created.

"That's an interesting name." Fabrizio forced a smile. "How is it pronounced?"

"Kee-lin, it's an Irish name, my grandmother's name."

"Give her to me," Cassie demanded taking Caelan from Meghan and gazed down at her tiny face.

"Hi, sweetie, I'm your auntie Cassie. You sure are a beautiful little thing, aren't you? You look just like your daddy."

"Cassie, please stop it," Meghan begged.

"Okay, that is the last thing I will say on the matter," she smiled at Meghan, then glanced back at Nathan. "When are you guys moving to Montana?"

"In a couple of weeks," Nathan muttered and glanced at Meghan. "Once she feels well enough to travel, and we straighten out Hayley's problem."

"How is that going?" Cassie questioned, between her cueing at the baby.

"Better than I thought." Nathan said offhandedly, his eyes glued to Meghan as she quietly talked with Fabrizio. Brody was standing to the side awkwardly, looking very disturbed. Nathan was pleased that Meghan was more interested in Fabrizio. If Brody had his way, she would stay in Dallas. "She was convicted of manslaughter, so her new sentence is five to ten years. She has already served sixteen months, so hopefully within the next few years, she will be out on probation."

"Well, I think I will get going," Brody announced after a few minutes of being ignored.

"Okay, thanks for coming. I will call you before we leave for Montana," Meghan smiled, totally clueless to Brody's pain.

He sighed and headed for the door. He had hoped she would have asked him to stay, but apparently she was more interested in Fabrizio. Once she moved away, his chances were majorly diminished. He waved goodbye and disappeared out the door.

"So what's going on with him? I get he is good looking, but jeez, Meg, he's kind of controlling. Did you see the looks he was giving Fabs? It's like he thinks something is going on," Cassie laughed at the thought.

"Nothing is going on. He's just a friend. Anyway he's not my type." She gave Fabrizio a sidelong look.

"Well, that's good because I still think Declan will come to his senses. Fabs and I will make sure of that." She gave him a sultry smile.

Fabrizio tensed slightly when Cassie rested her hand on his back and ran it up to his hair. He was getting himself into a very dangerous situation.

Meghan smiled and glanced up at Fabrizio, not noticing his facial expression. "I think the darkest days are over."

Fabrizio nodded and kissed her forehead softly, his heart exploding with joy.

CHAPTER SIXTEEN

The sun danced in the cloudless blue sky, distracting from the brisk June morning. Meghan parked her white pickup truck against the curb next to the red brick school. She smiled when Caelan's dark grey eyes scanned the area for a glimpse of her friends. Not a day went by since Caelan was born that Meghan did not feel a slight tug at her heart that Declan wanted nothing to do with his child. Their lives had been full and happy, but Meghan could not seem to get past the longing she felt for Declan and the love they once shared.

Meghan forced a smile when she noticed Caelan watching her with concern. "Mommy, you're making that face again."

"What face, peanut?" Meghan questioned as she reached over and brushed back a long black curl from Caelan's face.

Caelan's small shoulders rose in a shrug. "When you daydream."

Meghan smiled and bent to kiss her daughter on the cheek. "Well, I like to daydream."

"Uncle Fabrizio doesn't like it. He says you are silly and not happy with what you have," Caelan said casually and reached for the handle of the truck door.

"Fabrizio is the one that's silly." Meghan choked down the irritation that was building in her. Why would he make that comment to a child? "I am perfectly happy with my life. I have you, don't I? What more could a woman ask for?"

"Nothing, except maybe a new foal," Caelan giggled and opened the door. "Mommy, when is Molly going to have her baby, it's taking so long."

"Soon, peanut, this week sometime, the vet is pretty sure." Meghan jumped from the truck and met Caelan on the sidewalk.

"It's too bad I have to go back to school. What if it's born when I'm here." Caelan coughed slightly, her dark grey eyes looked up at Meghan with concern. "Maybe I'm not so well."

"You're fine," Meghan giggled and kissed her forehead. "Now get to class, you've already missed a week."

"All right," Caelan moaned and turned towards the side door of the old brick building. The playground was alive with noises as the children shrieked, laughed, and yelled. Calls of goodbyes from the parents were loud, but somehow muffled as Meghan adjusted Caelan's hat and zippered up her jacket.

"Keep your coat done up, Caelan. I don't want you getting chilled," Meghan smiled at the little girl and gave her a big hug.

"Okay, Mommy," Caelan smiled and took a step away but stopped suddenly. "Oh, Mommy, I need to get Hayley's autograph book." She lunged back towards the truck.

"Why?" Meghan questioned as she watched Caelan rummaging around on the front seat.

"She wants the actor's autograph," Caelan said, with little enthusiasm.

"What actor?" Meghan questioned, glancing around the school grounds.

"The new teacher's brother. Becky told me yesterday when she and her mother stopped by." Caelan tucked the book into her backpack.

"What's his name?" Meghan questioned as a slight ache filled her heart, the thought of Declan strong in her mind.

"Mr. Morrison, I guess."

Meghan could not help but laugh as Caelan crinkled her nose at her amusement. Meghan bent over and kissed Caelan's head, then turned her towards the school. "Have a nice day, peanut, and don't forget to get him to sign it, or Hayley will kill you."

Caelan blew a kiss to her mom, ran a few feet, then turned around, and waved goodbye, before she disappeared into a crowd of girls.

Meghan shook her head and climbed back into the truck. Her baby was growing up fast. Caelan was a blessing in her life, and she thanked God everyday for giving her such a precious child.

Caelan skipped into the class, her thoughts of the actor totally forgotten in the excitement of seeing her friends again. As she skipped through the door, she turned in response to an insult hurled at her by a redheaded boy, coming in the door behind her.

"It takes one to know one," Caelan retorted before she slammed into a pair of long legs. The laughter left the redheaded boy, and he ran frantically past to avoid the trouble.

"Sorry," Caelan blurted out, her eyes settling on a pair of dark grey eyes high above her. "I didn't mean to."

"No harm done, wee one," the voice was soft but very deep. "Are y' all right?" He squatted down in front of her, his hand landing gently on her shoulder.

"Yes," she smiled. "My mommy says that I am the clumsiest person she knows."

"Is that so?" Declan laughed and ruffled Caelan's hair, then straightened to his full height. He was very tall; Caelan had to look way up.

"Are you the famous actor?" Caelan blurted out, as the thought occurred to her, and her determination to have Hayley's book signed grew strong in her mind.

Declan laughed and smiled down at the child, slightly embarrassed by the remark. "Well, I'm an actor, but I wouldn't say I'm famous."

"Good," Caelan grinned. "Could you please sign this book for my housekeeper, Hayley?"

"Sure." Declan took the book from her and flipped through the pages. "Wow, this Hayley certainly has a good collection."

Caelan nodded and smiled up at him, sending a chill down his spine. There was something so familiar about her, but he could not put his finger on it. "My mommy says that Hayley is a stalker."

Declan laughed at her comment. "Doesn't your mommy want my autograph?"

"Oh no," her voice was slightly appalled. "She says that actors are arrogant jerks."

Declan was startled by the comment, but he could not help but chuckle. Children could always put you in your place. "Well, your mommy might be right, wee one."

"Good morning, Caelan," Mrs. Morrison muttered as she walked to Declan's side and glanced down at the little girl.

"Good morning," Caelan replied and focused on Declan, her eyes bright with excitement.

"I see you met my brother." Mrs. Morrison appeared apathetic.

"Aye, we've become fast friends," Declan chuckled and patted Caelan's shoulder, his gaze settling on his sister and her bizarre demeanour.

Mrs. Morrison noticed his expression and forced a smile and then returned her gaze to Caelan. "It's nice to have you back. How are you feeling?"

"Okay. My mommy said I'm fine now," she smiled and tucked the newly signed book into her backpack.

"Well, I guess she'd know." Mrs. Morison glanced around the room. "It must be nice having your mother as your doctor."

"Yes." Caelan crinkled her nose. "But everyone else gets suckers when they go to her office. I didn't get one while I was sick."

"Oh, how awful for y'!" Declan chuckled, drawing Mrs. Morison's attention back to him while he studied the little girl's face.

Declan had the oddest appearance to him, as if he was almost in a trance. As Moiré's hand landed on his shoulder, his gaze on Caelan broke, and he glanced over at his sister with a forced smile.

"Guess what, our mare is going to have a foal soon, and my mommy said that I can have it for my very own," Caelan blurted out, hoping to gain Mrs. Morrison's approval.

"That is wonderful," Mrs. Morison replied, only half listening to Caelan.

Moiré Morrison was a beautiful, dark-haired young woman, her eyes the colour of grey smoke, the family resemblance was definitely present. This was her first teaching position. She had only been in town a couple of months, after marrying the son of one of Montana's senators at her mother's insistence. Her husband's family owned a cattle ranch just outside the town. While the elder Morrison was in Washington, the son was expected to supervise the farm. Which, if the truth were known, Jason was more than happy to stay tucked away on the ranch, living his own life instead of the life his father pushed on him.

Moiré, however, hated the small backwoods town and craved the life of Boston society. She was terribly bored with her life in Pine Creek, and when the teaching position became available, Moiré jumped at the chance. How she hated the ranch and all the disgusting animals! She was definitely not a farm girl. All she could hope for was that the original teacher did not return in the fall so she could continue working as long as Jason felt the need to stay in town. Her mother hated the fact that she wanted to pursue a career in teaching; she wanted her to focus her efforts on helping Jason pursue a political career that he didn't want.

"Good morning, boys and girls," Moiré said loudly to settle the children and get the class underway; she hated to be off schedule. Moiré brushed back a shoulder-length black wave and wandered towards the front of the room. Her tall, slim body fit easily between the filing cabinets and the desk as she manoeuvred her way around the immaculately clean desk to her chair.

"Good morning, Mrs. Morrison," the students replied. Their voices were loud and cheerful, blocking out the shuffling of books and papers as the children removed their readers and prepared for the class.

"Today we have a special guest. I would like you all to meet my brother, Declan Montgomery. Who remembers what he does for a career?" Moiré waved her hand towards Declan, where he sat on a chair at the front of the room.

"My mom said he's a babe," a little blonde-haired girl giggled from the back of the room.

Declan blushed from the comment and ran his hand through his shoulder-length black hair. "Well, I'm glad your mam thinks that, but I'm an actor."

"My dad says you have to kiss girls all day," the redheaded boy in the front row grumbled, his eyes straying towards Caelan.

"I do get to kiss a few, do y' like to kiss pretty girls?" Declan questioned with a grin.

"Yuk, no way." The disgusted boy cringed and shook his head, then turned to Caelan and stuck out his tongue.

"Y' will change your mind as y' get older, and y' will be chasing the girls around, trying to get a kiss," Declan explained in a humorous tone, but he was agitated by the boy's treatment of his little friend. Caelan, however, seemed unfazed, and she turned her nose up at him with an air of arrogance, which he found rather amusing. Good girl, Declan thought as he watched Caelan treat the boy with distain.

"My dad said that your uncle Nat is a fagot, and he's going to hell," the redheaded boy whispered to Caelan, then stuck out his tongue again.

"Don't you say that!" Caelan screamed, jumped from her chair, and slammed her reader over the boy's head.

"Caelan! What in heaven's name are you doing?" Mrs. Morrison blurted out.

Caelan turned her angry face towards the front, before tears started to drip down her cheek. "He is calling my uncle names."

"That's no reason to smack him with your book, now go sit over there. You go as well, Lucas." Moiré's voice was cold and irritated.

"But she hit me?" Lucas batted his baby blue eyes at Moiré, trying desperately to appear innocent.

"Don't be playing me for a fool, Lucas Bracken, I know very well what you said, and you should be ashamed."

Caelan moved without complaint and rested her head on the desk, covering it with her arms. As Declan watched her, he could not help but feel sorry for the wee thing, after all, she was just defending her family. The redheaded boy did not seem upset in the least that he was sent to the far side of the room, and once there, he began to torment Caelan again.

"Laddy, I suggest y' leave the wee lass alone, or you'll have me to deal with," Declan said evenly, but his firm gaze let the boy know he was serious.

Caelan lifted her head, exposing her tear-stained face and smiled with thanks. The look in her eyes was so familiar and heart wrenching, he wanted to rush to her and console her. What was it about this child that made his heart flutter?

It was over an hour before Mrs. Morrison settled the children with their snacks, and they prepared to go outside for recess. Caelan, however, was sitting alone, pushing her grapes around her desk, her little face lonely and sad.

"Moiré, do y' need to leave the wee lass in the corner so long, she looks so sad," Declan questioned, his eyes still stuck on Caelan as the rest of the children began to leave the class for recess.

"She knows the rules, Declan. She is an island for the rest of the day." Mrs. Morison said coolly, his interest in the small child bewildered her. Declan never paid much attention to any child before, what was the fascination with this one?

When Moiré left the classroom to deal with a squabble in the hallway, Declan pulled his chair up next to Caelan's desk. "When I was a lad and I got into trouble in school, I got the strap," he said softly as her dark watery eyes settled on him.

"My mommy is going to be mad," Caelan sniffed and wiped at her eyes. "She told me I need to learn to control my temper."

"Aye," Declan smiled. "Y' are very volatile, but the lad was bothering y', I was watching."

"Can you tell her that?" Caelan's eyes pleaded with him. "She says I need to ignore him."

Declan forced a smile, not particularly wanting to get in the middle of a family issue. "Well, it's hard not to get upset when someone is bullying y'. I would have done no different if I were y'. He most likely bullies y' because he likes y'."

Caelan smiled with pleasure that he was coming to her defence. "That's what my uncle Nat says, but my mommy says that no good can come from having a temper."

"Is that so?" Declan smiled and leaned his elbows on her desk and rested his face in his hands. He was finding the little girl quite entertaining. She was the most beautiful child he had ever seen, her long black curls floating softly around her round face and her small button nose was slightly dusted with freckles. Her eyes were what attracted him the most, dark grey and shaped so perfectly, big and expressive, like a cat's.

"Mr. Montgomery." Caelan rested her little hand on his face, startling him. "You look just like my daddy. My mommy has his picture in her locket," Caelan informed him, her deep grey eyes sparkling.

Declan smiled, removed her hand from his face, and held it in his. "Well, wee one, I am proud to look like your da, he must be a very special man to have such a lovely daughter like y'." He patted her hand gently, then released it.

"I guess so, my mommy says so. He died a long time ago," Caelan answered, then glanced over at Lucas, who was listening to the conversation.

"I'm sorry," Declan soothed, then shot the boy a firm look. "But I am sure he is up in heaven watching over y' and is very proud of his wee lass."

"That's what my mommy says. She says he watches over us every day. She says that they were soul mates." Caelan crinkled her nose at

Lucas, then turned her little face back towards Declan, who was eyeing her grapes. "Would you like some?"

"Aye," Declan smiled and popped one into his mouth. "I love green grapes. Have y' ever eaten them frozen?"

"No," Caelan giggled, crinkling her nose at him as if he were crazy. "That's weird."

"I beg to differ, it's grand," Declan smiled and popped another grape into his mouth.

"My daddy loved grapes too," Caelan smiled. "My mommy told me so."

"Your mommy must have loved him a great deal." Declan felt slightly sorry for the child not to have the opportunity to grow up in a house that was apparently so full of love at one time.

Caelan's smile faded quickly as Mrs. Morrison headed towards them, looking particularly displeased.

"Declan, there is a reason why we call it the island. The purpose is to have her think about what she has done."

"I'm sure she's repentant," Declan smirked and stood hoisting the chair from the floor. He bent over towards Caelan and patted her head. "Be thankful she's not a priest with a strap."

"Priests don't have straps?" Caelan blurted out in confusion. "Father Brian never hits us."

"Well, I'm thankful for that," Declan smiled and rubbed her hair again.

"Caelan, your mother has been called, and she will be in after class. I suggest you figure out what you've done wrong."

"Oh, I already know what I did wrong, Mrs. Morrison. I let my anger get the better of me. I have to learn not to let the likes of Lucas Bracken get me cross. God will punish him for being a wicked boy when his time comes." Caelan smiled up at Declan when his head flew back, and he laughed. "That's what Father Brian told me last Sunday when Lucas pulled my hair and I kicked him in the leg during Mass."

Declan could not control his laughter. He buckled over and had to lean up against the wall for support. This child was a treasure, and he could hardly wait to meet her mother that afternoon, to see where she gets her fiery attitude.

Mrs. Morrison, however, did not find the humour in it and gripped Declan's arm. "That child has a mouth on her to equal the devil himself."

"Moiré, settle down, she's just a child," Declan soothed and gripped her arm, pulling her towards the front of the class. "You're starting to sound like Mam."

The comment startled Moiré, and she turned to Declan, slightly abashed. "I am," she sighed and sat in her chair.

Declan smiled and glanced back at Caelan. "She sure is a beautiful wee girl."

"She is, you should see her mother," Moiré commented absently, still wondering how she had turned into her mother.

"Well, apparently I look like her da," Declan chuckled and brushed back a piece of loose hair.

"You know, Declan, she does look a lot like you," Moiré teased as she watched him still eyeing the small girl. "Maybe that's what you find so enchanting about her."

Declan grunted with amusement. "Do y' think I have kids running about all over the states?"

"Well, you have dated a lot of women, you never know," Moiré laughed, then began to regroup as the children one by one returned to the room, their faces flushed from the fresh air and exercise.

Declan shook his head and settled back to last out the remainder of the morning. While the children practised their alphabet and drew pictures of apples for math class, Declan watched Moiré teaching their fresh minds. Caelan, however, rarely removed her gaze from Declan, and he found it quite unnerving, there was something so familiar about the child.

When the school bell finally rang at noon, the children scattered in mass confusion, collecting their coats and belongings. Declan let out a deep sigh of relief that he had survived a morning with so many children. As he turned, he noticed Caelan still sitting in her desk, her head resting on her folded arm, and he could not help but go to her.

"Are y' scared of what your mam is going to say?" Declan questioned softly as he pulled up a chair.

She nodded and sniffed slightly. "I'm more scared of Mrs. Morrison, she doesn't like me much."

"Sure she does," Declan soothed. "But she tends to be bossy sometimes. When she was a wee girl, she constantly tried to boss me about."

"Really?" Caelan smiled and straightened. "Because I really like her, and I don't like her cross with me all the time."

"I'll talk with her if y' like," Declan smiled but quieted when he heard Moiré's voice coming down the hall, accompanied by a second set of footsteps.

"I know she is just a child, but she needs to control that temper. What would have happened if she had cut the boy's head open? I would have had his mother here raising hell." Moiré's voice was calm as she relayed the events of the morning.

Meghan sighed and forced calmness into her demeanour. How could she be angry with Caelan when she gets that trait from her? "I know she shouldn't be hitting people, I will have a talk with her about this."

Declan stiffened at the sound of the voice. He knew that voice. It was Meggie's voice.

"I will have a talk with his parents too. He teases her all the time," Moiré commented; they were right outside the door.

"Why bother, I already have after last Sunday's encounter during Mass," Meghan said, with annoyance. Declan could hear the voice, but he was frozen in place as if the sound turned him to stone.

"That's my mommy!" Caelan blurted out, jumping to her feet and gripping Declan's hand. "You are going to tell them right, that he started it?"

Declan barely noticed the little hand gripping his and the pleading voice, but as she tugged on his arm, he stared down at the child. Meggie's child.

"Wee one, don't worry, I'll stand by y'," Declan smiled and squatted down in front of her, staring at her intensely.

"Hi, Mommy," Caelan blurted out as the footsteps stopped and the room went silent.

"Good God, Declan, what are you doing now?" Moiré questioned as she stared at him, he was hugging Caelan, and her little face was resting on his shoulder. When he turned his head towards the stunned women, his heart exploded.

"Meggie," Declan said softly, his heart was racing so fast, he was convinced it would leap from his chest if it were not her.

Meghan's eyes stayed stuck on the sight of Declan with his daughter in his arms. With the faces side by side, the resemblance was uncanny. She was fighting the urge to rip her child from his arms, but the sight of him filled her with such conflicting emotions.

"What are you doing here?" Meghan said weakly, her voice barely audible.

"Meggie it is y'?" Declan sighed with relief and stood releasing Caelan. Before he knew what was happening, he was taking another step towards Meghan.

Meghan could do nothing but stare at him, her eyes glazed over and speech seemed to be something she could not manage. Her knees gave way, and she swayed slightly as pure panic raced through her like a runaway train. Declan's hand reached out and grabbed hold of her arms to steady her, but before he could stop himself, he pulled her into his chest and wrapped his arms tightly around her trembling body.

"Declan," Meghan mumbled against his shoulder, her voice finally returning.

"Oh, Meggie, I have been looking for y' for years," he whispered into her hair.

Meghan's senses were so filled with him; she had temporarily forgotten where she was. All she knew was that she was back in his arms, and his strength and warmth was surrounding her. However, her attention refocused when she felt Caelan hitting her leg and calling her.

"Oh, Caelan," Meghan muttered as she lifted her head from his trembling chest and looked down at the little girl.

Meghan blinked a few times and pushed as far away as his arms allowed, keeping her eyes focused on Caelan. She could hear the commotion around them as the teachers began to gather, after waiting patiently all morning to meet him.

"Meggie," Declan muttered, glancing down at the little girl with the dark grey eyes, staring up at him.

"If you don't mind, may I ask what is going on here?" Moiré blurted out as the crowd began to enter the class.

Declan ignored Moiré, his gaze glued to Meghan's worried eyes, his hand resting on her face. "Oh, Meggie, where have y' been?"

"Here," she muttered, her teeth biting at her bottom lip. "I've been here."

Declan's hand slid down her face to her shoulder as the group of teachers began to surround them. He knew that they were there, but at that moment, he just did not care.

"Declan, these are my fellow teachers," Moiré blurted out, trying to get him away from Meghan. "You promised you would sign some pictures."

"Aye," he muttered, his gaze still stuck to the green eyes in front of him. "Don't go anywhere," he said firmly as he released her and turned towards the excited women.

Meghan's gaze stayed fixed on him, but she could not control the fear of him taking Caelan away from her. How did he find them? He must want Caelan very badly to track them down to this little town. She had not forgotten the conversation years earlier with Katie when she told Meghan that Declan wanted sole custody of her child.

Meghan was very aware of the teachers watching her, wondering what had just happened, but she did not intend to answer their questions at that point. Her hand had hold of Caelan's, her eyes still stuck in his grey gaze, and she began to back away from the group.

Declan noticed her movements, and he surged forward towards her, but the group surrounding him seemed uninterested in moving out of his way. They were almost to the point of frenzy with excitement, and they were determined to keep him with them.

"Meggie!" He could see the fear shooting from her eyes as she turned her head and pulled Caelan down the hall.

Declan still stuck in the mob of women, felt his stomach drop and the breath drain from his chest. He could not understand why she ran from him, and he certainly did not understand the fear in her eyes. He became agitated quickly, feeling her slipping away from him again. He had to find her; she could not get away again.

"If y' will excuses me, I have to find Meggie," Declan blurted out, pushing a piece of paper he just signed towards a woman who was gripping his arm.

"Declan, they have waited all day," Moiré said harshly. "Dr. Coleman will be there later."

"No!" His voice was sharp and forceful. "I need to find her now." He pushed his way through the crowd of teachers and parents that had gathered. "I'm sorry but—" His eyes were dark and filled with panic, which frightened Moiré.

"Declan," Moiré blurted out, gripping his arm and pulling him out of the classroom. "What is going on? How do you know Dr. Coleman?"

"Stop calling her that. Her name is Meghan, Meghan Montgomery."

"What?" Moiré blurted out and leaned up against the wall for support.

"She's me wife," Declan proclaimed, brushing back a rebel strand of long black hair.

"What?" Moiré stammered again, her words blocked behind bewilderment.

Declan said nothing and wandered down the hall, his destination unknown.

"Declan, what are you talking about? Is she your Meggie?"

"Aye, I have been searching for her for years." Declan scrubbed his eyes with the back of his hand. "Moiré, how old is Caelan?" Declan questioned with obvious anxiety in his voice.

"Five, close to it." Her brows crumpled in thought.

"Oh," Declan sighed and dropped to the chair that sat next to an empty classroom.

"Why does that matter?"

"I think she's me daughter," He muttered, dropping his face into his hands.

"Declan," Moiré chuckled at the absurdity of his comment. "I was just kidding earlier."

"This isn't a joke," Declan said sharply, but lowered his voice as one of the teachers' heads twisted, as if trying to get a better angle to eavesdrop.

"Her dad is dead." Moiré soothed, trying to calm her brother, unconcerned with her fellow teachers' presence.

"She has to be me child. She's Meggie's daughter." His voice cracked as he pinned her gaze in his. He glanced over at the woman still squatting down, shuffling the papers she had dropped. He sighed at the thought of her eavesdropping, and he stood and wandered down the hall away from her.

"Declan," Moiré called after him. "What are you going to do? Don't do anything you will regret."

"Regret, all I regret are the years I lost without Meggie and apparently me daughter."

"Maybe Caelan isn't your child," Moiré said carelessly, not noticing the expression in Declan's eyes.

"She has to be. She's the right age," Declan mumbled through his hands that scrubbed at his face as he leaned against the wall. The beige brick felt cold against his skin but not enough to cool the rising heat from his anger.

"She could have been pregnant when . . ." Moiré stopped when Declan's head shot around and his dark grey eyes pierced her like daggers. That expression she did not misread.

"Don't even say it! Meggie wasn't pregnant with another man's child. I was her first." Declan's voice was harsh and startled Moiré slightly. She had never heard him use that tone with her before, and she did not appreciate it.

"Declan, you only knew her for what, two days?"

"Six!" he snorted and marched down the hall, stopping before he reached the corner. "Why is it so hard for everyone to understand that I loved her?"

Moiré shook her head and rested her hand on his shoulder. "Six days?"

"Aye."

"Please think about this. How can you truly know someone in that short of time?" she sighed, trying to get him to think clearly. She could not believe this was happening all over again.

"I did," his eyes were ablaze as he stared at her disbelieving face. "She is me soul mate. I never felt so at one with anyone before her and never have since."

"What about Georgia?" Moiré blurted out, hoping to refocus him.

"Oh, dammit, I forgot about her."

"Georgia is the perfect woman for you."

"No, she's not!" Declan paused, eyeing his sister as if appraising her trustworthiness. "The only woman I have ever wanted to marry was Meggie," he confessed, staring sightless at the wall across the hall as if he could see something Moiré could not. "Moiré, I'm not like y', I can't marry someone because Mam wants it so," he mumbled almost to himself.

"Maybe you should have," Moiré sighed and removed her hands from his shoulder. She stumbled over to the window on the far wall, which overlooked the playground. "It's really not that bad. At least, I know he will never break my heart."

"No, y' did that yourself." Declan eyed his sister, then rested his hand on her shoulder. "Please understand that I loved Meggie with all me heart. I know Mam thinks that the O'Briens were behind the shooting, but if so, why haven't they come after either of us since then?"

"Mam is scared. When you were unconscious, she told me that Meghan and Liam O'Brien planned the whole murder to get rid of you."

"Christ!" Declan grunted and dropped his head to the wall. "That's not true, Meggie knows nothing about the decree or the land. I told Mam that."

Moiré shook her head, not understanding how he could hold on to his love for Meghan for so long, particularly now. What if Caelan was his child? She could not understand how any woman could be so selfish as to keep a father from his child. "Declan, what about Caelan?"

"Caelan." A slight smile curled his lips momentarily, but it faded quickly when the thought of not being in her life struck him. "All these years, Meggie kept her from me. What would possess her to do such a thing?" he mumbled.

Moiré's shoulders rose in a quick shrug. "Declan, I don't know Dr. Coleman very well, but from what they say about her here in town, well, she seems very reclusive."

"Well, do y' blame her, after being jailed for a crime she didn't commit? I'm sure she would rather stay away from people."

"That was so long ago," Moiré interjected. "And the charges were dropped. Since being here, I have never heard anyone mention it."

Declan eyed her with annoyance. "Moiré, stop it! Y' will not change me mind. I am going to get me wife and child back if it's the last thing I do."

CHAPTER SEVENTEEN

Meghan was panic-stricken by the time she returned home to her large two-storey Victorian house. The kitchen door was open alerting her that Nathan was inside somewhere. The large kitchen at the back of the house was empty, so she bolted down the hall towards her office.

"Nat, are you here?"

"Yes, what is all the yelling about? You'd think you've seen a ghost," Nathan commented as he exited the living room, with an arm full of firewood he had just cut.

"I have, Declan is here in town. I saw him at Caelan's school. He has come to take her away from me!" Meghan cried.

Nathan dropped the wood to the area rug and engulfed Meghan in his arms. "Calm down, Megs, we have been over this before. He can't just take her from you. The courts will not take your child away from you after all these years just because he's famous. Besides, how do you even know he wants her?"

Meghan's response was interrupted when a short burley man barrelled through the kitchen door, covered in blood, straw, and a nasty-smelling slime.

"Molly had her foal, and she's beautiful. You need to come down to the barn," Kevin rambled, running his hand across his short blond hair.

Meghan and Nathan eyed each other, then bolted out the kitchen door and across the lawn to the enormous red barn. Molly had been placed in the end stall simply because it was closer to the door to Kevin's apartment. Kevin boarded at the ranch year round so he could take care of the many horses Meghan had accumulated over the years.

The cement floor felt hard under Meghan's feet as she ran down the centre aisle, anxious to see her new filly. Molly was licking her to remove the remnants of the embryonic sack, her dark brown eyes fixed on the three faces peering into the stall. The Palomino filly's eyes also found the group, but its attention soon changed as it struggled to its feet. The scrawny legs of the filly trembled, causing her to sway from side to side.

Kevin eventually disappeared upstairs to his small apartment in the back of the barn. Meghan had offered him a room in the barracks where the kids and councillors slept during the summer camp, but he preferred the room in the barn. Kevin had become part of the family and spent most of his time with Hayley when their work was complete.

Declan was very anxious as he turned under the large archway at the beginning of what appeared to be a long drive, but no house was in sight. The black metal sign at the top of the archway spelled out Lost Eagle Ranch, and he had to stop the jeep to catch his breath. The memory of their wedding day and the story the sleigh driver had told them came flooding back. Did she still have the statue he bought her? Why would she use that name after running from him all those years earlier? What in the hell was wrong with her? Why was she behaving this way? The agitation was building in him as he recounted the afternoon and the way she behaved at the school, the way she looked when he was holding Caelan. Was Caelan his child or the man named Coleman's?

Enormous fields bordered the driveway framed by white fences. Horses frolicked across the lush green fields welcoming the arrival of spring. She had told him years earlier that she wanted to run a summer camp for special needs children at the ranch her grandfather had left her. Why hadn't he thought of it before now? Maybe he would have been able to track her down before now. He shook his head and focused on the large white Victorian house that emerged from the trees.

Declan slowed the jeep when he reached the main house, but he was so unsure of what he was doing, he almost turned around. He had been dreaming of the day that he found her for so long, but this was not the way his dream went. She was supposed to run to his arms when she saw him, not run away. He certainly did not expect to see fear in her eyes.

As he headed towards the big two-storey white house, he saw the wind chimes he had given her, so many years ago. They were hanging from a large covered veranda that wrapped around the majority of the house. A feeling of peace came over him. She must still love him if she had kept them for all these years.

The upper floor of the house divided into four wings that jutted out over the lower floor. A little window was visible, tucked up under the gable at the top of the house that appeared to be a small room in the attic. A rock chimney rose from three sides of the house adding a rustic charm to the grand structure. Flush against the house at the end of the veranda were blooming lilac bushes, the new blooms sending the fragrance drifting through the air towards him.

The railing and pillars on one corner of the veranda were engulfed in a large clematis vine, which covered the area with a mass of green foliage. A large flowerbed surrounded the veranda and came to a stop at the wide stairs, leading from the veranda to the flagstone path. The path weaved through the lush green grass, then separated with one path leading to the driveway and the other to the garage off to the side of the house.

Declan swung around towards the enormous red barn when he heard Nathan coming out, and a sudden chill ran the length of his body.

"Megs, I'll go get Caelan and tell her that her foal is here. I think she might be with Hayley and Anisha," Nathan shouted as he left the barn and headed for a smaller building off to the left of the barn.

Declan was quite relieved to see Nathan. If he was still around, then maybe there was no other man in her life. However, a chill ran down his spine as it occurred to him that maybe Nathan was the father of Caelan. The thought of Meghan being with another man made his stomach ache. He shook his head trying to clear it of his ridiculous ideas, but then the last name became clear. Nathan Coleman. Had she married him? What in the hell was going on? Caelan called him Uncle Nat. He felt his knees go weak as he began to stride over towards the barn, fighting the urge to turn around and leave, fearing her rejection.

As he got to the large opening in the barn, he could see Meghan inside standing by a stall, looking down admiring something inside. She was still as beautiful as she was the day they met. Her hair was much longer and still the beautiful auburn colour that he loved so much. He moved slowly and quietly across the floor until he was right behind her and then gently laid his hand on her shoulder.

She jumped slightly, then lifted her hand placing it on his. As her fingers touched his skin, a surge of excitement filled him with a sensation he had not felt since she last touched him.

"Oh, Nat, she's so beautiful," Meghan cooed, assuming it was Nathan behind her.

"Nothing's as beautiful as y'," Declan stated in a very soft voice.

Meghan recognized the voice and a bolt of fear shot through her. Excitement and terror tangled together, and she was unsure which emotion was going to be the victor. She slowly turned around and fought the tears that had built up in her terrified eyes and began to drip down her cheek.

"Please don't take Caelan away from me! She is all I have in the world," Meghan begged as she stared at him, fear exploding from her eyes.

"Take Caelan?" Her face once again betrayed her, as it had so often in the past, telling him that what he had suspected was true. Caelan was his child. He grabbed her trembling hands, holding them snugly against his chest. The feel of her hands on him was sending waves of ecstasy through his entire body.

"Is she me daughter?" he finally asked.

"Yes," Meghan sniffed and pulled her hands away from him.

Declan grabbed her arm, pulled her towards him, and engulfed her in his arms, letting her melt into him once more. She was so overwhelmed to be back in his arms, she had never felt so at one with anyone else. However, she knew that the moment would not last, he would soon get to his reason for being there, and she still was unprepared to deal with losing Caelan as she was, years earlier.

"I don't want to be the man who causes that look of pain in your eyes," Declan mumbled into her hair as he held her tightly to him for what seemed like an eternity. He was too afraid to let her go as he prayed all the years they had lost would vanish.

The moment was broken, however, when they heard voices coming towards them. Caelan's excited voice raising above all the other noises. Meghan pulled away and turned to wipe the tears from her eyes, not wanting Caelan to see her upset.

"Mr. Montgomery, what are you doing here?" A small voice from behind him spoke up, the sound piercing his heart. It was the soft sweet voice of his daughter, a word so foreign, yet so welcomed.

Turning towards the sound, he eyed Caelan with complete fulfillment, he was a father, and no one could ever take that away from him, Not even his mother. No matter what happened in his life, the child running towards him would be his forever.

"Are you here to tell her about Lucas?" Caelan crooked her finger at him, and he bent down towards her. "She isn't mad. I think you hugging her made her forget how bad I was."

Declan glanced up at Meghan, noticing her cringe from the comment. How much did the child know about their past? "Y' weren't bad, wee one, y' just have to stop letting that lad get to y'."

Caelan smiled and grabbed his hand. "Mr. Montgomery, since you're here, maybe you could come to the house for tea. I bet Hayley would make cookies for you."

Declan started to laugh at the expression on her face. "You're a delightful wee girl." He rubbed his hand across her head.

"Caelan, I don't think Mr. Montgomery wants to spend his time having tea with Hayley, he's a busy man," Meghan muttered, trying to keep him from having too much contact with her life.

"I'd love to meet this Hayley," Declan smiled. "But I don't suppose y' would care to join us, knowing the way y' feel about actors."

"Oops," Caelan muttered and covered her mouth with her little hand.

"Caelan, what did you say?" Meghan grimaced at the thought.

"Nothing y' haven't told me before, Freckles," Declan laughed at the remembrance of her comments at the lodge. "I'm not surprised that y' fill this dear child's head with the same opinions." Declan's voice was light, but she could hear a tone of annoyance building.

"Where is the foal?" Anisha bolted through the doors, stopping dead at the sight of the large strange man. "Who are you?"

Declan turned towards the little girl. Her dark mocha eyes and light brown skin enhanced her round face. "And who might y' be." He was curious.

"Anisha, she lives here," Caelan informed him as Anisha rushed to Meghan's side, her hands gripping onto Meghan's. "Please, Auntie Meghan, can I see the foal?"

"She's in the last stall, sweetie," Meghan smiled softly at the girl and bobbed her head towards the stall at the end of the barn. "Both of you go and look, just don't make a lot of noise, you'll scare Molly." Meghan however stayed, her gaze fixed back on Declan and his wonderful grey eyes. All her old feelings were surging upwards, setting her senses off balance.

Caelan smiled with glee and gripped onto Anisha's hand, but when she passed Meghan, she stopped and stared up at her. "Why were you crying, Mommy?"

"I'm just happy that the foal is born, you know me, I'll cry at anything." Meghan tried to explain, but her comment was cut short when Declan started to chuckle.

"I'm sorry." His voice light with humour as he watched her crinkle her nose at him. A wave of longing flowed through him at the sight; her little quirks still caused his heart to flutter.

"Mommy, can I show the kids when they come next time?" Caelan blurted out, not particularly interested in Declan's laughter.

"Sure, peanut. What are you going to name her?" Meghan questioned, directing her gaze on Caelan, hoping to calm her nerves.

"I don't know, maybe . . ." She put her little hand up to her face and taped her mouth with her finger. "Dallas."

"Dallas, why that?" Meghan questioned, her eyes back on Declan.

"Because that's where I was born, right? And that's where Uncle Nat is from," Caelan shrieked with excitement.

"I guess that would be a good name," Meghan said nervously, her eyes settling on Nathan, who had now entered the barn.

"Uncle Nat, her name is Dallas," Caelan said, turning to Nathan with excitement.

"That's great, darlin'," Nathan smiled, his brow rising with interest. What would Meghan do if Declan were to express interest in her again? He knew well enough Meghan had never lost her love for Declan, and with Caelan as a constant reminder, her thoughts had never strayed too far from him.

"Hi, Nat, it's good to see y'," Declan said pleasantly, as he moved towards him, his hand out in greeting.

"Hi, it's great to see you again. So what brings you out here?"

"Well," Declan's eyed Nathan curiously. He had always felt that Nathan did not approve of his relationship with Meghan, but now he seemed almost pleased to see him. "I came out to visit me sister and stumbled upon Meggie."

"It's a small world, isn't it?" Nathan forced an agreeable smile.

"Aye, it is," Declan sighed and glanced over at Meghan as she tried to occupy herself by watching the foal. He could see, however, that she was trembling. Was it out of excitement or something else?

"So, you didn't come to fight Megs for custody?" Nathan questioned, deciding to get right to the point.

"Why would I do that? Is that why she kept her a secret?" Declan's face filled with concern.

"You didn't know about Caelan?" Nathan asked, rather confused since he was with Meghan when she went to Los Angeles to meet with Declan's mother.

"No, how would I, she didn't tell me!" Declan's voice was slightly edged with annoyance as the thought occurred to him that Meghan did not intend to tell him he had a daughter.

"I think you two have a lot to discuss," Nathan informed Declan as he tried to absorb the fact that his mother had kept the information from Declan.

"Declan, please don't get too mad with her. She thought you knew about Caelan, and she had a good reason for not forcing her on you." Nathan tried to explain, hoping to avoid any impulsive moves on Declan's part.

"Good reason! What reason could possibly be good enough? She kept me from me own child for five years. I've missed out on her life," Declan said angrily, the thought of him having an heir that would secure his claim to the land over in Ireland filled his mind. That was something he had not thought about in a few years. Why was it strong in his mind again, or was it the sight of Meghan or just his anger? Whatever it was, he needed to calm himself.

As Declan's voice rose, Meghan could hear the tone and see the redness creeping up Declan's neck. She had seen the expression on his face before, and she did not want it prolonged.

"I think it's time we talked. I guess I can't put this off any longer," Meghan said, with forced calmness, grabbed him by the arm, and pulled him towards the house.

The silence was deafening, as they walked towards the house, neither being able to look at the other. Meghan's mind was spinning out of control as she tried to decide how to explain to him what happened that night and what his parents had done in the days and months to follow. Her heart was racing with fear, leaving her lightheaded and somewhat disoriented. When she stumbled, Declan glanced over becoming quite concerned as the blood drained from her face, leaving her skin almost grey.

"Are y' okay? Y' look rather pale," Declan questioned, turning towards her when she stopped and blinked at him a few times.

"I think so, I just feel weak," she muttered, right before everything in her vision blurred. Her hand flailed out in front of her, as she grabbed for a tree, but she missed and fell to the ground with a thud.

"Meggie!" Declan shouted and bent over her limp body. He scooped her into his arms, cradling her against his chest. "Meggie, wake up," he muttered as his hand swept across her face. "Please, Freckles." Declan was on his feet and trudging across the lawn towards the house.

"What's going on?" Hayley was already at the top of the porch steps by the time Declan noticed her.

"She fainted." Declan panted, glancing around for somewhere to sit down.

"Put her down on the swing, and I will get a cold cloth!" Hayley rambled, pointing frantically at the hanging swing on the porch. The excited girl disappeared into the house to fetch a cloth, leaving Declan alone on the swing with Meghan's limp body.

Declan sat down on the swing, laid her across his lap, and ran his hand through her hair stoking the soft area behind her ear. His voice was soft and comforting as he rambled until she slowly began to stir.

One eye slowly opened, then the other, her lashes fluttering slightly, trying to focus on her surroundings. A smile broke at the corners of her mouth as her dark green eyes settled on his face. He bent down and kissed her forehead, totally overwhelmed with the sensation of her skin under his hand.

"Here's the cloth." Hayley bounded across the porch, stopping suddenly, her mocha eyes focused on Declan. "You're Declan Montgomery," she blurted out.

"I know," he said, raising his dark brow.

"Oh my God, what are you doing here?" she babbled as her eyes danced with delight.

"I came to visit with Meggie. We're old friends." His voice was calm, but it definitely had an edge of worry to it. Why didn't this girl know about him, and come to think about it, no one in town seemed to be in possession of the information either. Meghan had apparently told no one of their marriage and the fact that he was Caelan's father.

"Meghan, you never told me he was coming. You're the actor that was in town?" Hayley rambled with excitement. "Does Caelan know you're here?"

"Hayley," Meghan blurted out as Declan's face filled with a grin. Meghan did confide in this girl, but why her and why only her?

"So, y' know I'm Caelan's father?" Declan questioned, ignoring Meghan's annoyance with her friend.

Hayley nodded, her eyes still glued to him. "I've known since she found out she was pregnant."

Declan's face filled with confusion and then he glanced at Meghan for an explanation. "Hayley was my cell mate."

"Oh!" Declan shuffled on the swing. "Well, it's nice to meet y'. I take it y' are the mother of the wee girl in the barn. She's a mighty pretty lass."

"Thank you." Hayley beamed and glanced at Meghan, noticing her gesturing her head towards the house.

"Well, I'll leave you alone, I'm sure you have plenty to talk about," Hayley commented, not wanting to leave the famous man on the swing. She was gazing down at Meghan cradled in Declan's arms and smiled.

"Thank you, Hayley, why don't you take some cookies to Caelan and Anisha, they're in the barn," Meghan said firmly, her eyes squinting with annoyance.

Hayley begrudgingly agreed, then disappeared into the house, leaving them alone to deal with the past, present, and possibly future.

"Meggie," Declan sighed as Meghan sat up and stared at him with a look of a lost deer. "I just need to know why?"

Meghan chewed at her bottom lip as she pondered his question. "Well, I . . ." She stopped, not knowing where to start. Should she tell him about his parents, his brother, or about Fabrizio? No, not Fabrizio, there was no need to drag him into the mess.

"Please, Freckles, I need to know why you would keep me daughter from me?" His voice pleaded with her, but she could hear an edge of anger rising.

"I tried to tell you, but your mother threatened me and . . ." Meghan stopped and gazed out over the pasture to the south. "I couldn't lose her to you or anyone else."

"What does me mam have to do with this? I want to know what made y' feel that y' had the right to keep me child from me?" he demanded.

"I was scared. Your parents convinced the judge not to grant me bail because she accused me of threatening her life. I was stuck in prison, Declan."

"I know!" His voice was even sharper. "Meggie, they dropped those charges. I came to the prison to see you after the trial, but they wouldn't let me in and then when I finally got permission to come visit during Sunday visiting hours, y' were gone. Where did y' go, why didn't y' come to me and tell me we were having a child?"

"I did, I came to Los Angeles, but your mother said that our marriage . . ." She stopped and bit her lip again. Why had she mentioned that, it was over years ago?

Declan stared at her for a moment, then sighed, trying to control his anger with her. "I can't believe that I would have married such a deceiving woman. I should have listened to me mam."

Meghan jumped from the swing, attempting to bolt into the house, but he had a grip on her arm before she made it three feet. She still had that flight instinct, he thought as he jerked her back towards him.

"Don't think y' are running from this," he grunted with anger. "We have to decide what we are going to do about our marriage?"

"What?" Meghan babbled. "I thought you had it annulled, I signed the papers that your mother gave me."

"Papers, what papers?" Declan questioned with confusion. "I never had it annulled."

Meghan stared at him, with pain shooting from her eyes. "Well, just make up new ones, and I'll sign."

"No!" he hollered, interrupting her comment. "It's not that easy now, is it? We have a child to consider." He had no intension of allowing her to blow him off so easily. "Y' are unbelievable. Did y' take your vows so lightly that y' can just disregard them so easily?"

"That was five years ago," she sniffed, completely overwhelmed with his response to her comment. "A lot has happened in that time and—"

"Well, if that is how y' feel. I will call me lawyer and make arrangement for Caelan."

"No, you can't take her from me," Meghan cried, the thought terrified her to her soul. "Please, Declan, I'll do anything, but please don't take her from me."

Declan's heart felt as though someone was ripping it from his chest. He knew he was causing her pain, yet he wanted to hurt her. However, he could not take Caelan away from her, anymore than he could give her up. He could barely think straight, and the last thing he wanted to do was to say something he would regret.

"I have to go," he blurted out having the overpowering need to put some distance between them, so he could straighten out his thoughts. "I know there is something y' aren't telling me. I'll give y' time to decide if your secret is worth losing your daughter over."

"Declan, please," Meghan cried. "You have to understand."

The pain was overflowing from her eyes. It was obvious that she was hiding something, but what? She seemed to be so frightened of revealing her secret she had kept inside for so many years.

"I can't be near y' right now. I'm scared of what I might say, but don't think this is over. She is me child too, and we are going to figure out a way to handle it. I won't go another day without her in me life."

"Come back for dinner?" Meghan was unsure why she asked, but it was too late to take it back.

"Aye." Declan turned and walked off the porch towards his jeep, leaving Meghan stunned by what had happened. She was not sure what he was going to do, he was so angry. Had she hurt him so deeply that he would never forgive her? Meghan watched helplessly as he drove the jeep down the driveway and out of sight.

CHAPTER EIGHTEEN

The sun was setting over the hills when Meghan walked out onto the porch to watch for Declan. It was still very warm, but there was a soft breeze coming from the west. She watched as the wind chimes swung in the breeze, the soft high tinkling sound she always found so comforting resonated through the air.

As the time ticked by, and Declan did not arrive as promised, she headed to the barn to check on the foal. She was hoping that it would occupy her mind and release the tension that had built to a bursting point.

She was half way across lawn when lights grew visible from an approaching car. A sharp tug of anxiety shot though her, freezing her in place like a deer caught in headlights.

Declan climbed from the jeep, and Meghan found it hard to take her eyes off him. He was wearing a Boston Red Sox baseball cap on backwards, giving him a very youthful appearance, along with a dark green T-shirt that hung loosely over the top of the tan shorts that exposed his long muscular legs dusted with black hair.

"Hi," she said, eyeing him in the fading light. "I thought maybe you weren't coming."

"I said I would, didn't I?" His voice was cool as his eyes scanned her light blue sundress judgmentally.

"Yes," she muttered, wishing he had not come. His aloof demeanour was ripping at her heart, and she was fighting the urge to run for the hills. "Come inside." She waved her hand towards the large deck.

Declan stared at her with a veiled expression she could not read. His hand rose towards her, but when she reached for it, he swung it towards the house. "After y'."

Meghan jerked her hand back unsure what to say after his deliberate refusal of her hand. She turned abruptly and walked quickly up onto the porch and through the front door without looking back.

Declan was determined to stay cool with her until she told him the truth, but he felt the warmth of the house instantly. Family pictures adorned the walls of the hall. A doll stroller filled to the brim with assorted stuffed animals sat against the wall next to the settee, and lying on the settee was a small pink umbrella. The staircase was the focal point in the foyer, as it graciously flowed to the second floor. The railing was constructed of thick oak, the lightwood matching the floor that stretched out in three directions. Off to his right, where Meghan was standing, was an office, the desk and tables cluttered with papers, and a doll was propped up in the chair overseeing the clutter. A hallway led to the back of the house and into a large room he assumed was the kitchen. A set of glass French doors off the front hallway led into the dining room, and he could see the reflection of the table in the mirror that hung on the wall.

He felt inner peace. When he was a small child back in Ireland, his houses showed evidence of children, a truck or boat lying about. However, once they moved to the mansion in Boston, that all changed. He and his siblings were not permitted to play anywhere but in their rooms. A nanny replaced their mother, and their father was away in Washington the majority of the time. Meghan had provided a warm loving home for his daughter.

Meghan gestured towards the large room off to his left, and he refocused and sauntered past her into the large living room. It was a big house, but it was laid out perfectly, giving it a very welcoming feel to it.

"Please sit down," Meghan muttered, her hand was trembling as she held it out towards the couch.

His mouth twitched slightly at one corner, as if he meant to say something, but he kept quiet as she moved across the room, away from him.

"Would you like something to drink?" Meghan asked nervously, fussing with her long ginger waves.

"A beer if y' have it," he muttered, his gaze left her and scanned the room, stopping on the baby pictures of Caelan on the fireplace mantle.

Meghan quickly moved through the opening at the other end of the living room, into the large kitchen at the back of the house where Nathan was raiding the refrigerator.

"Sorry, but I have no food in my fridge. I have nothing to feed Caelan. I'll be gone in a minute."

"Nat, you know they have a big building in town called a grocery store. They sell food there. Maybe you should check it out," Meghan said rather sharply.

"Why, when I can come here anytime I'm hungry?" Nathan joked, ignoring her tone as he filled his arms with food.

"Jeez, Nat, do you have enough? Maybe you should take the dinner in the oven too."

"No, thanks, darlin'. I want to live past tonight."

"Shut up. I'm sure it will be good." Her fears were dangerously close to the surface, and she was fighting to stay in control of her emotions.

"I can't believe you're cooking for him. Is that your way of dealing with the situation? By killing him off?"

"No, why are you so mean?" Meghan cried as tears began to fill her eyes. She contorted her face, trying to stop them from erupting, which drew Nathan's attention.

"Megs, are you okay?" Nathan lowered the stolen food to the counter.

"No," she muttered, wiping at her eyes. "He hates me."

"No, he doesn't. He's just upset." Nathan soothed, lowering his voice to a comforting murmur.

Meghan scrubbed her hand across her face and dropped to the stool in front of the long island.

"Megs, just tell him the truth. He will never understand why you kept Caelan a secret if you don't."

"God, how am I going to tell him?" she sniffed. "He doesn't think his family did anything wrong. And how do I explain my mother?"

"Simply," he whispered. "You don't need to go into detail."

She shook her head to regain composure and jumped from the stool. "I guess I either tell him now, or I will have to watch him glaring at me all night."

"Good. But if he doesn't like your explanation, you could always feed him that dinner," Nathan smirked, bobbing his head towards the oven.

"I'm sure it will be fine. Hayley said."

"Oh, Hayley made it? All you have to do is cook it. Well, don't burn it," he said in full smile.

Meghan shook her head at him. "I won't, I'm not an idiot you know."

"I never said you were. I just said you're a crappy cook," Nathan chuckled and walked with his armful of food towards the kitchen door. "Bye, darlin'. Good luck."

"Yeah, bye, and don't let Caelan sleep on the floor," Meghan shouted after him.

"Sure, darlin'," he replied, not listening to her orders.

Meghan grabbed two Guinnesses and headed back to the living room, where Declan was sitting, listening to the conversation in the kitchen. He was fighting hard to stay annoyed after hearing the pain in her voice while she talked with Nathan. The thought of being the person causing her so much distress was ripping at his heart, but he was still very angry with her for keeping Caelan from him.

"So, does Nathan live here with y'?" Declan grunted, his tone more hostile than he intended.

"No, he lives in that house across the yard, on the other side of the barn," Meghan mumbled, handing the Guinness to him and sitting down in the farthest chair from him.

"Oh," he sighed and eyed the bottle. She remembered he liked Guinness. Where had she gotten it? They did not sell it in town anywhere; he had checked.

"What store sells this?" he questioned, holding up the bottle.

Meghan shrugged and eyed his smirking face. "Dinner should be ready soon. Are you hungry?" She changed the subject, not wanting him to know that she had Nathan drive into Great Falls to buy it.

Meghan's face was still so transparent, and he knew right away that she had put some effort into obtaining the Guinness. That was a good sign. Now if he could just get her to tell the truth. What could be so bad? She was trembling, why was she trembling?

"Meggie, y' invited me here because y' have something to tell me. So tell me. I want to know what could possibly make y' keep Caelan a secret."

His smoky eyes were too intense. How was she to start? Could she stand those intense eyes filling with pity? She stood and walked over to the fireplace mantle, lifting Caelan's baby picture. She turned and stared at him, her long dark lashes fluttering across her sad green eyes.

"Meggie, just get on with it!" Declan said sharply, the anticipation was ripping him apart. "Please just tell me."

"Okay, the night we were shot."

"I'm really not interested in remembering that night. I have spent enough time thinking about it. Just tell me why y' lied to me."

"If you would stop interrupting me, I could tell you," Meghan snapped, directing her flaming eyes at him.

He flung his hands towards her in an annoyed gesture as he eyed her narrowly, waiting for her answer.

"I have to talk about that night," she continued. "That is where it started."

"Fine," he sighed with annoyance, but secretly enjoyed the sight of her flaring eyes. How her eyes excited him, almost as if they reached in and touched his soul.

"Well, why did you . . ." She stopped and eyed him with concern.

"Why did I what?" His voice was clipped.

"When Ian came into the room, you called him Rory." She eyed him to assess his reaction.

"What!" he growled.

"You told me it was your brother Rory. He's the one that shot you. Then Eliza, who we found out is my mother, came in. She watched while the man with the beard beat me. Then they framed me for murder. It was me they were after; you just got in the way. Then when Fabrizio questioned your mother about Ian being Rory, she said she was going to take Caelan, and I would never see her again. I couldn't lose her, she is all I have," Meghan blurted out and ran from the room, sobbing. She darted out onto the porch and down the stairs, into the night, with Declan close behind her.

"Meggie, wait!" Declan yelled as the reality of what she was hiding took hold of his spinning mind. It was all becoming clear to him. Was it Rory! God dammit, did his brother shoot him!

Meghan ignored his shouts and continued to run across the lawn, she could not face him. Why was he protecting the man that shot him?

Declan was gaining on her as she bolted across the lush grass towards a big apple tree. When she was within arm's length, he grabbed her around the waist, hauling her to the ground. She struggled to get up, but he would not loosen his grip. Her hands flew up and wildly swung at his head in sheer panic. She thrashed beneath him as she desperately tried to wiggle loose from his grip, causing every fibre in her body to burn with the heat of shame and terror.

Declan's heart was racing as he stared down at her. Her eyes were closed, blocking him out. What was she thinking? She must hate him.

"Meggie, please look at me," Declan asked softly, wanting to see her thoughts.

"Declan, let me go. Please just leave me alone," Meghan sniffed and covered her face with her hands when he released his grip on her arms.

"Freckles, please." He pried her hands from her face, resting his own hand down in replacement. "I'm sorry I don't remember. Are you sure I said that?"

A tremor slid through her at the sensation, she had always loved it when he held her face; his hands were so large and gentle. Slowly her eyes opened, and she stared up at him with pain and shame shooting from her beautiful big green eyes. He swallowed deeply, not knowing what to say to her to soothe her fears. He was overwhelmed by the fact that her own mother allowed someone to harm her. What did Meghan's mother have to do with Ian or possibly Rory? He was terrified that she was right, and Rory was the one that shot him. What was happening?

"Meggie, I don't understand why you think this is your fault?"

Meghan eyed him with worry. "It was a set up. I . . . ." Her eyes closed again. "It's my fault."

"Meggie, none of it was your fault." Declan soothed, trying to coax the rest of the information.

"It is. They were all there for me. Ian, my mother, and the other men." Meghan cringed as Declan stiffened on top of her.

"Ian? The man that was stalking y' years ago. That is who I said was Rory. So you think it was Rory stalking y'?"

"I don't know. All I know is that you called him Rory," She blurted out and sat up as Declan rolled off her. "He seemed very upset when he shot you. It is all still so hazy from that point on. I do know, however, that there were two other men there. One was big, bigger than the rest of them."

"Who was it?" Declan felt his stomach tighten. During the trial, he vaguely remembered her talking about the other man.

"I don't know. Eliza showed up just before the trial, but she said there was no one else there. But I know there was. Eliza said she had evidence to help the case, but Nathan did not want her testifying in case she changed her story again on the stand. He felt she was making up stories to frame me."

Declan sighed and wrapped his arm around her shoulder. "I'm sorry about your mam."

Meghan forced a smile and stared off into the distance. "I thought it hurt before that she didn't want me, but to discover that she is involved in a murder plot against me is horrifying. I live in fear, not knowing if they are coming back."

"That would explain the illusiveness here in town and the different name," Declan smiled as he put the pieces together.

"I took Nat's name. Everyone here in town believes that I got married before I moved back. They think Nathan is my brother-in-law," Meghan sighed, regretting allowing the lie to grow as big as it has. "I never saw any reason to change their minds at first, but as the years went on, the lie grew so big that I couldn't stop it. I just didn't know what to do."

"Well, that's what happens when y' lie." Declan's voice was slightly judgmental. "Eventually y' get caught."

Meghan nodded but did not make eye contact with him.

"The FBI tried to locate Eliza and Ian after the trial, but they seem to have disappeared. Fabrizio thinks they have left the country. He thinks that they are involved in a deeper conspiracy linked to the European mob." Her life was unravelling before her. "And there is no evidence of Ian ever existing, that's why Fabrizio thinks he is Rory."

"Fabs, y' still have contact with him?" Declan eyed her with interest; he had lost contact many years ago.

"Yes, he . . ." Meghan stuttered before Declan's attention switched to her earlier comment.

"What would this group want with y'?" Declan got preoccupied with his thoughts, and he felt the hair on the back of his neck bristle.

"Nat thinks it has to do with land I apparently own over in Ireland." She eyed Declan slightly as he twitched from her comment.

"Y' have land?"

"Yes, but my grandfather had it so well hidden that we haven't been able to figure out where it is. All we know is that it is leased out, and the money is funnelled through a bank account in the Cayman Islands. My grandfather's lawyer refuses to turn over the deed to me."

Declan's face had drained of colour as he listened to her information. "Meggie, how long have y' known about this land?"

"Well, Nathan suspected there was property in trust somewhere because the income began to show up in my trust fund. Actually just before I met you, Nathan began to suspect something wasn't right with my grandfather's estate."

"Hmm." Declan eyed her with interest. So she knew about the land, but what about the decree? Did she know that the land was in the hands of the O'Briens? But if that was the case, then how was she getting income from the estate? Something was not right; it could not be the same land.

Meghan flopped back on the grass and stared up at the stars. A few short days ago, her world was at peace, but now it is in shambles, and she was not sure how she was going to fix all the damage.

Declan watched her struggling with her thoughts, and it was ripping at his heart. Should he walk away from her? If he did, however, he would never know if what they had was still present. He never wanted to settle down with anyone, but five years earlier, he had made the decision to do so. At that time, his decision was fuelled by his need to take back from her, what was rightfully his family's. Now, however, his life had become filled with parties and travelling, and settling down had been the last thing he wanted for the last few years. But Meghan had been out of the picture. Now as he watched her staring up at the stars, he wondered if the need to be with her was just old emotions or something more.

Declan's lips landed softly on Meghan's forehead, causing her eyes to close and a quiet sigh too exited her. His lips lingered on her forehead before moving to her cheek and then to her trembling mouth. His hands slid across her cheeks into her hair, holding her head tightly, not wanting the kiss to end.

She wrapped her arms around his ribs, clinging to his back as tightly as she could, hoping that somehow it would stop the terrifying thoughts that were running through her head. Did he want her back, or was he only interested in Caelan?

After a few enchanting minutes, Declan slowly lifted his lips from hers and kissed her nose. "Oh, Meggie, why didn't y' tell me this before? I would have helped y' through it. Didn't y' trust me?" he sighed, brushing his thumb across her cheek.

"I tried, Declan, but your parents wouldn't let me near you," she said more softly than she intended to.

"Freckles, I'm sorry for that. I was unconscious for over two weeks, and when I came to, I couldn't remember what happened."

"You couldn't remember me," Meghan muttered as a statement, not a question.

"No," he sighed. "I felt a deep loss, but I couldn't understand why."

She nodded her head and raised her hand to his face. "Fabrizio snuck me into see you. He didn't believe that I shot you." Her eyes scanned his face, as her hand traced out the strong features. "I spent over an hour touching you and trying to memorize your face."

"Fabs is a smart man," Declan smiled and bent down kissing her nose. A smile curled his lips, and he pressed his face hard against hers. "I think I knew all along that y' were there, trying to bring me back. I'm sorry it took so long."

She forced a smile and closed her eyes. "It was horrible the way everyone treated me. I tried telling them that Ian did it, but no one believed me. After you remembered and told them what happened, the charges were dropped, but . . ."

"Meggie," he sighed and kissed her cheek. "I was so mad at y' for leaving me, I never gave any thought to what y' went through."

Tears slowly dripped out of the corners of Meghan's eyes and then grew into a strong, steady stream down her cheeks. Declan sighed and rolled to his side, pulling her into his arms and pressing his face tightly against hers. She sobbed hysterically over the life she had lost all those years earlier. His hand glided through her long hair, nudging its way through the tangles that had formed during her struggles. She pressed her head against him, too frightened to move. The strong thud of his heart, and his deep even breath was loud against her cheek as she desperately tried to think of a way to freeze time so the moment would never end.

As if in slow motion, his hands moved towards her face, suddenly gripping her with a desire he had not felt in a long time. His mouth twitched slightly, as if a smile was forming, but it never appeared. He was not talking, not smiling; he was simply staring at her with an unbreakable gaze. Meghan's brow rose ever so slightly as she fought the urge to break the silence between them and interrupt the trance he seemed to be in.

"Oh, Meggie," he finally muttered as he pulled her face towards his, wrapping his lips around hers. His kiss was intense and full of passion, causing her breath to catch in her throat. Her body surged towards him, with an overpowering sense of subservience. Even after five years, his kiss still forced any form of resistance in her to disappear and cause her to give herself to him completely. It was as terrifying as it was arousing.

His hands wrapped around her back, and he pulled her with him, positioning her on his chest. Her hair surrounded his face like a veil of amber, and her aroma was driving him into complete desire. He wanted her so badly; he could not focus on anything else.

Her bare shoulders were soft under his hands as he trailed his fingers down her arms to her hands that were gripping his face. His fingers slipped down her back as if they were reacquainting themselves with every inch of her, pressing slightly on every vertebra on their way down. One large hand settled on the arch of her back as the other moved back up her ribs to her shoulder. Suddenly he gripped his fingers around her upper arm, flipping her off him to the ground below. He rolled on top of her, imprisoning her under his large torso.

Her body trembled slightly as his hands slid up her arms, pinning them to the ground, his thumbs brushing gently across her wrists. Meghan squirmed slightly from the pressure on her wrist, but he merely lifted his head slightly, gazing down at her, his eyes piercing through her. His face was stern, and she was not sure what he was thinking, which slightly scared her. She could feel the desire in him, but it was different somehow.

Declan's face lowered towards hers; his kiss was hard and demanding, and his lips pressuring hers to part, allowing his tongue to flicker across hers. The large hands slid back down her arms, one hand continuing down her ribs, trailing tauntingly down her thigh. He needed her, and he needed her now.

She squirmed slightly as his hand slipped under her dress and moved back up her thigh with a persuasive force to her hip. In response to her movement, he pressed his mouth hard against her lips. His fingers gripped her panties and jerked them down her legs, startling her. Meghan involuntarily wrenched her hips away from his hand, reached down, and tugged at his arm.

"What are you doing?" Her voice shook as she pressed her other hand against his shoulder to push him away.

"Meggie, I need y', and I can't go another day without having y'." His eyes were filled with lust.

"Declan, I don't think we should," she muttered, continuing to push on his shoulders, but now with an edge of panic.

"Why?" he asked rather impatiently.

"I just don't!"

"Meggie, I have waited five years to be with y' again, and I won't wait a minute more." His lips landed on hers again, stifling any further complaint.

Meghan began to shift under him in a feeble attempt to remove him from her. She was not even sure she wanted him to stop. She had also been dreaming of feeling him within her for years, and her body was welcoming his touch.

"Meggie, please," he mumbled against her lips.

She wanted him as badly as he wanted her, she could not deny it. She nodded her head, then buried her face into his neck, feeling the rush of desire shoot through her veins. With her body relaxing to his touch, he moved his hand off her chest and unzipped his shorts. His hand moved back between her legs, causing a quiet moan in her throat as he stroked the dampening area.

A soft whimper left her lips as he spread her legs apart with his knee and thrust himself inside her. His head lifted, and he gazed at her with concern at the strange noise. The long dark lashes fluttered across the sea of green before they closed, completely blocking out his gaze. Damn, she was closing herself off from him, why wouldn't she look at him.

"Freckles?" his voice was soft and soothing in her ear. "Don't shut me out, let me see your desire for me, give yourself to me." His lips landed on hers with a reassuring presence. He buried his face into her hair, which was fanned out on the ground, simmering in the moonlight. His reaction to the sensation of being with her again was primal, and he took no care with her. His hands were hard against her skin as he groped and fondled her body.

Meghan responded to the attack with her own, her nails raking his back, her teeth nipping at his shoulder. But the battering continued, and she began to slip into a daze. The pain becoming unbearable.

"Declan, you're hurting me," she complained, but he continued with his attack, slamming into her pelvis with a need so strong he could not stop.

"Meggie," his breath was heavy.

When he didn't soften his movements, Meghan slammed her hands against his chest. "Please, Declan." Her voice was full of pain.

Declan gripped her arms, pinning her to the ground beneath him, his fingers digging into the soft skin too tightly. His mouth ravishing hers, forcing down any further complaint. Her body arched against his as he pushed her through the pain to a bursting point. As the tremors fanned out from her core, she screamed and collapsed to the ground beneath him.

Meghan lay silently underneath him; her face buried in his hair, smelling the familiar scent of his body, the combination of perspiration and the musky cologne he still wore. Tears were dripping out of her eyes as she struggled to control her conflicting emotions that were threatening to explode with a fierce vengeance. She had never experienced anything like that before, and she wasn't sure if she ever wanted to again. What had she done?

It was some time before he lifted his head and looked at her, and he didn't like what he saw. "What's wrong?"

"Nothing," Meghan muttered, not wanting him to think of her as a prude. After all, his sexual experiences had most likely been extensive over the last few years, and she didn't want him knowing that she had only been with one other man since him.

"Meggie, I'm sorry."

"Don't be." Meghan forced a smile and rested her hand on his cheek. "I just . . . well, I wasn't expecting this to happen. It's all right." She lied. All right was the far from where her emotions were at that moment.

"Be that as it may, I shouldn't have taken y' that way." He knew he had been too rough with her. She was most likely expecting the gentleness of their previous lovemaking, not the ravaging that he inflicted on her. "I'm sorry, that was very selfish of me." He unsealed their bodies and rolled off her.

"Declan, don't be sorry," Meghan sighed and rolled onto her side and stared at him. She was sorry, though. She had most likely built up their past lovemaking into an extraordinary event, however, what had just happened left her feeling empty and somewhat guilty.

"Meggie, ever since the first moment I saw y', I haven't been able to get y' out of me mind, and I know that our lives have taken different paths then we had planned, but I can't help but wonder." He stopped and kissed her forehead, trying to calm himself. "Well, I wonder if we would have had a large family and maybe a place like this, where we could putter around and just be us."

Her brow rose slightly as she watched him stare off into the darkness. "Is that what you want?"

"Aye, it is so peaceful here. I find LA so demanding, and the people never leave me alone. I can't even go shopping for groceries without someone taking me picture. I just want a normal life with me family."

Meghan smiled and rested her hand on his face. "Are the pressures getting to you?"

"Aye, I don't mean to complain because I know it comes with the job, and I do make excellent money, but sometimes, I wish I could just yell at someone and not have it show up in some rag magazine that I have gone off the deep end."

"Well, brace yourself for more scandal, I'm sure when word gets out you have a wife and child hidden away in the back country of Montana, it will be smeared all over the papers." Meghan cringed at the thought that her whereabouts could become public knowledge, and her peaceful life would be destroyed. She forced a smile hoping for calmness.

Declan's face lightened, and he leaned towards her and kissed her forehead. "No, they won't bother to print that. It's true."

Meghan let out a morose laugh and rested her head on his shoulder. "You're so funny."

He smiled and kissed her head, not noticing the worry that was building in her eyes. "How I've missed y'."

"I've missed you too," Meghan smiled, closed her eyes, and took a deep breath.

"Meggie, are y' all right?" Declan's voice was soft in her ear.

"Yes," she whispered, her hand resting on his face. "Declan, I need to know something, and I'm probably an idiot to ask this, but, when Caelan was born and I phoned the Malibu house, the number was changed."

"Aye," he interrupted. "I had to change it because someone from the National Inquisitor got a hold of it and was phoning me all the time trying to get an interview. Me management company number never changed though." His eyes studied her face. She already knew that, he could see it in her eyes.

"I know. I phoned there and left a message, but you never phoned." She stopped as a sharp tinge of anxiety shot through her stomach.

"I never got the message," he sighed. "I thought maybe y' never called because me mam accused y' of blackmailing me da. I never knew she talked to y'," he sighed and kissed the side of her head.

"She was so cruel to me. Even after I was cleared, I met with her, and she knows about Caelan or at least that I was pregnant."

"What?" he blurted out, his body suddenly ridged. "How could she?"

"After I left a message at your management company, your mother phoned me and arranged for me to meet her in Los Angeles. She told me you would be there. I was so excited to see you, but of course, you weren't there, just she and Georgia. Georgia told me that you proposed to her. They said I needed to sign the annulment papers. They told me . . ."

"What? What did they tell y', Meggie?" He gripped her face as the strain began to appear again.

"Well, I said I couldn't sign an annulment since we consummated our marriage, and being Catholic, I wouldn't do it," she sniffed and wiped at her eyes that were beginning to leak. "Declan, I was showing, I was so hoping that you would be there, I wanted you to see what we created, but you weren't there."

"Oh, Meggie, if I knew they were meeting y', I would have been there. I looked for y' for months." He soothed and rested his head against her.

"Your mother noticed, and I felt a sudden excitement that she would embrace me and her grandchild but . . ."

"But what, what the hell did she do?" He panicked and gripped her face once again.

"Declan, she told me to get rid of it. She said I would never inflict my bastard child on her family."

"Bloody hell!" he growled, his eyes sharp and angry. "I can't believe her."

"I told her that my baby wasn't a bastard because we were married." She gripped his shirt out of panic. "She isn't."

"No, Freckles, she isn't." Declan soothed, unclenching her hands from his shirt and lifting them to his mouth. "She's our daughter, and she's a Montgomery."

"Declan, did you . . . Well, did you and Georgia . . ."

"Get married? Is that what you're wondering? No, we didn't," he told her firmly, assessing the question in her eyes. Damn his mother, why had she interfered in his life to the extent she had? He knew she had accused Meghan of blackmailing the family, but he thought she gave up that ridiculous path, but apparently, she found a different way to destroy his life. "Freckles, I swear to y' that I have never proposed to any other woman, especially Georgia."

Meghan's brow rose slightly as a slight sniff exited her. She was trying hard to compose herself in the haze of uncertainty that surrounded them. "You don't love her?"

Declan held back the smirk as her eyes glistened with hope. "No, I told y' years ago, I didn't, and nothing has changed. She is just a convenient escort." Something shadowed his face that Meghan did not like. "But, I'm kind of trapped."

"Trapped? Why?" Her voice was higher and more panicked than she had intended.

"Well, her father is backing me da, and he is up for re-election in the senate. I promised him I wouldn't do anything to upset Georgia or her family until after the election."

"But that's not until the fall." She looked away as the words exited her mouth. What was she doing? He never said he wanted anything to do with her, so why was she planning their future?

"Aye," Declan smirked, knowing he had her again. She was his for the taking, and no one was going to get in his way again. He just needed to figure out a way to corral her until after the election.

CHAPTER NINETEEN

The house was eerily quiet after Caelan's departure to school, as if showing Meghan how life would be with Caelan gone to Los Angeles. She smiled at the remembrance of the afternoon and evening before when they took Caelan on a picnic and told her that Declan was her father. She took it surprisingly well. Meghan ran her hand across her chest as her breath caught, as the memory of making love to Declan came flooding back. He made her feel so loved, the way he did when they first met. It was the way she remembered it to be. Not the rough way he took her on the lawn a few nights earlier. Could they get back what they once had? Did he want her back as his wife? He did mention the rings he gave her all those years ago and the fact that they were at his parent's house in Boston.

Meghan rambled around the house for over an hour before she ventured out to the barn to check on Dallas and her mother. The beautiful palomino filly was up and exploring the paddock that Kevin had moved them into for the day. Her mane was sticking straight into the air like a Mohawk as she ran aimlessly around the paddock.

Meghan loved spending time in the barn; it was a place of refuge when she was young. As an adult, it brought her peace to be around the horses.

"I don't know how y' keep your hands so soft with the amount of work y' do around here." Declan's voice rose slightly with humour.

Meghan swung around and sighed at the sight of him. She wished he would stop showing up and setting her totally off balance. "Caelan's at school."

"Aye, I came to see y'," he smiled and moved towards her. His eyes settled on her bare arms and the large bruises that circled them. "Good Lord, did I do that?"

Meghan glanced down as his fingers gently brushed over the area. "Yes."

"Oh, I'm so sorry." He appeared horrified. "Was I holding y' that tightly or do y' bruise easily?" He could not believe he had hurt her.

"Both." She forced a smile and eyed him speculatively. "I have never . . ." She stopped to edit her thoughts. "You were a little rough the other night."

"I'm sorry." His eyes left her arm and settled on her face that was showing signs of stress. "But last night . . . Well, that was wonderful."

Meghan smiled bashfully as she thought about the night before, when they had made love. "Yes, it was incredible." She lowered her gaze to the ground, worried that she was weak when it came to him. All he needed to do was kiss her and she was jumping into bed with him. "But I think we need to slow down and think about what we are doing. I am glad Caelan took it so well when we told her that you were her dad, but . . ." She stopped as he gripped her arm.

"Meggie, if me Mam wouldn't have interfered and kept y' away from me," his voice was soft and nervous, "well, I was wondering if we would be together now, the three of us?"

"Declan, how am I supposed to know if we would have survived all the pressures of daily life, a great deal of marriages end in divorce," Meghan muttered and turned her back on him.

"Meggie!" he grunted and moved in behind her. "That's not what I meant, and y' know it."

She sighed and reached down for a bucket of oats that was at her feet. "I really don't think it matters now, does it?"

"I think it does!" he growled, spinning her around, dislodging the bucket, which flew across the barn floor, scattering oats in its wake. He paused slightly, looking at the mess, then refocused. "I need to know, I need to know if y' loved me."

"Of course I did!" she snarled as her anger built. Why wouldn't he leave the past alone? What happened in the past needed to stay there, for her sanity.

His grip on her arm was firm, but she did not attempt to pull away. The dark green of her eyes stayed focused on the dark angry grey of his, neither willing to break the stare and retreat. Declan suddenly yanked her forward and enfolded her in his arms, kissing her hard. His lips were demanding and possessive, causing her body to instinctively react and surge forward; pressing up against him with a need so strong, she could not fight it. The feel, the taste, the smell, everything about him drew her back into him, controlling her power to reason, to object.

"Meggie," he whispered against her lips. However, he halted his comment and wiped the tears off her cheek. "Are y' all right?"

"Yes." She bobbed her head and pulled away from him. "We have to stop doing that. I just don't want this to be all about sex."

"Aye." He softly agreed, seeing how he was hurting her.

Her eyes left him and scanned the scattered oats. "I better get this cleaned up before Kevin comes home, or I'll never hear the end of it. He hates a messy barn." She moved with purpose towards a stall at the end of the barn, returning with a large broom.

"Here, let me do that, I made the mess," Declan offered, holding out his hand towards the broom.

She happily agreed and handed over the broom, then set the bucket right. "I'll hold the dust pan."

"Y' mean the oat pan," he smiled, his brow rising with subdued humour.

She gazed up at him with a questioning eye. "What?"

"Well, if y' use a dust pan to pick up dust, then this must be an oat pan," he laughed and continued with his sweeping.

"You're such an idiot," she giggled and lowered the pan to the floor in front of the pile of oats. "Just sweep it in here."

"Aye," his voice was light and relaxed, putting her at ease. "Y' know, Freckles, I have to say that I have never seen a barn so clean in all me life."

She giggled and glanced around the space. Everything was in its place and the cement floor, other than the odd crack, was immaculately clean. The tools were stored away neatly, the straw was laid in the stalls with precision, and not a speck of oats or hay was on the floor other than the few pieces Declan missed in his sweeping.

"No thanks to you," Meghan giggled and pointed towards a clumping of oats still on the floor. "Your sweeping skills leave a lot to be desired."

"Hey, don't y' be criticizing me work now." He dropped the broom and lunged towards her, gripping her around the waist.

"Declan!" She shrieked when his fingers ran up her ribs. "Stop it." She was heaving forwards in his arms, trying to get loose, but he refused to release her.

"So, you're still ticklish," he laughed and continued with his attack. "It's good to have y' back." Her feet left the ground as he swung her up into the air, her legs landing in his arms. She shrieked and gripped around his neck, when he hoisted her again until she was cradled in his arms.

"Declan, put me down," she giggled and smacked her hand down on his shoulder.

Declan was laughing loudly at her facial expression, and he failed to hear the footsteps approaching, but he definitely heard the distinct sound of someone clearing his throat.

"Fabrizio?" Meghan blurted out as she too turned towards the sound. "What are you doing here?"

Fabrizio's dark brown eyes stayed fixed on Declan, who was still holding Meghan in his arms. "I came to check on you."

"Oh," she babbled and looked at Declan with pleading eyes. "Why?" she managed to say as Declan returned her to the ground.

"Hmm, hi, Monty." Fabrizio took a few steps towards them. "So it's true."

Declan caught the flash of worry in Fabrizio's eye and a smug expression crossed his face. "It's good to see y' again, Fabs." Declan's brow rose with mischief. "What's true?"

"Cassie told me you were here." Fabrizio's face filled with concern. The look on Meghan's face as Declan held her in his arms was devastating him. She still loved him. Dammit. He had run into Declan a few months after Meghan moved to Montana, and he lied and told Declan he didn't know where she was. That might have been a big mistake, but he thought Declan would move on and forget about Meghan. Over the years, he has held out hope that Meghan would one day return his love, but she never let him completely in. His mind was whirling, and he did not notice that Declan had released Meghan, and she was heading towards him, an odd expression shadowing her beautiful face. Damn, did Declan tell her he was trying to find her.

"Listen, sweetheart, I know it looks bad, but . . . Well, you were so vulnerable at that time and with what his parents had said, I thought that maybe he was just after Caelan," Fabrizio rambled, panic evident in his voice.

"What are you talking about?" Meghan stopped dead in her tracks, shock filled her eyes.

Fabrizio eyed Declan's smug face, then settled his gaze back on Meghan, who was also splitting her gaze between the two men. "You didn't tell her?"

"No," Declan's voice filled with anger. "I didn't realize that y' were dating me wife. I guess that would explain your reluctance in helping me find her."

"We're not dating!" Meghan blurted out, totally missing Declan's point.

Declan's brow rose slightly at the guilt that was evident in her eyes. "Meggie, why are y' lying to me?"

Meghan was backing away from Fabrizio and Declan, fear crossing her face. "We're not dating . . . We just, well . . ."

Fabrizio shook his head with annoyance at her dismissal of their time together. "That's great!"

"So y' are what Meggie, just fucking?" Declan growled.

"Don't be so vulgar, Declan. We're grown people and well . . . It's not like you wanted me!"

"So when did this happen? Before or after I asked y' if y' knew where she was?" Declan's voice was confrontational.

"You had no right deciding who I should talk to. I had the right to choose if I wanted to see Declan," Meghan cried as her anger exploded.

"I agree," Declan piped up, fuelling her flames.

"Shut up!" Meghan growled, turning her angry eyes on him. "Why must you be such a jerk?"

"Now, Freckles, don't get testy, y' know how much I love it when your eyes flare, do y' think it's wise to look at me in such a way, I might not be able to control meself."

Fabrizio had regained his composure, and his temper was beginning to flare. "I am not the only one that has been lying. Why would you keep this from me? How am I supposed to protect you if you sneak around behind my back?" He stopped before he said too much.

Nathan arrived at the door to the barn just in time to witness the fireworks. When he saw Fabrizio's truck pull up, he could not control the desire to watch him catch Meghan and Declan in the barn together.

"How long has he been here?" Fabrizio growled, stalking towards Meghan. "I talked to you yesterday, and you never mentioned that he was here?"

"I've been here a few days," Declan added helpfully.

"What?" Fabrizio flared. "Dammit, Meghan, you didn't think it was important to tell me he was here?" What the hell was happening?

Meghan took a step back from Fabrizio as he approached making a grab for her arm.

Declan gripped Fabrizio's arm and eyed him threateningly. "Keep your hands off me wife."

"She's not your . . ." Fabrizio's voice trailed off, the smug self-satisfied expression on Declan's face was clearly telling him that Declan had taken her. "You fucked him, didn't you?"

Nathan snorted a loud laugh at the question, completely enthralled with the drama unfolding in front of him. However, he quieted quickly when he saw the expression on Meghan's face. She was horribly ashamed.

"Fabrizio, it's just . . ." she stammered as tears began to drip down her face. "I didn't plan it."

Before she finished her sentence, Fabrizio lunged at Declan, knocking him to the floor of the barn. The large two men swung at each other, causing matching damage to the other before Declan managed to manoeuvre himself to the top of the pile and began pummelling at Fabrizio's face.

"Stop it, Declan!" Meghan screamed, jumping on Declan's back and wrapping her arms around his shoulders. "Please stop it."

Her pleading voice halted his attack, and he removed himself from Fabrizio, with Meghan still clinging to him.

"What the hell are you doing?" Meghan glowered and smacked his arm. "Dammit, this is all your fault."

"My fault, how do y' figure that, Freckles? If he hadn't kept me from y' years ago," Declan growled, gripping her hands to keep her from smacking him any further. "And if you wouldn't have spent the last five years fucking me best friend." His voice was accusing, but a note of disappointment was evident.

"Oh my God, Declan. I thought you didn't want me anymore. I was lonely, and Fabrizio was always there for me. You have no right . . ." Meghan grumbled and yanked her hands away from Declan and squatted down next to Fabrizio as he wiped his bleeding mouth with the back of his hand. "Fabrizio, are you all right?"

"No, I'm not all right, Meghan! How can this be all right? Dammit, I come back and find out that the woman I love is fucking her ex-husband!"

"Husband," Declan interjected.

"Shut up!" Meghan snarled at him. "And I would appreciate it if you two would stop saying I'm fucking everyone. I'm not a whore." Her voice chocked at the end.

Declan reached out and touched her face. "I'm sorry, Meggie, I was not implying that."

Fabrizio bristled from the look of love that crossed Meghan's face as she gazed at Declan. He had lost. "Dammit, Declan, I have spent the last five years keeping her hidden away, and now you are going to blow her cover. Do you realize the danger you have placed her in again?"

"I haven't placed her in danger." Declan was annoyed by the remark.

"Fabrizio," Meghan blurted out, following him out of the barn. "Please, Fabrizio, we need to talk about this. You have to let me explain."

Meghan turned back towards Nathan and Declan as they stood by the barn door, watching her begging Fabrizio to understand. Nathan forced the smile from his face when she stormed towards them. "Looks like one or both of us are in big trouble."

"Aye, I'll bet you're right," Declan mumbled, forcing back his smile.

"This was going to be hard enough, without you two idiots riling him up," Meghan scowled, coming to a stop dangerously close to them. "I . . ."

"Freckles," Declan's voice was soft. "I'm sorry I didn't mean for any of this to happen." Had he put her in danger, or was Fabrizio just angry that he was there. "I just wanted y'."

"It's always about what you want, isn't it, Declan?" she growled, throwing him for a loop. "Ever since I have known you, it's always been about you. You wanted to make love, you wanted to get engaged, and you wanted to get married. Well, look where that's gotten us."

"Meggie," Declan stammered. "I . . ." He had no argument. She was correct; everything always revolves around his wants and needs. No one had ever called him on that fact before. Her brow rose, awaiting his response, and he was struggling for something to say. "Well, I'm the man," he blurted out but quickly regretted doing so. Her mouth dropped open, and Nathan gasped at the comment. "Well, I mean . . ."

"I know exactly what y' meant!" Meghan snarled and turned to leave. "Why did you have to come back and throw my life back into chaos?" Her tone was panicked, her eyes glazing over. "It took me years . . ."

He waited a moment, but she did not finish her thoughts. "To what, Meggie? To forget me?"

"I never forgot you, I never did," she mumbled, her gaze lowering to the ground. Why did he still have such power over her? She had to get hold of her emotions, but as Declan gripped her arm, his fingers soft against her skin, she floundered with the right decision. One touch from him sent electricity shooting thought her, attacking her core, even after all the years, all the heartache. She needed Declan to go home, and it had to be soon.

Fabrizio was standing frozen in place, staring at her as she struggled with what was happening. He knew that if Declan ever returned, she would not be able to resist him. She had never stopped loving him, and Fabrizio accepted that just to be in her life. That might have been a mistake. He thought that was enough, but it clearly wasn't; he loved her and now he was losing her.

"Meghan, you are going to have to make a decision." He glanced over at Declan who was scrubbing his hand across his eyes in frustration. "It's him or me."

She could feel the piercing gaze of Declan, Fabrizio, Nathan, and she could not bear it any further. Once Declan released her arm, she bolted for the house, leaving the men staring after her.

"And she's off," Declan sighed, watching her dart up the porch stairs.

"What?" Nathan turned to Declan with a questioning gaze.

"She has a habit of bolting when she doesn't know how to deal with something," Declan said, offhandedly.

Nathan smirked, "You know her very well. Not many people ever notice that."

"I just seem to cause her stress." Declan watched Fabrizio as he headed for the house after Meghan.

The thought of Fabrizio being with his Meghan made him ache. However, that was the burning issue, was Meggie his? Caelan was, and she lived here, his daughter, so kind and loveable. She had accepted him with all her heart.

"Is everything all right?" Nathan questioned, breaking Declan's thoughts as he sauntered up to the fence, a large black Lab dancing at his side.

Declan shrugged, a look of devastation crossing his face. "I thought if I knew the truth everything would work itself out, but I'm more confused now than before. I'm not sure I can get past her being with Fabs," Declan sighed, still gazing at the large white house. "I know this is probably inappropriate to ask, but I need to know about Fabs."

Nathan sighed and gazed at Declan with agitation. "I won't lie to you, Declan. I believe she loves him on some level. Damn, this is tearing her apart?"

"Aye, and I'm to blame."

"I don't think you can burden yourself with all the blame. She has caused a lot of the problems as well. He is dating Cassie on and off for the last couple year, but Meg's keeps him on a string. I don't think she completely wants him, but she is scared to be without him. I'm not sure how Cassie deals with all this drama."

Declan shook his head and sighed. What the hell was going on!

Nathan squatted down to pat the large black Lab that sat panting at his feet. "You know, Declan, if you two are still married." He paused and glanced back at the house, then returned his gaze to the dog and scratched behind its ears. "Well, what's to say that you can't take back what's yours?"

Declan stared down at Nathan with slight amusement. "Y' think I should just walk in there and tell her that we're married, and she belongs to me?"

"I don't think that wording would do anything but put her on the defensive. You need to understand that she still loves you, but she was also very hurt and embarrassed by what happened."

"I wish I could change what happened, but I can't. Nat, tell me how to get her back. She told me she wants a divorce."

"Really, she never told me that." Nathan stood and threw a stick into the field for the dog to chase. "She is acting very strange."

"If y' had to guess who will she pick?" Declan questioned, not sure if he wanted to hear the answer. It was taking everything in him not to throw her into the jeep and keep driving until she and Caelan were far from everyone.

"I think her heart will choose you, but I think her head will choose Fabrizio. He's safe. She knows he could never get deep enough to hurt her."

"But I can," Declan sighed.

"Yes, but sooner or later, Fabrizio is going to have to put Cassie first. I don't think anything has happened between Megs and him since he started dating Cassie a few years ago, but he still seems to love Megs. I didn't realize how much though until today."

"This is so complicated," Declan mumbled and glanced back at Nathan. "Is Fabs good to her? I mean is she happy with him?"

Nathan sighed and threw the stick again that the dog had returned, "he is, he is a good man." Nathan's voice lowered slightly. "Other than his issue with me."

"His issue?" Declan appeared confused. "Y' mean that y' live here?"

"No, that I'm gay." Nathan stared at Declan awaiting a response.

"Aye, I know that. Why does that bother him?" Declan glanced at the house. "He didn't seem to have a problem with Colin."

Nathan stared at Declan with interest. "Who's Colin?"

"He's me little brother," a smile twisted Declan's lips. "He is dating a lad from my last movie. Me mam won't admit it though; she has a big problem with it, so Colin moved out to Los Angeles, and lives with me at the moment."

"My mom doesn't even know," Nathan laughed. "I figure what she doesn't know won't hurt her. She thinks Megs and I are together. Maybe that's what bugs Fabrizio, Megs pretends she's my girlfriend when my mom is around."

Declan eyed him sidelong. "How long do you think y' can keep that up. How did y' explain Fabrizio to your mam."

"Well I just said he was her agent that was checking in on her. My mom has only been here twice; I usually go out there to visit. My sisters know but that's it."

Declan started to laugh. "And Colin thinks he has it bad. Y' should come to LA to visit, there are lots of good looking lads for y' there."

Nathan smiled and scratched his head. "I might take you up on that, there are slim pickings around here."

Declan smiled and slapped his hand on Nathan's back. "Well you're welcome anytime."

Nathan smiled and watched Caelan bound from Hayley's car, her long black hair flying up around her face.

"Nat, I want to thank y' for being there for them," Declan smiled as he turned his gaze on the brown eyes of Nathan.

"No need to thank me, I would do anything for them," Nathan admitted.

"I know," Declan said as Caelan bolted towards them and jumped into Nathan's arms.

"Hi," Caelan shrieked. "We're going to the rodeo tomorrow, Uncle Nat. Are you coming?"

"Little darlin' I'm sure you'll have more fun without me there, you can eat chocolate," he laughed at the thought of how Meghan and Caelan hide the junk food from him.

Caelan giggled and rested her little hand on Nathan's face. "How did you know Mommy said that?"

Nathan's laugh accompanied Declan's. "This is your mother we are talking about, little darlin'."

Caelan nodded her head, then turned towards Declan. "Do you like chocolate, Daddy?"

"Aye, but not as much as your mam," Declan smiled with pleasure as Caelan leaned towards him, forcing Nathan to release her, allowing Declan to take her into his arms.

"Uncle Nat says we are poisoning our bodies by eating chocolate. But Mommy says he is nerot . . . nertotic."

"Neurotic," Nathan helped.

Declan threw back his head and laughed; these people were so down to earth, and the issues they had between each other were so comforting. He wanted to be part of this world, and he would not give up until he possessed Meghan again.

CHAPTER TWENTY

B y the time Meghan and Caelan arrived at the fairgrounds the next morning, it seemed that most of the town's residence had already arrived and were scurrying around the grounds with an unusually high level of energy. As they passed by a group of women, Meghan noticed she still seemed to be the topic of conversation when one of the women whispered something as she passed. It was very discouraging for her to know that her once peaceful life in town was shattered, and she would never be able to go anywhere again without being talked about.

The fair grounds were quite large for such a small town, but it was well used during the year with tractor and livestock sales. The large Quonset at the far side of the racetrack was used extensively for activities such as cattle penning and auctions. The field to the east of the Quonset where the rides had been set up was filled with excited children and parents scampering from ride to ride ensuring they sampled each one.

Meghan inhaled deeply, smelling the mixtures of fairground scents that entice people into over indulging in the variety of foods available. Meghan could not resist the small donuts, and she made a quick stop at the first booth she saw.

For over an hour, Caelan went on the rides, and Meghan made intermittent stops at the booths either to say hello to someone she knew or to look at what they were selling. She also could not fight the urge to purchase another bag of small donuts that she was eating when they stumbled upon Nathan, Hayley, and Anisha.

"Hey, darlin', where have you been? You were already gone when we left," Nathan said, eyeing the bag of donuts in Meghan's hand.

"I had to go into the office early this morning," Meghan said evenly.

"Oh, guess who I ran into," Nathan commented as the two young girls began to discuss the various rides.

"Who?" Meghan questioned, popping another donut into her mouth.

"Declan. He is here with his sister and her husband. Apparently, he is the guest of the mayor," Nathan smirked.

"Yes, I heard." Another donut entered Meghan's mouth.

"Why aren't you looking for him? He is trying to find you," Nathan asked, gazing down at the bag, noticing it was almost empty. "He said he was supposed to meet you here this morning, but he couldn't find you."

"He never mentioned it to me, and I'm not going to run around the grounds looking for him," Meghan said defiantly, her annoyance with Declan building.

"Megs, don't be like that. You're getting that 'I'm so offended' attitude, and it will only come back to bite you in the ass," Nathan warned her, reached his hand into the bag, and grabbed a donut.

"Nat!" Meghan snorted as she offered the bag towards Hayley. Hayley shook her head, and Meghan returned her gaze to Nathan.

"Megs, I mean it. Cut him some slack he's trying. He's had a lot to deal with in the past week. He's doing his best."

Meghan sighed and glanced around the area. "So have I! Anyway, when I finished talking with Fabrizio yesterday, Declan was gone."

"Well, what did you expect? He just found out you had been sleeping with his best friend," Nathan said softly so no one else heard.

Meghan bristled from the comment. If Declan reacted anything like Fabrizio, she wasn't looking forward to seeing him. Fabrizio had left the ranch and told her he was done. He was tired of being jerked around.

"Megs, I talked to him yesterday, and he really wants to make things work with you. He loves you, but he might just need some time to sort things out in his head."

"Nat, he doesn't even really know me. Once he figures out what a selfish bitch I am, he'll be gone too. I had a lot of time to think last night, and I know I did keep jerking Fabrizio along. I know I don't love him the way he wants me to, but I was too scared to be on my own. If

Cassie ever finds out how much time he spends at the ranch, she will never talk to me again."

Nathan rested his arm around her shoulder and turned her slightly away from the young girls. "Megs, you're not a bad person. You have made some selfish choices over the last few years, but Fabrizio made it very easy for you. He could have stopped coming to the ranch, but he didn't. He is just as much to blame. And as for Cassie, she knew from the beginning his feelings for you, and she chose to start a relationship with him. She chased him for years, Megs. I think you need to focus on Declan and leave Cassie and Fabs to sort out their own shit."

"Mommy, can we go see the bucking horses?" Caelan blurted out, breaking Meghan's thoughts.

"Sure," Meghan smiled and popped another donut into her mouth.

"So how many of those have you had?" Nathan questioned with amusement, his dark brown eyes glistening in the mid morning sun.

"I don't know," Meghan muttered and took Caelan by the hand.

"Two bags," Caelan announced as she turned to go.

Meghan crinkled her nose at her daughter. "Don't tell on me," she chuckled. "You know how Nat is about junk food."

Nathan's brows turned down at her comment, but he knew it was true.

"Are you three coming with us?" Meghan questioned as Caelan bobbed her head slightly, looking around Meghan, a large smile filling her little face.

"There's Daddy."

Meghan turned to see Declan heading towards her with a group of young girls trailing about ten feet behind him. He was wearing jeans and a dark blue cotton button up shirt, and he had the Red Sox's ball cap on, trying to disguise himself, but apparently, it was not working.

"Hi, I have been looking everywhere for y' two," he smiled, focusing on her long legs that were exposed under the khaki shorts she was wearing.

"Hi, Daddy," Caelan shrieked and ran towards him. He lifted her, balancing her easily in the crook of his arm, his lips landing gently on her cheek.

"So what are we doing today?" Declan questioned, looking down at Caelan's smiling face.

"We are going to see the bucking horses," Caelan informed him.

"Oh brilliant, I love to watch that." Declan's gaze moved to Meghan, the expression on her face disturbing him, her eyes were cold and dark.

Before Meghan could protest, he had lowered Caelan to the ground, gripped Meghan's hand, and pulled her towards the fence, away from the group. "All right, out with it."

"Out with what?" Meghan said curtly. "And I don't appreciate you dragging me around."

"I'll do what I want. You're me wife, and that means this lovely body belongs to me." His voice was taunting as he slipped his hand around her ribs, pulling her up against him.

"Declan, stop it. People are staring," Meghan protested as his lips landed on her neck.

"Oh, playing hard to get, are y'?" he laughed and yanked her up against him. "All I have to do is kiss y' right here." His lips landed on the nape of her neck, and she melted into him. "See, it works every time."

"You're a jerk," she laughed and smacked his chest. "I'm really going to have to break you of this arrogance you have."

Declan's lips twisted into a smile. "I'm not arrogant. I'm just right. So, are y' going to tell me why y' look so sad."

"I'm not sad. I'm just worried and sorry." Meghan gazed up at him.

His brow rose slightly. "Sorry for what? Could you be feeling slightly guilty about sleeping with me best friend?"

Meghan pulled away and leaned against the top rail of the white fence. "My only guilt is hurting him. At the time it started, I thought we were over. You have to understand that he was there for me. Brody was too demanding and . . ."

"Who is Brody?" Declan interrupted and leaned against the rail beside her.

"He is an agent with the FBI that helped with the murder case. He originally interviewed me but afterwards felt that I was being framed, but his colleagues were determined to put me away. He helped Nat and Fabrizio collect the evidence to help clear me."

"Did you have an affair with him as well?" Declan's voice sounded choked.

"No, he wanted too, but I just never liked him that way. I was still so in love with you that I couldn't even imagine being with anyone else."

"Except Fabrizio." He looked sidelong at her, his voice almost a whisper.

"Well, the weird thing is when I was with Fabrizio, I felt closer to you. I don't mean when we were . . . I mean, when he was just near me. I almost felt like you were going to come around the corner." She turned towards him. "The first time . . . well, I was so broken, and he kissed my forehead, and I don't know, I just needed him. I needed someone to love me."

"Oh, Meggie, I am so sorry that I caused you such pain. But we are together now and hopefully we can get past all the hurt. Hopefully we can start new."

"I would like to try," she smiled up at him.

"Me too. But I'll need y' to give up your wild ways," he laughed and kissed her nose.

Meghan crinkled her nose at him, then gestured towards the group. "Come on, Caelan wants to see the rodeo, and if we miss it, she will complain about it for months."

Declan grabbed Meghan's hand, turned, and led her back to where Nathan was standing with Hayley, while Caelan and Anisha tried their luck at a midway game. A judgmental gaze was evident on Nathan's face as he watched them approach, and Meghan grew annoyed.

"What?" Her tone was short and irritated.

"That was snappish," Nathan chuckled. "Remember what I told you darlin' and don't eat anymore of those donuts. You'll be wired for days." Nathan patted Meghan's bottom and wandered towards the girls.

Once Declan controlled his amusement, he glanced down to the bag of donuts still clutched in her hand. "Y' like those wee things, do y'?" he smirked.

"Yes, they are quite good," she smiled and popped another into her mouth.

Declan laughed at her facial expression as she defiantly chewed the deep-fried delicacy. "Well, are y' going to share or be a pig and eat them all yourself," he questioned.

Meghan smiled and lifted the bag towards him, and he snorted a chuckle as he looked into the empty bag. "Well," Declan muttered, "y' seem to have eaten them all."

"I guess I will have to buy some more," Meghan smiled with delight.

"Aye, but I think that Caelan and I should get our own bags," Declan teased and tweaked her under her chin.

"Good plan," Meghan grinned, not letting him bait her.

Caelan gripped Declan's hand and pulled him towards the grandstand. "Daddy, can we go now? I want to see the bucking horses."

"Aye, wee one, we can go right now."

"Daddy, what does 'aye' mean. You say it a lot."

Declan laughed and patted Caelan's head. "It means yes."

Meghan smiled, but it faded quickly when she noticed the short, rotund Mayor McGregor standing with a group of assorted people, their eyes all switching to Declan.

"Mr. Montgomery." The stubby arm flapped in the air with excitement.

"Oh, crap, there he is," Declan sighed. "I can't believe Moiré set this up. She's worse than me mam for hobnobbing with the political types." He wished he had not agreed to sit with them. When he had met the mayor a few days before, he found himself thinking of excuses why he could not dine at their home. Moiré was furious with him for snubbing the mayor and made Declan promise to sit with him and his family for the rodeo. Moiré used his euphoria over his reunion with Meghan to persuade him into this assuredly boring afternoon.

"Come, join me in my box," the mayor hollered, his movement towards them narrowing the distance.

"He has a box?" Declan whispered with a shocked expression crossing his face.

"He's important, remember. He has to have a box. What would the lowly town folk think if he mingled with them in the stands? I'm surprised I'm allowed to join you," Meghan joked but turned solemn as she caught the expression on his face.

"Meggie, y' sure can be sarcastic when y' want to be. Y' should be more gracious. He's a fellow countryman and all," Declan grinned, his lilt quite pronounced with the last phrase. He let go of her hand and adjusted his ball cap. "And by the way, y' weren't invited. You're crashing the party?"

"What?" Meghan swung around to face him. "They are the last family I would insinuate myself on. You are on your own with them. Come on, peanut, let's go find Uncle Nat."

A smirk grew across Meghan's lips as she watched Declan's shoulder slump forward with the dread of sitting with the mayor and his family. "Meggie, y' wouldn't abandon me with them, would y'? I'm frightfully shy, and I need y' there for support."

"You're so full of it," Meghan giggled as he gripped her arm, pulling her towards the gawking group. "Declan, I don't want to sit with them."

"To bad." Before she could protest any further, the group was directly in her path. The mayor's short, stocky frame at odds with the tall lean frame of his wife, who wore her hair pulled back into a twist on the side of her head. "They look like those two off the *Addams Family* cartoon," Declan said evenly, causing Meghan to laugh out loud.

"Oh great, their daughter Kaye is there," Meghan muttered, regaining her composure as the skeletor approached.

"What is it with y' and women named Kaye," Declan laughed and squeezed her hand slightly.

Meghan gazed at him, amazed that he would remember the problems she had with Kaye all those years earlier. "Oh" was all she said as the corners of her mouth rose slightly.

"I too remember everything," Declan whispered an impish grin, threatening to explode just before the small group arrived in front of them. Caelan backed up behind Declan's legs and wrapped her arms around one of them from behind when Andrew McGregor glared down at her with annoyance.

"Declan. May I call y' Declan?" he announced as he directed his narrow pale blue eyes on Declan.

"If y' like." Declan shrugged.

"We're glad y' could join us today," he smiled, causing the long tips of his moustache to curl up slightly, but as his gaze moved from Declan to Meghan, the smile turned into a solemn gaze.

"Dr. Coleman. It's nice to see you again," he muttered.

Meghan smiled but said nothing. Her hand was twitching in Declan's as the annoyed mayor stared at her.

"Well," mayor McGregor finally said, "this is me wife, Nan, me daughter, Kaye, and me son, Billy." He smiled towards Declan.

"Hi," Declan shook the hand of all three, then turned towards Meghan. "I suspect y' all know Meggie, and this is Caelan," he smirked, pulling her out from behind his legs and lifting her into the crook of his arm.

"Oh yes, we've met," The Mayor blurted out, unsure what to say next.

"Da!" yelled a short man with wavy blond hair, his arm waving excitedly in the air to attract his father's attention.

"Anthony, me lad, I thought y' weren't due back from Ireland until next month?" Mayor McGregor yelled back, his face lighting with delight. "How was your tour of historic buildings?"

"It was grand; there are so many wonderful old structures over there. It's hard to believe that they are hundreds of years old. I even went to a castle that had a picture of . . ."

"I'm Charles Murphy." The short heavy man with the wiry beard and beady pale blue eyes interrupted. He was rather harsh looking; it appeared that Anthony found him panhandling at the airport. "Sorry Charles," Anthony nodded his head towards the grubby man. Charles is the representative for a company looking to invest in Casino's here in Montana. So I invited him to spend a few days here with us. "This is my family." He introduced each member to a rough grunt and handshake from the man. "And this is our illustrious town doctor, Meghan Coleman." Anthony's voice was odd, almost as if the man should have known Meghan.

Murphy nodded his round head at her, his eyes settling on Declan, who still had his arm draped around her shoulder. "And y' are?" He finally spoke.

"I'm Declan Montgomery," Declan said, with a slight edge to his voice.

"Hmm," Murphy's eyes settled on the arm still clinging to her shoulder. "Would y' be the boyfriend then?"

"Husband actually," Declan said evenly.

"Well," the man muttered almost to himself. He glanced back at Anthony, his brow rising with what appeared to be interest.

"Is there a problem?" Declan questioned, wondering what the two men's interest was in whether he was the boyfriend or not.

"No," Anthony blurted out quickly. "I told Murphy on our way here that we had a beautiful doctor in town, and she wasn't married. I guess he is just upset that I was wrong."

Meghan smirked slightly at the thought of the men in the town so interested in her marital status. "Well, thank you for thinking of me,

Anthony, but I . . ." She stopped and gazed up at Declan. "I am quite content with my situation at the moment."

Declan's body was ridged, and his face was stern as he watched the man, not convinced of the reason for his interest. There was something else—a shadow, perhaps, in his eyes that was hiding the truth.

"Meggie, I think we best be off if we want to see any of the rodeo," Declan said, turning her towards the stands. "Thanks for the offer, Mayor, but y' seem to have gained two more people, so there is definitely no room for me now."

"But" was all that came out of the mayor's mouth before Declan was moving across the grass, Caelan tucked up in one arm and Meghan gripped tightly under the other.

"So what's with the son? Does he go back and forth to Ireland often?" Declan questioned with interest, thinking back to the exchange between the two men.

Meghan shrugged and glanced down at the rocky ground passing by under her feet. "I really couldn't tell you. I have as little to do with that family as I can. Why are you so concerned with that man?" she questioned as he lowered Caelan to the ground and leaned up against the rail that surrounded the racetrack.

"I don't know. There was just something about him that bothers me," Declan shrugged and pulled Meghan towards him. "While I'm in LA, if he stays in town," his eyes darted around the area, "please stay away from him."

Meghan giggled slightly at his worry. "All right."

"Meggie, this is serious. I don't like the way he was looking at y'. It seemed very depraved to me."

"Okay, Declan, I promise I won't go near anyone remotely associated with that family." She smiled, still not understanding his worry, but she had to admit she did feel a slight sense of gratification that he was so worried about her.

The rodeo passed by uneventfully; other than a few bumps and bruises, the cowboys exited the event rather unharmed. A few cowboys had gathered at the bottom of the grandstand to sign programs for the excited girls that followed their every move. Declan was quite relieved that their attention was directed elsewhere, leaving him to enjoy the afternoon with his family.

A loud ruckus from behind the stands drew Declan's attention as an apparent fight had broken out.

"Great, the Meadows boys are at it again," Meghan grumbled and headed towards them.

Declan grabbed her arm and jerked her to a stop. "Y' weren't planning on getting into the middle of that, were y'?" he questioned, his brow rising with disbelief.

"Yes, I'm going to break it up. They are my friend's sons," Meghan said, with determination.

"Meggie," he muttered, glancing back at the boys that were now punching each other. "I'll stop it."

"No, Declan, let me. You'll just make things worse." Meghan's eyes pleaded with him.

"Well, I'm staying close," Declan muttered, grabbing Caelan's hand, following closely behind Meghan.

"Okay, boys, that's enough!" Meghan said sternly as she arrived at the bottom of the bleachers. The three boys turned towards her, and two Meadows boys smiled with recognition, but the third she did not recognize, and he did not appear pleased with her interference.

"Hi, Dr. Meghan," Keith, the smaller of the two, said as he moved away from the group.

"Hi, Keith," Meghan frowned slightly. "You know you're not supposed to be fighting. If your dad catches you . . ."

"I know," Keith blurted out, wiping at the bleeding cut above his eye.

"Who the hell are y'?" questioned the young blond-haired boy. His appearance startled her, but she could not put a finger on it.

Meghan turned towards the boy with a cold stare but did not respond. Declan became worried at the movement of the boy, and he moved towards the situation standing just behind her.

"Keith," Meghan said, returning her gaze to him. "I want you and Danny to go to the Quonset so I can stitch up that cut you have over your eye."

"Yes, ma'am," Keith agreed, quite happy for a way out of the fight without looking cowardly. Their father being a retired judge, deplored fighting, and if he found out the boys were involved in yet another altercation, they would be in big trouble.

"Stay out of this, lady!" snorted the young man that appeared to be in his mid twenties. "They are going to finish what they started."

His thick Irish accent startled her slightly, and she turned her dark green eyes on the man. "You must consider yourself quite a man picking on boys younger and smaller than you." Meghan's voice held a definite tone of disgust.

The long lean muscles tensed on the young man as he stalked towards Meghan. His callused hands yanked at his white T-shirt that was splattered with blood from Keith's eye. Meghan eyed him nervously as he came closer, her eyes settled on the pale birthmark streaking his neck. A slight gasp escaped her mouth, and she backed into Declan.

"So, Dr. Coleman," he smirked. "The rumours of how beautiful y' are, are certainly true," he said as his eyes racked her long, slender body.

"I think it's time you left," Meghan said, forcing calmness into her voice.

"Y' can't order me about. I'm not one of your wee patients," he said smugly. "But I have to say it's a shame y' waste your time on children." He paused, letting his eyes inspect her body once again. "I think it's time y' look at a real man," he smirked and pulled at the waistband of his jeans.

"Don't bother, I don't deal with impotence," Meghan blurted out, quickly regretting doing so, when he lunged towards her.

She blinked suddenly when she felt a rush of air passing by her, and the next thing she was aware of was Declan kneeling on the back of the young man, his arm pinned behind his head.

Keith and Danny had jumped behind Meghan during Declan's attack, apparently slightly startled. Declan turned his annoyed face towards Meghan with a cold glare but said nothing.

Meghan's lashes fluttered across her terrified eyes, her breathing deep, trying to calm her nerves. Her attempt failed, however, when she heard a commotion behind her as two officers arrived and were pushing their way through the growing crowd, with the mayor and his family in tow.

"What's going on here?" a tall, balding officer asked, glancing down at Declan, who was still kneeling on the back of the stunned man. The older officer noticed the Meadows boys and sighed, "You two again?"

"He started it," Keith piped up in his defence, pointing at the man pinned to the ground under Declan.

The greying office looked down at Declan. "Let the boy up, and let's sort this out," he said, with disinterest.

Declan removed his knee from the back of the man but kept a tight grip on his arm as he yanked him to his feet, swinging him around to the officer.

"Well, you seem a little old to be fighting with these boys?" the officer commented.

He had assumed it was another of the town's teenagers they were fighting. The man grunted and pulled at his arm, trying to remove it from Declan's grasp.

"Let him loose," the older officer said. "But if you don't behave, you'll be in handcuffs."

Declan roughly released the man, then stepped in front of Meghan, in case the man intended to go after her again.

"All right, what happened here?" the greying officer asked, scowling at the Meadows boys.

"Well," Danny muttered. "He bumped into me and—"

"I was coming down the stairs, and I accidentally bumped into the lad," the man said in a calm voice. His eyes still fixed on Meghan, but his focus quickly changed as he noticed the short fat man standing with the McGregor family.

The officer shook his head with exasperation. "Boys."

"We're sorry," Danny muttered, looking at Meghan's frowning face.

Meghan shook her head at the boys. "When are you two going to grow up and stop all this fighting?"

The boys looked at each other, then both directed their gaze on Declan. Declan, however, did not intend to condone their behaviour.

"Don't look at me that way," he grumbled. "I was only protecting Meggie."

"That was amazing," Keith said, with excitement.

"Look, fighting is not something to be proud of," Declan said firmly.

The officer turned his attention to the blond-haired man. "Okay, sir, you are free to leave. But I suggest you go home and cool off."

"Don't worry, I'm leaving town. I accomplished what I came for," he smirked his eyes, running up Meghan's body to her face.

She blinked nervously and leaned up against Declan's back for safety.

"And what would that be?" the young officer questioned, not liking the tone of voice the man had used.

"I was just tracking down someone for a friend," he smirked, his eyes still fixed on Meghan.

Declan patted her hand that was clinging to his shoulder, tightening with every minute the man's gaze was on her.

The man grunted at the officers, then picked up his ball cap that Declan dislodged during attack, and then turned, disappearing around the bleachers.

"Okay, boys," Meghan said once he was gone. "You're coming with me to the Quonset!" she said, more resembling an order than a request.

"I think I should go with y'." Declan's voice left little room for discussion.

"I'll be fine," she smiled, turning to go, ignoring his annoyance.

"Meggie," he said firmly, gripping her arm, swinging her around to face him.

"What?" she questioned, quite startled by his tone.

"That man's been in prison," he said sharply.

"How do you know?" the greying officer questioned. "Do you know that man?"

"Did y' not see that tattoo of the cobra on his arm, it had the marking on the snake's head." Declan's annoyance and agitation was building when he realized no one else noticed. "It's the marking of a prison in Derry."

"In Ireland?" Meghan blurted out. It was happening again. "Declan?"

"Freckles." Declan, reading her facial expression, rested his chin on her shoulder, pressing his face into her ear. "Not now, we'll discuss this at home."

She nodded and focused on the two officers that were chattering amongst each other.

"I never noticed that," the young officer muttered and glanced in the direction the man went.

"I think, Mr. Montgomery's imagination is running away with him," Murphy said towards the mayor.

"Why is that?" Declan questioned, slightly annoyed at the tone the man had used.

"I saw no such marking, and I am accustomed to noticing every detail of people," Murphy said offhandedly, trying to dismiss Declan's suspicion.

"Is that right?" Declan's voice was slightly edged with hostility, and he turned towards Meghan, disregarding what Murphy had said, "I'll walk y' to the Quonset, Meggie, then I'm taking you home."

"All right," she agreed, worried about the collection of Irish men that had arrived in town. Last time it happened, she was shot.

CHAPTER TWENTY-ONE

The early evening was pleasantly warm as Declan walked up onto the porch and stood quietly listening to the peaceful sounds of the ranch. A horse was whinnying to a friend somewhere nearby, and the birds were chirping softly as they settled in for the night. He breathed deeply, inhaling the fresh scent of grass and flowers, quite pleased not to smell the scent of car exhaust or the clogging smell of the air in Los Angeles. He was home, and this is where he would stay.

Declan felt suddenly agitated, however, when he noticed Fabrizio's blue pickup truck up next to the garage. Why was he back? Dammit, why wouldn't he just realize that he had lost?

The door loomed in front of him, the barrier to his life; he was not going to lose her again. Years earlier, he had thought that he had only wanted her because she could restore his family's heritage. However, now after being with her again, he knew it was more. Had this wild redhead captured his heart? If so, she had done it years earlier; his feelings for her had only grown stronger since he arrived in the small town.

When he heard Fabrizio's voice inside, his decision was made, and he reached for the kitchen door with the appearance of belonging. He would belong, he told himself; she belonged to him and so did their daughter. This was his home now, and Fabrizio or anyone else was not going to come between them.

The locked door stalled his forceful entrance. Damn, now he had to knock. Fabrizio probably had a key. He cringed at the thought and banged on the door with determination.

Nathan was the one who came to the door, his face flustered and somewhat stressed. His nervous glance back towards the living room sent a shiver up Declan's spine. What was he hiding, were Meghan and Fabrizio in there or somewhere else.

"Nat, let me in," Declan hollered through the still closed door.

Nathan nodded and unlatched the lock, allowing Declan to fly through the door. "I'm glad you're here, Declan, she won't calm down."

"What's going on?" Declan questioned and took a step towards the living room and heard her panicked voice.

"Meghan, you need to calm down. Andy and I won't let anything happen to you." Fabrizio soothed, his hand brushing across her tear-stained face. "Please, sweetheart."

"Fabrizio, he will kill me this time. What about Caelan?" Meghan cried, her sobs catching in her throat.

"Andy is coming with four other agents, and the state police have every available officer looking for him." Fabrizio kissed the top of her head. "I promise, I won't leave you."

Fabrizio's chest was strong under her head, but she was not calming in the least. Where was Declan? Why hadn't he come over yet, should she phone him? How she wanted him with her, to hold her, and until he arrived, she would not be happy.

"Meggie," Declan's voice broke the silence, causing sudden stiffening in Fabrizio's body.

"Declan!" Meghan pushed at Fabrizio's chest, trying to get loose. "Let go!"

Fabrizio's grip suddenly released, and she threw herself at Declan, crashing into his solid frame, into his embrace. "Oh, Declan, he's coming after me," she wailed.

"Shh, Freckles, calm down." He kissed her forehead and stroked her hair. "This hysteria is not going to help matters. Where is Caelan?"

"Upstairs, with Hayley and Anisha," Meghan sniffed, her sobs lessening. "I can't tell her what is going on."

Declan nodded and rested his head against hers. "Is someone going to tell me what happened?"

"It's really no concern of yours," Fabrizio grumbled, the irritation clear on his face. "I suggest you leave, we don't need someone else to protect."

"I don't need your protection, and I'm not leaving," Declan snorted and glanced at Nathan.

Nathan was more than happy to fill Declan in on the information that Meghan returned home to a letter on her kitchen table that read we found you.

Declan's stomach dropped. "Do y' think it's from Ian?"

"Don't you mean Rory?" Fabrizio remarked with spite.

"You honestly believe Rory tried to kill me? I have a hard time believing that," Declan sighed and stared at Fabrizio.

"I do. Where is he now?"

"He is in Ireland. He's lived there for years." Declan scrubbed at his eyes. "Meggie, I think it's best that we leave tonight and go to Malibu," Declan muttered, the overwhelming need to get them out of the reach of Ian was strong in his mind.

"She is not going anywhere. For all I know, you are involved," Fabrizio grumbled and moved towards them.

"Christ, Fabs, y' really believe that? Y' have known me for years." Declan's head drooped, and he moved over to the fireplace and leaned on the mantle.

Fabrizio felt slight remorse accusing him, but then again, trouble seemed to follow Declan. Meghan was perfectly safe before he came around. If Ian and Rory was the same person, possibly one of Declan's family tipped him off.

"My partner is on his way with other agents, so we will catch the bastard this time," Fabrizio spoke forceful when Declan's face began to crumple concern.

"Is that so?" Declan mumbled, but before he could comment any further, he turned towards the front of the house. "Someone is coming."

Fabrizio eyed him with annoyance as Nathan glanced out the window, spotting a dark beige sedan heading down the driveway. The car came to a stop in the driveway, and three men jumped from the car and headed up onto the veranda. Fabrizio used to be grateful for Declan's sense of approaching danger, but now, it just irritated him.

"How did you know that car was coming?" Nathan questioned, his brow rising with vague surprise.

"I heard it," Declan muttered.

"You heard it? How could you have heard it?" Confusion shadowed Nathan's face as Declan turned his aloof eyes towards Meghan.

"I just did." Declan shrugged, not interested in explaining his ability to sense approaching danger.

Nathan looked at Meghan and flung out his hands towards her in a questioning manner.

"I don't know." Meghan shrugged. "He does the weirdest things sometimes," she mumbled and glanced over at Declan.

Fabrizio shook his head with annoyance and moved towards the door and his backup. "Andy, I'm glad you're here," Fabrizio sighed and slapped his partner on the back.

"Is red giving you a hard time?" Andy chuckled. "Where is she? Hey, red, your saviour is here."

Meghan turned just in time to see the expression of shock cross Andy's round face as he gazed at Declan. "Hi, Andy." The tone of her voice resembled guilt as she walked towards the tall, slender man. Andy's dark blue eyes studied Declan for a moment, then he focused on Meghan as she wrapped her arms around his neck. "So, red, did I miss something?"

Meghan looked puzzled by the question and shook her head, her eyes closing heavily. "It's a long story."

"Well, apparently, I have time. Come with me." Andy gripped Meghan's hand and pulled her into the kitchen.

Declan glanced over at Nathan, then back at Fabrizio and his two comrades standing facing him in a confrontational manner. Divide and conquer was their strategy, he decided, now that Meghan was escorted from the room.

An average-sized man with short grey hair and dark blue eyes was the first to speak. "Well, gentlemen, I'm Agent Cameron, and I need to know what your purpose for being here is?"

"I live here," Nathan grumbled and glared at Fabrizio. "In the house on the other side of the barn."

"Hmm, you're the friend," he muttered with disgust. "And you are?"

"I'm Declan Montgomery."

"His friend?" Agent Cameron chuckled, slapping Fabrizio on the back. "God, it's so hard to tell these days?"

"Yes, I am a friend of Nat's," Declan smiled smugly over at Nathan. "But me main purpose for being here is that I'm Meggie's husband."

Agent Cameron's blue eyes settled on Fabrizio at the same time that Agent Paxton, a tall, stocky bald man, gripped Fabrizio's arm. "Fabrizio, I thought."

Fabrizio shook his head at Agent Paxton. "She married him before they were shot, and apparently, neither one of them bothered having it annulled." Fabrizio's voice was harsh as he spoke, and the pain was very evident in his tone.

"I didn't want it annulled," Declan said firmly. "I married her because I loved her, and I have no intentions of changing me marital status anytime soon."

"Damn you!" Fabrizio snorted. "This is your fault."

"How is this my fault? It seems to me that the FBI and police departments should be accepting responsibility for allowing such a psychopath to disappear in the first place. Then to allow him back into the country, well, that's just bad form."

"If you hadn't shown up in town, the *National Interest* wouldn't be running a picture of you and Meghan on the front cover. He had no idea where she was, and now he has been provoked into action. She was in no danger from him before."

"You're so full of shit, no reporters have been here in town, and no one has taken a picture of Meggie and me together."

"It was from before," Agent Cameron said calmly, trying to settle the explosive situation. "Someone phoned in a tip that you had rekindled your romance." Agent Cameron held up the tabloid that was published that day, the headline screaming boldly across the top: *Declan Montgomery finds lost love in the foothills of Montana.*

"Bloody hell!" Declan grumbled and snatched the paper from Agent Cameron. "Meggie is going to freak."

"What am I going to freak about?" Meghan questioned, entering the living room through the doorway off the kitchen.

"This." Declan lifted the tabloid up towards her when she sat down on the couch. "I'm sorry, Freckles."

Meghan cringed, took the tabloid, and began to read the article. "How the hell did they get all this information?" She flipped the page and continued reading. "They don't mention Caelan. All they seem to know is the information from the past and that you are here." She glanced up at Declan, then at Fabrizio. "Thank God, they don't mention Caelan."

"Aye," Declan smiled softly. "But it won't take long for them to find that information. I would venture to guess that they have a reporter on the way here, and with all the gossips in the coffee shop, it won't be long before they have a book worth of information."

Meghan dropped her head into her hands and sighed heavily, she was cried out. "Declan, I'm sorry."

"Shh, Freckles, this isn't your fault. Obviously someone leaked the information." He dropped to the couch beside her and tucked a long auburn strand behind her ear. "It will be all right."

"What else could happen?" she muttered and rested her head on Declan's shoulder, totally forgetting Fabrizio and his cohort's presence.

"I think I will phone the chief. I'm interested in finding out his opinion on that young man from this afternoon. Maybe he can check out the mayor's son's new friend as well."

"Declan, are you saying that Ian is already in town and he is working with those men?" Meghan blurted out, sitting up straight, staring at him, her eyes wide with concern.

"I don't mean to scare y', Freckles . . ."

"Then don't!" Fabrizio growled, interrupting Declan's comment and sat on the other side of Meghan. "Listen, sweetheart, I know this is a lot to comprehend, but just let us deal with this. Why don't you go upstairs and lie down?"

"I don't want a rest. I want to get out of here," Meghan snorted and pulled her hand away from Fabrizio. How she hated it when Fabrizio treated her like a child. She jumped from the couch, leaving a gap between the two men.

Meghan dropped her face into her hands, shaking slightly as she contemplated the outcome of Ian's re-emergence in the country. "I have to get Caelan out of here. I don't want her anywhere near him."

"No, it's best if she stays here," Agent Paxton said firmly.

"We're not staying here. I'm taking Meggie and Caelan away from here." Declan jumped from the couch and moved towards Meghan as she stood against the wall clutching her face. "We're sitting ducks here, this place is too big. There are too many ways that maniac can gain entry into this house. I'm taking them somewhere where it's easy for me to protect them," Declan informed the agents as he grabbed Meghan's arm and pulled her towards him. "Go, get some clothes," he ordered.

"Sir, they are not going anywhere. If you're not going to cooperate, then I will have to ask you to leave."

"No, Declan, you can't leave, what if he is after you?" Meghan shrieked, grabbing onto his arm and shaking him frantically.

"Meggie, don't worry, I'm not leaving y'," Declan said firmly, his dark glare on Agent Paxton.

"We have everything under control. The police and agents are searching every road around here. He won't get within ten miles of the house," Agent Cameron said, trying to calm Declan, who was now pacing back and forth in front of the fireplace.

"I don't have a good feeling about this," Declan mumbled when Meghan stood in front of him, blocking his path.

"Declan, please, I'm sure they know what they're doing," Meghan begged, her dark green eyes soothing him somehow. How she managed to control him with just a look was beyond him, but she had that power, and she was using it now.

"We do, this isn't a movie. You're not the hero here," Agent Paxton said, with a tone of arrogance.

"Pardon me?" Declan snorted and turned towards the smug agent but stopped as Meghan rested her hand on his chest.

"Declan, please."

"That was uncalled for." Fabrizio glared at Agent Paxton.

"Well, I was just trying to get him to realize that we know what we're doing. We don't need some cocky actor telling us our jobs," Agent Paxton growled, defending himself, his voice lowering slightly, his eyes settling on Fabrizio's distressed face.

Declan wandered over to the fireplace and leaned on the mantle. He was not going to allow anyone to harm her ever again, and if it meant whisking her away in the middle of the night, he would.

"Y' said that rag came out today?" Declan turned and eyed Agent Paxton.

"Yes," Agent Paxton said offhandedly.

"Hmmm." Declan glanced over at Fabrizio, causing him to stir.

"What are you thinking?" Fabrizio questioned, recognizing the expression in Declan's eyes. He still knew him so well.

"If this just came out today, there is no way Ian could have mobilized all those people so quickly. I don't think the rag has anything to do with it. I think more is going on here, and I think those men today are involved. We should check out the mayor and his son. And definitely that bearded man, Charles Murphy."

"Murphy! Oh my God . . . Fabrizio. Murphy, it was him!" Meghan shrieked.

"Are you sure? Did you recognize him?" Fabrizio was by her side immediately.

"No, he didn't look familiar, but the name. His name was Murphy. That can be a coincidence." Meghan was shaking terribly.

Fabrizio tuned to Agent Paxton. "Go round up the mayor's guest."

Agents Paxton and Cameron disappeared out the door, and Fabrizio turned to Declan. "Listen, Monty, can we just call a truce? We both want the same thing, to keep Meghan and Caelan safe. I think if we work together, we can resolve this."

"Aye," Declan sighed and eyed Fabrizio. He missed him and their friendship. Could they ever get back what they had? He shook Fabrizio's hand and headed upstairs.

Fabrizio sat beside Meghan on the couch, his eyes fixing on her distraught face. He had not seen her so unglued in years. He felt a tug in his stomach as the reality of the situation hit him. He loved the fact that she needed him again. Over the years, since they had met, she became more independent and the longer she lived on the ranch with Nathan, the less she needed him. If he was honest with himself, he could feel the bond they had, turning from protection into more of a friendship than lovers. They had shared many wonderful nights together, but those had become few and far between over the last few years. He had always known her heart belonged to Declan, and he could never compete. Maybe it was time to let her go. He knew that Declan was the man she wanted, and he was a good man, but he didn't want to let her go.

"Sweetheart, I know you are going to be angry with me for saying this, but have you noticed that your life is always in an upheaval when Declan is around you?" Fabrizio's voice was soft; he did not want to put her on the defensive.

Meghan glanced up at him, her eyes bloodshot and puffy. "I've noticed that."

Fabrizio wrapped his arm around her shoulder and pulled her into his side. When she rested her head on his chest, he sighed deeply and dropped his head onto hers. How long was this moment going to last? Could he be the friend he used to be and let her go?

Andy had moved into the kitchen, allowing Fabrizio private time with Meghan; he was completely caught off guard by Declan's presence.

"Fabrizio, do you think that Ian is coming after me because of his family?" Meghan muttered, her hand idly playing with the buttons on his shirt.

"I think there is more going on." He kissed the top of her head, letting his nose linger in her hair.

Meghan shrugged and glanced back towards the kitchen. "There have been an awful lot of Irishmen in town. Andy McGregor showing up today with a business acquaintance he called him. Then the Meadows boys were fighting with a young man with an Irish accent. Declan said he had been in prison in Ireland."

Fabrizio's arms tensed around Meghan as he processed her information. "The man you said was in the room when you were shot, he had an Irish accent, didn't he? Rory has been in Ireland. I still think he is Ian. I just can't figure out how he got involved and why. Rory was always a punk ass kid, but to become a murderer . . ."

Meghan sniffed, turning her face up towards Fabrizio. "Declan is from Ireland, and what if he . . ."

"Sweetheart, don't even think that. Declan would never hurt you." He brushed a hand down her face resting it on her cheek. He could not believe that Declan meant her any harm. He had been friends with him for years; he would have known if Declan was evil. "You told me once that they all seemed interested in your locket. Has Declan ever expressed an interest in it?"

Meghan shivered and looked up at Fabrizio. "He told me that his grandmother has a locket with the same markings. And he commented on it a few days ago." She rested her hand on the locket as her mind whirled with worry. "What if he is lying to me?"

Fabrizio sighed with concern and stared down at Meghan. "If this has something to do with that locket, I don't think Declan knows about it." Fabrizio rested his lips against her forehead. "He loves you, Meghan." Fabrizio heard himself say quietly.

Meghan stared up at him with surprise. "I thought you didn't believe that?"

"I was being selfish. I honestly didn't think he would ever come back to you. After the shooting, he was different, guarded somehow, but now he seems to be . . ." His voice trailed off. "The man he used to be."

Meghan nodded and wiped away the tears that were dripping down her cheek. "But what if he isn't?" Meghan wrapped her arm across Fabrizio's chest, clinging to him for security. He was safe, and he would never hurt her. She could not understand what he was trying to tell her. Was he telling her to choose Declan? Had he given up on her too?

Declan's heart jumped into his throat when he arrived back in the living room and found Meghan wrapped in Fabrizio's arms, her eyes closed and her face pressed up against his chest.

"Caelan and Anisha are cleaning up," Declan muttered, trying his best not react to the intimate position he found his wife in. "I told her y' would come, tuck her in."

Meghan lifted her head from Fabrizio's chest, her eyes smouldering with green flames. Why was she looking at him like that? What had happened since he went upstairs? "Everyone is staying over tonight, so I need to get the bedrooms ready." Meghan directed her comment to Fabrizio, and then rested her hand on his face. "Thank you."

"You're welcome, sweetheart." Fabrizio kissed her lips softly, causing Declan to stir.

"You can sleep in the room at the end of the hall, or you could go back to Moiré's, it's up to you," Meghan said coolly and brushed by him on her way upstairs.

"Meggie?" Declan muttered as he followed her up the stairs to the hallway.

"That's your room." She pointed towards the open door, then darted up the set of narrow stairs leading to the third floor.

Meghan's voice flowed down the upper stairs as she attempted to get Caelan to clean up her mess and go to bed. Caelan was complaining at the prospect of having to go to bed, and Meghan was getting very agitated with her opposition. Declan could hear the anxiety in Meghan's voice and moved slowly up the stairs to the playroom, peeking his head in the door.

"Is there anything I can help with?"

"No, Caelan is just cleaning up before she goes to bed."

"Well, I guess I should help since I helped make some of this mess." Declan's voice trembled as he caught the look of distrust in Meghan's eyes.

Caelan looked at him with a smile of relief that she had some help.

"She doesn't need your help," Meghan grumbled, the sight of him setting her emotions into a tailspin. What was it he wanted from her?

"I want to. This is a very big room and will take her forever if she has to do it herself," Declan grinned at Caelan, then switched his gaze to Meghan and her distraught eyes.

"Declan, she knows that if she makes a mess, she has to clean it up," Meghan snapped, annoyed at his insistence to help.

"Meggie, don't be like that. Please just let me help her. I have nothing else to do." Declan felt his heart constricting; she wanted him to leave, to leave the house and his daughter.

"Fine, do what you want, you always do," Meghan growled and pushed by him and ran down the stairs.

"Meggie," Declan called after her but she continued down the narrow stairs and around the corner.

"Daddy, is Mommy mad at you?" Caelan questioned, her big grey eyes fixed on him.

"Aye, I think she is." Declan's voice filled with sadness, not sure what Meghan was angry with him for this time.

"Don't worry, she never stays mad for long." Caelan giggled and rested her hand on his arm.

Declan smiled at the wisdom of his little girl. She was so intuitive for such a young child. "Does Mommy get mad at y' a lot?"

"No."

Declan smiled, pleased with the answer and helped to clean up the large room. They put the books back on the shelves, the toys back in the toy box, the dolls back in the dollhouse, and the crayons and colouring books back on the little table by the window. He could not believe what a mess two children could make.

"Caelan, why do y' take out every toy in here. Why don't y' play with one thing at a time?"

"Mommy asks me that all the time."

"And what do y' tell her?"

"I don't know."

Declan's head flew back, and he laughed hard; she was a bright spot in his life, and he focused on that instead of the cold treatment he was receiving from Meghan. "Well, wee one, I think it will pass your mam's inspection."

"Good," Caelan sighed and began to play with the dollhouse.

Within seconds, she had all the pieces to the house on the floor again.

"Caelan, we just cleaned that up, what are y' doing?" Declan chuckled but looked towards the door when he heard footsteps.

"Not so easy, is it?" Meghan commented as she entered the room, staring at him, her eyes lifeless. "Moiré called, and she wants you to call her right away. She said your cell phone is off."

Declan sighed and moved towards Meghan cautiously; something was wrong with her. "Meggie, after I talk to Moiré, we need to talk."

"Fine, you can use the phone in my room if you want privacy. Everyone is still downstairs," Meghan muttered, her eyes staying fixed on Caelan, purposely avoiding Declan's gaze.

Declan forced a smile and wandered down the stairs and into her bedroom. Why was she brushing him off, telling him to go back to Moiré's? He could not help but wonder what Fabrizio had said to her while he was upstairs. Damn, he should not have left Meghan alone with Fabrizio, but he also could not be with her every second of the day, and if she did not believe in him enough not to be swayed by others, then maybe their relationship would never last.

Moiré's comments and attitude did nothing to improve Declan's mood, but when Meghan wandered into the room, her expression of disgust sent him over the edge.

"What the hell is wrong with y'?" Declan snorted as Meghan headed for her dresser after giving him a sidelong glance.

"Nothing, I was just surprised that you were still in here." She grabbed her brush and began to smooth down the auburn curls. "Are you done?"

"Aye, with Moiré but not with y'." Declan stalked towards her, causing her to step away.

Her withdrawal ripped at his heart, she was scared of him. "Meggie, what is wrong with y'?"

Meghan's eyes drooped with worry as she stared at him, trying to decide if she should tell him her thoughts. "Declan, why are you really here? What is it that you want?"

"I want y'." Declan forced a smile, trying to hide his anxiety. "I love y', Meggie."

"Do you?" Meghan took a step away from him and unfastened her locket. "Here, if you want this so badly, take it, but please leave before Caelan gets hurt."

Declan stared down at the locket, then his shocked eyes rose to hers. They were flashing with anger. "Freckles, I don't want your locket." She was figuring it out; damn, he was going to have to tell her something, but how much should he say, too much might scare her off. "I think it's time I told y' about something."

Meghan shuffled in place as if deciding whether to stay and listen. "Go ahead, Declan."

Declan sat on the bed and raised his hand out towards her. "It's a long story, so y' might want to sit down."

"I'll stand, thank you." Her voice sounded choked; she was scared he could see it in her eyes.

"You're right about your locket, it is . . ." he paused as she stepped backwards. "Well, it's your family's link to the past and to the future."

She shook her head and dropped to the chair on the far side of the room. "So you do want it?"

"No, not me." He forced a painful smile. "A man named Fergus O'Brien is the one that is after it I'm guessing, but I'm not sure why he wants it so badly. He is our cousin, Freckles, distant, mind y' but a relative all the same."

"What do you mean our?" Her eyes mirrored the terror that was in her voice.

"Meggie, we are distant cousins, about 450 years removed. Both our families originated from the O'Briens of Munster." He was determined to relay the information even though she was paling quickly. "My mother and you are two of the three descendants of the triad."

"The triad, what the hell are you talking about?" Meghan blurted out and jumped from the chair.

"Sit down first, Freckles, y' look like y' are going to pass out," Declan ordered and took a step towards her, but thought better of it and dropped to her bed, settling into his history lesson.

"In AD 976, our ancestor, Brian Boru, after the death of his brother, Mahon, became the head of the Dál gCais. After that through conquest of other Kingdoms in AD 1002, he established himself as, 'Ard Ri na hEireann,' High King of Ireland. After Brian's death in 1014, his descendants, the O'Briens, continued to rule the Kingdom of Munster until the twelfth century before their territory shrunk to the Kingdom of Thomond, which they would hold for just under five centuries.

"The downfall of the O'Briens began when King Henry VIII's wife, Catherine of Aragon, failed to produce him a son and heir. He tried to divorce her, but the Catholic Church in Rome refused to allow it. In 1541, King Henry VIII renounced the spiritual authority of the Pope, declaring himself head of the Church of England. After that, the problems grew in Ireland.

"In 1543, Murrogh O'Brien surrendered his Irish royalty to King Henry VIII of England. He was then named Earl of Thomond and Eamon was named Baron Briarmon. However, it came with a few conditions. They had to abandon their previous titles, and they had to adopt English customs and laws and pledge allegiance to the English crown. They also needed to abandon the Roman Catholic Church and convert to the Anglican Church of England. Eamon begrudgingly complied, wanting to keep his title, but secretly stayed a Papist. Eamon was married to Elizabeth, who was a relation of Gerald Fitzgerald, 15th Earl of Desmond."

Meghan stood and stared out the window but said nothing, so he continued.

"During Queen Elizabeth I's reign she enforced an act, prohibiting a member of the Roman Catholic Church from celebrating the rites of faith after the Pope excommunicated her. The punishment ranged from loss of property to death. So Eamon and his wife held mass secretly in a priest hole he constructed in a hidden room in the castle in fear of being found out. Now, Eamon had three sons, Michael who produced your branch was the youngest. William was my branch, and he was the oldest, and Colin, the middle son, was Fergus O'Brien's branch. In 1570, Michael, who was then twenty, realized that he would not inherit the estate or the title because he was the youngest, and he did something that changed the history of our family forever."

Meghan sighed when Declan paused, her head rising to meet his gaze. "How do you know all this?"

"Me Mam told me some of it, but I researched the majority of it." Declan forced a smile, not missing the expression of distrust crossing Meghan's face.

"How long have you known about this? Did you know that I was the third member of the triad when we were at the lodge?" Meghan questioned and glanced up at him.

"After I saw the locket I suspected that your family must have been connected somehow, but I wasn't sure. It looked so much like me grandma's but hers was not a locket. It had no back to it. When y' told me that your grandda gave it to y' and said it had been passed down through the years, I did some research and found that y' were a direct descendant."

"Why didn't you tell me this before? You have been lying to me all this time," Meghan snorted, her dark eyes pinning him for a response.

"I didn't lie, I just wasn't sure how to tell y'. But now I think y' need to know."

Meghan eyed him for a moment, trying to comprehend what he was telling her. "So what did Michael do that caused so much trouble?" Meghan was suddenly concerned with what her ancestor had done.

Declan smiled and continued. At least she was listening to the history and not bolting. "By 1570, Eamon and his wife Beth still owned their original estate due to political wangling on behalf of Eamon and his relationship with Queen Elizabeth. Eamon had been appointed the Earl of Briarwood a few years earlier by the queen because she wanted to reward his loyalty to her when all the other Earls were rebelling, especially Beth's relative the Earl of Desmond. It was in that year that Beth was told by a Gaelic seer that one of her sons would betray her. She believed that it would be Colin, the middle son, because he married an English courtier whose family was very loyal to the queen. At some point, she had identical amulets made for each son to protect them from harm. So they have been passed down to the oldest child ever since. Somewhere along the line, yours was made into a locket."

Meghan nodded and squeezed her hand tightly around the locket, her only link to the past. "But why is Fergus after mine if he has one of his own?"

"Well, from what I can figure out, he thinks that it will lead him to what Michael hid." Declan shook his head. "I'm getting ahead of meself." Declan glanced over at Meghan, her eyes glued to him, her face ghostly white. "Freckles, are y' all right?"

"No, I don't understand what this has to do with me." Her voice, soft and concerned.

"Well, Michael, after watching the Desmonds being killed and jailed over the last few years, decided to turn in his father for being a Papist to ensure that he would not lose his estate." Declan looked up when Meghan gasped.

"My ancestor did that? Why?" Meghan muttered, feeling ashamed of her ancestor.

"Greed, he wanted everything his father had, but when Queen Elizabeth was told, she was furious of Eamon's betrayal and as an example, he was brought to the Tower of London and beheaded." Declan continued, "She rewarded Michael by granting him the title of Earl of Briarwood and deeding him all of his father's estate."

Meghan stared at him in shock. Why hadn't she ever heard this family history before? Is this what her grandfather had been hiding?

"So this locket was passed down to me by a man who had his father killed?" Meghan stared at the locket, then discarded it on the dresser.

"Aye, but the thing was that Michael never thought things through. He thought his father would be jailed like Gerald Fitzgerald Desmond for a couple of years, and he would get some of his father's estate. It didn't dawn on him the consequences. Beth was heartbroken and died a few months later, which crushed Michael. He was so distraught that he spent the next ten years in solitude. Rumours that he had gone crazy spread throughout the country, and no one dared go near the cursed castle. His brothers disowned him after the death of their father, and he was completely alone. However, Colin demanded that Michael turn over the family jewels and the swords that belonged to their ancestor Brian Boru. Colin believed the sword held magical powers that protected Brian in battle. Colin was of the evil sort, and it is rumoured that he was overheard to say he wished he had turned his father in first."

"You really don't believe the sword was magical, do you?" Meghan blurted out, eyeing Declan with interest.

Declan was startled by the comment. "Well, it doesn't really matter what I think. If Fergus believes it, that might be what he's after. Michael hid it somewhere, and it has never been found."

"Well, I don't have it!" Meghan blurted out. "I have never even heard about this before."

Declan stood and stretched. "Meggie, I think we need a cup of tea before I tell you anymore. I'll bring some up for y'." Declan could see how distressed his story had made her, and he needed to calm things down.

Meghan nodded as Declan moved towards the door. "Please don't go anywhere, I need to finish."

"Don't worry, I want to hear the rest of this. Declan, could you bring up some cookies? I'm hungry," she smiled slightly when his brow rose with mischief as he wandered out of the room.

Fabrizio was nowhere in sight as Declan arrived at the bottom of the kitchen stairs, which was a great relief since his main goal was to get back upstairs to Meghan. With the tea in hand, he was back in her bedroom, but it was empty.

"Damn!" he muttered, placing the pot on the dresser with annoyance.

"Is that you, Declan?" Meghan wandered out of the bathroom, but she stopped, suddenly startled by his facial expression as he gazed at her pale pink satin tank top and matching baggy shorts. "I like to sleep in a tank top," she muttered, unsure what he was thinking.

"I see that, I like to sleep in me boxers." Declan watched her face fill with anxiety.

"Oh," she muttered and shuffled to the bed. "I just thought that this could be a long night, so I wanted to get comfortable."

Declan eyed her sidelong, then moved over to the bed with her cup of tea. "Y' look like y' could use this."

"Thank you," Meghan said softly, taking the cup from his hands. Her mind was spinning with turmoil over what had been happening over the day. She did not want to believe that Declan meant her or Caelan any harm. He claimed he loves her, but she had to be sure. "Declan, why are so many Irishmen showing up in town?"

Declan shrugged and sat down beside her, his hand resting on her locket she was now holding. He had been worrying about the same thing. "Well, I would venture to say that it has something to do with this." He lifted the silver locket from her hand. "I have to say it is almost identical to the one me grandma had except hers had a different insignia on the silver. I haven't seen it for years, but looking at yours, it almost looks like a puzzle piece."

Meghan sighed and gazed up at him. "Do you think that Ian is Rory?"

Declan eyed her with interest; he had been thinking the same thing. "Well, it is awfully coincidental that he goes back and forth to Ireland, and every time a group of Irishmen show up, so does his double." Declan scrubbed his hand across his eyes.

"So do you," Meghan muttered, not meaning to.

Declan jerked from the comment and glanced down at her. "Y' think I'm involved?" he sighed, as the realization of her attitude earlier became clear to him. That is what she and Fabrizio had been discussing, and he had most likely provoked her. "I guess in a way I am, since I'm one of the triad, and if Rory is involved, I wonder . . ."

"Declan, he's on his way here to kill us!" Meghan mumbled and leaned into him. "We need to hide."

"Freckles, calm down, I won't allow him to harm y'." Declan kissed the top of her head. He did not believe Rory would harm anyone. Something was not adding up.

"Do you want me to finish the story?" Declan eyed her with interest.

"Yes. I need to hear it." She forced a smile and made herself comfortable on the bed.

"Well, years went by, and Michael was rarely seen in public. However, one day, he showed up in town at the market. Everyone was staring at him like he was a leper and clearing a path as he walked. Some say he had the Boru sword in his belt, but that is just rumour. Anyway, he was just about to leave when from out behind a table walked the most beautiful lass he had ever seen. She had long flowing red hair, big green eyes, and a face full of freckles."

"Oh," Meghan's muttered and glanced up at his smirking face.

"I could be describing y'," Declan smiled and kissed her cheek. "Maybe that's why I noticed y'. It was like seeing a girl from a childhood fairy tale."

Meghan crinkled her noise, which made him laugh. "Anyway, Michael fell in love and married that girl and so your family continued."

"So what happened to the sword and the family jewels?"

"No one knows. No one has ever seen the sword again after that day, and the only piece of jewelry ever seen again was his mother Beth's ruby necklace that his wife Catherine wore on her wedding day."

"Wow, this is one incredible story. Are you sure it's not just a folk tale? You don't honestly believe that Fergus thinks I am hiding a magical sword, do you?"

Declan shrugged as a loud knock on the door broke their attention. Hayley's dark eyes peered through the door.

"Sorry," Hayley blurted out, eyeing Declan and Meghan's positioning on the bed. "I didn't realize you were . . ." Her dark gaze lowered to the floor.

"It's okay." Meghan bit her bottom lip. Why did she feel like a teenager who had just been caught with her boyfriend in her room? "What do you want?"

"Fabrizio wanted me to see if you were all right, and he wants to know if he can come up and talk to you," Hayley muttered, her gaze still stuck on Declan.

"Freckles, why don't I go back to the other room so y' and Fabrizio can talk," Declan offered, eyeing Meghan's stressed face.

"No, I'll go see what he wants." Meghan jumped from the bed and gripped Declan's arm. "Please stay here."

"Aye," Declan grinned wildly, but he was concerned with allowing Meghan anywhere near Fabrizio again; she seemed very open to suggestion at the moment. "Freckles, do y' want me to go talk to him?"

Meghan shook her head. "No, I'll do it. You know, after everything that has happened, he still cares for you a lot. When I told him I thought you . . . Well, he said that you loved me and would never harm me." She gazed back at Declan and sighed.

"He said that?" Declan was surprised. "He's a good man, that Fabs."

"Declan, I am so sorry that I am the cause of you two not being friends anymore," Meghan sniffed and rested her hand on his shoulder. "If I could do it all over again."

"Meggie, this is not your fault." Declan kissed her forehead. "Most of the blame falls on me mam's shoulder, convincing me that you shot me. If I might have been a stronger man, I would have figured out what she was doing long before I did." Declan's voice was apologetic. "I'm the one to be sorry."

Meghan smiled and rested her head on his shoulder. "Declan, mend the fences with him. You need him in your life."

"Aye. I have missed him terribly."

Meghan moved towards the door. "I am going to tell him the same thing." Meghan smiled and disappeared out the door.

Meghan was startled awake by an unfamiliar sound coming from outside her window. She jumped to her feet, seeing a disturbing light dancing across the pale cream wall.

"Oh my God! The barn is on fire." A loud shriek filled the room as she stood by the window, looking out in horror as bright orange flames ate away at the walls of the barn. "Molly and the foal are inside!" she shrieked and bolted out the bedroom door.

Declan was startled awake by her shrieks, and he was on his feet and at the door before she was down the stairs. "Meggie, wait," Declan shouted, slipping into his jeans and dashing down the stairs behind her. Nathan also had awakened to the commotion and was on his way down the stairs by the time Agent Cameron made it to the front door.

"What is going on?" Agent Cameron shouted to the departing backs of the two men.

"The barn is on fire," Nathan shouted over his shoulder, not stopping to explain.

The men were half way across the lawn when flames broke through the roof of the barn.

"Holy Christ!" Declan screamed as a terrifying panic surged through his body. "Meggie, where the hell are y'?"

Meghan was at the barn and found it engulfed in flames. The horses were whinnying and kicking at the stall door, with the knowledge that they were trapped. Meghan had no alternative; she needed to release the mare and foal from the inferno, or they would die. She covered her mouth with her tank top and ran into the smoke and flame-filled barn. Her mind completely focused on freeing the trapped horses. An obstacle course of flames and falling wood was before her as the fire attacked every inch of the grand structure.

Meghan darted back and forth as burning planks from the roof above began to fall in a defiant surrender to the flaming lady. She stumbled along the edge of the stalls until she arrived at the door trapping Molly and her foal in the inferno. The smoke was so dense, she struggled for breath and could barely see as she fumbled with the latch to the stall. When the latch finally came free, she pulled open the stall door, and Molly darted for freedom followed by her foal. In

Molly's excitement, she bumped into the stall door, sending Meghan flying backwards, her head slamming against the cement floor. Her last thought as the sharp pain fanned across the back of her head was that the roof was coming down.

Declan arrived at the barn as Molly and her foal bolted through the door, but Meghan did not emerge, and she was not visible through the impenetrable black smoke and flames that were shooting from the stalls.

"Meggie, where are y?" Declan shouted, but not waiting for a response, he darting in through the door, frantically searching for her, the smoke burning his eyes and throat. It seemed like a lifetime before he found the stall with the open door, but he could not see Meghan; the thick, heavy smoke was clouding his eyes.

Frantically, he groped the floor, on his hands and knees, trying to locate the woman he could not lose again. A shriek filled the darkness when his hand felt a piece of satin fabric, and he tugged on it until he found her legs. He was not sure if he pulled her towards him or if he had moved towards her, all he knew was that she was in his arms, her body limp and covered with soot. A primal fear in him emerged, that he had only experienced once before, the night Rory was pointing the gun at Meghan. Shit, it was Rory. His mind was in turmoil as the night they were shot played over and over again in slow motion as he struggled to his feet and staggered for the light of the open door.

With all the horrifying missions he had been on in his years of service with the Navy Seals, he had never experienced a fear as deep and terrifying as when Meghan was in danger. The dread he felt at the prospect of losing her again was more than he could endure.

Sparks were stabbing at his face and chest in a brutal attack as he got closer to the light of safety. The flames seemed to be subsiding as Nathan and Agent Cameron battled the aggressive blazing menace, armed only with garden hoses. However, the smoke surged up in retaliation to the attack, closing in on Declan and Meghan like a veil of black death. The impenetrable cloak was permeating his lungs in an attempt to smother him and take him as a prisoner of war. Declan, however, was well trained in the finer points of warfare and was determined not to become a casualty.

It was a horrifying sound as a large beam crashed to the floor behind him. He would have sworn the roof above him was moaning as the flames attacked its strength. The roof was coming down, and he needed to get the hell out of the barn. He struggled with every fibre of his being to reach the safety of the door, even though every muscle was burning from the weight of her limp body. His legs gave out as he took his last steps through the door, and he fell to the ground outside the barn.

Fabrizio was the one who carried her away from the barn and away from him, setting Declan into a panic. With what little strength he had, he pulled himself to where Fabrizio had her lying across his lap. Her face was blackened from the smoke, and her satin tank top was full of holes from burning embers.

"Thank God she's still breathing," Fabrizio mumbled.

As Fabrizio stroked Meghan's hair and face, she coughed and opened her eyes staring at him like a lost fawn; her deep green eyes were wide and questioning. "Fabrizio." Her voice was raspy. "Thank you."

Fabrizio forced a smile and kissed her cheek.

Meghan's eyes moved from Fabrizio to Declan's soot-covered face as he hovered over her. Her hand reached out for Declan's face. "You look like crap."

A morose chuckled exited Declan before he dropped his head down next to hers, pressing his face up tightly against hers. "Meggie, y' are going to be the death of me."

"So you've told me," she smiled, then glanced at the brown eyes above her. "Fabrizio, help me up."

"No, y' are staying put," Declan grumbled, noticing Hayley darting across the lawn in complete hysteria with blankets in hand.

Declan took the blankets from Hayley's shaking hand and laid one of the thick woollen blanks over top of Meghan's shivering body and wrapped the other around his bare shoulders.

"Are you guys okay? The Fire Department is on the way," Hayley babbled, assessing the situation, noticing it was Declan that was covered in soot, not Fabrizio.

"Aye, I think so," Declan said as he looked back down at Meghan. Her face was covered in soot, but he could see a cut on her forehead. "Are y' okay?"

"I think so. My throat is sore, and my eyes sting." Declan was staring at her with so much love in his eyes that everything around her seemed to disappear, and all she could see was him. Her hands instinctively reached out for him, begging him to hold her, to keep her safe.

Declan noticed the gesture and gathered her into his arms, pulling her from Fabrizio's lap. Fabrizio put up no resistance as the realization that he had lost shot through him like a burning poker. Declan risked his life to save her; maybe he loved her more than Fabrizio gave him credit for.

"Meggie, what the hell were y' thinking going in there like that? I have never seen such a reckless thing to do in all me life," Declan grumbled, once she was settled in his arm.

"I had to get Molly and her foal out. I couldn't let them die," Meghan muttered, her voice shaky. She was realizing how close she came to dying, and how much danger she caused Declan. She left him no alternative but to go in after her.

Declan shook his head and wiped his hand across his eyes. "I was so scared when I couldn't find y' in there."

"I'm sorry, I didn't mean to scare you. All I was thinking about were the horses."

"That's the problem, Meggie, y' didn't think. Y' just ran head first into a dangerous situation. I can't always be around to save y'," Declan scolded and wiped the soot away from her eyes.

Meghan jerked up, trying to get to her feet, but he gripped her arm, holding down. "Where do y' think you're going?"

"Let go!" Meghan pleaded as she turned her face away from him.

Declan gripped his dirty hand around her chin, turning her face towards him, and he saw total devastation in her eyes. "What is it?"

Meghan stared at him as if she were looking straight through him but didn't say a word.

"Meggie, tell me what you're thinking? You're scaring me."

"Nothing," she said as she pulled away from Declan. After all these years, she finally knew that he blamed her for the shooting. It was her fault; Declan was just caught in the crossfire. If she had handled the situation better instead of rushing into a relationship with Declan. Now she was doing it again, jumping head first into a relationship without thinking about the consequences. One of them was sitting only a few feet away.

Meghan's soot-covered face turned towards Fabrizio, and the pain was evident in his eyes. Why did she keep hurting everyone around her? She was a selfish being, only thinking about her feeling, not giving Fabrizio's feelings a second thought. Tears dripped down her face as she stared at Fabrizio, unable to break her gaze.

"Meghan, are you all right?" Fabrizio's voice was soft, noticing the expression on her face. Something had changed in her, and he was not sure if for the better.

"No," Meghan sniffed and forced herself to her feet, turning her back on both men.

"Meghan, when are you going to realize that he has brought nothing but misery to your life?" Fabrizio said sharply, deciding he had nothing to lose, and he planned to take Declan down with him.

"Don't y' dare try blaming this on me. I was the one that went in after her, if y' remember. I didn't see y' in there," Declan grumbled, his ego taking a hit.

"I wouldn't have let her go inside in the first place," Fabrizio growled.

"Shut up, both of you!" Meghan yelled as the two men continued to bicker with each other. "Just shut up, I can't take it anymore." Her voice sounded choked, as she forced down the sobs. "Please, both of you just stop it." She turned and bolted into the house as the fire department arrived.

CHAPTER TWENTY-TWO

The next morning, Meghan awoke to the birds singing on the porch railing, the morning resembling any other morning, but it was not. She was being held captive in her own house, her barn was destroyed, and she had come to the realization that she was constantly putting Declan's life in danger.

"Megs, can I come in?" Nathan's voice broke her thoughts as he peered through the door, his brown eyes filled with worry.

"Sure, come on in." She was sitting on the bed, still in her robe, brushing her hair as Nathan sat down on the bed beside her.

Declan was leaving his room and heard voices coming from Meghan's room. The anxiety that Fabrizio was with her pushed him towards her bedroom door. He was concerned with her state of mind after her reaction to him the night before. Why couldn't he control her, she was far too unpredictable, but that just made his feeling for her stronger. He shook his head, realizing that her unpredictability was the trait that had attracted him so strongly years earlier.

"Megs, are you okay?" Nathan questioned, laying his hand on her leg.

"No, what the hell is happening? Why did the barn start on fire?" Meghan sniffed.

"I don't know, but we do seem to be having a stroke of bad luck." Nathan soothed and patted her leg.

"This has been the worst week of my life," she snorted.

"Oh, Megs, just be thankful that no one was hurt."

"Yes," she sniffed.

"If the FBI hadn't arrived, Kevin would have been here at the ranch, and he might have been trapped upstairs in the barn, or what if it happened when all the kids were here?"

"Oh my God, I didn't even think about that."

"See, darlin', there is a bright side to everything." Nathan kissed the side of her head.

"I guess so," she agreed, but felt deep down that Nathan was wrong. Nothing was all right. She pushed Declan away, and she was dragging poor Fabrizio through hell, not to mention how her friendship with Cassie would survive if she ever found out Fabrizio still loved Meghan, and she was doing little to discourage him. How was she going to fix things, could she? She was not even sure if she wanted to. Maybe she would be better off if both men left, and she spent the rest of her life alone.

"Don't forget about Declan, you're happy that he is back in your life?" Nathan soothed, assessing the expression crossing her face.

Meghan shook her head and wiped her eyes. "He can't be in my life."

"Megs, what are you talking about?"

"Every time he is near me, he gets hurt. I can't bear to see him get hurt anymore because of me."

"Megs, you're being ridiculous."

"It's true. He almost died last night because I made a stupid decision."

"Dammit, Megs, would you snap out of this pity party and focus on what really matters?"

"What really matters, Nat?" Meghan's mind was so clogged with what had happened, she could not find any bright light.

"Caelan and Declan," Nathan snorted.

"Nat, don't you understand? I have put everyone I love in danger. Ian is on his way here, and we are all in danger. Look what I have done to Fabrizio. He has been there for me all these years, and he is dating my best friend. Why do I still lead him on? How can I be doing this to him and Cassie?

"Megs, please don't think that way. Cassie knew what she was getting in to. I know you have been struggling with your decision for the last week, and to be honest, I think you made the right choice.

You were never truly happy with Fabrizio, and he loves Cassie on some level, I'm sure of it. Everything will work out.

"You have never liked Fabrizio," Meghan muttered and leaned against Nathan's shoulder.

"Why should I? He is constantly trying to kick me out," Nathan grumbled.

"You like Declan though, don't you?" Meghan eyed him curiously. "You always have."

"That's because he's always treated me with respect," Nathan grinned. "Did you know his little brother Colin is gay? I wonder if he looks like Declan?"

Meghan laughed despite herself, "I have seen pictures, he's pretty cute. He has the same eyes and dark hair, he just a little shorter and thinner."

Nathan's brow rose slightly before Meghan smacked him on the arm. "Don't be getting any idea's"

"Don't worry Megs, I'm not going anywhere without you, you and Caelan are my family, and if I lose you, I would be devastated."

Meghan put her hand on his face and smiled softly. "Oh, Nat, I'm sorry. I shouldn't be telling you where you can go. I have no right."

"Darlin', that's not what I meant. What I am trying to tell you is that I think that you and Declan are meant to be together. I knew a long time ago that you could never love anyone as much as you love him. And fate has brought him back to you, and you shouldn't push him away."

"Nat, I have too much to worry about right now. I am just too tired to try anymore. I think it might be best for all concerned to cut them both loose. We could be by ourselves, Nat, you, me, and Caelan."

"Darlin', don't let him walk out of your life again. You'll regret it."

"It doesn't matter anymore." Meghan closed her eyes and softly sighed. She was so overwhelmed, she did not know what to think.

Declan felt his heart collapsing. Cut him loose, how had she come to that decision overnight? He was devastated that she turned to Nathan instead of him. Nathan gets to stay. Nathan was her best friend, maybe he owned her heart. If Nathan were not gay, would they be together?

Declan found himself outside on the porch, sitting on the swing. A deep sigh exited him as he watched the wind chimes blow in the early morning wind. Maybe it was best if he left and dealt with the issue of

Caelan from the safety of Los Angeles. He was finding it too painful to deal with Meghan.

Agent Paxton wandered through the screen door and stared at Declan with interest. He was impressed with the bravery Declan displayed the night before when he went into the barn after Meghan.

"Mr. Montgomery, I received some very interesting information regarding you last night," Agent Paxton questioned, breaking Declan's thoughts.

"Did y'?" Declan said, with little interest.

"I have. Fabrizio told me you were in the navy with him?" he questioned with interest.

"Aye, I was," he said evenly.

"Hmm. He said you were in an elite Seals unit?" Paxton questioned.

"Aye, I was."

Agent Paxton eyed Declan curiously as he gave his abrupt answers. "Well, what is the big secret?"

"There's no secret. It's just part of me past, and I don't particularly like discussing it."

"Oh. Why did you take a discharge?" Agent Paxton questioned with interest.

"I got burnt out," Declan sighed. "I wanted to live a normal life for a while, and when I was offered a job as a stunt man, I figured that was as good a job as any. At least, I would be in one place longer than a week."

"I guess seven years of chaos was enough?" Paxton smiled.

"Aye, more than enough. I joined because me parents wanted me to become a career officer, but I just got tired of seeing all the horrors of the world," Declan admitted. "I'm not tough enough not to let it get to me."

"I understand, I was in the missing children's unit for quite some time, but I had to transfer. I was at the point when we caught an offender that raped and killed a child. I wanted to jump across the table and strangle them. I couldn't take it anymore, so I asked for a transfer."

"Aye, I don't blame y'."

"Well, I'm going in to check on Meghan," Agent Paxton smiled. "I'm sure you can take care of yourself, but for my peace of mind, stay around the house."

"Aye, I won't leave the porch," Declan agreed.

Meghan entered the kitchen and found Agent Paxton sitting at the island drinking a cup of coffee. "So, Agent Paxton, what would you like for breakfast?"

"It doesn't matter, whatever you're making," he smiled, with an ease he did not have the night before.

Nathan was behind her, and he could not hold back the remark. "What she is making? That should be interesting."

"Funny, Nat," Meghan snorted and swatted at his shoulder.

"Well, you don't want to poison our guests? Why isn't Hayley cooking?"

"She's still asleep. I don't want to wake her, and anyway, I was just planning on waffles and eggs, I have some nice fresh farm eggs."

"Don't eat anything she cooks." Fabrizio's voice boomed through the air. "You'll regret it."

Meghan glowered at him, but settled quickly into getting the eggs from the fridge.

"Meghan, I'll eat whatever you cook," said the hungry Agent Paxton.

"Okay, but you're taking a big risk. That's why I don't eat here for breakfast," Nathan joked, not appearing disturbed by Fabrizio and his expression of annoyance. Nathan knew very well that his presence in the house was disturbing Fabrizio.

"What are you talking about, Nat? You are always here for breakfast," Meghan questioned, ignoring Fabrizio as well.

"Yeah, but I wait until you're gone to cook something myself," Nathan laughed and snuck up behind Meghan, gripping her around the waist from behind and kissing the side of her face.

Declan could hear them talking and laughing in the kitchen, and he was concerned that Fabrizio was with his Meggie. When he arrived in the kitchen, she was still in Nathan's arms, talking quietly with him.

"So what am I missing?" Declan's voice was filled with amusement as he eyed her positioning in Nathan's arms and the look of disgust on Fabrizio's face. Why did Nathan's relationship with Meghan bug Fabrizio so much?

"Oh nothing, Nat is just bugging me about my cooking skills," Meghan giggled as Nathan tickled her ribs.

"Oh, so how are y' doing this morning?" Declan asked, taking a step towards her.

"Fine." Her gaze settled on him, with the same hurt look she had in her eyes the night before.

"That's good." He knew that she was lying to him, and he was not sure if she was hiding it from him or the others in the room. He had obviously hurt her again last night somehow, and he realized he had to make her understand how much he loves her.

The phone rang, breaking his thoughts, and he watched Nathan move across the kitchen and lift the receiver. "Yeah?" he asked quickly.

"Declan?" asked the annoyed woman.

"No, it's Nathan."

"Get Declan, I must speak to him at once!" demanded the woman.

"Yeah, don't get your shorts in a knot, darlin'," Nathan said in a sarcastic tone.

"It's for you." Nathan handed the portable phone to Declan, then turned his attention to Fabrizio, who was appearing stressed that Declan was receiving calls at Meghan's house.

"Hello," Declan said calmly, his eye still on Meghan.

"Declan, what in heaven's name are y' doing there? Your sister said y' didn't come home last night. She said y' are associating with that wicked woman?"

"Mam! Stop it. I don't have to explain me actions to y'."

"Moiré said that y' have put yourself in harm's way again. Listen to me, get out of there right now." Katie's voice was raising with panic.

"No, Mam, I'm staying here. Meggie and Caelan need me, and I'm not leaving them." Declan lowered his voice and turned his back on the group in the kitchen. When his mother began to yell into the phone, he walked with the phone into the living room for privacy, leaving the curious group behind.

"Declan, this is not your problem, get out of there before y' get hurt again." Katie could not understand why he would not listen to her. It was happening again. Where Meghan was concerned, there was no reasoning with him.

"Darling, don't do this to me!"

"Y' did this to yourself. Y' destroyed any chance that I had for happiness. All these years, y' kept me from the woman I love," Declan yelled.

"I did it for y'. Y' were self-destructing around her. I had to keep y' apart for your own good."

"Me own good? It wasn't for my good, it was for yours. Y' ruined me life," Declan shouted again.

"I'm coming out there. Y' obviously have lost all common sense. I'll be there by this afternoon." Katie slammed the phone down.

"Bloody hell." Declan grumbled and dropped the phone to the coffee table. He realized how loud his voice was, and the last thing he wanted was to explain the call, so he went back out onto the porch to avoid the group in the kitchen. How he wished his relationship with Fabrizio had not disintegrated the way it had! He was his best friend at one time, the one person he could trust. Would they ever get their friendship back? He needed him.

Meghan watched him leave through the front door; his shoulders slouched forward with obvious distress. Her eyes settled on Nathan. She was not sure if she should follow Declan or not, but when Nathan bobbed his head towards the kitchen door, she knew what to do.

Meghan found Declan sitting on the swing, brooding over his situation. She walked nervously down the porch dropping down beside him, but unable to look at him, she glanced over at the pile of ash that was once her barn and shook her head.

"I can't believe that my barn is destroyed. What a week!" she sighed, unsure how to begin her apology.

Declan looked over at her and nodded. "That it has."

"What am I going to do with all those kids? They look forward to coming to camp and now," she sighed, her eyes still locked on the pile of blackened rubble.

"We'll think of something, maybe we can get some trailers or something," Declan said softly, reaching out and tucking a curl behind her ear.

"It won't matter much if they don't find Ian. I can't allow all those children to be in danger," she sniffed, her gaze settling on him.

"Meggie, when we were in the barn, I remembered the shooting, and I remember Rory shooting me. It was him, you were right. I don't think it's him causing these problems," Declan confessed and wrapped his arm around her shoulder.

"What do you mean?" Meghan blurted out.

"Well, the FBI agents keep talking as if Rory is a murderer, but we know it was an accident that he shot me, and I have seen him many times since, and nothing has happened. What has changed to make him hunt y' down now?"

Meghan shrugged and rested her head on his shoulder, glad that he now admitted it was his brother. "I don't know. I was wondering the same thing. Is it because of the article in the *National Interest*?"

Declan glanced down at her and sighed. "If I would have known this would turn out this way, I would have been a wee bit more discrete. Other than Georgia's da getting cross with me, I didn't think us rekindling our . . ." He flinched slightly not knowing what to call it. "Well, y' know what I mean."

"Yes." Meghan sat up and glanced at the pile of rubble once again. Why was this relationship so hard? Why couldn't they just say what they thought, without all the lies and secrets? She knew she had no more secrets, but she wasn't sure about him. "I guess when this is all over, you are going back to Los Angeles."

Declan's eyes mirrored a sadness as he stared at her. She seemed so anxious to get rid of him. "Aye, I have a lot to do there before I leave for Ireland to finish up filming."

Meghan smiled despondently. "How long are you gone for?"

"It should only be another two months."

"Oh," she mumbled, unsure what to say to him.

"Would you like to come with me? Well, I mean y' and Caelan," he smiled softly as he gazed into her eyes, but he could not control his emotions any longer. "Dammit, Meggie!"

She blinked from his sudden comment.

"What the hell is going on? I heard you talking to Nathan"

"I'm sorry," she muttered biting at her bottom lip. "I'm just scared."

"I know, Freckles." He soothed, tightening his grip around her shoulder, pulling her into his chest. "But please let me help y'."

"Declan," she cried against his chest. "I can't bear to see you hurt again."

"Meggie, I'm not going to get hurt," he said firmly. "Why can't y' understand that I would do anything for y'?"

"I do, I understand all too well what you would do for me," she sniffed, pressing her hand against the spot on his chest where the bullet pierced him years earlier. "Declan, you almost died because of me."

"No, it was because of Rory!" he snorted, gripping her hand, holding it hostage against his chest. "I am starting to think me mam organized the whole thing to keep you away from me, and it got out of hand. Rory went to your room, and he seemed surprised I was there. He thought I was out for dinner with me mam. Maybe he was just going to get the locket for me mam."

"I don't think it was your mom. There were more people in that room with Rory, and my mom and the big man wanted my locket. I think this had to do with me, and I think Rory was involved with them. Do you think he knows about what you told me last night?"

"It's possible, but my mam only told us about the folk tale about Michael meeting Catherine and that the lockets were passed down through the generations. I found out about the triad and sword legend when I was doing research."

Meghan sighed and glanced out over the field. "When you go to Ireland, is it okay if I come with you? Maybe I should sell the estate and then all this madness will stop."

"That might be a good idea." Declan was startled when the screen door flew open, and Fabrizio and his fellow agents headed towards them.

Fabrizio eyed their intimate positioning, then turned towards Andy. "We got a call that someone has broken into your house in Los Angeles, so Agent Paxton and Agent Cameron are heading out there. Andy and I are staying here until Ian is caught."

"Someone broke into me house? Was anyone hurt?" Declan sat erect on the swing, dislodging Meghan from his chest.

"No, your maid said that nothing was taken, just a note was left on the table," Fabrizio grumbled, his focus on Meghan. Fabrizio always knew that Meghan loved Declan more than she did him, but he had held out hope that someday she would give her whole heart to him. "Apparently there was no evidence of a break in."

"What did the note say?" Declan blurted out, missing Fabrizio's point.

"We can't discuss that right now, but it appears that the writer was trying to lead us away from Meghan. We believe that it is a diversion, so two of us are staying put. There has to be a number of people involved."

"Fabrizio, could it be that same group?" Meghan blurted out as the thought occurred to her. If Rory was involved with them years earlier, maybe he was still working with them. Her hand rested on her locket. "They are after me!"

"Calm down, Meggie, they will not get near y', I won't allow it." Declan soothed, hoping to settle her.

"Meghan." Fabrizio gripped her hand and pulled her from the swing. "You need to stay inside."

"He's right, Meggie," Declan agreed and pushed her towards the door. "I'll be in shortly."

Meghan eyed him with worry, then turned and went into the house. Once the door closed behind her, Declan turned to Fabrizio, with concern crossing his face.

"Fabs, I think we need to put the problems between us aside and work together. I think between the two of us we can control her and keep her from doing anything daft. You know how she gets under pressure."

Fabrizio nodded with agreement. "I wish things didn't turn out the way they did, Monty. I miss you."

Declan smiled and rested his hand on Fabrizio's shoulder. "I miss y' as well. Do y' think we can put this behind us?"

Fabrizio shrugged and glanced towards the kitchen door. "I don't know. I love her, and I won't apologize for that."

"I don't expect y' to," Declan sighed. "I never thought a woman would come between us."

Fabrizio nodded and shook his head. "Damn, I tried not to love her. I even started dating Cassie. She is a fantastic woman, and I love her, but I just look into Meghan's eyes, and I melt."

Declan started to laugh despite himself. "Welcome to my world. She has been doing that to me since the minute I met her." Declan's face went solemn. "I can't give her up."

Fabrizio leaned against the railing. "Neither can I."

"Well, I guess we have a problem then." Declan glanced around. "Fabs, why don't we leave it to her? Whatever she decides, I will respect."

"All right," Fabrizio agreed begrudgingly. Even if she chose him, she would never completely love him.

The two men shook hands and headed into the house.

Meghan strolled into her bedroom and across the cream-coloured carpet to her bed. Hayley had already changed the soot-covered sheets from the night before, her pale floral bedspread back in place. A deep sigh exited her as she contemplated the events of the past week. Her mind was whirling with her decision; it was fighting her heart, which had no reservations.

She jumped, slightly startled by the sound of the back stairs squeaking. "Nat, Fabrizio, is that you?"

Meghan got up quietly from the bed, crept to the door to her room, and peeked down the long narrow hall. The shadows that the midday sun cast were dancing across the wall as the trees swayed outside the bedroom windows. She stopped and listened to the creaking of the stairs coming up from the kitchen.

"Nat, is that you?" she said as she slowly peeked out the door.

"No, Doctor Coleman, it's me!" the young man from the fairgrounds growled and ran towards her, displacing the carpet runner under his feet. Meghan screamed hysterically and slammed the door.

The man was throwing himself into the locked door in a desperate attempt to gain entry, and the steady thump was terrifying her.

"Y' better open this door. I'm going to get in if I have to knock it down," he yelled and continued to slam into the door. The door was bending and heaving at the seams from the impact, mesmerizing Meghan.

Snapping back to reality, she searched the room for an escape. She ran to the window and pulled desperately on the latch and got the window half open before the door crashed in, with the loudest boom she had ever heard. She turned and came face to face with the young man and his gun.

"Well, here we are again. But this time, we're alone," he chuckled and took a step towards her.

"No, we're not. There are two agents downstairs." Meghan paused, wondering why Fabrizio or Andy had not come up after hearing the noise; it was loud enough. Where were they? She began to panic, her eyes darting around the room. "Declan will be back anytime, you better leave!"

"Don't count on it. But if he shows up, then I guess he can join the two men downstairs. Maybe this time your beloved Declan won't be so lucky. I have been waiting all day for those stupid agents to leave.

Unfortunately, they all didn't go, but it was very smart of me to send the other two on a wild goose chase, don't y' think?"

"What?" Meghan was frantically trying to comprehend what was going on. "What have you done to the agents?"

"Never mind!" He sauntered towards her waving the gun around angrily.

Meghan shifted over towards the bed, eyeing her exit over the large structure to the door.

"Y' are so beautiful! It's such a shame I have to give y' away."

He slowly moved the gun down her cheek to her neck. The cold metal muzzle stopped at her chest, brushing against her locket. His eyes raked her for a moment, then a wicked smirk curled his lips.

"Oh God!" Meghan cried as his hand reached up tearing the front of her blouse, exposing the upper curve of her breasts.

"I was told not to touch y', but I don't think y' will tell."

A shudder ran through her already trembling body, causing her knees to buckle slightly, but she caught her balance by gripping the large bedpost. Her once golden skin had turned a dreadful shade of grey, as the thought of him raping her filled her tormented mind.

She screamed and lashed out at him, slamming her fists against his chest. His fingers entwined in her hair, twisting her head back so her face was up towards his. She gagged as his lips pressed against hers with enough force to pry her lips apart, giving his tongue access to her mouth.

His loose hand grabbed her bra, and with one solid tug, the thin lace tore, and her breasts popped loose. Once free, he gripped it savagely, twisting her nipple between his thumb and forefinger.

Total terror was shooting through her, and she bit down on his tongue that was still darting around her mouth. A strangled moan exited him as he flung her back, his hand crashing across her face.

"Y' stupid bitch." His face was even more terrifying than it had been earlier.

"Please, just leave, no one knows you're here yet."

"Well, y' do . . . the agents downstairs won't be talking, but I guess this way was better than them dying in a fire," he snarled as he gripped her arm and pressed the gun back to her head.

"You started the fire in the barn?" Meghan shrieked.

"Sure, who else? I didn't realize that there were so many people here, and I didn't think y' would be daft enough to run inside a burning building. All I was trying to do was distract the agents long enough to grab y'." His mouth twisted into a wicked grin. "Luckily for y', your lover boy saved y' again. But he won't be able to help y' now," he gloated, but Meghan's attention became distracted by someone coming up the stairs. Was it Declan?

"Mommy, where are you?" Caelan called as she skipped down the hallway.

"Caelan, don't come in here!" Meghan yelled, but it was too late. Caelan was already standing at the door to the room, looking at the stranger, her grey eyes as big as saucers, and her long black curls hanging delicately around her tiny little face.

"Caelan, run, run and get Nat!" Meghan yelled, terrified for her daughter.

Caelan turned sharply and ran screaming down the hall to the back stairs. The man looked at Meghan with malevolence, then he turned and started after Caelan.

"No!" Meghan screamed. "Leave her alone." She grabbed the lamp off the bedside table and struck him across the back of the head with all the force she could muster, sending him collapsing to the floor, clutching his bleeding skull.

Meghan jumped over his back in an attempt to dart past his motionless body, but as she passed, his long arm reached out and grasped her ankle, causing her to plummet to the floor. She tried desperately to scramble to her feet, but he grabbed onto the back of her shirt and threw her backwards, slamming her into the wall. The sharp pain in the back of her head was excruciating, but she fought to stay alert. He had abandoned his pursuit of Caelan and was standing over Meghan, the gun pointed at her head.

He shook his head with annoyance and squatted down in front of her, pressing the gun up against her temple. She could feel the cold steel shaking against her as he stared at her, his steel blue eyes filled with rage.

"Y' just don't learn, do y', y' stupid bitch."

"Please, don't kill me. She needs me."

"Don't worry, I'm not killing y', you're coming with me." His hand grasped her breast again, giving it a ruthless twist.

308

"I'm sure y' will enjoy this, darling. I have been told I'm a brilliant lover," he said with a smug tone as he started to undo his pants.

"No!" Meghan screamed in terror.

"Get the fuck away from her!" Declan yelled as he materialized in the doorway, pointing the shotgun from the hall closet directly at the young man.

The man spun around, lifting his gun towards Declan. "Well, if it isn't the big movie star."

"Put the gun down. It's over," Declan told him as he scanned Meghan's condition. "If y' have hurt her, I swear I'll kill y'."

"Well, big hero, I don't think y' have the balls to pull the trigger."

"Y' are already in enough trouble, are y' sure y' want more?"

"Don't be such an imbecile. I will never stand trial in this country. I have too many connections."

"Put the gun down. I don't want to have to shoot y', but I will!"

"Go ahead, hero. I bet y' won't have the balls. But I do. Say goodbye to him, Meghan," he yelled as he tightened his finger on the trigger.

Meghan wedged her eyes closed as a shriek of anguish exited her. Her heart was beating furiously with terror as she wondered who would shoot first.

A loud bang rang out and time seemed to stand still before she reluctantly opened her eyes, to see the young man collapse to the floor in a pool of deep red blood. Declan was stationed in the doorway with the shotgun smoking in his trembling hand.

He laid the gun down in a peculiarly regimental fashion, then rushed to Meghan and scooped her up into his arms, pressing her firmly against his chest. She was shaking uncontrollably, and it took every fibre of his strength to hold her still.

"Meggie, it's over."

She buried her head into his chest and held onto him for dear life, but within seconds, she heard a low grown from the doorway. She jerked around, her eyes settling on the lifeless body, and then she scanned the room, spotting Nathan in the doorway. He was holding a shotgun in his hand as he surveyed the scene in the war zone, which was once her bedroom.

He sauntered over and kicked at the motionless body to make sure he was not going to spring up like a jack-in-the-box. When he kicked the gun away from the man's hand, it skidded across the room, hitting the opposite wall.

"Are you both okay?" Nathan questioned, his tone strangled, to say the least.

"Where's Caelan?" Meghan was frantic, her voice pitched and fearful.

"She's okay. She's locked in my house. The cops are on their way." Nathan glanced over at Declan, but he shook his head directing Nathan to stay quiet.

"Is he dead?" Meghan asked as her eyes rested on the nightmare of a man lying on her bedroom floor.

"Yeah, I think so. There is a pretty big hole in his chest," Nathan reported, giving him another kick.

Declan's eyes left Meghan and settled on the man sprawled on the floor, blood running down his ribs and landing as crimson raindrops on the once pale cream carpet. He started to tremble at the sight; realizing how close he came to losing Meghan again.

"Declan," Meghan whispered, clutching his face and brushing her thumbs in a caressing circular motion across his cheeks.

"That bloody bastard! He had to push me." Declan's voice was shaky but terrifyingly harsh. "He hurt Meggie, I couldn't let him live."

"Declan, she's all right," Nathan said, gripping his arm, trying to refocus him. "Look, she's right there."

Declan's dark gaze settled on Meghan's worried face that was within inches from him. The corners of his tense mouth turned up, and he dropped his head into hers.

"Oh, Freckles, if anything were to happen to y'," Declan sighed, his breath hot on her face. "I don't know what I would do."

"It's all right now," Meghan sniffed, trying to control her own fears. "It's all right," she repeated.

"Come on, you two, let's get out of here and wait for the cops," Nathan ordered, worrying that they both were going to go into post-traumatic shock. Declan nodded and helped Meghan to her feet, but she stumbled as she leaned on her foot.

"I must have twisted my ankle." Meghan bent down to rub it, but Declan scooped her up into his arms and gingerly passed by the lifeless body, out into the hall.

"I'll check on things in the kitchen and then I will go stay with Caelan. Take her into the living room," Nathan said as calmly as he could, before disappearing into the kitchen.

"Aye," Declan mumbled at Nathan's departing back. He was terrified about how he was going to tell Meghan what he found in the kitchen when he entered the house.

Declan lowered her to the couch, then flopped down beside her, and brushed a renegade strand of auburn hair from her face. A deep sigh filled the room as he dropped his head back into the couch with a mixture of relief and fear.

"Meggie, this has got to stop." Declan sighed, knuckling his eyes.

"I'm sorry," Meghan sniffed and swabbed at her own burning eyes. "This is what I was afraid of."

"Shh, Freckles, I'm not blaming you." Declan slipped his arm around her back, pulling her towards him. "I meant almost losing y'."

A soft sob exited her as she broke down in the safety of his arms.

"Meggie, there is something I must tell y'." Declan's voice sounded chocked even to him. "Fabs . . ."

"What happened to Fabrizio," Meghan shrieked and tried to get off the couch but was held firm by Declan's strong hand, "and Andy, he shot them, didn't he? That's why he wasn't concerned with them catching him. Oh God!"

"Freckles, calm down, Nat is checking on them. I'm sure he has already called an ambulance if . . ."

"Declan, Fabs is still alive." Nathan's voice bellowed from the kitchen.

"I have to go to him. Please let me go," Meghan cried, struggling in Declan's arms.

"All right, Freckles, but it's pretty nasty," Declan sighed, totally caught up in her emotions.

She forced calmness into her voice as she entered the kitchen. "I need some towels and get my medical bag from my office. Did you call the ambulance?" Her gaze settled on Nathan.

"Yes, darlin', they should be here soon." He soothed and went for the medical bag.

"Declan, can you hold this against the wound and hold it tightly?" Meghan ordered, then groped under Fabrizio, feeling for any more holes. "How could he have shot them without me hearing it?" she rambled, trying to think of something else. "There must have been a silencer on the gun, I can't remember if it had one." Her mind was in control, her training taking over. "Oh, crap, here is another hole. The ass shot him in the back."

Declan rolled him onto his side, still holding the cloth snugly against the first hole. He didn't speak as he watched Meghan calmly pressing a towel to the bullet wound in Fabrizio's back.

"Fabrizio, listen to me. You are going to be all right, do you hear me?" Her voice was surprisingly firm. "I want you to focus on my voice and stay with us. The ambulance is on its way."

The police officers were the first to arrive, then the fire department and ambulance. The house resembled a war zone: bodies littering the floor, blood splattered everywhere. Declan pulled Meghan away from Fabrizio to allow the paramedics to remove him from the house. They were driving him towards Great Falls, meeting the medic-chopper en route. The coroner had arrived and was bagging the bodies, while the chief of police, Randall Hildebrand, corralled Meghan and Declan into the living room for questioning. An officer had gone to Nathan's house to question him and Caelan.

Meghan dropped to the couch and laid her head on her knees, her hair falling down around her face, covering it like a veil of flames. The sun was bringing out very red highlights in her hair, and it was shimmering like fire under the afternoon sun.

"Meghan, are you all right?" Randall questioned, resting his hand on her hunched back, his other hand sliding across his thinning hair.

"Yes," Meghan sniffed. "I'll be better when I find out that Fabrizio is all right."

"So, who did the damage?" Randall questioned his dark eyes settling on Declan's agitated face.

"Everyone except the agents," Declan muttered, his knuckles scrubbing at his brow. "The boy shot the agents, then went after Meggie. I found them up in the bedroom, and he was about rape her." Declan shuddered and glanced through the glass doors and watched the yard fill with State Police.

"That was the man from the fair grounds," Meghan sniffed and directed her eyes out the window. "He was sent after me by someone. He said he had to take me."

312

Declan shook his head and eyed Agent Paxton that had just arrived back at the house. "I thought y' said it was Ian O'Brien that was after her?"

"No, that's not Ian," Meghan said sharply. "I think I would be able to recognize him."

Agent Paxton grunted and turned towards Declan with a questioning eye. "Well, it was a good thing you were here, Mr. Montgomery."

"Aye, I was outside when Caelan ran from the house, screaming." Declan closed his eyes, not wanting to remember the fear on his daughter's face.

"My only complaint is that I couldn't kill the bastard myself. I can't believe he managed to take out both Andy and Fabrizio," Agent Paxton grumbled.

Meghan let out a loud sob as her body began to shake once again. "This is entirely my fault."

"No, Meggie." Declan was on the couch beside her and cradling her in his arms. "I told y' before, more is going on than we know. This man just didn't show up here in town by accident. And what about the birthmark?" Declan cringed at the thought. Was it possible that this man could have the same birthmark as his brother? It had to be possible, since the man upstairs was not Rory. Who were all these men, and were they connected to Fergus O'Brien?

"Where is his gun now?" Randall questioned Meghan and tugged at his pants, tucking his shirt around his overflowing stomach.

"Nathan kicked it across the room." Meghan lifted her head, exposing her tear-stained face. "After he came into the bedroom."

The officer listened to the explanation of the events that ended with two dead and one in critical condition. Meghan and Declan's accounts of the events matched up with what Nathan and Caelan told the officers, which pleased the chief.

It was hours before the crew of FBI agents and police officers removed all the bodies from the house. The authorities seemed convinced that Declan acted in self-defence, and they were in no hurry to vilify him for killing the man that killed one of their own.

When Agent Paxton gave them permission to leave, Meghan glanced over at Declan with distress. "I can't stay here tonight."

"Aye, I will take y' and Caelan somewhere." Declan soothed.

"Could we go to Great Falls? I want to see how Fabrizio is doing," her eyes pleading with him. "I need to phone Cassie, she needs to know."

He had already planned to take her there, knowing she would not be happy otherwise, so it was no hardship to agree. "Aye, Freckles, I'll take y'. We can leave whenever y' are ready."

CHAPTER TWENTY-THREE

The soft Irish sun was breaking through the clouds as Meghan and her entourage jumped out of the cab in front of an old stately manor in the seaside town of Kinsale. Meghan was amazed at the array of colours of the building that lined the narrow streets. Purple, orange, green, and blue, there wasn't a colour that wasn't used. The thing that amazed her the most was that a building could be a block long, but it could be four different colours, depending on the residents' colour of choice. Almost every window had a flower box, and the Irish flag flew everywhere. It was a stunning little town. The town slopped down the hill towards the water and the small harbour on the River Bandon, which flowed out to the Celtic Sea. She was so excited to explore the incredible little town.

Declan was in town, filming a movie and wanted Caelan to come stay with him, so Nathan and Meghan thought it would be a great opportunity to track down the property she owned and sell it. Declan believed that the family castle was located on the west coast of County Claire, but he had never been there. Cassie tagged along, to be with Fabrizio, he had been acting very strangely since he had been shot. The FBI placed him on injury leave, but he was going stir crazy at home. When he found out that Meghan and Nathan were going to Ireland, he insisted on going along with her for protection but ended up going with Declan.

The grey stone structure in front of them was covered with vines and mosses that had wrapped themselves around the building for the last hundred years. Windows divided into small squares of bevelled glass allowed the mid afternoon sun to shine through into the countless rooms. The large grounds surrounding the building were well manicured and decorated with rows of hedges and a variety of fragrant flowers that filled the air with the scents of summer.

Meghan took Caelan by the hand and anxiously wandered up the cobblestone path that weaved aimlessly through the flower gardens and under a stone archway that was precariously perched on a four-foot-high wall of similar stones. The moss and vines had almost engulfed the stones over the years and appeared to be what held the structure together.

The sweet smell of heather filled Meghan's nostrils as she hurried up the path, scanning her surroundings, but not noticing any of the small details. There would be time for closer examination later, all she could focus on was Declan, and the long month she had spent apart from him. Their visit to Boston to see his parents turned into a battle when Declan confronted his mother and Rory about Rory being the one that shot him. Rory swore it was not him and that Meghan was brainwashing Declan. She thought that Declan was convinced that it was Rory that shot him, but he decided to let Rory think he was mistaken, and she became worried. Katie had confronted Meghan when Declan was talking with his father, and she repeated her threat to take Caelan from her if she proceeded down the path of accusing Rory. Declan assured her he had no intentions of leaving her or taking Caelan from her, but when he said Rory was going with him to Ireland, Meghan found herself mistrusting him. She could not understand why he was ignoring the fact that Rory shot him years earlier and was involved with whoever tried to kidnap her. Meghan left Boston, took Caelan to Dallas to stay with Nathan's parents, and told Declan she needed time to think. Now he seemed to have rescinded his invitation for her to join him and only asked for Caelan. She would have to occupy her time with Nathan, searching out her ancestry while Caelan spent the month with Declan, touring Ireland.

The wind was blowing her long fiery hair around her face as she walked up the stairs to the large wooden door. Her hand swept up and brushed the waves back from her face, and she turned to Cassie and Nathan with impatience.

"Are you coming?" Meghan questioned as they wandered slowly up the path to the stairs, their demeanour light and relaxed.

"I see why Declan loves it so much here." Cassie waved her hand towards the lush green garden. "It's fantastic." Cassie found the plant life surrounding her extraordinary, and she was in no hurry to get into the manor.

"We will be there in a few minutes." Nathan sat down on the bench next to where Cassie was examining the cones of a Black Alder tree.

Meghan smiled wearily, her stomach churning with anticipation; she turned her attention back to the large heavy door that opened into a large foyer. A magnificent chandelier hung in the middle of the room, about twenty feet up, overseeing the white polished marble floor adorned with a Celtic insignia in the centre. Mauve settees were placed around the fireplace, and on the far wall was a set of doors that were opened to the large patio out the back. A small pub was visible to her left, and it seemed quite busy.

Caelan excitedly tugged on Meghan's arm and drew her attention to the majestic wooden staircase that wrapped around the far wall on its way to the second floor. Meghan's heart stopped at the sight of Declan standing on the balcony at the top of the stairs, carrying on a conversation with Fabrizio, Colton Barrett, the actor she had met at the lodge years earlier, and a couple of women she did not recognize. Every time she saw Declan, it was the same—everything else around her disappeared.

Meghan watched for a moment as Declan smiled and laughed at what the others were saying, and she could not help but smirk as he brushed back a long black clump of hair that kept falling across his face. A group of older ladies were sitting on a grouping of chairs on the far side of the balcony that appeared to be a small library. They didn't seem interested in the collection of actors, but a young girl standing a few feet away was taking selfies and trying to get Colton in her shot.

Caelan pulled loose with impatience and ran up the stairs towards him. "Daddy!" she shrieked half way up the staircase, manoeuvring herself one big step after another, passing the people in her way.

Declan's eyes left the group and darted towards the stairs, hearing her calls. "Caelan," he screamed, moved away from the gawking women, and ran towards his daughter. "Ah, wee one, I'm so glad to see y'." He lifted her into the air above his head, then lowered her into his arms, and kissed her on the forehead.

Caelan giggled and put her hands on his face. "Daddy, I got to fly in a plane again, but they didn't let me go see the captain." Caelan crinkled her nose with disappointment the very same way Meghan always did, which caused Declan to laugh.

"Aye, I guess the stewardess wasn't in a big hurry to do Mommy a favour," Declan smiled and kissed her again on the head.

"I know. I like it when you are around, Daddy, because people do what you ask."

Declan was startled by the comment and worried that Caelan was already realizing that his celebrity could get her what she wants. During the last month, he had made the decision to return to the ranch with his girls, that is, if Meghan would have him. He enjoyed the time he spent in the quiet town; he almost felt normal.

"Where's Mommy?" He looked anxiously towards the stairs when she had not arrived. After their big fight in Boston, their relationship seemed strained, and when he talked with her on the phone over the last month, she was very distant. Maybe it was a mistake not to tell the FBI that he believed it was Rory. She believed he was choosing his family over her.

"Down, there." Caelan pointed her little hand towards the bottom of the stairs.

Declan's eyes followed her finger, and he grinned wildly when he saw Meghan staring up at him. "I thought Uncle Nat was coming too." Had she come alone, maybe she was willing to give their relationship another chance.

"He's outside with Auntie Cassie," Caelan said offhandedly, not too concerned with the rest of the travelling group.

Declan cringed that she had brought Cassie too, but then, she could occupy Fabrizio so he could spend time with Meghan alone. His attention was drawn back to the group he was talking with when Colton inquired about Caelan.

"This is Caelan, me beautiful wee daughter," Declan introduced her to the group. Colton and the tall shapely blonde woman smiled pleasantly, but the dark-haired woman seemed unimpressed, as a scowl crossed her narrow face.

The blonde woman's pale blue eyes settled on Caelan, and she questions about her trip, but the dark-haired woman's eye never left Declan as he glanced down to the lobby, noticing Meghan was still standing by the luggage. The woman's hand landed on Declan's arm, drawing his attention back to her.

"Declan, can I catch ride with y' to the set tomorrow?" Her sultry lips turning up into a sweet smile.

"I can't say, it depends if Caelan and Meggie are coming. I might not have the room," he said offhandedly, his eyes settling back on Meghan who had not moved.

"You can come with me, Deirdre." Colton's sky blue eyes crinkled with amusements. He ran his hand through his shoulder-length blond hair, awaiting her answer.

"Oh, do you have room for me?" Lydia's pale blue eyes almost pleading.

"Sure I do," Colton grinned. "I always have room for a beautiful woman." Colton winked at Lydia, causing her to blush.

Declan was preoccupied with the fact that Meghan hadn't come to him. If she was not going to come to him, he was going to her.

"Fabs, hold me wee one." He handed Caelan off to Fabrizio and bolted down the stairs, leaping two at a time towards her, his smoky eyes a blaze as he descended the long staircase. Meghan began to move towards him, and as they reached each other's arms under the chandelier, he grabbed her around the waist, pulling her up into his arms, her feet leaving the ground. His lips were strong on hers, forcing her to give what he demanded and her total surrender.

He could feel his body pulsing with the anticipation of making love to her, to feel her soft skin under his hand, to have her soft lips on his skin. It had been an extremely long and arduous month without her, and his body ached for relief.

Meghan's hands explored his face, brushing across the light stubbly beard back into his long hair. Her desire for him was stronger than ever. She could hardly control herself, her body pressing up against him, the need to have him surrounding her, his strong arms holding her close to his broad chest, overpowering her mind.

"Oh, how I've missed y'," Declan mumbled against her lips, his one hand sliding up her back to her hair.

"Me too," Meghan panted as she leaned her head against his shoulder, sliding her arms around his back, holding him tightly.

"Look, how curly your hair is," Declan chuckled, twisting the auburn curls around his finger.

"It's the dampness in the air. It's a mess, isn't it?" Her dark green eyes settled on him, stirring his lust again.

She had to stop looking at him the way she was, or he would explode on the spot. In all the years since he had known her, no other woman had been able to shake him to his soul the way she had. History had ordained them to be together and fate had ensured it.

"No, it's not. It looks nice," Declan said absently, rolling the curls around his finger, his mind occupied with his providence. "I've got so much to show y' now that you're here."

Meghan smiled and kissed his cheek. "So you're happy I'm here?" she asked tentatively. After asking him for space last month, she was unsure if he was still interested.

"Aye, of course, I'm pleased. I knew you would come around, y' love me, Meghan Montgomery, and you can't fight it." Declan grinned and lifted her left hand and kissed her knuckles just above the rings. "I see y' are wearing these."

"Yes, why wouldn't I?"

"Well after what we left Boston, I wasn't sure, y' were pretty upset."

Meghan smiled a soft sweet smile. "I'm sorry I was so crazy about your decision. If it were my brother, I probably would have done the same."

"I'm sorry too. I shouldn't have dropped that on y'. I just think he wasn't going to tell me anything, and if y' are positive that someone else was involved, this is the best way to find out who it is. He has been back over here for a few weeks, but I haven't been able to get anything out of him, and I haven't seen him with anyone. Maybe he's not involved anymore. He didn't seem to know anything about the lad I shot at the ranch."

Meghan nodded and glanced up at Fabrizio. Maybe it was over, nothing had happened since that day and even Mayor McGregor seemed oblivious to what happened. "Do you remember Agent Brody Spencer?" Meghan's eyes settled on Declan. "Well, he is now the director, and he came out and personally interviewed the mayor and his son. He concluded that they had nothing to do with the man you shot."

"Hmm, well, we can talk about this later; all I'm interested in right now is being with you."

Fabrizio had decided that they had had enough of a reunion and was on his way down the stairs with Caelan tucked up in his large arms.

"Boo, good to see you." Fabrizio bent over and kissed her cheek on his arrival. "Declan, I think you two better move this to a bedroom, you seem to be attracting a lot of attention." He glanced up to the balcony.

Meghan followed Fabrizio's gaze and noticed the gathering of people staring down at them. Colton sported his usual grin, but the two women standing with him did not seem as happy to see her.

"Declan, why are they glaring at me?" Meghan questioned, her hand instinctively resting on his arm.

Declan glanced up at the women. "Those girls? I don't know." He shrugged casually, returning his gaze to Meghan.

"Boo, you have interfered with their attempts to pick up your husband," Fabrizio laughed and lowered Caelan to the ground.

"They weren't trying to pick me up," Declan grumbled with defiance, slightly annoyed that Fabrizio was trying to rile Meghan.

"They were too. How naïve are you?"

"They know I'm married. I was telling them that Meggie and Caelan were coming." Declan looked at her with an attempt at ignorance.

"Monty, Deirdre grabbed your hand." Fabrizio continued to goad Declan.

"Aye, she was looking at me ring!" Declan said strongly, giving Fabrizio an unusual glare, almost trying to quiet him.

"Sure, that's what she said." Fabrizio could hardly keep from laughing at his friend's denial.

"You were holding her hand?" Meghan questioned, with a slight smile.

"No. She was holding mine." Declan's mouth rose to one side, but his eyes still held the appearance of guilt.

Meghan crinkled her nose and glanced back up into the faces still peering over the balcony. Declan cringed as he watched her face suddenly harden with the recognition of one of the women that just arrived on the balcony. In an explosion of anger, she turned on him with confusion and rage shooting from her eyes.

"Declan?" Meghan blurted out, directing her gaze back on the woman. The bleached blonde hair was shorter, but she could not mistake the anorexic frame of the woman. It was Kaye, her nemesis all through college. She fought for breath as her eyes settled on Declan's guilt-ridden face. "What?"

"Meggie, calm down," he soothed, taking her hands in his. "I didn't want to tell y'."

"How long has she been here?" Meghan whispered fiercely interrupting his comment, keeping her voice deliberately low.

"About a week." Declan tried to smile, but her face was so disturbing that he could not manage it. His hand landed gently on her cheek, and he could feel her twitch slightly. "Freckles."

"So what else has he been doing while he was here on his own?" Meghan asked sharply, directing her gaze on Fabrizio.

"Not much, he's been pretty good I guess," Fabrizio grinned at Declan, realizing the trouble he was in. He was still rather weary of Declan's relationship with Meghan. He was worried that Meghan was going to get hurt if Declan discarded her like he did most women. Declan also repeatedly claimed he needed her, but Fabrizio had not heard him say he loved her. Did he or was it just the fact that Declan wanted to take her away from him out of spite. On the other hand, since they arrived in Ireland, Declan, to his knowledge, had not been with any other woman. This was a large departure from his normal behaviour.

"Hey, I've been very good," Declan snapped rather grumpily, disturbed by what Fabrizio was implying. "Meggie, I would have told y' when she got here, but I knew y' would react like this, and I didn't want y' stewing about it for a week."

"Why is she here?" Meghan grumbled as her anger started to change to worry.

"Well, it turns out Deirdre is her cousin on her father's side. I guess she is here visiting, and she said she is looking forward to Cassie coming," Declan said, almost nonchalantly.

"Oh great." Meghan's brow rose ever so slightly. He could see the worry growing in her eyes as she turned and glanced at Caelan, who was now across the room at the desk with Nathan getting their room keys.

"I'm going to get my key," Meghan mumbled and pulled away from Declan's grasp.

"Meggie, don't y' blow this out of proportion, nothing happened," Declan said firmly, gripping her arm, turning her towards him.

"I know," Meghan said evenly, but her eyes were telling quite a different story. She had not thought about Kaye in a few years. The last time was when she reappeared after Meghan was released from prison. She told Cassie that she was staying on a small Greek island to rest and did not want to be disturbed.

Declan griped her face in his hands and kissed her forehead. "Meggie, I swear to y'." Her finger rested over his mouth halting his comment.

"I know," she whispered. "I know."

A relieved smile filled Declan's face as he rested his forehead against hers. "Please don't be cross with me, I was hoping she would have left by now, and y' wouldn't have to see her."

"I'm sorry, I don't know why I got so jealous," Meghan muttered against his lips.

"Sure, y' do. Y' told me once, remember? But y' can be assured that I have avoided her as much as possible," Declan grinned.

"It's just the thought . . ." Meghan closed her eyes heavily.

"Freckles, y' have nothing to worry about. I will never betray y'." Declan kissed her lips softly. His feelings said in a kiss.

CHAPTER TWENTY-FOUR

It was mid afternoon when the group arrived at the large stone castle called Briarwood Manor on the West coast of Claire. It was larger than she had expected, spanning over 10,000 square feet. The old brick walls were well constructed but showed signs of neglect. However, the grounds that slopped down to the sea, surrounding the castle were immaculate. It was laid out like a park, with rows of hedges and a great number of flowerbeds surrounding a large reed-lined pond. Two large gargoyles stood guard on the top of the building in-between the two large turrets. It was a very odd-shaped structure, with areas jetting out into all directions and doors on the top floor opening to the ground below. The graveyard on the far side of the property drew Meghan's attention, and she turned and headed towards it.

"Do you think our ancestors are buried there?" Meghan whispered.

"Possibly," Declan muttered as he pushed open the gate. He glanced back in the direction of the castle, but it was quite far away, and no one seemed to be around. "Let's have a look."

Caelan shook her head and sat down on the bench outside the fence as Meghan wandered through the gate heading towards what appeared to be the oldest gravestone. She knelt down on the damp grass and wiped away the moss from the face of the stone. She gasped when she read the name. Eamon O'Brien 1523-1570.

"It's him. Eamon's grave." Meghan slid across the grass to the grave next to it, and it read Elizabeth O'Brien 1532-1571.

One by one, they found every descendant down the line until they came to Caelan Delaney. Meghan dropped to the ground by the grave and ran her hand along the stone. "Caelan Delaney, beloved wife and mother 1931-1956. This is my grandma," Meghan muttered and looked across the graveyard at Caelan, who was sitting on the bench watching them. She glanced up at Declan as he watched her with a soft expression.

"Y' found where y' are from. Your family?" Declan's voice was soft. He rested his hand on her shoulder as she continued to sweep her hand across the gravestone.

"I wish I knew about this place before Papa died. He would have liked to lie beside her," Meghan sighed but a content smile crossed her face.

"Aye."

"Well, should we see who your tenant is?" Nathan commented as he raised the copy of the deed to the estate that he had found in the county records. Meghan was definitely the owner, but her grandfather had granted a fifty-year lease to the occupants, which only had ten more years on it.

"I feel bad for ditching Cassie and Fabrizio," Meghan muttered as she wandered towards the castle. "She would have loved to see this."

Declan sighed and grabbed Caelan's hand. "Well, to be honest, I didn't want Fabs tagging along. He doesn't need to know all our secrets."

Meghan sighed and followed Nathan to the large wooden front door that was at least ten feet high.

The door swung open, exposing a short elderly man, his wispy hair grey, unkept, and short. His large nose was covered in small red veins, and his eyes were cloudy from cataracts.

He gave the group a once over before his gaze settled on Meghan. A large grin spread across his weathered face. "Catherine, y' came home?" He lunged towards Meghan and surrounded her in his frail arms.

"I'm not Catherine. I'm Meghan Montgomery," she smiled and wiggled loose from his grip.

"What is all the commotion out here?" A short, heavy woman waddled towards the door but stopped dead in her tracks at the sight of Meghan. "As I live and breathe."

Meghan turned to Declan who was looking as bewildered as she was. "Hi, I'm Meghan Montgomery. I believe my grandfather leased you this house."

The two elderly tenants looked at each other, then back at Meghan. "Y' are Mick Delaney's granddaughter? Well, come in, come in," he repeated and moved over into the foyer and began wandering down the hall.

"Oh, how exciting this is!" the elderly woman chirped, and she closed the door behind the group. "Y' must see this. Oh my heavens," she rambled and followed behind them into the great room.

Meghan gasped when she looked up at the enormous painting hanging over the fireplace. It was the spitting image of her. The woman's long auburn hair tied back, exposing a large ruby necklace. Her small nose was dusted with freckles, and her large green eyes danced with life from the canvas. The rest of the group stood staring at the picture as Meghan turned to the old man.

"Who is that?" Meghan blurted out.

"It's y'," the old man stated confidently.

"Oh, y' old fool, that's not her. It's Catherine O'Brien. She's been dead for over four hundred years," the woman scolded. "I'm Mrs. Anthony O'Brien and the daft old man is me husband." Her hand swung out towards the old man. "We lease the land and buildings from your grandda. We were so excited to live in the O'Brien family home." She turned to the young woman that entered the room. "Julia, can you fetch some tea for our guests?"

Julia stared at Meghan a little too long before she turned and left the room.

"So, would y' be related to Fergus O'Brien?" Declan questioned as an uneasiness shot through him. What had he done letting her come to this castle?

"Aye, we are distant relations. All the O'Briens come from the same clan. Did you know that?" The man wandered over to the table and lifted his pipe. "Fergus used to come to visit every once in a while, but he is old and feeble now. His son came a couple of times to explore the rooms and corridors. I don't particularly care for him. He broke holes in a couple of walls, so I won't let him back in."

"Why did he do that?" Meghan blurted out. "Was he looking for something?"

"Aye. I imagine he was looking for the Boru sword," the old man said before his wife interrupted him.

"Y' daft old fool. Why must y' babble on about that old folk tale? We have lived here for forty years, and y' have searched every nook and cranny of this house. There is no sword or jewels." The woman was annoyed.

Meghan glanced over at the old woman and smiled. "Yes, my grandpa lived here for most of his life, and I have never heard anything about that," she lied, causing Declan to glance over at her.

"Aye, the only weird thing in this old home is all the weird rooms and passage ways to nowhere." The woman chuckled and sat down in a chair by the fireplace, waving the rest to do the same. They all found a seat, and the woman cleared her throat. "I don't know how much you know about your distant relation that lived here, but he was crazy as a loon. He thought that the ghosts of his parents were haunting him, so he started to build hidden rooms and passageways that went nowhere in hope of fooling the ghosts. It was that woman, his wife Catherine, that stopped all his madness. He loved her so." The woman looked at Meghan, who was now glancing at Nathan's stunned face.

"It's amazing how much you look like her, Megs," Nathan muttered and stared at the painting.

"It's uncanny," the old woman comments before Julia returned with the tea.

"Well, I think that she was a sidhe come to reclaim the power of the sword," the old man blurted out.

"Agh. Y' and your crazy thoughts. I sometimes wonder if y' have not gone a little daft. Catherine was no sidhe."

"Then tell me this, where did she come from? The legend says Michael saw her at the market. No one knew who she was, and he had the sword with him. That's why she was there. She probably came to reclaim the sword. Maybe Michael was not worthy to possess it. I'm sure that's why it hasn't been found here."

The woman made a guttural noise at her husband. "Oh, stop filling the heads of these fine people with your crazy talk. She was no more a sidhe than I."

"What does the sword have to do with the sidhe?" Declan questioned with interest.

"What's a sidhe?" Meghan blurted out.

"Oh dear girl, the sidhe is a fairy. They live up on the hill under the Hawthorne tree in the fairy ring. They come down here and cause mischief, and sometimes they bring magic." He grinned a toothless grin.

"Ah, y' old fool." The woman shook her head with annoyance.

He turned the grin on her, then glanced over at Declan. "It is said that the fairies forged the Boru sword and gave it to Brian. The sword made Brian very powerful, and some say that's why he lived into his seventies. That was very old for that time."

The old man was in his glory telling the old tales. His wife, however, was getting annoyed. She abruptly stood and suggested they take a tour of the castle, which ended his tales. They went room by room and were shown every weird hallway and door that opened onto a wall. All the doors on the upper floor that led to the outside were nailed shut, so no one walked out to their death.

"I'm so pleased that y' came to visit today, Meghan. We are taking good care of your estate, but we are old and can't get around well anymore. We have hired a nice young man to take care of the grounds." She rambled on their way out the side door of the castle.

"How far does the property go?" Nathan questioned as he glanced over the field that seemed to go on forever.

"It goes right down to the sea. The cliffs are full of caves that lead quite far under the property. When I was a lad, we would row our boats into them. I bet a large ship could fit into some of them." The old man's face was filled with distant memories. "I don't think anyone ventures into them these days. Me hired man keeps people from trespassing on the property."

The group wandered the property for about an hour before they said goodbye to the elderly couple and headed for the SUV.

"That was the weirdest thing I have ever seen," Nathan commented once they were back in the car. "You own the coolest castle."

"Is that ours?" Caelan blurted out. "Can we live there?"

"No, the O'Briens live there, and that's fine with me!" Meghan glanced over at Declan. "I think some of those caves lead right into the castle. I remember Papa getting drunk one night, and he was talking to his friend and telling him about the house he grew up in and how there were secret caves under the house leading to the ocean."

"Hmm," Declan grunted. "Why wouldn't the old man know that, or did he and just didn't want to tell us for some reason."

"We'll I don't see why he would hide that. He didn't have a problem talking about the fairies that live up the hill," Meghan laughed and tweaked Caelan's nose. "I bet you would love to see one of those."

"Oh no, y' don't want to see a sidhe. They bring nothing but trouble," Declan blurted out, but did not finish his comment when he noticed the shocked looks on Meghan and Nathan's face.

"What?"

"You believe there are fairies. You think his story is true?" Meghan giggled at the absurdity.

"Well, I don't believe his story, but as for the sidhe, I believe that. Old myths are based on fact," he grunted and turned his attention to the road.

Meghan sighed and thought about what the old couple had said. They had told her pretty much the same story that Declan had told her back at the ranch. Was it the true history or just an old folk tale? Well, it was best to leave it alone and leave the old couple to spend the rest of their lives there.

CHAPTER TWENTY-FIVE

It was early morning when Declan jostled Meghan awake from her restless sleep. "Meggie, y' have to get up if y' and Caelan are coming to the set today."

"I'm up," Meghan mumbled, squinting through sleepy eyes. She was determined to stay as close to Declan as possible with Deirdre lurking close by.

"Y' don't have to come. I just thought y' might like to see Blarney Castle. It is a spectacular old castle." Declan climbed off the bed and headed for the bathroom.

"I do, I'm getting up right now." Meghan yawned, her eyes closing again.

Declan laughed and moved over to the high canopy bed and pulled back the large olive green down duvet. "Freckles, get up!"

"Yeah." Meghan rolled onto her back and looked up at him with one eye open just enough to make out his face. "If you're going to wake me at the crack of dawn, you are going to have to let me get some sleep," she grunted with a half smile.

Declan smiled impatiently, grasped her hand, and pulled on her arm until she was sitting up, slumped over towards him. "Get up, or I'll tickle y' out of that bed."

"Fine, I'm going," Meghan muttered as she stumbled to the floor and into the bathroom behind him.

Declan pressed up against her back, resting his head on her shoulder as she brushed her long auburn hair and stared into the mirror as if seeing something he could not. "What are y' thinking about?"

Meghan was startled when his lips landed on her cheek. "I was just wondering about Colton and Kaye. After dinner last night, they seemed pretty happy with each other."

Declan shrugged and kissed the nape of her neck.

"How long have they been dating?" Meghan turned in his arms and nuzzled his neck.

"I didn't realize they were dating. I just thought Colton was doing her."

"Well, that's a nice way of putting it," Meghan giggled and slapped his shoulder.

"What would y' rather me say, he's fucking her?"

"Declan!" Meghan grumbled and pushed away slightly, but his hands stayed firm around her.

"Well, that's all it is. This is Colton we're talking about," Declan laughed slightly. "If she keeps his interest longer than a week, she's doing well."

"Hmm. You don't seem to think anything is wrong with that." Meghan turned and moved over to the shower, turning on the spray.

A grin curled Declan's lips as he watched her fussing with her brush. "Well, Freckles, I can't say I was any different before I met y'."

Her eyes settled on him as he moved towards her. "Did you sleep with a lot of women?"

"A good many," Declan smirked, missing the flash of anxiousness in her eyes. "But none of them could compare to y'," he laughed and grabbed her around the waist, hoisting her into the air.

"You're such a liar," Meghan grumbled but could not help but smile as she caught the expression of love in his eyes.

"I am not," Declan grunted, putting forth a good impression of being offended.

"Haa," Meghan snorted a chuckle as he lowered her to the ground in front of him. His lips capturing hers, stifling any further comment she might have.

"Deirdre was wrong. I do know what I have in you." Meghan's green eyes were ablaze as she focused on him. She couldn't help but wonder if he felt that Deirdre's comment the night before was correct.

"Aye, Freckles, I know y' do," Declan smiled and kissed her forehead. "Deirdre and Kaye were just being nasty. Meggie, I don't care what they think."

"Do I embarrass you in front of your friends?" Meghan questioned as she turned and faced the mirror but kept her eyes on his reflection.

"No, and they aren't me friends." Declan slid in behind her, wrapping his strong arms around her shoulders from behind. "I love the way y' are."

Meghan sighed and rested her head back against him. "But I am trying to you, aren't I?"

"Aye, y' are." His arm tightened around her as she stirred. "But that is what I found so attractive about y' when we first met. Y' have such a good sense of humour and always say things that shocked me. I never want y' to lose that."

"Really?" Meghan turned in his arms, gazing at him, the gold flecks in her eyes shining brightly.

"Aye." Declan watched as she forced a smile to her lips, something was still bothering her; it was illuminated in her eyes. "What's wrong, Freckles? Y' seem upset."

"I wish it didn't bother me so much what people think of me." Her voice was quiet and soft.

"Don't worry about those women. They were just after Colton and y' got in the way. When y' are around, Colton only wants to flirt with y'," Declan chuckled, trying to dismiss her worry.

"Kaye and Lydia maybe, but I think that Deirdre was more interested in you," Meghan grumbled, not appreciating him dismissing her feelings. She could not forget the previous afternoon when she stumbled upon Declan, Colton, and their harem of women, sitting in the pub.

"Y' think so?" The corners of his mouth twitched, but he held the smile back when he caught the expression in her eyes. She was concerned, and that was evident. Did she think that he was having an affair? Is that what she was anxious about? After all, he didn't tell her he was going to the pub, but it was just with Colton. He had no idea that the women were going to show up.

"Yes, Deirdre was definitely focused on you, twirling her hair and smiling," Meghan grunted, amazed that he did not notice. "You are out of touch!" She moved away from him back into the bedroom.

"Hey, don't y' walk away from me in the middle of a discussion." Declan grabbed her arm and dragged her back towards him.

"What discussion?" Meghan questioned after catching her footing.

"About Deirdre's love for me."

"You're enjoying this, aren't you? You can't tell me you never noticed her eyeing you," Meghan grumbled and pushed at his chest.

"Y' did?" Declan's smile broke.

"Yes. She was blatantly obvious. If I hadn't walked in, she . . ." Meghan stopped, not sure what the expression on his face meant. He seemed almost proud of himself.

"Aye, I did, I just didn't care. Why would I even notice her when I have a beautiful vivacious wife like yourself?" Declan leaned forward to kiss her, but she pulled away. "Freckles, if I paid attention to every woman that looked at me, I would be exhausted."

Meghan shook her head with amazement, but he was right, it came with the job. Declan could not go anywhere without people staring at him. They were either trying to decide if it was really him, or they were ogling him.

"Come on, enough about that woman. We need to have a shower." Declan shoved her towards the warm spray.

A spectacular reddish orange glow was appearing on the eastern horizon as the group drove towards Blarney Castle. They had not been in the SUV five minutes before Meghan fell asleep on Declan's shoulder. His lips landed on her forehead as a gentle ache rippled through his heart. How he loved her, he never thought that anyone could fill the void inside him, but she did. He was going to savour every moment with his family.

"Monty, I thought I would warn you, Deirdre is going to be there today." Fabrizio disturbed his thoughts, but when Declan glanced towards the front seat, he could see Fabrizio's eyes in the rear-view mirror.

"I know," Declan mumbled offhandedly.

"Well, I know how she irritates Meghan. I just thought you would like to be prepared," Fabrizio said warningly.

"Aye, she does seem to push Meggie's buttons, doesn't she?" Declan chuckled, running his hand across Meghan's cheek. "But Meggie needs to calm down."

"Declan, why don't you just tell Deirdre you're a happily married man, and you have no interest in her?" Cassie interjected in Meghan's defence.

"Aye, I am happily married," Declan agreed, kissing Meghan's sleeping head. "I just didn't want to hurt Deirdre's feelings. She hasn't done anything other than hang about me all the time."

"Yes, but soon she might, and it could cause you problems." Fabrizio's voice was concerned.

"What do y' mean by that? Do y' think I would cheat on Meggie?" Declan grumbled, insulted by Fabrizio's comment.

"No, that's not what I meant. There is just something about that woman that I don't trust. She sets off my radar," Fabrizio grumbled back and glanced over at Cassie's concerned face.

"Aye, Meggie gets the same feelings from her. I'll be careful," Declan agreed.

"Declan, I have known Meg for a long time, and she needs to feel loved, and if she feels that she is losing you, she might do something stupid," Cassie warned. "She is very impulsive and has poor judgment sometimes."

"Aye, I've noticed." Declan glanced down at Meghan's peaceful face. "She means everything to me, and I don't intend on doing anything to lose her."

"Good," Cassie sighed and glanced over at Fabrizio. "It's just that she has been through a lot over the past few months, and I don't think she has dealt with any of it. I'm scared that one day she is going to wake up and realize that Andy died protecting her."

Declan nodded and stared out the window for a short moment. "Was she close with Andy?"

Cassie nodded. "I think she cared about him very much. She always had him over for holidays with us once he and Fabs became partners. She is avoiding thinking about what happened. I guess we can be thankful that Fabrizio is still alive." She rested her hand on Fabrizio's shoulder. "Please keep an eye on her, Declan. When she snaps, it's not going to be pretty."

"Aye, I will," Declan agreed.

The sun was casting its first glow of light on the fields as they pulled up to the castle passing through the enormous amount of security. Cassie had drifted off to sleep about ten minutes before they reached the castle.

Declan was starving and impatient to eat breakfast, and he jostled Meghan's shoulder, causing her to moan, but she did not open her eyes.

"Should we wake them?" Fabrizio questioned, eyeing Cassie's sleeping face.

"No, let them sleep for a while. We won't start filming for another hour or so." Declan gently rested Meghan against the door.

"What about Caelan?" Fabrizio glanced back at the little girl with her Barbie gripped tightly in her hand.

"She can come with me to the trailer while I get me makeup and costume on," Declan informed him as he lifted Caelan and headed for the castle. "Are y' hungry, wee one?"

Caelan nodded her head. "So is Barbie, Daddy, can I have cereal today?"

"I'm sure they will have something y' like," Declan chuckled and tussled Caelan's hair.

Meghan was startled awake about an hour later when she heard a commotion outside of the SUV caused by Cassie, trying to get past the security guards that were stationed around the entrance. After tidying herself in the mirror, she jumped out of the car into the early morning sun. The ever-present clouds were white and full, resembling large soft cotton balls placed throughout the sky.

"What's wrong, Cass?" Meghan questioned Cassie, who was still arguing with the large, neck-less man.

"I was telling your friend here that the castle is closed to tourists today, we're filming a movie here today," he grumbled but forced a slight smile when he recognized Meghan.

"I know. I'm Meghan Montgomery, Declan's wife," she said with a friendly smile.

"Oh yes, I recognized you, Mrs. Montgomery, go right in." He blushed and waved them past the other guards. "Sorry for the inconvenience."

"That's okay, you're just doing your job," Meghan smiled and turned towards Cassie.

"Don't you get sick of this?" Cassie appeared rather annoyed that she had been harassed.

Meghan shrugged settling in behind a group of people heading towards the castle.

The massive stone castle that stood ahead of them was breathtaking, its large tower looming over the abundance of lush greenery surrounding the outer walls. The landscaping around the castle was perfectly manicured with flowing flowerbed and large trees. There were a number of gardens to explore and Meghan especially wanted to see Rock Close with its waterfalls, druid caves and alters and the witch's kitchen. Cassie was almost vibrating with excitement about exploring the fern garden and the recently discovered ice house, but where she planned on heading first was the Poison garden.

The castle was damp but surprisingly bright, as the light streamed in from the windows high on the moss covered walls. Meghan wanted to find Declan and Caelan before they started to explore, so they headed through the castle to a large meadow on the other side. When the two women exited on the other side of the castle, they found a mass of people standing around, listening to an older man wearing a baseball cap, explaining what he wanted them to do. The amount of people gathered to listen was enormous—at least, two hundred. Most were locals from neighbouring towns that were lucky enough to have been chosen to portray ancient warriors in the battle scenes.

As they passed by a group of women in the back of the crowd, they eyed them momentarily but quickly refocused on the director when they realized that Meghan and Cassie were not actors.

"Meghan." Deirdre's voice stuck pins into Meghan's stomach. Why was that woman always around? Well, at least she knew that Declan must be close by if Deirdre was there. Meghan turned and forced a smile to her reddening face. It took every ounce of self-restraint she had not to knock the invasive woman to the ground.

"Deirdre." Meghan voice was calm and surprisingly friendly. "Have you seen Declan?" Of course she had seen Declan, she probably spotted him the minute he arrived.

"Yes, he is over filming his scene. He should be done in about an hour or so."

"Thank you." Meghan turned towards Cassie and crinkled her nose with annoyance.

"Let's go, Meg," Cassie piped up, hoping to help her friend to get away from Deirdre before Meghan blew.

Meghan nodded and smiled with mischief before turning around to face Deirdre. "I don't suppose you know where our daughter is?"

Deirdre shrugged and glanced over at the blond man sauntering towards them. "I haven't seen her. Why isn't she with y'?"

Meghan glanced over at Cassie and rolled her eyes at the tone Deirdre had used. Her resemblance to Kaye was striking, and Meghan realized that the bitchy personality must come from Kaye's father's side of the family, since her cousin Deirdre is exactly like Kaye. "Declan let me sleep for a while. He kept me up late last night, and then woke me up earlier this morning," Meghan smirked, her point hitting Deirdre like a sledgehammer.

Deirdre's face showed the anxiety clearly, but she managed to refocus. "Before y' run off to relieve your husband, I want y' to meet someone."

Meghan sighed, but could not think of any excuse to get away. The last thing she wanted was to meet any of Deirdre's friends.

Deirdre swung her hand out towards the tall handsome blond man that was now at her side, his pale blue eyes focused on Meghan. "Meghan Montgomery, this is my friend, Liam O'Brien."

"Hello." Meghan forced a smile as she recognized the name. His pale blue eyes were too sharp and too focused on her.

"Hello." His hand went out towards her in greeting.

Meghan gripped his hand and felt a shudder run down her spine. Something was so familiar about his face, could this be the Liam that Declan talked about, their relation? "It's nice to meet you, but I must excuse myself."

Liam's hand tightened around hers when she tried to pull away. "Mrs. Montgomery, I understand y' are here visiting from the United States?"

"Yes," Meghan muttered and glanced over at Cassie, who was being completely ignored. "This is my friend Cassie," She blurted out, trying to direct the pale blue eyes off her.

"Nice to meet y'." Liam finally released Meghan's hand and gripped Cassie's, his eyes switching to her. "What are two beautiful ladies doing out on their own?"

Cassie smiled with pleasure, not sensing anything odd about the handsome man. "We're just looking around at this beautiful castle."

"Would y' like a tour?" Liam released Cassie's hand and directed his gaze back to Meghan.

"No, thank you, I have to meet my husband," Meghan blurted out, backing away from the man. His eyes now focused on her locket. Oh God, it was him.

"Could I interest y'?" He glanced over at Cassie, a smile curling his full lips.

Cassie's brow rose with interest. He was damn good-looking, she thought as she eyed his tall muscular frame. His wavy blond hair was blowing slightly in the wind, the golden streaks shining with warmth. Her lustful critic of him was thwarted however when Meghan's hand gripped her arm.

"No, she needs to meet her boyfriend," Meghan's voice was demanding. "Cass, don't do it," Meghan whispered to her friend.

Liam smirked, his hand rising towards Meghan's hand, pulling it from Cassie's arm. "Are y' her guardian?" He kept hold of Meghan's hand. "You're a mighty pretty governess."

"I'm not her governess," Meghan mumbled and pulled at her hand, but he kept a tight grip and took a step towards her, his eyes lowering to her chest and her locket. "That's a lovely locket y' have there."

"Thank you," Meghan muttered and glanced around the area, looking for Declan. Why did she wear the locket? It seemed every time she came in contact with an Irishman, they were attracted to it.

"Did y' buy it here in Ireland?" Liam's hand reached out and lifted the locket from her chest. His hand resting against her skin.

"No," Meghan blurted out and jumped back, her hand covering her locket in a protective manner.

"Where did y' get it?" Liam questioned, again his eyes smiling with delight.

"My grandfather." Meghan backed away another step as Liam turned towards Deirdre, exposing the right side of his neck and the russet birthmark streaking down his skin.

Liam noticed Meghan's facial expression and lifted his hand to his neck covering the mark. "Does me birthmark offend y', Mrs. Montgomery?" Liam's voice was taunting, which surprised Meghan.

"No, it's just my brother-in-law has the exact mark on his neck." Meghan bit her lip, wondering if she had said too much when Liam's face lit with pleasure.

"Oh yes, that friendly man, Rory Montgomery, I didn't put the names together."

Meghan cringed and glanced over at Cassie. So Rory was involved with this man, but it shouldn't surprise her since Rory was the first Irishman obsessed with her locket. "I have to go."

Liam smiled and slightly bobbed his head towards her. "It was lovely meeting y' ladies. I hope we can meet again."

Meghan forced a polite smile, gripped Cassie by the arm, and pulled her towards a group of extras.

"Meg, what are you so freaked out about?" Cassie blurted out when they were far enough away.

"That man seems so familiar, and I don't like the fact that he knows Rory," Meghan sighed when she spotted Fabrizio heading towards them with Caelan tucked up in his arms. "Good, there is Fabrizio."

Cassie turned and a smile hit her eyes. His big powerful body swaying as he walked, Caelan appearing to be weightless in his arm. "Hi."

"Hi, I'm glad I found you two. Caelan and I are going to see the Blarney stone." Fabrizio kissed Cassie, but his attention swung to Meghan as he caught the expression on her face. "What's wrong with you?"

"She's freaked out over that man." Cassie mocked and turned back, but Deirdre and the man had vanished.

Fabrizio turned and saw nothing, then returned his gaze to Meghan, her face still distressed. "Did you know him?"

"It was Liam O'Brien, but I'm sure I have met him before. He seemed familiar, but I couldn't place him. I need to see Declan," Meghan blurted out, not wanting to tell Fabrizio about her locket. She was not sure how much he knew about the locket, and her and

Declan's ancestry. If he found out, he would have her in protective custody within the hour.

"He's filming right now. Come with me, he's meeting us there when he's done," Fabrizio said firmly, gripping her arm, turning her in the direction he was originally heading.

Meghan did not argue and followed quietly behind Fabrizio and Cassie to see the famous piece of Irish folklore that is known throughout the world. Meghan remembered reading an article about the Stone of Eloquence years before in which it said that anyone who can accomplish the feat of kissing the stone will be rewarded with the "gift of eloquence."

"I'm going to kiss the stone," Meghan informed them as she wandered up behind Fabrizio.

"Are you sure? I don't think we could handle it if you gabbed any more than you already do." Fabrizio's tone was sarcastic as he tickled Meghan under the chin.

"Funny," Meghan snorted and followed him up the staircase.

"Did you know that this is the third castle to be built on this site, it was built in 1446, by Dermot McCarthy," Cassie blurted out trying to get Fabrizio's attention back on her. "The legend says that in 1314, the McCarthy clan supplied four thousand troops to Scotland to fight in the battle of Bannockburn. Robert the Bruce, High King of Scotland was so grateful he sent a piece of the legendary Stone of Scone to the McCarthy King." Cassie glanced over at Meghan as she began her climb up the 125 stairs.

"It sat in the castle for over one hundred years before King Dermot McCarthy saved a witch from drowning in Blarney Lake. The witch was so grateful that she revealed the secret of the stone to Dermot. He wanted to keep it a secret, so he had it placed high up on a dangerous point on the castle wall for all the future kings. In 1560, Queen Elizabeth I ordered Cormac McCarthy to surrender and pledge his elegance to her, but the golden-tongued McCarthy always managed to talk his way out of it. The queen is said to have gotten mad and said 'that is a load of Blarney', that's how the stone got its name."

Fabrizio stared at Cassie in amazement. "Did you just get all that off that pamphlet?" He bobbed his head towards the pamphlet in her hand.

"No, I did some research before we came." She grinned, happy to have his dark brown eyes on her. "It's also said that in 1646, Oliver Cromwell sent his soldiers to attack the castle, but once inside, they found that the McCarthy clan had disappeared out of the three secret caves in the bottom of the castle. They took all their valuables with them, including the family's priceless gold plate. It is said that it was thrown into Blarney Lake so the English could not get their hands on it. Legend says that once the plate is recovered from the lake and returned to Blarney Castle, the McCarthy will again rise to the throne of Munster."

Meghan smiled at the story, it made her think of her own history, and all the legends that surrounded her family. Ireland certainly had no shortage of legends.

The climb up the spiral stone staircase was long and cramped, and once on the wall of the castle, she felt rather weak. "I didn't know it was up here," Meghan muttered cowering next to Fabrizio.

"It's over there," Fabrizio laughed, pointing down the long narrow wall path. "Just don't look down."

Meghan swallowed hard and clung to Fabrizio as they moved down the narrow wall. No matter what direction she looked, all she could see was the ground far below. By the time they reached the hole in the wall, she was drained.

Cassie, however, was annoyed that when Meghan was around, Fabrizio hardly noticed her. She had hoped that over the last few months, his love for her would overpower his love for Meghan but some days she was not sure.

The stone formed one of the massive lintels helping to support the castle's parapet, and to get to the stone, she would have to hang upside down through the gap in the wall.

"Are you still going to do this?" Cassie questioned, looking down the opening to the murder hole below, then eyeing Meghan as she leaned up against Fabrizio.

Meghan looked down and shuddered at the distance to the ground. "Hmm. That's quite far down."

"You don't have to do it," Cassie chuckled with amusement.

"No, I am," she said firmly. "I just won't look down."

"Well, this should be entertaining to watch," Fabrizio joked and wrapped his arm around Cassie's shoulder, pulling her into him.

Meghan shook her head and knelt down on the hard stone floor in front of the gap. She examined the gap for sometime before she sat down and started to bend backwards into the hole.

"Shit, Boo, you're going to kill yourself, let me help." Fabrizio moved in beside her and held her by the waist as she manoeuvred her shoulders down the hole. She started to giggle as she got further down the hole, and her body shook from the laughter.

"You better hang on tight, Fabrizio, I don't want to go head first down this hole." Meghan kept sliding herself down, her eyes fixed on the large stone ahead of her, as she got closer and closer.

"Oh don't be so dramatic Meg, there are metal bars down there. You won't fall down the hole. "Cassie grumbled, her eyes stuck on Fabrizio holding onto Meghan's waist.

"Well, that's an interesting position." Declan's voice filled the hole as he came up behind them with Colton.

Colton smiled as he glanced at Meghan's outstretched body lying on the ground under Fabrizio's hands, her golden brown tummy exposed as well as the lower portion of her pale pink lace bra as she stretched her body further down the hole.

"Fabs, let me help her," Colton blurted out, squatting down beside Meghan, resting his hand on her stomach.

"No, and stop gawking at me wife," Declan snorted and pushed at Colton's shoulder, removing his hand from Meghan, then nudged Fabrizio out as well.

"What are you two doing up there?" Meghan questioned impatiently, feeling the movement on her skin.

"Nothing, just hurry up and kiss the damn stone and get back up here so Colton can put his eyes back in his head," Declan grumbled; he was growing tired of Colton's overt behaviour towards Meghan.

"You two are such boys!" Meghan snorted and wiggled one more time, then leaned towards the stone.

Colton's eyes widened with excitement as her shirt rose further up her chest. Declan grunted at him and pulled the shirt down, covering her exposed lower breasts. "Meggie, hurry up, he's going to jump y' any minute."

"Fine, I'm done, help me back up." She started to wiggle her way back up through the hole as Declan pulled on her ribs carefully, removing her upper body.

"This is not supposed to be a peep show," Meghan grumbled when she sat up and pulled at her shirt but was distracted by the costumes that the two men had on. "Speaking of peep shows, it's a good thing you boys aren't Scots, because from here, I can see right up your skirts." Meghan giggled and pushed herself to her feet, brushing the dirt off her tan-coloured shorts.

"They're not skirts, they're tunics." Colton corrected her.

"Oh, pardon me," Meghan laughed as she surveyed the outfits.

The mid thigh tunic with a band of embroidered trim around the bottom was covered by a pleated saffron shirt over top. The warrior outfit was finished with a thick leather belt worn over top of the shirt and a long sword hung through a loop on the side of the belt. They were both bare legged but had little slipper-type leather shoes covering their feet. Declan's costume differed slightly; he was wearing a dark red sash across his shoulder that tied at his hip.

Declan laughed at Meghan when she turned to him with a content smile on her face. "Pretty proud of yourself that y' did that, aren't y'?" he grinned and kissed her lips softly. "I must say it was very brave."

"That was hard and look how far down it is," Meghan grumbled, not appreciating his mocking tone.

"Aye," Declan laughed eyeing the hole. "I'm quite surprised that y' made it this far." He nodded back towards the long narrow wall they crossed.

"Don't be too impressed," Fabrizio piped up. "I think her finger imprints are still in my arm."

"Shut up," Meghan snorted and turned towards Declan's smirking face and began eyeing his hair that was pulled back into a ponytail, tied with a suede sash. "So they want it long so they can tie it back."

"Aye, sometimes it's flowing about me face." Declan winked at her and pulled her towards him, then kissed her thoroughly.

Meghan was amazed at the number of people wandering around the castle as the lunch break wound down. Everyone seemed to have somewhere to be as the crowd quickly moved in all directions. The only ones not in a hurry seemed to be Declan, Colton, a handful of minor cast members, and Deirdre. She was lingering close by, of course, with the tall blond man she had insisted Meghan meet earlier. There was something eerie about the man; the sight of him made the hair on the back of Meghan's neck stick up. Declan noticed Meghan standing by the trailer, watching Kaye and Deirdre talking with O'Brien.

"Meggie, I don't think I appreciate y' staring at other men," Declan mumbled and nuzzled the nape of her neck from behind.

"That's the man that I met earlier." She swung around to face Declan. "He gives me the creeps."

Declan's dark eyes settled on the man with some recognition. "He looks familiar, what's his name?"

"His name is Liam O'Brien." Meghan pressed up against Declan as his arms tightened around her.

"Liam O'Brien?" Declan's voice was hard and cold.

"Yes." Meghan gasped as he tightened his grip around her, squeezing the breath from her lungs. "Declan, you're hurting me."

"Sorry," he said offhandedly, loosening his grip. "What did he want?"

Meghan shrugged and glanced over her shoulder at the man whose back was now turned towards them. "Deirdre said he was a friend of hers. She introduced us." Meghan focused back on Declan's worried face. "He was interested in my locket, though."

"Christ," Declan mumbled louder than he had meant to.

"Is he the Liam that is the third member of the triad?"

"Freckles, I want y' to stay with Fabrizio while I'm filming today," Declan ordered without answering her question.

"Why?" she questioned, not liking the expression on his face.

"Because I said so!" His voice was cold and demanding. "Please don't question me on this."

"All right," Meghan sniffed, fighting back the tears. Why was he talking to her like a naughty child? She pushed away slightly and gazed at him with worry and anger fighting for supremacy. "What are you hiding now?"

He was startled by her comment and gazed at her, forcing calmness to his face. "Nothing, Freckles, it's just that every time someone shows interest in your locket, trouble soon follows." Meghan nodded but said nothing. She knew more was going on, and once again, Declan was hiding something from her, but she decided to agree with him for the time being. Tomorrow he would be on set, and she would find a reason to stay at the hotel so she could go and research the locket more in-depth. During her previous search of the church records, she had authenticated Declan's original story about the origins and the family link, but she found little about Michael's family line after the marriage. She needed to search the records in the town's records for the answers. Tomorrow she would find the answers.

CHAPTER TWENTY-SIX

Meghan waited an hour after Declan left for the day, to ensure that he had not been held up in the lobby or out in the garden, before she snuck down the hall to the stairs. Fabrizio was seated in the lobby, his eyes scanning the area, obviously planted there to keep her under wraps. Dammit, how was she going to get past him? He would never let her go to the church now. Liam had spooked Declan to the point of denying her any freedoms. The entire evening before, Declan never let her out of his sight; even when she went to the lobby to buy a chocolate bar, he accompanied her.

She was going to find out the whole story, and if sneaking out of the manor was the only way, she would. She went down the back stairs and out the servant's entrance.

The air was crisp and damp as the low cloud cover was threatening to open and saturate her, but the town's people were going about their business without concern for the inevitable shower they could receive at any moment.

Meghan's attention was drawn to a group of women bickering with each other as they exited a store across the street. The sign over the blue door read, *O'Leary's Jewelry* and in small letters underneath was written, *specializing in historical jewelry*. The little store nestled in lower floor of a very old stone building almost beckoned out for her. Why hadn't she noticed that store before?

Meghan jerked open the front door, causing a small bell to ring alerting the owner inside.

"Good day, Miss." Welcomed an elderly man, tucked in behind a glass display case.

"Hi," Meghan responded as she looked back to see if Fabrizio was anywhere in sight.

"What could I help y' with today?" the man smiled, causing his weathered wrinkled skin to crease deeply around his eyes.

"Well, I was hoping you could help with my locket," Meghan asked, studying his face.

"Is it broken then?" Then man waved her towards him, obviously having no intentions of going to her. "I've old bones, lass, and can't move about like I used to."

Meghan smiled and moved towards him, taking a seat across the table from him and his collection of small watch parts.

"I've been trying to piece this together all morning, but I seem to have misplaced a small piece, could y' have a peek on the floor, lass, and see if y' can see anything."

Meghan forced a helpful smile and scanned the floor, bending over to appear observant, even though she had no interest in spending her time helping the old man search for lost watch parts. "I don't want to take up too much of your time, but I would appreciate it if you could give me some information about my locket. Your sign says you specializing in historical jewelry."

"Aye, I do. Let's have a look, shall we?" He reached out his weathered hand, palm up.

Meghan eyed him tentatively, then removed the locket, and laid it in his hand. "I would like to know what the insignia on it means. It disturbed someone yesterday, but he wouldn't tell me what it meant."

"Oh well, dear, let me have a look." He slipped on his glasses that hung around his neck on a chain.

The aged man lifted the locket to his face and studied it with great care, his hand trembling slightly. His face began to fill with a mixture of excitement and something close to terror as he looked at the locket from every angle.

"Where did y' come by this?" he asked, forcing calmness into his voice.

"It was my great-great-grandmother's," Meghan responded, raising her brow towards him.

"Oh" was all he said as he turned it over in his hands and studied the back, flipped it again, then flicked it open and examined the pictures. "Your family?" he smiled as he looked up at her over his glasses. Recognition crossing his face.

"Yes, my husband and my daughter," Meghan smiled proudly.

"Have you been out to Briarwood Castle?" The man glanced over his glasses.

"Yes," Meghan said simply.

"So I suppose they showed you the painting. Y' are the spitting image of Catherine."

Meghan nodded but said nothing.

"May I remove this picture to take a peek underneath?" He resumed his examination of the locket.

"Sure, I guess so," Meghan answered, rather curious to find out what the man was looking for.

"If I am correct, this amulet was one of three. See this part here." He pointed to the small tail of silver out of the knot and the indented piece on the other. "This is where the three connect to make one. This was turned into a locket at some point very later on, maybe to disguise its true identity."

The man lifted a pair of tweezers and moved his shaky hand towards the picture of Declan. He pulled out the picture and placed it on the counter, then lifted the locket up to his face once again. "Aye, there it is," he said as a large smile filled his face.

"What is it?" Meghan blurted out.

"The mark of the Dál gCais tribe." His breath was catching in his throat as his eyes settled on her. "Lock that door, lad." He bobbed his head towards the young boy that had come down from the long staircase at the back of the room.

"Why, what are you doing?" Meghan panicked as the old man clasped his hand closed on the locket and stood.

"Come with me, I have something to show y'."

Meghan grimaced and glanced over at the young boy, who was now heading towards her and the old man. "Y' stay here, lad, and place the 'back in five minutes' sign in the door."

Meghan eyed the boy of about twelve. His curly brown hair was long and covering his face. "Aye, Granda."

The man stopped inside the door at the back of the shop and gestured towards a set of steep stairs leading to what she assumed was his living quarters. "I'll follow y'. I don't move so swiftly." His hand again waved up the stairs.

Meghan took each step slowly, her hesitation evident to the old man. "By the way, lass, I'm Adam O'Leary."

"Meghan Montgomery," She said simply, but wished she hadn't when she entered the stale-smelling apartment of the man.

The sun was shining through the dingy lace curtains, illuminating the immense dust particles that were floating around the room. The spacious room was filled with books, more books than she had ever seen in one place before. Some appeared extremely old. The table up against the wall was stacked high with papers and scrolls, browned with age, and on the wall directly behind it was a large chart.

The man wandered over to the chart and raised his glasses back to his face. "See right here, miss, this amulet belonged to this family."

"So, it is from the O'Brien family?" Meghan moved closer to the chart.

The old man's eye brow rose slightly. "Well, I see y' know a little about the origins. So why bring it to me?"

"I saw the sign, and I wanted to find out if my information was true. This locket seems to draw people's attention, so I wanted to be sure of its history," Meghan muttered, following the flow chart of ancient families.

"Well, that mark inside is the mark of a chieftain. Brian Boru, to be exact. Y' said it was your great-grandmother's?"

"Actually it was my great-great-grandmother's on my grandfather's side. He said that it was his ancestors from the 1800s." She wanted to see if he would relay the same historical information that Declan had told her months earlier.

"More about 976 would be me guess." His excitement outweighed his fears as if he had discovered a missing piece of time.

"It's that old?" Meghan gasped at the date.

"This amulet was one of three that when placed together formed the pommel of a very powerful sword. This sword was said to have been forged by the sidhe for Brian Boru himself." He glanced up at Meghan when she gasped.

"I heard this before. From Mr. O'Brien at Briarwood. But his wife said he was crazy. I tended to believe her."

"Oh no, lass, it is very possible." The old man pulled a book off the shelf and flipped to a drawing from AD 1012 that depicted the sword of Boru. "See this part, right here is the piece y' have. Your piece is the anchor, the most valuable. Your amulet is the one that represents the unity of the three powers. This piece here with the three lines is the three rays, and it represents the male and female energy. And this last one that looks like a three-legged man represents the progress of man. When the three are put together, they form a perfect circle. The legend says that when they are linked together, they hold the key to where the sword of Boru is hidden."

"But that's just on old wives tale!" Meghan blurted out.

The old man eyed her with interest. "Y' don't believe there is a sword? There is a good number of people who believe that it is hidden in Briarwood Castle. That's why he made so many hallways and hidden rooms."

"Well, if it was there, don't you think someone would have found it by now?" Meghan still did not believe in the mysterious sword.

The man shrugged and looked back at the family lineage. "This amulet would make y' the descendant of the youngest son, Michael."

"I believe so," Meghan muttered and sat down in the chair that the man pulled out for her.

"The legend says that when the three become one, the sword will wield the power of the Gods."

Meghan stared at him as the information sunk in. This got more convoluted the more she heard.

"Let's do some research, shall we? I have records from every church in the country, and we should be able to trace this linage right to y'."

Time seemed immeasurable as the two heads stayed lowered, their eyes scouring the documents in front of them. Mr. O'Leary seemed very acquainted with the flow chart of Meghan's family tree and had little trouble pointing out the path to her.

"This is where the family is lost. When this Caelan Delaney was killed, her husband Mick took their son and left for America in 1956. The church no longer kept track of them." O'Leary muttered, raised his glasses, and scrubbed at his eyes. "My departed wife, bless her soul, was very astute at keeping records, but she passed on before she could find out where that branch of the family had vanished to."

"My grandfather never came back here nor did my father. I know that much," Meghan sighed.

"They wouldn't dare with the O'Briens after them."

"The O'Briens?" Meghan's voice sounded shrill. "That's the man that was interested in my locket yesterday, the man that Declan says we are related to."

"He's related, all right."

A high-pitched ring startled Meghan, and she pulled her cell phone from her purse. "Hello?"

"Meg, it's me." Cassie's voice was almost a whisper. "Where are you?"

"I'm at a jewelry shop down the street."

"Declan is on his way back to the hotel. He is going to freak that you're not here. It's almost five."

"What?" Meghan eyed her watch with panic. "If he finds out I took off?"

Meghan shoved the phone in her pocket and jumped from the chair. "Thank you for your help."

"Miss, please, stay away from the O'Briens." O'Leary's voice was gruff with worry for his new-found friend.

"Why?"

"They are evil like their forefathers before them. They are the spawn of the devil himself. Please just heed me words. They will bring nothing but anguish to y'."

"Thank you for your help," Meghan said, backing down the stairs. "May I come back tomorrow and read some more of your papers?"

"Aye, and miss, please be careful!" he begged as she turned at the bottom of the stairs. With a quick thank you and a wave, she was out the door.

Cassie's call had panicked her, and she knew she needed to get to the room before Declan returned. Her only problem was that if Fabrizio spotted her out of her room without him, she was busted. Meghan ducked behind a clump of bushes in the back garden, when she noticed Cassie and Caelan being followed by Fabrizio. Damn, she should have gone through the front door. There was nothing she could do until they wandered off. She planted herself on the ground and peered through the holes in the shrub. Fabrizio was agitated, that was plain to see as he continually turned, eyeing the path leading to the front door of the manor. What was he watching for, her leaving or someone coming in?

Meghan sighed when Cassie sat down on the grass and settled Caelan onto her lap for a hopefully short lesson in botany.

"Meghan, I need to talk to you." Rory stumbled across the grass towards her.

Meghan cringed and glanced over at Fabrizio; he apparently had not heard Rory. "You are not supposed to be near me?" Meghan blurted out impatiently, her eyes straying back to Fabrizio.

"I now, but it's really important, and I don't know who else to talk to," Rory told her with an air of urgency in his voice that startled her.

"Fine, what is it?" Over the past few weeks, she had seen him a few times. He still had not admitted that he was Ian, but he made no attempt to be near her anymore than necessary. Declan was convinced Rory was deep into something, but he could not figure out what.

"I can't tell you here, where are you going?"

"Back to my room, why can't you just tell me? You know if Declan catches you talking to me alone."

"I know." Rory's voice was sharp. "Damn. Would you just listen?"

"Fine," Meghan grumbled and stood up. "But if you want privacy, we need to get away without the guard dog spotting us."

Rory followed her gaze and chuckled slightly. "A prisoner, are you?"

"Something like that," Meghan grumbled. "Go distract him, so I can sneak around the back way."

Rory sneered at her but did as she requested and wandered over to Fabrizio, immediately annoying him. Meghan used the split second that Fabrizio's attention was on Rory to dart to the row of hedges, then up the front steps of the manor.

Meghan debated heading straight to her room, but a twinge of guilt caused her to wait for Rory and hear what he had to say. The minute she saw his face, however, she regretted that decision. Nothing Rory was involved in could possibly end well.

"I just wanted you to know that Liam O'Brien is . . . Well, he is upset that you and Declan have been snooping into your past." Rory's voice sounded choked even to him.

"Why is he concerned we will discover he is related to us," Meghan muttered and eyed him for a reaction.

"How do you know that?"

"Well, Declan told me some of it and the rest I found out doing research. It wasn't that hard to piece together."

"So you know about my relationship with the O'Briens. That would explain Declan's attitude," Rory sighed.

"Rory, what the hell are you talking about? What relationship?"

Rory dropped to a mauve chair by the big window, covering his face with his hands. "Meghan, it was me that tried to steal your locket years ago."

Meghan was startled by the admission. "I know."

Rory glanced up, his face confused. "But you said you were wrong."

"Declan told me to stop pushing and see what you were up to." Meghan forced her fears down her throat.

"So Declan thought it was me as well, he has never trusted me?" Rory scowled and stood to face her.

"Apparently, for good reason," Meghan mumbled and glanced out the window, spotting Fabrizio wandering back and forth. "You shot him."

Rory nodded and followed her across the lobby. "I always knew something was different about me and the way my father treated me. So six years ago, I came over here to search my family's history." He paused and glanced over at her when she stopped by the front desk to retrieve her messages. "I found out something that I have never told anyone before."

"Rory, just tell me what you found out," Meghan grumbled, getting tired of his speech.

"Liam O'Brien is my brother," Rory blurted out and gripped her arm when she backed away from him. "He is my half-brother," he repeated with an underlying fear in his eyes.

Meghan eyed him with confusion as she tried to sort out the logistics of what he was saying. "How can he be your half-brother? You would have to have the same mom. Or dad?" she questioned, not grasping what he was saying.

"Meghan, his da is my da. You always thought I was nothing like Declan and now you know why," he said, trying hard to make her understand.

"Oh my God, are you telling me that your mother had an affair on your dad?"

"Yes." Rory struggled to find the words "She had an affair with Fergus O'Brien." He finally blurted out.

"Shit." Meghan dropped to the chair, her hands cupping her face. This can't possibly be happening, no wonder Declan's father had such an aversion to Rory. He must know that Rory is not his son.

"Meghan, you can't tell Declan."

"Why? I can't keep this from him." The last thing she was going to do was lie to Declan about this. She was convinced that Rory's relationship tied into all the troubles that followed her around.

"You have to. I don't want my parents to find out that I know. It would break my mam's heart."

"So that's why your family moved to the States?"

"Well, that was part of it. I guess the whole town knew I was his son when they saw this damn birthmark."

"Yeah, Liam has an identical one. Rory, if he is as dangerous as they say, you could be in danger." Meghan glanced over at Rory, and it struck her that he could be lying to her once again. "Rory, why did you want my locket?"

Rory was startled by the question but gained control of his facial expression. "Liam wanted it. When Kaye showed up here with Deirdre and started rambling about a friend of her cousin that had an amulet which was passed down from generation to generation, Liam and Fergus freaked out. They thought your line had died out. Fergus was in the process of going to court to get possession of the estate."

Meghan sighed, clutching the locket in her clenched hand. She needed to talk to Declan about this, more was going on then he was telling her. Declan must have known that the locket's insignia holds the key to finding the sword if he had done such extensive research as he claimed. She found out just by talking to a jeweler.

"Meghan, I would avoid him if I were you. He wants that locket, and he doesn't seem to have any boundaries on how to get it. I'm leaving in the morning; I want no part of him or his father." Rory turned and headed for the staircase.

"Well, he's not getting my locket," Meghan said defiantly as she followed behind Rory, contemplating his admission. "Rory, is Kaye involved in this?"

"No, I don't believe so. She was just the one that tipped him off. They were having an affair years ago, and I think she's still in love with him. She follows him around like a puppy dog."

"That figures," Meghan grunted and stared at Rory. "I better get back to my room before Declan gets back."

Meghan sighed and headed towards the stairs to retreat to her room but was stopped in her tracks when a group of people headed towards them.

"Rory and Meghan, I'm so glad I finally found y'," Deirdre blurted out, darting quickly across the room, her long black hair flying up around her.

"Oh shit," Meghan whispered towards Rory as her eyes settled on Liam O'Brien and Kaye heading towards them behind Deirdre.

"Hello, Rory, it's good to see you haven't left the country," Liam clasped Rory's shoulder, his voice smug with a tone of threat.

Rory nodded his head but said nothing, his eyes staying fixed on Meghan's face that was filling with panic.

"So, Mrs. Montgomery, we missed y' at the castle today. I was hoping we could talk more about your amulet," Liam said, seemingly uninterested in Rory's silence.

"Why?" Meghan questioned inadvertently, moving her hand up to cover her locket.

A twisting terror was filling her with the realization that Rory was in closer contact with Liam O'Brien than he was telling her. Liam appeared to know Rory was leaving for home or had he just guessed. No, Rory was keeping him apprised on his whereabouts, that was obvious. When would he tell his brother that Meghan is in possession of a lot of family information?

"I'm very interested in the historical relevance of the markings." Liam's voice was loud and drew her attention back to him.

"I'm sure they are nothing. It's just a worthless knickknack," Meghan mumbled, terrified that Rory was going to expose the truth to his brother.

She could feel her face flushing under Liam's scrutinizing eyes and her first instinct was to back away and run, but she was not sure what that would accomplish other than alert him to the fact she knows the origins of the locket.

"Y' could be right. But y' wouldn't mind if I took a look, would y'?" Liam questioned with a tone of demand.

"Well?" Meghan mumbled as his large hand reached out and lifted the locket from her chest.

His mouth twitched slightly as his hand brushed against her soft skin, when he flicked the locket open. The picture of Caelan was still intact, but she hadn't put the picture of Declan back in properly, and O'Brien lifted it with his thumbnail, revealing the clan seal on the back of the amulet.

His eyes slowly rose to meet hers, his golden brow lifting slightly as he stared at her, probing deeper and deeper into her mind. She could feel every drop of blood flowing through her face as his eyes quizzed her for information. Panicking, she lifted her hand to remove the locket from his hand, but he closed his hand around hers, his blue gaze still fixed on her terrified eyes.

As Meghan tugged at her hand, he nonchalantly released her hand and the locket, letting Declan's picture drop to the floor. She gasped and bent down, grabbing it from the marble floor with O'Brien's eye never leaving her. When she straightened after pushing Declan's picture back into its place in the locket, she found O'Brien smiling at her with amusement.

"So, Mrs. Montgomery, could y' tell me again where y' got that amulet?" Liam questioned, taking a step towards her, completely invading her personal space.

"It's none of your business. Now, if you will excuse me, I have to go," Meghan blurted out and backed away from him, hitting a solid form behind her, causing her to jerk around quickly. Declan was standing quietly behind her, glaring at O'Brien, his eyes cold and aggressive as he stared at the large muscular man.

"Declan!" Meghan sighed and dropped into him.

"Meggie, I have been looking for y'." Declan wrapped his arm around her in a protective gesture.

"Well, well, if it isn't the pretty boy," O'Brien sneered, eyeing Meghan's positioning in Declan's arms.

"Liam O'Brien, I see y' haven't changed much. Y' still appear to be a bully," Declan snarled with a note of disgust. "What seems to be the problem here?"

"There's no problem," O'Brien responded smugly, his pale blue gaze settling on Meghan as she pressed up against Declan's chest.

"Then I suggest that y' keep your hands off me wife," Declan ordered in a firm but calm voice. His grip around Meghan was tightening the more she stiffened in his arms. He couldn't help but wonder how much information she was in possession of, and if she had discovered his original intentions.

"If you think y' have beaten me, Montgomery, you're mistaken. This changes nothing," Liam said coolly, bobbing his head towards Meghan.

"Y' stay away from me wife," Declan blurted out, his voice sharper than he intended.

O'Brien snorted a snide laugh and turned to leave. "Your da thought it was over when he married your mam." A smirk curled his full lips as his eyes settled on Rory. "But he was wrong too."

"O'Brien, I'm warning y', come near me family, you'll regret it." Declan tensed slightly, as a dread that the past was going to explode at any time filled him. When it did, how was Meghan going to react? Would she ever forgive him for lying to her?

"Well, we must be going. It was grand talking with y' again, Mrs. Montgomery." Liam wrapped his long muscular arm around Kay's narrow frame. "Good evening to y'." He looked back at Declan, an evil expression crossing his face. "Don't think this is over." Then he lumbered across the lobby with Kaye tucked under his arm.

Meghan had been abnormally quiet on the way back to their room, she knew that more was going on than she was being told, and anger was building in her.

Declan slammed the door, deciding to go on the attack and distract her. "Meggie, what the hell were y' doing leaving the room? Did I not tell y' to stay here?" Declan questioned, his voice on the verge of yelling.

"Yes, but . . ." she stammered, being caught off guard by his attack. "But I wanted to go to the church."

"I told you to leave it alone, didn't I?" he was yelling then. "I told y' not to dig into the past, I told y' to let it alone."

"Declan," she babbled, taking a few steps away from him. "Why are you getting so mad?"

"Because y' defied me!" he snorted and had to turn away from her, unable to look at her terrified face. "Y' just don't understand what is going on."

"Then maybe you should tell me, because you obviously know him, and he knows that Rory is—" she blurted out before she could stop herself.

"Meghan!" Rory blurted out with panic exploding in his tone.

"Rory, if y' have got her into some kind of trouble, I swear I'll kill y'," Declan snorted as he moved towards him.

"No, I haven't," Rory replied trying to defend himself. Rory took a step backwards and glanced over at Meghan with distress. The last thing he wanted was for Declan to find out his connection with Liam. How he wished he had never come to Ireland the first time. His life would be so much more settled. He would not be looking over his shoulder all the time, wondering when Liam was going to materialize, wanting him to do some dirty work. If he had not gotten involved all those years ago, Declan would never have met Meghan, and he would probably be married to Georgia right now, and they all would be safely tucked away in the warmth of the California sun.

Meghan's eyes stayed glued to Rory's pale face. "I think you should tell him."

"Meghan, please," Rory interrupted her.

"Rory, what the hell are y' trying to get her to hide for y'."

"Declan, I really think you would be better off not knowing," Rory said, with a note of finality.

"Tell me!" Declan shouted, glaring at Rory and took a menacing step towards him. Suddenly he turned and directed his glare at Meghan. "Are y' going to tell me the truth or not?"

Meghan gazed at Declan, then back at Rory; she did not want to hurt Declan by telling him the truth, but she did not like keeping secrets from him either. The decision was tearing at her insides as she struggled to decide what to do.

"Rory, either you tell him or I will," Meghan finally said with a firm voice.

Rory frowned and looked directly at Declan, realizing that the truth was going to come out, so he may as well confess. "I know why Pop hates me so much."

"He doesn't hate y'."

"Well, he hates the way I came into the world then." Rory felt his stomach churning as he watched Declan's dark grey eyes fill with distrust.

"For Christ's sake, would y' stop talking in riddles and just tell me?" Declan snorted.

"Liam O'Brien is my half-brother. Ma had an affair with his father, and I was the result of that," Rory blurted out and took two steps backwards.

Declan dropped to cream velvet couch, slouching over in shock, his hands clutching his face. "This is unbelievable."

"Declan," Meghan muttered, moved in front of him, and placed her hands on his shoulders. "You can't tell your parents that you know. Your mother would be devastated."

"Aye, I won't," Declan sighed, pulling her close to him. His head rested against her stomach, and his arms wrapped around her hips. She could feel his body shaking under her hands as he tried to deal with the horrible information he had just heard. "Why didn't she ever tell us?"

"Declan, why would she? It's not something she would want everyone to know." Meghan bent down and kissed the top of his head.

"Oh, Freckles, how could she do that to me da?" Declan lifted his head towards her and pulled her down onto his lap. Was that why his father had such a wandering eye? Was he so hurt by her betrayal that he felt it was his right to roam into other women's bedrooms? His life was a mess and the more he found out about his family, the more bleak his life seemed to be becoming. Meghan was not going to understand his lies, and she was going to be devastated.

Meghan sighed and looked over his shoulder and out the window. She could feel her pain, his mother's pain, and his pain, rushing through her at an uncontrollable speed. She closed her eyes and leaned her chin on his shoulder. "I don't know, Declan. But we don't know what really happened, and I don't think we should . . ." She stopped as his cold grey eyes focused on her.

"There is no excuse for betrayal!" Declan snorted, still caught up in his own betrayal. He felt terribly guilty, and his reaction was showing it.

Meghan stirred on his lap, as his eyes stayed glued to her face. "I'm not saying there is. But you shouldn't judge people without knowing what really happened." She soothed. "Anyway it's not like your dad has been completely faithful to her."

His glaring gaze stabbed her with anger. "That's not the same thing."

"Oh really?" Meghan growled and pulled away from him. "Cheating is cheating. Are you saying it's all right for a man to do it but not a woman?"

Declan didn't misread the expression on her face, and he was on his feet and in front of her with two strides. "I don't know what I'm saying, Freckles, please don't misunderstand me. I would never cheat on y', but I have just become accustomed to me da's behaviour I guess."

Meghan said nothing in response; she was trying hard not to cry. It sickened her that he was so complacent about his father's exploits but was completely appalled with his mother's.

"Meggie, it's just that she produced a child with another man," Declan blurted out, trying to settle her tormented eyes. "How could any man live with that?"

"I guess the same way a woman can live with the fact that her husband is sleeping with every woman in Washington," she snapped back, quite surprised she was taking Katie's side on the issue. "We don't know what happened and I am not judging her. I have no right." Meghan's voice was harsh.

Declan watched her wander over to the window and glance down at the street. "If Liam O'Brien is half the man his father is, I don't doubt she had little say in the matter."

"Meggie, what are y' saying, that y' find the man attractive?"

"No!" she lied. "I'm saying he seems to have some power, I don't know how to explain it, but he freezes you with fear, almost hypnotizing you."

"Hmm." Declan didn't like the direction this conversations was going. Something took place in the lobby between her and Liam, and he could sense it was not going to turn out all right.

Declan could hardly keep composed with all the thoughts flying through his mind. If Fergus and his mother did create Rory, is that what O'Brien meant when he said his father didn't win. A shudder ran through him as the thoughts of Liam's blue eyes scanning Meghan with a lustful gaze flashed through his mind. His face was beginning to show signs of concern as his brows crumpled slightly.

"Meggie, whatever is going on over here is getting out of control. I don't trust that man," he said, grabbing her shoulders and pulling her in front of him, his gaze was directly on her fear-filled eyes. He had to get her away from O'Brien before he dropped the bomb, leaving their lives together in shambles. "I want y' and Caelan to go home."

"No! I'm not leaving you," Meghan said, thrusting her face into his neck.

"Meggie, it's not safe here. I don't want y' getting hurt."

"I'll send Nat and Caelan home, but I'm not leaving you," She told him, with determination in her voice.

"Meggie, please."

"No!"

"Declan, you might as well be whistling jigs to a milestone," Rory remarked with a humorous tone.

Declan grunted with amusement at his brother's intervention with something his father used to say about his mother. Lifting Meghan's head away from his neck, he looked into her determined eyes. "Okay, Freckles, tomorrow we're sending Caelan home. But if anything else happens, y' are going too."

"Okay," she agreed and wandered towards the bedroom. "I'll phone Nat and let him know what's going on."

She returned to the sitting room and noticed that Rory had left. "Where did Rory go?"

"He left. He is going home tomorrow. He is scared for his safety." Declan sighed.

"Well, he should be if he is caught up the O'Briens."

"Meggie, I think it's best if we try to avoid the O'Briens for the remainder of our stay here. Relation or no, he's not someone we should involve ourselves with." Declan's voice sounded chocked, and he wondered if Meghan picked up on his distress.

"The man at the jewelry store said to stay away from them as well, he said they were the spawn of the devil," Meghan rambled.

"How does he know the O'Briens?"

"He doesn't know them personally, he just knows about them, and they scare him. However, he knows about my locket. The old man at the castle was right it did belong to Brian Boru."

Declan appeared stunned by the information. Maybe he didn't know. "Meggie, it didn't belong to Brian Boru, it was made by the Normans. That old man was daft."

"According to the writing from that time, it was."

"I have never read anything about this before." Declan shook his head and turned towards her, his face, expressionless. "Where did y' find out all this information? I mean, did O'Brien tell y'?"

"No, the jeweller down the street. You should see all the books and papers he has, my gosh, some date back to the 800s," Meghan rambled, trying to get all the information out quickly. She opened the locket and pulled out his picture, exposing the mark. "See this mark, it is the insignia of the Dál gCais tribe, Mr. O'Leary feels that this amulet is the one in the writings. He said it is one of the three that makes up the pommel of the sword. He even had a picture."

Declan examined the mark and shrugged. "How do y' know that is what that mark is? It just looks like an imperfection in the silver," he questioned, rubbing his finger across the small mark on the backside of the amulet, hoping he could discourage her from continuing with her search. He was starting to believe that his mother was right, and the O'Briens would do anything to keep him from gaining control of the estate.

"Because it matches the description of the one in the writings, and it dates back to that time."

Declan eyed her with interest. He always knew she longed to belong to something, to a family, but she seemed almost euphoric with the knowledge of her ancestry.

"Hmm." Declan was now chewing his lip, trying to decide how best to proceed. Maybe it was best to abandon his plan all together and be content with the knowledge of who he is. Take Meghan's lead and bask in the knowledge that his ancestry dates back to the time of Brian Boru. Leave the O'Briens to have their precious estate, go back to the States, and live his life with his beloved Meghan.

CHAPTER TWENTY-SEVEN

I t had been a week since Caelan and Nathan left for the safety of the States, and Declan had become very distant and cold towards her, and she had decided to return home, which was apparently what he wanted.

The group was down in the dining room having breakfast, mulling over the plans for the day; Declan had to go shoot his last scene, and Fabrizio had promised Cassie that they would go sightseeing.

Meghan had no interest in doing either; she simply wanted to get packed for her return home. "I have decided to go home today," she commented, interrupting Declan and Fabrizio's discussion.

"What?" Declan's dark eyes rose towards her, his brows crumpling slightly.

"I said I'm going home. It is clear that you don't want me here, and I have just become a burden on Fabrizio," Meghan said as calmly as she could, but she could feel her eyes glazing over.

"Meggie," Declan grumbled, annoyed that she would wait until everyone was around before she told him she was leaving.

"I think I'm going to pack," she muttered, pushing her chair back from the table. "That way, everyone can do what they want, without worrying about guarding me."

"Meggie, y' are not going by yourself. Wait until tomorrow. I'll go with y'," Declan ordered, getting very agitated at her insistence.

"No, you still have a lot to finish up here, I'll be fine anyway. O'Brien hasn't been anywhere around since that day in the lobby. Obviously, whatever he was interested in, he has forgotten about. I guess with Rory gone home, he lost interest."

"Meg, just come to Lough Gur in Limerick with us," Cassie pleaded, noticing the redness streaking up Declan's face as he glared at Meghan.

"I've already seen the Neolithic settlement there. I don't want to see it again. I'll just go to the airport and catch the first plane out."

"Meggie, why are y' being so difficult?" Declan questioned impatiently.

"I'm not trying to be difficult. I'm just so sick of being a prisoner."

"You're not a prisoner, I just want y' to be safe, and I don't want y' by yourself," He informed her softly, trying to convince her.

"Tell you what, Declan, I'm staying around town today. Why don't I look after her?" Colton offered, with a look of excitement filling the sky blue eyes.

"I don't need to be looked after. I'm not a child," she snorted at Declan, getting very annoyed with the way she was being treated.

"Y' do!" Declan snapped back at her, then looked over at Colton, his eyes studying him as if he was deciding if he were capable of taking care of his precious possession. "Y' can't let her out of your sight!" he ordered, still eyeing him.

"Hey, don't worry, I won't," Colton said, with an air of confidence.

"Good then, it's settled," Declan informed Meghan, with demand in his voice. He knew that she was strong willed, but there were times that she was very hard to handle, and he found himself getting annoyed at her easily these days. "And as for y' going home, we will discuss that when I get back."

Meghan's face filled with a mixture of annoyance and pain as she stared at Declan while he finished his breakfast. She could not believe that he was treating her this way; she would have been better off going home with Caelan. Maybe that was the point he was trying to prove, after all, he did want her to leave with Nathan and Caelan.

Meghan was feeling very uncomfortable with the way the people at the table were watching her every move, even Cassie seemed to be in on the conspiracy to stifle her movements. Suddenly she stood, threw her napkin down on her plate, and moved towards the door of the dining room.

Declan's face crumpled with annoyance as she darted across the floor. "Bloody hell, that woman is going to be the death of me," he snorted and leapt to his feet following her into the lobby.

She was halfway up the stairs by the time he caught up with her. She noticed him chasing her up the stairs, and she began to jump two steps at a time to reach the top and escape to their room.

"Dammit, Meggie, would y' stop?"

"Leave me alone," she snapped and ran down the hall to their room.

Declan intentionally let her stay ahead of him, knowing there was nowhere she could go to get away from him. She reached the room and fumbled with her key card as her hands shook with emotional distress, but finally she flung the door open and bolted inside, swinging it closed behind her.

Declan shook his head as he reached the closed door; he wasn't sure what she felt she was accomplishing by slamming the door shut. He opened the door and found her standing by the window glaring at him, her eyes narrowed and her arms crossed in front of her.

"Freckles, what are y' doing?" he asked with a tiresome tone.

"Just leave me alone," she mumbled, moved away from the window and walked towards the bedroom but was abruptly cut off by his long muscular arm when he slammed his outstretched hand against the wall in front of her. She turned to look at him, and he slammed his other palm against the wall on the other side of her, trapping her between them. His body was close to her, but purposely not touching her, his gaze forceful and annoyed.

"Declan, move your arm!" Meghan demanded, standing motionless against the wall, rather fearful of him.

"No, y' are going to listen to me for once in your damn life," Declan shouted.

Meghan's eyes widened as he hollered at her in a tone she had not heard him use before. "Declan, don't you yell at me!"

Declan's hand moved from the wall to her face, and he pushed his palm firmly up against her chin, gripping his fingers tightly up around her jaw. "Meggie," he snorted as he tightened his grip.

He was squeezing her face hard enough to cause her hands fly up and pull at his arm. "You're hurting me." She squeezed out of her puckered mouth, her nails digging into his muscular forearm.

Declan's intense gaze broke, and he looked rather startled for a moment, then released her face and slammed his hand back on the wall beside her. "I'm so angry with y' right now, I could . . . ," he muttered through his teeth.

"You could what?" she snorted, trying to provoke him. "Hit me?" She raised her dark brow waiting for a response. "Go ahead, your brother already has!"

"Bloody hell, Meggie," he replied as his eyes darkened from her comment. "Y' know I would never hit y'." He could feel his blood boiling as he looked into her eyes, and he could not understand how he could simultaneously want to beat her within an inch of her life and throw her to the floor and make love to her.

Meghan's body relaxed at his comment, but she was still uncomfortable with his large arms trapping her to the wall. "Please, move your arm," she asked again.

"No, that I won't do until I get y' to understand that y' need to stay with someone."

"No, I don't. I'll be fine."

"If it's Colton that's bothering y'?"

"It's not Colton, I don't mind spending time with him, but I don't want to be treated like a child."

Declan lifted his hand back up to her face, and she jerked her head away at the remembrance of his hurtful grip moments earlier. He was startled by her response to his touch, but nevertheless, he grabbed her face again. This time, his touch was his familiar gentle presence as he gazed into her questioning eyes.

"Meggie, I'm not trying to punish y', I just don't want anything to happen to y'. I love y' more than anything, and I couldn't bear it if I lost y' again," he told her softly as he bent down and kissed her forehead.

Meghan smiled softly, her gaze trapped in his, and she saw the love overflowing from the dark grey orbs. "Nothing will happen," she repeated to him again.

"Dammit, Meggie, why can't y' understand?" he muttered, getting annoyed again. "Do I have to handcuff meself to y' and drag y' with me?"

"No," she could see he was not going to give up on the subject. "Fine, I'll stay with Colton," she mumbled, with a sigh of retreat.

Declan's eyes widened with amusement when he heard her concede defeat, and a large grin grew across his face. "Good," he replied, bent over, and placed his mouth around hers. His hands slowly moved across the walls towards her, his body pressing her up against the wall.

She could feel his heart smacking up against her chest as he leaned against her, his hands still pressed firmly on the wall next to her head.

"Freckles," he whispered against her lips as he pulled his head slightly away from her. "Please trust me."

Her lashes were fluttering frantically over her distrusting eyes. Why was he hiding something from her? She knew very well that he was terrified that O'Brien was going to try and harm her, but he refused to tell her why.

"Y' don't trust me, do y'?" Declan questioned, his gaze sharp and accusing.

"I do," she babbled, stiffening under him. "I do."

"Meggie?" he sighed and jerked back from her, leaving her pressed up against the wall. "Now you're lying to me."

Of course, I am lying to you, she thought bitterly. The fact that he was lying to her grew clear in her mind, and she turned on him like a caged animal. "Well, you're lying to me!"

"What?" he blurted out, his brow crumpling with annoyance.

"More is going on than you are telling me. You sit up at night, with Fabrizio whispering, then you disappear for hours at a time. What is happening?"

"Freckles, it's nothing you need to worry about," he said softly. "I will handle it."

Before she could respond, a loud knock on the door broke the tension slightly.

"That must be Colton," Declan said evenly, forcing calmness in his voice.

"Here I am, my beauty, are you ready for an exciting afternoon?" Colton teased as he sauntered into the room with an air of playfulness.

Her brow rose slightly, then her eyes settled on Declan as he stood by the door still looking rather agitated.

"I hope you like churches," she said tauntingly, her gaze still stuck on Declan. "I have more research to do."

"Meggie, you're not going to that church!" Declan growled as he stalked towards her.

"Yes, I am!" she muttered, taking a step away from him, to put more distance between them.

"No, y' stay here. I don't want y' out running about the streets."

Meghan's eyes narrowed with annoyance. "Why can't I go to the church, I will bring Colton with me?" she questioned in a short tone.

"Dammit, Meggie, y' could try the patience of a saint!" Declan snorted as he tried to control his anger. "I thought we agreed on this. Y' are to stay here with Colton," he ordered, gripping his fingers tightly around her upper arms.

"No, I agreed to stay with Colton. You didn't tell me I couldn't go to the church. What's the big deal?"

"Meggie, I will only tell y' this once. Y' stay here with Colton and don't go to the church. Do I make meself clear?" he demanded with a fierce tone of authority.

Meghan glared at him with defiance, then swung her arms trying to release his grip.

"Hey, you two, this is getting out of control. Don't worry, Declan, I will take good care of her, I promise. We will go for a drive or something," he intervened, trying to calm the lovers.

"Fine!" Meghan blurted out as she continued to glare at Declan.

"Meggie, I mean it, do what I ask. Please," he added as an obvious afterthought.

Her eyes softened, but the anger was still flaring when he kissed her forehead and turned to leave the room.

"I love y'," his voice was soft but firm.

"Whatever," Meghan muttered, turned her back on him, and moved towards Colton.

Declan stood staring at her, rather upset at her response, but Colton nodded towards the door, coaxing him to leave.

"Declan, she'll be fine. Deal with this when you get back," Colton said, with a note of reassurance.

"Aye." Declan backed towards the door, his eyes still fixed on Meghan. "Meggie?"

"Declan, just go. I'll be a good girl and do what you say," she mumbled as she turned back towards him. "Go have fun with Deirdre."

"What?" Declan jerked around, his eyes aflame. "What did y' mean by that? Are y' accusing me of something?"

"Do you have something to feel guilty about?" Meghan's voice cracked at the end of her comment. Damn she wanted to be so aloof about her suspicions.

Declan snarled and moved towards her. "I don't have time for this now, Meggie. I have to get to the set."

"Go then." She waved her hand dismissively towards the door to their room. "I'm sure Colton will keep me entertained." Her hand rested on Colton's shoulder and slid down his back to his waist.

Colton jerked from the sensation and the expression crossing Declan's face. "She'll be fine, Declan, just go to work. I won't let her out of my sight."

Declan forced a painful smile, not liking the expression in Meghan's eyes. It was something close to chaos, and when she had that look, she always did something foolish. "Meggie, I love y'."

Meghan turned her back as the door closed. Why didn't he deny he was having an affair with Deirdre? Was he? Meghan had no proof, only her gut instincts, and they were usually right. He smelled of Deirdre's perfume when he came back to the room the night before. He had not made love to her since Caelan left, and she was tired of him turning her down. Deirdre's smug demeanour over the past week was not helping his case either.

"Okay, how about we go for a drive?" Colton questioned, grabbing her hand, trying to chase the pitiful expression from her face. "You need a coat."

"Why?"

"Meghan, don't start to argue with me. I'm not afraid to take you over my knee. As a matter of fact, I probably would enjoy it," he smirked and pulled her into him, wrapping his arm around her shoulder.

Meghan slipped out from Colton's grasp, shrugged into her cream-coloured leather jacket, and followed Colton through the lobby that was a bustle of activity as the crew left for the day. Meghan waited out on the path as Colton chatted with a tall lean man that came through the door just behind them.

A deep sigh filled her as she watched Lydia heading down the path towards her. Meghan hadn't seen her in over a week, and she wasn't in a terrible hurry to see her now. The advice Meghan had given Lydia on how to draw Colton's attention worked, but in his regular style, he discarded her only a few short days after the romance began, and Meghan felt guilty putting her in that position.

"Hi, Meghan," Lydia smiled as she came to a stop in front of her, letting her eyes rest on Colton's lean frame.

"Hi," Meghan responded with a friendly smile as Colton headed downstairs towards them.

"Hi, Lydia. How are you today?" Colton asked politely, stopping at Meghan's side.

"Fine, thanks. Are you going to the set?" Lydia asked hopefully, but her eyes narrowed soon after, when Colton leaned up against Meghan and pulled a leaf from her auburn curls.

"No, we're going for a drive," Colton said, directing his dark blue eyes towards Lydia.

"Oh?" Lydia's voice trembled slightly; a distinct tone of disappointment was evident.

"He's babysitting me today," Meghan informed the upset woman.

"Oh, don't make it sound so horrible. How bad can it be, you get to spend the whole day with me?" Colton joked and wrapped his arm around Meghan's shoulder, completely oblivious to Lydia's pain.

Meghan frowned slightly at his comment. What was wrong with him? Could he not see how hurt Lydia was? Was he so immune to feelings that he couldn't see what was right in front of him? "Do you want to come with us?" Meghan asked to ease Lydia's pain and cause Colton some of his own.

"No, sorry, this is a two-person trip," Colton interrupted quickly, running his hand back through his shoulder-length blond hair.

"Why?" Meghan grumbled as his hand settled on her shoulder. She stared into the dark blue eyes and wondered if it was Colton she was cross at or if she was transferring her anger with Declan onto him. This was Colton after all, and he made no pretence about his relationships. His reputation was notorious, and any woman that got involved with him knew at best all she would get was a few good nights. Lydia, however, didn't seem to have the heart for it. She wanted more.

"You'll see, now stay here, I'll be right back," Colton ordered before disappearing into the parking lot.

"I'm sorry," Meghan apologized with a sincere smile. "He's just babysitting me."

"Sure," Lydia forced an unsure smile, her eyes scanning Meghan with distress. "Can I ask you something?"

"Sure," Meghan smiled, her eyes scanning the surrounding area, looking for Colton to return.

"Well, Deirdre seems to think that you and Declan got married for other reasons than love. That's why she and Declan—" She stopped abruptly when Meghan's brow began to crumple. "Sorry I—"

Meghan fought hard to keep her face from showing what she had been thinking for the last week. More was going on than Declan was willing to admit, and she did have the feeling he married her for more reasons than loving her. "Deirdre has a vivid imagination." Meghan forced a smile, praying that Deirdre was making it up. What if that was where Declan had been disappearing to, he certainly had not been spending the nights making love to her.

"So, are you and Colton having an affair?" Lydia blurted out, wanting to know the answer. "It's just that you are the only woman he wants to spend time with. I mean, other than in the bedroom."

"No, we aren't." She forced a smile. "I guess he is not worried about me wanting anything from him, since I am happily married," Meghan added for her own piece of mind as well as Lydia's.

Lydia nodded, her eyes scanning the area.

"I'll work on him for you. He will have no option but to listen to me, trapped in a car with me all day," Meghan blurted out, trying to end the conversation, but the women's attention was drawn to the street when they heard a honking horn, and Colton's loud voice calling for Meghan.

"Well, I better go," Meghan mumbled as she headed down the cobble stone path and under the archway.

Lydia followed closely behind, hoping to get one last opportunity to talk with Colton. They both came to an abrupt stop out on the sidewalk and stared at the mode of transportation Colton was intending to spend the day on.

"Your ride, my beauty," Colton said from the padded seat of a motorcycle, as he patted the seat directly behind him.

Meghan stared at the black Harley and shook her head. "Are you out of your mind? I'm not getting on that thing," she blurted out as she watched him looking particularly sexy on the bike, his feet planted on the ground for balance, and his arms stretched forward holding onto the handlebars.

"Come on, get on," Colton laughed, holding out his hand towards her.

"Colton, I'm not getting on that. It's not safe," Meghan cringed, a tone of fear in her voice.

He grunted, knocked the kickstand down, climbed off the bike, and sauntered towards her with a spare helmet gripped in his hand. Stopping directly in front of her, he pulled the helmet down over her head as she stood staring at him. He smiled with amusement and stuck his hand up to her face, tucking her long ginger curls into the sides of the large heavy headgear. She was so beautiful, he could hardly control himself. Be patient, old boy, your time will come.

"You're the one that wanted to spend the day with me instead of Fabs and Cassie. Now you are going to have to pay the price," Colton laughed, trying to force down his desire. Maybe this was not such a good idea watching her for the day. She was all his, with no one around to interfere. He shook his head and dragged her towards the bike. "See you later, Lydia," he hollered over his shoulder.

Once at the bike, he flipped his leg over and sat down, still hanging onto Meghan's hand. "Okay, my beauty, get on."

"Colton, I'm scared," Meghan whispered, her voice slightly trembling.

"That's okay, just hang on tight," Colton smirked and pulled her closer to the bike.

Meghan sighed with worry, but she flipped her long leg over, sat down on the seat behind him, and wrapped her arm around his waist, clinging tightly to his body.

"You are scared, aren't you? If you squeeze me any harder, you'll cut off my circulation," Colton moaned.

"Don't complain. This was your idea," Meghan snorted and wiggled her body right up to his, hoping for some feeling of security. Colton grunted with arousal, feeling her pressing against his back.

As they left the crowded streets of the town and headed down the small road, Meghan began to relax as the bike seemed to take on a smooth rhythmic motion. The feel of the wind on her face gave her a freeing sensation, exfoliating all her fears and anxieties of the past few days. Colton's "fly by the seat of his pants" attitude had managed to dim the fear of the unknown.

It was a peaceful hour drive down the road before Colton turned off onto a side road and pulled up beside a beautiful little brook. Meghan climbed off, her legs slightly wobbly as she tried to adjust to the stable ground finally under her feet.

Colton took her by the hand and led her down to a grassy area beside the brook, then sat down and pulled her down beside him. The small brook weaved its way through the long grasses and reeds lining the banks, singing a soothing song as it flowed over the rocks. The birds were peacefully singing from the bushes bedside them as the two sat quietly soaking in their surroundings.

Meghan glanced over at Colton's relaxed face and sighed wishing that Declan could be this relaxed. He was terribly high-strung over the last few weeks, and she felt him pulling away.

"This is very pretty." Meghan took off her coat and lay back in the grass, gazing up at the clouds that were slowing moving across the pale blue sky. "When I was little, I would try and figure out what the clouds looked like," she muttered keeping her eyes fixed on the billowing clouds, trying to arrive at a place in her mind where she could find peace.

"I did too." Colton lay down beside her on the lush grass. "Look, that one looks like a dog," he said, pointing towards the sky.

"Yeah, and that one looks like an alligator," she replied.

"That one looks like a motorcycle with a chicken on the back," Colton smirked towards her.

"Very funny," Meghan snorted and smacked his chest with the back of her hand.

Colton grabbed her hand and held it on his chest. "Meghan, why did you ask Lydia to come with us today? Were you scared to be alone with me?"

"No, should I?" Meghan giggled, enjoying the soothing feeling of his thumb stroking her palm.

"No."

"I asked her because she likes you." Meghan turned her head towards him, a soft smile curling her lips.

"I know," he mumbled, overwhelmed with the expression on her face. She was so beautiful, and he wanted her with every fibre in him.

"Don't get so excited," Meghan giggled, completely missing the desire in his eyes.

"Well, she's nice enough. She's just not my type," he said evenly.

"Oh, what's your type?" Meghan's green eyes stayed fixed on him. Did she want him the way he wanted her? Is that what she wanted to hear?

"You." He glanced over with an intense gaze.

"Yeah, right," Meghan snorted with a tone of amusement.

"Meghan, I know you think that I'm just teasing you when I flirt with you, but I'm not." His voice was far too intense, and she panicked.

"Colton?" She stopped, not knowing how to respond. Lydia seemed to be more astute than Meghan had given her credit for.

"It's okay, I know you love Declan, and I know he loves you. I just wanted you to know how I felt." He was eyeing her intently as he slid his hand up her arm, stopping at the bend of her elbow.

Meghan smiled nervously, finding the attention from this handsome man frighteningly welcome. As her better sense took hold, however, she pulled her arm from him and crossed it across her chest with the other, hoping to close herself off to him.

"Colton, if I ask you something, will you tell me the truth?" Meghan turned to him, anxiety filling her green eyes.

"I'll do my best," he grinned painfully, she wasn't responding to him the way he hoped.

"Well, I was wondering if Declan, well, is he having an affair with Deirdre, and I only ask that because he has been disappearing a lot lately and Lydia said."

"Meghan, calm down." Colton soothed, brushing his hand across her face, carrying a rebel red curl back behind her ear. "I can't say for sure, but I have seen them together a few times in the last week."

Meghan's eyes closed painfully as her heart threatened to explode. Why did this keep happening, why couldn't she keep a man happy enough so that he didn't have the need to make love to other women?

Scratchy whiskers brushed across her face, and Colton's lips were on hers without warning. Her eyes shot open and squinted at the face that was inches from hers.

"Meghan, I wish I was the one that met you first," Colton admitted, gazing into her terrified eyes.

"Colton, we can't do this." Meghan pressed her hands onto his shoulders.

Colton grabbed her hands, pinned them to the ground under his strong hands, and gazed down at her. "Please, Meghan, make love to me. No one needs to know."

"No, get off me," she shrieked with fear.

"Meghan, I need you, I have from the first day I saw you. Please just once."

"Colton, please don't." Tears began to drip out of the corners of her eyes and run down her temples into her hair. She feared he was going to rape her, and there was nothing she could do.

Colton was startled by the tears and realized that he had pushed too far. He had obviously terrified her with his advances. "Meghan, I'm sorry. I didn't mean to scare you. I just thought that you were attracted to me." He released her hands, then kissed her cheek.

"That's not the point, I'm a married woman, and I love my husband," Meghan blurted out, quite confident that her husband did not have the same morals.

"Even though he—" Colton stopped what he was saying, not willing to cross the line. A smile curled his lips as he decided to bide his time. With Declan's recent behaviour, she would soon either leave him or turn to another man, and he would be waiting. She exposed her attraction to him, and once free of her chains to Declan, she would be his.

With great restraint, Colton rolled off Meghan and sat up. He had hoped their afternoon would be filled with lovemaking. She was so beautiful, so desirable but, apparently, not ready.

"I would like to go back to the manor. I need to get packed," Meghan said abruptly, standing and brushing the grass from her shorts.

"You are still leaving tomorrow?" Colton panicked, not wanting her to leave.

She nodded and turned towards him. "I don't see any point in staying here any longer. Declan obviously has no time for me, and he would be happier if I went home."

"Meghan," Colton sighed, rather remorseful that he helped fuel a rumour that he didn't know was true or not. From everything, he knew about Declan and how he felt about Meghan, he couldn't imagine Declan risking everything to make love to Deirdre, but that is what he appeared to be doing. "Come on, I'll drive you back."

It was late afternoon when Meghan and Colton arrived back at the manor. Meghan noticed that the streets seemed to be unusually quiet for that time of day, when the shops were usually full of people doing their shopping.

"It's pretty quiet out today. I wonder why?" she questioned, still glancing around.

"You're starting to sound like Declan. I'm sure it's nothing." Colton comforted her as they walked under the large stone archway.

Meghan stopped abruptly when she saw Liam O'Brien sauntering towards her with Kaye walking quickly behind him, trying to keep up. A menacing grin filled his broad face as his eyes settled on her. "Mrs. Montgomery, there y' are. I have been looking for y' all day."

"Why?" Meghan questioned, backing up into Colton's arms.

"Well, I need y' to come with me," Liam ordered softly, his grin to confident.

"No!" Meghan snorted with defiance.

"Now we could do this the easy way or the hard way. Which is it?"

"You're not taking her anywhere!" Colton's voice was stern, but he was terrified as he watched three men surrounding them.

"I think I am," O'Brien said smugly.

Meghan shuddered as she noticed the men surrounding them from all sides, but what terrified her was that they were all carrying guns. "Colton, they have guns," she whispered to him.

"I see that," Colton replied back, tightening his grip on her.

"Liam, what the hell is going on?" Kaye questioned as she too noticed the guns.

"It's none of your concern," he said evenly. "Take her to the car." He bobbed his head towards a young blond man who gripped Kaye's arm and dragged her away.

"Now, Mrs. Montgomery, I don't want to have to hurt your friend, so I suggest y' come with me quietly."

"Meghan, run!" Colton hollered as he flung her behind him, shoving her through the archway to the road. He turned to follow her, but a hard thump to the back of his head caused him to collapse to the ground.

"Colton!" Meghan shrieked as she watched him fall. Her eyes rose to the man that hit Colton, and he was heading towards her with an annoyed expression crossing his face. Instinct took hold, and she twisted around and ran down the street, screaming with all her might.

Her retreat was halted, however, when a tall wiry man jumped out from behind a hedge directly in front of her, causing her to stumble backwards. Within seconds, the short stocky man that was chasing her had hold of her arm and his gun to her head.

"Mrs. Montgomery, why did y' have to do it the hard way?" Liam questioned, as he sauntered up to her, gripping her arm and tugging her towards him.

"Let go of me!" Meghan snorted and tugged at her arm to release it from his grip.

"What do y' think you're going to accomplish by this behaviour?" Liam smirked and dragged her back up the street to the awaiting car. After he flung her through the open door, he climbed in beside her, squishing her between him and the sweaty stout man.

"Where are you taking me?" Meghan questioned, realizing that she was trapped.

"Y' will find out soon enough. Now shut up," Liam ordered as he shoved her away from him over to the short stocky man beside the other door. Meghan shuddered and sat up straight in the middle, trying to stay away from both men that seemed intent on holding her hostage. Her eyes slowly returned to the man beside her as the recognition of where she had seen him before took hold. He was the man that Andrew McGregor introduced her to at the fair.

She gasped loudly as the man turned towards her. "Dr. Coleman," he muttered with a slight smirk.

"What do you want?" Meghan questioned again, her voice shaky, her eyes staying focused on the man.

"Y'," O'Brien said evenly, watching her staring at Murphy.

"Me, why do you want me? What possible reason could you have to want to kidnap me?" she questioned, returning her gaze to O'Brien since he seemed to be the one in charge.

"Would y' shut up!" he snapped. "For Christ's sake y' could talk the teeth out of a saw," Liam muttered as he glanced down at the locket resting on her chest. His golden brow rose with interest, and he placed his hand on the locket, deliberately resting his hand against her skin.

"Don't touch that," Meghan snapped, lifting her hand up, trying to grasp her locket.

"I'll touch what I please," Liam snorted, smacking her hand away.

Meghan could feel his fingers brushing against her skin as he gazed at the locket intently, studying every small detail. Suddenly his hand jerked back with the locket firmly between his fingers, and she felt the chain tear away from her neck as he moved his hand away from her.

"Give me that back!" she shrieked.

"Y' will not be needing it anymore. These people will no longer be part of your life."

"Give it to me!" Meghan cried, reaching over him, trying to grab his hand that he slipped into his pocket with the locket. Liam started to laugh as she climbed on top of his legs and pulled at his arm. "Give it to me."

"I'll give y' something if y' don't get off me," he informed her as she stopped her attack and looked at him, her eyes full of tears.

"Please," she begged, with a tone of despair.

"Maybe when y' do what I want, I will give it back." Liam placed his thick hand on her face and wiped the tears with his thumb. "Now get off me lap." He pushed her back between him and Murphy.

Meghan stared at him, fear exploding from her eyes as the car sped through the town and out onto the long road leading into the horizon. She was terrified as she saw the town getting further and further away, Declan was getting further and further away.

"What do you want from me?" Meghan questioned once again, deciding she was dead anyway, she may as well find out why.

O'Brien sighed with annoyance, then scratched his well-trimmed golden beard. "Well, if y' must know, I want to marry y'."

"What? I'm not marring you."

"Aye, y' are," Liam smiled and rested his hand on the side of her head.

"No, I'm not!" she snapped, slapping at his hand, but he did not move it.

"Do y' think y' have any choice in the matter?" he questioned her, his brow raised with interest at her bravado.

"I'm already married," Meghan muttered, an air of finality ringing in her voice.

"Aye, that y' are. Don't think that has escaped me. But don't y' worry, that problem will be dealt with," Liam laughed and leaned over and kissed her cheek.

"What do you mean by that?" Meghan snorted, her mind filling with horror. Her hand swung up, but Liam had hold of it before she made contact with his face.

"Never y' mind," he told her, patting her leg with his loose hand, apparently not bothered by her attack.

Meghan pulled her leg away from his hand as he began to run the large thick hand up her leg. He eyed her with amusement as she tried to avoid his touch.

"Don't y' worry, me love, y' will soon be me wife, and me hands will be what y' long for."

"Don't count on it," Meghan snorted, pushing his hand off her leg again.

"Y' stupid bitch, mind your manners around Mr. O'Brien," snapped the balding man beside her, as he grabbed her hair, shaking her head violently.

"Let her go!" Liam snorted at Murphy. "Y' will not be hurting her, unless I say so," he said, gazing at Meghan, as the tears built up in her eyes and began to drip down her face. He grinned, then turned and looked out the window at the lush green fields that they passed by on the way to their destination.

CHAPTER TWENTY-EIGHT

Colton slowly stirred when he heard voices calling to him, as he lay on the ground in a daze. His hand immediately rested against the large gash to the back of his head as the pain shot through his skull. The sound of the ambulance arriving jolted him into alertness, and he sat up and frantically scanned the surrounding faces that were hovering over him.

"Meghan," he shouted "Where are you?"

The onlookers glanced around to find out whom he was calling for, but no one came forth. "Meghan," he called again, this time with a more urgent tone in his voice.

"I don't think she's here," a man told him as he bent down trying to calm Colton.

"She has to be. Where is she?" Colton pushed himself to his feet and started to stumble and fell back to the ground as the paramedics arrived.

"Be still, sir," ordered one of the paramedics.

"What happened here?" asked the Garda arriving on the scene.

"My friend, she's gone. They took her," Colton shouted at the constable.

"Calm down, sir. Tell me who's gone." The Garda's voice was professional.

"Meghan Montgomery. They took her."

"Sir, what are y' talking about, who took her?" the Garda asked as he scanned the growing crowd.

"Liam O'Brien. He and his men took her and hit me over the head," Colton snapped, getting very annoyed at the man.

A loud moan came over the crowd, and many of them started to back away and leave the area. They were frightened to be around with O'Brien involved.

"Why are you still standing there, go get her back," Colton snapped.

"If O'Brien has her," the man lifted his hat and scratched his head, "I'd imagine he'll come to y'," he said evenly, then he turned and walked away.

"What the hell is going on here? Why aren't you going after her?" Colton hollered at the Garda as he walked back down the path towards the street.

Fabrizio and Cassie had stopped by the town where Declan was filming and picked him up on their way back to the manor, arriving to find the commotion outside in the garden. Declan moved quickly into the crowd to find out what was happening when he noticed Colton sitting on the stretcher with a paramedic applying a compress to the back of his head. Colton was still screaming at the Garda's back as the man disappeared through the gate.

Declan bolted towards Colton with primal fear surging through him, his eyes darting around the crowd searching for Meghan. "Colton, where is she?"

"I'm sorry," Colton said, knowing he had lost the most precious thing in Declan's life, and he would be devastated.

"Sorry for what?" Declan asked, not wanting to know the answer.

"He got her. I tried to stop him, but one of his men hit me from behind. God, I'm so sorry."

"No, no, Meggie!" Declan screamed so loud, his voice echoed off the heavens and bounced back to earth, scaring the nesting birds out of the nearby trees. He was hysterical as he spun in circles, searching the crowd, screaming her name, hoping that Colton was wrong.

"Monty, calm down, we'll find her," Fabrizio told him with hesitation in his voice. He knew that if O'Brien had her, she was in grave danger.

"No, he doesn't have her. He can't," Declan babbled as he stood shaking with fear. Suddenly he bolted up the stairs of the manor and ran full speed across the lobby and up the long staircase to their bedroom. Once at the door, he flung it open and darted through the sitting room into the bedroom.

"Meggie, where are y'?" Declan shouted over the enormous lump that had developed in his throat. "Bloody hell, Meggie," he cried as he fell to the ground and covered his weeping face with his hands.

Fabrizio and Cassie had followed him up the stairs; Cassie was herself in hysterics as she ran into the room and threw herself on Declan's hunched body.

"Declan, we'll find her. We have to." Cassie sobbed on his shoulder.

"Cass, I can't lose her. I can't. Why didn't she listen to me? I told her to stay in the manor."

"Because she's Meghan," Cassie said, with a tone of anger in her voice.

"Declan?" Colton said, with hesitation as he entered the room after being patched up. His face was full of distress as he stood staring at Declan, his sky blue eyes filling with tears.

Declan's head jerked towards Colton, his eyes cold and hostile as he stood and moved quickly across the room. He lunged at Colton with extreme anger, but Fabrizio grabbed him by the arm and pulled him to a stop, halting his attack.

"Monty, that's not going to help." Fabrizio's voice was as firm as his grip on Declan's arm.

"Colton, y' promised me y' would take care of her," Declan said, on the verge of tears again.

"I know, I'm sorry. I tried. There were too many of them."

"Y' lost me Meggie," Declan mumbled as he collapsed into the arms of Fabrizio, who was still holding onto him.

"Monty, snap out of this! You have to be strong if we're going to be any help to her," Fabrizio told him in a stern tone.

"Aye." Declan tried to compose himself; he knew very well that emotions must be pushed down in situations such as these, and he also knew that if O'Brien was the one that took her, her life would be in danger.

"Declan, I don't know what she has gotten herself mixed up in, but he wanted her pretty badly. There were six of them, and they all had guns, she's in big trouble," Colton informed them.

"Are you sure it was O'Brien?" Fabrizio asked, trying to get all the information.

"Yeah, it was that guy that Deirdre and Kaye have been hanging around with. Actually Kaye was with him."

"What? Why the hell would she be involved with this!" Cassie sounded completely shocked. "I'm calling her!"

The night dragged by as they waited for any news on Meghan's whereabouts. Cassie could not track down Kaye or Deirdre. The Garda were under the conclusion that Meghan left on her own accord, and they were not going to carry out any investigation. Declan had left determined to search for her, he felt that someone in the town must have seen something, but Fabrizio insisted on staying put in case O'Brien called with any demands. Fabrizio felt he wanted Meghan for something and that they would find out the purpose for the abduction soon enough.

It was early morning when Declan arrived back at his room to find Cassie, Fabrizio, and Colton in the sitting room, still waiting for the call. Declan avoided their combined stares, dropped his coat on the cream chair, then slumped into the bedroom and fell to the bed.

His eyes settled on Fabrizio. "No one is saying anything. This whole damn town is scared of him," Declan mumbled with exhaustion, his Irish lilt stronger than usual.

Cassie glanced up at the strange voice, he seemed like a complete stranger, his eyes dark and sunken, his hair messy, and his face unshaven. He appeared to be a hobo off the street. He looked horrible, and her heart was wrenching with terror and sadness.

All these people in this room, these friends were in her life because of Meghan. What if Meghan was no longer around? Her best friend gone? Cassie sighed and glanced over at Fabrizio. And what about him, was she just convenient because of Declan and Meghan, was she just the accessory to the perfect foursome so Fabrizio could stay in Meghan's life? He was just as upset as Declan, and he hardly spoke to her all night. She shook her head to clear her thoughts; it was time to worry about Meghan, not her.

Cassie dropped down beside Declan on the bed and forced a painful smile, a mixture of compassion and fear clearly visible. "Declan, she'll be okay." Did he hear how dishonest she sounded?

Declan sighed and pulled her towards him, cradling her in his arms, pressing her head against his chest. "Aye, I have to believe that or I'll go crazy. The last time I saw her I was yelling at her." He closed his eyes, trying to erase that memory from his head. "What if she . . ."

"Declan, she won't. She loves you, and she knew that you were just looking out for her. Don't torment yourself with those thoughts," Cassie cooed, trying to reassure him, but truth be told, she had no idea what Meghan thought. Meghan had been so unpredictable the last few weeks that even Cassie could not understand her.

Declan sighed deeply, then opened his eyes, the dark grey surrounded by small red lines. "She thinks I had an affair with Deirdre. I never denied it. I was so cross with her."

Cassie cringed and lifted her head slightly. "Did you? Sorry," she blurted out, reading his facial expression.

"That would explain her behaviour lately." Cassie glanced out at Fabrizio, who was paying little attention to them, while he paced back and forth by the window. "Declan, I warned you that she was going to break down. Her guilt over what happened to Andy is most likely what is fuelling her thoughts."

Declan nodded and slid his hand through Cassie's long blonde hair. "When I saw her at the school that day, I thought I had gone mad. I spent years looking for her, who would have thought a forced trip to visit me sister would bring me right to Meggie. It's like everything that happened to me in life was all preparing me for her. I love her so much that life without her wouldn't be worth living."

"Declan, please don't give up. She's alive." Cassie stared into his eyes that were within inches of hers. She felt rather guilty at the sensation he was causing her as he stroked her hair, but she justified staying in his arms by believing that it was helping him.

Declan nodded and kissed her forehead, then rolled onto his back. "I'll kill him if he has done any harm to me Meggie." Declan's voice was soft and not directed at Cassie. He made the comment for his own benefit, not Cassie's.

Cassie leaned on her elbow and stroked his hair, his body shaking under her hand. "Declan, try to relax and get some sleep," she whispered, her fears surging closer to the surface.

Another hour passed before the phone finally rang, causing the group to jump to their feet and run to the phone, Declan arriving first.

"Hello?" Declan blurted out, adjusting the receiver to his ear.

"Mr. Montgomery, I'm so glad I caught y' in. I seem to have something of yours."

"What the hell have y' done with her? If y' have hurt her, I swear I'll kill y'."

"Now, Mr. Montgomery, is that anyway to talk to the person who holds your wife's life in his hands?"

"What do y' want?" Declan forced calmness into his voice, swallowing hard to push down the bile.

"Well, like I said, I have something of yours, and y' have something that belongs to me."

"What do I have of yours?" Declan muttered and glanced over at Fabrizio.

"Me amulet. I want that amulet."

"Meggie's locket?" Declan heard the group gasp at his comment.

"No, it's my amulet. And I want it tonight, or she dies."

"Fine, where?" Declan questioned, fear building inside him while he listened to the directions to the old cottage with the thatched roof and the green shudders and door, five miles off the road to Glenbeigh.

Declan hung up the phone, ran into the bedroom, and started to search through her dresser, looking for the locket. He was getting agitated, pulling out every piece of clothing, but he could not find the locket anywhere.

"What the hell has she done with it?" Declan rambled, panic strong in his voice.

"Are you sure she didn't have it on?" Cassie questioned. "She rarely takes it off."

"He said she didn't have it."

"Declan, she had it on. I saw it," Colton informed him, appearing terribly guilty.

"Are y' sure?" Declan eyed Colton momentarily taken aback by the expression on his face. He had never seen Colton so stricken.

"Yes, I saw it when we were at the brook. Maybe she lost it there." Colton was hoping that his actions had not put her life in danger. What if it had fallen off as she struggled to get away from him?

"Colton, can y' go back there and check it out and see if y' could find it?" Declan asked, not particularly worried how it might have fallen off.

"Sure, I'll go right now." Colton headed for the door, feeling terrible that he had tried to seduce his friend's beloved Meghan under his nose.

"I'll come with you, Colton. If the two of us look, it won't take so long." Cassie followed behind him, wanting to do something before she went crazy.

"Be careful and make sure no one is following you." Fabrizio kissed her lips softly. "I mean it, Cass."

"We will." Cassie forced a smile and turned towards Colton, but looked over her shoulder at Fabrizio. Should she say the dreaded words? He hadn't, maybe now was not the time to declare her feelings for him. The hell with it, she turned and ran to his arms. "I love you, Fabs."

Fabrizio smiled and kissed her cheek. "Remember what I said."

Cassie flinched but managed a weak smile. He wouldn't say it or couldn't. She needed to calm down and focus on Meghan. Whether Fabrizio loved her was not important at the moment.

The day was spent arranging the rescue of Meghan later that night. Fabrizio tracked down some underground guns through an employee of the manor who seemed to have connections that were rather unseemly but nevertheless convenient.

Cassie and Colton were on their way back to the manor after having no luck finding the locket. Cassie stared out the window, her thoughts stuck on the condition of the grass where Meghan and Colton had spent the afternoon.

"Colton, something has been bothering me," Cassie questioned, noticing Colton was unusually quiet since they left the brook, almost melancholy.

"What would that be?" Colton responded nonchalantly, his eyes still glued to the road.

"What were you and Meg doing in the grass?" Cassie's voice shook slightly at the question. Something had been going on with Meghan over the last few days, and she was concerned that Colton had something to do with it. If Meghan believed Declan to be having an affair with Deirdre, did Meghan retaliate by having sex with Colton?

Colton glanced at her rather startled, then forced a guilty smile and turned back to the road. "Nothing, we were just looking at the clouds."

"Colton, you're lying." Cassie eyed him curiously, his face was flushing quickly. "Shit, you didn't."

"No!" He blurted out.

"Well then, what the hell happened? The grass looked pretty packed down for just lying there?"

Colton sighed, realizing that Cassie was not going to drop the subject, and if he explained it to her now, maybe he could convince her not to say anything to Declan.

"I kissed her and . . . well, it doesn't matter because she wouldn't let me, and she got really upset with me," Colton rambled, unsure why he said so much. Women never turn him down, and he wasn't very secure with the fact that Meghan blew him off.

"Jeez, Colton, why would you try to sleep with your friend's wife?" Cassie snorted, shaking her head at him.

"Because I love her." Colton's eyes glazed over.

"What?"

"I do, I have for years, and if anything happens to her, I will never forgive myself."

"Colton, this is unbelievable. Is that how you lost her? Did she take off on you when you got back to the manor?"

"No, we straightened everything out. I apologized, and she said she forgave me. When we got back to the manor, O'Brien was waiting for her. I threw her behind me and out the gate and then turned after her, but someone hit me on the head. I don't know what happened after that."

"I'm sorry for attacking you. This is just becoming a nightmare. I can't lose my best friend. I just can't." Cassie covered her face with her hands and cried.

The sun was starting to set over the western hills that had been overtaken by lush green ferns. A dilapidated old stone fence encircled the small cottage, scattered rocks lying next to the fence, leaving gaps in the once strong barrier.

Declan cringed as the thought of how similar the farm appeared to be to the home he grew up in so many years earlier. Large lush trees were surrounding the small cottage, and the emerald green door and shutters were a stark contrast to the white plaster of the cottage. The overgrown grass was damp on their feet from the earlier rain storm. As the sun descended over the trees, the soft glow that shone across the small reed-filled pond behind the house seemed almost hypnotic.

How simple life was back when Declan was a child! His dream to become a soldier was all he worried about. Every day, he would run from home into town to attend school, then run back over the five kilometres to ready himself for the academy. His friends teased him out the window of the school bus as it passed by him, filled with all the neighbouring farms' children.

That seemed so long ago, his life passing before his eyes as he scanned the area praying to find Meghan alive. His experience in the Navy Seals was gnawing at him, telling him that she was most likely already dead, and this meeting was a trap, but his heart was telling him to follow through with O'Brien's orders. Once again, he regretted ignoring his parents' warning about bringing her to Ireland. He never thought that the O'Briens would go this far, if Rory hadn't stirred up the past. Declan shook his head; blaming Rory for what has happened was pointless, and if he was honest, it was his fault. He put Meghan in danger, and now he must do all he can to get her back.

The small slope on the east side of the cottage provided a panoramic view of the house and surrounding area, and Declan headed towards the path through the thick fern bed that allowed small animals passage.

"Monty, I have a bad feeling about this," Fabrizio muttered and gripped Declan's arm before he wandered too far into the ferns.

Declan nodded and swept the area again with a judging eye. "She's here somewhere. I can smell her perfume."

Fabrizio eyed Declan speculatively, then bobbed his head towards the house. "Did you notice that the grass in front of the cottage has been walked on recently?"

"Aye, I saw that," Declan agreed, then bent down in front of him. "Someone's also been up here. This plant has recently been broken.

The stem is still damp." He stared up the path. "We need to get out of the open."

"Let's check out the cottage." Fabrizio turned and pulled his gun from the back of his waistband.

"Fabrizio, she's close, I feel it." Declan stopped as the scent became weaker the farther away from the ferns he got. He turned and eyed the ferns again, his intuition screaming to him. The ferns were large and high off the ground, maybe two or three feet, a perfect place to hide a body. Declan cringed, was she dead? Her body discarded on the hill somewhere. He stood completely still, eyeing the ferns, but not a sound was being made; everything was eerily quiet.

"Meggie," Declan yelled. "Where are y?"

"Monty?" Fabrizio scolded. "What are you doing?"

"Sorry, I know she is here somewhere." He could feel her, damn, where was she?

"Declan, please help me!" Meghan's voice filled the air. "Please, I'm in here."

Declan swung around and bolted towards the cottage, his heart pounding with terror. Fabrizio, however, had not moved, his neck prickling with distrust, and he grabbed hold of Declan as he passed.

"Monty, it's a trap."

"No, it's Meggie, she needs me," Declan yelled and broke loose of Fabrizio's grip.

"Monty, it's too easy. Don't go in there," Fabrizio yelled, too late, Declan was already through the door. "Dammit."

Fabrizio shook his head and ran into the cottage after Declan, knowing he was risking his life, but he needed to cover Declan's back, they were brothers of sort, vowing to protect the other, no matter the danger to them.

The two men had only just disappeared into the cottage when O'Brien dragged Meghan up from the fern bed, where they had been lying, watching Declan and Fabrizio arrive. Meghan struggled against the ropes at her wrists, the gag in her mouth suffocating. Liam glanced down at the struggling woman and laughed a cruel sound.

"Say goodbye to your husband, me love." A smug grin curling Liam's lips, he wanted her to witness the house blow so she would believe that Declan and Fabrizio were dead. Liam's hand ran down her tear-stained face, then he yanked the gag from her mouth.

"Declan, get out, it's a trap!" Meghan shrieked just before a thunderous explosion rocked the house, blowing it apart like matchsticks and clay.

"D-E-C-L-A-N!" Meghan shrieked, watching in horror as the pieces of the cottage fell to the ground in a mass of rubble.

"Well, show's over." O'Brien informed her and pulled at her arm.

"No . . . Declan . . . Declan!" A bone-chilling scream exited her as she pulled away from Liam and ran towards the pile of debris. Liam grunted with annoyance and ran after her, grabbing her tightly around the waist as she heaved forward trying to break free.

"Let me go! Damn, you let me go!" Meghan snorted and kicked back at Liam's shins.

"Okay, me patience is wearing thin with y', woman. You're coming with me now."

Liam picked her up, flung her over his shoulder, and carried her towards the car that was heading up the road towards them. Meghan kicked wildly at Liam and screamed for Declan as she scanned the rubble for any signs of movement, but Liam seemed unfazed by her attack.

The driver opened the car door, and Liam flung Meghan inside with annoyance, then climbed in beside her, slamming the door shut behind him. Meghan struggled to get to the other door, but with her hands still tied behind her back, she was unable to open it. Panic, rage, and terror flowed through her as she slammed her head against the window, shrieking Declan's name. He could not be dead; she could still feel him.

Rory seemed almost catatonic as he sat in the front seat facing forward, realizing just what his half-brother was capable of. He should have gone home, why he made the detour to say goodbye to Fergus and Liam. Now he was trapped, linked to the murder of his brother, the brother he loved and admired, growing up. The brother he envied as an adult. How was he going to explain to his mother that Declan died, and he helped set the trap? He knew Declan well enough to know that when it came to Meghan, he was impulsive and sometimes unwise.

Liam took advantage of that, setting the trap for Declan to run head first into, and he did just that. Declan's love for Meghan got him killed, and now Rory was on his own to survive, to convince his new family that he was trustworthy and devoted to them. He felt like he had entered a mafia family, only to be released upon death. Death, maybe he would be better off dead, all he could think about was his mother. She would never speak to him again.

"Rory, you son of bitch, why won't you help me, he's your brother," Meghan screamed as she turned her hysteria towards the front seat and kicked at the back of Rory's head repeatedly.

"Me love, settle down," Liam ordered, gripping her arm and pulling her back towards him.

"Let go of me, you bastard!" Meghan screamed, slamming her head into his chest. Liam sat quietly for a moment, letting her repeatedly smack him until she finally stopped from exhaustion. She flopped to the seat beside him, curled up into a ball, and sobbed.

Liam's face turned sympathetic, and he reached over, brushing the hair off her face, stroking it behind her ear. Meghan jerked away from him, causing him to smile with amusement. He was quite fascinated with the fight she had in her and how strong her spirit was.

CHAPTER TWENTY-NINE

The small dark room, covered in filth, was getting very damp and cold, and she was feeling her life slipping away. Rory appeared to have changed from a prisoner to a welcome guest since the day of the explosion a week earlier. He was permitted to visit Meghan on a regular basis. Maybe he was not a prisoner in the first place.

Now Rory was back in her face, pushing her towards marrying Liam O'Brien. Why was it so important to Rory, it was almost life or death. Meghan also could not understand why Liam was so determined to marry her. He must have more women than he could handle. Kaye had said that he was one of the richest men in Ireland. Why did he want Meghan? He had her locket, what more did he want?

"Meghan, you need to listen to me. Declan is dead, you have to accept that!" Rory pushed again, annoyed that he was getting nowhere with her. Could she not understand that she did not have a choice? She was trapped in the castle, and whether she liked it or not, she was never going home.

"No, I would feel it if he was. He's not dead," Meghan sniffed, her mind whirling with questions.

"You have to stop this," Rory said, shaking her slightly, trying to get her to focus on her options.

"No." Meghan sobbed uncontrollably, she knew very well that she had no choice, but she was damned if she would marry him willingly.

"Listen, it's time to face reality. You need to think about yourself now." Rory's voice was raised with agitation. Why wouldn't she agree? The gold digger she was, he thought Meghan would jump at the chance to marry his rich half-brother.

"Rory, let me out of here. I have to go find Declan."

"You know I can't let you out," Rory grunted and slammed his fist down on the table. "Dammit, Meghan, just say yes."

"No!" Meghan pushed the chair to the small window, climbed on top, and peered out the grime-covered glass. "Where are we?" The view from the turret gave a perfect view of the grasslands below that surrounded the castle and flowing down the valley to the Atlantic Ocean; she knew that much, they were on the south-western coast of the island.

Rory glared at her and ignored her question. "Meghan, you will marry Liam and whether you do it the easy way or the hard way is up to you. He is rich and powerful, and he will get his way."

"What about Caelan, Rory, she is your niece. Do you not have any feeling for her? What is going to happen to her with both her parents gone?"

"I'm sure if you cooperate, Caelan can come here and live with you. Liam's not an animal, he's just a man that needs you to be his wife." Rory watched rather uneasily as she picked up a fork and began pressing it against the wall, trying to bend the prongs back.

"Why? Why is it so important?" Meghan sniffed but stayed focused on bending the fork.

Rory shrugged and eyed her appraisingly. "He likes you."

"Ha," Meghan snorted and turned to him after she managed to bend three of the four prongs.

"What are you doing?" Rory grunted, eyeing the mangled fork.

"I'm making something to pick the lock," Meghan snorted and moved towards the large wooden door. She glanced back at Rory, crinkled her nose with disgust, and then stuck the single prong into the lock. "If you won't help me, I'll get out myself. All you need to do is find Cassie and tell her where I am. She'll call the police."

"No police will come. Liam has connections everywhere," Rory laughed, almost in awe of Liam. "Meghan, there are three more locked doors between here and the outside. Are you going to pick all of them?"

"Yes, if I have to," Meghan muttered as she moved the fork desperately around in the hole. "Shit, this isn't going to work," she snorted as she slammed her head into the door. "Rory, you are the only one who can get me out. They let you come and go as you please."

"No, they don't. They watch every move I make. The only reason why he lets me anywhere near you is he thinks that I am helping him with you. If I can't convince you to marry him, my usefulness will be up."

"It doesn't matter anyway because Declan isn't dead," Meghan sniffed with desperation.

"Meghan, we both saw the house blow up. There is no way he could have survived that explosion."

"Rory, I would feel it in my soul if he was dead. I know with all my heart that he's not."

The discussion was cut short when they heard the clanging of the door down the corridor. The loud footsteps came closer, and the hair on the back of Meghan's neck rose as she listened to the rhythmic smacking on the stone floor.

"Meghan, I suggest you do as he says. It won't be that bad."

Meghan grimaced at him as he moved over to the door. She stood watching with terror in her eyes as the thick wooden door slowly opened, and the muscular man stood staring at her with amusement on his face.

"Mrs. Montgomery, are y' enjoying your stay here at Kerrybrook Castle?" O'Brien's voice was cordial but slightly mocking.

Meghan crinkled her nose at him, her eyes full of terror, but she said nothing.

Liam's brow rose slightly at her silence, then he glanced around the dirty room. "So, Mrs. Montgomery, are y' ready to discuss your future?" A devilish grin curled his lips, as if he knew she had no choice but to give into his demands. He highly suspected she wouldn't want to spend too much more time in the turret.

"No!" Meghan snorted at him, her ability to reason greatly damaged by her sorrow.

Liam grunted with amusement, then nodded towards Rory, who left the room promptly, shutting the door behind him. As the heavy door slammed shut, Meghan felt an overwhelming sense of hopelessness come over her.

"I'm glad to see that your time here hasn't stripped y' of your spirit." Liam moved towards Meghan, a devilish glimmer in his eyes.

Meghan backed away until she hit the hard stonewall, then quickly scanned the room for a path around Liam. He smiled as he watched her from under his thick golden brows, while her eyes darted back and forth, desperately searching for a way out of her nightmare.

"There's nowhere to go. Y' may as well relax," Liam said softly as he walked towards her, noticing the mangled fork in her hand.

"Don't you come near me!" Meghan snapped and slid along the cold stonewall towards the door that hadn't been locked. Suddenly, her face hardened, and she flung her hand up, pointing the one-pronged fork at him.

Liam eyed her with delight, wondering how she figured that she could protect herself with the fork. "Mrs. Montgomery, we've been through this before. I don't plan on hurting y'. I need y'," he told her with a gentleness in his voice that startled her.

"I'm not marrying you!" Meghan's brows puckered towards her nose as she glared at Liam in disgust.

"Why, your husband's dead, so y' have nothing holding y' back."

"I don't love you," she said defiantly.

"So, I don't love y' either. We just need to be wed."

"Why?" she muttered.

"I told y' before, y' will find out in good time."

Meghan was terrified, realizing she had no way out, and if she didn't marry him, she would be trapped in this turret forever. Rory obviously was not intending to help her and Declan, well, if he wasn't dead, he must be terribly hurt, and as that thought came to her mind, she could feel the tears seeping out the corners of her eyes and rolling down her cheeks.

Liam moved towards her and lifted his large thick hand towards her face, sliding his fingers across her cheek, wiping the tears away. With his other hand, he gripped her arm tightly to keep her from trying to stab him with the fork.

"Y' need not cry, me love. All y' need to do is agree to marry me, and I'll let y' sleep in a proper room tonight." He slid his hand up to her clenched fist and yanked the fork from her hand, then released her arm.

Meghan turned her back on him as panic set in, knowing that her only way out of this turret was to agree to marry him.

"If I agree," she said, turning back towards him. "I won't sleep with you."

Liam began to grin at her. "No, not until we wed. But it's not the sleeping I'm looking forward to," he said, with a large smile on his face.

Meghan shuddered at the thought of him touching her. She had to figure out a way to get away from this horrible place before he forced her to marry him.

"So y' agree to marry me?"

She nodded at him, her tears streaming down her face and bouncing off the dark dirty stone floor. Her throat constricted to the point of silence, so even if she did want to speak, she would not be unable to push the words through her throat.

She was shaking with fear as Liam approached her again and grasped her by the arm. She flinched from his touch, and he grunted at her rather annoyed at her aversion to him.

"Y' don't think much of me, do y'?"

"No!" she sniffed nervously but kept her eyes fixed on him.

"Y' will, one day. I will be a good husband to y'," Liam boasted, rubbing the back of his hand up and down her arm.

"Don't' do that!" Meghan snapped, jerking her arm away from his touch.

Liam grunted with an annoyed grin, took her by the arm, and escorted her with slight force out of the dingy room she had called home for over a week. His touch was making her nauseous, and as she imagined him running his hands on her skin, she shuddered involuntarily. If she could not find a way out of this castle before the day of the wedding, she would be trapped in a marriage to this horrible man forever.

As they descended the stairs out of the turret, she could smell a distinct sweet odour of heather that was blowing in from the fields surrounding the castle. It was a welcome smell after a week of smelling nothing but musty rotting fabric.

As they passed by one of the small windows that encircled the large turret, she glanced out over the horizon. She could not believe that no one was looking for her. How could someone just disappear, and the authorities not look for them? This should be the first place they would look. Maybe everyone thought she was dead, and no one was looking for her.

Meghan's head was in turmoil by the time they reached the main floor. She scanned the room and made a mental note of all the exits, hoping that she could take advantage of one of them. Getting an overwhelming urge to run as they passed by a large set of doors, she jerked her arm loose and bolted for the doors across the hall.

Liam darted after her and caught her before she got hold of the knobs. He swung her around towards him, and her face exploded with sharp pain as his large hand smacked down on her cheek.

She raised her hand in an attempt to retaliate, but his hand swung up, gripping her wrist with extreme pressure and holding it tightly in front of her. He pulled her towards him, grabbing her by the hair, his face moving towards hers.

"Y' are such a spirited thing. Y' excite me so much, I could take y' right here." Liam pressed his mouth around hers with a forceful presence, causing Meghan to gag and pushed at him with her loose hand. That action only served to arouse him more, and he kept his mouth tightly on hers until she stopped struggling. His hand gripped her bottom, forcing her towards him, giving him the opportunity to rub his pelvis against her. He suddenly jerked her back and eyed her as she gasped for air.

"One day, y' will welcome me touch!" Liam panted, lust overflowing in his eyes.

Meghan gazed at him with blank eyes; she feared that there was no way out of this hell that had become her life.

Liam dragged her up the stairs to a long hallway lined with lamps along the white plaster walls. Pictures of his ancestors hung methodically on the walls leading to her new room that would be her jail cell until she marries this awful man.

Half way down the hall, she heard a door open and a short heavy man exited with a painting easel and brushes.

"I'm going to paint, okay, Liam," the man smiled and eyed Meghan, his soft blue eyes smiling with delight.

"That's fine, Tomas." Liam's tone was surprisingly gentle; he obviously cared for the man.

"Hi, I'm Tomas. I live here." The dark-haired man raised his hand towards Meghan.

"Hi, Tomas, I'm Meghan," she said softly back, realizing that he had some form of mental disability.

"Will y' watch me paint? I paint good."

"I'm sure you do. But you'll have to ask Mr. O'Brien if I can," Meghan responded, raising her brow towards Liam, hoping to be allowed.

"Liam, can she, please?" Tomas begged, his pale blue eyes pleading his brother.

"No, not today, maybe tomorrow." Liam smiled at the young man. "Go find Ayden, he'll watch y' paint."

"Okay, bye." Tomas hurried down the hall clumsily, trying to carry everything he was carrying.

"Come along," Liam grumbled, the sternness returning to his voice as he pulled her towards the end of the hall.

When they came to a door at the end of the hall, he took out a key from his pocket and opened the door, hurling her inside. The door slammed behind him with a sense of finality.

"Is this to your liking?" he asked, as if he were a bellhop at a hotel.

"I would rather be home," Meghan responded weakly.

"Now, Meghan, this is your home. Y' promised me y' would behave." Liam shook his head, amazed with her resolve. She was going to be a challenge that was plain to see. He was not accustomed to women turning from him with disgust, which made her all the more appealing.

Liam moved closer to her, and his large forearm, covered with curly blond hair, reached out, and his large hand gently touched her arm. His grip was gentle now as he led her towards the window.

"Y' have a very nice view from up here."

The window offered a view of the garden below and out to the coastline in the distance. The fields surrounding the castle led to the ocean on the west side and up into the hills on the other. Not a tree in sight on the west side as the grassy fields wandered down towards the ocean, an island visible in the distance.

"Yes, it's beautiful," she said, trying not to agitate him. "What is that island?"

Liam's brow rose slightly. "It's Valencia Island but don't think that information will help y', my love," he chuckled as she crinkled her nose at him. He could apparently read her thoughts as easily as Declan.

So they were in Kerry. How was anyone going to find her on the other side of the island from where she was last seen? Why had she not listened to Declan; if she did, he would be alive, and she would most likely be safe at the ranch by now. Her thoughts strayed to Colton, her concern for his well-being overpowering. "What happened to my friend? The one your man hit."

Liam shrugged and glanced out the window. "I don't know."

Meghan cringed and glanced back out the window. She swallowed hard, trying to force down the bile that was surging upward. What if Colton was dead too, three people dead because of her, and what happened to Cassie? Had she gone back to the States or was she still in Ireland?

Meghan's eyes caught sight of a small blond boy of about seven playing in the yard with an uncooperative tabby cat that apparently didn't appreciate being shoved into a small motorized jeep. The boy's attention was diverted when Tomas exited to castle with his easel and sat down by a row of hedges. As the little blond head disappeared between the hedges, then reappeared out the other side, Meghan glanced up at Liam.

"Who is that boy?" she questioned as she watched Liam eyeing the child with delight.

"Ayden," he said evenly.

"Is he the son of one of your staff?" Meghan pushed, her natural curiosity coming forward.

"Meghan, stop asking so many questions," Liam said calmly as he turned back towards her.

He smiled softly and ran his hand up her arm. She could feel it sliding across her shoulder and up her neck, coming to rest on the red mark on her face from where his hand made its impact.

"I'm sorry for that. I didn't mean to hurt y'."

Meghan's eyes narrowed at his comment. She was finding him reprehensible as he was attempting to seem companionate. "It didn't bother you to kill my husband, though, did it?" she flared at him like a caged animal.

"I didn't kill anyone. That was an unfortunate accident." Liam shoved her back onto the large feather bed. He climbed on top of her and ran his hand to the back of her head, pulling her towards him, pressing his lips onto her mouth. She started to push frantically at his shoulder, then lifted her knee, ramming it upwards, but he seemed to sense her intent and swung his hand off her arm, grabbing hold of her leg before it made contact. His reflexes were quick and accurate like

Declan's, and she found herself idly wondering where a man would learn those traits.

As suddenly as the assault started, it stopped, and Liam sprang from the bed, leaving her shaking with terror as she lay looking up at him. "I'll not take y' by force."

"Oh, how respectable of you!" Meghan's voice was shaky as she moved herself to the other side of the bed.

He grinned at her with amusement, then turned to leave the room. "I will, however, have y' once we're wed." He closed the door behind him, and Meghan fell to the bed and sobbed uncontrollably.

CHAPTER THIRTY

The next morning was a bright fall day, even with the ever-present cloud cover still lingering in the early morning sky. Meghan rose from her bed and slowly shuffled over to the window to widen the gap in the curtains. As she looked out the window, she noticed two men dressed in chief whites out in what was left of the garden, picking herbs, with the little blond boy holding the basket for them. Meghan gripped the window and tugged, trying to open it to holler to the men; she tugged with every fibre in her body, but it wouldn't open.

"My God, this place is a fortress," she mumbled as she scanned the room for something to break the window. She picked up the chair over by the fireplace and ran to the window. She heaved it up over her head, but her motion was stopped by the sound of a voice at her door.

"You're wasting your time. Y' won't break that window. It's strong glass," Liam said from the doorway.

Meghan glared at him and flung the chair into the window, and it bounced off the glass and sent her crashing to the hard tile floor. She was dazed from the sudden fall, and she struggled to get up as Liam leaned down lifting her to her feet with his large strong hand. She sighed deeply as he gently pushed her tousled hair off her face.

"When are y' going to resign yourself to the fact that y' aren't leaving here?"

For the first time in her life, Meghan could not cry. She was so deeply drained from what was happening; she was numb as she stared at him with her eyes dark and distant. She pulled her arm from his hand, moved across the room, and flopped into the other chair by the fireplace. Liam lifted the chair she had thrown and carried it over

401

to where she was sitting. He sighed slightly with exasperation and sat down beside her.

"Meghan, once y' are me wife, I will let y' out of this room. But I need to marry y'."

"Why, why won't you tell me?"

"Soon, me love." Liam rested his hand on her leg.

She sighed and gazed at him with hopelessness. "Once we're married, what are you going to do with me?" she asked, with fear in her voice.

"Love y' I hope. If y' be a good wife, then I'll keep y' around, but if y' continue to try to escape . . ." A cold smile filled his face.

Meghan lowered her eyes to the floor and squeezed them closed tightly, hoping she was having a bad dream and it would go away. "You're going to kill me, aren't you?" She shuddered at the thought.

"Well, that would be an option." He looked at her, his head tilted to the side. The expression on his face seemed uncomfortable with that option. "But I don't want to harm y'."

"But you will if . . ." She quickly regretted asking that question.

"Aye, I will." He raised a brow and started to grin. "But if y' behave, I won't have to. Meghan, y' will have a nice life here. Y' can come and go as y please, and y' will have servants. Y' can entertain and do all the things y' have ever dreamed of," he rambled, trying to convince her.

"All I have ever dreamed about was being with Declan," Meghan sighed and closed her eyes, running her hands across her face as if somehow the scrubbing motion would erase what was happening to her. Unfortunately, when she opened her eyes again, Liam was still sitting next to her, watching her curiously.

"I promise that no harm will come to y' as long as y' do what I ask." Liam stood and moved towards the door. He turned and looked back at her big, green eyes, gazing at him, and he couldn't help but smile at her. The door shut behind him leaving her alone again.

Meghan sat nervously in the enormous library, glancing back and forth between the door and the two gun-toting men that were standing by the wall. The numerous bookshelves lining two walls were stacked full of books and from what she could see from her position on the couch, they appeared to be everything from the classics to modern mysteries. On one side of the room was a scattering of couches giving her the impression that this room was used to entertain small groups of guests. Across from her was a large chair positioned almost overseeing the room as if whoever sits there lords over the room's occupants.

Meghan was not sure what the purpose of her presence was since the men simply insisted she accompany them with no explanation. When she tried to inspect the books, she was told to sit down and be quiet but over ten minutes had passed, and she was becoming anxious.

"What's going on?" Meghan questioned again towards the short fat Murphy.

"Be quiet!" Murphy snorted and turned his attention to the steps coming down the hall; then he and the other man stood at attention, waiting for the approaching person.

Meghan could feel the tension building in her stomach as she stared at the older man that entered right before Liam's large frame.

The greying man's pale blue eyes settled on her terrified face as he headed towards her. "Well, descriptions of your beauty have not been exaggerated," he smiled and grabbed her hand.

She jerked her arm from his touch, but he held it firm and kissed the soft skin of her hand, then lifted his face to hers, with a smirk building across his broad face.

"So how is Katie?" he questioned with interest, his strong Irish lilt rather soothing.

"Pardon me?" Meghan muttered, surprised by the question.

"I asked how Katie is doing."

"She's fine," Meghan blurted out, backing away from him, realizing that he was Fergus O'Brien. Her panic was fuelled when Rory entered the room and sat in a chair by the fireplace, appearing comfortable in the room.

"Oh, Rory," Fergus smiled. "Come here to me, I am in need of your help."

Rory moved tentatively towards Meghan, unsure how she was going to react to him. She looked terrible, her hair was messy, and she had dark sunken eyes. She obviously had little sleep since her arrival. What had he done? As much as he disliked Meghan, no one deserved to be held prisoner, and with his knowledge of his new family, she was unlike to be leaving, alive anyway.

Meghan glowered at him and backed away from the two men; she was unsure where to go, but her instinct was to get away from Fergus, he terrified her. Her movement, however, was halted by Fergus's bony wrinkled hand on her arm, digging his fingers into the flesh of her upper arm.

"You're hurting me," Meghan complained, eyeing the group of men in the room. All determined to keep her hostage.

"Good," Fergus laughed rather cruelly. "Now sit down!" he snorted and flung her back towards the chair, causing her to stumble slightly and fall to the floor, completely missing the chair.

"Da!" Liam shouted as he ran to her trembling body. "Y' don't need to be so rough with her."

"Watch your tone with me, lad," Fergus snorted and sat down in the large armchair by the fire. "Come here, girl," he said firmly, crooking his finger at her.

Meghan inadvertently slid backwards on the floor. "No, leave me alone." She managed to push through her clogged throat.

Fergus's face crumbled, causing the abundance of wrinkles to deepen into vast crevasses. "Bring that girl here to me!"

Liam gripped her arm firmly, pulling her to her feet, staring down at her with a reassuring smile. "Come along, me love."

Meghan said nothing, but her lashes were fluttering across her eyes with anxiety as she tried forcing the tears back that were threatening to explode. Liam's behaviour was confusing, and his father's was terrifying.

"Sit down, me dear," Fergus said gently, the annoyance gone; he had adopted the tone of a caring father. "I want y' and Rory to listen to me."

Rory moved over to Meghan and stood by the chair, resting his hand on her shoulder. Meghan jerked forwards to remove the hand, disgust filling her.

"Still the superior bitch I see," Rory grumbled, his ego taking a hit. He had told Fergus and Liam that they had a good relationship, and she was making a liar out of him.

"Shut up, Rory, you disgust me, you spineless coward," Meghan snarled, her dark eyes piecing him.

Coward? Is that what she thought of him? Is that what his family would think? After all, he did play a part in his brother's death, and now he was too afraid to help Meghan escape. Not that his mother would care either way about Meghan, but his father would be very upset. He had taken quite a liking to Meghan and Caelan.

When Rory refocused, Liam had moved towards them and was now leaning over towards Meghan. "Would y' be more comfortable, me love, if Rory sat over there?" Liam took her silent glare as a yes and bobbed his head towards the chair next to Fergus.

Even in this family, he was ordered around like a dog. Dismissed until he was needed for something. He forced an agreeable smile and dropped to the chair, his annoyed eyes settling on Meghan as she watched Liam moving away from her and over towards the bar area.

"Liam has told me that y' are the granddaughter of Mick Delaney?" Fergus began, uninterested in the dynamics of the group he had assembled.

"Yes," Meghan muttered, keeping her eyes directed on the floor.

"Hmm," Fergus made a guttural sound, then continued, "Let me tell y' a story." His face was cold and tired looking as he settled into the large chair. Murphy and his partner were now leaning against the wall, and Liam was over at the bar pouring snifters of brandy.

"Ireland was invaded by the Celts in approximately AD 400, the strongest of the tribal groups being the Gaels, introducing the Gaelic culture to the Island."

Meghan nodded her head in agreement, panic surging through her as he continued with the history lesson.

"So it is said that a Celtic sorcerer forged a magical sword that would protect the bearer from any harm. That sword ended up in the hands of Brian Boru."

She was learning more about Irish history than she wanted, and the more information she found out the more trouble she seemed to be in. "I was told the sidhe forged the sword?"

Liam snorted a laugh and glanced over at her. "I find it hard to believe that y' would believe that story."

A snarl grew across Fergus's lips. His eyes left Meghan's face and settled angrily on Liam. "Liam, y' are going to have to teach her some respect not to interrupt me."

"Aye, Da," Liam smirked, watching her with interest, not knowing if she was too stupid to realize she should not be interrupting, or if she was just so stubborn that she would always push the line.

"As I was saying," Fergus snarled and glared back at Meghan, "that sword, depending on what form of the story y' believe had a powerful amulet embedded in the pommel."

Meghan gasped, understanding where his story was going.

Fergus eyed her with annoyance and continued, "After Brian's death, it was passed down through the generations until your ancestor Michael stole what was rightfully mine, and now I want it back." A crooked smile filled Fergus's weathered face. His pale blue eyes began to come to life under the long unruly grey brows. He nodded as Liam handed him a snifter of brandy, then turned his attention back to Meghan.

"Me love," Liam said softly, handing Meghan a snifter. She settled her dark green eyes on Liam and took the glass in her trembling hand. He smiled softly, then turned and handed a snifter to Rory.

"Well, technically, it should have gone to Andrew's line, he was the oldest," Meghan blurted out, unsure why she did. Fergus shot her an annoyed glare, causing her to adjust herself further back on the chair. A large hand came down on her shoulder, and she flinched as the fingers dug into her skin.

"Me love," Liam said coolly. "Keep quiet."

Meghan swallowed painfully and gazed over at Rory, who was watching her with worry shooting from his eyes.

"May I continue?" Fergus questioned sharply in her direction. "I see you have done some research. Then I won't bore you any further with the history lesson."

She nodded and took a deep breath, trying to calm her exploding nerves.

"Anyway, the estate stayed in your family's line, as I'm sure y' know," he sneered towards her. "Your grandda thought by moving to the States and leasing out the estate, I would give up me quest to get it."

She nodded with acknowledgement but said nothing.

"Since the estate must be passed down to the oldest male or the oldest female, if no male child is produced, the estate now belongs to you. The decree states that only descendants of Eamon can inherit the estate. It also states that if a descendant of Eamon enters into marriage with another descendant, the child of that union would complete two-thirds of the triad. At the moment that consists of y', meself, and Katie."

"Oh my God," Meghan blurted out as it became clear to her what Liam was after.

"What the hell!" Rory said, with shock glancing over at Meghan. "We are related?"

"Yes, you didn't know that?" Meghan blurted out, her eyes switching to Liam.

"No," Rory snorted and jumped to his feet. "What the hell is going on here? How did you know that?"

"Declan told me," Meghan muttered, biting her bottom lip. "But he didn't tell me about the decree. Why the hell didn't he tell me that?"

"Y' two don't understand what is at stake here, do y'?" Fergus said coolly.

"No," Meghan sniffed, fighting back the tears. "If two heirs have a child . . ."

A grin grew across Fergus's face as she put the pieces together. "I think you're finally understanding, it love."

"It's an heir you are after?" Meghan blurted out and turned towards Liam.

"Aye, me love, I'm surprised your late husband didn't tell y' about the heir. That's why he married y', after all. I'm just surprised he hasn't gotten y' pregnant yet."

"That's not why he married me!" Meghan snorted, jumped to her feet, and wandered aimlessly around the room before Liam halted her movements, pulling her against his large chest and holding her securely. She struggled slightly, but settled quickly when Fergus's booming voice began to speak again.

"You're not as stupid as this line seems to be!" Fergus grumbled, glaring at Rory.

"You want me to have a child with Liam?" Meghan questioned, not wanting to hear the information.

"Aye, that is why y' will marry Liam and join together what was rightfully ours and with Rory being part of this family now, we have all the bases covered."

Meghan cringed at the thought and squirmed slightly in Liam's arms. Was he right about Declan, and did he only marry her because he wanted control of the estate? Is that what his mother was so upset about? His mother, she was still the heir.

"But Rory isn't . . ." Meghan halted her comment, not wanting to say anymore.

"He wasn't the eldest son," Liam finished for her. "Then it was a bit of luck that your husband met with an unfortunate accident."

Meghan became enraged at Liam's comment, how could he be so nonchalant about killing? As the remembrance of the explosion rocked her mind, she became hysterical and turned on Liam with the ferocity of a wild animal. Her hands flew towards his head, unsure how it would help, but she cared little. Her only thought was to hurt him as badly as he hurt her. Unfortunately, as usual Liam's reflexes outmanoeuvred hers, and he gripped her hands holding them to his chest, his eyes full of laughter.

"Me love." Liam shook his head at her, unsure why she continued to try to hit him. She must know how futile her attempts are and that she is only wasting energy. "Y' are exasperating."

"Let go," Meghan snorted and tugged at her trapped hands. "I could kill you."

"I'm sure y' would try, but I doubt y' would succeed," Liam laughed and kissed her nose, allowing his lips to linger. "I do, however, enjoy the fire y' have in y'."

Meghan crumpled her nose with disgust and wiped her nose on the sleeve of her shirt with defiance, causing Liam to laugh harder. She was funny he thought as he watched her eyeing him with subdued rage brewing beneath the surface of her eyes. She was going to blow soon, and he was looking forward to experiencing her in all her glory.

"Enough!" Fergus snorted over at the two. "Boy, get her under control, you're just encouraging her disrespectful behaviour."

"Aye, Da," Liam smirked, then stared down at Meghan with a wide grin. "You're getting me in trouble."

"I don't care," Meghan said sharply.

"I don't imagine y' do," Liam chuckled, then turned his attention back to his father who was staring at Rory's blank face. "But believe me, I'm the better alternative."

"I tried to solve this with your grandmother. She was a beautiful woman, but she married your grandpa and had a child with him," Fergus injected as Liam whispered and blew into Meghan's ear. "Me men went to kill your grandfather and da, but they killed your grandmother by accident. Your grandfather escaped with the child. I thought that your line had died off, but luckily for me here y' are"

"You killed my grandmother? That's why Papa was so scared for me to find out about the estate." Meghan was in such shock as everything spun in her head.

"Aye, when I produced Rory with Katie, I thought that I could claim the estate with the family merging, but Katie wouldn't leave her husband, and well, then y' surfaced." His face became distant and somewhat sad.

Meghan's body began to tremble as the dread of what was going on in Fergus's head took hold. Fergus cleared his throat and stood abruptly, causing everyone in the room to jerk slightly. "Now that the elder brother is taken care of, Rory is the sole heir for that line."

"Oh," Meghan muttered as a tremor ran through her. "So when Katie . . ." She stopped and directed her terrified eyes on Fergus. "Oh God, you're not?"

"No!" Fergus said with a slight smirk.

"He's not what?" Rory questioned.

"How stupid are you, Rory?" Meghan snorted, squirming in Liam's arms once more. "Dammit, would you let go of me?"

Liam laughed but did not release her. "I don't think so."

"Meghan, what is going on?" Rory questioned again.

"Your mother," she said sharply. "She is the heir until."

Rory's face, suddenly understanding, changed direction and turned towards Fergus. "Oh no, you can't hurt my mam."

"I'm not going to hurt Katie," Fergus said, with exasperation. "I love her."

"Love?" Meghan muttered to herself, not realizing how loud she said it.

"Meghan," Liam muttered into her ear, pressing his face up against hers. "I suggest y' watch your tongue. Y' will find me da a great deal less tolerant than I."

Meghan nodded slightly and took a deep breath while he continued to press his bearded face against her, his lips brushing across her skin.

"Now," Fergus started again, after refilling his snifter. "As I suppose y' have figured out that a son produced by y' and Liam will inherit the estate."

"Yes." Meghan nodded as he moved towards her. She took a step backwards, pressing up hard against Liam, realizing she was safer with him than with his father. "But why is that land so important to you? You obviously are very wealthy. Why is that estate so important that you are willing to kill over?" She knew what they were after, but she wanted to see if they would tell her.

Fergus came to a stop directly in front of her, resting his bony but large hand on her face. His blue eyes fixed on hers and held her gaze firm. Even with the extensive wrinkles, she decided that he must have been a handsome man when he was younger. He had the same bone structure as Liam and almost the identical eyes. The red birthmark streaking down the lower portion of his neck seemed to have faded with age, but it was definitely a carbon copy of the one his two sons shared.

"Y' know why, don't you?" Fergus smirked, moving his face towards her. She jerked back, smashing her head into Liam's shoulder, and Liam stepped backwards, pulling her with him as annoyance filled his reddening face.

"Da, that's enough!" Liam snorted.

"Don't worry, me boy, I was planning on letting y' marry her."

"This can't be happening," Meghan cried as she dropped to the ground beside the couch. She leaned forward burying her face in her legs as the tears exploded from her eyes.

"Me love, don't get upset." Liam soothed as he moved towards her. His large hands lifted her effortlessly to her feet and then he deposited her on the couch. "Stop your crying."

She sniffed a few times but managed to stop the stream as she looked at his annoyed face. "All this hysteria is not going to change your life. Y' will marry me, and y' will share your bed with me. It should not be long before we produce a son and heir and ensure my family's heritage. And once we are married, I will have control of the estate, and you will evict those two old idiots so we can search for . . ."

"Liam!" Fergus blurted out. "That's enough!" His brows crumpled with anger.

"Search for what? The sword?" Meghan decided to go on the offensive.

Fergus eyed her with interest. "So you do know." He gripped her face in his boney hand. "Did your grandda tell you its location?"

"No, he never told me anything about it. Declan told me the story, but he said it's an old wives' tale," Meghan sighed when Fergus released her face.

"Well, if Mr. Montgomery believed it to be a wives' tale, why did he marry y'? His family also has a great deal of money. I made sure of that." Fergus's question scared her.

"He married me because he loves me," she said, more for her peace of mind than for them.

"No, he didn't, he married you to fulfil the prophecy," Liam laughed.

"Liam!" Fergus snorted.

"Oh, Da, we may as well tell her," Liam smirked at Meghan. "The prophecy states that when the three become one, the power of the sword will be revealed."

"Isn't it the bearer will wield the power of the Gods?" Meghan blurted out. She was completely overwhelmed with what was happening.

Liam started to laugh. "So y' do know more than y' were letting on."

Meghan cringed. "Well, I heard that statement before, but I didn't understand it until just now. You are trying to merge the family into one." She glanced at Rory, who was looking completely confused. Apparently, they kept him in the dark.

Fergus smiled and sat back down in his chair. "So I thought I had started the process with him, but I neglected one small item. It also states that the child must be a legal heir. That would mean it needs to be born in wedlock. The original plan was to have Rory marry you and produce an heir but luckily you had such an aversion to him that I had to send Liam after y'."

"But Rory isn't your eldest son?" Meghan questioned, settling her eyes on Liam. "Were you going to knock him off?" She bobbed her head towards Liam.

Liam appeared agitated by the question. His eyes settling on his father for an answer.

Fergus glared at her, then glanced over at Liam. "Luckily, it didn't come to that. This way is better anyway. Rory is so daft you probably would have produced an idiot."

Meghan opened her mouth to respond, but the door flew open at the other end of the room and broke her thoughts.

Fergus turned towards the door and glared at Kaye as she stood in the doorway. "Get out, this is a meeting that doesn't concern y'."

"Well, I just came to tell Liam that I'm leaving," Kaye said, with slight disdain as she wandered across the room towards Liam.

Her eyes settled on Meghan and a slight amount of worry flashed in them. "Could I talk with Meg for a moment alone?" Kaye questioned Liam.

"We are right in the middle of something," he said coolly. "Could this not wait?"

"I'm sure I can help." Kaye raised her narrow blonde brow.

Liam gripped Kaye's arm, dragged her to the corner, and began telling her something that seemed important. She nodded her head as he talked but was unable to get a word in. Meghan watched curiously but was unable to hear what was being discussed. Fergus had disappeared from the room along with the two gun-toting men, leaving her virtually unguarded.

A rush of excitement filled her as she eyed the unguarded patio door at the end of the room. With Liam occupied with Kaye, that only left Rory to stop her, but would he? She shrugged slightly and slowly began to move towards the doors. Her anxiety built the closer she got to the door without being noticed, and she could feel the blood rushing through her like a burning fire.

She swallowed hard as her hand reached for the door; Rory was watching her but made no sound, and Liam's back was still towards her. She could see the muscle tensing in his shoulder at something Kaye said and at that moment, she gripped the knob and flung the door open. She was through the door and on her way across the stone patio before Liam had even turned. The stones were uneven and hard under her feet, but she pushed on towards the rows of hedges surrounding the large patio.

When she reached the grass, she was slightly relieved, but her fears built again when she heard Liam's voice behind her and getting closer.

"Going somewhere?" The man stepped out from behind the third row of hedges blocking her escape.

Meghan screamed, turned on her heels, and darted between the hedges before the man could get a grip on her. Unfortunately, the change in direction allowed Liam to catch up, and he was only a few steps behind her calling for her to stop. Panic surged through her, not allowing her to give in to her common sense that he was going to catch her and she kept running. She could feel the muscles in her thighs burning under the strain. However, the pain of Liam's large frame knocking her to the ground quickly overshadowed the pain in her thighs. His body lay heavily on hers crushing the air from her lungs as she struggled to regain her senses. Her legs were throbbing and her back was cramping with sharp pains.

"Get off," Meghan begged, hitting at his chest.

"Me love, why did y' do that?" Liam said with annoyance. "I was hoping that I could trust y'."

A scowl grew across her face as she watched the lightly bearded face staring down at her. "Please let me go."

He sighed deeply and jumped to his feet. His hand lowered towards her to help her off the ground, but she refused his help and struggled to stand on her own.

"Life will be much easier for y' if y' just realize that y' belong to me now, and this is your home." A slight smile filled Liam's face as he watched her brushing the dirt from her ripped shorts and blouse, totally ignoring his comment. "Were y' this much trouble to Mr. Montgomery?"

"Much more," she said evenly and turned towards the house with him on her heels.

He made no attempt to touch her, and she made no further attempt to flee. Obviously, she needed a plan and just running was not the way.

"Me love, Kaye would like to have a word with y'," Liam said calmly as they returned to the room. Rory was now gone, and the room was empty apart from Kaye.

"Fine," Meghan grumbled calmly as she watched him leaving the room through the door to the hall.

"By the way, me love," a smile filled his face as he turned back to her, "me men are outside that door, so if y' are planning on trying that again y' will be shot."

She shuddered slightly and glared at him. "You can't kill me," her voice was firm, but her face was slightly timid. "You need me."

"Aye," he laughed. "You're no fool, but nothing is stopping them from beating y' senseless."

She cringed as he turned shutting the door behind him. "Kaye, you need to find Cassie and tell her where I am," Meghan blurted out once he was gone.

"I will," she agreed. "But, Meg, with Declan gone, maybe you would do well by marrying Liam."

"Why?" Meghan questioned sharply.

"Well, he's very rich, and he is gorgeous. And he will treat you well," Kaye said, trying her best to convince Meghan to accept Liam. "I know from experience."

"If you like him so much, why don't you marry him then?" Meghan snorted and turned her back on Kaye.

Kaye grunted as Meghan swung around, Kaye's eyes filled with a mixture of worry and disdain.

"Do you remember when I told you that your locket meant nothing?"

"Yes."

"Well, I lied. When I told him about it, he freaked," Kaye sighed with what seemed to be disappointment.

"Well, he sent Rory after you, do you remember you met at my party?"

"Yes." Meghan swallowed painfully as the pieces started to fall into place. "You are in on this whole thing?"

"Yes, Rory was supposed to get you to come back here with him, but he is such a freak that you instantly disliked him. Then Cassie invited you to the lodge so Liam thought that Rory could take you from there."

"How does Declan fit into this plan?" Meghan growled at the thought of Declan lying to her.

"He didn't, as far I know. Liam told me to suggest the lodge to Cassie, but I don't think he knew Declan was there. Apparently, he just wanted to have a place that was remote so Rory could get you to fall in love with him. But, unfortunately Declan met you and for some reason, married you before Liam got a hold of you. Somewhere along the way Liam's plans changed and my life fell apart." Kaye glanced around the room. "This should have been mine."

"Oh God," Meghan muttered. "How could you do that to me?"

"Stop being so dramatic. I was just helping a friend. I had no idea he was going to take it this far," she grumbled.

"You had no idea he would kill Declan?"

"What?" Kaye blurted out.

"You heard me."

"He didn't kill Declan, he was killed in an explosion."

"Who do you think set off the explosion?" Meghan snorted.

"Meg, you need to listen to me," Kaye said quietly, directing her eyes on the door. "Just marry him and pretend that you're happy. He will eventually let his guard down, then you can leave."

"Kaye, I can't marry him," Meghan cried as the tears welled in her eyes.

"Meg, you have to. He is really a kind man," Kaye assured Meghan, realizing to what extent Liam was willing to go to posses Meghan.

"Are you insane?" Meghan blurted out. "He killed Declan, he kidnapped me, and you think he is kind?"

"Has he hurt you?" Kaye questioned. "He won't."

Meghan glared at her with a mixture of terror and hatred. "Kaye, you are the last person I would take advice from. You have done nothing but purposely try to hurt me since the day we met."

"Well, you deserved it," Kaye snorted. "Meghan, the ever sweet and kind. I was so tired of everyone always saying how wonderful you were. And you had no clue, did you?"

"No clue about what?"

"That everyone you come in contact with adores you. Dammit, every man on campus wanted you, and you spent your whole time with Nat."

"He's my friend," she muttered, turning her back on Kaye's annoyed face.

"Friend?" Kaye snorted. "That just made you more desirable because you were unattainable."

"Why are you telling me this now?" Meghan questioned as she scrubbed her hand across her face. "I have enough to deal with at this moment than to worry about what happened in college."

"I'm telling you this because if you weren't so blind, you would have seen this coming."

"How would I have seen this coming?" Meghan snorted.

"You are so clueless when it comes to men, aren't you? Didn't you see the way Liam was looking at you when you met him at Blarney Castle?"

"I met him before, the week I met Declan," Meghan muttered and watched for Kaye's reaction.

"What?" Kaye's voice sounded panicked.

"He was at the cast party at the Spring Mountain Hotel." Meghan eyed Kaye's shocked face. Obviously, she was only told what Liam felt she should know.

Meghan crumpled her nose and turned away, dropping to the couch by the fireplace; she was so overwhelmed, she was speechless. She had noticed him staring at her, but she paid little attention to it. She assumed it was because of his interest in the locket. The last month passed before her, and she tried to recall everything that had happened since the day she met Liam.

"What could I have done differently?" she finally questioned.

"You could have stayed away from him," Kaye scowled, jealousy showing in her eyes.

"Stay away from him? He was the one that kept coming after me," Meghan snarled hurtfully; she was almost pleased that she was causing Kaye such distress after everything she had done over the years.

Kaye shook her head with exasperation. "Why did you even come to Ireland after what happened at your ranch?"

"What?"

"How do you think Liam found you?" Kaye waved her hand in dismissal. "By a fluke of luck that idiot from your town went to the castle and started rambling on about beautiful Dr. Meghan Coleman who looks just like the picture of Catherine O'Brien."

"Anthony?" she muttered, shaking her head with disbelief.

"Well, you can thank him because that's how Liam found you again," Kaye grunted and drained the contents of Rory's discarded glass of brandy.

Meghan lowered her head burying it in her knees. "This is unbelievable. He has been tracking me all these years."

"Yes," Kaye said sharply. "And if you would have stayed back in the States, he probably would have left you alone," she sighed and sat down across from Meghan. "But he took one look at you again and decided that he must have you and here you are."

"I don't think so. They are after a lot more than you know. This has nothing to do with his attraction for me?"

"Meghan, me love," Liam's deep voice boomed into the room. "When are you going to understand that decree is only part of it?" he smiled and wandered towards her.

Kaye glared at her and stood in Liam's path, resting her narrow hands on his broad chest.

"Liam, why don't you just let her go home? She has no interest in your damn land. Send her home and marry me."

A slight grin grew across Liam's face as he gazed down at Kaye's pleading face. "Aye, well, my dear, as much as I love having y' in me bed. Y' are of no value to me otherwise."

"No value?" Kaye snorted, but his fingers over her mouth, halted her comment.

"Don't y' be saying anymore," Liam snorted, his eyes narrowing at her.

"I'm sorry," Kaye said softly. "It's just that I want you so badly, I'm just upset."

"Well, come with me, and y' can show me how much y' want me," Liam said smugly as he dragged Kaye towards the door.

Meghan stayed seated on the chair watching the two depart. She sighed with relief that his attentions would be elsewhere, and she was safe for a while.

She stayed in the room for over an hour wondering what she should do. She knew guards were placed at both exits, so she had no hope of escaping, and she had no idea when someone was going to return her to her room.

Her mind had finally settled into slight calmness, and she stood and wandered to the bookshelf deciding to find something to occupy her time. She was tired of thinking about what was happening to her, she needed an escape.

Fergus's collection of books and memoirs was quite impressive, and she found herself being lost in the excitement of finding an interesting book. Her thoughts, however, were broken when she heard the door from the hall open and loud footsteps heading towards her.

"I see y' like to read," Liam said with interest.

"Yes," Meghan said evenly.

He stopped at her side and gripped her arm. "It's time y' go back to your room. I have to take Kaye back to town."

Liam ushered her back to her room, and she was surprised that someone had been in cleaning while she was gone. A tray was left on the dresser filled with shampoo, soap, and other hygiene products for her use. He waved his hand towards the bed and the royal blue cotton dress laid out across the quilt.

"I thought you might like to clean up," Liam smiled, glancing at her ripped clothing.

"Thank you," Meghan said quietly. "Liam, doesn't it bother you that your father was planning on killing you if Rory married me and had a son?"

Liam shrugged and looked out the window. "Well, I don't believe all that crap about the sword. I agree with you about it being a wives' tale. So I wasn't too concerned. And if he tried to kill me, I would have taken him out first. It's not like I didn't know what he was up to. He's an old man who is little more than a figure head in this family. I'm in charge."

"Oh," Meghan muttered, a sadness filled her. What kind of life must he have lived knowing his dad would kill him at any minute?

Liam smiled and kissed the side of her head. "I'm pleased to see that y' are concerned for me, but don't worry, me love."

"I'm not worried," she said defiantly. "So if you don't believe in the prophecy, then what do you need with me?"

Liam laughed, "I said I don't believe in the legend of the sword. I still want to posses the estate. It is more valuable to me than you will ever know," he smirked and walked over towards the door. "I'll be gone a few days, so y' will have to stay up here." With a quick grin, he was gone out the door, leaving her alone.

CHAPTER THIRTY-ONE

M eghan stood by the window, gazing off over the fields towards the shoreline as she had done every day since she was locked in the room.

"Why hasn't anyone come for me? Why hadn't Kaye told someone?" she mumbled to herself as she leaned against the window frame.

The young man with the chief's hat was out in the garden picking herbs again from the dying plants and looked up towards her window and smiled. She waved at him, but he made no other attempt at acknowledgement.

Meghan frowned and moved away from the window and fell into the chair in front of the fireplace. She should not be surprised that Liam did not provide her with firewood; he most likely thought she would burn the house down.

The room was very barren other than the large four-poster bed, the old bureau and the table and chairs around the fireplace. She picked up the brush from the table and dragged it through her tangled hair. She was a mess. Her hair was matted, and her clothes were covered in dirt from the turret room and rolling in the grass days before.

She lifted the blue dress that Liam had left her, trying to decide if she should put it on. Changing into the dress was one more step away from her old life, and that terrified her. A soft smile grew across her face as she thought about Declan and their discussion about vanity years before. He was right; she was a bit vain, she decided, as she felt the overwhelming need to tidy herself. In the past few weeks, she had no interest in grooming, but today she was feeling rather frazzled, and a shower was needed.

After her shower, she patiently tugged at the tangles in her hair and thought about what Fergus had asked her. Her grandfather talked very little about Ireland, but he did sing her a song every night before she went to bed.

> Deep down in the bellies of the gargoyles two
> Lays a secret no stranger can share
> A secret that will lead to the treasures of Boru
> This destiny is yours alone to bear
> When midday strikes the eyes glow bright
> Showing us the way
> As keeper of the key, we are the entrusted light
> As Lord and King we must not ever stray

Could that be the information that Fergus wanted? She sat erect on the bed when the remembrance of the two large gargoyles at the front of Briarwood castle filled her mind. Could those be the gargoyles in the song? Was her grandfather trying to ensure that she remembered the information without telling her directly what it meant?

She was startled by her thoughts, when she heard the familiar soft knocking on the door. "Tomas," she shrieked as she ran to the door and sat down against it. Tomas was Liam's younger brother and the bright spot in her day as he would visit her every morning and talk to her through the door.

"Miss Meghan, are you there?"

"Yes, Tomas."

"Miss Meghan, Liam is having a party this week, but he said I can't go."

"I'm sorry, Tomas, but maybe you could stay and visit me. I can't go either."

"How come y' can't come out of your room? Y' have been in there a long time. Are y' still being bad?"

"No, Liam has . . ." Meghan started to say but realized it would accomplish nothing by telling him. He obviously never leaves the castle either, and if he started to bother Liam or Fergus, his life could be in danger. No, she would have to find another way out.

"Is Liam mad at y'? He locks me and Ayden in our rooms if we have done something bad."

"I'll get to come out soon, I'm sure. Don't worry, Tomas, I'm fine."

"Okay, Miss Meghan."

"Tomas, who is Ayden?" Meghan asked with curiosity.

She had asked Liam on many occasions, but he either totally ignored her question or he answered very vaguely. Her natural instinct to be fully informed was driving her crazy, and she figured Tomas would give her the information.

"He's me nephew," Tomas said with excitement.

"Your nephew? Do you mean he is Liam's son?"

"Aye."

"Oh," she muttered, unsure what the big secret was. Why is Liam so secretive about this? "What happened to his mother?"

"She died," Tomas said with a hint of sadness.

"Oh, I'm sorry to hear that. How long ago?"

"A couple of days ago."

"Oh." Meghan could feel the blood drain from her face at the thought. What the hell was going on? He didn't seem to have a wife when she arrived. And if he had a wife, what was Kaye doing there? A shiver ran down her back when the thought that he or Fergus had killed Ayden's mother filled her mind.

Meghan sat on the cold floor for over an hour listening to Tomas's stories about the rabbits outside in the garden. He told her all about how he paints the rabbits every day, along with the ocean, the trees, the flower, the manor, and anything else he saw fit. After he ran out of things to tell her, he said goodbye and quickly rushed down the hall to create more masterpieces in the early morning sun.

The morning was dragging by, and Meghan was getting very anxious wondering what happened to the mother of the child. The shower did nothing to soothe her frazzled nerves and the blue-flowered dress she was wearing only served to remind her that she lost control of her life.

Meghan had been trapped in the manor for over three weeks now and in this room for at least two weeks of that, and she was to the point where she was longing for company, and it didn't matter who it was. She was even finding Liam's presence a welcome one, but now she was not sure if she wanted to see him. What if he killed his wife? If so, how long did she have before he got what he wanted and killed her?

The sun was shining brightly through the autumn haze of clouds when the young man came in with her lunch. He was still quiet as ever and didn't offer any attempt at communication.

"Is Mr. O'Brien coming home today?" Meghan questioned the tall thin man.

"No," he said abruptly, placing the tray on her table.

"When will he be home?" He had said he would be gone only a few days, but it had been almost a week.

"I don't know, miss." He turned quickly and exited the room.

Meghan frowned as the door shut, and the room was quiet again. She was going crazy from the silence of the cold drafty room, and she only picked at the food left on the table. She still didn't have her appetite back; her stomach was still in turmoil.

How she longed for Declan and her darling Caelan. Her worry for Caelan was mounting with every day she was trapped there. What would Nat and Cassie tell her if she never returned home?

Her thoughts were disturbed when she heard the door slam shut. She jumped to her feet and swung around to see Fergus smiling menacingly at her.

She eyed him cautiously as he came towards her. His arms were moving loosely at his side, he seemed to have a very light demeanour, and she actually found him less threatening in some way.

His hand rose to her arm and gripped it tightly as he pulled her towards him. "Y' missed me, did y'?" he asked as he ran his hand down her back and rested it on her bottom.

"No, I . . . ," she snorted, pulling away from him suddenly frightened of him again.

"Where is Liam?" she questioned, trying to break his focus. "Why hasn't he come home yet?"

"He's been busy. I left and came home early so I could spend some time with y'," Fergus grinned, his pale blue eyes sparkling beneath the wild brows.

Meghan's heart was racing as he ran his hand down her face to her neck, and she pulled back from him as total disgust raged through her. A cold expression filled his broad wrinkled face.

"Leave me alone, you animal," Meghan sniffed.

"Y' are a bitchy wench, are y' not?" Fergus snorted, heading towards her. "Y' have no problem bedding me son. Why don't y' want the real lord of the manor."

"I haven't slept with your son," Meghan said weakly, backing towards the bathroom.

"Don't lie to me, wench. He wouldn't be so infatuated with y' without y' giving him a little taste."

"You're disgusting!" Meghan mumbled as panic filled her. Her back hit the wall; the bathroom door was still ten feet away.

When his hand gripped her arm, her knee hit his groin; he didn't have Liam's sharp reflexes. A loud moan left his lips as he fell back on the bed clutching his damaged crotch.

Murphy ran into the room and stood staring at the groaning man. His gaze left Fergus and settled on Meghan who was now pressed up against the wall, heading for the bathroom.

"Take her to the turret." Fergus pushed through his moans.

Murphy seemed hesitant to follow the order. "I don't mean to question your order, sir, but your son would not like this."

"I don't care what that fool would like," Fergus snarled harshly after regaining some composure. "She is a vicious disrespectful wench, and she needs to be taught her place." He straightened on the bed, glaring at Meghan, who was now being held by a tall sinewy man that entered the room. "Put her in the manacles."

"What?" Murphy questioned.

"Y' heard me!" Fergus ordered sharply.

"But . . ." Murphy argued, but stopped when he noticed the look of annoyance building in Fergus's eyes. "Right away, sir."

Liam had returned home to find Meghan's room empty, and he was enraged. How had she gotten out of the room? Did she escape or had his father taken her somewhere? The men would have never allowed her out without Liam or Fergus's approval. His damn father must be entertaining her again, he thought as he stormed through the castle towards the library. Liam hated the thought of his father anywhere near Meghan, after his last encounter with her. His father may be old, but he would have no trouble forcing himself on Meghan, and that thought made him cringe. She was his woman, and no one else was going to touch her again.

It took over an hour to track Meghan down; all anyone knew was that she was moved. Fergus's guard was reluctant to tell Liam where Fergus had hidden her, but after he was threatened with his life, he lost all loyalty to Fergus and revealed to Liam that she was placed in the turret the morning before.

Once Liam arrived at the turret room, he found her guarded by a man Fergus trusted over all the rest of the men. He himself preferred Murphy, and once finding the man asleep at his post, he knew why. The man was leaning back in the chair, resting peacefully, with his feet propped up on a small decrepit wooden table. Liam's hand swung out knocking his feet to the floor with excessive force.

"Where the hell is she?" Liam growled as the man abruptly awoke.

"In there," he said, with obvious surprise at Liam's appearance. "Your father said to leave her in there until he returns," the man mumbled, rubbing at his eyes. "At least, she stopped screaming."

"Open the damn door!" Liam yelled as panic surged through him.

The man seemed unsure if he should, but with Liam's reassurance by throwing him against the door, he did as asked.

Liam's eyes widened as he stared at Meghan's limp body hanging from the manacles attached to the stone wall. Her chest had fallen forwards, and her arms were pulled backwards towards the wall where her wrists were chained. The large metal manacles were locked around her wrist, but they were obviously too large, and she could remove her hands, so chains were also binding her wrists.

"Christ!" Liam muttered and ran to her, pushing her up against the wall. Her eyes fluttered, her gaze settled on him with distress.

"Liam," she sniffed. "Please."

"Meghan, I'm so sorry he did this to y'." Liam soothed as he turned towards the tall thin man. "Where are the keys?"

"Here," he said, wandering over with a large set of keys in his hand. "I don't think your father wants y' to release her. He was pretty upset when he left here."

"How long has she been here?" Liam growled, yanking the keys from the man. He propped her chest up against his, then fussed with the lock trying every key on the ring.

"Since yesterday afternoon."

"Damn him," Liam muttered as her first arm dropped landing solidly on his shoulder. Once the other arm was free, she fell heavily into him. "Me love, are y' okay?"

"No," she cried as she tried feebly to stand but was unable to find her balance.

He lifted her into his arms, pressing her firmly against his chest. "You'll be fine, me love. I'll take y' back to your room," he said softly as he stormed from the room past the somewhat concerned guard.

They were out of the turret and half way across the main hall when he spotted his father and Murphy heading towards him.

"Ah, so y' have the wee wench," Fergus snorted, fixing his glare on her lifeless face.

"Don't y' ever lay a hand on her again," Liam snorted, knocking into his father as he passed.

"Don't y' use that tone with me, boy," Fergus said coolly.

"I'll use whatever tone I please, and if y' harm her again, I swear I'll kill y' meself."

"Y' keep her under control, boy, or I will," he said and turned away.

Liam glared at his father, then turned to Murphy. "Ring Dr. Murray and tell him to get here right away," he said firmly, then continued on his way to her bedroom.

She was trembling terribly when he laid her on the soft bed and covered her with the quilt. She made no attempt to move, but her eyes stayed fixed on him as he moved around the room with distress. He returned from the bathroom with a small basin and a washcloth and sat on the bed beside her. She put up no resistance when he took her hand and began swabbing the raw marks around her wrists.

"I called for a doctor," he said softly. "To make sure nothing is wrong in your chest."

"Thank you," she said with laboured breath. "I am finding it hard to breathe."

"Oh," he muttered, resting his hand on her face. "I'm sorry he did this to y'."

Her eyes fluttered, then closed heavily as the thought of what happened came flooding back. "He'll come after me again."

"No, he won't," Liam said firmly. "He'll not get y' alone again."

"He . . ." Meghan stopped and opened her eyes fixing them on him.

"What happened?" Liam questioned as he tucked back her long curls behind her ear.

"He came in here after you left and wanted . . ." She cringed at the thought. "He wanted me to have sex with him, and he grabbed me, and I kicked him in . . ." She broke her gaze as his face began to fill with humour.

"Got him in the bullocks, did y'?" he laughed slightly. "Well, that will teach the dirty old bugger."

Meghan turned her head away, not finding the humour in the situation. He was no different from his father, she thought, other than he was hiding behind the veil of marriage for his rape of her.

"Don't worry, me love. I won't leave y' alone here again when he's around."

"Thank you," Meghan said quietly; at least, that was one less person she had to worry about.

The next week was relatively quiet with Liam stopping in to check on her every hour or so. She hadn't seen Fergus since, and she was glad of that.

The morning was showing promise for a beautiful day as the sun slowly rose over the eastern horizon casting a fabulous glow on the garden below. Within the hour, the yard below was filled with people scurrying around with tables and chairs. A catering truck backed up to the vestibule doors, and two men unloaded tray after tray of prepared food. She banged on the window, but unfortunately no one looked up. They just kept going about their work, preparing for the party that the O'Briens were having.

Liam had informed her that they were hosting a party, but he had also told her that she was not attending. He didn't trust her to behave, so all she could do was stand by the window and hope that someone looked up and saw her.

Her thoughts were broken when she heard the door open, and Liam's hard footsteps coming closer. She swung around and started at him as he sat down in a chair by the fireplace.

"Y' look lovely this morning," he said pleasantly as he glanced up at her. He rested the folder he had in his hands on the table and gestured towards the other chair. "Come sit."

She hesitantly wandered to the chair, very concerned with what he had in the folder. Marriage license, she assumed. What if she could not bring herself to sign it? She sat down gripping the arms of the chair, trying to think of an excuse not to sign the dreaded forms.

"What's that?" she blurted out, unable to control her worries.

"It's our family tree," he smiled, quite pleased with himself. "I thought you might like to see it for yourself."

She eyed him sceptically, then glanced down at the paper on the table. His large finger was pointing the line down from Eamon O'Brien through her ancestors to her. Kaye seemed to be correct in her account of the last few years, because the tree was complete, and it included Caelan.

"How long have you had this?" she questioned sharply, lifting the page with Caelan's name and clutching it to her chest.

"I have known about you for many years now," he grinned. "Do y' not remember meeting me at a party in Colorado years ago?"

"Yes, I remember meeting you," she mumbled, remembering the night Declan brought her to his cast party with great clarity.

A grin curled his lips as he watched her face crumpling in thought. "I couldn't take me eyes off y' that night. Y' were so beautiful."

Meghan eyed him with irritation but said nothing.

"I tried to obtain y' that night, but y' were too well guarded," he grinned. "It has been a long five years I have waited to have y'."

"You were trying to kidnap me back then?"

"Don't be upset with me, I have not kidnapped y' I have brought y' home," he said, placing his hand on her shoulder. His touch made her quake, but she was painfully aware that the only way out of the room was through him. She repeatedly swallowed, trying to clear her throat that seemed obstructed.

"Liam, were you trying to kill me?" She questioned abruptly. She had been thinking about everything she had learned in the last weeks.

"Well, at first Rory was supposed to marry y' and get y' pregnant, but y' wanted nothing to do with him, and he seemed incapable of securing y' on his own, so I had to intervene."

"Oh God!" Meghan muttered, cupping her hands around her face.

"Don't worry, me love, I changed the plans the night of that party. When I looked into these eyes." His fingers rested at the corner of her eye. "I saw something in y', and the thought handing you off to Rory sickened me. He was supposed to remove you from the lodge, not shoot anyone. Because of him, I lost y' for five years."

"So Kaye was right? If I would have stayed in the States, you would have left me alone."

"No," he said abruptly. "I was coming after y', but luckily your husband brought y' to me."

"But Kaye said."

"Kaye is wrong. I wanted y', and once I found y' again, I wasn't going to let anything stop me from having y'." He looked rather uneasy as his fingers brushed across her cheek. "But that idiot brother of mine almost destroyed me plans."

Meghan gasped at the mention of his brother.

"Y' do realize that Mr. Montgomery killed me brother James, do y' not?" Liam questioned, but he knew the answer by the expression on her face.

Meghan shook her head and forced a soft smile. "I'm sorry about your brother."

"No, you're not," Liam said firmly. "But I don't suppose I can blame y', after all, he did try and rape y'."

Meghan nodded and closed her eyes, hoping to calm herself.

"Don't fret, Meghan, I got me revenge on your husband. I don't hold y' responsible in anyway."

Meghan nodded, deciding to play the cards she was given. At least, she knew he had no intentions of harming her, and sooner or later, he would lower his guard, and she could escape and get back home to Caelan.

Liam stood and wandered over to the window and stared out over the horizon. "Everything worked out for the best, don't y' think?"

"How so?" Meghan questioned, wondering where he was going with his thoughts.

"Well, since your husband felt so strongly about coming out here to claim his land, he walked right into the trap."

"Declan didn't know anything about the decree," Meghan blurted out in his defence.

"Sure he did. That's why he married y'. He knew the minute he saw your amulet he would pursue y' until he possessed y'. We knew that he wanted to claim the land and the title, and having y' as his wife and producing an heir would ensure it would return back to his family."

"What title?" Meghan blurted out. This was getting worse with every bit of information she received.

Liam eyed her speculatively. "Are you saying y' don't know that y' are the 14th Countess of Briarwood? When we have a son he will be the 15th Earl of Briarwood. The government of Britain still holds jurisdiction over the title, but here in Ireland it is a courtesy title in name only, the Irish government doesn't recognize it."

Her head was spinning with what Liam was saying; it had to be a lie, Declan would not have married her just to gain control of a piece of land and a courtesy title. She shook her head, then buried it in her hands.

"Me love, don't be sad, everything will work out, and y' will be happy here." Liam's hand rested on the side of her face.

Meghan pulled her face from his hand and jumped from the chair. "Liam, if you love me, you would let me go home to my daughter."

"You will be free to come and go once you give yourself to me, heart and soul," he muttered, following behind her.

Meghan sighed, knowing she would never love him. How was she going to get back to Caelan, and if she did, would he hunt her for the rest of her life? Was her only way out to make this man think she loved him? And if so, she would have to live with him for the rest of her life pretending to love him, letting him touch her.

"Liam, I am so lonely, and I miss my daughter," she confessed, in the hopes he would feel some level of compassion for her.

"Well, Meghan, once y' marry me we can send for her, and she can live here with us."

"Really?"

"Aye, I don't like to see sadness on that pretty face of yours." He turned her towards him, resting his hand on her face again. She closed her eyes as she found it hard to watch him touching her.

"When?" She stopped, not ready for his response.

"When is our wedding day? Is that what y' want to know?"

"Yes," she replied hesitantly.

"Two weeks. By then, the investigation into your late husband's death should be complete, and y' will be free to marry me," he said evenly.

"Liam, is the boy your son?" she questioned abruptly, wanting to know if she was also inheriting a son in the deal.

His brow rose slightly. "What boy?"

Her eyes narrowed. "The boy that always plays in the garden, the one that is out there now."

"Well, if y' must know, Ayden is me son," he smiled and glanced out at the boy playing with the golden retriever in the garden below her window.

"Where is his mother?" she blurted out before she could stop herself.

"Me love," he sighed with exasperation. "She is gone."

"Oh. I'm sorry," she muttered, swallowing hard. "When?"

His face hardened, and he turned from her. "A while," he said with a tone of finality.

Meghan realized that she should stop pushing and glanced out the window, watching the small boy. He ran up to the caterers and helped carry a chair to the large canopy that was set up on the edge of the house.

"He is a handsome little boy," she commented, almost to herself.

"Aye, he is," Liam admitted proudly as he moved in behind her.

She smiled softly and tried to move around him, but he blocked her path. His hands slid around her back, pulling her towards him again, and he gently kissed her. She kept her eyes closed trying to see Declan; she wanted to go home so badly, she was willing to let this man touch her.

Not sensing any resistance from her, he scooped her up in his arms and carried her to the bed, but her eyes abruptly opened, however, when she felt the bed underneath her and him on top. She gasped and pushed at him as he leaned towards her, his pale blue eyes intent on her.

"Stop it!" she shrieked as she hit at him, realizing she wasn't as willing to let him touch her as she thought.

He looked down at her with a half grin on his broad face. She could see the glimmer of his teeth through the short golden beard. "So this is how y' are going to be," he said, pushing himself off her.

"What do you mean by that?" she snapped, feeling her fight returning to her.

"You're going to be a tease."

"No. I'm just not ready. My husband just died and I . . ." She stopped and pushed herself to the other side of the bed as far away from him as she could get.

"Y' feel like you're being unfaithful?" he asked, with an amazing sensitivity.

"Yes."

"Well, don't y' worry, I will honour your feelings until our wedding night," he said as he turned to leave the room.

"Liam," she blurted out.

"Aye."

"Could I go outside? I need some fresh air."

He looked at her with an amused look. "Y' don't give up, do y'?"

"It's just that I haven't been outside for weeks," she pleaded.

He eyed her for a moment, then began to smile. "Aye. I will take y' outside for some air, but if y' try to bolt, then y' won't be allowed out again."

"Okay. I promise," she said, realizing that her best chance at freedom was to gain his trust.

"I'll get y' a coat. It is quite nippy out today."

Within minutes, he was back with a beautiful blue ruana made from hearty wool. It had a full hood, lined with velvet, and the neckline clasped with a silver Celtic knot hook. He dropped it on the bed and turned to leave the room.

"I'll be back in five minutes to fetch y'."

She smiled at him graciously, relieved that he wasn't planning on staying while she changed. She slipped into a red dress with a small-flowered pattern that tied up the front of the snug bodes. It was quite long and covered most of her lower legs, which suited her fine. "The less he can see of me the better," she mumbled.

She heard a knock on the door, and it flung open, exposing the short stocky man standing in the hall.

"Mrs. Montgomery, y' are to come with me. I will take y' to O'Brien," Murphy grumbled, with no expression on his face.

Meghan slipped on her cloak and followed the balding man out into the hall. He grabbed her by the arm, causing her to flinch. With a scowl towards her, he continued to pull her down the hall. He spoke not a word to her all the way to their destination, which suited her fine since she had no interest in making small talk with him either.

The back patio was surrounded on three sides by flowerbeds and on the far edge, rows of hedges edged the cobblestone sitting area.

"Miss Meghan," Tomas called as he ran over to her with great delight that she was out of the room. "Y' were good?"

"Yes, apparently," Meghan smiled at the excited man, as his pale blue eyes sparkled underneath his dark brows.

"Miss Meghan, look what I painted today." He held up a painting of a wren sitting on the hedge in the garden.

"That's beautiful, Tomas." Meghan's smile was genuine when her eyes settled back on Tomas.

"I know. I am going to sell me paintings and make some money to buy y' a present."

"That's very nice, Tomas, but you don't have to buy me anything."

"I want to. You're me friend," Tomas said, with exhilaration building on his face.

"Don't worry about it, lady. This retard won't be able to sell that crap."

Meghan's arm swung up, and it came crashing down on the round face with a force she didn't know she had. "Don't you talk about him that way!"

Murphy turned to her and eyed her up and down from under his overgrown brows.

"You'll make a fine mistress of the manor," Murphy grumbled with a smirk as he took a threatening step towards her.

As Meghan backed away around the corner of the manor, Murphy slowly moved towards her and thrust up his stubby hand towards her face. Meghan jumped back out of the reach of his hand, but backed into a large object. A muscular arm came from behind her, and the large hand gripped the fleshy arm heading for her head. She turned suddenly to find Liam standing up against her, with his arm extended around her.

He raised a brow at the aggressive man. "Murphy, don't ever lay your hand on her again," Liam ordered with a nod before the man turned, disappearing into the building, unwilling to face Liam's wrath.

"I thought y' promised y' wouldn't try to bolt?" Liam smirked, gripping her arm.

"I wasn't, I just didn't want him touching me!" Meghan snapped, rather annoyed that these men kept groping at her.

He smiled at her softly. "Thank y' for defending me brother and don't y' be worrying about him. He'll be dealt with."

"Well, I hope so. He shouldn't talk about Tomas that way," Meghan grumbled.

"Y' really care about Tomas, don't y'?" Liam smiled and rested his hand against her cheek.

"Yes, he is a lovely person," Meghan mumbled, pulled away, and moved over to Tomas, hoping to console him after the mean-hearted comment from Murphy.

Liam watched Meghan softly talking and smiling at Tomas, her delicate hand resting on his shoulder in an affectionate manner. He was realizing that she did care about his brother, and it brought hope to him that maybe in time she would grow to love him as well; then there would be no need to keep her locked up in her room.

"Meghan, come with me," Liam ordered gently as he took her by the arm, led her to the table, pulling out the chair for her.

"Well, at least, you have some manners," Meghan said sharply as she dropped to the chair, flipping her cloak up to avoid sitting on it.

"If y' give me a chance, you'll see I'm not the awful man y' think I am." Liam gave her a sidelong glance.

Meghan grunted at him but was unable to control the smile at the corners of her mouth.

"I had some tea brought down for y'." Liam waved his hand towards the white ceramic tea pot and the matching cups.

"Thank you." Meghan tried to be polite. The feeling to run was overwhelming, but what Paddy had said stuck in her mind. *A windy day is not the day for thatching.* She began to smile at the remembrance of how Declan made fun of his father's Irish sayings when they were visiting his parents in Boston.

Liam noticed her smiling and tilted his head towards her.

"I hope that smile means that y' have decided to behave yourself?" he said, half grinning at her.

"Yes," she mumbled. For now, she thought to herself. Her trip to Boston seemed so long ago now, but she couldn't help but agree with Katie that coming to Ireland was a dangerous mistake. Katie must have known about the decree, the estate and Declan's desire to regain the title of Earl of Briarwood. That must be why she was so against their marriage.

"Good." Liam poured her a cup of tea and watched her glance around at the grounds.

Meghan was trying to survey the grounds to find the best way to get off the property when she found the right time to leave. She looked down the path through the autumn hedge and then across the fields.

Liam was talking about something that she was not paying much attention to, since she had her own thoughts going through her head. She would glance back at him every moment or so and flash a polite smile.

After about half an hour of this behaviour, Liam got up and slid in behind her. He brushed her hair off her shoulder and placed his hand on her cloak, pulling it over slightly, exposing her lower neck and shoulder. His head dropped to the nape of her neck, and his lips rubbed against her skin, causing her to grimace at his touch. However, she didn't move, but her eyes closed tightly, trying to block out what he was doing.

Liam lifted his head and slipped his hand down her shoulder towards her breasts, causing Meghan to jerk forward and jump to her feet, sending the table top over end and the refreshments smashing to the ground. She swung around with her hand raised towards his face, but as usual, he grabbed hold of her wrist with his razor sharp reflexes and held it tightly to the side of her.

"Y' are going to have to stop trying to slap me! I find it very unappealing," Liam laughed.

"I don't give a damn what you find unappealing!" Meghan growled, trying to pull her arm away from him.

Liam stared at her with pleasure. "The more y' fight me, the more it makes me want y'." He grabbed the back of her head and yanked her towards him. His lips were around her mouth like a suction cup as she struggled to free herself. He released her hand, allowing her to hit at his arms and chest. After a few blows, he pulled her close to him and ran his hand down her back to her bottom, gave it a slap, then pushed her away from him with slight force. Meghan stumbled backwards but braced herself on the chair.

"Y' like it better when I'm gentle with y', don't y'?" He winked.

Meghan raised her hand to slap him, but thought better of it and lowered it to her side and sighed. She could feel all the fight she had left abandoning her. Liam smiled smugly and turned to the mess she had created.

"Y' are a destructive thing, are y' not?" Liam commented as he shook his head at the shattered tea set.

Meghan did not respond; she stood quietly looking at him with little expression on her face. What was she going to do? He wasn't going to let her out of his sight until the wedding, and she couldn't marry him.

"Liam, I told y' to control her. What the hell is she doing out here with guests coming in an hour?" The hoarse voice filled the air.

Meghan swung around to the voice and began to back away as Fergus headed towards her. She swallowed hard as his long bony hand reached for her arm. She jumped back, knocking into Liam but managed to avoid the old man's touch. Liam's arm slid around her waist, and she turned abruptly, so she was pressed right up against him, her face buried in his chest.

"Don't let him touch me," Meghan begged, wrapping her arms around Liam's ribs, feeling safer with him than the father.

Liam kissed the top of her head and lifted his face towards his father. "Da, I told y' to leave her alone. She is going to be me wife, and I won't have y' disturbing her."

"Y' are so blinded by this girl that y' can't see what's happening," Fergus began warningly. "She will run the first chance she gets, don't fool yourself about that." Fergus glared at Meghan, who was still pressed firmly against Liam's chest.

"Da, this is really no concern of yours. Y' told me that I must marry her, and that's what I will do. So I suggest y' stay out of it."

"Girl," Fergus said sharply. "Look at me."

Meghan made no attempt to move but Liam pried her loose and turned her towards his father. She inadvertently took a step backwards stumbling into Liam once again.

"Me love, calm down," Liam said softly, gripping her shoulders.

"Let this be a warning to y', girl," Fergus snorted and took a step towards her. "If y' do anything that causes me a minute's worry, I will kill y' meself. Decree or no."

Meghan stared at him, unsure what to say. "If you kill me, you . . ."

"Me love," Liam's voice was strong and hard in her ear. "I suggest y' don't push him. I can't protect y' every minute of the day."

Meghan shuddered slightly at his comment but kept her eyes focused on Fergus. His face was hard and evil as he watched her struggle with what to do next.

"Y' have become more trouble than you're worth, but me boy here seems to have taken a fancy to y', but we could always accomplish our goal with your daughter."

"No, you leave her alone, you disgusting bastard," Meghan screamed.

Fergus's bony hand slammed across Meghan's face with a driving force. "Don't y' ever talk to me like that again."

"Da!" Liam snorted as he turned her in his arms and glanced down at her tear-filled eyes.

Meghan was fighting hard to stay calm but was losing the battle as the thought of Fergus hurting Caelan overpowered her common senses. She swung around suddenly in Liam's arms and lunged forward towards the old man, knocking him off balance. Fergus landed on the ground with a thud, and Meghan fell on top of him swinging her fists at his head.

"You bastard, I'll kill you before you touch my daughter," Meghan repeated a couple of times before she felt Liam's large hands gripping her arms and yanking her from his father.

"Damn," Liam said, with slight amazement. "You're a wild lass," he muttered, placing her behind his large frame. "Da." His hand lowered towards his father who was now sitting up trying to regain his composure.

Fergus's face quickly turned from shock to rage when he heard muffled laughter coming from the edge of the patio. The two men seemed somewhat amused at the attack, but quickly quieted when they noticed Fergus's gaze on them.

"Take her back to the turret!" Fergus snorted and gripped Liam's hand for assistance in standing.

Meghan panicked at that, turned and ran towards the row of hedges. Liam snorted and turned on his heels and darted after her, catching her easily before she made it off the patio.

"Meghan," Liam grunted pulling her to a stop.

"Let go. I'm not going in that room again," Meghan shrieked as he pulled her back towards him. "Please, Liam, I can't, I'll behave."

"No, me love," Liam said calmly. "You're not. I will deal with me da, but I suggest y' don't try attacking him again." He could not control his smile, he found her so entertaining. "I do have to admit, though, y' have more courage than any man I know."

"Why?" Meghan questioned, her voice shaking as much as her body.

"In all me years, I have never seen anyone attack me da," he laughed slightly. "I haven't even had the courage to physically attack him."

"Oh," Meghan muttered, directing her gaze on Fergus, who was standing with two men, waving his arms furiously in her direction. "Liam." Her voice trembled slightly.

"Aye, me love." Liam followed her gaze, then pulled her tightly into his arms. "Don't be worrying. He'll not harm y' or your daughter as long as I'm around."

"Thank you," Meghan sniffed as his arms tightened around her, holding her hostage to his chest.

Liam glanced down at her tear-stained face and a slight grin filled his lips as they headed towards hers with determination. As they landed on hers, her eyes caught sight of Fergus, and she decided at that minute that her best bet to protect herself and Caelan was give into Liam. With Declan and Fabrizio dead, her only chance of survival lay with Liam.

She felt Liam pressing hard against her as she returned his kiss. Her eyes were glazing over with disgust, but she did not pull away, allowing him to kiss her with abandon. She noticed Fergus move away from them as they kissed, but her eyes were drawn to something in the hedge; it appeared to be the dark grey eyes of Declan peering through the browning leaves of the hedge. A slight gasp exited her, and her eyes blinked frantically, trying to focus, but her movement caused Liam to halt his kiss.

He glanced around the area noticing his father's absence and assumed that is what caused her reaction. A slight smile grew across his lips as he eyed her with interest. "What is upsetting y', me love?"

"Nothing," Meghan blurted out, her eyes glancing over his shoulder and the empty hole in the hedge. "I was just pleased to see your father leave."

"Were y' now?" Liam's lips headed towards her again. "I guess he felt we needed some privacy."

Meghan jerked from the comment and forced calmness into her voice. "Yes, why don't you go get us some tea, and we can have . . ." His finger landed on her lips, halting her comment.

"Nice try," Liam muttered, his brows crumpling slightly. "Do y' think that I'm a moron? You're not being left alone out here to escape."

"I wasn't going to escape," Meghan said as calmly and sweetly as she could. "I . . . well." She bit her bottom lip, trying to find the right words. "Other than your father's presence, well, I am actually starting to enjoy it here. You know with Tomas, he is very good company, and I care for him a lot and . . . ," she was rambling out of control, but he stayed quiet and listened. "And well, I have become . . ." She stopped and rested her hands on his face. Her stomach began to churn at the thought of what she was doing. "And well, I am finding myself, well, you are very attractive, and I . . ." She stopped, unable to say anymore.

"Are y' saying that y' want to stay with me and be me wife?" Liam questioned, an excited grin filling his lips.

Meghan forced a smile and nodded, unable to respond. Liam laughed and pressed his lips against her with a driving force.

"I knew y' would come around if I gave y' time," he grinned as he lifted his lips from her.

"Liam," Meghan blurted out. "Once we are married, can we go back to the States to get Caelan?"

"Aye, me love, I wouldn't want her growing up without parents." Liam's voice was surprisingly caring. "Cheer up. I promise y' will have a nice life here. I'll be very gentle with y'," he smiled smugly and led her back towards the house.

By the time they returned to her room, she was at the point of emotional exhaustion. She was terrified that her mind was playing tricks on her, and she could feel her life slipping away.

"Do y' feel better now that y' have had some fresh air?" Liam smiled, softly kissing her nose.

"Yes." She moved towards the window and watched the activity below.

"I'm having some company over this afternoon, so I won't be back to see y' until tonight. I hope y' don't get lonely," he smirked as he moved towards her. His hand quickly moved onto her face, and he looked into her eyes. "Meghan I do care for y'. It won't be a loveless marriage." He bent down and kissed her softly on the lips, then turned towards the door. When he looked back at her, a large smile filled his face. "And don't y' be worrying about me lovemaking either. I'll bring a smile to that pretty face."

The door slammed behind him, and once she was sure he was gone, she tugged on the door knob, but he had locked her in again. Despair engulfed her as her body slid down the door until her bottom hit the cold tiled floor. She covered her face with her hands and cried as she had never cried before.

CHAPTER THIRTY-TWO

Meghan had been sitting by the door, crying for a short time when she heard activity outside in the hall. Thank goodness, Tomas had come to see her; she needed to hear his cheerful voice.

"Tomas, is that you?" she called through the door, but he did not answer.

Panic surged through her that it was Fergus, and she scanned the room, looking for a hiding place, deciding that behind the dresser was her best bet. Why had she called out to Tomas? Now whoever was at the door knew she was inside. Her terrified eyes watched the doorknob moving back and forth as someone was trying to gain entry.

"Boo, are you in here?" The deep voice asked, the dark brown eyes peering in through the small opening.

"Fabrizio!" Meghan shrieked and stumbled to her feet.

"Meggie!" A loud panicked voice blurted out from behind Fabrizio, and the large figure bolted across the room.

Meghan's emotions exploded, and she began to back away as the thought of what she had learned since her arrival at the castle became clear in her mind. Declan stopped suddenly as he watched her cowering up against the wall, terror shooting from her eyes.

"Meggie, it's me," Declan blurted out, his voice cracking with worry. "What's wrong?"

She bit her bottom lip, her eyes darting from him to Fabrizio. "You want to kill me?"

"What?" Declan gasped moving towards her, his hand outstretched. "Meggie, y' know I would never hurt y'. I love y'." He felt his stomach churning, wondering what ideas O'Brien had filled her head with over the past few weeks.

"I know," Meghan muttered. "I know that you married me to become more powerful than Liam."

"Freckles," Declan whispered, his voice soft and concerned. "I married y' because I love y', that's all that matters right now." His voice was becoming slightly panicked. "We have to leave before someone finds us."

"Meghan, he's right, we need to go," Fabrizio said firmly, glancing down the hall.

"I . . . I don't know if I can trust you," Meghan muttered, her eyes glazing over with obvious pain and confusion. Her heart was telling her to go to him, but her mind was telling her that he was a danger to her.

"Well, you don't have any choice at the moment!" Declan growled. "It's me or him."

Her eyes darted around the room, and she realized that she did not have any choice at the moment. At least, Declan would take her home, and then she could decide what to do about her sham of a marriage.

"All right." Meghan reached her trembling hand towards his outstretched hand.

His fingers clutched hers with slight force, and he pulled her towards him crushing her up against his chest. Her body was stiff and unwelcoming, but she stayed pressed against him as he stroked her hair down her back.

"Let's go," Fabrizio whispered fiercely. "We don't have much time."

Declan nodded and pulled Meghan towards the door.

"I will make sure it's clear," Fabrizio whispered and quietly moved down the stairs and peered in both directions.

Fabrizio waved; then they quickly moved down the hall. Fabrizio was giving Declan bizarre hand signals all the way out of the castle that Meghan had no understanding of, but Declan seemed to comprehend them. The two men crept with stealth across the grounds like cats on the hunt. Meghan was following behind them, trying to be as quiet as she could, but she was tripping over her feet in her panic.

Meghan was startled by a large orange tabby that jumped out of a shrub as they moved down a set of steps near the back of the garden. She jumped back and knocked over a large flowerpot that crashed to the ground with a horrendous bang. Declan swung around and glared at her freezing her in place.

"Bloody hell, Meggie, be careful!" Declan scolded, his dark brows crumpling with annoyance.

"Sorry," she sniffed as he propelled her towards the hedges.

"Miss Meghan, where are y' going?" Tomas questioned, popping up from behind the hedge, his paintbrush in his hand.

"Tomas," Meghan blurted out, her eyes scanning the area for Liam.

"Is that man hurting y'?" Tomas's stout body moved towards them threateningly.

"No, he's helping me. He's taking me back to my daughter."

"To Caelan?"

"Yes, Caelan, remember I told you about her." Meghan could feel her panic rising. She knew how much Tomas worshiped Liam, and she wasn't sure how he was going to react.

"Meggie, we have to go," Declan ordered, tugging on her arm.

"Are y' coming back?" The complete expression of sorrow that filled Tomas's eyes caused a pang of sadness to shoot through her. She knew that she was the only person in the castle that paid him any quality attention.

"No, Tomas, please don't tell," Meghan begged, not wanting to lie to him. With his mental development, he would spend the rest of his life waiting for her to come back if she told him she would.

"Y' don't like Liam, do y'?" Tomas commented, with surprising understanding.

"Tomas, I just want to get back to Caelan." Meghan's voice was sharper than she intended. She needed to get him to understand before he alerted the entire castle to her escape.

"Okay, Miss Meghan. I won't tell Liam, but I want to give y' something," Tomas said, reaching into the pocket of his overalls. "I know how much y' wanted this back." He handed her the silver locket. "I was going to give it to you tonight."

Meghan's eyes filled with tears as she held it in her hands. "Thank you, Tomas," she said as she leaned over and kissed his cheek.

"Meggie, come on," Declan snapped, tugging on her arm. "Someone's coming."

"Goodbye, Tomas. Keep up your painting. You are wonderful at it."

"Thank you, Miss Meghan," Tomas yelled after her as she ran with Declan towards the hedge.

Declan did not let go of her hand until they were safely concealed in the shrubs, then he turned and glared at her.

"His yelling is going to get us caught," Declan growled, his jealousy bubbling to the surface. She had developed feelings for members of this family and that infuriated him.

"How did you expect to get away from him?" Meghan snarled through her teeth. "He gave me my locket back," she whispered, glancing down at the silver locket, her only link to her heritage.

Before Declan could comment, Fabrizio's hand landed on his shoulder warningly. Fabrizio could see the change in Meghan and was not sure provoking her would serve any purpose other than get them caught. She obviously had developed relationships, and the way she was clinging to Liam earlier, he was not sure if she wouldn't prefer to stay at the castle.

Meghan gasped when two men appeared from the far side of the building and glanced from the shattered pot to Tomas. Declan covered her mouth with his hand, his brow flickering with annoyance. When his angry smoky eyes returned to the men, they were interrogating Tomas.

"Tomas, did y' do this?" The tall sinewy man growled, his hand smacking across the back of Tomas's head.

Tomas gripped the back of his head, a look of sorrow crossing his childlike face. "No."

"Then who did? And who were y' yelling at just before we got here? Your father is going to be furious if y' have let those neighbour children play here again."

"Liam said it was all right if they come and play with Aiden." Tomas defended himself, completely forgetting about Meghan and the two strange men.

Meghan held her breath praying that Tomas would not give them away. "They have distracted him, he might blurt something out." Her voice was barely audible as she tugged on Declan's shirt. "He is like a small child."

Declan eyed her sidelong, then returned his gaze to Tomas and the angry men.

The heavy man shook his head and kicked at the broken vase. "Y' know your brother will be angry about theses flowers. He had them planted for that damn woman."

The thin man laughed and bent down to pick up the pieces. "Aye, I have never seen him fuss over things before. He even made me wash down the patio this afternoon before the princess came down for tea."

Meghan flinched as Declan's grip tightened around her hand.

"Liam loves Miss Meghan," Tomas muttered and glanced towards the hedge that they were hiding behind. "He is going to be so sad when he finds out."

"Finds out what?" The stout man snorted, his gaze firm on Tomas.

"Nothing." Tomas flustered and stumbled away towards the castle.

"Tomas, y' idiot, get back here and tell me what y' meant." The man gripped Tomas by the arm and smacked him across the back of the head a few times.

Meghan felt her heart sink, knowing that they would beat the truth out of him, and she began to stand. Declan yanked her arm pulling her to his side.

"Meggie, what are y' doing?" he growled.

"They will hurt him," she sniffed, her eyes switching back and forth from Declan to Tomas.

"So?" Declan had no compassion for any member of the O'Brien, and his lack of caring enraged Meghan.

"Please stop hitting me," Tomas begged, trying to shelter his head with his canvas. "It hurts."

Fabrizio gripped Declan's arm and bobbed his head towards the direction they were originally heading. It was time to leave whether they were spotted or not. The horses were only a hundred feet away, hidden in the trees.

Declan nodded and yanked on Meghan's arm, drawing her attention back to him. Her eyes were cold and distant when she gazed at him, and it stabbed at his heart. He should have expected no different from her that she would develop feeling for the kind man who had the misfortune of being born an O'Brien. He seemed mentally no older than an eight-year-old and Declan had no right judging him so brutally.

As Fabrizio crept to the edge of the hedge, Declan handed Meghan over to him. "Fabrizio, take her, I'll cover y'."

Fabrizio eyed him narrowly, annoyed he was altering the plans. "We can make it to the horses. We don't want to attract too much attention."

"Aye, I won't," Declan assured him, glancing back at Tomas; he was crumpling to the ground as the two men repeatedly struck him.

"Go." Once Fabrizio and Meghan disappeared around a row of hedges, Declan jumped to his feet. "Leave the lad alone. Do y' feel mighty beating on someone so defenceless?"

Both men stopped their attack and stared at Declan with shock. Their eyes settled on each other, then simultaneously they bolted towards him.

Declan was around the corner and on Meghan's heels before the two men even arrived at the hedges. Declan gripped her hand and propelled her behind him. They had almost made it to the horses when a tall sinewy man jumped out from a row of hedges in their path. Declan abruptly stopped, and Meghan smashed into his back, unable to stop as quickly.

Declan's stance was aggressive as he eyed the man trying to decide what action to take. He sensed movement behind him, and he spun surveying the approaching men. Three, those odds were a little out of balance, and Meghan was certainly going to be no help. Fabrizio had disappeared into a glade of trees at the edge of the cliffs not noticing the men surrounding Meghan and Declan, so he was on his own.

"Fabs, I could use some help here," Declan said calmly as he steadied himself for the attack as the men approached.

The sinewy man lunged at Declan, and without warning, Declan's elbow swung up, clipping the sinewy man in the chin, sending him flying backwards to the ground. Declan spun, gripping Meghan by the arm and shoving her behind a hedge, sending her crashing to the ground.

The lean man arrived first, lunging at Declan as his back was turned, but Declan's leg swung around and crashed into the man's ribs, which caused him to collapse to the ground, holding his chest.

The stout man pulled out his gun as he struggled towards Declan, his short stubbly legs not strong enough to carry the heavy body at great speeds. When the man got within ten feet, Declan took two steps towards him and lunged into the air, his foot heading towards the man's chest. When he made impact, the stout man collapsed to the ground with Declan landing on top.

Declan, however, was on his feet before the sinewy man grabbed him from behind, the muzzle of his gun pressed against Declan's head. The stocky man smirked as he regained his bearings and moved in front of Declan, his eyes filled with disdain.

"Mr. O'Brien isn't going to appreciate y' stealing his wife," the man snorted through his dark beard.

"She's not his wife, she's mine," Declan snapped back, seemingly unaffected by the cold steel muzzle to his head.

"Shut up!" yelled the man as he struck Declan in the stomach.

"Declan!" Meghan shrieked as she jumped to her feet and moved towards him.

"Meggie, get back!" Declan yelled as the third punch made its impact.

The stocky man turned towards Meghan with a grin growing across his face. "Come here, and no one will get hurt."

"Meggie, stay where y' are," Declan shouted as he leaned back on the man that was holding him from behind, his feet left the ground and smacked against the man's back while he was turned towards Meghan, knocking him to the ground. Declan then suddenly jerked forwards, flipping the man behind him over his back to the ground. The lean man was on his feet and heading towards Declan, but his back was turned. Meghan grabbed a thick stick that was lying on the ground, and slammed it across the man's pimpled face, just before he reached Declan, sending him crashing to the ground.

"Shit, Monty, you're a one-man demolition team," Fabrizio joked, heading towards them with three horses.

"I could have used a little help," Declan snorted, but then noticed the man lying on the ground at his feet, his face covered in blood. His eyes settled on Meghan with surprise. "Nicely done Meggie." He smiled and grabbed her by the arm and dragging her towards Fabrizio. "Get up, Meggie," he ordered, pushing her towards one of the horses.

"Horses, what's wrong with a car?" Meghan questioned, looking rather concerned.

"Be quiet and get on, we don't have time to argue," Declan snapped at her.

Meghan eyed him with annoyance but did what he said and mounted the chestnut mare. His attention never left Fabrizio until they finished discussing the direction to take. She could feel the damp sea air surrounding her and the aroma of salt filling her nose with the familiar smell of the beaches back home and she started to ache for Caelan again.

"Declan, how is Caelan?"

"She's fine. I talked with her yesterday. She told me to tell y' that Nat is letting her walk her foal," he told her as they quickly galloped away from the castle.

"I hope he's helping her. She could get hurt," she blurted out.

"I'm sure he is, Freckles. Don't be worrying about that. We have enough to worry about right now." Declan couldn't help but smile, some things never change; she was still so high-strung.

"Oh, how is Colton? That man hit him with the gun."

"He's fine," Declan grumbled, a little annoyed that she was thinking about Colton. He suspected something had happened between Meghan and Colton that day she disappeared, and looking into her eyes, he could see it.

They rode for over two hours before they reached the top of the hill from where they could see the whole countryside for miles in each direction.

"We should be safe here until dark," Fabrizio muttered, then dismounted and tethered his bay gelding to a large aspen.

Declan was off his horse and over to where Meghan had come to a stop instantaneously. "Are y' okay?" He lifted her off her mare and lowered her gently to the ground.

"Yes," Meghan muttered, her gaze on him slightly hostile.

"What's wrong?" Declan grumbled, his annoyance rising.

"Nothing," Meghan blurted out and moved over towards a pile of rocks that were a few feet away. She needed to put some distance between them before she said something she would regret.

"All right, we are going to clear this up," Declan said, firmly gripping her arm as she turned away from him.

She turned on him, the pain evident in her eyes. "Why? Why would you do something like this to me?"

"Freckles, I'm sorry I didn't tell you, but I swear to y' that I married y' because I loved y'. The fact that y' were the heir to the land had nothing to do with it."

"So you did know!" she snarled and pulled at her arm he was still gripping tightly.

"Yes," Declan admitted softly, his eyes lowering to the ground. She knew now, he had to think fast to explain his behaviour.

"Since when?" Meghan questioned with concern, the tension in her building.

"Since I was young," he said with slight shame. "I didn't want to tell y' that part because I had no intentions of making claim on the land," he lied.

"So you pursued me for the only purpose of marrying me and producing an heir so you could take my estate and title and find the sword?"

"No, not exactly. I don't believe the sword exists," he mumbled. "I fell in love with y', Freckles, I swear."

"Declan, tell me the truth!" Meghan growled as her hand brushed across her face, swabbing at the tears.

"I phoned me ma and told her that I was going to ask y' to marry me, and I thought that she would be happy, but instead, she freaked out. She told me that I was signing me death warrant, and I should get as far away from y' as possible."

Meghan buried her head in her hands. "You would have never married me if . . ." she sniffed and began to back away.

"Meggie, don't," Declan blurted out, grabbing her trembling hands. "I love y', I do."

She could feel his hand tensing around hers as she stared at him, unsure what to think. She did not want to believe that he only married her to gain control of the estate. He had more money than he needed, and he certainly did not seem to believe the story of the sword.

"Well, Liam claims to love me too, and I . . ." She blurted out almost cruelly. "He . . ." She stopped as Declan's face hardened.

"Meggie, do y' love him?"

She eyed him critically but did not answer. She felt the overpowering need to hurt him as badly as he hurt her.

"Meggie!" Declan snapped. "Tell me!"

"What does it matter?" Meghan said evenly.

"It matters because y' are me wife," he snarled. "I can't believe that you would betray me."

Anger surged through her like a bomb exploding deep in her soul. "Me? I guess you screwing Deirdre doesn't count. God, you are such a hypocrite."

"I didn't touch Deirdre, she disgusts me," he babbled, somewhat shocked from her comment. "I would never do that to y'."

"Then why were you spending so much time with her? I'm not an idiot. I could feel you pulling away from me," Meghan sniffed and sat down on the grassy hillside, pushing away the small rocks near her legs.

"Oh, Meggie," Declan sighed and dropped to the ground by her side. "I was trying to get information from her about what Liam was up to."

A slight tremble ran down Meghan's spine when he laid his arm around her shoulder. "Please believe me. I don't know what more to say."

"There is nothing more to say, is there?" Meghan muttered and jumped to her feet. "When we get back home—"

"Don't!" He was on his feet and had hold of her arm before she could finish her sentence. His worst fears were filling his head that she had fallen in love with O'Brien during her captivity at the castle. He could not help but recall how she clung to him on the patio; she felt safe with that horrible man, that was evident, and now her trust in him was broken.

"Declan, please let go," Meghan muttered, tugging at her arm.

"Fine," he blurted out as his pride took hold. "If you want to be with O'Brien, I won't stop y'. I'm sorry we took y' from your love nest."

Meghan's eyes narrowed as she stared at him with amazement. "I don't want to be with him. What the hell is wrong with you? I don't want to be with either of you. I will not be the prize in the power struggle you two seem to be having."

His hand released her arm more forcefully than she appreciated, and he turned and stormed over to the rock and dropped down to the ground with rage exploding from every fibre in him.

Meghan turned and ran towards a clump of aspens, not noticing Fabrizio sitting under a tree, trying to avoid their fight. His hand reached up, gripping her arm, pulled her down beside him on the heather.

"Meghan, don't be mad at him. He's just upset." Fabrizio soothed, completely disillusioned from the whole meltdown of Meghan and Declan's relationship. Meghan loved Declan so deeply that she always held out hope that he would come back to her. If a love that deep can't endure, then what love can? Fabrizio had grown up in a shattered family; his father left when he was small, and his mother went from one man to another. Fabrizio was left to raise his little brothers, Tony and Nick. Declan's love for Meghan filled Fabrizio with hope that he too could find such a love but now even Declan could not keep his life from falling apart, he too was throwing it away. Maybe his relationship with Cassie would not last either. He wasn't even sure if he loved her completely. His feeling for Meghan was still so strong.

Meghan stared at Fabrizio momentarily, her emotions tangled in a mass of fear, anger, and sorrow. "Fabrizio, I trusted him. I believed that he loved me."

"He does, Boo," Fabrizio soothed, his voice low and sincere. "I have known him for a long time, and I know without a doubt that he loves you with all his heart." It was killing him to push her back towards Declan. Maybe this was his chance again.

She shook her head and wiped at her blurry eyes. "I don't believe it."

"You don't or you won't?" Fabrizio questioned, his tone seemingly annoyed. "Meghan, don't push him away. He loves you, but he is also very arrogant, and I don't know how much his ego will take. He already believes you slept with O'Brien."

"I didn't," she blurted out. "I . . ."

"Shh," Fabrizio sighed, he was actually pleased to hear her admit that. The thought of her in bed with that despicable man made his skin crawl. His feelings for her were still so strong. "Boo, he risked both our lives going into that castle to get you when we did. I wanted to wait until the party was under way, but he was terrified that O'Brien was taking you back to your room to . . . Well, after the kissing on the patio, he figured . . ."

"I know what he figured," Meghan grumbled. "That is exactly what I was trying to do. I wanted Liam to think I cared for him so he would stop locking me in that room and I could get back to Caelan."

Fabrizio nodded, his hand smoothing down the back of her hair. "It's just when he saw you kissing O'Brien . . ."

"What did he expect me to do? I thought he was dead, and I needed to get home." Meghan stifled a sniff and wiped her eyes.

"I don't know, but I had to hold him back when he was watching. The look on his face was frightening. I've never seen him so enraged," Fabrizio whispered, wrapping his arm around her shoulder, pulling her up against his chest. She was trembling, and his heart ached for her. Why was Declan pushing her away after everything he went through to get her back? She loved Declan completely, that was obvious, and Fabrizio was finding it hard to suppress his hostility at Declan's stupidity. If she was his woman? Fabrizio shook his head; what was he thinking? She wasn't his woman, she was Declan's, and he needed to get them off this disruptive path. He loved her too much to see her in this much pain.

"We're not going to get through this," Meghan mumbled quietly to herself, but Fabrizio heard.

"Meghan, please don't think like that. You love him."

"I do, but I am having a hard time believing that he didn't just marry me to bond two-thirds of the triad," Meghan sniffed and wiped at her eyes.

"So you would rather believe O'Brien than Monty?" Fabrizio's voice was edged with anger; had she fallen in love with O'Brien? Would that mean that she would move here, and he would never see her again? "Meghan think about what you are saying."

Meghan cringed at that comment, wondering why she would choose to believe Liam, a kidnapping murderer over Declan, the man she loves with all her heart.

"You're right, Fabrizio, I have made a big mistake." She stood and brushed the dirt off the back of her floral red dress.

Fabrizio forced a smile and watched her moving towards Declan with caution. She belonged with Declan; he knew that she would not be happy with any other man.

"Declan," Meghan called quietly as she stopped in front of him, where he paced back and forth in front of a grouping of rocks. "I . . ."

She stopped when he turned his back on her, his face cold and distant. "We will get y' into town safely, then y' are on your own."

"What?" Meghan blurted out, quite startled by his comment.

"I have had enough. Y' were right. I just married y' to get at the land. Why else would I marry someone like y'?" Declan's voice was husky and painfully cruel as he turned his dark eyes on her.

Tears clouded her eyes as she processed what he said, and as it registered, her hand flew up slamming across his face with all the strength she had. "You bastard!"

Declan's eyes filled with surprise, and his hand ran across the impact sight, then without warning, he reached out, grabbed her by the arms, and shook her slightly. "Y' stupid bitch, I'm glad to be rid of y'." His eyes were locked on her tear-stained face as she tried to pull her arms loose.

The words became trapped behind the lump in her throat as total despair surged through her. She shook her head, trying to stop the terror running through her. "I hate you, why didn't you just leave me alone? I was happy. I had a nice life with Caelan and my friends." She sobbed, unable to complete her sentence. "I hate you!" She repeated.

"Good!" Declan snorted and released her arms, pushing her slightly away from him, and she stumbled backwards into Fabrizio, who was heading towards them to stop their destructive argument.

"Monty, stop it!" Fabrizio yelled, gripping Meghan around the waist to keep her from falling over. "What the hell is wrong with you?"

Declan glared at Fabrizio but said nothing as he turned his angry face away from them. He could feel his heart being ripped from his chest, but he knew that as long as they stayed together, she would be in danger. Maybe if he could get her to go back to the States, Liam would give up on his quest to possess her. The loss of her would be a price he would accept to ensure her safety.

Meghan was trembling terribly as Fabrizio wrapped his arm around her, allowing her to sob against his chest. Declan had moved away, unable to hear the sound of her crying over what he had said. The thought of hurting her was tearing him apart, but he needed to ensure her safety.

"Boo, come over here," Fabrizio sighed, pulling her towards the patch of heather. "You need some rest."

"No," she blurted out, pulled away from Fabrizio, and ran towards the tethered horses.

"Meghan, get back here!" Fabrizio yelled as she grabbed her mare and mounted quicker than he thought possible. He had forgotten how experienced she was around horses.

"Meggie, wait!" Declan snorted and darted towards the horse, grabbing onto the bridle.

His sudden actions spooked the mare, and she reared up a couple of times before she broke loose from Declan's grip. Once loose, she reared up once more, then bolted towards the trees, dislodging Meghan. Luckily, the heather cushioned her fall as she plummeted to the ground.

Declan was at her side instantaneously, his hands on her face, scanning her for damage. "Are y' hurt?"

"What do you care?" Meghan snorted and took a swing at his head, but his reflexes won out, and he had hold of her wrist before she made contact.

"Stop it," Declan growled, squeezing her arm tightly.

"Let go of me!" Meghan shrieked as tears exploded from her tortured eyes. "Please just let go."

"I will, if y' promise to stay put. We can't have y' taking off, putting all our lives in danger."

Meghan scowled at him and pulled at her arms once again, and this time, he released them, pushing her back down to the ground. "Stay there!"

Meghan's eyes were stinging from the tears, and her heart was aching as she lay with her head pressed up against the damp ground. Declan grunted and handed her saddlebag to her, and she begrudgingly tucked it under her tear-drenched head.

Fabrizio wandered up and rested his hand on Declan's shoulder as he hovered over Meghan seemingly to keep her from running off. "Monty, I'll stay with her. I think you need to calm down."

Declan nodded with agreement and disappeared in the trees on the far side of the clearing. Once out of sight, Fabrizio sat down beside her and sighed heavily, not knowing what to say to erase all the horrible things they said to each other.

"When he thought you were killed in the explosion," Fabrizio began explaining that night and the horror Declan went through.

The sun had completely set when Declan started to stir. He was groggy and somewhat dazed as he stumbled to his feet and looked down at Fabrizio who was lying beside him about twenty feet away from the destroyed cottage. He rubbed the back of his head and bent down to check Fabrizio's pulse, and he sighed with relief as he felt a pulse. He was just about the shake Fabrizio when the remembrance of what had happened came rushing back.

"Meggie!" Declan shrieked, turned, and gazed in shock at the pile of rubble. "Bloody hell," he screamed and darted over to the debris, throwing the shattered pieces of the cottage around, trying to find her.

"Meggie, where are y'? Meggie!" Declan kept repeating as he threw one piece after another searching through the shattered cottage. His body was shaking with terror as he searched from one side to the other, and he was getting more frantic the longer it took.

"Monty, she's not here. She never was." Fabrizio staggered towards Declan, rubbing at his back.

"She is, I heard her calling me." Declan choked back a sob as he continued to dig through the debris.

"Monty, it was a trap. She wasn't here. Come on, let's get out of here."

"No, I can't leave her. She needs me, she trusted me with her life. I can't let her down."

"Monty, listen to me. She wasn't here, it was a recording of her voice. They wanted us in that house so they could blow us up. He doesn't want you around. We need to go."

"Fabrizio," Declan moaned, falling to his knees. "I can't live without her."

Declan crossed himself, clasped his hands together, and prayed. "Heavenly Father, please don't take her from me again. She is me heart and soul. Why would y' give her back to me only to take her away? Please don't take her from me again," Declan pleaded, his voice low and terrified.

"Monty, come on!" Fabrizio ordered, grabbed Declan by the arm, tugged him out of the debris, and led the numb man across the yard to their car.

Meghan sat quietly listening to Fabrizio's account of the events that night, and she couldn't help but wonder what had changed in Declan's heart. If he was truly devastated, then why did he tell her such horrible things?

She slowly closed her eyes and listened to the birds chirping around them and the rustling of the dying leaves as the wind gently moved through the trees. She had to stop the horrible thoughts her mind was determined to pursue, the torturous thoughts of how she had been gullible enough to believe that Declan loved her. Fabrizio's information was in stark contrast to Declan's present behaviour, and the way he was treating her now was all she could think about.

Fabrizio was running his fingers through her hair, pulling it back over her ear in steady soft movements, the feel of her skin pleasant to the touch. How fragile she seemed at the moment, her normal fire seemed to have been extinguished by Declan's cruel words. He had reduced her to the way she was after the shooting.

Declan's eyes stayed fixed on his friend as he cuddled with his wife. How he hated the sight of her in anyone's arms, including Fabrizio's. How safe she appeared wrapped in Fabrizio's strong arms! What the hell was happening, she was his woman, not Fabrizio's! Declan grunted and kicked a small rock, sending it flying into the brush.

Fabrizio caught the stricken expression on Declan's face and knew he needed to intervene. Once he heard Meghan's rhythmic breathing, he glanced down, her face was relaxed and quiet. Slowly lowering her to the ground, he cushioned her head with the saddlebag, then took out a blanket from the other side of the bag and covered her.

The sun was setting over the western horizon when Fabrizio approached Declan. The sun was dancing off Declan's ebony hair as he sat against a tree, his hands covering his face, the sadness very evident in him.

Fabrizio was completely agitated by Declan's behaviour, and he knew that he better settle himself or he would only manage to get Declan on the defensive.

"What are you doing?" Fabrizio questioned, forcing calmness into his tone.

"What do y' mean?" Declan asked in a short tone, his head lifting from his hands.

"I mean, why are you treating her that way? What did you expect her to do?" Fabrizio's voice protective and hostile.

"Well, I didn't expect her to jump into his bed!" Declan snarled, his emotions erupting to the surface. Had O'Brien touched her, taken her the way only he should? That thought tormented him.

"Monty! You know she didn't do that." Fabrizio shook his head, by the expression on Declan's face, he knew exactly what Declan thought.

"Do I?" Declan grumbled and glanced down at her sleeping body. "Fabs, the thought of that bastard touching her sickens me."

"She says she didn't have sex with him, and I believe her. Dammit, Monty, you know she is incapable of lying without it showing on her face. She is telling the truth."

"She was kissing him."

"She was trying to stay alive, why are you punishing her for that?"

Declan grimaced at the sight of Fabrizio's disapproving gaze. "Stay alive. That is the point. I knew what would happen if I married her and O'Brien found out. I knew that he would most likely come after her, and I still went ahead. I'm a selfish bastard, and I don't deserve to have her."

"Monty," Fabrizio piped in, interrupting his rambling. "You had no idea that he would go after her."

"Aye, I had a good idea that he would want her for himself. I just didn't expect him to try killing everyone in his way."

"Would he have killed her?" Fabrizio questioned with concern. "He seemed quite fond of her."

"That's what she thinks. He would have no problem killing her, and I'm sure once he got possession of the land, he would discard her immediately."

"Then why are you telling her to go back to him?" Fabrizio questioned, unsure of Declan's rationale.

"She won't, I know her well enough to know that she finds him repulsive, but she can't stay with me either. She will never be safe as long as we are together. O'Brien will always see us as a threat."

"Monty, what are you saying? You can't let her go. You love her."

"That's why I can't put her life in danger any longer. I shouldn't have married her, and I definitely shouldn't have brought her to Ireland." Declan shook his head sadly, then wandered away.

CHAPTER THIRTY-THREE

The sun was almost completely obscured by the western fields, setting the sky ablaze with orange and red streaks. A promise of a new magnificent day. A new day, a day to wash clean all the sorrow and pain this day had brought with it.

Declan's eyes never left Meghan's sleeping face as he perched on the rocks, his heart aching with worry that she would never forgive him for all the cruel things he said to her. As he watched, her peaceful face suddenly began to crumple with terror, and her body began to tremble.

"Declan, Declan!" Meghan screamed and sprang to a sitting position, looking around frantically, an expression of terror crossing her face.

Declan was at her side in seconds, cradling her in his arms before she could get off the ground. "Meggie, I'm right here."

"Oh," she shuddered looking at him, true fear in her eyes. "Please, don't hate me," she begged.

"I don't. I'm sorry that I acted that way. I didn't mean the things I said."

Her body was trembling as he held her, trying to think of some way to explain why he said the things he did. He knew that he hurt her terribly, but he had no choice, he needed to keep her and Caelan safe, and if the only way was having her hate him for the rest of his life, he would make that sacrifice.

"Meggie, it will be okay. Fabrizio and I will get y' home safely."

She abruptly pulled away from him as what he was saying took hold. "You meant what you said, that you shouldn't have married me, didn't you?"

His stomach dropped, and he forced down the lump that was exploding in his chest. "Aye."

Meghan jumped to her feet and stared down at him, her eyes glazing over with sorrow. "I understand. I'm sure we can get a quick divorce when we return."

He made a grab for her hand, but she turned and wandered over to the horse with the illusion of rummaging through the saddlebag.

"Meggie, we don't need to discuss this right now," Declan muttered as he watched her pulling her pants and a clean shirt from the pouch.

"If it's all right, I'm going to change out of this dress. I'm getting cold."

A slight smile curled his lips. "That's why I brought them."

"Thank you." Meghan's voice was soft as she ducked behind a clump of pine trees to change.

Declan's eyes followed her until she was completely out of his sight. It cut to the bone that she was sheltering herself as she changed, but he had to accept the fact that if he continued on the path to keep her safe, she would pull farther and farther away from him.

Once out of sight of Declan, Meghan leaned against a tree and let her emotions loose. He did not love her, after everything they went through to be together, all she sacrificed. Damn him, why did he need to ruin her life? Meghan wiped at her eyes and forced her pride to swell to the surface. If that is what he wanted, she was not going to give him the satisfaction of knowing how devastated she was. She too could be cold and detached.

"Did Rory tell you where I was?" Meghan questioned calmly as she trudged back through the bushes dressed in the pair of jeans and the red cotton shirt covered by the blue ruana that O'Brien had given her.

"No, I haven't seen Rory since he left Ireland," Declan muttered, an odd expression filling his face.

"He didn't leave Ireland." Meghan's voice was causal as she stuffed the dress into the saddlebag. "He lives at the castle."

"What?" Declan blurted out and moved towards her at a quick pace.

"I thought you knew. He is living with his dad and brothers," Meghan said coolly, almost with malice. "He was helping Liam convince me to marry him."

Declan's brow rose slightly, and he eyed her with interest. "Rory wanted you to marry O'Brien?"

Meghan nodded, turned away, and moved with purpose towards the rocks, not wanting to be too close to him. "Yes, our wedding was planned for two weeks." She pushed a loose strand of hair from her face and glanced back over her shoulder. "I guess Liam will be pleased that you don't want me any longer."

Declan stiffened with worry, his gaze settling on her oddly calm face. "What's that supposed to mean?"

Meghan shrugged, bent down, picked a little purple flower from the heather, and sniffed the fragrance deeply. "Nothing, I'm just saying that with you out of the way, it will make Liam's pursuit much easier."

"Meggie, y' aren't seriously considering going back to that mad man, are y'?" he snorted and gripped her arms, giving her a slight shake.

"Well, I don't really have a choice. He has made it perfectly clear that he plans on marrying me, and I can't fight him on my own," she muttered as his hands began to tighten around her upper arms. "And I have Caelan to consider. He promised me that she could come and live with us."

"Meggie!" Declan growled. "You are not going back to that man, and y' are definitely not putting me daughter anywhere near him."

He was now shaking her quite forcefully as panic surged through him.

"Declan, you're hurting me," she complained before he slammed her to the ground.

"You're not going anywhere near that man," Declan snorted and kneeled down in front of her, gripping her arms once again.

"What do you care?" Meghan blurted out cruelly, her eyes glazing over with sadness. "You don't want me, so I don't think you have any right to tell me what to do. I have to look after myself, and if I go back to Liam, I will."

"No!"

"Why, are you worried that he will gain too much control? Is that all you two think about is that damn piece of land. I know Liam and Fergus want it because they believe that the stupid sword is hidden there somewhere, but I don't understand what your need to have it is," Meghan growled, tugging at her arms that were still trapped in his large hands.

"I want it because it belongs to me family, and my descendants have the right to their legacy.

"A deadly legacy I'd say," Meghan blurted out. "That damn land will bring anyone who owns it nothing but heartache and death."

Declan snarled, jumped to his feet, and paced back and forth for a few minutes. "Meggie, I have decided not to divorce you," He blurted out calmly as if it was not an important comment. "Instead, we will stay married. That way O'Brien will not be able to steal from me what is rightfully mine."

Meghan bit her bottom lip as she stared at him, unsure what to say. She had no intentions of returning to Liam and only told Declan that to try to jolt him into realizing that he loved her, but instead, she seemed to have locked herself into a marriage with him and he apparently had no love for her whatsoever.

"No," she blurted out. "I will not stay in a loveless marriage with you. You have made it perfectly clear that you don't love me, and you never did."

"Meggie," he whispered as he bent down in front of her again. "I."

"Please let's not drag this out any longer. I think what I will do is . . ." She stopped, unsure what to do.

Declan rested his hand on her face, the pain in her eyes overwhelming him. He could not believe that he was hurting her so intensely. "Meggie, I'm so sorry."

Before she could respond, Fabrizio had moved towards them, looking quite anxious. "We better get moving, it's dark enough now, and if we want to get to the truck by morning, we need to leave now."

Declan nodded and jumped to his feet, lowering his hand towards Meghan. As his large hand engulfed hers, she felt a tugging at her heart that was so bitterly painful, she found it hard to control her fears.

The night was exceedingly dark and cold as they rode towards safety, no one speaking, no one breaking the deadly silence of the night. The dew was settling in Meghan's hair, and she was shivering from the bone-chilling dampness, but she stayed quiet, unsure if Declan would care or not.

She gazed over at Declan, her eyes drooping from exhaustion. Did he care, did he ever care, or had everything been a lie? How could she have been so stupid not to have known he was using her? Fabrizio warned her years earlier that Declan was not the man he claimed to be, that something else was going on, but she chose to ignore his warning. Fabrizio, the man that truly loved her, why had she pushed him away? Now he was pushing her towards Declan, had Fabrizio fallen prey to Declan's lies as well? She wasn't sure who she could trust. She needed to get home to Nathan.

Declan did not like the expression on her face as she gazed at him. What was she thinking? For the first time since he met her, he could not read her face. What had happened to her over the last month? Had she changed that much that she was a completely different person? A closed off, unreadable person. What hellish things had the O'Briens done to her to break her, to force her into submission? Liam obviously ingratiated himself into her trust, so it must have been the father. She seemed terrified of Fergus, cowering against Liam in complete fear.

Declan's gaze switched from her to the horizon, unable to see her face any longer. It was killing him.

Meghan fought back the tears and huddled further under her cloak, pulling the hood up around her head. She thought living with the O'Briens as Liam's wife was the worst thing that could ever happen to her, but she was wrong. Living with the knowledge that Declan didn't love her was far worse.

"How are you holding up, Boo?" Fabrizio questioned, his voice soft and slightly uncomfortable.

"I'm fine," Meghan claimed, trying to keep her teeth from chattering. She was freezing, but she was too proud to admit it to either of them.

Declan's gaze settled on her with disbelief, but he said nothing, his expression lifeless.

"How much longer is it until we get there?" Meghan questioned, directing her eyes on Fabrizio. "And where are we going?"

"We are going to a small inn to meet up with Cassie, then we will get the hell out of this country."

"Why is Cassie still here?" Meghan blurted out.

"She wouldn't leave until you were safe. She's a good friend to you, Meghan," Fabrizio smiled.

"She always has been," Meghan said softly. "I can always count on her."

Declan's brow rose slightly at the comment, but he continued to stay quiet. It had been over two hours since his last words, and Meghan was beginning to find his silence stifling. She sighed and focused on the rhythmic sound of the horse's hooves pounding against the damp ground.

As an hour passed, she felt her horse begin to stumble every few feet, as if slipping or tripping over something in its path. She stopped the mare and dismounted to examine the problem, but as the problem became evident, she began to worry.

"She's cut her leg," Meghan muttered, wondering if she had done the damage when she bolted into the trees earlier that night. "I can't ride her any longer. It's too much weight for her to carry."

Meghan grabbed the reins and began to walk towards the men and their mounts, but she did not stop, instead she continued walking in the direction they were heading. Declan grunted and rode up beside her and stared down at her while she continued to walk.

"Meggie, why don't y' ride with me?" Declan gestured his hand out towards her.

"I'm fine," Meghan said evenly, keeping her eyes focused on the horizon.

Declan grunted again and pulled his horse back a couple of paces behind her, allowing her to continue on her path. He decided to wait patiently until she tired, before he forced the issue.

To his amazement, she had been walking for over an hour before she slowed; she however did not stop. He caught up to her, and to his surprise; her face was crumpling with pain.

"Meggie?" Declan blurted out, jumping from his horse and gripping her arm. "What's wrong?"

"Nothing," Meghan blurted out, forcing calmness to her face.

"Something is wrong; you're as pale as a ghost." Declan muttered pulling her to a stop.

"I'm fine!" she argued. "I'm just a bit dizzy."

"You've done enough walking for tonight!" Declan grumbled and pulled her towards his horse. "You will ride."

"Declan!" Meghan complained, not wanting to give in to him, but she had to admit she was not welcoming the thought of walking any longer. She had sharp pains in her stomach, and the recollection of the sensation sent fear shooting through her.

"Meggie, just get up!" Declan ordered, quite worried with her colouring.

She nodded and climbed up onto the large black gelding, but as she straddled it, she began to crumple with pain.

"Meggie, what's wrong?" he questioned, gripping her leg to keep her from falling off.

"I have a pain in my stomach," she admitted as she wrapped her arm around the area in question. "I'm all right. I think I just pulled something."

"Hmm," Declan muttered, his hand gently stroking her leg with the gentleness she had felt from him so often in the past. "Do y' think y' can ride?"

"Yes." She nodded, her dark green eyes ablaze. Was she pregnant? Her timing couldn't be worse. If she was, how was Declan going to react? Did he even want another child now? What if it's a boy? Would the child that bonds two-thirds of the triad be a threat? Caelan was a threat, and they didn't seem bothered by her. Meghan shook her head trying to clear her thoughts. She had to push them to the back of her mind. She needed to get home and away from the O'Briens and their damn family feud.

Meghan stared at Declan, her heart breaking at the thought of not having him in her life. She could not understand why one minute he seemed to love her, then the next, he could be so distant. She sniffed and pulled the deep blue ruana hood over her head.

"Meggie, it will be okay," Declan whispered, a deep sigh exiting him. All he wanted to do was hold her in his arms and rewind the day.

As the pickup truck weaved down the road towards the inn, Declan closed his eyes and drifted off into overly needed sleep. Fabrizio was mumbling something to himself, and Meghan turned to him and smiled.

"Pardon?"

"I was just saying that they built this road as the donkey wandered."

"What?" Meghan started to laugh.

"It's so winding, why the hell didn't they just build it straight?"

Meghan grunted a laugh, turned her eyes to the front window, and stared out over the horizon. "I hope you know how much I appreciate you two coming to get me."

"I know, Boo, I would do anything for you." Fabrizio stopped before he said too much, how he wanted to make things right.

"Fabrizio?" Meghan glanced back at Fabrizio, her eyes glazed over. "What happened? I mean, what did I do to . . . ?" She looked away, unable to phrase her question properly.

Fabrizio's hand landed on her leg. "Meghan, just hang in there, everything will be all right."

Meghan sniffed and wiped at her eyes that were now leaking again. "Liam will come after me again, and if I'm going to be on my own . . . Well, I think I will sell the ranch and move back to Canada."

Fabrizio's hand tensed slightly at her comment. "Why there? I didn't think you had any connections to Calgary anymore."

"Well, I really don't. Except for my mother's cousin."

"Your mother? I thought we settled this years ago. That woman is toxic?"

"She is my mother." Meghan's voice sounded guarded, as if she was waiting for him to be disapproving.

"Meghan?" Fabrizio shook his head. "She is the one that told the police that you shot Monty. Have you been in contact with her? Have you given her anything?"

"I'm not an idiot." Meghan was offended by Fabrizio's comment. "I haven't seen or heard from her since that day in court."

Fabrizio eyed her, then glanced around her at Declan, who still appeared asleep. Fabrizio found himself questioning Eliza's timing once again. Where had she been all those years before, and was it just an accident that she came in contact with Rory? That would be something he would have to research when he got home. The thought of anyone taking advantage of Meghan irritated him.

"Nathan tracked down a cousin in Calgary. I have become quite close with her. She is younger than me, but it's nice having family."

"How do you know she is trustworthy?" Fabrizio's voice sounded judgmental, which was not his intent.

"I don't know, but she hasn't even met Eliza and her father, who is Eliza's brother, hasn't had any contact with her since we left Calgary," Meghan sighed. "I just don't want to be alone," she grunted, with almost an angry tone. She tucked back the long dark strand of hair behind Declan's ear and shook her head. "I should have used more common sense."

"You're not alone." Fabrizio soothed, patting her leg. "I'm not leaving you."

"Until you get me home." She stared out the window, trying to see her future. "Fabrizio, before we leave for the States, can I phone home? I might want to go to Dallas."

"Dallas?" Fabrizio questioned, his voice rising slightly. "Why?"

Meghan glanced over at Declan when she felt his body flinch, but when her eyes settled on his face, it seemed calm and undisturbed.

"I will stay with Nat's parents until I decide what to do with the ranch. I obviously can't go back there since Liam knows about it. Nat can bring Caelan to meet me if he is not already there."

"Oh, Boo," Fabrizio sighed. "He really screwed up your life, didn't he?"

"Yes," she sniffed. "I wouldn't care if he truly loved me, I would do anything for him, but the fact that he just married me to get at that land is destroying me."

Fabrizio shook his head, unsure what to say; he knew that Declan loved her, but he had to keep his word to Declan and not tell her the truth.

"Do you think Liam will go after you again even if you are out of Ireland?" Fabrizio questioned, wanting her point of view since she was the one that spent the most time with him.

Meghan nodded and glanced back at Declan to ensure he was still asleep. "Yes, he has been tracking me for years now apparently. He sent Rory after me." She looked up at Fabrizio with a questioning gaze. "He was supposed to marry me, and then, when I had a child, they were going to kill me and Declan?"

"What?" Fabrizio blurted out.

"Well, with Declan dead, Rory is the heir, and with Fergus being his father, that gives them two-thirds as long as Rory stays with them. Rory is weak, and he will let the O'Briens control him. But then I wouldn't have anything to do with Rory so Liam came after me and was planning on forcing me to marry Rory. But when Liam saw me at the party years ago he decided to change the plan and marry me instead."

Fabrizio's brow rose slightly. "Does Monty know about this?"

"No," she muttered. "I never had a chance to tell him, he was too busy dumping me."

Fabrizio grunted and looked around her to Declan. "So Liam felt it was better to marry you than let Rory do it."

Meghan blushed slightly. "Well, he said that when he looked into my eyes that night at the party he couldn't let Rory have me. I guess the plan was to kill me after I produced an heir for Rory. But, Liam said the thought of killing me now is painful."

Fabrizio chuckled slightly as a grin curled his lips. "Meghan, your doe eyes will save you every time."

"My what?" she questioned with surprise.

Fabrizio began to laugh at her facial expression. "When you look at people with those eyes, you totally entrance them. If you ever figure out what you're doing, you could be dangerous."

Meghan broke her gaze on Fabrizio when she felt Declan's body shaking slightly. "You're not asleep?" she grumbled, wondering how much of the conversation he was listening to.

"No," he admitted, opening his eyes one at a time. "I woke and heard Fabs talking about your eyes."

She crinkled her nose and turned towards Fabrizio, not wanting to look at Declan's smiling face. Pain was flowing through her that he could be so nonchalant towards her after breaking her heart.

"So what were y' two talking about?" Declan questioned, sitting up straight and stretching largely, his arms brushing up against Meghan.

"Nothing," she said quietly and adjusted herself away from him slightly on the seat. The space in the cab of the truck was snug, her being wedged between the two large men.

Declan's brow rose slightly, but as Fabrizio shook his head, Declan decided not to push the subject. He had heard the majority of the conversation anyway; he just wanted to see if she would tell him about O'Brien, and more importantly, her decision to return to Canada.

CHAPTER THIRTY-FOUR

The seaside town was a picturesque collection of houses dotting the hillside painted in colours of browns, dark greens, and burnt reds. The large trees occupying most of the area appeared to have been there for hundreds of years, standing up proud and tall over the town site. As they came over the hill, the harbour lay out in front of them with a mass of small fishing boats and a few larger steamers. The town's welcome sign claimed settlement during 1602, but from some of the ruins scattered along the roadside, the area dates back to the Vikings.

The sun was fighting hard to break through the clouds as they arrived at the cottage. Fabrizio jumped from the truck and ran into the small white plaster building, and within seconds of his disappearance, a loud shriek resonated out of the building. Cassie bolted through the door, her long blonde hair flying up around her face, her arms stretched outwards towards Meghan.

"Thank God, you're okay?" Cassie cried, her eyes filling with tears, her arms tightening around Meghan's trembling frame.

Meghan stood shaking in Cassie's arms. The realization of what everyone else was going through in her weeks of captivity hit her hard. "I'm so sorry, Cass."

"What are you sorry for?"

"For scaring everyone."

"Meg, don't be so silly, you couldn't help it. It's not like you chose to be kidnapped by a brutal killer."

"He wasn't that bad," Meghan sighed.

"Meg, I can't believe you are defending him. Don't let Declan hear you say that," Cassie whispered fiercely.

"I'm not defending him. He didn't hurt me, that's all."

Cassie shook her head and smirked at her friend. "If there is even a drop of goodness in someone, you will find it, won't you?"

Meghan shrugged and looked towards Declan and sighed.

"Meg, he was devastated when he thought he lost you. I was terrified for him. I thought he was going to kill Colton for letting O'Brien take you."

"It wasn't Colton's fault," Meghan blurted out, somewhat startled by the fact that everyone felt so strongly about Declan's love for her.

"Meg, why did you leave the manor?" Cassie questioned, wondering why she would put herself at risk.

"We went for a ride. It wouldn't have mattered anyway. Liam was inside the manor, looking for me when we arrived."

"Meg, did you tell Declan about your trip with Colton?" Cassie asked, her blonde brow raising with interest.

"No, why?" Meghan was not sure what Cassie was getting at.

"You know, what Colton did."

"No, and I'm not going to." Meghan's tone was dismissive and firm.

"Not going to what?" Declan questioned as he came up behind the women.

"Nothing," Meghan quickly told him, focusing her eyes on Cassie.

"Meggie, what are y' hiding now?" Declan asked, raising his brow. It was back, he could tell she was lying to him. A wave of relief washed over him before he settled back into finding out what she was hiding. "We have enough problems, don't y' think?"

Cassie felt an instant discomfort with her presence there and moved over towards Fabrizio, leaving Meghan to fend for herself with the problem.

"Nothing," Meghan muttered, her eyes wide and filling with pain.

Declan took her by the arm and led her into the small bedroom, determined to find out what she was deliberately keeping from him. Was it something to do with O'Brien?

"Meggie, I know you're keeping something from me, so let's have it," Declan asked again firmly, but this time he had hold of her arms.

"It's nothing, we were just talking about Colton," Meghan informed him evenly, glancing around the small room in the cottage, the old bed and dresser occupying most of the room.

"He made a pass at y', didn't he?" Declan questioned, his brow rising slightly.

Meghan's eyes widened with surprise, and she stared at him momentarily. "How did you know?"

"I just guessed. I know he has feelings for y', and I figured if I left y' two alone that he would try something," Declan smirked, quite proud of the fact that he was correct.

"Well then, why did you leave me alone with him?" Meghan snorted, feeling rather like the lamb being led to the slaughter.

"Well . . . I knew that y' would turn him down, so I wasn't too concerned." Declan's mouth rose into a one-sided grin.

"Well, what if I didn't?" Meghan mumbled and forced her angry gaze on him.

"Are y' saying y' took him up on his offer to sleep with him?" Declan's brow rose ever so slightly as he tried to remain calm. What the hell was she doing? Was she trying to bait him or was she telling the truth? This was getting out of control. Why did he think she was having sex with every man she came in contact with? He needed to control his jealousy. It was eating him alive.

"No!" Meghan snorted. "I'm just saying. Well, it was pretty arrogant of you to put me in that position in the first place." She flipped her head and turned towards the window. "Anyway, what I do with Colton or anyone else is of no concern to you, remember."

Declan stiffened from the comment and slammed the door to the cottage shut, causing Meghan to swing around with the appearance of a trapped terrified animal.

"Y' are going to listen to me!" he began forcefully. "You're me wife, and it does concern me, and I will not have y' . . ." He stopped as her face crumpled with anger.

"You will not have me what?" Meghan snorted. "Declan, you think I slept with Liam, don't you?" He stayed quiet, but his face told the story. "You do," she sighed and turned her back on him. "I'm not sure why I should justify this, but I never had any sexual contact with him other than him kissing me." She swung back around, her eyes dark with anger.

"Well, that's not how it looked to me!" Declan raged, unable to control his emotions any longer. "Hugging and kissing him. Dammit, Meggie!"

Meghan recoiled at the comment and turned her back on him. "I thought you were dead!" Her voice was hard and sharp.

A deep grunt left his mouth, and he grabbed her from behind and shook her slightly. "So y' thought y' would throw yourself at a vile killer?"

"Get your hands off me!" she cried and swung around to face him. "God, I hate you. You make me love you, and then discard me like an old shoe. You are the most cruel, uncaring man I have ever met."

The anger on his face changed to horror at her comment, but before he could reply, the door opened, and Fabrizio's worried face peered inside.

"I got a hold of Inspector Maloney, and he wants to meet with us. Do you two need some time?" Fabrizio's eyes narrowed, his condescending gaze fixed equally on both of them.

"No!" Meghan blurted out. "I think we know where we both stand." She swung around, her gaze settling on Cassie's worried face. "I would like a shower, though."

"Fine," Declan grumbled, pushing past Fabrizio and Cassie, leaving Meghan alone again.

She shook her head at his departing broad back, dropped to the bed, and covered her face with her hands.

"Meg?" Cassie was across the room before Meghan could respond. "What is going on?"

"It's over," she sniffed and wiped at her eyes. "He never loved me. He just married me . . ." She stopped as the words lodged in her throat.

"What are you talking about, he loves you," Cassie argued as her eyes settled on Fabrizio for support, but he simply shrugged his shoulders, unsure what was happening.

"That's what he wanted us to believe." Meghan stood and glanced around the room as if searching for something. As her eyes settled on her purse that was sitting beside a small suitcase, she moved towards it and pulled out her passport. "I need to get home to Caelan. I have to explain to her. How could I have been so stupid?" Meghan began to sob and fell into Cassie's open arms.

Declan could hear her sobs, and it was ripping at his heart. Why couldn't he get past the sight of her kissing O'Brien, and why couldn't he believe her when she said she did not make love to him? His jealousy and guilt was eating at him, causing him to make bad decisions. The fact that he put Meghan and Caelan's lives in danger was all he could think about, and he swore he would never place them in that position again. He needed to get her home and then somehow convince O'Brien that they wanted no part of the estate.

Declan heard the shower shut off, and the pull of her lured him into the room, even though he knew that he should keep his distance. He had hurt her so deeply that she hated him. Those words pierced his soul like a scalding knife. How could he have let things get so out of control?

The room was very small with a metal-framed bed and a rickety old dresser, which took up the majority of the space. The lace curtains that hung down over top of the white roll up blinds were blowing in the breeze through the open window. Declan closed the window, pulled down the blind, and scanned the room.

The blue ruana was lying on the bed along with her clothing, and the sight of it made his skin crawl. How she could have kept that gift from that monster was beyond him. Maybe she did have feeling for O'Brien, and she was afraid to admit it. After all, she had spent a month with the man, maybe she had fallen in love with him.

The door squeaked as it opened, and he turned towards the noise startling Meghan when she exited the bathroom. A look of unease crossed her face, and her flushed skin was easily seen, since the towel barely covered her body.

"Declan, what is it you want?" Meghan said, coolly trying to hide her discomfort. His eyes were scanning her with an appearance of lust, and she was fighting hard not to just drop the towel and allow him his desires. That thought however changed as quickly as his facial expression and the remembrance of how he felt about her was evident in the cold grey eyes.

"I came to tell y' that we have a couple of hours before we'll be leaving, so y' should get some sleep," he said evenly, trying not to let his eyes settle on her long, damp legs.

"Thank you." She forced a calm smile. "I am pretty tired."

After an uncomfortable silence, she shifted towards the bed and sat down, then eyed him dubiously. "Are you waiting for something?"

His brow crumpled with annoyance at her dismissive tone. "I'm waiting for y' to lie down!" he said sharply and yanked the chair away from the wall and dropped down into it facing the bed. "And if y' think I'm leaving y' alone, you're out of your mind."

"I would prefer to sleep without you staring at me," she grumbled and lay back in bed, throwing the sheet over her. Her hand slipped under the sheet and exited with the towel, then she discarded it on the floor beside the bed.

Declan's brow rose slightly as an uneasy arousal filled his entire body. How he wanted her, how he needed her, how he loved her, yet he could not have her. He closed his eyes, trying to force himself to focus on the mission at hand and not on Meghan and her naked body not five feet from him. His only purpose now was to get her back home.

Meghan flopped onto her side, her back to him, trying to control her emotions. How she wished he had come to her when she climbed into bed. She had fully expected him to be unable to control himself and be on her within seconds of removing the towel, but he seemed completely uninterested in her, and that sent a cold tremor up her spine. Had she been that unappealing to him all along and had he simply been acting all those months, pretending to find her desirable? Tears began to drip out of her eyes, and she tried to lessen the sounds of her sniffles by burying her head in the pillow.

Declan was aware she was crying, but he stayed in the chair, watching her back jerk every few minutes as she sobbed quietly. Should he go to her, hold her in his arms, and tell her how much he loved her? Would that solve anything or make things worse? He did not know.

The gleam of the sun sparking through the window woke Meghan midmorning, her thoughts dazed and unclear. After a painful stretch, she glanced around the small stuffy room, spotting Declan asleep in the chair beside the bed. His chiselled face appeared relaxed, the long, dark lashes resting peacefully against the tanned skin. Her breath still stuck in her chest at the first sight of him, and the thought of his true feelings for her ripped at her heart.

It was unfathomable to her that he could have fooled her so completely. She truly believed that he loved her with all his heart, but apparently, his greed was his driving force. She flung back the sheets and the comforter that Declan had apparently covered her with after she had fallen into her devastating sleep. She knew she had only covered herself with the sheet.

His orders to stay put in the room filled her head, but the conflicting emotions she had forced her from the room and out into the soft autumn sun after she slipped into clean clothing.

Her options spun in her head; she could stay with Declan until he got her back to the States and Caelan, but then what? Would Liam come after her, and if so, would his rage be more than she wanted to experience? If Declan had no intentions of staying with her, would she be able to keep herself and Caelan safe? Should she go back to Liam and claim Declan forced her away against her will? How would Liam react, would he trust her enough to allow her freedom to come and go? If so, she would be able to bring Caelan over to Ireland.

She searched her soul for the answers, and she kept coming back to the safety of Caelan. That is what was important, and if staying and being Liam's wife was what it took, she would do it.

"Meg, what are you doing out here? I thought Declan said to stay in the inn." Cassie's voice, slightly edged with annoyance, broke her thoughts.

Meghan turned her tear-stained face towards her friend. The only person she felt she could trust with her thoughts. "Cass," she sniffed before collapsing into Cassie's arms.

"Meg, what's wrong?" Cassie soothed, rubbing her hand down the long auburn curls. "Where is Declan?"

"Sleeping," Meghan sniffed and lifted her hand swabbing at her eyes. "Cass, I need your help."

Cassie dropped to the bench, and Meghan collapsed beside her, pulling her legs up in front of her, her arms clutching them close to her chest. "Tell me what's wrong."

Meghan sighed heavily, then proceeded to inform Cassie of the events over the past month and what had transpired the night before.

"Are you saying you would be better off staying with that animal?" Cassie cringed at the expression on Meghan's face; she had already made up her mind. "No, you can't do that."

"I don't have a choice. Caelan and I will never be safe. He will find me and what if he hurts Caelan? I can't risk that, especially since Declan doesn't want me."

"Meg, you must have misunderstood him. He loves you. I believe that in my soul." Cassie pleaded with her friend to use common sense. "When he found out O'Brien took you, he was frantic, I was scared for him."

Meghan shook her head and wiped at her eyes. "I have made up my mind. This is best, Cass, once Liam trusts me, I will be able to come and go."

A tremor ran down Declan's spine at the determination in her voice, as he listened to the conversation from his vantage point behind the potting shed. He loved her more than he had realized, and the feeling of complete loss ripping through him was confirming it. What he had done in the past to wangle her into marriage and then more recently ripping her away from a man that loved her was the past. What he needed to concentrate on was the future, and how he was going to keep her safe.

"Meg," Cassie said firmly, drawing Declan's attention back to the conversation. "Come home with me." Cassie soothed. "Fabs will get us all home safely and then we will worry about what you are going to do. Nat has Caelan at his parents' ranch in Texas. She should be safe there for now."

"Good," Meghan sniffed, regaining some composure. "How am I going to tell her that her father . . ." She paused and stared at Cassie, with sorrow shooting from the watery green eyes. "Cass, she is going to be heartbroken that he doesn't love her."

"Meg, he loves her. Don't convince yourself he doesn't. I'm sure he does."

"Damn, he's a bastard!" Meghan snarled. "I hate him for what he has done. My life was perfect before he showed back up."

Cassie's brow rose slightly. "Do you really believe that?"

"Yes!" Meghan growled in defence of her comment. "I was happy, and we were in no danger. Now I'm being hunted by a man who would kill everyone in his path. And as for Declan, I don't think he is too different."

"Meg, what are you saying? Declan wouldn't kill anyone," Cassie blurted out.

"He killed Liam's brother at the ranch," Meghan whispered, gripping Cassie's hand. "And then yesterday he beat up three men. I have never seen so much rage before."

Cassie cringed at her remembrance of how he lunged at Colton at the inn the night Meghan disappeared. "Meg, he was like that when O'Brien kidnapped you. The way he looked at Colton, I thought he was going to kill him. If Fabs hadn't been there, I think he would have hurt Colton."

Meghan glanced around the area and then stared at Cassie with worry. "I haven't told you this, but . . . Well, Liam and his dad are after more than the estate."

Cassie swallowed hard. "What else is there?"

"A sword. There is legend that says that Michael O'Brien had it and hid it somewhere in Briarwood Castle. It belonged to Brien Boru, and I think I know where it is."

"How?" Cassie's voice filled with interest.

"Do you remember that stupid song my grandfather would sing, the one about the gargoyle?"

Cassie nodded her head and rubbed her temples. How was she mixed up in this nightmare?

"I think the words to that song lead to the hidden room."

"Did you tell Liam about this?" Cassie's voice lowered as if someone was lurking nearby.

"No, but apparently my locket . . . Well, it was an amulet, and someone added the back piece. But once all three are put together, they create a key that opens the door. Each stone's insignia is a clue to the location as well"

"This is unbelievable." Cassie shook her head, "Are you going to tell Declan?"

"No, he knows about the legend, and he claims he doesn't believe it. I will not give him one more thing to try to get away from Liam. If Liam wants that sword, let him have it. But he needs my locket." She pulled the locket from her pocket. "He has the other two."

"Two? Where did he get Declan's mother's from?" Cassie questioned. She could not believe what was happening. It was like a bad murder mystery.

"Fergus gave them money, a lot of money, to leave Ireland and give him the locket. I don't think Katie knew about the sword and the family jewels at the time she gave away her locket, but they definitely know about them now," Meghan smirked and glanced over at the cottage; she thought Declan was still inside. "Fergus loves Katie. He agreed to allow her to leave, and he gave her enough money to start a new life in the States. That's where all their money came from."

"So Fabrizio was right about their money," Cassie sighed. "I thought maybe he was making that up. Do you think Declan knows where his family's money originated?"

"I don't think so. But who knows with him? He is such a liar." Meghan jumped to her feet and turned towards the front door of the inn. "I need to phone Nat and see what he thinks I should do."

Cassie nodded and walked with Meghan towards the manager's office to place the call.

Fabrizio had heard the last few minutes of the women's conversation and was very concerned with the expression on Declan's face. He had never seen him looking so stricken, and it worried him. "Monty, what's going on? Did you only marry her to get control of the estate?" Fabrizio finally asked, wanting to know if he was putting his life and the life of the women at stake, just for Declan's sense of family heritage.

"At first," Declan sighed. "But God help me, I love her, Fabs. I do."

"Then tell her that. She must be completely heartbroken to even consider going back to O'Brien."

"I can't," he rubbed his hand across his face. "She deserves better."

"Better how, O'Brien?" Fabrizio snarled. "You're letting your pride get in the way of your common sense. Dammit, Monty, you know what will happen if he gets a hold of her and produces a male heir."

"I know that will knock Caelan out, and O'Brien's heir will be two-thirds of the triad," Declan grumbled.

"Yes and then he will kill her."

Declan shook his head with exasperation. "I don't believe that," he said, not wanting to face that fact.

"What the hell is wrong with you? He will, is that what you want?" Fabrizio hollered, his anger completely exposed. "You're a damn fool."

Declan grunted and shoved at Fabrizio. "Shut up, Fabs, I have me reasons."

"Selfish reasons!" Fabrizio yelled and shoved Declan back. "Whether you like it or not, I'm not letting Meghan go back to that man, and I'm certainly not letting Cassie get into the middle of danger."

Declan raised his hands in retreat and wandered towards the manager's office to check on the women.

CHAPTER THIRTY-FIVE

The cold barrel of the gun pressed forcefully against Meghan's temple, halting her movements. Her terror-filled eyes caught sight of Cassie as a tall lean man gripped her arm, his gun to her head.

"Well, look who we found," Murphy grumbled, his sweaty hand gripping Meghan's arm.

"Let go of me," Meghan shrieked, tugging at her arm.

"Shut up, y' bitch. He had us out looking for y' all night." Murphy's voice was raspy from a lack of sleep.

It's too late she thought, Liam must be somewhere close, it was now or never. "Oh, Murphy, thank God, it's you," Meghan muttered. "They took me away. Please take me to Liam."

"Meg?" Cassie blurted out with confusion, her eyes scanning Meghan's face for her reasoning.

"Cass, it's okay, Liam will help us." Her eyes begged Cassie for understanding. This was their only way out at the moment.

Cassie nodded and followed behind Meghan and Murphy, the gun still pressed against her head. A feeling of dread filled her as they were taken down the small embankment towards a long dock and warehouse.

Meghan, also feeling concerned, stopped and yanked on her arm. "Where are you taking us, Murphy, I want to see Liam."

"All in good time, sweetheart," his hand slid down her face. "First, we have some questions for you, and you better have the right answers."

"Liam will be very angry if you hurt me or my friend," Meghan blurted out, unsure why she did.

"Get inside!" Murphy snorted and flung her through the door. "I'm getting very tired of your attitude. I think y' need to be taught a lesson."

Panic surged through Meghan, and she swung around and darted for the door, screaming for Declan and Fabrizio. It did not surprise her that Declan was the first person that came to mind when she was threatened.

"Damn stupid woman!" snorted a man that jumped her before she got past the door. "I'll teach y' to disobey Mr. O'Brien." He flipped her over and slapped her face. "I could kill you right now."

Meghan struggled to get out from under him, her arms flailing at his head, her legs kicking wildly. The man slapped her again, hard enough to rattle her teeth, her head slamming back to the hard cold cement floor.

She blinked repeatedly, trying to regain her focus on her surroundings. The large room was dirty and smelled horrible, a mixture of rotting fruit and vegetables and a distinct smell of fish. Hadn't anyone ever cleaned the place. She thought as she turned her head to the side, noticing the grunge she was lying in?

A cockroach scurried by her face, stopping only to wave its antennae towards her, but when she screamed, it seemed uninterested in sticking around.

Where was Declan or Fabrizio, why were they not around? Why did she leave the room? Panic surged through her, and she was painfully aware that the last thing she wanted was to be taken by Liam again. She wanted Declan, and she wanted to go home.

"Declan, help me," Meghan screamed as loud as her voice would allow.

"Shut up," Murphy snorted, dragging her to her feet after he dislodged her attacker. His eyes scanned her bruised face, then settled on the stocky man. "Why didn't y' listen to me? I told y' that Mr. O'Brien didn't want her harmed."

"She's fine," the man blustered, wiping at his pants that were slightly soiled from the dirty floor.

Murphy's brow rose at the stupidity of the man, then shook his head and focused back on Meghan. "Mr. O'Brien is waiting for y'."

The door at the back of the warehouse opened, and Liam bolted through the door followed by three more men, one of them Rory. Why couldn't he travel with only two men, why did he constantly have five or six with him? she thought angrily.

"Meghan, me love, why are y' so upset?" Liam's voice echoed through the warehouse.

"Here she is," Murphy growled, shoving her towards the large frame heading towards her. "I'm telling y' she is more trouble than she's worth."

"Y' don't know what she's worth, Murphy, and I suggest y' don't be questioning me." Liam's voice was laced with threat, but his hands were gentle as he clasped them to her arms.

"Liam, he was going to kill me," Meghan blurted out, trying to take advantage of Liam's anger with Murphy. She threw herself into Liam, pressing her head against his chest.

Liam eyed her with slight amusement. "Don't think I didn't hear y' calling for Mr. Montgomery." He kissed the top of her head as she tried to pull away, but he had a tight grip on her waist. "But I suppose y' can be forgiven."

She nodded and glanced up at him, but the expression on his face changed from pleasure to concern. Her face was bright red and her lip was cut and bleeding. "What happened to your face?" he questioned, stroking down the wild waves that were full of debris from the warehouse floor.

"Ask him," Meghan muttered, her eyes glancing towards the man Murphy called Williams.

"Y' did this to her?" Liam's voice was surprisingly calm before a slight smile curled his lips. "Giving y' some trouble, was she?"

"Aye," Williams relaxed slightly. "She was trying to escape, so I knocked her to the ground."

"Did y' slap her?" Liam questioned. His voice was still calm.

"Aye," the man said proudly, ignoring the warnings of Murphy. "And I'd do it again, Mr. O'Brien, if y' asked me to."

"Hmm." Liam rested his hand on her face, his thumb brushing across the cut lip.

It seemed to be in slow motion as Liam's arm rose towards Williams, the gun gripped in his hand. "I believe I asked y' not to harm her." His voice was calm but cold as he pulled the trigger, firing a bullet straight into the heart of Williams.

"Oh my God!" Meghan shrieked as she watched the young man fall to the floor, blood oozing from his chest. She glanced up at Liam with horror shooting from her eyes.

"Feel better now, me love?" he smiled as if he did not notice the dead corpse on the floor.

"No, you killed him," Meghan muttered and glanced over at Cassie whose face had gone completely white. "Liam." Her knees began to dissolve under her, and her head spun with terror.

"Me love, don't be upset with me, I did it for you. I will not have anyone harming y'." His eyes scanned the men that were all looking rather stricken. "Let that be a lesson to y' all. When I say something, it is to be done."

His attention returned to Meghan's ashen face, and he rubbed his hand across her skin. "Come along, me love, it's time to go home."

"She's not going anywhere!" Declan's voice rose above the rest. "O'Brien, let her go." His voice was harsh, his gun rose towards Liam.

Declan eyed Meghan's positioning in Liam's arms and cringed. What was she doing? Was she planning to go back to the horrible man? Jealousy reared its head, and he became enraged totally throwing his ability to reason into a tailspin.

"Well, Mr. Montgomery, it's nice to see you, alive," Liam smirked and kissed Meghan's head. "But unfortunately, I must be going, I'm taking Meghan home."

"You're not taking her anywhere," Declan growled as Fabrizio arrived on the scene, his gun up against the hostile men of O'Brien's. For the first time, Declan noticed Rory and the gun he had pointed towards Cassie.

"Bloody hell, Rory, what are y' doing?"

Rory looked stricken, but his eyes stayed fixed on Declan. "It's over, just let her go."

Declan glared at Rory, but his attention changed as he noticed Meghan's eyes glued to the dead man lying in a pool of blood on the floor.

"One of yours?" Declan said evenly, bobbing his head towards the body. He was not sure how the man died, but he was almost positive that Meghan or Cassie had not done it. "Killing off your own man? That's an odd thing to be doing to instil loyalty."

Liam glared at Declan, then a wicked smile curled his lips. "Aye, well, the lad struck Meghan, and I will not have her harmed." He kissed her head. "I don't suppose y' would argue that point."

"No," Declan agreed, his gaze back on Meghan's terrified face. "And on that thought I'll be taking me wife and going."

"I don't believe y' will be. She is coming with me. What do y' think, me love, should I kill him right now or are you coming with me?" Liam questioned smugly.

"I'll go with you, Liam, just please leave them alone," Meghan begged, tugging on his shirt. "Please just let them go."

"Meggie," Declan gasped at her agreement to leave with O'Brien. "Are y' mad? You can't go with him."

"It's all right, Declan," she begged, her eyes pleading with him. "Please, I don't want you hurt."

Declan shook his head with agitation. "Meggie, just come here and stop this foolishness," he grumbled.

"Y' think y' have any say in this matter?" Liam chuckled. "Drop your guns, or I'll shoot the blonde." He nodded his head towards Cassie.

"No, you fucking Irish bastard," Meghan shrieked and yanked loose of Liam, catching him off guard. She flew towards Cassie, screening her from Murphy's gun. "I won't let you kill her."

"Meggie," Declan muttered, his eyes widening at her actions. He never would have suspected she would put Cassie's life before her own.

"Meghan, me love," Liam smirked, apparently amazed at the same thing. "Y' really need to stop being so unpredictable. Y' could get hurt."

"Liam, please just let them go. I promise I'll go with you. I want to go with you," she begged, completely overburdened with the thought of Cassie being hurt because of her.

"Me love, if y' are just coming with me to spare their lives," he gripped her chin in his hand and lifted her face towards him, "I'm not sure how this benefits me."

Meghan swallowed hard forcing down the bile that was pushing its way up her throat. "I'm coming with you because I want to, Liam." Her voice was as soft and sweet as she could force it. "Why would I want to go with him when I could stay at the manor with you? I like it there other than your dad."

Liam's laughter broke her comment. "Aye, the feeling is mutual." His eyes settled on Declan's angry face. "But that still doesn't solve the problem. You're still married."

"I'll get a divorce."

"Meggie, what are y' doing?" Declan blurted out, completely overwhelmed with her comments.

"Monty," Fabrizio squinted at him, seeming to understand what Meghan was doing. "Let her go."

Declan's dark gaze settled on Fabrizio, then back to Meghan. "All right, take her, I want nothing to do with her, or that bloody land."

Meghan felt her heart drop; she was not sure if he meant what he was saying or not. She wanted to be the one to end it, not him. Her pride needed it. "I want you, Liam, I want to marry you."

Liam's face lit up with her words, in total contrast to the expression that was present on Declan's face. "All right, me love, let's go home." He gripped her around the waist and turned her towards the door.

"Liam, I need to say goodbye," Meghan said softly, stopping and glancing back at Cassie, then at Declan. "Please, he won't stop coming after me unless he understands."

"All right, me love, but only a minute." Liam kissed her lips hard, but she stayed completely still, not wanting him to realize how disgusted she was from his touch. "Make it quick." He released her and patted her bottom as she calmly headed towards Cassie.

"Get the hell out of this country," she whispered into Cassie's ear as she hugged her. "No matter what happens, just get out." She kissed Cassie's cheek and glanced over at Declan. "He needs to go home to Caelan."

Cassie nodded and wiped at the tears that were exploding from her eyes. "Meg, be careful."

"I will, he'll trust me soon. It will be all right." Meghan forced a smile and wandered towards Declan with apprehension. She could see the annoyance in his eyes, but there was also something close to terror. Could he really love her?

"Meggie, don't do this. Fabs and I can take them out," Declan whispered into her hair as he engulfed her in his arms. "Please."

"Declan, I can't let him kill you. Please just let him take me. Everyone will be safe," she sniffed, her arms tightening around him in an unconscious grip for security.

"Freckles, you listen to me. Get him to let Cass go, then wait for me signal, then jump behind the crates."

She gazed up at him, tears dripping down her face. She shook her head. "I can't."

"Meggie, please, Caelan needs you. I need y'. I love y'," he whispered.

She jerked away from him and slapped her hand hard across his cheek. Now was a great time to tell her that, she thought. Her mouth gaped open, the words trapped behind subdued anger. "Why now?"

"Always," he said softly, ignoring the stinging cheek. "Please."

"All right, enough of this. Meghan, it's time to go." Liam gripped her arm and pulled her away from Declan; however, her eyes never left him.

At that instant, she made her decision. "Liam, before I go, I want Cassie to be allowed to leave. I don't trust him." She bobbed her head towards Murphy. "If anything were to happen to her, I would never be able to live with myself, and Caelan needs her and . . ."

"Shh." His finger landed on her lips. "You're always asking for something." A smile curled his lips as he looked into her pleading face. "Aye, I can't refuse y' anything."

"Thank you." Meghan forced a smile and watched as Murphy shoved Cassie towards the door on the far side of the warehouse.

Cassie glanced at Fabrizio as she passed him; he bobbed his head towards the door, then gave her a quick wink. She turned back to look at Meghan, then darted through the door and out of sight.

"Happy now?" Liam chuckled and kissed her nose.

"Yes," she smiled with relief; at least, Cassie was safe.

"Good, because I don't like to see this pretty face saddened." His hands cupped her face, and his lips landed on hers.

How she wished he would stop doing that! She knew she could not fight him, but the urge was strong. Once his lips left hers, she glanced over at Declan, his face reddening quickly with rage.

"Well, Mr. Montgomery and friend, we'll be leaving, once we're gone, I suspect you'll be leaving the country." Liam smiled a wide toothy grin. "Come along, me love, I can't wait one more minute, I'm taking y' home to bed."

Declan jerked slightly before he caught himself. It took every ounce of self-restraint he had not to make the move to early. He needed Meghan to get to the crates; if anything happened to her, he would never forgive himself. What would have happened if he had told her the truth the night before, would they be safely tucked away in their room right now? No, he thought O'Brien would still be after her, the location would just be different for this showdown.

Meghan's heart was thumping against her chest as she stumbled beside Liam as he dragged her towards the door and away from Declan. What was Declan waiting for, why was he letting Liam take her? She glanced over her shoulder, assessing the situation. Declan's eyes were on her, but Fabrizio was eyeing the four men still in place with their guns fixed on Fabrizio and Declan. Four against two were not good odds she thought, and she would be no help controlling Liam, he out powered her; she had found that out early in her captivity. Rory was following behind them, his face crumpling with distress as he glanced back at Declan.

Time suddenly stopped as Declan's voice echoed through the warehouse. "It's thatching time, Meggie." She understood exactly what he meant and, in the confusion of the next few seconds, managed to pull loose of Liam and jump behind a pile of crates.

She scrambled between and around them until she was out of Liam's reach. He would have to climb in after her or leave her. Would he risk being caught in the gunfire to recapture her?

Her question was answered when he leaped over the first crate and attempted to force his broad shoulders through the space she had disappeared. A few choice curses left his mouth when he realized he was too large to fit. She let out her breath and huddled down into her hiding place, but her safety was short lived when she noticed Murphy tugging on Liam's shirt and pointing towards the far side of the warehouse where streak of flames shot up the wall.

Liam cursed again and kicked at the large crate, his head shaking with dismay. "Meghan, the warehouse is on fire. Y' need to come with me," he said loudly, his voice surprisingly full of fear.

She could see Declan from her vantage point, his eyes switching from the door to the three men held up behind a pile of skids across the room. Her ears were aching from the sound of gunfire and the bullets were coming dangerously close to her, causing her to lay flat against the floor. What should she do, would the gunfire stop if she went to Liam, but after her attempted escape, would he be angry with her? Would

Declan be killed and what of Fabrizio, they were putting their lives on the line for her, so she had better follow Declan's plan.

The room was quickly filling with smoke, but at least the gunfire had lessened, she could only hear three distinct guns. Whose were they? Her lungs were clogging with the thick black soot, and her eyes were burning. The sound of the crates moving to one side had stopped and so had the gunfire around her; all she could hear was the crackling of wood and metal.

"Declan?" Meghan blurted out, her mind disoriented. Where was everyone? Had they left her behind? She covered her mouth with the sleeve of her jacket and crawled towards what light she could see. She assumed it was the door that Cassie had gone through, but at that point, all she wanted was to get out of the inferno.

"Meggie, where are y'?" Declan's voice was panicked and loud behind her. "Meggie?"

"I'm here," she screamed, scanning the murky room. "I'm here. Declan, please help me."

"Freckles." His hand was on her arm, and before she could respond, she was propelled towards the light, her leg moving faster than she expected. "It's going to blow, they planted explosives."

Liam had no intensions of allowing Declan and Fabrizio to live and probably Cassie for that matter. She was most likely just outside the door. God, where was Fabrizio? Did he have Cassie? Or was Fabrizio dead?

"Cassie, where is Cass?" Meghan blurted out, terror exploding through her.

"I don't know," Declan panted, tugging on her with more force. "Freckles, hurry up, we need to get out."

The dock was a welcome sight, but Declan continued to pull her along behind him towards the water. She gasped with relief when she caught a glimpse of Cassie's long blonde hair flying up around her head as she ran beside Fabrizio. The end of the dock was dangerously close, and Fabrizio did not seem to slow down. Cassie, however, stopped and glanced back towards the warehouse as if judging something. Her decision was made, however, when Fabrizio gripped her hand and tugged her into the water.

"What the hell?" Meghan blurted out, her heart skipping with worry. She glanced back at the warehouse. It was fully engulfed in flames, the thick black smoke spilling towards the clouds.

"Meggie, don't look back," Declan ordered, pulling her towards the spot where Cassie and Fabrizio had plunged into the cold bay. "It's going to blow."

A thunderous explosion from behind her caused Meghan to turn, and she lost her footing and fell, landing with a thump on the slippery salt-covered dock. A cloud of black and orange flames was heading towards her, and she stumbled to her feet while Declan tugged on her to get her up.

"Bloody hell, Meggie," was all she heard before she felt her body flying through the air and crashing into the ice-cold water.

She thrashed around under the water as the black and orange cloud of fire fanned out over her, depositing burning chunks of wood and debris down around her. Sharp objects sliced through the water, hitting her head and ripping at her body; the pain was excruciating and causing her to lose cautiousness.

The cloud retreated as quickly as it came, and Meghan was struggling to get to the surface, but it seemed to be getting farther and farther away. Her eyes were getting heavy, and legs were slowing from exhaustion.

As she strained to keep her eyes open in the bitterly cold water, she felt a sizeable grip on her arm, pulling her effortlessly up towards the light.

She closed her eyes and awaited the bright lights from heaven that would accompany the angel that was pulling her to the sky. She felt her face break through the icy grip of the water and a hand on her skin. When she opened her eyes, she saw a pair of grey eyes directly in her sight. She shook her head, blinked and looked again at what she was seeing.

Declan was staring at her with fear exploding from his eyes. "Meggie, are y' okay?"

"What?" she asked, rather confused.

"Are y' okay?" he asked, shaking her in the water.

"I thought you were an angel."

"Oh shit, now she's seeing angels." A deep sarcastic voice bellowed from behind her. She turned her head to see Fabrizio swimming up to them, with Cassie holding onto his back.

"Oh, that's brilliant, y' two are okay," Declan sighed with relief and pulled Meghan towards him.

She wrapped one arm around his neck and slicked back his long black hair with her other one. "You really need to get this cut," she sighed, wiping back the mass of hair off his face.

"Bloody hell, Meggie, you're unbelievable," Declan laughed, all the tension of the last few days seemed to have vanished from her eyes, and the pure love was back.

"Meggie, I'm sorry," Declan whispered into her hair as his lips landed on the side of her head.

"So am I," Meghan sniffed, pressing her face against his. She was unsure what he was apologizing for, but she did not want to ask. All that mattered to her at that moment was that he was holding her. However, that was also what frightened her. His touch, his caress was all that stood between her love and desire for him and her common sense. What common sense, it was gone again, stolen by the touch of his lips to hers.

"Give me your hand." A deep unfamiliar voice broke her thoughts. She glanced up at the firefighter that was leaning over towards her, his hand outstretched. A startled expression crossed her face before Declan assured her it was safe to accept the assistance.

Once the group was out of the icy water, the firefighter handed Declan a blanket, and he quickly wrapped it around Meghan, holding her tightly while she shivered in his arms.

"Declan, you're cold too, you need this!" Meghan opened the blanket and attempted to wrap it around him.

"Meggie, keep it on, I know how y' are with the cold. I'll be fine until they bring another blanket," Declan ordered and dragged her down the docks towards the fire trucks.

Declan eyed Meghan sidelong for a moment, then a roar of laughter exploded from him. "Fooking Irish bastard?" His voice was full of amusement.

Meghan gazed at him and grimaced. "Well?"

"I can't believe such foul words can come out of a mouth so pretty." He kissed her lips and smacked her on the bottom. "You've a sharp tongue, Meghan Montgomery."

Meghan crinkled her nose at him, but his attention suddenly switched to a body lying on a stretcher with a number of EMS personnel surrounding it. Declan's face had gone completely white at the sight, and before Meghan could question him, he darted towards the man.

"Rory?" Declan screamed and dropped to his knees beside the stretcher. "Bloody hell."

"Declan, I'm so sorry. I never thought it would come to this." Rory's voice was soft and weak. "I just wanted to find out where I belonged. I just wanted someone to love me."

"I love y'," Declan muttered and gripped Rory's pasty hand. "Rory, y' are me brother, I have always loved y'."

"Declan, please forgive me. I can't die knowing y' hate me."

"Oh Rory, I could never hate you. What happened to y'?"

Rory forced a smile to his face. "I couldn't let him hurt you again. I told Liam that I would not help him kill you again. I ran back inside to help, but I didn't get out in time."

"I thought someone was shooting at Liam's men from the other side of the room." Declan squeezed his brother's hand. "Thank y', Rory."

Rory nodded slightly and closed his eyes. "Please tell ma and da that I love them and tell Moiré and Colin to stop all their fighting and get along. Life is too short."

"Rory, y' can tell them yourself." Declan's voice constricted with despair.

Rory forced a morose laugh. "It's ironic that it takes Liam to bring us to a place where we can express our feeling for each other."

Declan grunted and wiped away the tears that were dripping down his cheek.

Meghan rested her hand on Declan's shoulder and glanced down at Rory, her face ashen. "Rory?"

"Meghan, I'm so sorry for everything I have done to y'. Please forgive me." Rory was fighting to keep his eyes open. "Please."

Meghan nodded her head, unable to speak. She knew from the expression on the paramedics' faces that he was dying, and from the amount of blood soaking his shirt, it was inevitable. "You should get him to the hospital," Meghan blurted out even though she knew he was not long for this world. "He needs blood."

"Meghan, please don't fret. I know I am dying. The explosion blew me to pieces. Luckily these nice men covered me up." His laugh was soft and low.

Meghan choked back a sob as Declan dropped his head onto Rory's chest. "Come on, little brother, y' are strong."

Rory's hand slowly rose and rested against Declan's head. "Declan, go home, and let him have it. Declan, just be happy." The hand went limp and slid down the black hair, landing solidly on the stretcher.

"Rory?" Declan cried and shook his brother slightly. "No . . ."

"Declan." Meghan rested her hand on his shoulder once again, but this time he dislodged it and pushed her away from him.

"If y' had just stayed in the room."

Meghan stumbled backwards, quite shocked from his comment. Her eyes glued to his angry face.

"Monty, I don't think we should be lingering here." Fabrizio grabbed Declan's arm and pulled him away from Rory. "Call this number, and they will make the arrangements for him." Fabrizio scrawled down Declan's parents' number on a piece of paper. "Monty, we can call them and let them know, but we need to get out of this country."

"Aye." Declan's eyes were still glued to Rory's lifeless face. "Goodbye, brother."

Meghan wanted nothing more than to hold him and console him, but after he pushed her away, she was scared to attempt a connection again.

When the paramedics draped the sheet over Rory's face, Declan's gaze broke, and he began to scan the area. His eyes settled on Meghan as she leaned up against a pile of crates, shaking uncontrollably. What had he done? Why did he blame her for what happened? It was Rory who put himself into the path of danger by attempting to have a relationship with the O'Briens.

Meghan noticed his gaze on her, and she turned away and headed towards the inn. "Fabrizio, I think we all need showers before we go anywhere."

Fabrizio nodded and gripped Cassie's hand. "We will all shower in my room. Then we are leaving for the airport."

CHAPTER THIRTY-SIX

The chaotic murmur of the airport was a welcome sound as they rushed through the doors towards the ticket counter. Meghan was finally starting to warm after showering and changing into dry cloths at the inn. She was still rather shaken and worried about the safety measures that Declan and Fabrizio were taking. They must still be in real danger, they were being so cautious.

"Okay, let's go to the gate, our plane leaves in an hour," Declan informed Meghan as he grabbed her arm and dragged her towards the departure gate.

"Declan, you don't need to tug on me. I'm coming," Meghan scolded him, feeling rather like a rag doll he was dragging around.

"Sorry, I didn't mean to hurt y'," Declan mumbled but did not release her arm.

"You're not hurting me. I just don't want you dragging me around like a prisoner," Meghan grumbled, pulling at her arm to release it from his grip.

"Meggie," He snorted as he stopped and glared at her.

"What?"

"Don't start with me. We need to get to the gate and get on that plane. Why are y' being so difficult."

"I'm not."

"Aye, y' are."

"I just want to walk on my own," Meghan snapped, pulling at her arm again.

"Fine," Declan muttered through his clenched teeth and released her arm, then stood glaring at her.

Meghan rubbed at her arm where his fingers had been gripping her and then she snarled and turned towards the gate. Declan shook his head and followed close behind her, so close in fact, she could feel his breath on the back of her neck. She was finding it hard to deal with the fact that he blamed her for his brother's death. Maybe it was best if she disappeared into the crowd, allowing the rest of the group to go home to safety.

"Meggie, here's your ticket," Declan said evenly as he handed her the ticket.

"Thanks," Meghan muttered, trying to avoid his cold dark eyes. It was back, the dead expression, the uncaring gaze.

Meghan sighed and rested her purse and carry-on baggage on the table for the security to scan. Her eyes stayed lowered to the ground, unable to look at Declan.

Cassie noticed her first as she headed towards them with an expression of complete devastation on her weary face.

"Meg, what's wrong?" Cassie's voice was soft but tired. She was wishing now that she had gone home a month ago. She was not cut out for all the danger that followed Meghan around. Who would have thought that the quiet redheaded girl that was an outcast in school would have grown into a woman that men were willing to kill to posses?

Meghan did not miss the expression in Cassie's eyes, so she forced a smile and moved over to a chair by the window and watched the rain drizzle down the glass.

Cassie eyed her departure, then turned to Fabrizio and shrugged at Meghan's attitude.

Fabrizio grunted with annoyance as he watched Declan sit a few seats away from Meghan and scrub at his eyes. Declan looked exhausted, his eyes dark and sunken. He had not slept more than a few hours a night since she disappeared, and the tension was certainly showing. Declan was making poor choices; one of them was his behaviour towards Meghan. What was he doing, screwing her around so horribly? Did he not see the sadness in her eyes? Did Declan not see what he could lose? Meghan was incredible, kind, funny, intelligent, and most of all, loving. She is the perfect woman, a woman that any man would give up everything to posses. Maybe even friendship.

"Fabs?" Cassie's voice was concerned as she stared at him, his eyes glued to Meghan. "What is going on?"

"Pardon?" Fabrizio looked back to the beautiful woman at his side. The woman that stuck by him, supported him through the last month. He smiled at the sight of her and wrapped his long arm around her narrow shoulder.

"Nothing, sweetheart." Fabrizio kissed her cheek. "I was just wondering what he is doing." He bobbed his head towards Declan.

Cassie forced a smile, knowing it was not Declan that Fabrizio was staring at like a lovesick puppy, it was Meghan. What was happening to her life? Meghan had changed over the last month, become more guarded somehow. At the warehouse, Cassie wasn't sure if Meghan cared for Liam or not. Now Fabrizio seemed preoccupied with her best friend. Cassie did not miss that it was Meghan Fabrizio was focused on at the warehouse; he seemed furious that O'Brien was kissing her, almost jealous. Fabrizio's expression had not been too different from Declan's.

All those weeks they spent together in Ireland before she was kidnapped, all the times Declan had Fabrizio escorted Meghan somewhere. Had Fabrizio fallen for her again?

"Fabrizio, what's going to happen when we get home?" Cassie questioned, resting her head on his shoulder, hoping she was wrong.

Fabrizio shrugged slightly, his gaze settling back on Meghan. "I think he will go after her again. He loves her, Cass, I'm sure of it. Declan doesn't want to believe it, but . . ." He stopped his comment and watched Declan as he got up and went to the window in front of where Meghan was sitting. "The way O'Brien held her, kissed her, it was sickening." Fabrizio's voice was husky with disgust.

Cassie cringed and forced calmness into her demeanour. She had nothing to worry about. Fabrizio was just concerned for a friend, that's all Meghan was, a friend.

"Cass, you know Meghan better than anyone. Does she have feelings for O'Brien or was she just pretending?" Fabrizio glanced down at Cassie, awaiting her answer.

"She loves Declan, she always has," Cassie assured him as well as herself. "Meghan has been through a lot in her life, and she has developed a strong survival instinct. I wouldn't be surprised if she had O'Brien completely convinced she had feelings for him. She would do anything to get back to Declan and Caelan."

Fabrizio nodded, his gaze settling back on Declan who had now sat down in the chair next to Meghan. He appeared so uncomfortable, so unsure of what he should do that Fabrizio chuckled.

"What are you laughing at?" Cassie questioned, sitting up and following his gaze.

"Those two. Look at them. I have never seen Declan so uncomfortable before," Fabrizio sighed, deciding to focus on his relationship with Cassie; she, after all, was a fabulous woman in her own right. "I guess it's all the excitement."

Cassie sighed and glanced over at the quiet couple. "I really don't think I like living like this," Cassie said softly. "I can tell you that I could never be married to a soldier. I hate this feeling of dread."

Fabrizio eyed her curiously. How did she know that he was thinking about rejoining the services? He had to admit he loved the rush, the excitement of tracking and removing hostages from their captures. When he and Declan served in the elite unit, he thrived on the high he received from outsmarting the terrorists.

Declan watched Meghan as she stared out the window, and he could not help but review the events of the last few days. Rory's final words be happy were haunting him. Be happy. How could he be happy? Rory was dead, and he had hurt Meghan repeatedly. What could he possibly say to her to get her to forgive him?

Meghan could feel Declan watching her, but his silence was unnerving. Why wasn't he talking to her, why was he just staring at her? Her hand slipped into her pocket and exited with her locket clenched between her fingers. "I can't believe that such a small piece of jewelry could start such chain of misery," she whispered, examining it from all sides. She flicked it open and brushed the picture of Caelan with her finger.

Declan blinked when her eyes settled on him. He felt his heart tighten at the expression in her eyes.

"Meggie," Declan's hand rested against her cheek, but he had no idea what to say to her. Everything that had happened was his fault. "I'm so sorry."

Meghan's eyes settled on Declan with worry. What was he doing now? "What are you sorry for?" She wanted to know.

"For everything. For blaming y' for Rory's death, for telling y' I didn't love y'." Declan gripped Meghan's hand and lifted it to his lips. "I love you, Meggie, and I'll be damned if I am going to fight it anymore."

Meghan's eyes filled again, and the tears ran down her face. His eyes were so sincere, his voice so true. Maybe he did love her.

"I know it's going to take a lot for y' to forgive me for what I did. I have made plenty of mistakes, but loving y' isn't one of them." His hand swept across her cheek, brushing away the stream of tears cascading down her skin.

The realization of how deep her love for him actually was scared him slightly, but it scared him more not to have her, to possess her completely. She belonged to him, and no one was going to take her away again. She owned his heart, and he needed her, he loved her. It felt fantastic to admit his love for her to himself and to her. The expression in her eyes the moment he said it crushed him completely. No woman had ever looked at him the way she did, no woman could ever reach into his soul the way she does.

Meghan closed her eyes, pressing her face into his hand. "Do you realize that we spent almost five years apart and nothing happened to either of us? Then we're back together for a week and all hell broke loose again, and it hasn't stopped. We're a magnet for trouble when we're together."

"Aye, we do seem to attract trouble." His tone was not as light as he intended. "But I would rather deal with the trouble than live without y'."

Meghan eyed him speculatively, why did he keep bouncing back and forth with his emotions? "Declan, I'm sorry for all the trouble I've caused."

"Freckles, this isn't your fault, I'm to blame. If I hadn't wanted to prove me mam wrong, this would never have happened."

Meghan sighed and looked out the window at the tarmac and watched as the rain beat against the windows with excessive force. "I just want to get out of here and get home."

"I know, Freckles, me too," Declan agreed kissing her on the forehead. She was going to fall apart, he could see it in her eyes. They could not get on that plane soon enough. Hopefully, once in the air, she would sleep, the feeling of safety would hopefully return.

He hated seeing the fear in her eyes; he wondered if he had left Pine Creek without her, left before the media got involved, would she be safely tucked away in her nice warm house with Caelan. He tried to imagine his life now; it was the middle of October, by now his mother should be preparing for her yearly Thanksgiving feast, and in less than a month, she would have forced him into proposing to Georgia at the dinner. His father needed her father's support. Would he have selflessly helped his father or would he have bolted?

He shuddered at the thought of spending the rest of his life with Georgia Preston. Her beauty could not mask the shallow arrogance she possessed, the complete superiority she felt towards people. Georgia treated the household staff like scum under feet, where Meghan embraced her housekeeper as a friend. The two women were completely different, but both completely in love with him.

He was blessed, he decided to have a woman like Meghan love him. She didn't appear to give her love that freely, and when she bestowed it on someone, it was a lifelong bond. Nathan was one of the lucky few, but he would never hurt her as Declan had. Yet, after all the cruel and horrible things he had done, she still loved him, still yearns for him, and that thought tugged at his heart. She was his destiny, and he would risk his own life for hers.

The heavy rain had dwindled into a fine mist that hung over the airport like a veil, causing Meghan to shudder from the bone-chilling dampness. She brushed back her long auburn hair and leaned against the large window, looking out over the tarmac. Their flight out of Ireland back to New York had been delayed due to the heavy rain, causing her anxiety to build as she longed to get home and see Caelan.

Cassie startled Meghan's thoughts when she grabbed her arm and turned her towards her. "Meg, are you okay?" she asked, brushing back her long blonde hair.

"Yes, I'm fine. I'm just thinking about what has happened since we arrived in Ireland," Meghan sighed.

"Meg. It will be okay. The plane will be leaving soon, and we will get home," Cassie smiled softly as her dark blue eyes flickered with worry.

Meghan forced a smile and glanced back over towards Declan, fixing her dark green eyes on him. "Look at him. He seems so at easy now."

"He does, doesn't he? I wish Fabrizio would relax," Cassie muttered, glancing back at Fabrizio, who was sitting nervously next to the wall, his brown eyes darting back and forth keeping watch on all of them.

Fabrizio was finding it hard to relax, knowing that they would not be safe until they were on the ground in New York and away from O'Brien's reach. He was so programmed to keep his eyes on Declan that he was finding it hard to keep track of Meghan and Cassie's movements as well. The Navy Seals had given Fabrizio and Declan the acute senses that have kept them alive to this point, but he couldn't relax until they were all back in the States safely.

Meghan turned back to the window and watched as the mist floated down from the dark sky with a peaceful soothing effect. Her eyes widened and a gasp exited her lips as she caught a reflection in the window from the security check across the hall. She turned abruptly and saw a tall solid man with short blond hair, wandering down the hall towards her. As she scanned the area, she caught sight of at least five armed men surrounding him as they moved closer, scanning the faces in the crowd.

"Declan," she blurted out, with a tone of fear.

"Aye," he smiled, his grey eyes fixed on her.

"Look." Meghan pulled on his arm and directed her gaze towards O'Brien.

Declan's face hardened, and he instantly reverted into his military behaviour he had been exhibiting earlier that day. "Fabs," he hollered towards his friend that was still sitting across the room.

Fabrizio recognized the tone of voice and jumped from the chair, displacing Cassie. He looked down at her annoyed face, grabbed her arm, and dragged her out of the chair towards Declan and Meghan.

"Declan, he's blocking the exit," Meghan muttered as her eyes started to fill with tears.

"Meggie, calm down. Y' can't get upset," Declan ordered, grabbing her hand ushering her towards the far end of the room. Declan turned back to assess O'Brien's position and could see that he had spotted them and had his men fanning out, trying to surround them.

"Bloody hell!" Declan snorted as he began to run down the hall, pulling Meghan along behind him. Fabrizio and Cassie were directly behind them as they passed by departure gate after departure gate and found no other exit.

"There has to be an emergency exit here somewhere," Fabrizio snorted as he scanned the hall in front of them.

Meghan was panting with exhaustion as Declan pulled on her arm with such a force, she felt her legs would buckle, and she would collapse to the ground. Declan abruptly stopped and spun around, causing her to trip into the wall with a thud. He pulled her back to her feet with one smooth movement as he scanned the area.

"There's no exit," Declan muttered as he directed his grey gaze on an empty departure gate. "Come on." He dragged Meghan through the doors and down the long ramp.

Once at the end, they came to a stop and looked down at the ground. "That's quite a drop," Declan muttered, as he seemed to be trying to decide if they could jump without breaking every bone in their legs.

"You're not thinking we should jump, are you?" Meghan blurted out, looking down at the ground below.

"Well, it's jump or go back and try to get past O'Brien and his men." Declan eyed her with agitation.

"Declan," Meghan muttered, her voice full of fear. Liam was never going to stop hunting her.

"Meggie. It will be okay." Declan soothed, kissed her forehead, and climbed down the side of the ramp.

When he reached the bottom of the ladder, he assessed it was approximately a fifteen-foot drop to the ground. Meghan watched with amazement as he dangled from the last rung, then released his grip and dropped the remaining seven feet to the ground, landing on his feet like a cat. Meghan batted her eyes as she watched him raising his arms towards her, coaxing her down the side of the ramp.

"Meggie, come on," he gently ordered.

She knew she had no choice, now that he was on the ground, so she mustered up all her courage and climbed onto the ladder. As Meghan reached the last rung, she glanced up; Cassie was right above her, with Fabrizio sliding down the side towards her. He stopped at Meghan's side and wrapped his legs around the last rung, then dropped down hanging from his bent legs.

"Meghan, give me your hands," Fabrizio ordered, bending at the waist and looking up at her. She was startled by his positioning and stared at him with amazement. "Boo," he snapped, waving his hands towards her.

"Meghan, hurry up, I can hear them coming," Cassie hollered as terror shot through her. How the hell did she get into the middle of this nightmare?

Meghan closed her eyes and reached her hands out towards Fabrizio who grasped them firmly in his large strong hands. She shrieked with terror as she felt him tug on her, displacing her from the rung and swinging her downwards.

When she felt Declan's grip on her legs as he pulled her to the ground, she felt almost euphoric, as if she was in a dream, and this man was her saviour. Declan, however, was not in the same dream and released her immediately, his arms swinging back up to grab hold of Cassie, who was dangling from Fabrizio's hands.

Once Cassie was safely in Declan's arms, Fabrizio leaned back up, grabbing the bar with his hand, flipped his legs down, and dropped to the ground with the same smooth motion that Declan displayed.

Declan had hold of Meghan's hand once again, and she found herself propelled at speeds her legs were not meant to travel. Every muscle was burning from the exertion as they darted across the wet tarmac to a fence on the far side of the airport.

O'Brien and his men stopped at the edge of the ramp eyeing the ground with annoyance. They apparently did not intend to make the drop. O'Brien shoved at one of his men with irritation, then turned and ran back up the ramp to find another way to the ground. His behaviour was holding true when they didn't shoot at the fleeing group. Apparently, he still needed her alive.

Meghan sighed with relief as she watched him disappear up the ramp. At least, they had a head start on the man that had been terrorizing her for the last two months.

Once at the fence, Declan stopped and turned to Meghan, one side of his mouth rising in a smile. "I can't believe y' did that, Freckles. I thought Fabs was going to have to push y'."

"Well, I didn't have much choice now, did I?" Meghan snorted, crinkling her nose at him as she tried to catch her breath.

"Aye, I guess not," Declan laughed, remembering how scared she was of heights. He bent down and kissed her damp forehead, then pulled her towards the fence. "I'll help y' over." He glanced over his shoulder as the tarmac glowed with red and blue. "Bloody hell," he grumbled at the three Garda cars heading towards them.

Fabrizio's attention settled on the approaching cars as Declan hoisted Meghan over the twelve-foot high fence that she awkwardly managed to climb over and scale down the other side.

There was no time to discuss the direction to head, and once over the fence, the group was on the move again towards the road leading back into town.

"There's a cab," Fabrizio shouted and darted into the middle of the road, with his hands up in the air in front of him. The cab screeched to a stop on the rain-drenched road, and the driver bolted from the car, screaming hysterically, his words blurred by the thick Irish accent.

Fabrizio grabbed the little fat screaming man and flung him into the large ditch beside the car, giving Declan the opportunity to jump into the back seat. He was startled to see an elderly couple gazing at him, with terror exploding from their faces. However, when Meghan jumped in on top of Declan's legs, their expression turned to interest.

"Hi," Meghan blurted out as Declan turned his head away, pulling down his dark Boston Red Sox ball cap to cover his face.

The elderly woman eyed Meghan with curiosity, then quickly switched her attention to the front seat as Cassie and Fabrizio entered the vehicle.

"Please don't hurt us," the terrified woman begged as Fabrizio drove off, leaving the stunned cabby crawling up the muddy embankment, screaming at the departing car.

"We won't, don't worry," Meghan smiled softly, trying to console the couple that were now scrutinizing the soaking wet quartet. "We just need to get to town."

The grey-haired woman turned her gaze on Declan, who still had his head turned away from the couple, trying to avoid recognition. "Have you done something illegal?" questioned the woman, still gazing at Declan.

"No," he muttered, still keeping his head turned.

The elderly man turned his squinty blue gaze on his wife. "What did he say, dear?" he shouted, evidently hard of hearing.

"He said he didn't do anything illegal," she shouted back into his ear.

"Oh. Are they going to rob us?" he hollered.

"No," Meghan blurted out. "We just needed to get into town, and then we will leave you alone," she muttered, gazing up at Cassie.

"What was the big rush, dear? I'm sure another cab would have come along," she questioned with interest, realizing that they were in no danger.

"Well, we couldn't take that chance. Someone is . . ."

"Freckles, that's enough," Declan snorted, still keeping his face turned towards the window.

"Sorry," she muttered and smiled slightly at the woman, then looked up at Fabrizio, who was scanning the area to find somewhere they could deposit the couple.

He saw a tavern ahead, and he came to a stop, jumped out, and opened the trunk to remove their luggage. He opened the back door and pulled the man out to the curb. His wife followed quickly behind and stood staring at Fabrizio with disbelief.

"Welcome to Ireland," Fabrizio said, bowing towards them, then jumped back into the cab, and drove off at great speeds down the road.

"Welcome to Ireland?" Declan laughed, turning his head towards Fabrizio.

"I couldn't think of anything else to say," Fabrizio laughed so hard, the car began to swerve from side to side on the slick road.

Declan shook his head and turned to Meghan. "What were y' going to do, tell her our whole life story?" he smirked.

"No!" Meghan crinkled her nose at him in annoyance. "I was trying to keep her calm."

"Well, they didn't seem too scared of us. I actually think they were rather disappointed that we weren't terrorists," Declan laughed and deposited Meghan on the seat beside him.

Meghan grinned as she pulled his hat up so she could see his handsome chiselled face. He smirked and lifted off his cap, brushing back his long black hair, then replaced the hat on his head.

"What are we going to do now?" Meghan questioned, with fear building in her gut.

"We need to get a different vehicle," Fabrizio commented as he pulled into an alley behind a small hotel.

"Are we going into that hotel?" Cassie questioned.

"No, we're getting out and walking to the car rental agency down the street." Fabrizio muttered as he wiped the steering wheel clean of prints. Declan was busy with the door handles and any other surfaces that they might have touched.

Once finished, Declan grabbed the open edges of Meghan's denim jacket, pulled her towards him, and kissed her forehead.

"Meggie, remember when I said that I would rather live with the trouble that follows us around than live without y'?" he smirked.

"Yes." She squinted at him. "Are you changing your mind?"

"No. I was just thinking that I should be careful for what I ask for," his smile was wide and lit his grey eyes. "As exciting as this has been, I don't think I want to spend me whole life doing it."

"Exciting?" Meghan snorted and smacked his arm. "You're finding enjoyment in this?"

"Well, I wouldn't say enjoyment, but I like the rush," Declan grinned and kissed her forehead.

"Monty, enough of that," Fabrizio snorted, bobbing his head towards the car rental agency. "We need to get out of here."

"Fabrizio, I think I know a way to get out of this country safely," Declan informed him with a slight smile as he followed Fabrizio up the street.

"Good, fill me in after we get the car."

The Volvo was waiting outside the building for the group, and once inside, Declan began to explain his plan. It involved them heading up to Northern Ireland to the area, where Declan's father, Patrick, was from, called Ballymena. Declan's aunt Amy was married to a Catholic man named Michael Flynn, who was rumoured to have had connections to men that were once members of Irish Republican Army.

"Declan, are you out of your mind? We are in enough trouble, we don't need to be getting mixed up with the IRA," Meghan snorted, as they pulled away from the curb.

"Meggie, calm down. I don't plan on getting caught up with them, and as far as I know, they are not involved anymore. I just figure that Uncle Mick hates O'Brien as much as we do and would be willing to help us get out of Ireland. He already knows most of what's going on. He is the one that helped us locate the residence in which O'Brien had y' stashed."

"Well, he's family, wouldn't he just help us without involving the IRA?"

"I don't know how far O'Brien's reach is, Meggie. He managed to get through the security at the airport fully armed." Declan raised his brow and glanced at Fabrizio, who was listening carefully as he drove.

"Oh God, I never even thought about that. How did he do that?" Meghan muttered and leaned into Declan, feeling rather fearful.

Declan shrugged and turned back to Fabrizio, with worry building in his eyes. "Fabs, I don't know another way."

"Well, let's just see what your uncle has to say. It's one thing to give you information, but I don't think he will be too impressed to have relatives showing up at his door with a man like O'Brien on their heels." Fabrizio glanced back in the rear-view mirror and eyed Declan as he consoled Meghan.

"Liam is never going to stop coming after me, is he?"

Declan sighed and rested his head against Meghan's. "I don't believe so, Freckles."

CHAPTER THIRTY-SEVEN

The group split up in Belfast, where Fabrizio and Cassie headed for the airport. The plan was for Cassie to fly back to New York, and Fabrizio was going to notify the FBI of what had been happening. Fabrizio wanted to get Cassie home and out of the reach of O'Brien. The worry was that he would use her as leverage against Meghan if he caught them. To their knowledge, Meghan was his main target, so hopefully, he would continue after Meghan, leaving Cassie to go for help.

They suspected the Garda had a leak allowing O'Brien to locate them easily, so going to them was out of the question. Fabrizio was convinced that that was how O'Brien found them at the inn. There was no way he could have just lucked out and found them. O'Brien showed up within hours of his call to Inspector Maloney of Garda. Declan placed a call to Maloney, informing him that they were heading to Dublin to meet up with him, so hopefully that would lead O'Brien in that direction.

The little plaster house was exactly as Declan remembered, untouched by time. The rolling hills behind the house flowed into the overgrown fields, the small amount of sheep were apparently unable to keep up with the growth.

When the solid dark wood door swung open, Declan was startled at the appearance of his aunt and uncle. They had aged. He had expected them to age, but his memories were from childhood, and he almost expected them to appear unchanged by time. His aunt Amy was still very slender, and her hair was short and curly with streaks of grey.

Uncle Mick was thin and frail, his grey hair combed over the bald spot on his head.

Once Declan eyed the frail frame of Uncle Mick, he wished he had not involved him. They didn't need this in their life.

"It's great to see y', lad." Mick grabbed Declan and hugged him tightly.

"Aye," Declan grunted from the pressure around his ribs. "I'm sorry it's under these circumstances, though. We were planning on coming up north once the movie was done, but those plans changed," Declan smirked and pulled Meghan through the door towards his relatives. "This is Meghan."

"Good day to y', Meghan," Amy smiled and hugged Meghan's thin frame. "Y' look exhausted, dear, come sit down, and I'll get you some tea." Amy floated down the hall towards the kitchen.

"Thank you, that would be lovely," Meghan smiled and followed her.

"Wow, this kitchen hasn't changed," Declan said with shock. He was surprised they had not updated the kitchen since he left.

"I suppose y' feel we should have kept up with the times." Mick's dark blue eyes glimmered after noticing Declan's facial expression.

Declan shrugged and pulled out the chair for Meghan, then dropped down beside her at the large maple table. A mischievous grin curled his lips, and he bent down, looked under the table, and then laughed. "It's still there."

"Aye." Amy grey eyes filled with a mixture of humour and annoyance. "Y' and Eamon were rascals I must say. He was here last week with some lass he met in Belfast, and he pointed out that his famous cousin's name was carved under the table."

Declan roared at the thought of Eamon using his mother's table as a tourist attraction. Eamon was always the ladies man, being almost thirty and still not married. He was almost as bad as Declan in that regard, and Katie was quick to point it out.

"So is this the same lass he brought with him to visit me when I first arrived?"

"No, I believe she was a new one," Mick laughed. "I believe he and your brother Colin will be bachelors for life." Mick's face suddenly darkened. "I must tell y' again how sorry I am about Rory. It's a shame that the lad got caught up in this."

505

Declan sighed and eyed Meghan with worry. He could not get that moment out of his mind when he blamed her for Rory's death. The expression in her eyes devastated him. Had she forgiven him for his cruel comments? She appeared to have, but when he watched her, the hurt was still present. If the tables were turned, would he have forgiven her? Probably not.

"Aye," Declan finally said and eyed his aunt. "Have y' talked with me mam?"

"Aye, she called yesterday and asked if I would track y' down," Amy smiled slightly. "Unfortunately, I can't call her and tell we found y' in case our phones are tapped. I assume that they will be watching us, if they are not already."

Declan sighed and lowered his gaze. "I'm sorry to put y' in this position. Maybe it is best if we left."

"Don't be daft, lad. We are kin, and I will not turn me back on y'." Mick focused on Amy as she poured the tea. "I called Eamon this morning, and he is on his way here. He has more connections than I do."

Meghan bristled at the thought but said nothing. She was not sure if she wanted to get involved with the IRA, no matter how inactive they had been of late. She watched Mick and idly wondered if he had killed any innocent people over his years as a soldier in the IRA. Declan had told her many stories from his uncle's day, and most she found reprehensible. But this man seemed very kind as he interacted with them, and Declan loved him dearly. Amy was a kind motherly type, doting on them since they arrived, which caused Meghan slight shame that she had judged them so unkindly before her arrival.

"So O'Brien has decided to marry y' and produce an heir instead of killing y'?" Mick's voice startled Meghan back to the conversation.

"He apparently decided that years ago." Declan filled him in on the details of the past.

"Well, that's a lucky break for y', lass," Mick grinned and sipped his tea.

"Why is that?" Meghan cringed and glanced over at Declan, wondering how she was lucky.

"Meghan, dear, y' are a big threat to O'Brien, you're lucky you're not dead," Mick sighed and directed his gaze towards Declan. "And so are y'. You're still in danger. He needs y' dead."

"Aye," Declan chuckled. "It's not from a lack of trying on his part."

"Declan, this isn't funny," Meghan grumbled.

"I know, Freckles." Declan soothed, then glanced over at Mick and rolled his eyes letting him know that Meghan was being dramatic.

"Well, lass, the thing we need to focus on now is how to get y' home. Then we need to find a way for y' to take control of your estate and oust the leasers." Mick bit into the biscuit Amy had laid on the table.

"I don't want that damn land," Meghan snorted before Declan's hand rested on her leg warningly.

"Well, that's too bad, lass, because you're stuck with it."

"I know," Meghan sighed and covered her face with her hands. "Fergus has already explained this to me. I can't sell it, and I can't give it to anyone. It has to be willed down through the pure line."

"Aye," Mick agreed and glanced over at Declan. "So the question is what do we do about that? I've heard that O'Brien uses it to smuggle drugs into Ireland from South America. There are hidden coves and caves perfect for hidden small ships. Apparently, the Vikings used them during their time here on the island. From there, he has the perfect location to transport it into Europe," Mick suggested. "And you can bet that tends to upset me acquaintances." His overgrown brows crumpled with agitation. "So that is one of the reasons why they are willing to help y'. They would rather y' have possession of that land."

"Why do they care what Liam is doing?" Meghan muttered, trying to understand what Mick was telling her.

"Are y' saying that they don't like him smuggling drugs in because they are against it or they don't like the competition?" Declan questioned, getting concerned with the direction the conversation was heading.

Mick scrunched his greying brows in thought. "Well, lad, let's just say that they don't want him doing business," he commented with a note of finality.

"Why not?" Meghan questioned, knowing she was pushing the line, but she didn't care.

"Meghan, dear, I think that's all y' need to know," Mick frowned at her.

Meghan sighed and lifted her cup of tea. She gazed over the rim at Declan and slowly sipped, trying to calm her exploding nerves. "Great, so I have a drug lord killer trying to marry me," she muttered against the rim of the cup.

"He needs more from y' than marriage," Mick announced, with a tone of worry.

"He needs me to give him a child, I know," Meghan muttered, her frayed nerves exploding. The teacup dropped from her fingers to the table with a crash, splattering the hot dark liquid on everything in its path. "Dammit," she cried as she tried desperately to clean up her mess.

"It's okay, dear." Amy soothed as she jumped up and wiped the table with the tea towel from the sink.

"I'm sorry," Meghan blurted out, the tears dripping down her face.

"Meggie." Declan stood and moved in behind her, sliding his arm around her shoulders with a comforting grip.

"Declan, what if he figures out about Caelan?" Meghan sniffed, assuming he was thinking the same thing.

Declan jerked and glanced down at her. "What do y' mean, Meggie?"

"She is the legal heir of both of us." Meghan looked over at Mick.

"Aye," Mick said, scratching at his grey stubble that was covering his face. "It would. I'm surprised he wouldn't know that unless . . ."

"Unless what?" Declan questioned with panic.

"Unless he doesn't know that Caelan is your daughter," Mick said, bobbing his head up and down as he contemplated the thought.

Meghan turned her gaze on Declan with a puzzled look filling her face. "He seemed to know everything about us."

"Hmm." Declan moved over to the window, staring blankly out at the foothills in the distance behind the cottage. "Meggie." His tone was soft but somewhat concerned. "Who is listed as Caelan's father on her birth certificate?"

Her eyes widened at the question he never thought to ask before. "Nat."

"What? Why would y' put him down?" Declan questioned sharply.

"Because," Meghan snorted rather defensively, "you . . ." She stopped and removed her gaze from his irritated face. "I was so hurt that you didn't want us," she sighed at the thought.

"Oh, Meggie," Declan sighed and moved towards her, resting his hands on her shoulders. His hands gently rubbed her tense muscles as he stood quietly, contemplating what she said.

"It's probably for the best, Declan, if they don't think that Caelan is your child, they will leave her alone," Mick said with confidence. "An heir produced by the both of y' would place the power of the triad in the hands of two families. That's what the O'Briens have been trying to do. First Rory, then with Meghan."

"Mick!" Amy's voice was harsh. "That is not to be discussed."

"We already know that Fergus is Rory's biological father," Declan sighed and glanced over at Meghan.

"Oh, for heaven sakes!" Amy gasped and turned to Mick. "How did y' find out. Your mother is going to be devastated."

"Rory told me." Declan eyed his aunt. "Bloody hell, Da knew this was going to happen? Why didn't he tell me the truth that the O'Brien's were killers? This all could have been avoided."

"Now don't blame Paddy for this, lad. He was just doing what he thought was best," Mick defended his brother-in-law. "I talked to him last week, and he regrets not letting y' know how dangerous that family is."

"Mick's right, Declan, we all have some blame here," Meghan mumbled and scrubbed at her eyes.

"Aye?" Declan's gaze settled on Meghan.

Meghan settled in to explain what Rory had been up to since she was kidnapped. She didn't like hurting Declan, but she wanted him to know everything. She told them everything she had learned at the castle, but she left out the information about the possible hiding spot of the fabled sword. The last thing she wanted was for them to decide that was worth going after.

"So, Rory was after your portion of the estate?" Mick shook his head. "I always knew that lad was trouble."

Declan nodded but didn't speak.

Meghan breathed heavily as what was happening was becoming clear. "So when Declan and I die, if we don't have a son, Caelan will have more control of the triad than Liam's son."

"His son?" Declan blurted out. "He has a son?"

"Yes, his name is Ayden. He's a nice little boy."

"Well," Mick muttered. "We were unaware he had a child."

"You didn't know?" Meghan said with shock.

"No. How did y' find out?" Mick questioned, his eyes glued to her with interest.

"He told me," Meghan said calmly. "Well, I . . ." A smirk filled her face. "I asked him every day who the boy was."

Declan laughed at the thought of her tormenting O'Brien. "Y' nagged him until he told y'."

"I guess," Meghan chuckled. "He wouldn't tell me who the mother was, but Tomas said she died."

"Hmm," Declan muttered, getting up and wandering over to the stove to refill the teapot, not wanting Amy to have to get up and move again. "How old is the boy?"

"I don't know, about six or seven. He looks just like Liam, except he doesn't have the birthmark."

"Well, this changes things a bit," Mick said with a bit of interest. "If the boy Ayden is Liam's eldest son, he inherits Liam's third. Any child he sires now would have no claim unless Ayden were to die without leaving an heir."

"He wouldn't kill his own son," Meghan blurted out. "He loves him."

"Aye, he would," Mick said with a cold tone. "If he is anything like his da, he would."

"He's not," Meghan said in his defence, more scared for the small boy than concerned about Liam's reputation. "He wouldn't kill him. He couldn't," she babbled out of control.

"When Rory was born and proved to be Fergus's, he tried killing Liam, but his wife at the time hid Liam away until Fergus promised not to harm the child," Mick informed him. "I believe y' see where I am going with this, Meghan, Liam's life depends on whether he can produce an heir with y'."

Meghan gasped at the thought. "Liam knows about that. When Fergus was telling me about his plan to have Rory marry me, I asked if he was planning on knocking Liam off."

Mick eyed her with shock. "Y' asked Fergus that? What the hell did he say?"

"I believe his words were it didn't need to come to that."

"What the hell does that mean?" Declan's voice was shocked.

"Well, since Rory wasn't a legal heir, he couldn't fulfill the prophecy." Meghan covered her mouth when she realized what she said.

"Y' know about the prophecy?" Mick asked, his brow raising with interest. "There is also the issue with the sword. Fergus believes it exists, and he has been trying to find it for years."

"What prophecy?" Declan said, with growing concern. She obviously found out some information she chose not to share with him.

Mick eyed Declan, then sighed. "I was thinking that was what Fergus's driving force was. I know Liam is just more interested in the estate itself."

"What the hell are y' two talking about?"

Meghan cringed and decided she was going to have to tell him. "I just didn't tell you at first because I wasn't sure what your true motives for marrying me were. But the prophecy is when the three become one, the bearer of the sword will wield the power of the Gods'."

"Bloody hell," Declan blurted out. "So are y' saying that Fergus is trying to breed the three descendants into one? That's what he needed Rory for."

Meghan nodded and glanced over at Amy's shocked face. "But Rory was born out of wedlock, so he can not be the true heir. That's what Fergus meant when he said it didn't come to that."

"I believe she is right, Mick," Amy blurted out. "That would explain why O'Brien is so determined to marry you. Was he married to his boy's mother?"

"I don't know," Meghan muttered, he never said he was married before.

"Well, I could see the point if Rory was the one producing the child with Meggie, but a child between Liam and Meggie will no more fulfil the prophecy than Caelan does. What is Fergus going to gain from this?"

"Peace of mind, because it could be accomplished in the next generation. Katie has provided a good number of children to choose from. Fergus will be long dead, but if Liam is driven to fulfill the prophecy there could be trouble in years to come."

"This is never going to end, is it?" Meghan sighed and lowered her head to the table.

It was quite some time before Meghan stopped shaking, and Declan loosened his grip on her. His gaze settled on Mick who was talking quietly with Amy about something that seemed quite serious.

Declan's hand rubbed across her shoulder with a soothing presence, but he said nothing. He was not sure what to say that would be any help to the situation. Declan's head was spinning as he contemplated the information. If Rory knew he was an O'Brien years earlier, that would explain his involvement in attempting to steal Meghan's locket years earlier. Damn, how could he have been so blind not to figure this out years before? Rory wanted the inheritance for himself. He set Declan up.

"I can't believe Rory was so conniving," Declan grumbled as the thoughts became clear.

"Oh, Katie is going to be horrified," Amy mumbled, totally missing the point that Rory had actively helped his new family to destroy his old one. "I told them that this secret would blow up in their faces."

Mick grunted dismissing Rory's involvement, then turned towards Declan, avoiding Meghan's gaze.

"So do y' have any ideas about how we are going to get out of here?" Declan questioned, deciding to drop Rory's involvement; he would deal with that when they got home. He couldn't think about his brother or his death now.

"I think it was a good idea for y' to split up and get out separately. It is easier for us to get two of y' out than four," Mick suggested. "If we move y' around, leaving a slight trail, then your friends could leave without notice. It is Meghan he is after."

"Well, what are we going to do? He came after us at the airport. He got through security, fully armed," Declan reminded him. "How powerful is he anyway?"

"Very," Mick sighed. "We haven't been able to figure out his sources, but he always seems to be one step ahead of us and the Garda."

"Great," Declan muttered, flopping down on the chair beside Meghan and scrubbed his face with his hand.

"I think the best bet would be to send y' by ship to Scotland, then y' could drive down to Heathrow and fly home from there. There is no possible way he could get through security there." Mick began to flip through his phonebook, searching for an acquaintance with a boat.

"Hmm," Meghan mumbled, not confident of anything now.

"Here is a fellow, but I don't know him well. Eamon, however, knows the man well. He went to school with the son. Strange family they are, though, the boy moved to London with his mam and knows nothing of his father's doings."

Meghan eyed Mick with interest. Did he feel that the IRA was somehow a family business that was passed down to the sons, and if so, was his father one of the first members?

Mick was nodding to himself, not noticing Meghan's gaze on him. "Aye, when Eamon arrives, he can make the arrangements." Mick's dark gaze settled on Declan again. "Declan, y' are going to need to disguise yourself somehow. Y' are far too recognizable. Your hair can stay long, but y' need to grow that beard out and that baseball cap has to go."

"Me hat? Why?" Declan questioned, glancing at his hat that was hanging on the hook by the kitchen door.

"Because everyone knows y' wear that hat," Mick smirked.

"What?" Declan asked, rather confused about the issue of the hat.

Mick rose from his chair and moved towards the large hutch by the pantry. He pulled open the second draw down, lifted out a magazine, and laid it on the table in front of Declan. The picture was of him standing outside the inn, wearing the Boston Red Sox baseball cap with the caption overhead. "Local boy returns home."

"So, I'm wearing the hat in one picture," Declan laughed.

Mick snorted a chuckle and flipped open the magazine to the story and pointed at the other four pictures of him with the cap on.

"Y' have it on in every picture in the magazine except for this one," Mick said, tapping his finger on a picture of Declan at the opening for his last movie, and his hair was quite short.

"Luckily the hat hides your hair in these pictures taken over here, so most people won't know y' have long hair, and that beard, it conceals your face somewhat," Mick finished, eyeing Declan.

"He has to keep the beard?" Meghan moaned.

Declan laughed at her disgust. "Would y' rather be the mother of O'Brien's child or live with a beard for a while."

"Declan!" Meghan snorted. "You're not funny."

"Aye," Declan grinned. "I know, Freckles, I'm just trying to lighten the tension."

Meghan frowned and grabbed the magazine and stared down at the pictures. "Luckily, you have Georgia on your arm in this one."

"Aye," Declan chuckled. "At least, no one will expect me to be dragging around a feisty redhead."

"Yeah, funny," Meghan grumbled, taking a swing at his smug face, but as usual, he had hold of her arm before she made contact.

By the time Eamon arrived, O'Brien had been spotted up north. It wouldn't be long before he arrived in Ballymena, so time was of the essence.

"Well, if it isn't me, cuz," Eamon's large frame slammed up against Declan's, "you're always in trouble, are y' not?"

"Apparently," Declan chuckled and slapped his cousin's back. "It's good to see y' again."

Eamon's attention left Declan, however, when he noticed Meghan across the room, helping Amy with the lunch dishes. "Well, well." He released Declan and moved with purpose towards the women.

Meghan gazed at him with surprise; the resemblance to Declan was amazing. He was a little shorter and not quite as broad as Declan, but he looked more like his brother than Rory or Colin did. His hair was short and lighter, his face was slightly narrower, but the eyes were identical, smoky grey.

"Ma, it's great to see y'," Eamon smiled and gripped the little woman, hoisting her in the air.

"This is Meghan, your cousin's wife, so behave yourself," Amy grumbled to her excited son.

"Oh, that's too bad," Eamon grinned, his eyes still glued to Meghan. "Well, I can see why O'Brien decided to marry y' instead of kill y'."

Meghan cringed and turned to Declan, who was right up at her side. He was getting tired of men she encountered hitting on her.

"Eamon, I'm not in the mood to battle with y' over me wife," Declan grumbled as he watched Meghan eyeing his cousin.

"Oh, a wee bit worried, are y', cuz?" Eamon gripped Meghan's hand and kissed it. "I must say that y' are very lovely."

"Thank you," Meghan giggled at the reaction Declan was displaying; she was sure he was jealous.

"All right, enough of this. We need to get organized." Declan gripped Meghan's hand and pulled her towards him.

Eamon laughed a deep cheerful sound, then moved over towards the table. "Da, me friend can take them across the channel the day after tomorrow. So we need to hide them until then."

Mick nodded and glanced around the kitchen. "We can't keep them here. O'Brien will have this house under surveillance any time if he hasn't already. We need to move them right away."

"Aye," Eamon grinned. "Tell y' what, we'll send Declan up to Derry to stay with Cousin Brendan, and Meghan can come home with me."

"Not bloody likely," Declan snorted and moved towards the table. "Meggie is not leaving me sight."

"Don't let him fluster y', me lad, he's just teasing y'." Amy moved past her son and smacked him across the back of the head.

"I'll bet." Declan eyed his cousin and could not help but smirk. Why was he getting so jealous? He knew exactly why, every man he knew would gladly take Meghan from him. Even Fabrizio. He had not missed all the secret glances and the tension in Fabrizio when he was around Meghan. What power did Meghan have over men? Georgia never held this power. She was a very beautiful woman, one of the most perfect faces he had ever seen, but she seemed to repel men. Even he grew tired of her.

Meghan's grip on Declan's arm brought him back to the discussion that was still deliberating separating them.

"Declan, I'm not leaving you. Please don't make me go by myself." Meghan's voice sounded terrified, her eyes darting from him to his cousin to his uncle. "Please, if Liam catches me, and you are not there."

"Shh, Meggie, I'm not leaving y'." Declan kissed her forehead. "We stay as a package."

Meghan smiled and rested her head against his shoulder. The feel of him under her cheek was reassuring. He was the only man that ever made her feel completely safe. She felt so blessed to have him in her life.

"Meghan dear, why don't you come with me and have a wee nap while the men discuss the plans? Y' look terribly tired and quite pale."

"I am." Meghan nodded and released her grip of Declan. "Is it all right?"

"Aye, Freckles, go lie down. I'll be in shortly to tell y' what's going on. Try and sleep," Declan whispered softly, then rested a gentle kiss on her lips.

As the afternoon passed and turned into evening, Meghan and Declan were being moved from the warm and familiar house to an old mill a few miles down the road. Eamon's sources told him that O'Brien was already in town, and his father's house was under surveillance. That would mean that the pair would need to be removed very carefully. Eamon was sure that they were not seen entering, so O'Brien's men had no idea if they were in the house or not.

Mick eyed the fields outside his home and was once again thankful that he remained on the farm instead of moving into town. The house was old, dating back to the 1600s. A time when being a Catholic meant disgrace, ridicule, and death. During that time the inhabitants of the house had the forethought to build a tunnel leading from their cellar under the field to a small knoll in a densely forested piece of land. Mick never told anyone of the tunnel he found years after he moved into the house. He was not sure how many of the old timers of the town knew, but no one ever mentioned it. He had used it a number of times to elude the army when they were on the hunt for IRA members.

Declan was amazed when Mick opened the hidden door revealing the tunnel. He had no idea that it existed. Meghan, however, was not as excited and cringed slightly as she peered into the dark abyss.

"Don't tell me y' are scared of small spaces too," Declan laughed as she backed away from the tunnel.

"No, I'm not. It's just that it's so dark. Are there bugs in there?" Meghan voice sounded choked.

"I would imagine," Mick said evenly, not interested in Meghan's phobias.

Meghan eyed Declan's smirking face and decided to suck it up and try not to cause a fuss. "If I get bugs in my hair, will you pick them out?" Her eyes stayed fixed on Declan as she took the flashlight from Mick.

"Every last one of them," Declan chuckled and kissed her nose, then shoved her towards the tunnel.

"All right, so y' will meet me at the mill on the other side of the creek," Eamon said firmly, directing the attention back on him. "There is a small shack on the far side. Wait inside until I come for y'. It might be a while I'll have a tail to lose I'd imagine."

Declan nodded and slapped his cousin on the back. "Be careful, Eamon."

"Aye, y' too," Eamon grinned. "But if anything should happen to y', do I get custody of your wife?"

Declan laughed and eyed Meghan. "There is no one I would trust less with her than y'. She's too precious to leave to the likes of y', Eamon Flynn."

"Oh, so that's how it is, Cousin," Eamon grumbled and scrubbed his eyes. "What's to say I won't just leave y' at the mill and stay at the pub and get wasted?"

"Aye, well, Cousin, we're kin, y' wouldn't betray kin, would y' now?" Declan's lilt was stronger as he spoke to his cousin.

"No, I guess I wouldn't," Eamon laughed. "But heed me warning, cuz, if you ever let the lovely lass out of your sight, she'll be mine."

Declan roared at his cousin's comment. He was almost as blatant as Colton was about his attraction towards Meghan. It was Fabrizio that concerned him. He hid his feeling for Meghan, which could only mean that they were stronger than Fabrizio was willing to admit.

Declan pulled Eamon to the side. "If something should happen to me, promise me y' will get her home. Do anything y' have to." Declan's voice was harsh.

"Aye, I will." Eamon was serious, the teasing a few minutes earlier ending. "Don't y' worry, Declan, I won't let y' down."

"I know," Declan smiled and hugged his cousin. "I'll see y' at the mill."

"Aye." Eamon agreed and watched Declan and Meghan disappear down the tunnel.

CHAPTER THIRTY-EIGHT

The deserted mill was run down, the walls were full of holes, and half the roof was missing. Eamon had not yet arrived, and Meghan was getting concerned. Declan, however, seemed unfazed by their surrounding, and the time it was taking Eamon to appear; he knew it could take a while.

It was cold and damp, but it was safe and unknown to O'Brien. The only ones that knew where they were are Mick and Eamon. The Garda had not been notified and wouldn't be until they reached New York.

The cold wind was screaming through the holes in the walls, slightly blowing the straw that was covering the floor over into the far corner of the mill. It was horribly run down; most likely it had not been used for many years. Abandoned by the company whose land they trespassed on. "Meggie, what are y' doing?" Declan questioned as he watched her rummaging through the backpack that Amy had packed for them.

"Well, if we have to sleep here tonight, I thought I would try and find the blanket she put in here," Meghan muttered, not looking up from the bag. "I'm freezing. I don't know why we can't stay at Mick's. What if the owners find us?"

Declan sighed and moved towards her, sensing her fears. "Freckles, it's going to be okay. I'm sure the owner is long gone, and if not, he won't be checking anything in the storm that's raging outside," he whispered into her hair and pressed his stubbly face against the side of her head. Meghan leaned heavily back into him, and he could feel the slight tremors in her body as he held her.

Meghan sighed, "I'm sorry for complaining, I'm so scared." She leaned into his chest.

"Meggie, I promise I won't let anything happen to you." Declan comforted her as he rubbed his hand through her hair, pulling at the tangles.

"It's not me I'm worried about. It's you." Meghan gazed at him with worry.

"Me?" Declan's voice was filled with shock.

"Yes, he wants you dead." Meghan moved out of his arms and laid the blanket down on the straw.

"Meggie," Declan sighed and stood watching her as she flopped to the blanket, pulled her knees up in front of her, and wrapped her arms around them the way she always did when she was upset. A smirk slightly graced his lips as he thought about how predictable she was with her responses to things.

Meghan's eyes stayed focused on the straw as she rocked back and forth deep in thought, Declan leaned over a half wall and watched her as she struggled with her thoughts.

"Declan," Meghan finally muttered through her teeth that were chewing at her lower lip.

"Aye." His eyes settled on her with sudden panic; whatever she had to say he was not going to like.

"What if I . . ." Meghan paused. "What if I let him catch me?" she finally said.

"Are y' mad?" Declan snorted and darted towards her, dropping to the blanket in front of her, his hands gripping her shoulders.

"No, he won't hurt me. But if he catches us, he will kill you," Meghan rambled as tears filled her eyes.

"Meggie, he won't catch us." Declan's hands were gripping her face, trying to calm her.

"What if he does? I couldn't live with myself if you die because of me. It would be better if . . ."

"Don't even think that. I'm not letting y' give yourself to another man to save me life. I would rather die than think of y' in the arms of O'Brien," Declan growled, his jealousy surging upwards.

"But—" His lips on hers halted her comment.

"Freckles, you're not doing it," Declan said firmly and engulfed her in his arms.

A deep sigh exited her, and she closed her eyes, pressing her face firmly into his chest. The fear of losing him again was overwhelming, and she could feel her stomach churning with terror.

"Declan, what if I went back?"

"Meggie, stop it," he snorted.

"No, listen to me. What if I went back?" she said, with a surprising calmness in her voice. "What if I killed him?"

"What are y' thinking? Y' can't kill him. You'd go to jail if his men don't kill y' first." Declan's voice was loud and full of panic as he shook her shoulder, trying to get her to listen to him.

"So what, he's trying to kill you," she shouted back, not quite sure why she was yelling, but she couldn't help herself.

"Meggie killing someone isn't easy to do or to live with. Even if y' don't go to jail, y' will have to live with it for the rest of your life," Declan said calmly and pulled her back into his arms.

"I don't care. I would rather live with that than live without you," Meghan cried and tried to squirm from his lap.

"Freckles, please listen to me," Declan begged, tightening his arms around her. "Y' can't kill him."

He could feel her body trembling in his arms as she thought about what she had been thinking. "Meggie, it's going to be okay. We'll get out of here in a few days, you'll see."

"What if this friend of Eamon's can't help? What if he won't?" Meghan's voice sounded almost foreign to her; there was so much fear coming through.

"I don't know. But for now, let's just concentrate on the fact that he will." Declan soothed, kissing the top of her head.

"Do you think we can trust him?"

"Well, Mick and Eamon trust him, and I trust them, so that's the best I can tell y'," Declan smiled, then pressed his lips against her trembling mouth. "Anyway," he said, lifting his lips off hers. "Mick said that this fellow has had dealings with the O'Brien family before, and he apparently has a good reason to hate them. So, at least, we have that going for us."

"I'm just not comfortable getting involved with someone so heavily involved in the IRA," Meghan muttered as she leaned her head into his chest.

"I know, Freckles, but they're willing to help us. Every time we try and involve the Garda, O'Brien seems to find out where we are. He must have connections everywhere."

"How can that be possible? He's a drug lord for goodness sakes. Everyone seems to know it, why won't they arrest him?"

"I don't know, I guess it's like the mafia families back home. He keeps his hands clean and lets his men take the fall."

"But he kidnapped me," Meghan snorted. "Why won't they listen to me?"

"I don't know," Declan sighed, unsure of the reasoning himself. "But for now, let's just keep them out of it." Declan paused for a moment. "I can protect y', don't you worry."

"Declan, when are you going to tell me why you and Fabrizio left the Navy Seals?" she questioned. He was so well trained and she wanted to know what happened to make him leave. Cassie told her that Declan took a discharge, but Fabrizio never told her why.

Declan appeared guilty about something he should have told her long ago. "Meggie, I just didn't think y' wanted to hear it."

"Declan, please tell me," Meghan begged as he deposited her on the blanket and wrapped his arm around her.

He sighed and sat beside her, pulling her onto his lap, wrapping her in a blanket. "Are y' sure?"

"Yes."

"Well." He locked his eyes on the wooden door as he decided how to start. "I was eighteen when I enlisted in the navy. I wanted to get away from me parents. Even back then, me mam was trying to arrange me a marriage. That girl was worse than Georgia."

As he closed his eyes, Meghan watched the dark lashes twitch against his golden skin. "I was in the navy for four years when I was asked to join the Seals. They felt that I had the physical aptitude," he grinned.

"Well, you do have that," Meghan smiled back and ran her hand across his chest, tracing the strong firm muscle that was still as toned as it was when they first met.

"Aye. Well, I actually was very excited about the possibility of making it, and when I graduated through training, I was quite proud. It's not everyone who can be a Seal," he smiled, gazing sightlessly at the wall. "Anyway, once in the unit, I met Fabs, he was me bunkmate."

"Oh you have known him that long?" Meghan muttered, realizing where their strong bond came from.

"Aye. Since I was twenty-two," he smiled. "Fabs is older than me by a couple of years, and he certainly used that against me." His eyes refocused on her as he stretched his arms out in an uneasy manner. Then one settled on her lap and the other loosely sat on her shoulder.

He continued to talk about his days in the Seals and all the missions that they were sent on, which gave her insight into his ability to deal with dangerous situations. She was fascinated with his descriptions of some of the events of his missions that were never even mentioned in the news. Obviously, more goes on in the world than the common person ever hears about.

"So near the end of me fourth year, we were sent to Somalia to help take down a terrorist group that was threatening to overthrow the government there at the time," he sighed. "The American compound there was under siege, and we needed to evacuate the ambassador and staff."

She gazed at him with interest seeing the tension building in his eyes. "Declan," she started to say, but he kissed her quickly and continued.

"Well, we had just about everyone out, but the ambassador himself and his aide. But as we were loading him into the chopper, the outer wall was penetrated, and all hell broke loose. One of the men in our unit ran to the side of the building and began to shoot at the approaching mob. Fabs threw the ambassador into the chopper and told the pilot to take off before the mob reached them. The chopper was in the air when they rounded the corner, and the commander ordered us to retreat to the house to hold off the mob. Well, it was so loud and chaotic," he muttered almost as an apology. "I was scared," he admitted.

"Declan, who wouldn't be?" Meghan said softly, resting her hand on his face.

"No one, I suppose," Declan smiled softly, relieved she was understanding. "We made it to the house and knocked out the windows and . . ." He stopped and licked his dry lips. "Well, the commander told us to start shooting and we did. I unloaded the whole clip in me MK20 and reloaded and did it again and again," he shuddered. "By the time the whole thing was over, one of our guys was dead, and the compound was littered with bodies. I think most of the mob retreated." His eyes glazed over as he stared into her dark eyes.

"Meggie, when we left the house to survey the compound . . ." He broke his gaze, lowering his eyes to the ground. "The people lying on the ground, well, they were just lads." His voice shook with distress. "Young boys, maybe fifteen or sixteen."

"They were all kids?" she questioned with surprise.

"No, well, not all of them, but quite a few. Only some had guns. The majority of them only had sticks," he admitted.

"Oh my gosh," Meghan muttered under her breath. "Well, then who was shooting at you?"

"I don't know, but someone was. It's just that we shot at kids." Declan buried his face in her hair. "I killed kids."

"Oh, Declan, how would you have known? They were shooting at you, and they . . ." She stopped and glanced at him with a slight grin. "What was that saying 'Big Boys' Rules', if you pick up a gun, someone's going to die."

Declan snorted a laugh. "It figures y' would remember that movie with your precious Harrison."

"Well, it's true, though. What were they thinking attacking an American compound anyway?" she questioned, ignoring his comment.

He smiled softly content that she didn't think he was horrible. "Well, after that I just couldn't do it anymore. So I got a discharge."

"So that's when you started acting?" she commented, remembering him telling her that he started out as a stunt double, then a director was so impressed with him that he gave him a small role in the film and the public loved him and his career took off from there.

"Aye, and that decision pissed off me mam. She said I was a quitter and going into a shameful profession such as acting. It was an embarrassment to her."

Meghan shook her head and forced back a laugh. "Your mother has never been a good source of support and encouragement, has she?"

"No, she never likes anything I do. She feels me only purpose in life is to embarrass her."

Meghan giggled and rested her hand on his face. "That's what Rory thought too."

Declan eyed her but made no comment. He knew that Rory got the worst of his treatment from his father, but his mother felt the sun rose and set on Rory. Her love child. Declan shivered at the thought, Did his mother love Fergus O'Brien?

"Fabs left shortly after that and started up his security company. But when I needed someone, I hired him because I trusted him," Declan smiled and kissed her nose. "I don't know how y' do it, Freckles, but I was terrified to tell y', and somehow y' have managed to put it into perspective."

Meghan's brow rose slightly. "Well, I certainly can't judge you for anything that happened in a situation like that. You were sent into rescue people, and you were being shot at. What were you supposed to do, let them shoot you?" She shrugged.

"I guess not," he agreed. "No, it's not that we did anything wrong. It's just I couldn't deal with the fact that we were fighting children. I just couldn't do it anymore."

"It's okay." Meghan soothed, rubbing the hair at the back of his head.

Declan eyed Meghan, her eyes soft and loving, her smile warm and welcoming. His wife, his love. "God, how I love y'!"

"I love you too," Meghan muttered. Her life was beginning to fall into place. Everything leading up to this moment a rehearsal for this moment when he trusted her completely, loved her completely.

The wind had picked up and was screaming through the small holes in the walls of the mill they had taken refuge in. Meghan was startled awake by a loud thumping noise on the far side of the mill, and she bolted upright on her makeshift bed in the straw. Her eyes darted to and fro in the dark damp night, trying to determine what the sound was. She noticed the blanket beside her was empty, sending her into complete panic.

"Declan?" she called but was barely audible over the howling wind. She wobbled to her feet and stumbled to the edge of the stall. "Declan, where are you?" she called again as her eyes filled with tears.

She was feeling rather flushed and dizzy as she staggered to the door of the mill, not seeing any sign of him. Her breath was laboured as she leaned heavily against the doorframe, swabbing the beads of perspiration running down her face. What was wrong with her, she couldn't be getting sick? Why now? She was fighting to stay standing, but voices from the far side of the mill had drawn her curiosity.

The rain must have been falling for sometime because when she stepped out of the mill, the grass was sopping under her feet. The chill in the air was bitterly cold, and she wrapped her arms around herself, trying to preserve any heat she had left.

Her heart was beating at a rapid pace as she slowly wandered around the side of the mill to find a few men standing by the back door. The drenching rain luckily shadowed her from their view as she jumped back around the corner before they noticed her.

"She's in there. I heard her calling him," A low voice said.

"She was calling him?" She heard the recognizable voice of Liam.

"Aye. It sounded like she is looking for him."

"Okay," O'Brien paused. "He's probably not in there, but don't take any chances. Go in and get her and bring her out here to me. And for Christ's sake, don't hurt her."

Meghan felt her stomach drop as she tried to decide what to do next. Her eyes darted around the area looking for somewhere to hide, and she decided to head for the road. Her mind was in turmoil as she stumbled through the shrubs down towards the road, unsure of where she was going.

Without a sound, Meghan was grabbed from behind and dragged behind a large bush. Shrieks exited her as she struggled and kicked back at her attacker. Her feet left the ground, and she smashed them back repeatedly into the legs of the large figure behind her.

"Shut up," a low voice said, unrecognizable through the wind and the rain that was slamming into the branches and what was left of the leaves on the trees and shrubs.

"Let go!" she shrieked, continuing to struggle from her attacker.

A large hand cupped over her mouth as the man pulled her back farther into the trees. She was hysterical as she struggled to free herself from his grip. Once deep into the trees, the man dropped to the ground, pulling her down with him, then spun her around to face him.

"Eamon!" Meghan blurted out as he removed his hand from her mouth. "Christ, what the hell are you doing here?" she panted, trying to catch her breath.

"Keep your voice down," he snorted.

"Where is Declan?" she questioned as she started to panic.

"Shh, he's okay. He went back to the mill to get you. What the hell are you doing wandering around out here?"

"I was looking for him. I woke up, and he was gone." Meghan tried to hold back the tears that were right below the surface. "Liam is here."

"Meghan, calm down." Eamon soothed. "We figured as much. You have to stay here. I need to go let Declan know where you are."

Meghan sighed and crumpled to the ground with distress. She was shaking not only from the fear, but also from her clothes that were drenched down to her skin, allowing the bone-chilling dampness to seep into her body.

"Meghan, I need to go get Declan. Please stay here and don't move or make a sound. I don't want anything to happen to you."

"Okay," Meghan whispered as she glanced after him, but he was gone, leaving her alone in the dark cold night.

She curled up into a ball, trying to calm her nerves that were exploding with terror that, once again, O'Brien had found her, and she was beginning to believe that they were never going to get home. The sound of the rain splattering down around her was obscuring any other sounds in the night, and she was finding it frightening that someone could be right behind the bush, and she wouldn't be able to hear them. She was to terrified to move as she lay curled up under a bush that she had crawled under, trying to keep some of the rain off her.

It was over half an hour before Declan crashed through the bushes into the clearing after Eamon to find it empty. "Bloody hell, where is she?" Declan muttered, his eyes darting around the area.

"I don't know. I told her to stay put," Eamon grumbled, annoyed that she didn't listen to him.

"Damn that woman. Why doesn't she ever listen?" Declan's voice was full of terror. "What if he got her?" he muttered as he began to wander towards a clump of shrubs that appeared to be disturbed. He dropped to his knees and peered under the dead foliage.

"Meggie, what are you doing?" Declan questioned with relief as he watched her staring at him with a blank expression on her face.

She was curled inwards, with her arms wrapped around herself, and her head was resting on the wet ground. Her eyes stayed focused forward but showed no sign of recognition.

"Oh God, Meggie," Declan blurted out as he reached in and touched her face.

Her skin was clammy and quite hot under his trembling hand. As his hand touched her face, she jerked from the sensation, her eyes focusing on him.

"Declan," Meghan shrieked so loud that the sound startled Declan, and he fell back onto the dirt.

"Christ, Meggie, be quiet," Declan snorted as he regained his positioning beside her. He reached under the bush, lifting her out, and she lay limp in his arms. Her eyes seemed distant and glazed over as they looked out of the flushed face.

"Eamon," Declan called over his shoulder. "I think she's sick."

"She was fine when I left her." He ran over and bent down beside them, resting his hand on her face. "She has a fever. We need to get her somewhere warm and dry."

"Where? O'Brien has the mill surround, and all our dry clothes are in there along with the blankets your da gave us," Declan muttered, trying to find a solution.

"We are heading up to me cousin Brendan's, he lives in Derry."

"Derry?" Declan muttered.

"Aye, we don't have much choice. She's in no condition to do anything at this point. We need to get her out of the rain. Da said he would meet us up there when it's safe."

"Okay, where did y' park the car?" Declan questioned, suddenly realizing Eamon must have driven to the barn.

"About a mile up the road to the north. It's hidden in a clearing, off the road."

"Well, let's get moving then," Declan announced, standing up and adjusting Meghan in his arms.

"Are y' going to be able to carry her that far?" Eamon questioned, watching Declan struggle with her limp body.

"Aye. I don't have much choice, do I?" Declan smirked slightly. "But she sure is heavy when she's dead weight. Don't you dare tell her I said that."

Eamon chuckled and moved through the bushes towards the car. It was a rough hike across the fields, climbing over the small stone fences along the way to reach the car, and Declan was to the point of exhaustion. He stopped and dropped to the ground, heaving for breath and shaking his arms, trying to remove the burning sensation.

"I'll carry her for a while," Eamon offered as he leaned down, resting his hand on Declan's slumped shoulders.

"Eamon, what have I done to her?" Declan sniffed and wiped at his damp face.

"What do y' mean?" Eamon questioned, not quite sure what Declan was referring to.

"Why did I bring her to Ireland? If I hadn't been so selfish and listened to me da, she would be safe at home right now."

"Y' weren't being selfish. Y' wanted your wife with y'. Who would have known this would happen? Shit, it's like something out of one of your movies. I have lived here all me life and have known O'Brien for years. I never thought he would go this far," Eamon smirked, patting his shoulder.

"If anything happens to her," Declan muttered into her hair as he buried his face into the mass of wet tangles.

"She's going to be okay, it's probably just the flu." Eamon soothed. "Let's just keep moving." He lifted Meghan from Declan's arms and adjusted her into a comfortable position against his chest. She stirred slightly from the movement, pressing her face against his neck.

Within minutes, they were on the move again, through the dark damp night. The rain had subsided, but the air was still very damp, and the ground was soft and marshy under their feet, making the travelling difficult.

Eamon abruptly stopped after about fifteen minutes and adjusted Meghan in his arms with a peculiar appearance to his face.

"What's wrong?" Declan questioned, stopping beside Eamon and glancing around the baron field in search of what was disturbing him.

"Nothing," he said, with a tone of amusement. "But I think y' need to carry her for a while."

"Why, is she getting too heavy for y'?" Declan joked as he slapped Eamon's shoulder.

"No," Eamon laughed. "She's kissing me neck."

"What?" Declan questioned as he moved forward and stared down at Meghan, whose face was pressed against Eamon's neck.

"Oh," Declan muttered. "Exciting y', is she?" His voice was accusing as he watched Eamon trying to adjust her away from his neck.

"Actually, she is," Eamon admitted, the enjoyment he was receiving from her lips suckling his neck was sending him over the edge. "Here, take her."

The Volvo was a welcome sight and once inside, Declan laid Meghan across his lap, removed her wet jacket, and draped it over the front seat.

"She's so hot," Declan mumbled, resting his hand on her forehead.

"She'll be fine when we get to Derry. We'll stop at a drug store and get some Tylenol."

"I'm so sorry, Freckles. What was I thinking?" Declan muttered. "We should have thought of something else. She's not strong enough to survive in these conditions."

"Who are you calling a weakling?" Meghan's voice was quiet, but the sound caused both men to startle.

"Meggie," Declan blurted out, gazing down at her flushed face.

"Declan, where are we?" Meghan questioned, batting her eyes trying to focus on her surroundings.

"We're with Eamon, and we're heading to Derry to meet up with Mick's cousin," he informed her as he rubbed his thumb back and forth across her cheek; he was relieved to see her awake.

"Liam was there?" Meghan mumbled, trying to get up, but Declan held her firm across his lap.

"I know, and he was accompanied by a group of armed men that were searching the mill. Did he see y'?" Declan asked calmly, but the pressure he was using to restrain her was telling a different story.

"No. I heard him talking outside the mill. They didn't see me because of the rain."

"Well, it's a good thing y' left when y' did."

A grin grew across her face. "I guess you're not going to yell at me then."

"No, I'm too tired," Declan smirked and bent down and kissed her forehead, letting his lips linger on her burning skin.

"Declan, I'm so cold," she muttered as she pulled her legs up to her stomach, forming a ball. His eyes scanned the back seat, looking for something to cover her with but saw nothing.

"I know, Freckles. You have quite a fever, but we'll be there soon." Her skin was burning up, but she felt cold. She was shivering, that could not be good.

"Can I change in to dry clothes?" Meghan sniffed, trying to sit up.

"No, we have nothing to change in to. We couldn't get back to the mill, so all our cloths are gone."

"Oh," she muttered and gazed up at him, her eyes big and glassy. "Well, I guess we will have to go shopping."

"Freckles," Declan laughed, his white teeth flashing through the dark beard.

"You know, you look like a mountain man," she mumbled as she focused on the beard.

Declan laughed loudly. "Well, I guess I don't need to worry anymore about y' if you're complaining."

"Declan," Meghan mumbled as she closed her eyes. "I am so cold."

"Meggie." Declan gently jostled her shoulder, but she lay motionless, and fear began to shoot though him. "Meggie, wake up."

Declan's voice was panicked. "Eamon we have to get her to a hospital."

"I don't know if that's a good idea," Eamon glanced back at her lifeless body and felt his stomach tighten. His heart was telling him to take her to the hospital, but his mind was screaming no.

"I don't care, I won't let her die," Declan moaned and buried his face into her hair.

"Well, we'll be at Brendan in a few minutes, it's just over this bridge, and we'll see what he says." Eamon's tone was final as he stopped the car in front of the red brick row house.

The tall extremely thin man wrapped in a housecoat that opened the solid wood front door surprised Eamon. His lofty frame was hunched from age and bad posture and his long grey hair was draped around his face like a veil.

"Cousin Brendan?" Eamon questioned with concern, he had not seen him in years.

"Aye, Eamon, are y' daft?" Brendan smiled, exposing his missing front teeth. "Sorry for me appearance," Brendan apologized, noticing Eamon's eyes stuck on his mouth. "I was too tired to put in me teeth," he grinned, exposing the pink gums.

"That's all right. I know you weren't expecting us tonight," Eamon apologized. "Before I get them out of the car, Meghan has a bad fever. I think it's from being wet and cold, but I'm not sure." Eamon glanced back at the car. "Declan wants to take her to the hospital but . . ."

"But if she goes there, O'Brien will surely get his hands on her," Brendan finished for him.

"Aye, that's exactly what I was thinking." Eamon smiled slight that Brendan was on the same page.

"Well, bring her in here. I'll call Dr. McGuire. He just lives down the street. He's trustworthy." Brendan waved his hand welcoming them into his house.

CHAPTER THIRTY-NINE

It was early morning when Meghan opened her eyes and glanced around the small damp room still not lit by the morning sun. Her surroundings seemed almost grey, and she blinked repeatedly trying to clear her eyes.

Her eyes were drawn to the heavy object on her pelvis and the dark head of Declan fast asleep on her hip. She ran her hand through his long dark hair as she tried to figure out where they were and how they got there.

The bed she was in was a narrow single bed covered in a thick floral down duvet, which she was finding pleasantly warm. Declan was sitting in a large chair with his head resting on her hip, and it looked like a terribly uncomfortable position.

"Declan," Meghan mumbled and jostled his shoulder trying to wake him.

"Aye." Declan sat up abruptly, eyeing her with shock. "Oh, Meggie, you're awake?" A smile filled his face and his hand rested on her forehead. "How do y' feel?"

"Fine."

"Well, your fever has broke. So that's good," Declan smiled, his bloodshot eyes, staying fixed on her face.

"Did I have a fever?" Meghan inadvertently raised her hand to her forehead. "I seem okay now."

"Aye, y' were pretty hot. The doctor said it was 105 degrees. He gave you some medicine last night."

"Where are we?" Meghan pushed herself to a sitting position.

"We're at Brendan's house in Derry."

"Hmm. Declan, Liam was at the mill. He almost caught me." Meghan scanned the small room. It must be in the loft, it was small, and the roof sloped down towards the window. The wallpaper was a paisley pattern, appearing to have been applied years earlier. The wood floor was covered with a small area rug, and the chair Declan was sitting in was large and cumbersome, the gold fabric worn with age.

"Aye, I know. Eamon and I were outside when we heard the car approaching. I was actually behind them when they were standing outside the mill."

"Oh," she muttered. "They went inside."

"Aye, I know," Declan smirked, reading her expression and knowing she was going to explode.

"Declan, you let him go in after me?" Meghan snorted as she swung her legs to the edge of the bed.

"Stay in bed, Freckles," Declan ordered, stood up, and sat beside her on the small bed.

"Well." She pushed, not appreciating his light demeanour.

Declan chuckled at her facial expression. "Well, I figured they wouldn't hurt y', so I was going to ambush them on the way back to the car." His mouth rose to one side. "I may be skilled at fighting, but I'm not stupid, and five men with guns against me aren't very good odds."

"Yeah, I guess not," Meghan smiled and flopped back to the bed.

Declan stood, removed his pants, and then climbed into bed beside her, adjusting her so they both fit on the small bed. He was pressed up against her back holding her tightly against the length of him.

"Declan, stop poking me," Meghan giggled.

"Sorry, Freckles, I can't help it," he laughed as he adjusted himself, then pressed his face against hers. "I'm so glad you're okay. I was so worried."

"Declan." She turned to face him, pressing her body against his for warmth. "I was so scared when I woke up and you were gone."

"I'm sorry I didn't mean to scare y'. It's just when Eamon showed up, we went outside, so we didn't wake y', and then we heard O'Brien showing up. I went back to the mill to get y', and Eamon was covering me back."

"I know he scared the hell out of me when he grabbed me," Meghan smirked, slightly nuzzling her nose into the base of his neck.

"Aye he told me. He says y' kick pretty hard," Declan chuckled. "Y' know, Freckles, I think I should teach y' some self-defence moves."

"That might be a good idea," she laughed and ran her fingers through his tangled hair.

"Meggie, I'm so sorry I got y' into all this," Declan whispered, placed his hand on her face, and brushed his thumb up and down her cheek.

"Declan, this isn't your fault or mine. We just seem to attract trouble." She smiled slightly at him, then pressed her face into his neck. "I don't care what happens as long as you're with me."

"Me too, Freckles," he sighed and pressed his head against hers. "I was so scared that you weren't going to get through this."

"It was just a fever," Meghan chuckled and kissed the smooth skin of his neck, just below the beard line.

"Aye, but you were so out of it." A smile curled Declan's lips as he felt her sucking at his neck.

"Y' know, Freckles, y' were kissing Eamon's neck when he was carrying y'." Declan eyed her for a reaction.

"Was I?" she muttered, pulling her head out and gazing up at him. "Hmm."

"Y' don't seem too concerned by that?" Declan chuckled nervously.

"Well, I was dying, remember? I can't be held responsible for anything I did," Meghan smirked, sensing Declan's concern. He was slightly jealous, that was obvious. In some ways she was flattered, but other ways, she was slightly scared. How controlling was he going to get? "Declan, you really need to stop being so jealous of other men. I don't want any other man. I love you." Her lips pressed back into his neck and suckled his skin.

"Aye, I know y' do, Freckles."

"Declan." Meghan glanced up at his content face.

"Aye." Declan kissed her nose that was now up at his face.

"I really hate this beard," Meghan smirked, raised her hand, and pulled at the long dark whiskers.

A loud laugh exited him as he eyed her amused face. "So you've told me." His lips landed on hers with a secure force as his arms slipped around her, pulling her against the length of him.

"Declan, I don't think that I'm in any condition," she smiled as she felt him throbbing hard against her thigh. She squirmed slightly, but he held her close to him.

"Don't worry, Freckles, I'm not planning on ravaging y' today. I do have some restraint," he laughed.

"Hmm. Well, if you don't stop poking me with that thing," she laughed.

"Oh, getting aroused, are y'?" His brow rose slightly. "I guess that's a good sign. I don't think if you were dying, your body would waste its time on such thoughts."

"I guess not," Meghan giggled and pressed her body into his; the feel of the long firm muscles surrounding her was comforting.

"Meggie, stop it," Declan grabbed her hips and adjusted her away from his pelvis. "I can't be held responsible for what happens if y' keep doing that." A slight demand was in his voice.

"Sorry," Meghan smiled brightly. "I couldn't help myself."

"I think I will let you get some sleep," Declan muttered, released her, and climbed out of bed. "Do y' think y' could eat?" A loud laugh left him. "Well, that's a stupid question."

"Hey," Meghan snorted and took a swing at his smirking face, but his hand had hold of her arm before she made contact.

"Well, are y' hungry?" he questioned again, ignoring her annoyance.

"I guess I could eat something," she muttered, trying to keep a straight face. "How long are we staying here?"

"I'm not sure. We didn't really discuss that last night. I was so worried about y'." He bent down and kissed her, then turned to leave. "I'll be back with some breakfast."

"Declan," she giggled, her brow rising with amusement. "Do you plan on putting on pants?"

"Oh." He was quite startled as he glanced down at his bare legs. "I guess I should put some on. I don't know if there is a woman in the house."

"Declan?" Meghan questioned, sitting up and swinging her legs around to the side of the bed. "Do you think we're safe here? Maybe we should . . ." She stopped and crinkled her nose in thought.

"Freckles, I think we're okay for now. It's Mick's cousin, and he trusts him, so we have to take his word for now." Declan soothed as he sat on the bed beside her, pulling up his jeans. His lips landed on her forehead as he stood up.

"Y' stay in bed." He gently ordered as he swung her legs back onto the bed. "Y' need to be healthy if . . ."

"If we have to run again?" Meghan questioned, knowing he stopped what he was saying so he would not worry her.

"Aye. I don't want to frighten y', but we have to be prepared for anything. O'Brien seems intent on possessing y', and he will stop at nothing." An impish grin filled his face as he watched her eyes fill with fear.

"What are you finding so funny?" Meghan snorted and tugged at the floral comforter that he had replaced over her body.

"Well, I was just thinking I must have done something right somewhere, because I'm the one that is lucky enough to possess y'."

"Possess me?" Meghan questioned, with slight annoyance. "No one possesses me."

"Oh, I beg to differ," Declan smirked as he leaned towards her. "I possess y' totally," he said, with an air of arrogance.

"No, you don't," Meghan snorted, pushing at his shoulders that were heading towards her along with his puckered lips. "Get away from me."

"No." His lips landed on hers with delicate accuracy, sending tremors of passion through her body only to be outdone by the sensation his hands were causing on her skin.

"See," Declan lifted his lips off hers, "I possess y' totally, heart and soul, and y' can't deny it." His mouth rose slightly to one side. "But don't feel bad, Freckles. Y' possess me too."

"I know," Meghan smirked, grabbed his face, and pressed her lips to his once more.

A soft knock on the door startled her from her dozing, and she glanced up to see a short tiny woman coming through the door with a tray of breakfast.

"Good morning, deary." A smile warmed the weathered face. "I'm terribly sorry that I didn't welcome y' last night, but Brendan didn't see it fit to wake me," she mumbled as a scowl of disapproval for his actions filled her face.

"That's okay. I don't remember anything from last night anyway," Meghan smiled and eyed the tray of food.

"I'm Aisling," she said, with a large smile, exposing her large white teeth that were almost too large for her face.

"That's a beautiful name," Meghan smiled, the woman was pronouncing it *Ashlin,* but she was sure it wasn't spelt that way. That would be a wonderful name for her baby, that is, if she is actually pregnant. "I'm Meghan," she smiled, happy to see another friendly face. "I have to admit I was a bit nervous about showing up on your doorstep."

Aisling smiled and laid the tray on the bedside table, then turned to Meghan, and laid her hand on her forehead. "I see your fever has broken," she muttered as she fussed with the sheets. "Oh heavens."

"What?" Meghan blurted out with worry as she eyed the shocked expression on the woman's face.

"Oh, sorry, I didn't mean to startle y', deary." She flushed slightly. "It's just that when Declan told me what you would like for breakfast," she paused and scanned her body again with interest, "well, I though y' must be a sizeable lady."

Meghan started to laugh. "What did he tell you I wanted?" she questioned, looking at the tray filled with eggs, bacon, pancakes, and toast.

"More than that," Aisling laughed. "He says he's never seen a woman eat as much as y'."

"Well, that's because he only knows actresses, and most of them are as big as my leg and never eat," Meghan laughed as she adjusted herself on the bed. "One day, it will probably catch up with me, but until it starts, I'm enjoying myself."

"Good for y', deary," the grey-haired woman smiled. "I don't worry much about what I eat either. As y' can see, I'm rather skinny," she said, pulling at her loose-fitting clothes.

Meghan smiled and reached for the tray with anticipation of eating a hot meal for the first time in days. "Aisling, where is Declan?"

"He said he had some errands to run. So he and Eamon went with Brendan into town."

"Oh, he left me alone?" Meghan questioned with worry.

"No deary, you're not alone," Aisling informed her as she glanced out the window, as if looking for something.

"What's out there?" Meghan questioned, jumping from bed and dashing towards the window. She glanced out at the two young men that were at the front of the house, painting the metal fence that didn't appear to be in need of repair. "Who's that?"

"Marty and Simon," Aisling said evenly, closing the curtains when the boys glanced up at the window. "Y' better get back to bed. Y' don't want to wear yourself out," Aisling smiled as she ushered Meghan back to bed.

Meghan watched as Aisling settled her thin frame into the chair next to the window. She appeared to be staying for a while.

"So Mick is Brendan's cousin?" Meghan questioned for lack of anything else to talk to her about.

"Aye," she smiled and pulled her knitting from the bag she brought in with her. "I like to knit while I visit, if that's all right with y'."

"That's fine," Meghan smiled and turned her attention to her breakfast.

Aisling was quiet for some time before she cleared her throat. "So, Brendan tells me that O'Brien fancies y'."

"Apparently," Meghan mumbled, not too sure what the expression meant that was clear on Aisling's face. "Why?"

"Well, I suppose y' already know this, but the O'Briens usually get what they want. Brendan says that the lads that are to help y' out are pretty connected, if y' get me meaning."

Meghan shuddered. "Connected, how?"

"Well, let's just say they have as many connections as O'Brien. I don't ask, that way I can't be held responsible." Aisling glanced back out the window. "I was terribly angry when Brendan introduced the lads to the life, but Brendan said they needed to ensure a life for themselves. Brendan grew up in severe poverty on the bog side of Derry, and he witnessed some horrendous things. I was lucky enough to have grown up in Galway. Me parents weren't rich, but we had more than most."

Meghan nodded and settled back to listen to Aisling's story. It was better than worrying about where Declan had gone.

"When Brendan was ten, he was walking to school with his elder brother Hugh, and they were stopped by four members of the army. Did y' know, they walk back to back, down the street, to keep an eye on all directions?"

Meghan shook her head.

"Well, they did, not so much anymore unless they feel there is danger about. Anyway, the soldiers stopped the boys and questioned them about where they were going. Hugh apparently looked like someone they were looking for, a soldier in the IRA, so when Hugh couldn't produce identification, they grabbed him and said they were arresting him. Hugh panicked, terrified of what was going to happen to him, and he bolted." Aisling paused and took a deep breath.

"The damn soldier shot Hugh right in the back. Gunned him down in the street like a dog. Brendan screamed and ran to Hugh, he couldn't believe what had happened, and before he got to his brother, he felt the bullet of the soldier ripping through his shoulder.

"Oh, it must have been a horrible sight, two young boys lying in the street in a pool of blood. Brendan fell next to his brother, and he watched as the life drained from Hugh. 'Squirt,' Hugh mumbled to Brendan, 'y' be strong and make sure y' take care of yourself because no one else will. How I'm going to miss seeing y' grow up, y' were actually becoming a pleasure to be around'. Hugh died that day, never to see the age of fourteen." Aisling shook her head, her eyes fixed on Meghan's watery gaze.

Meghan could feel the tears dripping down her cheeks. What a pitiful story! Yet Brendan's story was not unique. How many young men have been killed over the last hundred years? Too many on both sides of the fight. Life was so hard, so many people touched by terror and tragedy.

"It's funny what sets a person on the path, either for good or evil. I'm not saying Brendan is evil, mind y', but he is capable of some horrible things. I believe it all started that day. He has never forgiven the British government for killing his brother. That's how he sees it, that they sent their army over here to kill innocent boys." Aisling shook her head. "So much tragedy."

"It's hard to imagine, I grew up hearing about all the problems in Northern Ireland, usually with a British slant on the whole tragedy. Growing up in a country where war was just something that happened elsewhere, I never could understand how neighbours could fight each other. But over the past few weeks, I can see how someone would be willing to kill to keep his family safe, and what he perceives as a threat is what he has witnessed time and time again, growing up."

"Aye," Aisling smiled and took a sip of her tea. "Y' know, Meghan, children have to be taught to fear and hate. They are not born with such burdens. The hate and fear of the British government has been passed down through the generations. The oppression that faced our forefathers has been visited on the sons. Every generation feeding the flames, teaching their children what they have learned. Unfortunately, Brendan's generation grew up facing the oppression and fear and he hates," Aisling sighed.

"When he was about thirteen, an older lad he knew from the street approached him. He wanted him to carry pieces of a gun to an assigned meeting place, then meet up with another few lads and assemble it and pass it off to the lad in charge. By the time he was fifteen, he was already leaving bombs about the town. Of course, he was always instructed where to leave them."

Meghan swallowed hard and tried hard not to show the complete horror she was feeling. Why was Aisling telling her that her husband was a young terrorist?

"Anyway, I'm not trying to frighten y'. I just wanted y' to understand why Brendan is the way he is. I'm not saying I approve of the things he does, but I don't interfere. I don't ask, and he doesn't tell me." Aisling stood and lifted the tray with Meghan's half-eaten breakfast. "Are y' finished?"

"Yes, thank you," Meghan smiled. "It was delicious."

"Thank y'. Now get some rest, later this afternoon, y' can come out into the garden while I weed. I would love the company."

Meghan smiled and watched the woman disappear out the door.

The door to the room flew open, and Declan stood in the doorway, appearing quite proud of himself. His smug grin was too much for

Meghan. She had been worrying for hours, wondering where he was, and now he showed up appearing to have had no concern for her fears.

"Where have you been?" Meghan cried and sat up in bed, her terrified eyes piercing him.

"I was out meeting some of Brendan's friends," Declan grinned wildly as he dropped to the bed beside her.

"You smell like beer and smoke," Meghan complained, taking a swing at his face as it headed towards her. "You went to the pub and left me here by myself."

"Y' weren't alone, Freckles," Declan chuckled and glanced towards the window.

"Oh you mean those two boys out there?" Meghan questioned, her nose crinkling with concern. "I don't like the fact that we are dragging so many people into this."

"Aye, well, it can't be helped. We can't do it on our own," Declan grinned, lifting a couple of large brown bags onto the bed, dismissing any further comments or concerns. "I wasn't just sitting in the pub, y' know, I did get y' something."

"What?" Meghan's attention switched to the bags as he knew it would. She was like a child when it came to presents.

"Y' are so greedy," Declan laughed as her hand lunged out towards the bags, and he pulled them out of her reach.

"Declan, let me see," Meghan complained, making another grab for the brown bags.

"No, y' can wait." His mouth twisted into a crooked grin. "I will show y' one thing at a time. Then I will be expecting y' to be very grateful."

"Hmm," she muttered, flopping back down to her pillow.

Declan laughed loudly as he watched annoyance filling her face. "Okay, first," he muttered, pulling out a pair of jeans out of the bag. "I got y' a couple pairs of pants."

"Wonderful," she smiled, snatching them from his hands, flipping them over in examination.

"Then I got y' some pretty shirts." He pulled out three shirts and dropped them on her lap.

"What else?" Meghan questioned greedily as she sat up and examined the shirts.

"Y' don't think that's enough?" Declan laughed at her expression.

A smirk filled Meghan's mouth. "Those bags aren't empty."

"Y' are just like a child," Declan chuckled and reached into the bag once again. "Okay, I also got y' a lovely dress." Out came the blue cotton dress and a pair of beige sandals.

"Very nice," Meghan smiled with approval. "You're doing great so far. Everything is very nice, and you even got the right size."

"Aye, well, I'm a very informed husband." Declan's voice was cocky.

Meghan giggled as she held the dress up to herself. "Well, you're lucky you didn't get them too big after what you told Aisling this morning."

"She told y', did she?" Declan couldn't control his laughter, he was busted. "Aye, well, I know that body so well, I couldn't very well get the size wrong now, could I?"

Meghan smirked and began reaching for the bag again.

"Hey, I'm not finished," Declan snorted and batted at her hand.

She crinkled her nose and pulled her hand away. "Hurry up."

"Fine, the last thing I got you I think y' will like," he said evenly as he glanced down into the bag. "I spent a lot of time looking for this. And I had a big decision to make on the colour." He smiled as he watched her sighing with impatience. "Well, they had a green one that would go with your eyes, and a blue one, but I thought no." He glanced back down in the bag. "The red one was very beautiful, and I figured that it matched your fiery personality," he smirked and gazed at her. "But I had quite a hard time deciding between the red and green."

"Declan!" Meghan snorted with impatience at his rambling.

He chuckled slightly and reached into the bag. "Well, I finally decided on the red one," he grinned wildly as he pulled out the bright red rauna.

"Oh my gosh," Meghan blurted out. "It's beautiful." She pulled it from his hands and held it up in front of her. The red wool was soft and warm in her hands, and the red velvet hood had a small drawstring that collected in the middle at the sliver Celtic broach.

"Thank you."

"You're welcome, Freckles," he smiled. "I told y' I would get y' one after I threw out the one O'Brien gave y'."

"I thought that you were just saying that to shut me up," Meghan giggled and nuzzled into the soft fabric.

"Well, I partly was," Declan admitted with a grin.

"Well, this one is much nicer anyway. I love it."

"Brilliant," Declan smiled and kissed her forehead. "If y' get dressed, I'll take y' for a walk if you're up to it. Maybe tomorrow we could go see the walls of Derry."

"That would be nice. But do we have time to sightsee?" her question hung in the air as a loud knock on the door stopped her comment.

Declan jumped from the bed and swung open the door to find Fabrizio standing in the hall, with an amused smile.

"You're back?" Fabrizio laughed.

"Aye." Declan stepped back, letting Fabrizio into the room.

"Hi, Boo." Fabrizio shut the door behind him and headed towards the bed. "How are you feeling?"

"Fine," Meghan smiled as she gathered up the clothes and put them back into the bags. "What are you doing here? Where is Cassie?"

"She's fine, she's back in New York. She is going to see agent Paxton for help," Fabrizio said calmly.

"Why did you leave her alone? He could get her," Meghan's voice was panicked.

"Well, I figured you needed me more. It's you he is after, not Cassie. I'm here to help Monty get you home safely." He turned to Declan.

"I see you got your shopping done," Fabrizio smirked and sat down on the bed beside Meghan, resting his hand on her forehead.

"Aye. What's with y'?" Declan questioned, not understanding Fabrizio's amusement.

"You haven't talked to Brendan since y' left the pub, have you?" Fabrizio's brow rose slightly.

"No."

"Well, he apparently is very annoyed with you." Fabrizio let out a loud laugh, kissed Meghan's cheek, and turned his attention to Declan.

"Why?"

"He can't understand why you would go shopping for a woman." Fabrizio eyed Meghan, then glanced up at Declan's amused face.

"What?" Meghan blurted out.

"He thinks that you must be woman." Fabrizio could hardly control his hysteria.

Declan shook his head with a slight smirk. "He's just like me da."

"Yeah, well, he wouldn't stop moaning about you leaving the men in the pub to go shopping for woman's clothes," Fabrizio laughed hysterically.

"Well, she needed some clothes," Declan snorted, getting rather offended by Brendan's opinion. "What was I supposed to do, let her walk around in the ripped ones she has?"

"Hey, don't get mad at me. I'm just relaying the information," Fabrizio announced.

"Aye, I'm sorry," Declan sighed. "I forgot how some of the older men here think."

"I guess leaving your pals sitting in the pub to go shopping for the little woman is a big insult," Fabrizio laughed.

"Apparently," Declan chuckled. "Well, I guess I will have to prepare meself for the ribbing," he smirked as he put the bag of clothes on the floor.

"Well, if you're a woman, I suppose you won't be needing this beautiful creature any longer." Fabrizio's arm snaked around Meghan, pulling her up against him. "I'm mighty lonely since Cassie is gone."

"Don't y' get any ideas," Declan grumbled, unsure if Fabrizio was kidding or not. He was convinced that Fabrizio still had feelings for Meghan, and he had to fight hard to control his jealousy.

Meghan giggled and rested her lips on his cheek. "Well, I guess I could be a cheap substitute for Cassie. Would you like that?" Her voice was playful, sending Fabrizio's desires for her into turmoil. Why did he start this, he should never have touched her, the feel of her intoxicates him.

"Too much," Fabrizio whispered so quietly, she could barely hear him.

Meghan sensed something in Fabrizio that she hadn't felt in months, and she pulled away forcing a smile. "Well, I won't burden you with such torture again."

Fabrizio smiled and released her from his grip. "It wasn't torture." He jumped from the bed and looked back down at her. "It was pure pleasure. Now I remember how you control him so well." Fabrizio patted Declan on the shoulder as he passed. "Brendan wants to see you when you have a minute."

"Aye," Declan smiled and closed the door behind Fabrizio. "He still loves y'."

"He does not," Meghan giggled, hoping Declan was wrong. "He loves Cassie, and she loves him."

"Oh, Meggie, y' are like a magnet. I believe I'm going to have to lock y' up when we get home."

"Well, count yourself lucky that you are the man I love."

"Aye," he laughed and kissed her thoroughly. "See what trouble y' cause me, woman."

The air was damp but reasonably warm as Meghan wandered down the front walk towards the two men that were now putting the second coat of paint on the small metal fence surrounding the red brick row house.

"That's going to be the nicest-looking fence around," Meghan commented as she came to a stop beside the two young men.

"Aye," said the tall blond boy.

Meghan's brow rose slightly as she watched the two scanning her with interest. "So are you friends of Brendan's?" she questioned.

"Aye, ma'am," said the short, stocky redhead.

Meghan grunted at their abrupt answers, then turned towards the gate to the street, but a sweaty hand on her arm halted her movement.

"I'm sorry, ma'am, but we can't let y' leave the yard," said the redheaded Simon.

"Why not?" Meghan snorted, pulling at her arm.

"We have our orders," Simon muttered, pulling her back towards him.

"Orders?" Meghan's voice wavered with concern at the tone of voice he had used. These boys were obviously placed at the house to keep an eye on her.

"Aye, ma'am," Simon said, still clinging to her arm.

"Please, let go of me," Meghan asked, tugging at her arm.

"Y' should go back inside, ma'am, y' are getting rather cold," Simon said, totally ignoring her attempt to free herself. His blue eyes slowly scanned her jeans and thin blouse covered by a thin woollen button-up sweater.

"I'm fine," Meghan muttered with defiance, staring directly at him.

He was about her height, maybe a tinge shorter, but he was quite broad at the shoulder and had enormous rough hands. He obviously used them extensively in whatever type of work he did, but she was sure painting fences was not his career.

"Ma'am, please just do as I say." Simon's tone was becoming sharp.

Meghan's eyes were narrowing at his tone, and she was becoming frustrated with his insistence for her to go inside. "No. I want to go for a walk."

Suddenly the blond man broke into hysterical laughter. Meghan's eyes left Simon's face and settled on Marty, who was still laughing.

"What are you laughing at?" she questioned as her eyes flaring with interest.

"Well, I didn't believe him when he told me that you would . . ." He stopped, unable to push the rest through his laughter. "He is so big, and I figured y'."

"What are you talking about?" Meghan snorted, still tugging at her arm.

"Your husband said y' wouldn't do as y' were told," Simon muttered, glaring over at his hysterical friend. "He said y' never do."

"Hmm," Meghan muttered, scrunching up her nose. "Well," she stammered for the words to defend herself. "Well, I don't see why I can't go for a walk."

Simon began to shake his head at her. "If I were your husband, I would have taught y' who's boss long ago," he snorted.

"Who is boss? I take it you are still single," she snorted.

"Aye," he muttered, his brows scrunching to the middle of his face.

Meghan grunted a chuckle. "Are you planning on holding on to me forever, or are you going to let go?"

Simon sighed with exasperation. "Ma'am, please, I don't want Brendan getting annoyed with me."

"He won't. I'm sure he wouldn't mind me getting some fresh air."

Simon's face began to enflame with annoyance. "Did your husband not tell y' to stay inside?" His voice was getting louder with agitation.

"Yes, but . . ."

"Then get back inside," Simon snorted as he flung her towards the front door. "Damn woman."

"Don't talk to me like that," Meghan snorted as she caught her balance and faced him with defiance.

"He said y' were the most bull-headed woman he's ever met," Marty laughed, causing a long strand of blond hair to fall down his face. His hand swept across the young attractive face. "I think he was right."

"Bloody hell, Marty, don't encourage her. If she gets away from us and O'Brien—"

"O'Brien?" Meghan panicked at the name. "You know about that?"

"Aye," Simon admitted, the redness in his face slightly fading. "He has been spotted in Derry."

"Oh," Meghan muttered and dropped to the steps.

"Ma'am, don't concern yourself. Y' are well protected as long as y' stay here," Marty told her as he moved towards her. "Anyway, he won't come into this part of the city."

"Why not?" Meghan questioned, not understanding the reasoning.

"Well, he's not Catholic, ma'am. This is the bog side of Derry. A devil as well known as him would not show his face on these streets."

"Oh," she muttered. Her mind was whirling with worry and also confusion about the way of life in this beautiful but troubled country. "I want to find my husband," Meghan mumbled as she began to shake.

"He will be back soon. They went to arrange transportation," Marty informed her as he sat beside her, placing his long narrow hand on her shoulder.

"What kind of transportation?" Meghan questioned.

"A boat. They are hiring a fisherman to take y' to Scotland, then y' can drive down to London," Simon mumbled as he glanced around the area.

"Oh, I knew that," Meghan sighed as she rested her face in her hands. She could feel his hand gently stroking her back, and she turned to look at his very young face.

"How old are you?" she questioned, out of curiosity.

"What?" Marty asked, quite startled by her question.

"You just look very young. I was wondering." She stopped and bit her lip. "Well, I was wondering why you would be in this line of work?"

"This line of work?" he laughed. "Y' don't think painting is a proper job?"

Meghan's face filled with a smug smile. "You're not a painter."

"Y' don't think so?" His mouth twitched slightly.

"No."

"Why not?" Marty questioned, quite interested in her reasoning.

"Well, I have never seen painters take four days to paint ten feet of fence." Her brow rose slightly.

"Aye well," Marty laughed.

"Marty!" Simon snapped, trying to keep his chatty friend quiet.

"You never told me how old you are?" Meghan questioned again, ignoring Simon's annoyance.

"Twenty," Marty smiled, exposing his large white teeth.

"Twenty?" she repeated and shook her head, thinking about the twenty-year-olds she knew back home that were busy at university partying and enjoying their youth. This young boy had obviously been raised with danger all his life and still enjoyed life. "Are you related to Aisling?" Meghan questioned.

"Aye, how did y' know?" Marty laughed.

"You look like her," Meghan commented as she stood up from the steps.

"She's me aunt," Marty admitted, following her into the garden.

"Ma'am, where are y' going now?" Simon snorted as he came up behind her.

"Nowhere," Meghan scowled at him as he grabbed her arm again.

"I don't want to have to tell y' again. Get into the house," Simon grumbled, dragging her towards the front door.

"You don't have to be so rough. I'm going," Meghan snapped.

"Meggie, are y' giving these lads a hard time?" The low amused voice came from behind her.

She swung around to find Declan, Fabrizio, and Brendan heading through the gate towards her.

"No, don't worry, they have been very good jailers," Meghan snorted, still tugging at her arm that was trapped in Simon's hand.

"Well, I see that," Declan commented, his eyes settling on Simon's hand.

Simon released his grip when he noticed Declan's gaze on him. "She . . ."

"She's been giving y' a hard time," Declan finished, noticing Simon's worried eyes landing on Brendan.

"Aye," Simon admitted.

"Well, I told y' she would," Declan laughed, settling his gaze on her annoyed face.

"Declan," Meghan muttered, crinkling her nose at him.

"Freckles, when are y' going to learn to listen to me?" Declan questioned sharply as he moved towards her.

"Declan, me lad, y' are going to have to get control of her if y' are going to get home safely," Brendan announced, his eyes narrowing as he glared at her.

"Aye," Declan muttered. "Meggie, come with me." He gripped her arm.

"Declan, don't talk to me like that," Meghan muttered through her clenched teeth.

"Meggie!" Declan's voice was cold and firm.

"I'm not ready to go inside," Meghan announced, setting her chin into a stubborn pose. She was getting very annoyed at the attitude of these men.

"Meggie, I'm not telling y' again," Declan demanded as his face began to redden.

"No!" Meghan snapped and swung around, but with his grip still firm, she stumbled a few steps.

"Dammit, Meggie!" Declan pulled her back towards him. "Why won't y' obey me?"

"Obey you?" she questioned, quite startled by his comment.

"Aye." His eyes were flashing, but she couldn't read the reasoning behind his comments. His outer demeanour appeared angry, but his eyes were filled with amusement.

"Declan?" she muttered, her eyes still trapped in his grey gaze.

"Meggie," he said through his teeth. "Please," he added as an obvious afterthought.

"Fine," Meghan muttered and allowed him drag her into the house.

He was quiet until the door to their bedroom shut behind him. "Christ, Meggie, what do you think you're doing?" he questioned.

"What am I doing? Since when are you such a chauvinistic pig?" she snorted.

His face broke and loud laughter exploded from him, his body shaking uncontrollably. "Y' are going to be the death of me."

"What the hell are you finding so funny?"

Declan finally settled after a few moments of hysterical laughter and dropped to the bed.

"Meggie, I'm sorry, but Brendan thinks that y' are too wilful." His brow rose slightly. "I'm not sure I disagree with him."

She scowled and went over to the window and gazed out at the group of men still standing in the garden.

"Freckles, I'm begging y', please just make it appear that y' listen to me," he laughed with a delightfulness she hadn't heard from him in a long time.

"I listen to you," she said evenly. "Most times," she added.

"I know," he chuckled. "But Brendan thinks that I have no control of y', and he thinks that makes me weak."

"What?" she snorted.

"Well, he is under the opinion that women are to obey and serve their men." A slight smirk grew across his face. "And there are times that I would have to say . . ."

"If you were going to say that you agree with him," Meghan muttered and pressed up against him.

"Well," he laughed. "Aisling seems very devoted to him. She cooks and . . ."

"Declan," Meghan snapped and smacked his chest. "You knew what you were getting, and if you are changing your mind, that's too bad."

"Aye, I did," his infectious laugh was getting louder. "But sometimes."

"Don't you dare!" Meghan laughed as she swung around, moving away from him.

"Hey, don't y' walk away from me," he snorted a chuckle and grabbed her arm, pulling her towards him.

"Meggie, I know it's going to take every ounce of self-control y' have, but y' need to listen to me." His face was remarkably solemn as he gazed at her.

Meghan stared at him, her big green eyes ablaze. "Fine," she sighed with retreat.

"I knew from the first day I met y' that y' were going to be the death of me," Declan laughed, quite content with his choice of wife. This wife of his was always a delight.

"Yeah, well," she smirked. "You still married me, though."

"Aye, I like the challenge," Declan laughed, engulfing her in his arms. His lips gently landed on hers as he dragged her towards the bed.

"Now since y' promised to obey me," a large grin filled his chiselled face, "take your clothes off and get on that bed, woman," he ordered, with a tone of amusement, his hands slowly unbuttoning her blouse.

Meghan stared at him, her body trembling. This was the first time since she was abducted that he initiated intimacy. She had attempted a few times in the past week, but he always turned her down, claiming he needed to stay alert.

What had changed? Did his meeting with Brendan's friends go that well that Declan was now relaxed enough to focus on making love to her? Whatever it was, she didn't care, all she knew was she wanted him. She wanted to feel her body pressing against his warm strong frame as he filled her completely.

"Oh, Meggie, it's been too long," Declan groaned into her hair as she suckled the nape of his neck. She smelled so good, felt so soft under his hand. This wife of his, what a wonder! Everything about her intrigued him, excited him. Why was he so blessed to have her in his life, to be the man she loved?

"Declan, I love you," she whispered in his ear as if she had been reading his thoughts.

Declan said nothing, his only response was to lift her into his arms and carry her towards the small bed. It was hard enough sleeping on the tiny bed with her, let alone making love, but it must be done. He couldn't go another day without fulfilling his needs, his need for her.

Passion erupted on the oversized single bed that their hosts claim was a double, but at that moment, it did not matter. They would occupy one space on the bed as they linked together reacquainting themselves with each other.

CHAPTER FOURTY

The early morning sun shone brightly through the small stain-glass window, casting a colourful glow across the oddly shaped room at the top of the house.

Aisling was sewing, and Meghan was sitting on a small settee, reading a mystery novel she had found on a bookshelf in Brendan's study. A week had passed since they arrived at Brendan's and Aisling's, and their plans were finally in place. Angus's boat was in dry dock longer than anyone expected and that left them stranded at Brendan's. Not that Meghan minded terribly much, she was enjoying the company of Aisling. She was an extremely lovely woman, and Meghan found herself confiding in her as if she was her mother.

"Aisling." Meghan glanced up from her book as Aisling finished her rendition of By Yon Bonny Banks. "Do you believe in fate?"

"Aye, child, I do," Aisling smiled, her eyes leaving the quilt she was sewing. "I believe everything happens for a reason."

"Me too," Meghan smiled. "And I'm sure glad I met you. Do you think that we could keep in touch once I get home?"

"Oh, I'd love that, dear, you're like a daughter to me," Aisling grinned bashfully. "I do hope y' will come back one day and bring your dear Caelan with y'. I feel as if I know her from all your stories."

"I'd like that. You could always come to visit us, we could go to Malibu and stay there for a while."

"Aye, California, I've always wanted to go there and meet some movie stars." Aisling blushed slightly as the words exited her mouth. "I know that Declan is a movie star, but he seems more like one of the lads, no airs about that boy."

Meghan laughed but covered her mouth quickly, not wanting to spoil Aisling's impression of Declan. She was right; he had changed a great deal over the last month, the arrogance that once surrounded him was gone, and he seemed genuinely grateful for the help he was receiving from everyone.

Aisling eyed Meghan for a moment, then returned her eyes to her work. "Y' know who I would really like to meet? It is Harrison Ford."

Meghan giggled. "Me too."

Aisling smiled and picked up a small patch. "Do y' like this pattern, Meghan?"

"Yes, it's beautiful, you are very skilled. I could never sew like that."

"Aye, well, it comes with practice. I was thinking I would send it with y' for Caelan."

"Really?" Meghan's voice filled with glee, this woman was more motherly and loving than her own mother ever could have been.

"Aye, and when that child is born," she bobbed her head towards Meghan's tummy, "I'll send another."

"How did you know I was pregnant?" Meghan muttered, completely caught off guard. "I mean, I'm not even sure myself."

"Y' have a glow to y' that only women with child have," Aisling smiled and focused back on her quilt.

Meghan giggled slightly, relieved to have someone to talk to. She still had not told Declan of her suspicions, why cause him anymore worry? "The first day I met you, when you told me your name . . . Well, I thought it would be a lovely name if I had a girl."

"Aye, I would be honoured if y' named the wee bairn after me."

Meghan smiled, jumped from the chair, and hugged Aisling. "If it's a girl, her name will be Aisling."

"Grand, and I'll be Granny Ash," Aisling grinned, her large white teeth brightening her pretty face.

Meghan nodded and glanced out the window. Andy and Marty had finally finished the fence. Where had they gone, they were no longer in front of the house? She shrugged and moved back over to the settee.

"I had a child once." Aisling looked up from her knitting. "But he died when he was three. He would be forty-two next spring."

"Oh, I'm sorry," Meghan muttered.

"Thank y', dear, but it was a long time ago. I have grown accustomed to the emptiness. I must say having you around is like having me own daughter. I'll be sad to see y' go."

Meghan smiled, but the doorbell rang, and caused the two women to startle. Meghan's eyes settled on Aisling at precisely the time the bell rang again.

"Well, someone is impatient." Aisling clicked her tongue with disapproval. "Brendan is taking his nap, so I best see who it is."

Meghan nodded and followed her to the top of the stairs. She went no further, knowing she was to stay out of sight until Aisling told her it was all right. Only certain people were privy to the pair's whereabouts.

"Who could it be at this time of day? Everyone knows Brendan enjoys to have a midmorning nap right after breakfast. The damn fool who wakes him . . ." Her voice cut out as she reached the bottom of the stairs.

Meghan glanced down the stairs when she heard a strangled yelp coming from Aisling as she bolted towards the stairs.

"Meghan, hide yourself." Aisling's voice sounded terrified.

Before Aisling made it up the first flight of stairs, the door crashed in and loud screaming filled the house. It was the gun shot, however, that Meghan focused on, the gun shot that sounded dangerously close to where Aisling was.

Any common sense Meghan had was ignored as she bolted down the stairs towards the ruckus. She came to a dead stop and almost tripped over Aisling, pulling herself up the stairs, blood streaming from her back.

"Oh, Aisling," Meghan cried as she scooped the woman into her arms. "Who did this to you?"

"I did." The gruff voice of Murphy flowed up the stairs.

Meghan screamed and dragged Aisling up the stairs as fast as she could. Panic rushed through her as she pulled Aisling's weakening body into a bedroom next to the stairs. She wasn't sure what she was going to do, but she just knew she needed to help Aisling.

"Meghan, me love, where are y' hiding?" O'Brien's voice was close, possibly right outside the door.

"Aisling, I need to hide you."

"No, child, hide yourself. I'm done in, but y' need to get away. I wouldn't want anything to happen to my precious Aisling." Aisling's trembling hand rested against Meghan's tummy. "Please, Meghan, save yourself."

"No, I'm not leaving you," Meghan argued before the door flew open, exposing Liam's smug face.

"I can understand why y' keep running from me, me love." He shook his head and sauntered towards the two women.

Meghan found it hard to breathe, her eyes switching from Aisling to Liam to Murphy who was standing in the doorway, his gun pointed towards them.

Liam noticed her agitation and bobbed his head towards the two men directly behind Murphy. "I'll deal with the ladies, y' go find Montgomery."

"Liam, please," Meghan sniffed, her terror dangerously close to the surface. She knew only Brendan was in the house, but they would find him.

"Me love, don't be scared of me. I don't plan on hurting y'," Liam smiled through the short golden beard. His eyes settling on Aisling. "Ah, it's a shame she got in the way."

"Leave us alone," Meghan cried, covering Aisling with her body. "Brendan, they're coming after you."

Liam sighed and shook his head. "What do y' think that's going to accomplish?"

"Hopefully he'll get out of the house," Meghan sniffed, her head buried in Aisling's grey curls. "Hang on, Aisling, you are going to be all right."

Liam eyed Meghan sceptically. "How long have y' known this woman?"

"Long enough," Meghan snorted, her dark piercing gaze settling on Liam. "And if she dies . . ."

"Well, if y' wouldn't have run away, none of this would be happening," Liam scolded and pulled her to her feet, dislodging Aisling to the floor.

"Let go," Meghan cried as she struggled desperately to get back to Aisling. "Don't hurt them," she screamed just before first shot rang out.

The sound of shouting voices filtered down the stairs before two more shots rang out. The heavy footsteps moved across the floor. The fourth shot rang out, and a terrible thud resonated through the floor, then the footsteps were on the move again. Meghan looked desperately past Liam with hope, but it was quickly dashed as Murphy appeared on the landing.

"Oh God," Meghan cried as her legs gave way under her, and she collapsed to the floor in a heap of distress and terror.

"Brendan?" Aisling's voice was weak and sorrowful. "Child, is it Brendan?"

"No, it's Murphy." Meghan choked back the tears. "Aisling, please don't give up." Meghan tugged to get loose, and Liam obliged and released her, allowing her to crawl to Aisling.

"Any sign of Montgomery?" O'Brien asked Murphy.

"No, he's not in the house," Murphy sighed, his head shaking slightly with dismay. "The bastard got Freddy."

Liam waved his hand with dismal of the loss and turned towards Meghan who had the pillowcase off of the pillow, and had it pressed up against Aisling's shoulder, where the bullet had penetrated. She stripped off her belt from her jeans and fastened the pillowcase to Aisling's shoulder.

"Meghan," Liam muttered as he kneeled down beside Meghan, wrapping his arm around her ribs. "It's time to go, me love."

"No," Meghan cried as she hit at him as total terror raged through her.

"This is not an option that y' have," Liam warned and pulled her to her feet.

"O'Malley, take her to the car. I'm going to leave a note for her husband. I wouldn't want him worrying," Liam laughed as he flung her towards the tall young man.

"Let go," Meghan screamed as O'Malley's thick sweaty hand gripped her arm. "Aisling, be strong."

O'Malley had her down the stairs and to the door before she heard Liam's voice. "Leave the woman be, if she survives, it's her choice."

"But she can identify us." Murphy's voice was concerned.

Liam laughed a cruel sound. "She won't make it through the night. I just don't want Meghan blaming me for her death."

Murphy snorted a laugh. "Your da is right. That woman has y' tied in knots. Maybe she is a sidhe sent to retrieve the sword, just like old man O'Brien from the estate thinks."

Liam shook his head at the stupidity of the comment and heading down the stairs.

The garden was eerily quiet as O'Malley dragged Meghan kicking and screaming down the path towards the road. He was too strong; she could not break his grip. What was she going to do? She could not go back with Liam. If he got her into that car, she was trapped again.

She was startled by a loud grunt from behind her, and she swung around and watched Declan casually throwing the limp body of the man behind them to the ground. O'Malley had also turned and quickly lifted the gun to Meghan's head.

"Don't move or she dies," O'Malley said sharply, pushing the barrel tightly against Meghan's temple.

"Now, we both know that y' aren't going to kill her," Declan smirked as he lifted the gun he had in his hand towards O'Malley.

"Aye, I will," O'Malley snorted.

"No, y' won't. Your boss would be terribly annoyed if y' harm her. He needs her, and we both know it."

"Aye, y' may be right, but he doesn't need y'," O'Malley sneered, removing the barrel from Meghan's head and pointing it at Declan.

"Aye, true enough," Declan smirked as he pulled the trigger. The bullet hit O'Malley dead centre in the forehead, and he dropped like a brick to the ground.

Meghan stood motionless, staring at Declan with complete shock. She couldn't believe that he would shoot a gun at someone so close to her.

"Declan," she muttered and stared down at the lifeless body.

"Meggie, go with Fabs," Declan shouted as Fabrizio materialized out of the trees and grabbed her by the arm.

Declan swung around to face the door when he heard the shouting coming from inside. "Meggie, go now," he shouted again.

"No. I'm not leaving you!" Meghan screamed, struggling against Fabrizio.

"Dammit, do what I'm telling y'! This ends today!" Declan snorted as panic surged through him. There was no way O'Brien was getting his disgusting hands on her again. He would die before he let that happen. He stole one last glance at Meghan before he dashed through the front door. His wife, his love. He would keep her safe.

"Meghan, come on," Fabrizio said, firmly pulling her through the gate and down the street towards the car.

"Fabrizio, we can't leave him there," Meghan cried when he pushed her into the small silver Volvo.

"Boo, it will be okay. He wants me to get you away safely, then I'll come back for him."

"No, we can't leave him all alone. Liam has already killed Brendan and the young boys," Meghan shrieked and tried to climb back out of the car.

"What?" Fabrizio suddenly stilled.

"He's all alone," Meghan cried. "Fabrizio, please."

"How many of them are there?" Fabrizio questioned abruptly.

"Just Liam and Murphy. Brendan shot one, and Declan got the other two outside," Meghan rambled as Fabrizio shoved her back into the car.

"Okay, it's okay," Fabrizio reassured her as he jumped into the car.

"Fabrizio," Meghan screamed, staring helplessly out the back window as the car pulled away from the curb.

"Meghan, if anything happens to you, he would never forgive me. I have to do what he asked." Fabrizio glanced back in the rear-view mirror, hoping he was making the right decision.

It seemed to take forever for Fabrizio to return to the small cottage where he deposited Meghan in before returning to Brenda's' to retrieve Declan. The cottage was suffocating, but she was determined not to disobey Fabrizio. He made her promise that she would not leave the cottage.

The quaint cottage was well taken care of. The owners must not have been away too long from home. She had no idea who lived there, but from the pictures on the mantle, she managed to piece together a life for her illusive hosts.

The young girl in the lovely emerald green Irish dancing dress smiled from the picture, overjoyed with the trophy she held in her hand. The two boys, however, did not appear to be as pleased with the whole experience. Their faces showed compliance, most likely appeasing their mother.

She would have to enrol Caelan in dance when she returned home. She loved to watch Irish dancing; the music and the grace of the dancers always enchanted her.

She wondered idly if the little girl danced around the living room for her parents. Did her father sit in the large rocker by the fireplace and tap out the beat of the reels on the maple floors? Did her mother sit on the sofa by the window, knitting and humming along with the music to the jigs?

The three bedrooms at the back of the house were spacious, the little girl's room filled with dolls and books. The room was neat and organized, waiting for her to return home. The boys' room sported large oak bunk beds and a desk on the wall under the window. One side of the room had a telescope and maps charting the stars, the other filled with toy trucks and trains, two boys so different. Which one was the stargazer? Was it the older boy, the boy with the golden hair?

Did this family know that their house was being used as a hideaway for her? Should she leave a note of thanks? She shook her head and wandered back towards the window, trying to glance outside without exposing herself to the outside world.

Another hour passed, and Meghan had been anxiously pacing back and forth still horribly terrorized from what had happened earlier. The death that surrounded her was horrifying. What happened to Aisling and Brendan, but most of all, what happened to Declan?

Her heart skipped a beat when she heard a car approaching. Who was it? Fabrizio's warnings filled her mind. "Stay hidden," he told her at least three times before he left. "Don't leave the house and stay away from the window."

"Thank goodness," Meghan muttered. Her breath caught in her throat when Fabrizio jumped from the driver's side and hesitantly moved towards the door. Her eyes left him and fixed on the passenger side, but the door never opened.

"Fabrizio?" Meghan's voice shook slightly. "Where is he?"

"Oh, Boo, I'm sorry," Fabrizio mumbled and moved towards her.

"No!" Meghan lunged towards the car. "No, Fabrizio!"

"Meghan," Fabrizio muttered, grabbed hold of her around the waist and pulled her into his chest.

"No!" she cried. "No, not Declan!"

"Meghan, I'm so sorry."

"Damn you, Fabrizio. Why did you leave him?" Meghan screamed and slammed her fists into his chest.

"I'm sorry," Fabrizio repeated, letting her smack him over and over. His heart was breaking for her.

"Oh, Declan," Meghan sobbed and finally collapsed into Fabrizio's chest, hoping that somehow he could change the outcome.

Fabrizio surrounded her trembling body, wrapping his arms tightly around her as he led her towards the couch. What was he going to do? This poor woman curled into him, sobbing uncontrollably, clinging to him; he was now her only safety net.

"Meghan, I promise I will do everything in my power to keep you safe. I will get you home and then . . ."

"Then what, Fabrizio?" she snivelled, her heart collapsing in her chest. "I'm alone."

"No, you're not. I'll never leave you. If you want, I'll move to the ranch and live there with you and Caelan. I will never leave you, Meghan." She was his now. His responsibility, his reason for living at the moment. He would never let her down.

"Fabrizio, are you sure he's dead?" Meghan finally questioned, wiping at her eyes and gazing up at him, the hope he was wrong strong in her eyes. She appeared not to have heard a word he had said. Why didn't she comment on him living at the ranch, had she even heard him?

"When I got back to Brenda's' the Derry police had arrived, and the bodies had already been taken to the hospital."

"Then how do you know?" Meghan rested her weary head against Fabrizio's chest and stared up at him. How safe she felt, this man that continually risked his life for her! What would happen now when they got home? Their relationship was always at arm's length because of her love for Declan. She never let him completely in. But now he was with Cassie; she would not get in the middle of that. Cassie loves him.

"Because the officer told me that they found two bodies upstairs, four in the garden, and one in the kitchen."

"So?"

"Meghan, the one in the kitchen," Fabrizio paused and turned away from her. "The man in the kitchen, they said was big with long black hair." He turned back around. "O'Brien's blond, and Murphy isn't tall."

"This can't be happening. It has to be a horrible mistake," Meghan cried and buried her face into his chest. "Please, Fabrizio, tell me it's a mistake."

"Meghan, listen to me. The Derry police want us to come and identify the body." Her pleas ripped at his heart. How lucky Declan was to have a woman love him so completely! Did Declan even realize what he had in her?

"We can't, what if it's a trap, and Liam is there?" she blurted out. "He'll kill you."

"Boo, calm down. O'Brien has gone back down south." Fabrizio soothed and kissed the top of her head. She was concerned for him. How wonderful that felt!

"How do you know?" Meghan sniffed.

"Because I talked to Eamon, and he says his sources claim that O'Brien and Murphy were spotted in Ballymena this afternoon. Eamon thinks that he'll stay put for a while and wait to see if we show back up at Mick's."

"Fabrizio, what are we going to do?" Meghan sighed, turning over the decision making to Fabrizio. All she wanted was for someone to walk her through the rest of her life. A life without Declan? How was she going to survive?

"We need to make our move now. We have to go get Monty's body and get home before O'Brien feels safe to come out of his hole again. Eamon is meeting us at the boat tomorrow, and we will stick to that plan to get you home." Fabrizio rested his face against the top of her head. How sweet she smelled, how soft she was curled up against him, her fingers playing idly with the buttons on his shirt like she had so often in the past!

She was not undoing them or making any advances towards him, but just having her in his arms was causing him discomfort. How disloyal he felt, he still loves his best friend's wife. Declan trusted him, making him promise to take care of her if anything happened to him, and well, death was something.

She was his responsibility now, and he needed to suppress his guilt and his desire and focus on how he was going to get her home. What would happen when they got back to Montana needed to be pushed to the back of his mind. He could not deal with what Cassie would say, and he certainly did not want to think about how Meghan would react.

The hospital was relatively quiet as Meghan and Fabrizio wandered down the hall towards the morgue to identify the body of Declan. Meghan was feeling rather faint and somewhat dazed as she passed sightlessly by the security station and down the hall. The walls had a greyish appearance to them as did everything else in her view. The day seemed to be playing out in slow motion.

The door opened abruptly, and a short thin man with a stark white cloak stood staring at them solemnly. He nodded his head, then moved slightly, allowing them to enter the sterile white room. Meghan blinked repeatedly, trying to adjust her eyes to the drastic skew change from the dull grey to the extremely white facade of the sterile room.

"Are you here to identify the body of the unknown victim?" he questioned as he stopped at his desk.

"Yes," Meghan mumbled.

"And what's the name?" the cloaked man asked as he lifted his pen.

"Declan Patrick Montgomery," Meghan sniffed and wobbled back into Fabrizio's arms.

"Meghan, are you okay?" Fabrizio questioned, holding her tightly.

"No. No, I'm not," she snorted. "I'm never going to be okay again."

"Meghan, please calm down, let's just get this over with," Fabrizio said calmly, leading her towards the long silver shelf.

As the cloaked man pulled the ghostly white sheet back slowly, Meghan gasped as everything around her faded to a calm blackness.

The next thing she was aware of was Fabrizio shaking her, calling her name repeatedly.

"Fabrizio," Meghan shrieked as she began to recover. "It's not him."

CHAPTER FOURTY-ONE

The sky was clear and dark, the air crisp as they pulled up to the cottage hoping to regroup and find out what had happened to Declan. Meghan jumped from the Volvo and gazed up at the multitude of star shining brightly in the dark night.

"Fabrizio, where could he be? What if Liam has him?" Meghan sniffed.

"I don't know," Fabrizio mumbled and pulled the bag of groceries out of the back seat. "Let's just have something to eat and then I'll call Mick."

"Maybe I should contact Liam. If he has Declan, I'm sure he'll tell me."

"Meghan, you're not calling him. If he has Monty, he will contact us."

"How?" she questioned, with panic.

"Through Mick. He knows he is in contact with us. That's how he tracked us down at Brendans'."

Meghan sighed and glanced up at the clear, star-filled sky. "This is unbelievable. We have to find him."

"Boo, we'll find him. Either way."

She turned, looking quite shocked at his comment but decided not to respond as the fear of what he meant surged through her like a scalding knife. She became very agitated, and she dropped the bag of groceries she was carrying.

"Boo," Fabrizio muttered as he ran to her side, helping to gather the contents of the torn brown bag. "It's going to be okay."

"No, it's not," she cried. "He's probably hurt. Liam's men are probably beating him as we speak."

Meghan collapsed into Fabrizio, her arms clinging around his ribs, hoping that somehow everything was a bad dream. A bad dream she would wake up from soon.

"We don't even know if O'Brien has him. Don't work yourself up until we know for sure." Fabrizio kissed the top of her head.

"Then where the hell is he?" Meghan screamed and pulled away from him and threw the apple she had in her hand at the wall of the cottage, causing it to splatter into pieces.

"Oh, Meghan," Fabrizio sighed and engulfed her in his arms. "We'll find him. If it's the last thing I do."

Meghan pressed her head against Fabrizio's chest, squeezing her eyes tightly shut. "Fabrizio, I'm so scared."

"I know, sweetheart, but please trust me when I tell you that I will never leave you alone." Fabrizio's voice was soft but clear in her ear as he pressed his face against her head. He had to stop the feelings welling up inside him again, why was he feeling this way? He loves Cassie, he was sure of it. Was it just the fact that she was the centre of the mission? He always loved the thrill of a dangerous mission.

"I can't wait," Meghan blurted out, pushing from Fabrizio's arms. "I'm going to find Liam and get Declan back."

"Meghan, are you out of your mind! If you go there, he'll kill Monty, and you will be stuck with him," Fabrizio said, sharply pulling her back towards him. "I'm not letting you anywhere near that animal. God, Meghan, it sickens me to think of the way he was slobbering over you!"

"Fabrizio," Meghan cried as the feeling of utter helplessness overtook her.

"And what if O'Brien doesn't have him?" Fabrizio paused, trying to back out of his previous statement. "Monty will kill me for letting him get his hands on you."

"Fabrizio, please, I can't stand by waiting. What if he's hurt?" Meghan cried, tugging on her arms to free herself from his grip.

"I'm not hurt." A soft deep voice spoke from the doorway.

"Declan!" Meghan swung around, managing to get a quick glance at the figure looming in the door.

Fabrizio instantaneously released her from his grip, and she lunged towards Declan, slamming into him, her sobs loud in Declan's ear.

"Meggie, are y' okay?" Declan soothed, kissing the top of her head.

"Declan," she muttered as she blinked repeatedly, trying to focus on his face. "I was so scared you were dead. Is it really you?"

"Aye, it's me," Declan chuckled and rested a kiss on her trembling mouth. "I'm sorry for scaring y'." He soothed, rubbing her hair behind her ears. "I didn't want to stick around there and try to explain what happened to the Derry police."

"Declan!" Meghan blurted out, once her senses regrouped. "You let me think you were dead. We went to the morgue to identify your body. I can't believe you would make me do that, you big jerk," she snorted.

"Meggie," Declan chuckled. "Calm down."

"No!" Meghan pushed away and wandered past Fabrizio, who was leaning against the wall of the cottage, somewhat shell-shocked.

"Freckles, please." Declan soothed, following a few paces behind her.

"And poor Fabrizio, he had to come with me, and I blamed him for this and you knew and you let us go through that," she rambled as she headed for the path that led to the back of the cottage.

"Meghan, stay here," Fabrizio told her as she took a step to get around him.

She turned and stared at Fabrizio, somewhat annoyed at his silence. "Are you just going to stand there and let him get away with this? You were going to get stuck looking after me, Fabrizio, you were willing to throw away your life for a promise made to him, and this is the way he treats you."

"Meghan, please calm down. Monty wasn't trying to hurt us," Fabrizio muttered. So she did hear him, but she didn't understand his meaning. Thank goodness, she didn't realize he meant he wanted to be with her again. Declan's eyes were set on him almost accusingly after Meghan's comment. Did Declan know he still had feeling for Meghan, and is that the reason for the expression on his face?

Meghan grunted and stormed past Fabrizio with Declan close on her heels.

"Monty, she's had a long day." Fabrizio reminded him as he passed by.

"Aye, I know. Fabs, I'm sorry to have scared y'."

"I understand. You couldn't very well hang around, waiting for the possibly crooked cops to show up."

"Aye." Declan patted Fabrizio's shoulder and eyed him momentarily. This friend of his loves his wife. What had transpired over the past few hours! He watched Fabrizio holding Meghan, promising her his everlasting loyalty. "I need to get Meggie, but I think we need to talk."

Fabrizio forced a smile and bobbed his head. "Go get her, she needs you, Monty."

Meghan was sitting on the grass, her legs pulled up in front of her like she had done so often in the past when she was frightened and upset. She was slightly shaking as the light from the moon danced across her, casting a hypnotic glow.

Declan's approach was cautious, and he dropped in behind her, straddling his long legs around her. She slightly jerked as his hands wrapped around her, pulling her trembling body into his chest.

"Meggie, I'm sorry, I wasn't trying to scare y'. I just couldn't stick around that house."

"Declan, I thought you were dead," Meghan cried, resting her head back against his shoulder.

"I know, I'm so sorry," Declan sniffed, the tears started to fill his eyes.

His face pressed up against the side of her head, his tears dripping into her hair. He was so overwhelmed with what had been happening. He could have lost her again. She was willing to risk her own life, by going back to O'Brien to save him. What if he hadn't gotten to the cottage when he did, would she have snuck away to go back to O'Brien? Would Fabrizio have been able to stop her? Declan believed he would. The sound of Fabrizio's voice when he told Meghan he was disgusted by O'Brien touching her sounded jealous, mirroring Declan's thoughts.

What if he had died, would Meghan have returned to Fabrizio for support? Would they become lovers again? He cringed slightly at the thought of sharing her with Fabrizio, but as the thought of Fabrizio filled his mind, he had to admit he would prefer Fabrizio being the one she was with instead of O'Brien. However, Fabrizio kept Meghan from him for five years. What would their lives be like if he hadn't interfered? Would they have had more children, a boy maybe?

Declan's hand inadvertently slid down, resting on Meghan's tummy. He wanted more children, a house full, as a matter of fact. That was something they never discussed other than a few times, when he joked about it.

Meghan felt his hand sliding across her stomach, and she wondered if she should tell him of her suspicions. Would he be happy or annoyed at her bad timing? Maybe it was best not to tell him.

"Meggie, will y' promise me something?"

"Anything," Meghan sighed, the feel of him surrounding her causing a relaxing sensation.

"Well, if anything were to happen to me . . . Well, I want y' to stay with Fabrizio."

Meghan turned to Declan, resting her hand on his face. "I did, I listened to everything he said. I didn't want to do anything that would put you in danger."

"No, Meggie, I mean. Well, I want y' . . ." His eyes left her and settled on a clumping of gorge bushes across the yard, the moonlight outlining the lumpy shapes.

"Declan, what is it?" Meghan turned so she was facing him.

"I just want to know that y' will be safe and loved," Declan smiled a painful grin. "I know that Fabrizio, well he'll be good to y' and."

"Declan what are you saying?" Meghan blurted out. "That you want me and Fabrizio . . ."

"Aye," Declan interrupted the rest of her question. "I want y' to be with Fabs."

"Declan," Meghan mumbled and squirmed in his arms. "I can't do that again. First of all, Cassie loves him and second."

"Meggie, I have been watching him, he cares for y' a lot, and I believe more than he does for Cassie. He would leave her for y', especially if I asked him to."

"Are you out of your mind!" Meghan grumbled and tried to pull loose of him. "That has to be the stupidest thing you have ever said."

"Meggie, listen to me. If I die, I want to know that it is Fabrizio that is touching y', not . . ."

"Not who? Liam?"

"Aye. Fabs will always protect y'."

Meghan shook her head, her flaming eyes glued to Declan's agitated face. "So you think it's better to ruin Cassie's and Fabrizio's life?"

"Aye," Declan admitted without any remorse. "And it wouldn't ruin Fab's life. Were y' not listening to him early, expressing his love for y'?"

"What are you talking about?" Meghan snorted, he was unbelievable, and his jealousy was out of control.

"Don't worry, sweetheart, I will never leave you," Declan mimicked Fabrizio's voice. "What do y' think he meant by that?"

"That he would always be my friend," she grumbled and rested her hands on his face. "Declan, I love you, and I don't want anyone else. You need to get that through your thick head." Meghan rapped on his forehead.

Declan couldn't help but chuckle at her facial expression. She was funny, this wife of his. How he loved her! "All right," Declan conceded. "I'll leave it alone for now."

"Good," Meghan smiled and kissed him softly, then glanced up at the stars. "Declan, do you see that star?" she whispered, gazing up into the northern sky.

He glanced up in the direction her finger was pointing and saw two stars so close together; they looked connected.

"Aye, I see," he said softly.

"That must be our star," she smiled. "I have never seen it before tonight."

"Hmm. I guess if our fate is in the stars, we will be okay," Declan grinned rather tauntingly.

"I don't think this is a good time to mock me, Declan," Meghan muttered, lifting her face towards his.

"Aye, I guess not," Declan apologized, kissing her nose.

The night air was cool and damp, but neither made any attempt to move inside, apparently both too overwhelmed with the events of the day. Meghan's eyes were closed tightly as she leaned heavily into Declan's chest, not wanting to move and feel the separation of their bodies. Declan's long muscular arms were wrapped around her, one around her ribs under her red rauna and the other across her chest in a very protective grasp.

"Who was that other man that we identified?" Meghan finally asked as her natural curiosity took hold.

"He was their neighbour. He just came through the door at the right time."

"At the right time? What are you talking about?" Meghan questioned sharply.

"Well I . . ." Declan sighed and pressed his head against hers. "I went into the house, I didn't realize that Brendan and Aisling . . . Well, I began to go into the kitchen when O'Brien and Murphy jumped out from behind the counter. They had their guns pointed at me, and I was trying to decide which one to shoot first, and O'Brien was looking so smug that I chose him, figuring that at least I could die knowing y' were safe from him."

"Oh, Declan," Meghan sniffed, lifting her hand and resting it on the long wiry whiskers on his cheek.

"Well, so much for the best of intentions because me gun jammed, but just as O'Brien began to pull the trigger, the back door flew open, and this tall dark-haired man came flying into the kitchen. O'Brien swung around, and the gun went off, and in that split second, I made me escape out the front door. I ran down the street and climbed onto a roof of one of the neighbours' sheds until I saw O'Brien and Murphy leaving. The Derry police were there within minutes of their departure."

"So what did you do?" Meghan questioned as she turned slightly to see his face.

"Well, I waited until I could get down off the roof without being seen, and I came here to find y' and Fabs, but y' had already left for the hospital."

"Oh," Meghan sighed. "So if that man hadn't walked in?" She shuddered. "You would be dead."

"Aye, I think so," Declan muttered into her hair. "Meggie, I was so scared for you at that instant. If I was gone, O'Brien would have no one to stop him from taking y'."

"Declan," Meghan said sharply, trying to avoid thinking about his comment. "What the hell were you doing shooting that man with me so close?" she snorted as she thought about the man with the bullet straight through his forehead.

"Aye, well," Declan smirked.

"Well what?"

"I knew I wouldn't hit y'." Declan chuckled at her annoyance. He knew it wasn't funny, but his emotions were out of control.

"How did you figure that, you haven't shot a gun on a regular basis for years?"

"Oh, I have," Declan smiled. "I have been practising every day since you disappeared. I figured I would be in need of me old skills."

"Declan," she muttered. "Why didn't y' tell me?"

"Well, I didn't want to worry y'," Declan said softly and kissed the side of her head. "Y' tend to get rather hysterical over things."

"I do not!" Meghan grumbled.

"Aye, y' do," Declan laughed and gripped her hand as it headed for his face. "I'm not arguing with y' about this any longer. We have other things we need to be discussing."

"What things?" Meghan questioned, turning to face him.

Declan grinned and kissed her forehead. "How we are going to get home?"

CHAPTER FOURTY-TWO

A silence hung over the harbour that unnerved Declan; no activity was evident and even the birds seemed absent. The hair on the back of his neck was prickling with warning. They needed to tread carefully; something was wrong.

The smell of fish and salt was mixing with a slight scent of gasoline and filling Meghan's nose as she wandered slowly behind Declan, her hand trapped in his. She could feel his unease but was too scared to question him.

As they stepped onto the lower dock, a handful of weathered fishermen came into view, and Declan relaxed slightly. All seemed well, the men were busy folding nets and unloading their catch from that morning. However, Declan still felt slightly uneasy and glanced over at Eamon, but he seemed calm enough.

The sun was still quite warm, considering the amount of fall cloud cover that lingered in the mid-October sky, and Meghan allowed herself to be swept away in the beauty that surrounded them. The small harbour was full of fishing boats, some with bright colours adorning their hulls.

"This is so beautiful," Meghan muttered as she glanced out over the water shimmering with green, blue, and golden shades mixing together in the soft flowing waves.

"Aye, it is," Declan agreed offhandedly, not completely listening to her, the majority of his attention was directed at the people lingering around the docks.

His eyes settled on the short, gnarled man standing on the deck of a small, rather rickety boat. The nets had seen better days, and the barnacles on the side were overtaking the hull.

Meghan blinked repeatedly as the worry of the seaworthiness of this boat took hold. "Declan, please tell me that's not the boat."

"Aye, I believe so," Declan sighed and squeezed her hand. He glanced back at Eamon, who nodded with agreement but seemed focused on something across the dock.

"I'm not going out to sea on that thing," Meghan complained, adding to Declan's stress.

"Shh, Freckles, let's just talk to the man." Declan soothed as he tucked her under his arm.

The old man spotted the group coming and hollered something to someone below. Fabrizio, hearing the shouting, stopped abruptly and rested his hand on his gun that was tucked down the back of his pants. Declan in the same moment had shoved Meghan behind him, and he too had hold of his gun awaiting the arrival of whoever was below deck.

"Declan, what is it?" Meghan questioned, she had seen the behaviour in the men enough in the past month to know they were on the defensive.

"Shh, Meggie," he whispered quietly.

"Ahoy, there," yelled the older man. "Y' must be Mick's friends."

"Aye." Declan hollered back. "And y' are?"

"Me name is Angus," he smiled, exposing his poor dental hygiene. "Oh, Eamon, there y' are." His demeanour relaxed when he saw Eamon step out from behind Declan.

The man turned abruptly as a young blond man arrived on deck from below. Declan tensed slightly as he watched the young man's every move as he headed towards Angus.

"This is me son, Ryan," Angus yelled to the tensed men, noticing the expressions on their faces.

"Y' never mentioned your son." Declan glanced at Eamon and moved cautiously closer to the boat.

"I never expected him to be here. He just flew in from London last night, and I thought I would take him with us so I have company on the way back." Angus bobbed his head towards Eamon. "Y' remember Ryan?"

"Aye, he's all grown now," Eamon smiled with recognition.

Declan stopped at Fabrizio, his eyes questioning. "What do y' think, is he trustworthy?"

"Aye." Eamon nodded.

"Well, just to be safe." Fabrizio paused and gazed back up at the two men "Why don't I go aboard and check out the boat to ensure that no one else is aboard? You stay here with Meghan and keep your eye on those two until I'm finished."

"Aye."

"Angus, if it's all right with y', me friend would like to come aboard and check out the boat before I bring me wife aboard," Declan informed the man.

"That would be fine," Angus smiled. "After everything y' have been through, I don't blame y' for your scepticism."

"Da, what is the problem?" Ryan questioned with concern. "I thought they are tourists y' are taking for a tour."

"Ryan, that's enough," Angus snorted and glanced around at the other fishermen on the dock.

"Meggie, please stand right behind me so I can feel y' against me back," Declan whispered as he reached his loose arm around and pulled her right up against him "Put your arms around me ribs."

"Why?" Meghan questioned but, nonetheless, did what she was told.

"Thank y'," Declan whispered, patting her hands that were locked around his chest. "Now don't move until I tell y'."

Fabrizio slowly climbed the ladder and boarded the small boat. He shook Angus's hand, then reached out towards Ryan. Ryan eyed Fabrizio dubiously, then took his hand with hesitation.

Fabrizio smiled reassuringly and nodded towards Angus. "Would you two please stay here where Monty can see you, while I have a look around?"

"Why? What the hell is going on?" Ryan questioned again.

"Ryan!" Angus snapped. "Please just be quiet. I will tell y' when we are away from this dock."

Ryan's attention settled on Eamon as he climbed aboard after Fabrizio.

Declan's attention was drawn to a group of men that were sitting by a small boat a couple of skids down. The men were trying very hard to appear busy, but they seemed to be very interested in what was happening with Angus's boat.

"Meggie, I'm going to move towards the boat. Please stay right behind me," Declan said, resting his hand on her hands.

He could feel the tension building in her as he pulled her slightly, so her body was just slightly beside him. His slow movement towards the boat was watched carefully by the men he was concerned about, which confirmed his suspicions.

"Declan," Meghan whispered. "What's going on?"

"Meggie, just stay calm and do as I say." He patted her shoulder softly. "Once Fabrizio says it's okay, I want y' to get up that ladder as fast as y' can. Then take cover."

"Okay," Meghan mumbled with fear.

They were right by the ladder when Fabrizio reappeared leaning down over the railing. "Looks clear," he said as he focused his gaze in the direction Declan was gesturing with his eyes.

"Boo, give me your hands," Fabrizio said calmly.

Fabrizio reached down, grabbed hold of her outstretched hands, and yanked her up with Declan gripping her waist, shoving her up towards him. Then with amazing speed, Declan was up the ladder and on deck. Angus had also spotted the men, and he had untied the ropes mooring the boat to the dock before Declan and Meghan had even boarded.

Two of the men stood and headed towards Angus's boat, as the other two jumped into the boat they were sitting beside. Fabrizio pushed Meghan behind the wall of the cabin on the other side of the boat, then returned to Declan's side.

No sooner had the engines started the shouting began.

"Stop right there!" yelled the tall dark-haired man. "Y' are all under arrest."

Angus paid no attention to the man, pulled away from the docks, and headed out into the channel.

"Da, what are y' doing?" Ryan yelled. "The police want us to stop."

"Those aren't the police, me boy," Angus said coolly, annoyed that his son was so dense.

"Get down," Declan yelled as he saw the man pull a gun from inside his coat.

The sound of bullets hitting metal and wood was deafening, as Meghan stayed huddled behind the wall, waiting for instructions. She watched as the dock drifted farther away, and the shooting slowed. She was beginning to panic as the boat grew quiet, and all she could hear was the creaking from somewhere below deck.

Unable to control herself, she crawled to the corner and peeked her head around, and a loud shriek exited her as she saw the small boat within one hundred yards of them and approaching quickly.

"Meggie, stay down!" Declan shouted, noticing her.

"Declan."

"Meggie!" Declan snapped, but his gaze switched to Angus, who was climbing up a small hole in the back of the boat with a long black case tucked under his arm.

"Do y' know how to use one of these?" Angus grinned at Fabrizio.

"I sure do," Fabrizio laughed and pulled out the long metal rocket launcher from the case. "Where did you get this from?"

"Aye, well," Angus grinned. "Y' never know when it might come in handy."

"Jeez, Da," Ryan snorted as he slid out of the cabin, dragging his leg behind him. "What the hell have y' gotten us into?"

"Me boy, you've been shot?" Angus said, darting towards his son. "Bloody hell."

Ryan fell to the ground as the blood drained from his already pasty white face. Meghan crawled over to him and ripped at his pants, exposing the small hole in his upper thigh.

"Christ," Meghan muttered, lifting his leg, looking for an exit wound, which she found just above the back of his knee.

"Who the hell are you people?" Ryan snorted, pushing at Meghan, trying to get her away from him. The young boy was terribly scared and unsure what was happening around him.

"It's okay, I'm not going to hurt you," Meghan soothed, reaching into her backpack and pulling out a long scarf. "I just need to control the bleeding," she informed him as she tied the scarf around his leg.

"Here, me boy, have a swig of this," Angus said as he handed him a small silver flask. "This is your brother's friend Eamon and his cousin." He bobbed his head towards Declan.

Ryan gladly drank the whisky provided by his father as Meghan rummaged through the first-aid kit Angus had also brought with him from the galley.

"So you're the actor that drew the wrath of the O'Briens?" Ryan's wiped at his mouth to clear away the whisky that was dripping down his chin. "Me older brother told me of your misfortune."

"Y' have talked to your brother?" Angus grumbled.

"Aye, but he didn't tell me that y' were getting involved, Da. Y' know that the police are just waiting for y' to break the law so they can nab y'."

"They aren't going to catch me, lad. Eamon will run interference."

"Don't be worrying about those men, young Ryan, the lads are no police." Eamon patted Ryan's shoulder.

"Aye, that's a fact," Declan muttered. "The last thing we wanted was to put your da in danger."

"Well, that's what you've done," Ryan snorted and eyed Meghan as she moved back towards him, crawling across the deck. "If me brother would have told me that y' were planning this . . ."

"That's exactly why he didn't," Angus growled and gripped his son's shoulder. "I know y' feel me lifestyle is reprehensible, but these nice folks don't deserve to be hunted by O'Brien, and if I can help them in any way, I plan to."

"This is going to sting a little, but it will clean the wound," Meghan smiled calmly, trying to end the discussion. She was feeling terribly guilty that she put yet two more lives in danger.

The young boy clenched his teeth and closed his eyes when she poured the antiseptic over the hole in his leg. The thick wad of gauze she attached seemed to be containing the bleeding for the moment, which was encouraging, at least, no major arteries had been ruptured.

"Have you had a tetanus shot lately?" Meghan questioned him as the colour began to return to his face.

"No," Ryan muttered, taking another sip from the flask.

"When you get home, you need to go get one. Just in case," Meghan smiled softly. "And you should get an X-ray to see if the bullet hit the bone, the bullet came out at a weird angle."

Meghan was so enthralled with her patient that she had temporarily forgotten about the other boat and the rocket launcher Fabrizio was aiming at the approaching craft. Her attention, however, was drawn back to the problem when a loud shrieking noise resonated from the back of the boat, and within seconds, a loud explosion rocked their boat as if they were caught in a squall.

The jolt of the blast sent her flying backwards into the railing, smashing her head against the thick wooden rail. Her skull exploded with shards of pain that fanned out from the back of her skull to the front with extreme force. She staggered to her knees, her hands gripping her head, as the flames from the boat shot into the air, and chunks of wood and debris dropped into the ocean, where their pursuer's boat used to be. What was left of the boat was burning brightly on the water, casting an even brighter glow than the one presented by the afternoon sun.

"Declan," Meghan shouted as she glanced around, unable to see him.

"Aye," Declan popped up from behind at pile of fishing nets. "Wow, that was spectacular."

"Are you insane?" Meghan snorted, but her attention was drawn to the small spots filling her view.

"No, Meggie, did y' not see it?" Declan muttered, running to her side. "I haven't seen anything blow like that in a long time."

"Declan, there were people on that boat," Meghan grumbled, her eyes frantically fluttering, trying to clear the growing spots.

"Aye, I know." Declan's voice was cold, not noticing her eye movements. "People that were trying to kill us."

Meghan crinkled her nose at him and turned her attention back to the burning shell of a craft. "How many more people are going to die before we get home?"

"Oh, Meggie, please don't cry," Declan soothed, wiping the tears that were now running down her face.

"I don't know how much more of this I can take?" Meghan sobbed into his chest, closing her eyes, hoping it would help.

As Declan held her tightly, he glanced over her shoulder at Ryan, who was now sitting up against a crate, looking somewhat shell-shocked.

"Are y' okay, lad?" Declan questioned, with a soft smile.

"Aye." Ryan nodded, still clinging to the flask.

"Freckles, y' did a fine job of patching up the lad," Declan whispered into her hair.

"I know," she muttered into his chest.

"No confidence problem here I see," Declan chuckled and kissed the side of her head.

"Some day I could throttle you," Meghan snorted and smacked his chest.

"Aye, well, that will have to wait. I need to get y' home, Freckles," Declan laughed and released her, causing her eyes to open, or so she thought. All she could see was blackness.

"Declan!" Meghan shrieked and groped out in front of her, trying desperately to find something to cling to.

"Meggie, what is it?" Declan dropped down in front of her, the panic in her voice terrifying him.

Her hands hit him frantically, then gripped his arm with panic. Her face was terrified, and her eyes seemed erratic and unfocused.

"Declan," Meghan cried, groping around his body for his face. "I can't see."

"What?" Declan blurted out.

"I can't see." Meghan cried and began to tremble. "I hit my head, and I can't see."

"Bloody hell," Declan muttered, cradling her in his arms. "Calm down, Freckles."

"Dammit, this can't be happening, not now," Meghan sniffed and pressed her face hard against Declan's chest. It was as if they were cursed.

Declan cradled Meghan until the dock was in view. Scotland, then home. His heart was racing with hope; maybe it would be easy from here on in. It was a risk taking Meghan to the hospital; however they couldn't let Meghan's injury go unchecked. O'Brien would never think they would go to a hospital, Declan assured himself. How could he know she hit her head? Declan sighed confident in his decision and pressed his head firmly against Meghan's.

"Monty, we have a problem." Fabrizio's agitated voice broke Declan's thoughts.

"Damn, look at them all," Declan grumbled as he glanced around the crates at O'Brien, surrounded by approximately ten armed men, standing in the middle of the dock.

"How many are there?" Meghan questioned quietly.

"Ten or more," Declan muttered. "If we dock, we're going to be slaughtered."

"Declan." Meghan's hand groped at his face. "Can't we use one of those rocket things to blow them up?"

"No, Meggie," Declan chuckled slightly at how easily she changed her opinion of killing people. "They cause too much damage, and there are other people and boats that would be hit. We can't hurt innocent people."

"Can't we turn the boat around?" Meghan questioned.

"We don't have enough petrol to get us to another port," Angus said as he peered over the rail.

"This can't happen again," Meghan cried. "I won't let everyone on this boat die because of me. How the hell does he keep finding us?" Meghan blurted out. "It's like he has a tracking devise on me."

"No one's going to die, Freckles, calm down," Declan said softly, kissing her forehead but he stiffened as a thought came to him. "Meggie, where is your locket?"

"In my pocket, why?"

Declan lifted the locket from Meghan's hand when she pulled it from her pocket, and he began to examine it from all sides. As he studied the inside, he noticed something wedged behind the picture of him. His stomach tightened as he picked out the small tracking chip glued to the wall of the back portion of the locket. "Bloody hell!"

"What is it?" Meghan mumbled. "What's wrong?"

"He put a tracking chip in the locket. I wondered how his brother managed to get hold of this so easily. I guess the plan was to give it back to you so he could keep track of you. But how did he know you would get away?"

"Well, probably because I tried running twice before, but he caught me. Maybe he just wanted to be sure I never got away. He knew I would never willingly leave this locket behind."

"Bloody hell, that is how he always finds us."

"That's how he is zeroing in on us. This chip can be tracked from a satellite, like the one in the phones. He can track this locket to within a two block radius." Fabrizio muttered taking it from Declan and examining it.

"I'm going to go to him," Meghan said, with remarkable calmness.

"No, you're not!" Declan snorted. "We have been through this before, Meggie, I won't let y'."

"Declan, listen to me. He won't hurt me, and maybe I can get him to take me to the hospital."

"Meggie," Declan sighed.

"Please. You can come for me when it's safe. I will tell him that you and Fabrizio are dead, and he will lower his guard."

"Meggie, how are y' going to convince him of that?" Declan questioned, she was incapable of telling a lie, it showed clearly on her face.

"I don't know," Meghan sighed. "But it's the only way. You can track me with that. I will put it in my pocket and then you can follow me. Let's use it against him."

"Freckles, what if he . . ." Declan stopped and pressed his bearded face against her. "God, the thought of that man touching y'."

"This could work, Monty. He is not going to hurt her, and if we can follow using the chip," Fabrizio's interjected.

"Declan, it will be okay," Meghan mumbled. "I can't let you guys die, and Angus and Ryan don't deserve this."

"Okay," Declan sighed, not seeing any other way out of the situation. "But what if he doesn't take y' to the hospital?"

"I'm sure he will. I think he does care for me," Meghan soothed, hoping she was right.

"What if he finds the chip or asked about the locket?" Declan questioned as he thought about every possible scenario that could go wrong.

"I'll tell him I left the locket on the boat with my clothes. Then if does take me back there, I could maybe sneak away and find the tunnel to Mick's house." What if she was wrong and he takes her into hiding? Declan may never find her. This could be a risk that backfires, and she might end up spending the rest of her life with Liam O'Brien as his wife and lover. She shuddered involuntarily at the thought of him touching her, but she couldn't bear to think of more people dying because of her.

"Meggie, are y' sure y' want to do this?" Declan questioned. "We could try shooting our way out of this."

"Yes, I'm sure."

The plan was quickly set into place. Declan, Fabrizio, and Eamon stayed hidden as Angus helped Meghan into a life jacket. Then the boat would pull away but return once O'Brien left with Meghan; then they would follow from a safe distance. It should not be too difficult to find a car to appropriate.

"Meggie, I love y', and I promise I will get y' back." Declan ensured her, kissing her on the forehead as she sat down beside him.

"I know you will." Meghan forced a reassuring smile. "I love you."

"Stay calm," Declan gently ordered.

"I will," she smirked slightly. "Well, at least, I don't have to look at him."

"Meggie," Declan laughed nervously, trying to hide his fear. What if he lost her, what if O'Brien takes her to a different hospital? What if Fabrizio can't track the chip?

Declan's hand rested on her trembling face. "When y' get into the water, don't panic, the jacket will hold y' up. He'll pull y' out, I'm sure of it."

"Okay," Meghan sniffed. "If something should go wrong. Come to the castle, he also has a place in Galway somewhere."

Declan kissed her head. "I'll find y', Meggie, I promise." He could see the unease in her eyes, she was terrified, but she still put her life at risk to protect the others. Maybe this was not such a good idea, maybe he should stand up and start shooting, hoping that they could kill all the men before they were killed. Not likely since most of them carried machine guns.

As Declan pressed his lips on hers, his beard scratching up against her face. Meghan giggled when he removed his lips and she raised her hand to his face pulling at the whiskers.

"I hope when I get my sight back, this will be gone," Meghan chuckled, trying to soothe her fears.

"Me too," he smiled. "Okay, Freckles, it's time."

"Bye," Meghan sniffed as tears began to fill her eyes.

"Bye." Declan kissed her forehead and gripped her hand tightly "I love y', Freckles."

"How could you not?" Meghan pushed through her clogged throat.

Declan grunted a solemn chuckle, still holding her hand so tightly, she could not pull away. He was terrified to release her into the hands of O'Brien, and he pulled her back down onto his lap and wrapped his arms around her.

"Monty, she needs to go now, or they will get too suspicious," Fabrizio informed him gently.

"Meghan, it's time," Angus said, reaching for her hand.

"Okay," she said calmly.

Meghan pushed herself from Declan and looked down in his direction. "I'll be okay. I promise."

Declan nodded with agreement as she turned towards the bow of the boat with Angus, but she couldn't see him. Her face crumpled at his silence, and she turned back around in his direction.

"Declan," she muttered quietly. "You're my destiny, you'll find me."

"Aye," Declan sighed, grabbed her hand, and kissed her knuckles. "I will see y' soon, me everything."

With that, she pulled her hand away and walked away from him with Angus clinging onto her arm. Declan watched as she disappeared around the front of the cabin, and he could feel his heart being ripped out at the thought of letting her go.

"Okay, love, I am going to make it look like I'm forcing y'," Angus said softly. "Let's give the bastard a show."

"Okay," Meghan muttered and forced a smile. "Angus. Thank you for everything."

"You're welcome. Just please take care of yourself," Angus whispered as he tugged on her arm.

"I will, I promise."

"It's time; start screaming like I'm hurting y'," Angus smirked as he yanked her towards the railing.

"Let go!" Meghan shrieked at the top of her lungs.

"No, y' wee wench, I have had enough of this. Your man didn't pay me enough for this," Angus yelled as he hoisted her above the railing.

"All the best, love. God bless y'," Angus whispered. "Now be gone with y'," he shouted as he flung her into the cold water.

The icy water engulfed her as she hit with quite a force. The reality of what she had done took hold, and she started to panic. What if Liam did not come after her, would she freeze to death? She had no idea which direction the shore was. She floundered in the water, listening to the shouting going on back and forth. She could hear Angus's boat moving away from her slowly, and male voices coming from the other direction. She turned towards the voices and started trying to swim.

"Meghan, me love, are y' okay?" She heard over the rest.

A sigh exited her as she realized that it was Liam, and he was heading towards her.

"Help me," Meghan screamed, waving her arms in the direction of the voice. "I can't see."

"I'm coming," Liam yelled as he got closer.

She felt a large hand on her arm, and she groped around, trying to find the body that it was attached to.

"Me love," Liam muttered as he engulfed her in his arms. "Are y' okay?"

"No, I can't see." Meghan was terrified, and her emotions were assisting her in her charade. She was relieved that her panic was taking over because she was unable to lie without her face giving her away.

"Come on, I'll get y' to the dock." Liam pulled her along with him as he swam effortlessly through the fidget water.

Meghan stayed motionless, but when she felt two hands gripping her arms and hoisting her out of the freezing water, she panicked. "Let go!" she shrieked when the strong hands wrapped a blanket around her shoulders, keeping a grip on her.

"Stay still." The deep voice grumbled, his grip tightened on her shoulder.

"No, let me go!" Meghan yelled as she stumbled to her feet.

"Meghan, where are y' planning on going?" Liam soothed as his hands landed on her face.

"Liam," Meghan muttered, recognizing the voice. "Please, let me go, I have to go to the hospital."

"Why?" Liam questioned, looking into her blank eyes.

"I can't see," she said, trying to pull away from him.

"Me love," he sighed. "What happened?"

"Your bloody men did it," Meghan snorted. "They killed . . ." She stopped and started to cry.

"They killed who?" Liam questioned, with a smirk filling his face.

"Everyone," she cried. "They killed Declan and Fabrizio and . . ." She stopped and slouched down to the ground, burying her face in her hands. "And that man we paid to bring us here threw me overboard. He said he didn't want any more trouble."

"Well," he said smugly. "I guess I'm all y' have now."

"No," she cried, her face still buried. "I have to get to the hospital. I need my eyesight back."

"All right, me love, I will take y'." Liam soothed, kissing the top of her dripping head.

"Liam," she muttered.

"Aye," he questioned, wrapping his arms around her trembling body.

"I need to find Declan's body," she muttered. "That man threw them overboard."

"Meghan, I'm not wasting time searching the channel for his body. He will float ashore somewhere," he laughed cruelly. It could not have ended any better if he planned it. She was blind and helpless, no one to help her. She needed him now, and she knew it.

"No," Meghan screamed, continuing on with her drama, Liam was buying her story, and she could hear it in his voice. "I need to find him."

"Me love, I said no!" Liam snorted as he stood up, pulling her to her feet, tiring of her hysteria. "Now, let's go."

Liam dragged her towards the car, but she stumbled, clumsily tripping on everything in her path. He had to ensure she wasn't playing him again. She was a cunning woman, and he loved her for it but distrusted her for it as well.

"Liam, you're hurting me," Meghan cried as she tripped over a rope, lying across the dock. Her legs gave out from under her, and his grip on her arm was the only thing that kept her from plummeting to the dock.

"Sorry," Liam muttered softly, gripping her around the waist and pulling her up against him. "I just wanted to make sure y' weren't fibbing to me."

"About what?" Meghan snorted, trying to appear offended.

"That y' couldn't see," he laughed. "Me trust in y' has been greatly diminished in the past month."

"You never trusted me in the first place," Meghan said defiantly.

"Aye," he chuckled. "But y' are a clever little lass, and y' could be up to anything."

"You think I blinded myself on purpose?" Meghan snapped tugging on her arm.

"No, as unpredictable as y' are, I don't think even y' would go that far," he smiled.

"Thanks for the reassurance of my common sense," Meghan muttered, the tension lessening. The plan was working; Liam did care enough to take her to the hospital. Now all she needed to do was wait until Declan and Fabrizio rescued her.

Liam started to laugh at her comment, completely unaware of the trap she was setting. He lifted her into his arms and kissed her lips softly. "I'll carry y' to the car. I wouldn't want y' to damage anything else on this lovely body."

CHAPTER FOURTY-THREE

The emergency ward in the hospital was bustling with a variety of minor injuries, but Meghan's injury was serious enough to ensure she was placed in an examination room right away. Liam pushing the issue could also have contributed to her speedy placement; the nurse seemed intimidated by his large size and loud booming voice. Whatever the reason, however, Meghan did not care, she was just happy to have a doctor examine her.

The woman in the next bed was watching Liam and Meghan curiously as Liam held her close to his body. Meghan sat quietly on the bed waiting for Declan to come for her. Until then she needed to pretend she was Liam's loving wife. She wanted the doctor to examine her.

"What are ye in for?" The thin woman questioned as she looked down her long nose.

Meghan moved her head in the direction of the voice. "Are you talking to me?"

"Aye," she smiled a wide friendly smile.

"I hit my head and lost my eyesight," Meghan informed her.

Liam squeezed her arm that was tucked under his, trying to keep her quiet.

"Oh, you poor dear," the woman said with sympathy. "I cut my hand."

"Oh," Meghan muttered.

Liam scowled at the woman as she continued to watch them, but the inquisitive woman seemed unfazed.

"I must say ye are a lovely couple," she commented.

"Thank y'," Liam blurted out before Meghan could say anything. "I'm a lucky man." His lips landed on her cheek, and his mouth slid across her face to her ear.

"Remember what I told y', me love. I wouldn't want to involve your daughter in this," he whispered.

Meghan swallowed painfully and nodded, forcing a smile. Her eyes closed tightly, hoping that the nightmare would soon be over.

"Well, what can I do for ye today?" A short stalky doctor questioned as he arrived at the bed and pulled the curtain closed, blocking out the nosey woman in the next bed.

"Me wife hit her head, and she lost her eyesight," Liam informed him in a calm voice.

"I see," the doctor said. "Can you get off the bed, sir, so I can take a look."

"Aye," Liam smiled.

"So ye fell," he questioned Meghan.

"Yes, I slipped on the dock and fell into the water. I think I hit my head on the side," she muttered nervously.

Hmm, his eyes focused on Liam, then turned back to Meghan. "Are ye here on vacation then?" he questioned.

"Aye, we're from Ireland," Liam piped up.

"Well, ye sound more like you're American," the doctor smiled towards Meghan, exposing his small flat teeth. His light flickering from one of her eyes to the other.

"I'm Canadian actually," Meghan smiled. "But I live in Ireland with my husband." She forced out of her mouth.

"So how do ye like Scotland? Have ye been out, sightseeing much?" the doctor questioned as he examined her eyes.

"It's beautiful," Meghan said softly. "But we haven't seen much yet."

"Well, I'm glad to say that ye will be able to see more." He patted her shoulder. "Everything looks fine in your eyes. I would venture to say that ye just have some bruising to your brain. Your sight should return in a day or two."

"So she can come home then?" Liam questioned.

"No, I would like to get a CAT scan to take a look and see what's going on. I will schedule it for later today. But I want her to stay here for tonight. If she hit her head hard enough to lose her sight, she could have more damage than we can see."

"Oh," Liam said with worry. "Okay."

"I will have the nurse take y' to a room."

The hospital room she was settled in was drafty and eerily quiet now that the flirtatious nurse had left the room. The nurse apparently found Liam attractive, and her remarks were blatantly obvious when she suggested that Liam leave Meghan alone for a rest, and he could sit out at the nurses' station and fill out the paperwork. Unfortunately, Liam didn't seem to be interested in her and, to Meghan's dismay, chose to stay at her side.

"Liam, maybe you should go see if that nurse needs any help with the paperwork," Meghan's voice was suggestive.

"Nice try, me love, but I'm not leaving your side." Meghan could not help but giggle at the thought of the woman trying to seduce him away from her.

Liam's brow rose slightly at the sound; he had never heard her giggle before, and he found the sound appealing. "She is a beautiful woman." He glanced out towards the nurses' station and the petite blonde nurse. "Big blue eyes and long blonde hair." His voice softened. "But I must say I prefer redheads with big green eyes and freckles." His finger tweaked her nose.

Meghan smiled at the comment, but as the reality of who said it took hold, she became solemn.

Liam's hand slid through her hair, rubbing gently at the back of her neck. He loved the feel of her under his hand, she was so soft. Kaye was the woman that had shared his bed on and off for the last few years, and as attractive as he found her, she was hard and rather unappealing when undressed. His hand slid down the soft skin of Meghan's arm to her hips. She was lying on her side, one arm tucked under her head, the other resting on her hip. Liam could not control the urge to caress the curve of her narrow waist, his fingers sliding up her ribs and resting against the curve of her breast.

"Liam," Meghan grumbled, batting at his hand. "Someone could come in."

"So." He leaned against her and kissed her cheek. "You are so beautiful, even with the taste of salt on your skin."

Meghan crinkled her nose at him, the strong scent of salt water and sweat surrounding Liam had not gone unnoticed by her. How she wished he would leave her alone so she could sneak out of the hospital! She was not sure where Declan was, but she was confident that he wouldn't be far away.

"It's good news that the CAT scan showed just minor bruising," Liam muttered into her hair, trying to break the silence.

"Yes," Meghan sighed and moved her head slightly away from his face.

It was good news that there was no more damage to her brain. She was concerned about the impact causing an aneurysm, but fortunately her scan was clear. She knew that her eyesight would return soon, and she was thankful for that. Hysterical blindness, the doctor called it. Now if she could just stay calm until Declan arrived.

"Me love, tomorrow when we leave here, how would y' like to go to Venus?" Liam questioned, his lips landing on her cheek.

"What?"

"Well, I was thinking that we could get married there," Liam smiled and kissed her lips.

She started to tremble as his comment became clear in her mind. "Liam."

"Now, don't start this again, Meghan," Liam whispered against her lips.

"I guess I don't have any choice," she muttered quietly.

"No I guess, y' don't," Liam laughed and slid his hand down her neck to her chest. "I can hardly wait for y' to be me wife."

His hand slid under her smock and slid gently across her breast, his thumb brushing her nipple.

"Liam, please," Meghan begged, batting at his hand.

"Me love, when are y' going to relax? I promise y' will enjoy me touch." His lips were on her again. She found the experience terrifying, not being able to see him and his movements, but it was the shock of where his hands and lips were going to be next that scared her more.

Her question was answered when she felt his body pressing against her as he pushed her onto her back, crushing her under him. He was kissing her again with abandon his hands greedily taking what he wanted. Meghan began to tremble as he pulled her smock down her shoulders exposing her breasts. His head lowered and his mouth surrounded her breast, his tongue explored its way around her firm skin.

"Liam, someone could come in," Meghan begged, her stomach churning out of control. She pushed at his shoulder, trying to remove him from her. Panic began to set in when he was immovable. She thought that while in the hospital, she was safe from his advances, but apparently, he had no concern about a nurse catching him.

"Liam, please," Meghan cried.

He snorted a heavy sigh and lifted his head from her breast. "Meghan." His voice was gruff with annoyance. "No one is going to come in, the nurses are busy."

"I don't care, get off me." She forced authority to her trembling voice.

Liam grunted, but surprisingly removed himself from her and rolled onto his side and stared at her with interest. "Y' have got a lot of bravado. You're in no position to be demanding anything and yet y' do. What is even more disturbing is that I give in to y'," he laughed and kissed her nose. "I believe me da is correct in his opinion of y'."

"And what would that be?"

"That y' are a fairy and have put a spell on me," Liam chuckled and ran his hand across her face back into her hair. "That's the other reason I think we should not return to the castle anytime soon. I'm worried what he might do to y' for escaping."

A tremor ran through her, not only from the thought of his father, but the possibility that he would whisk her away somewhere, and Declan would be unable to find her.

Liam noticed the stress on her face and brushed his cheek against hers, his lips up against her ear. "Me love, what if we went back to the States and got your daughter first, then we could travel for a while?"

She sighed with relief and relaxed slightly; at least, if he took her back to the States, she could get help.

"Liam." Meghan turned her head in his direction and forced calmness into her voice. She needed to play him now, and she needed to be convincing.

"Aye." Liam kissed her nose, enjoying the closeness. She had never relaxed with him this way before, she was almost settled.

"Thank you for saving me." Meghan forced a smile.

"You're welcome, me love. I told y' that I would never let any harm come to y'."

Meghan took a deep breath and rested her head on his shoulder, hoping to lull him into a false sense of security.

"That man that took us on the boat," she muttered, lifting her head towards his face. "He was a member of the IRA."

"Aye, I know," Liam laughed. "Y' seem to have surrounded yourself with dangerous people."

"Well, Declan said . . ." She stopped and sighed. "He said that they would help us."

She turned onto her side and pressed her body against his. "He said he would protect me, but he didn't, all he did was get himself killed and leave me with a man that dumped me into the water," Meghan snorted, trying to give Liam the impression she was angry.

"Well, I guess he wasn't as smart as he thought," Liam chuckled.

"This is all his fault," Meghan muttered, closing her eyes, not that it made much difference since she still could not see anything. "That man threw a blind woman into the freezing water," she muttered, almost to her herself. "What kind of man would do that?"

"A horrible one," Liam commented, his voice remarkably consoling.

She shuddered slightly at his comment and bit her lip, holding back the comment that she felt he was just as horrible. He would have no trouble doing the same thing to anyone. Her only saving grace at the moment was that he needed her.

"Liam, do you think they will come after me and try to kill me?" Meghan questioned, knowing that there was no possibility of that happening, but she wanted to see how he would respond.

"I don't know, me love, but don't y' worry, I won't let them harm y'." His lips landed on hers as he wrapped his arms around her trembling body. She forced herself to stay calm and let him hold her. She knew her only way to get away from him was to make him think she felt he was her only protection.

"This is nice," Liam muttered, pressing his head against hers. He was enjoying her against him. She was not pulling away; he was not sure how long it would last, but he was going to hold her as long as she let him.

It had been a couple of hours before the door opened, and a tall man in green scrubs came through the door pushing a wheel chair.

"Mrs. O'Brien," said the deep voice. "The radiologist is concerned with something on your last scan. He wants ye to have another one."

"Oh," Meghan muttered, pushing out of Liam's arms that were still wrapped around her. "Okay."

Liam sat up and eyed the tall man. "I'll come with y'," he said firmly, pulling her to the side of the bed. His mouth went to her ear. "Behave."

She smiled and slid her arms around his neck as he lifted her from the bed. He carried her to the man and placed her gently down in the wheel chair.

The man adjusted his thick glasses, then pushed Meghan through the door of her room. As they walked down the hall, Murphy and another man began to follow closely behind, causing the tall orderly to turn and watch them curiously.

"I'm sorry but only family past this point," he announced, closing the doors on the two men.

Liam appeared somewhat nervous but continued on his way behind the orderly.

"What showed up on the scan?" Meghan finally questioned.

"I don't know, ma'am. I was just told to come and fetch ye."

"Oh," Meghan muttered, gripping the arms of the chair tightly.

"Don't worry, ma'am, I'm sure it's nothing major." He soothed. "So you are an American?"

"No, I'm Canadian," Meghan replied.

Liam was now at her side, gripping her hand snugly in his.

"Oh," the man said as he eyed her hand being squeezed in the large hand of O'Brien's. "Do you live in Canada?"

"No," she said simply.

"Hmm. I have a friend that lived in Canada. He worked on the rigs just outside Calgary."

"Oh," Meghan muttered as the voice heavily disguised in a Scottish burr became clear. It was Fabrizio. They were here to take her home.

"Did you know that Calgary was named after a town in Scotland?" she questioned. "Colonel James MacLeod's mother lived there. That's where he got the name from."

"I didn't know that," Fabrizio smiled, she knew it was him. Now all he had to do was get her away from O'Brien.

Liam glanced down at Meghan, wondering how she would know that piece of Canadian history, but he did not question her because he didn't want the orderly questioning their relationship.

"Meghan, me love, please don't talk this poor man's ear off," Liam said firmly.

"I don't mind," Fabrizio said. "I find it pleasant talking with people."

"I'm sorry if I talk too much. Apparently, that is a flaw that I have."

"I wouldn't call it a flaw," Fabrizio chuckled. "I might call it trying."

"Yes, I have been told that," she smirked.

Liam's hand was now squeezing her hand tightly, trying to get her to stop talking. He was getting agitated that she was going to blurt something out to this talkative man. Meghan sensing she had pushed it too far, quieted and faced forward until Fabrizio stopped the chair by a small room.

"Well, we're here," Fabrizio announced, lifting a clipboard off the wall.

"Okay, sir, if ye would just have a seat over there, she'll be done in a flash."

"Can I wait with her until the technician is ready?" Liam questioned, peering into the room.

"Well, I don't see why not," Fabrizio said evenly. "But ye will have to step outside during the scans. We can't have ye exposed to the radiation."

"Fine," Liam agreed as he entered the room after Meghan and Fabrizio. Fabrizio helped her to the narrow table and lifted her on top. She stretched her legs down the length and lay back with a deep sigh.

"I'll be back to fetch ye once you're done," Fabrizio said as he left the room.

"Liam, are you in here?" Meghan questioned.

"Aye, me love, I'm right here." He sat down on the bed beside her.

"I'm scared," Meghan commented, trying to stay calm.

"Me too," he admitted. "But I'm sure whatever it is, they can fix it."

"I hope so," Meghan muttered, wondering when Declan was going to arrive.

They sat quietly for a few minutes before a short brunette woman entered the room. "Good afternoon."

"Hi," Meghan said, moving her face in the direction of the voice.

"So are ye ready?" she questioned, moving towards the bed. "This shouldn't take too long, sir. If I could just get ye to step outside into the waiting room."

"Aye. What's wrong with her?" Liam questioned, with worry.

"Well, I saw a dark spot on the scan, and I just wanted to check it again," she smiled reassuringly. "It's probably nothing, but better safe."

"Aye, I'll be right outside," Liam sighed as he left the room.

Meghan sat upright on the bed, trying to jump off when she heard the door close. "Where is he?" she blurted out.

"Shh, come with me." The woman's voice sounded panicked.

Meghan gripped the woman's arm and followed her across the room to a small door that was concealed by the curtains.

"Here, go through there," she muttered as she opened the door and disappeared down the hall.

"Declan?" Meghan whispered as she groped her way down the hall.

"Meggie, thank God," Declan muttered as his hand grabbed her around the waist.

"You're here," Meghan cried, resting her head against his chest.

"Meggie, we have to go before he realizes something is wrong," Declan ordered as he dragged her down the hall.

"Declan," Meghan muttered as she tripped over her feet. "I still can't see."

"Oh, sorry," Declan apologized and hoisted her into his arms, hoping to speed up their escape. The hallway was unfortunately not deserted, and the staff began to watch them with interest. "Meggie, people are staring."

"Just ignore them and keep going, Declan, I want to get out of here," Meghan whispered into his ear. "Please, just keep going."

Declan forced calmness into his demeanour. She sounded terrified, and he was not going to let her down; he was going to get her home safely. "Aye, Freckles, don't worry. I'm not leaving y' again."

The end of the hall was within a few steps when he heard a female voice filling the hallway. "Excuse me, sir, where are ye taking her?"

Declan swung around and glanced at the small blonde nurse. "Meggie, it's a nurse."

"Ignore her, Declan, get me out of here," Meghan panicked.

"Mrs. O'Brien, what is going on?" Her voice was getting closer.

"Declan!" Meghan shrieked. "Go!"

Declan did not think twice, he was through the emergency exit before the nurse had a chance to react. The loud screams from her, however, were clear as she yelled for security.

The stairs were narrow, and Declan was finding it hard to run down them with Meghan in his arms, but he had no choice; it would be slower with her trying to manage them.

"There you two are," Fabrizio grumbled as his eyes settled on Declan's flushed face when he passed him and bolted out the doors, Meghan still tucked up in his arms.

"Aye, we're busted, let's go," Declan yelled just as the security sirens went off. "Damn."

Meghan breathed deeply inhaling the fresh air that surrounded her. "I thought I would never get away from him," Meghan sighed as Declan placed her in the back seat of the black sedan.

"Meggie, put your head down and rest," Declan told her as he covered her body with a blanket, then jumped in next to her. "Stay down until I tell y' it's safe."

Meghan nodded but said nothing, the panic in Declan's voice telling her the whole story. They weren't out of the woods yet. That damn noisy nurse. Why did she have to be in the hall at that exact minute? She would go straight to Liam, and he would be after them again. The nurse would describe Declan, and then Liam would know she was lying to him. If he got hold of her again, he would certainly punish her.

The security guards were stopping cars leaving the parking lot; apparently they had been notified what to look for. There were at least six guards at the entrance—four checking the cars, the other two standing with their hands on their guns. Why did her leaving the hospital merit such concern? How much pull did Liam have anyway?

"Bloody hell!" Declan grumbled as he glanced around the area. He would be seen if he tried to sneak her out of the car. "How could they have organized this so quickly?"

"Monty, I don't think it's us they are looking for. They seem to be checking everyone coming and going," Fabrizio bobbed his head towards an old guard heading towards the gate with the nurse in tow. "It's just bad luck on our part. That is the guard that is here to stop us."

The nurse was the first to arrive at the security station; her mind whirling with worry. "Excuse me, sir," Nurse Leanne called when she spotted a tall dark-haired man, his dark glasses and ball cap obscuring his appearance.

"Yes." Director Brody Spencer turned towards the woman as she bolted across the parking lot.

"A woman was kidnapped from the hospital." She panted as she arrived in front of him.

"When?" Brody immediately moved towards the woman. "Who was it?"

"Mrs. O'Brien." The nurse glanced up at Spencer, shocked by the American accent and the FBI badge attached to his jacket. "She was carried out of the hospital by a large man with long black hair and a beard. Oh the poor dear being blind and all."

Brody felt his stomach churn, who the hell had her now? Was it Fabrizio or Declan or someone else? Dammit, how did he keep missing her, first at the morgue, now here? "This Mrs. O'Brien, what does she look like?" he asked just to ensure it was her. But who else could it be? The caller told them that O'Brien had her and was taking her to the hospital.

"She is very tall with long red hair." The nurse turned up her nose slightly. "Her husband seems very nice, and he is going to be very upset."

"Where is he?"

The nurse shrugged. "I guess still in the waiting room. I didn't want to notify him until we got her back. I saw the vagrant that kidnapped her, and no good can come of it."

Brody gripped the nurse's arms, hoping to refocus her. "What did the man look like? Tell me again."

The nurse looked startled and glanced over at the other man, now listening to the explanation. "He was big, maybe a little taller than y', long black hair, and a beard. I believe he had grey eyes. She was yelling for her husband."

"Really?" Brody took a step backwards. "She was yelling for O'Brien." He felt sick; the description sounded like Declan, but if it was, why was she screaming for O'Brien?

"Aye, she kept yelling Declan," the nurse blurted out. "She sounded scared."

Brody shook his head. What the hell was happening "When was this?"

"Not more than five minutes ago." She glanced back at the line up of traffic "I would say they are in that mess somewhere."

Brody glanced back at the traffic and bolted towards the cars, his eyes scanning in every window; she was close, he could feel her.

"Something is happening," Eamon blurted out, knowing that Fabrizio and Declan could not see the big man heading towards them. "That man, I think he is with the police, he has changed the focus of the search. Damn."

Fabrizio's view was obscured by the large delivery truck in front of them. He could not see the man. Declan shook his head and glanced back at Meghan's terrified face. "Fabs, we're getting out."

"What?" Fabrizio glanced over at Declan who was eyeing the surrounding area.

Declan glanced up at Eamon. "See that truck? Pull up as close as possible. We are going to slip out the door and under that truck. Then y' can pick us up down the street. Remember that parking lot two blocks away?"

Eamon nodded as Declan assisted Meghan into slipping on her jeans and her red ruana that he had brought with him from the boat. "Meggie, once we are on the other side of the truck, we are going to cut through those trees and walk calmly down the street. Y' can't trip on anything."

"I'll try," she muttered, trying to stay calm. "Liam is going to be furious. He will have everyone out looking for me. It is not just the police. He has at least six men with him here at the hospital," Meghan mumbled as Declan opened the car door.

Declan nodded, then focused on Eamon. "Five minutes."

Eamon nodded and turned his attention back to the guards that had pulled out a large man with a beard from a truck about ten cars ahead of them. "Declan, it's you they are looking for, get going."

"Aye," Declan slipped under the truck, pulling Meghan along with him, followed by Fabrizio.

Their departure seemed unnoticed, and once out onto the street, Declan wrapped his arm around her waist, and the three of them walked calmly down the street. Meghan leaning into Declan for balance, mimicking his rhythm.

"Declan, is anyone following us?" Meghan whispered.

"No," he said calmly. "We are almost to the parking lot. Eamon should be out of the hospital parking lot by now. We will just go sit on that bench and wait. It's obscured from the street by the shrubs."

Declan sat down on the cement bench, pulling Meghan down next to him, her head resting on his shoulder. "Declan, what is going to happen when we get home? Liam will stop at nothing to get me back."

"Well, I will stop at nothing to keep y'," Declan's grinned and kissed her head.

"I'm serious, this isn't funny!" Meghan was slightly annoyed at the lightness in his voice.

"I know, Meggie. But let's just worry about one thing at a time. We need to get home first. I think, though, we will go to Malibu for a while. Caelan can go to school there."

Meghan nodded but said nothing.

Once they were back in sedan, Meghan lay down across the back seat, hoping to have a short nap. She was exhausted; it had been an extremely long day, and now that the sun was setting, she was finding it hard to stay awake. They were only hours away from getting home.

Fabrizio turned and eyed Meghan curiously. Now that they were safely on the road to London, his thoughts turned to the sight of her wrapped in Liam's arms. Why was she snuggling with that vile man? He knew it was not any of his business, but he couldn't help his feeling. He was frowning when he removed his gaze and returned it to the road, forcing the thoughts from his mind.

"What's wrong, Fabs?" Declan questioned, noticing his facial expression. "Why are y' looking at Meggie like that?"

"No reason," Fabrizio mumbled, trying to avoid answering.

"Are you wondering why I was lying in Liam's arms on the bed?" Meghan blurted out, remembering her positioning when Fabrizio arrived.

"Well, as a matter of fact, I was," Fabrizio admitted, deciding since she brought it up, he would force her to explain her reasoning.

"I was trying to make him think I was mourning Declan and he was consoling me. I thought that if he felt he was comforting me and I was turning to him, he would lower his guard. Apparently, it worked because he left me alone in the room," Meghan rambled, her voice defensive. She knew that Declan would still be upset, and she couldn't blame him. She wouldn't appreciate it if he was snuggling with another woman, whether he was trying to save his life or not.

"Aye, I guess it did," Declan muttered, purposely keeping his eyes fixed on the road ahead, trying not to see her lying in O'Brien's arms.

"Declan, please don't be angry. I had to make him think that I was scared and alone."

"Aye, I know, Freckles," Declan soothed and glanced back at her. The expression on her face ripped at his heart, and he couldn't allow her to feel guilty over what she had done. He cradled her against him. "I'm not cross. I'm just glad that you're okay."

"Me too." A large yawn exited her as he gently ran his hands through her hair, and within minutes, she was fast asleep.

Declan sighed deeply as he watched her beautiful face relax into a calm existence. "Fabrizio, I don't know how much more of this I can take, it's fucking mad."

"It is." Fabrizio shook his head, fighting off the exhaustion and glanced over at Eamon as he drove through the night. "Monty, I don't know if this is the time to bring this up, but I thought I would warn you."

"About what?" Declan questioned, with slight panic in his voice.

"Well, when I went in to get her, she was curled up in O'Brien's arms." Fabrizio's tone was almost apologetic.

"I know, Fabs, she already told us that," Declan said sharply, not wanting to hear it again.

"Well, it wasn't so much that, it was the expression on his face." Fabrizio glanced back towards him. "He loves her."

"What?"

"I really believe he does. His face was resting on hers, and he looked so content. God, it was sickening."

Declan glanced down at her face and brushed his fingers across her soft skin. "The thought of that man touching this skin makes me nauseous."

"I have to tell you, I don't think this will be over even if we get her home." Fabrizio's voice was full of worry.

"Well, let's worry about that when we get there," Declan said sharply, not wanting to think of that problem.

"Fine, I'm just warning you," Fabrizio grumbled, annoyed that Declan was ignoring the problem. "I see what she meant, though, when she said he was gentle with her."

"What?" Declan snorted.

"He was very caring, and he seemed truly worried about what the problem with the scan was. If I didn't know better, I would have believed that they were a happily married couple."

"Fabs!"

"Monty, I not saying this to hurt you. I just think you need to know where he is coming from. This is not just about getting that estate back. He loves her, and that makes him even more dangerous. Think how you feel when she was with him." He glanced back, watching Declan's face crumpling with worry. "I'm sure that's how he feels when she is with you."

"She's me wife," Declan snorted.

"Yes, she is. But he thinks she belongs to him, and he will do anything to get her back," Fabrizio said firmly.

"Bloody hell," Declan muttered.

"Monty, when we get to back to London, I'm going to see if I can get a hold of Paxton again. I don't know why, he isn't taking my calls. We need to get her into protective custody."

"Aye," Declan sighed, this nightmare had to end soon, or he was going to collapse.

CHAPTER FOURTY-FOUR

The dark clouds that hovered over the city dulled the morning sun. Declan prayed that it was not an omen of how their day was going to go. He glanced down at Meghan's sleeping face, so peaceful! If he watched her long enough, he could almost block out the past few months and imagine waking up to her in their bed at the ranch. Caelan's little voice filling the house with chatter and laughter.

By the time they arrived at the US Embassy in London, Declan's nerves were shot, and he was exhausted, not having slept for over twenty-four hours. If he got any resistance from these men, he was going to snap.

"Okay, let's get this over with," Fabrizio muttered and jumped from the car. "I'm ready to get home."

"Meggie," Declan said quietly as he jostled her shoulder. "Wake up, we're here."

Meghan began to blink as she slowly regained consciousness. A smile curled her lips as she reached up and touched his face.

"Hi." She stretched deeply, bending her neck back and forth. She blinked a few times and sighed deeply. "Everything is still so blurry."

"That's okay, Freckles, it's only been a day."

"I know, but I was just hoping that it would be better by now."

"Well, it's better than yesterday, isn't it? At least, y' can make out objects."

"Just the outline," she muttered, closing her eyes with worry.

"Meggie, it's going to be okay." Declan soothed as he pulled her from the car. "Here, put on your rauna, it's cold out here."

"Where are we? This isn't the airport," she questioned, not hearing the familiar sounds that usually accompany an airport.

"No, it's the US Embassy, we are here to meet with the FBI agents." Declan soothed as he led her towards Fabrizio, who was standing at the door to the large building. "We are going to try and get a hold of Agent Paxton."

"Oh yes, I forgot. Maybe this isn't a good idea. Maybe we shouldn't trust anyone," Meghan blurted out with panic. They thought they could trust the Inspector from The Garda, and that turned out to be a huge mistake. Common sense told her that he was only one man in the agency, but her trust in people had been greatly damaged over the past month. She would have never imagined that they would have had to resort to the violence and lies that accompanied it.

"We are going to have to take that chance," Declan said calmly, interrupting her thoughts. "These people are FBI agents that Fabs works with."

"Then why wouldn't they help us before?" Meghan grumbled, thinking back to the disinterest she received a few weeks earlier when she called. "I hope we can find Agent Paxton, I don't think they will help if we don't."

"Well, let's just see."

"Okay, cuz, this is where I say goodbye." Eamon nodded his head towards the building.

"Aye, thanks for everything," Declan hugged his cousin and smiled. "Maybe next time I see y', it will be under less dangerous circumstances."

"Aye, but it's been exciting," Eamon grinned and hugged Meghan. "Take care, love."

"I will try. Thank you," Meghan smiled and moved back towards Declan when Eamon released her from the hug.

His hand went out to Fabrizio. "You're a good lad to have around. Me cousin is lucky to have y' as a friend."

Fabrizio nodded and shook his hand. "Thanks for all your help."

Eamon nodded and wandered up the street. "I'm meeting a lad at the pub," he laughed and disappeared around the corner.

Declan laughed and then ushered Meghan through the front door. The security at the door was tight, and each of them were frisked and checked completely, then sent through the metal detector. Declan informed the guard of their purpose, and they were ushered down the hall into a small room. The security officer sitting next to a door at the end of the room looked up, her green eyes settling on the dishevelled group.

Declan felt uneasy at the expression on her face as the guard from the front door whispered something to her. They both glanced at the group, then the woman guard nodded and disappeared into the back room.

Time seemed to drag as they sat patiently waiting for a man named Agent Anderson to see them. The guard seemed quite put out by their arrival, and she was watching them intently as they sat talking amongst themselves.

Her eyes were mostly settling on Declan, who with his long beard and very long hair looked like a hermit that had just emerged from exile after years of hiding. Meghan had tripped over just about everything in her path during her entrance into the office, appearing to be intoxicated. Fabrizio, the best of the three, was looking very sleep deprived, the dark circles under his eyes giving him a dark dangerous appearance, but to the guard, he seemed the least likely to go on a shooting rampage.

She was nervously fussing with papers on her desk when Declan approached and leaned his large body over her desk, resting his arms on the counter that ran across the top.

"I'm sorry to bother y', but I was wondering how much longer Agent Anderson was going to leave us sitting here," Declan smiled a toothy grin, easing her discomfort slightly.

"I'm not sure sir." She forced a smile. "I'll check for you."

She jumped from her chair and darted into the back room, leaving the three of them still waiting.

"I think you scared her, Monty," Fabrizio laughed.

"I can't help it. I was just asking her a question," Declan smirked. "I'm not used to women running in fear from me."

"Well, if you look anything like you did the last time I saw you," Meghan laughed, "I don't blame her."

"Now listen here, Freckles," Declan complained as he moved towards her with mischief in his eyes. "I think that I have had just about enough of your complaining."

"Yeah, and what are you going to do? Beat up a blind woman?" Meghan giggled as she watched the blurry blob heading towards her.

"No," Declan said evenly as his hand slipped around her ribs, and without a word, he ran his fingers up her ribs forcing shrieks out of her mouth.

"Stop it!" Meghan shrieked as he continued his attack. "Declan!"

"I want y' to apologize for saying I look like monster," Declan laughed, pushing his fingers deeper into her ribs.

"No, stop it." Meghan's voice was loud and excited as she squirmed under his hands.

"Stop right there!" A loud angry voice yelled from the doorway, from where the guard had disappeared.

Declan looked up, startled by the voice to see three men standing in the room with guns pointed directly at him.

"Well," Declan muttered as he slowly removed his hands from Meghan and raised them into the air.

"Declan, what is it?" Meghan blurted out.

"We seem to have attracted attention."

"Shut up, and move away from the woman," The tall greying gentleman snorted. His dark brown eyes were narrow and aggressive as he stared at Declan.

Declan nodded with agreement and stood still, holding his hands in the air. "There seems to be a misunderstanding here. This is me wife, and I was just tickling her."

"Shut up and move away from the woman," he said again.

Fabrizio stayed seated as he watched a short well-built man keeping his gun aimed at him. "We are here to talk to Agent Anderson," Fabrizio informed them lifting his hands out in front of himself. "I'm Agent Stagliano with the FBI."

The tall man ignored Fabrizio and waved his gun towards the wall. "Get up against the wall, both of you."

"Declan, what is going on?" Meghan questioned, blinking, frantically trying to bring the blurry figures into focus.

"Meggie, just stay calm," Declan said evenly.

Meghan, of course, could not, and she bolted to her feet and headed in the direction Declan's voice was coming from. Her legs hit the coffee table, and she staggered towards the young agent by the reception desk.

He grabbed her by the arm to steady her, and she panicked from the unfamiliar touch.

"Let go of me," Meghan screamed, tugging at her arm. "Declan, where are you?"

"Meggie, calm down," Declan said calmly, his eyes darting around the room, assessing the situation. Damn, had they made the wrong decision? A dread filled him that O'Brien was on the other side of the big door. Why the hell didn't they just go to the airport?

"Shut up," the greying man said, heading towards Declan.

The man holding Meghan tugged her towards the door to the back room, with her fighting him every step of the way. "Let go of me." She kicked back against his shins.

"Where are y' taking her?" Declan shouted and took a step towards Meghan and the agent. "She can't see, you're scaring her."

"Stay where you are," the greying man yelled.

"Declan, help me," Meghan screamed as she tried desperately to pull away from the young man. It was happening again. Liam was there.

"Let go of her!" Declan shouted, his eyes fixed on Meghan's terrified face. He grunted and shoved the greying agent that was next to him, and he bolted towards Meghan, but a solid thump against the back of his head stopped his movements. He stumbled slightly but managed to grab hold of Meghan before he fell to the floor.

Meghan felt Declan's hands slipping off her arm, and she groped, frantically trying to find him. "Declan," she shrieked as she thrashed around in the young man's arms.

"Christ, what are you doing." Fabrizio yelled moving towards the situation.

"Stay back," hollered the greying man, changing his focus off Declan's crumpled body to Fabrizio.

"What the hell is going on? This is Declan Montgomery, and we came to get help getting home, and instead, you attack us," Fabrizio hollered.

"Sit down!" the man shouted. "I want everyone to be quiet."

The man began to look rather anxious about the whole situation, and he glanced down at Declan, who was now sitting up, clutching the back of his head where the gun made impact.

"Declan, where are you?" Meghan called again, her eyes darting around the room with panic.

"Freckles, I'm here," Declan muttered, trying to stop the nauseating spinning in his head.

"Let go," Meghan cried as she again started to wiggle in the young man's arms.

The greying man nodded and the young man released his grip on her and she stumbled towards Declan. Her hands were waving frantically out in front of her, trying to locate him.

"Meggie," Declan said, raising his hand and gripping her wrist when she was in reach.

She dropped on top of his legs and groped at his face. "Are you okay?" she cried.

"Aye, I'm fine. Just a wee bump," Declan muttered into her hair as she wrapped her arms around his neck.

"Are they going to kill us?" Meghan whispered into his hair.

"No, we're not going to kill you, ma'am," the sharp voice of the greying man blurted out.

"Then what are you doing?" Fabrizio questioned with annoyance. "Christ, I have never seen such incompetence in all my life."

"That will be enough out of you," the short man snorted. "What did you expect us to do when you show up here, looking like terrorists?"

"Terrorists?" Fabrizio snorted.

"Calm down, everyone," the greying man said evenly. "Let's take this into my office and figure out what is going on."

Meghan was still clinging to Declan, with no intentions of releasing her grip on him.

"Meggie, y' need to get off me legs so I can get up," Declan said calmly and kissed her forehead.

"Are you okay to stand?" Meghan questioned, groping at his face. "You might get dizzy. Hang on to me," she ordered as she stood and gripped his arm.

He stood up and wrapped his arm around her shoulder, leaning on her for support. She was right. He was still a bit dizzy and wobbly on his legs.

"Here, Monty, I'll help," Fabrizio smirked. "It's literally the blind leading the blind," he laughed.

The three were deposited in a small office with the young man, while the other two men disappeared down the hall. Meghan stayed on

Declan's lap on the chair, holding the icepack to the back of his head as Fabrizio paced anxiously back and forth in front of the window.

"We would have been better off just taking our chances at Heathrow," Fabrizio muttered, almost to himself.

"Aye. At least, we know O'Brien won't rough up Meggie," Declan smirked and grabbed her hand that was heading towards his head.

"O'Brien?" the young man blurted out. "Do you mean Liam O'Brien?"

"Aye," Declan said, directing his curious gaze on the man.

The man eyed them for a moment, then turned to the door. "Don't leave this room," he ordered before darting out the door.

"Well, that name seemed to spark him into action," Declan laughed. "Maybe we should have dropped it earlier."

"Declan, this isn't funny," Meghan scolded. "We should get out of here."

"I think she might be right. They don't seem interested in helping us, and the longer we wait, it gives O'Brien more time to figure out where we are. We need to get home tonight."

"Aye." Declan agreed. "Let's go."

Fabrizio opened the door and peered out into the hall assuring that no one was in sight. Then out of habit made hand gestures to Declan who took Meghan by the arm and moved towards Fabrizio. Their departure from the office was almost complete when they heard a deep voice from behind them.

"Where are you going?" The deep voice resonated down the hall.

"Home," Declan said firmly, turning to see the greying man standing behind them.

"Well, I would like to talk with you before you do," he asked, with a friendly tone.

"Oh, now y' want to talk?" Declan grunted.

"I'm sorry for earlier, Mr. Montgomery, but you caught us off guard, and your behaviour was rather aggressive."

"Well, y' were scaring me wife," Declan countered, not interested in accepting the man's apology.

"I know. I'm sorry for that. Please, would you come back inside?"

"Why?" Declan questioned, involuntarily tightening his grip around Meghan.

"There is someone that needs to talk with you," Agent Anderson smiled and gestured back towards his office.

"No, Declan, it's Liam. Let's get out of here," Meghan shrieked, her fear exploding from every fibre of her body.

Declan had a tight grip around her waist and was pulling her backwards towards the emergency exit. "There is no one we need to talk to, we'll be going."

"Meghan." Brody Spencer's voice filled the hall. "I'm so happy you're all safe."

"Director?" Fabrizio blurted out, his face turning towards the voice.

Declan's grip was still tight around her waist; he was unsure what was happening. His eyes were switching from Meghan to Brody to Agent Anderson.

"Fabs, that's the guy from the hospital." Declan bobbed his head towards Agent Spencer. "The guy checking the cars."

Brody's dark blue eyes settled on Fabrizio. "You saw me, why didn't you get out of the car?" He glanced back at Meghan pressed up against Declan.

Fabrizio sighed and relaxed slightly. "I didn't see you, Director, and I was a running on adrenaline. What the hell, I have been calling Paxton for weeks."

Brody cringed, "Cassie phone and told me what was going on, but I always seemed to be one step behind."

"Well, welcome to our nightmare. O'Brien always seemed to be one step ahead of us. He has some pretty strong connections." Fabrizio lowered his voice.

Brody smiled and moved towards them, his eyes settling back on Meghan. "Meghan, are you all right?" His hand reached out to her.

"Yes," she smiled and took a step towards him, her hand groping out in front of her.

Brody gripped her arm and pulled her into him, surrounding her in his long arms. "I'm so glad you are okay. I checked on Caelan and Nathan, and they are fine. Cassie is there with them. I have agents out there watching them."

"I wish I would have thought of calling you," Meghan sniffed as she pressed her head against his shoulder. "It has been a hell of a couple of months."

"You should have. Did you think because I am the director now, I wouldn't help?"

Meghan shrugged and sighed. "I'm sorry. It's been a long time since I've seen you, it just never crossed my mind."

"Why didn't you go to the police?" Brody questioned, his accusing eyes settling on Fabrizio's exhausted face.

"We did!" Declan snorted. "But they kept informing O'Brien of our whereabouts." Declan glared at Brody; it suddenly struck him that he was the FBI agent that was helping Meghan through the trial. "O'Brien obviously had a great number of connections. He found us everywhere."

Brody nodded and released Meghan, allowing her to go back to Declan. "We have felt for years that he had moles in some agencies here in Britain."

"You have known about him for years?" Declan questioned, with shock.

"We didn't know that he was the one after Meghan. We would never have put her life in danger. Apparently, something you had no problem doing."

"Stop it!" Meghan grumbled and put her hand up towards Declan to stop any further comment from him that she knew he was ready to throw back at Brody. "This isn't going to get me home. I want to go home."

"Aye, Freckles." Declan's voice was soft and comforting, his hand soft as he gripped her hand, pulling her back towards him.

Brody glowered at Declan, then turned and whispered something to Agent Anderson. He could not believe Fabrizio was taking this reunion so lightly. He had not been so gracious to Fabrizio when he found out of their relationship.

"All right, we need statements from all of you, then we will get you home," Agent Anderson spoke up and waved towards the office down the hall.

It was over an hour by the time the group had explained what had happened in the past month. Meghan sat quietly tucked under Declan's arm for most of it, just giving her input in areas that Declan was unsure of. The agents seemed very interested in the whole experience, and they kept glancing back and forth at some of the things Declan was saying. He was purposely leaving out the fact that they blew up a boat, not wanting to drag Angus into it. He did, however, admit to killing the man that had the gun to Meghan's head and shooting at the men in the warehouse.

"Well," Agent Anderson said, scratching his greying hair. "The fact that O'Brien was trying to kidnap your wife might sway the authorities in your favour, but the fact remains that you and Agent Stagliano killed or wounded at least five men between you. And you, Agent, were supposed to be on medical leave," he muttered, leaning back in his chair with concern, his eyes settling on Fabrizio. "And with the fact that the two of you were Navy Seals, and you are also an FBI agent . . ."

"It wasn't them," Meghan blurted out. "It was me, I killed those men."

"What?" Brody snorted. "Meghan, what are you saying?"

"I'm saying I did it, so if anyone is going to be arrested, it's me." Her voice was surprisingly calm.

"Meggie," Declan grumbled. "She's fibbing, I'm not sure why, but she killed no one." Declan stared at her with amazement.

Brody grunted and paced back and forth. Meghan was obviously going to use herself to shield Declan. His original intention was to have Declan arrested and held in London long enough for Fabrizio to get Meghan back home and erase all the brainwashing that Declan had obviously put her through. If he pushes the issue, she might be dragged into the whole turmoil, and O'Brien might just get his hands on her again.

"Why don't we put them in protective custody and ship them home with the navy? That way, they will be accessible," Brody grumbled, deciding not to sacrifice Meghan to try and help Fabrizio out.

"Accessible for what?" Fabrizio questioned, rather concerned at the tone of voice.

"To testify when we get enough evidence to arrest O'Brien. You, Agent, will need to explain your actions to the board."

"Don't you have enough now?" Meghan questioned irritably. "He keeps kidnapping me. That's a crime. And he killed Brendan and Aisling."

"Well, the kidnapping maybe." He turned and went to his desk. "But you said that a man named Murphy killed Brendan. The woman is in the hospital, she will be fine."

"Really?" Meghan shrieked and turned towards Declan. "Thank God."

"Aye," Declan sighed and kissed Meghan's forehead.

Brody refocused and turned to Fabrizio, who seemed to be the only one listening to him at the moment. "O'Brien can only be held as an accessory to the murders. But we are more interested in his other activities."

"Y' mean the drug smuggling?" Declan questioned.

"You know about that?" Brody blurted out.

"Aye, we have, for a while."

"Really?" Agent Anderson said dryly. "And how did you come across that information?"

Declan eyed him warily. "Well, Meggie owns a piece of land that he leases from the couple Meggie's granda leased it to. Well, he uses it to . . ." Declan stopped as he felt her quivering under his arm. "Are y' okay, Freckles?"

He twisted his head in her direction. She was pressing her face against his chest with her eyes tightly shut.

"Meggie?" Declan questioned again.

"What?" she muttered in a shaky voice.

"Are y' okay?"

"No. No I'm not," she growled, sitting poker straight. "I have been sitting here listening to this for over an hour, and I don't know why. Obviously, they have no intentions of arresting him, but they were quick to point out that you could be arrested for killing the bastards that were trying to kidnap me and force me into a life with that son of a bitch."

"Meggie, calm down." Declan soothed, pulling her into him.

"No," she snapped. "I'm not calming down. This is ridiculous. It wouldn't surprise me if they think that we are somehow connected with his drug-smuggling ring. I'm surprised we haven't been strip-searched yet."

"Meghan, I think you're blowing this out of proportion. We don't think that you are involved with his activities. We were just curious to know how you found out. I'm sure it's not something he told you while he had you locked in his castle," Brody said calmly. She had changed since he last saw her. She was bitter and aggressive. What the hell had O'Brien done to her, or was it Declan's influence that changed her?

"No, our IRA connections told us," Meghan snorted.

"Meggie," Declan snapped.

"Now, we're getting somewhere," Agent Anderson smirked and leaned forward in his chair. "You have IRA connections, and who would that be? The group's activities have been very quiet for some time now."

"It's not like she makes it sound," Fabrizio piped up to cover up the information she just blurted out. "We just met a man in a pub in Derry, and he told us about O'Brien's reputation. We just figured he was with the IRA because he didn't seem scared of O'Brien like everyone else."

"Hmm," Brody grunted, directing his gaze on Meghan, who had her head pressed against Declan's chest again.

She sighed with worry and reached out for Declan's hand that was clenched into a fist, his thumb nervously rubbing back and forth across his forefinger. She knew when he was doing that, he was anxious, and she grabbed his hand to stop the motion.

His gaze dropped to her hand, and a slight grin grew across his face. He kissed her head, then returned his gaze to Brody.

"Okay, I guess you have told us all you can. Or will," Brody added as an afterthought. "Let's get you home. If we have any more questions, we can get the answers from you there." Brody stood and left the room.

Declan stood and stretched his long body; his hand reached down and lifted Meghan to her feet. Her eyesight was still extremely blurry, and as the day went on, her eyes were beginning to burn from the strain of trying to focus.

"How are your eyes?" Declan questioned, noticing they were quite red and irritated.

"They sting quite a bit. I think I should get some sun glasses," Meghan sighed, her hand reaching for his face, but a scowl twisted her lips when her fingers brushed across the beard. "Oh, I almost forgot about that."

"Oh, Freckles," Declan laughed and turned towards the curious Agent Anderson. "Y' wouldn't happen to have a razor I could use?"

"I think I might be able to find one for you," Agent Anderson chuckled. "I get the impression she doesn't like the beard."

"Not in the least," Declan laughed. "And it will be a long flight home if I have to listen to her complain about it."

"Well, anything I can do to ensure your peace," he smiled and disappeared out the door.

Declan turned to find Meghan scowling at him. "What about your hair?"

"Meggie, that can wait until I get home," he chuckled.

"Fine," she smirked. "Just get rid of the beard."

"Aye," he agreed.

The plane was waiting on the tarmac as promised, the American flag prominently displayed on the fuselage.

"Well, that's a beautiful sight," Fabrizio commented, his eyes focused on the plane.

"I'd say," Declan smiled and wrapped his arm around Meghan's shoulder when she stood up beside him. She rested her head on his shoulder and stared at the long object that appeared to be a plane. They were going home, finally. Her hand rested on her stomach, and a smile curled her lips; now she could finally tell Declan about the baby, little Aisling. Her heart lightened with the knowledge that Aisling was going to survive. Meghan was pleased with that news; at least someone survived O'Brien's killing spree.

Declan and Fabrizio both jerked around when they heard a loud voice coming from behind them.

"Well, if it isn't the big famous movie star and his sidekick," yelled the large black man heading towards them.

"Samson, y' son of a bitch," Declan shouted as he left Meghan's side and darted towards the man dressed in navy Seal fatigues.

Meghan was a bit worried with Declan's sudden departure and began turning in circles, trying to decide which form belonged to him. Fabrizio had also moved towards the man as Declan gave him a quick embrace.

"God, it's good to see y'," Declan said, smacking the man's back as he released him from his embrace.

"So how the hell are you, Monty?" Samson questioned Declan as he finished hugging Fabrizio.

"Better now," Declan admitted, relieved to see his good friend.

"Got yourself into a bit of trouble, did you, bro?" Samson laughed as he glanced towards Brody and the other FBI agents that were standing next to the car.

"Aye. We did," Declan smiled.

Meghan could not hear Declan's voice over the drone of the engines, and she started to move towards a group of men standing next to the plane, assuming that it was Fabrizio and Declan.

"Meghan, where are y' going?" Brody yelled, loud enough to draw her attention.

Meghan turned in the direction of the voice, relaxing slightly as Brody gripped her arm.

"Meghan, don't wander off." Brody took her by the hand. "Come on, I'll get you settled on the plane."

"Where is Declan?" Meghan questioned, glancing around the area, slightly concerned. "I'm not going anywhere without him."

Brody grunted and glanced over at Declan. "He's just over there."

Declan smirked as he watched the annoyance fill Brody's face; obviously, Meghan was giving him a hard time. "And that would be the cause of me problems."

"Well," Samson grinned, eyeing Meghan's long lean frame. "She sure is a pretty problem."

"Aye, she is," Declan agreed as he darted towards her.

Brody was still trying to encourage her onto the plane when Declan arrived at their side. "I'll be taking me wife now, if you don't mind." Declan's voice was confrontational.

Brody glowered at him but released her from his grip. Meghan, however, made no attempt to move towards Declan; she was annoyed that he would leave her alone.

"Declan, don't leave me alone," Meghan muttered, with annoyance filling her face.

"I'm sorry, Freckles," Declan smirked, raising his brow towards the men. "Meggie, I would like to introduce y' to a good friend. This is Martin Samson."

Meghan turned towards the two blobs and forced smile to her face. She was not sure which one was Samson, so she stuck her hand out in the middle of the two. "Hi."

"Hello," Samson said with an amused tone and took her hand in his.

He was watching her curiously as her eyes moved towards his face but seemed unfocused. His gaze left her face and settled on Declan's with a questioning look.

"Meggie had an accident, and her eyesight is a wee damaged at the moment," Declan explained, noticing the expression.

"Declan, do you have to tell everyone?" Meghan muttered, crinkling her nose at him.

"Well, you're looking at everyone like they're from another planet. I think that they can tell something is wrong," Declan laughed as he kissed her nose.

Samson laughed at Declan's comment and turned to Fabrizio. "So why don't you fill me in on what you three were up to, to rate getting flown home by the navy?" Samson pushed Fabrizio's shoulder away from Meghan and Declan.

"Sure," Fabrizio agreed as they headed towards the plane.

"Declan, how do you know that man?" Meghan questioned as the voices drifted away.

"He was in our Seal unit," Declan grinned widely, knowing for the first time since the whole nightmare started that they were actually going to get home.

"Oh, so everything is going to be okay?" Meghan sighed, pressing up against him.

"Aye, Freckles, I think it is," Declan assured her, wrapping his arms tightly around her body.

The plane's engines were comforting as Meghan sat next to Declan, resting her head on his chest. She could feel his rhythmic breathing as he slept for the first time in almost two days; he finally felt safe.

Samson came back from the front of the plane and sat down next to Fabrizio after gazing at Meghan's positioning in Declan's arms. The long muscular arms were wrapped around her as she cuddled against him. Samson shook his head and gazed over at Fabrizio.

"So anytime you want to come back?" Samson smirked.

"Funny you should say that," Fabrizio responded with a smile.

"Are you seriously thinking about re-enlisting?" Samson questioned, an excited grin crossing his face.

"I am, I miss it," Fabrizio admitted and glanced at Meghan's peaceful face. It was amazing to him how strong his feelings were for her, and he felt he needed to get away from her. However, was re-enlisting the right move?

Meghan sat quietly listening to the men discussing Fabrizio's possible return to the Navy Seals, and she had to bite her lip to keep herself from interjecting her opinion. It was really none of her business what Fabrizio does, other than the fact that he was dating her best friend and his decision would affect Cassie's life. However, her only focus right now was to get home and see her daughter. She closed her eyes and tried to ignore the conversation.

"So, do you think Monty wants to re-enlist?" Samson questioned glancing in Declan's direction.

"No," Fabrizio said lowering his voice. "He has other priorities right now."

"Oh," Samson smirked. "The little woman?"

"Yeah." Fabrizio's eyes settled on Meghan, her eyes were still closed, but was she listening carefully to the conversation, which had now become of interest to her?

"So when did he get trapped?" Samson laughed. "I never thought I'd see the day."

"Me neither," Fabrizio chuckled. "But he was doomed from the minute he laid eyes on her."

"Poor Monty," Samson muttered gazing at Meghan. "But at least, she's pleasant to look at."

"Yes, she is," Fabrizio agreed with a slight smirk. "But she's a handful."

"I can imagine. We were warned about her by the agents," Samson laughed and adjusted himself in the seat.

"You were?" Fabrizio questioned, concerned with what he was told.

"Apparently, O'Brien was frantic when she disappeared from the hospital, and he even went so far as to go to the authorities."

"I can't believe he would expose himself that way," Fabrizio blurted out and shook his head. She was never going to be free of that man.

"Well, he did. Agent Anderson said he was terrified that she was wandering around, lost," Samson smirked. "They feel that any woman that could captivate a man like O'Brien could manipulate any man into getting what she wants."

"Hmm," Fabrizio muttered. "Meghan's not like that. She wouldn't purposely do anything to hurt anyone."

"You don't think? She managed to snare Monty." Samson's laugh was mocking and annoyed Fabrizio.

"Yeah well, he's not trapped. He loves her." Fabrizio's comment was more in defence of Meghan. "He is lucky to have her."

Meghan began to stir, unable to keep her emotions under control any longer. She opened her eyes and stared directly at Samson. Her vision was still blurred, but she could tell from the voices which one he was.

"Well, she's awake," Samson smiled towards her.

"Yes," Meghan muttered, with annoyance building in her eyes.

"Boo," Fabrizio said calmly, noticing the expression. He was as good as Declan at reading her face.

"What?" she said, sharply turning her gaze on him.

His mouth twitched as he watched the anger threatening to explode. "Calm down."

Meghan's nose crinkled with annoyance, but as Brody's voice filled the cabin, she settled. She glanced up in the direction of his voice, then back at Samson.

"Meghan, you look tired. Why don't you come up front and lie down, let the men talk?" Brody reached out for her hand. He had been listening to the conversation and was wondering why Fabrizio was defending her relationship with Declan, and why was he calling her that stupid name.

"I'm fine here," Meghan muttered, not wanting to leave Declan alone with Samson in case he talked him into re-enlisting.

"I need to talk to you." Brody gripped her hand and yanked her to her feet. "Come with me."

"All right," Meghan sighed and allowed him to pull her to the front of the plane.

"Well, that was intense." Samson glanced back; Brody now had his arm around her shoulder. "Monty better be careful. I think that agent is after his wife."

"He was," Fabrizio whispered. "Years ago he told me he found her attractive, but then I . . ." Fabrizio stopped what he was saying.

"Then you what?" Samson's brow rose ever so slightly.

"Well, it's a long story, but she and Declan parted ways, and Meghan and I dated for a while."

"Really?" Samson chuckled. "What a cozy group we are!"

Fabrizio laughed but kept his eyes on Meghan and Brody; he was not going to give him the opportunity to insinuate himself into her life. He was a womanizer, she was too vulnerable now, and it would not take much to push her over the edge. The minutes ticked by while Brody talked with Meghan, soothing her into compliance. Fabrizio became irritated when Brody kissed her cheek and rested his head against hers. He was making his move. Fabrizio jumped to his feet and was at Meghan's side before Brody had a chance to react.

"Boo, it's time to put the drops in your eyes." Fabrizio's voice was full of authority.

Meghan nodded, pulled away from Brody, and reached out for Fabrizio, her hand resting on his face. "Fabrizio, you must be tired, why don't you go to sleep?"

"I'm fine, Boo," Fabrizio smiled, the feel of her hand on his cheek exciting him. "Once we're home, I'll sleep. I'm too wired right now."

Brody bristled from the caring that was evident in Meghan's voice; he was still annoyed that Fabrizio had gotten in his way years earlier. "So what's with the name?" he asked lightly, not wanting to show his annoyance. He did not want Fabrizio know of his attraction to Meghan. He might tell his wife.

"Oh well, it's a long story, but he started it years ago, when I thought I saw a ghost," Meghan giggled and bumped up against Fabrizio. "I'm not sure if I appreciate it, but I guess I'm stuck with it."

"You are, Boo," Fabrizio laughed and wrapped his hand around her shoulder.

Brody grunted and turned away but looked back over his shoulder at Meghan talking with Fabrizio, her hand sweeping across his face in examination. "Fabrizio, your eyes are puffy, you are exhausted."

"Boo, I'm all right, I swear to you." Fabrizio kissed her head. "Please stop worrying."

"All right." Meghan wrapped her arms around Fabrizio's ribs and rested her head against his chest. "Fabrizio, I just want to thank you for everything. I don't know what I would have done without you."

"You're welcome," Fabrizio sighed. How he wanted to kiss her! Should he? One small peck on the lips, that would be all right. No, it would not, he decided, she would never be his again; her heart would only ever belong to Declan. Fabrizio satisfied himself with a kiss on the head and led her back to Declan.

Meghan curled into Declan on her return, his arms snaking around her ribs, pulling her tightly against him. The safety she felt at that moment was overwhelming, and she never wanted it to end. Her fingers slid across his check, back into his hair, tucking a long black strand behind his ear. She smiled slightly, placed her finger on his mouth, and began gliding it softly across the full bottom lip, causing him to twitch slightly from the sensation. His lips were still so ticklish; even when he slept, he twitched when they were touched.

Fabrizio and Samson were watching her exploring his face as if she had never seen it before and a mischievous smile crossed Samson's lips as he watched her tormenting Declan's lips.

"She's going to wake him and from what I remember, he doesn't wake up in a good mood," Samson whispered to Fabrizio.

Fabrizio shrugged, his eyes fixed on her long slender fingers stroking Declan's face. "I don't imagine he would mind terribly, being woken up by her," Fabrizio chuckled, shaking his gaze from her to Samson.

"Freckles, if y' don't stop arousing me, y' are going to have to face the consequences," Declan smiled, opened one eye, and gazed at her.

"Is that a threat?" Meghan giggled and brushed his lips once again.

"No, it's a promise." Declan opened the other eye and grabbed her face in his hands, his lips taking hers, causing her to melt into him, totally forgetting about the two men watching.

Declan's left eye opened, and he gazed at the laughing men as he slowly removed his lips from hers. "Are y' finding this entertaining?"

"Well, I was hoping to see more, but . . ." Samson pushed through his laughter. "Monty, if I hadn't seen it for myself, I would never have believed it."

"Aye," Declan smirked when the realization of what was coming filled his mind. "Well, I guess I forfeit."

"Yeah, and I will make sure you pay up," Fabrizio laughed and smacked Samson on the shoulder.

Meghan was listening to the conversation, but she did not understand what they were talking about; it sounded very ominous, and she was beginning to worry. "Declan, what do you have to forfeit?"

"Ah well," Declan smirked. "Years ago, we made a bet. The first one to enslave themselves to a woman . . ." He stopped as Meghan's face crumpled with annoyance.

"Damn, Monty, you've done it now," Samson laughed and elbowed Fabrizio with amusement.

"Meggie," Declan soothed.

"Enslaved? Is that what you think you are?" Meghan snorted, pushing out of his arms.

She jumped to her feet and stumbled past Fabrizio and Samson, groping her way to the back of the plane, where she found empty seats. Declan watched as she dropped to the seat with frustration. He shook his head and glanced over at Fabrizio with amusement flowing from his eyes.

"Sometimes I wonder if it was worth it," Declan laughed as he stood, not wanting to leave her by herself with Brody lurking at the front of the plane.

Fabrizio laughed and shook his head, his eyes settling on Meghan. "Yeah, well, you knew she was volatile."

Declan smiled, then turned back to Samson. "Well, go get them and let's get this over with."

"I'll be right back," Samson laughed, jumped to his feet, and darted to the front of the plane.

Meghan had calmed by the time Declan dropped to the seat beside her. His lips teasingly suckled her neck as she batted at his head. "Freckles, don't be cross. I don't think that, it was just a silly bet made years before I met y."

Meghan crinkled her nose and turned her head towards the small window. Her emotions were beginning to overtake her, and he could not blame her. She had been through more than most people could have survived over the last two months, and they both knew it was not over. Declan could tell by the expression on her face when O'Brien's name was mentioned that she knew he would still come after her.

"After everything that we have been through, you . . ." Meghan blurted out after a few minutes of silence; she was not quite sure what she was so upset about, but she couldn't stop her emotions from erupting to the surface like an out-of-control volcano.

"Meggie," Declan sighed, kissing her forehead. "Y' know I don't think that way. I love y'."

"I'm sorry, it's just that I heard that man talking to Fabrizio, and he . . ." She stopped and gazed in Fabrizio's direction.

"He what?" Declan pushed.

"He said that I trapped you, and he said that the agents told him I was a conniving woman that could manipulate any man," Meghan sniffed, not particularly impressed with their description of her.

Declan threw back his head and laughed at the information. "Aye, well."

"Declan, this isn't funny. People think I'm awful."

"No, they don't, Freckles." Declan changed his voice to sound consoling. "I told y' this before that you have some power over men."

Meghan grunted and turned her head towards the window once again. "Do you think that I manipulate people?" she muttered.

"No, I think y' are a very strong woman with your own mind," Declan smiled and placed his hand under her chin, lifting her face towards his. "And I think that y' don't let anyone push y' around anymore. Me included."

"Then why did the agent say that?" Meghan grumbled as tears filled her eyes. "People think I'm . . ."

"Meggie, don't worry what the agent thinks. He is just threatened by y'." Declan bent down and kissed her lips. "Some men are intimidated by strong women because they are not confident enough in themselves. It has nothing to do with y'."

"Are you embarrassed by me?" she questioned, fixing her big green eyes on him.

"No, Freckles. That's what I loved about y' from the day I met y'. That y' had a mind of your own," he smiled and kissed her nose, resting his forehead against hers.

"Declan . . ." Meghan sniffed and gripped his face. "I don't want any more secrets between us."

"All right." He kissed her nose. "But I don't believe I have anything else about me that y' don't know." Her eyes, however, told him that she did. "Meggie, is there something y' need to tell me?" He glanced up at Fabrizio, who was watching them intently. His stomach began to tighten with worry.

"Yes," Meghan muttered and tightened her grip in his face. "I just want you to know that I never planned this, but since it happened," she paused when she felt him flinch, "Declan, please don't be cross with me."

"Meggie, y' are scaring me. Just tell me what it is!" His voice was agitated.

Meghan gripped his hand, spreading out his fingers over hers. Her hand was trembling as she rested his open hand over her belly. "Say hello to your child."

"What?" he blurted out louder than he had intended, which drew the attention of everyone on the plane. Samson was on his way over to them when Fabrizio gripped his arm.

"Stay here for a minute." Fabrizio didn't like the sound of Declan's voice. She had told him something that shocked him.

"Meggie, are y' telling me that y' are pregnant?" Declan voice was trembling. "Who is the father?"

"Declan!" Meghan snorted and took a swing at his head. "Who do you think! Dammit!" Meghan tried to jump to her feet, but Declan yanked her back down to his lap. "Meggie, I just meant. Well, how long have y' known?"

"Well, I don't know for sure. But I have missed my cycle for three months." Her voice was low, trying not to allow anyone to overhear the conversation. "It's yours, Declan. I haven't been with anyone else for over a year."

"Are y' not on birth control?" Declan questioned, unsure why he was questioning her opinion.

"I was using a diaphragm before. I can't use the birth control pill. When we . . . Well, we never used anything the first few times." She was beginning to wish she had never told him. Why was he accusing her of misleading him? "This isn't just my fault you know. You could have used something," she snorted as her pride took hold. "Don't worry, after everything that has happened over here, I'm not expecting you to be burdened any further."

"What the hell are you talking about? Y' think I am not going to take responsibility for me child?" His voice was angry, and she was relieved she could not see his eyes. "Dammit, Meggie, y' are the most exasperating woman I have ever met."

Brody moved towards the pair when he heard Declan yelling at her. This behaviour was the exact description people gave at the trial that they were always fighting, which made him wonder why she was so intent on staying with him. Why did she constantly want conflict in her life?

"Meghan, is everything all right?" Brody broke into the conversation. "I think maybe you should come up to the front with me."

"Director, this has nothing to do with y'," Declan growled, his eyes dark and angry.

"It does when you are yelling at her that way." Brody reached down and gripped her hand. "Come on, Meghan."

"No, we need to finish this." Her face turned towards Declan. "I'm not asking for an answer right now, I just . . ."

"The answer is that I have no intentions of allowing you to raise me child without me," Declan grumbled.

"Are you two still arguing about that!" Fabrizio grumbled as he came to pull Brody away from their conversation.

"I'm not talking about Caelan," Declan sighed, his dark eyes settling on Fabrizio. "I'm talking about my child she is carrying."

"Declan!" Meghan blurted out; totally horrified that he would purposely tell Fabrizio that information. "I can't believe you."

"You're pregnant?" Fabrizio tried to control his emotions. He forced a smile to his face. "That's great, I'm so happy for the two of you. Who else knows? Does Cassie? She is going to be so excited," he rambled, doing his best to seem pleased.

Declan could tell he was lying, but after all that had happened and with the knowledge that Fabrizio was one of the only people he could trust with his life, he decided to let the past go. Meghan made her choice, and Fabrizio seemed willing to accept it. He had mentioned Cassie in his rambling, so he must be planning on keeping her in his life. Cassie was a great girl, and she would make Fabrizio happy.

"Freckles." Declan gripped her hand and pulled her back onto his lap as the group moved away to give them privacy. "I know this is not something you want, but I do. I'm sorry I reacted the way I did, but I do want this child."

"Really?" Meghan sniffed and rested her face into his hair. "Because I have dreaded telling you. I wanted to share it with you so many times. Aisling said I should pick the right time."

"Aisling knows?" Declan sounded shocked. "You told her and not me?"

"She noticed. I don't know how, but she knew, and I wasn't going to lie to her," Meghan sighed and pulled her face from his hair. "I'm sorry."

"Don't be, Freckles. It has been a long couple of months, and with everything that happened, well, it's probably best that I didn't know. If I did, I certainly would not have allowed y' to jump off the boat."

Meghan chuckled and rested her hands on his face. "So you didn't mind losing me, but the baby?"

"Meggie, it wasn't the fact that I was willing to lose you. It is the fact that if O'Brien ever found out y' were carrying me child . . ." Declan shivered. "There is no telling what he might have done."

Meghan nodded and rested her head against Declan's shoulder. "It's all right now."

"Aye, Freckles," Declan smiled and glanced over at Fabrizio and Samson. "I'm going to be a da again."

Samson eyed Fabrizio, then grinned and moved quickly towards the pair, the scissors, in plain view, clutched in his hand.

"I'm so happy for both of you," Samson laughed. "But now it's time to pay up," Samson blurted out, lifting the scissors into the air.

"Well, Freckles, I guess y' better take one last look at me, because I'm in for it now," Declan laughed fixing his eyes on Samson. "Samson is ready with me punishment."

"Declan?" Meghan panicked, glancing in the direction of the blobs. "What is he going to do?"

"Well, I have to pay the price for losing the bet," Declan said evenly.

"No!" Meghan wrapped her arms around his body. "I won't let him hurt you."

"Meggie," Declan laughed. "They aren't going to hurt me."

"Well, Monty, I think that she might just be worth all the trouble she causes you," Samson laughed as he watched Meghan clinging to Declan, trying to shelter him from the approaching men. "I'm not sure how she thinks she can stop two grown men, but I have to say it's admirable. She's got guts."

"Aye, she does," Declan laughed. "She's one of a kind."

Meghan lifted her head from his shoulder and turned towards the group of men that now surrounded them, but she didn't release her grip.

"Freckles, I suggest y' get off me now. I would hate for anything to happen to that gorgeous hair of yours." Declan pried her hands loose.

"My hair?" Meghan questioned as he deposited her next to him.

"Aye. That's what the penalty for forfeiting is. I lose me hair, shaved right to the scalp," Declan smirked and glanced up at Samson. "I'm really not sure why we made that bet. Since our hair at the time was quite short."

"Declan," Meghan muttered, a smirk curling her lips. "They are cutting that hair?"

"Aye."

"Thank God," Meghan blurted out, grabbing a long clump of hair.

"Bloody hell, Meggie, at least y' could act a bit sympathetic." Declan laughed loudly at the expression on Samson's face. Shock was what it was.

"Oh sorry," Meghan giggled and rested a delicate hand on his face. "I'm crushed."

"Hmm, I'll bet," Declan grunted a laugh and turned towards Samson. "All right then, get it done."

"Meghan, would you like to do the honours?" Samson smiled, handing her the scissors. "You can make the first cut. But I want to buzz it off myself."

"Freckles, are y' sure y' can see clearly enough? I don't want y' lobbing off me ear," Declan smirked as he watched her gripping the scissors in her hand.

"I think I can feel the difference between your hair and your ear," Meghan grumbled and snapped the scissors shut on the hair. The long chunk of hair was still clutched in her hand when she handed back the scissors to Samson. "I'm keeping this."

"What for?" Declan questioned with a smirk, his head shaking slightly.

"As a souvenir of your subservience to me," Meghan said wryly, glancing in the direction she thought Samson was.

Samson immediately roared at her comment, "Monty," his head shaking in disbelief. "I'm not sure if I envy you or pity you."

"Aye, well," Declan smirked. "I'm not sure sometimes meself. Now stop talking and get it over with."

Meghan stood up and found her way to Fabrizio as he held out his hand to guide her. He rested his arm around her shoulder as she leaned into him.

"How come you never did this to him before?" Meghan questioned, with interest.

"Well," Fabrizio chuckled. "For one thing, he needed that hair for his movie."

"And the other?" Meghan pushed, hearing the enjoyment in Fabrizio's voice. She was surprised she had never heard of this bet before now.

"Well, I couldn't fault him for falling in love with you," Fabrizio smiled and kissed the top of her head. "You're one hell of a woman."

"That she is," Declan agreed as he stood and brushed off the loose hair from his shirt. "Well, Freckles, come to your new man."

Meghan took his hand and allowed him to lead her towards him. "Wow, it is just like a baby's head," she giggled as her fingers slid along the smooth skin. "Your head is shaped just like Caelan's."

"Well, I must say, I'm regretting getting rid of me Red Sox hat now," Declan grumbled and kissed Meghan's forehead.

Declan rested his hand in Meghan's belly and rubbed the flat stomach in a circular motion. His life was falling into place. Meghan belonged to him, and no one was ever going to come between them again, not O'Brien or Fabrizio, not even his mother. He had lived with her and without her, and he knew in his soul that he would never be truly complete without her in his life.

"Meggie, I got y' something. I was going to wait until we got home, but I think y' need it now." Declan reached into his pocket, his fist clenched around something in his palm as he pulled it from his pocket.

Meghan gripped his closed fist. "What is it?" she sounded scared, what did she think he had in his hand? Declan swallowed painfully and slowly opened his fingers, spreading out his hand, exposing a small eagle pendant attached to a gold chain.

Meghan's eyes widened with amazement as she felt the eagle, its wings outstretched as if in flight. Her eyes rose to meet his gaze, and he could not help but smile as he watched her eyes glaze over with tears.

"Declan, it's beautiful," she mumbled, lifting it out of his palm and raising it towards her face.

"I got it at the jewelry store across from the manor the day before y' disappeared. I went to talk to the old fellow about the locket, and he said that y' should not wear it. So I thought if I got y' this, y' would wear it instead, and we could lock that cursed locket up."

Meghan smiled softly and closed her eyes. "I think you're right. This is a fresh start, and I love it."

"Here, let me help," Declan chuckled as he watched her fumbling to attach it around her neck. He brushed her hair away from the back of her neck and latched the chain. "There, it looks fabulous." His fingers slid under the pendant, lifting it to get a better look.

"Meggie, me lost eagle, you are the only woman I will ever love."

"Declan." Her voice was choked as he brushed the tears off her cheek.

His head lowered to her neck, and he kissed the pendant. "You're me everything," Declan whispered against the lips of the woman he loved. "Promise me, you'll be mine forever."

"I promise!" she pledged, leaning her tousled auburn hair against the strong welcoming chest of the man that she loved with every fibre of her being. Now and forever.

AUTHOR'S NOTES

While writing this novel, I did a large amount of research into Ireland's history, traditions and myths. Even though this is a work of fiction, some of the people mentioned are true historical figures. Brian Boru (*Brian Bóruma mac Cennétig*) for example lived from 941—April 23, 1014. He is considered the last great King of Ireland. The information I give in this novel about him and his descendants is historically correct and confirmed through a number of sources. Eamon O'Brien is where the fiction begins, and down through his descendants. The legend of the sword is also fiction. While discussing Eamon's life, I mention King Henry VIII, Queen Elizabeth I, and Gerald Fitzgerald, 15th Earl of Desmond, and of course, these people are all historical figures. I encourage you to go to your local library and research these individuals.

Ireland has a rich history of myths and one of those is about the sidhe or shee. They are a fairy people that rule the Otherworld, who, are believed to be the Tuatha De'Dannan's, who were concurred by the Milesians, and then went underground. Many different forms of sidhe are described in the ***Book of Leinster***. This is a medieval Irish manuscript complied ca. 1160 and is now kept in Trinity College in Dublin. The myths are many and differ slightly depending on the source, but you can decide for yourself.

Another legend of Ireland is the history of Blarney Castle. The legend I tell in this novel is the most agreed upon in the sources I used. As in all legends, it is based in facts but sometimes is skewed in the translation and in the re-telling, becomes more romantic.

Ireland is a beautiful and magical country that everyone should take the time to visit and explore.

Typos and Terminology

Despite the due diligence of my fantastic copy editing team, a number of friends who read the manuscript in bits and pieces, and the obsessive re-reading by myself, there could be a few typos. My hope is that you can enjoy the content all the same.

Dál gCais—were a Gaelic Irish tribe, considered to be a branch of the Déisi Muman, who were powerful in Ireland during the 10th century.

Ard Rí na hÉireann—which means High King of Ireland. Some of the figures were historical and others legendary, but all either had or claimed to have had, lordship over Ireland. There are a great number of Irish writings, which show an unbroken chain of High Kings ruling over Ireland going back thousands of years.

An Garda Síochána—which translate to guardian of the peace. Garda can be used when describing the police force or a single person—this position is similar to officer, deputy, trooper and constable. The police station is called a Garda station.

CPSIA information can be obtained at www.ICGtesting.com
Printed in the USA
LVOW13s1913160414

381976LV00006B/1032/P

9 781490 725000